# Operation Selector

*To Lesley
Slainte!*

HULTA GERTRUDE

authorHOUSE

AuthorHouse™ UK
1663 Liberty Drive
Bloomington, IN 47403 USA
www.authorhouse.co.uk
Phone: 0800.197.4150

© 2018 Hulta Gertrude. All rights reserved.

No part of this book may be reproduced, stored in a retrieval system, or transmitted by any means without the written permission of the author.

Published by AuthorHouse 03/13/2018

ISBN: 978-1-5462-8899-2 (sc)
ISBN: 978-1-5462-8900-5 (hc)
ISBN: 978-1-5462-8917-3 (e)

Print information available on the last page.

Any people depicted in stock imagery provided by Getty Images are models, and such images are being used for illustrative purposes only.
Certain stock imagery © Getty Images.

This book is printed on acid-free paper.

Because of the dynamic nature of the Internet, any web addresses or links contained in this book may have changed since publication and may no longer be valid. The views expressed in this work are solely those of the author and do not necessarily reflect the views of the publisher, and the publisher hereby disclaims any responsibility for them.

# Contents

Part 1: Misinformation ..................................................................1
Part 2: Transient Killers ............................................................129
Part 3: Duel Of The Champions ..............................................248
Part 4: Auribus Teneo Lupum ..................................................387
Part 5: The Hang Fire ...............................................................507
Part 6: The Closest Thing To Justice ........................................516

*This book is dedicated to the memory of Chloe Sarah Lynn 1977 – 2018. Rest in peace.*

*My thanks and acknowledgements go out firstly to a much apreciated proof reader. You'll notice that out of deference to their great work, I have misspelled a word in this tribute. I now task you to find it. You are much prised.*

*Lastly they go out to my family and friends who have had to put up with me whilst I worked on this project. I would also like to thank anyone who chooses to read this work.*

## Part One

# Misinformation

The money had arrived, all of it. From that distance, Satiah couldn't be sure if it was real or counterfeit, but it hardly mattered. Concealed behind what flimsy shrubbery there was out on the alpine tundra, Satiah lay on her front, and the telescopic sights of her projector magnified the distant for her. She scrutinised the area closely. Her brown eyes wide, her breathing even, she watched as the group of twelve men waited in open view, about five hundred metres further down the mountainside. They were guarding three crates crammed with Essps in cash form.

It was supposed to be a million, but it wasn't as if she could just slip in and count it at her leisure. She had been told that these men, on behalf of a rich entrepreneur, were illegally purchasing females from a slave dealer. This was to be the payment. There was more to it than that, but she'd not been told more. Her job, as a Phantom Agent of the Coalition, was simple. *Prevent the transaction from taking place. Oh yes... they would get a payment all right, she told herself.*

The dealer had been designated for termination. His death was imminent. That was someone else's job. Strictly speaking, this wasn't an official operation but rather a briefly cobbled-together assignment. Satiah didn't much care how they worded it... so long as they paid her. She wasn't sure who the men waiting with the money were. Just mercenaries hired to perform the most hazardous part of the deal? People that the businessman, whoever he was, deemed *expendable*? She doubted they were even aware of the true nature of the deal. Too bad for them; it would turn out to be a death-pact either way.

So the bait was there and *here*, unless her ears deceived her, came the game. The sound of a ship approaching made her glance up, her eyes evaluating it. The ship, a freighter, was coming in to land. The pickup. She'd expected a warning of its approach from Kelvin but she dismissed its absence as rather pointless. It's not like she couldn't hear a spaceship coming for herself. The ship whipped up the cold breeze and she shivered as it howled around her, thrashing her long orangey red hair into a frenzy.

She squinted instinctively, remaining still and keeping her eyes on where it was meant to land. If they bothered to scan before they landed, they would not be able to sense her. She was shielded from any normal scanners. As she had predicted - frankly, as *anyone* could predict - the ship came in to land within metres of the men and the money. A grim smile creased her pale face as she aimed. The ship was slowly turning, trying to get their landing ramp to face the men... exposing the engines to her. They were landing as any sensible pilot would, just as she had anticipated.

"In your own time," she murmured, to herself. They used to say that in the old days when she had been trained. Her hand flexed, her finger stroked the trigger readily. A little to the left, a little more... and...

Satiah pulled the trigger, launching the SRED, or short-range exploding device, with a smoky whoosh. It sailed rapidly forward, slamming into the exposed engines and detonated.

The ensuing chain reaction caused on the spot obliteration to the ship *and* to the men standing mere metres from it, in less than a second. Protected from the flash by the sights, Satiah watched to be sure she'd got everyone. Debris burned, and vegetation too. The mushroom cloud rose slowly into the air and away on the breeze. Some additional wreckage crashed to the ground noisily after it had been flung away by the force of the blast. Still she waited. Nothing moved. She let out the breath she'd been holding in and stood slowly.

The bolt struck her projector instead of her, otherwise she'd have known no more. As it was, with a shriek, she pitched over backwards from the kinetic force that the bolt had imparted. She barrel rolled a few metres and then began to crawl away, unsure where the shooter was. Another laser bolt hit a rock close to her, accompanied by the high-pitched mechanical squeak of high power as she crawled, and she could hear shouting coming from the North.

She reached a larger boulder, the one she'd deliberately stayed close to for just this sort of contingency. She rose into a crouch while drawing her pistol in her usual style and stole a cautious look over it. Three armed men were running. Zigzagging toward her, simultaneously, so as to hamper any attempt she made to bring them down. There was also another, in the treeline beyond - maybe sixty yards away, and he fired at her a third time. *Where* had they come from? Was this a set up? She tapped her earpiece; she needed to get out of this *now*!

"Kelvin, I need to hightail, *right now*!" she requested, wondering which way would be best to run. No answer. "*Kelvin*!" Still nothing. She made herself calm down and think tactically. She fired a shot over the rock to buy time. She aimed at nothing but she wanted to slow down the men approaching her. An answering shot hit the rock.

She got back onto her belly and began a rapid commando crawl in a line directly away from her pursuers. She set her earpiece through a brief diagnosis program to see if it was still functioning. It could be a problem at Kelvin's end, or she might be blocked. He *hadn't* warned her of the ship's arrival… the significance of his silence dawned on her. She couldn't rely on him coming to her rescue *this time*. She reached an outcropping of many huge boulders together and scrambled in among them. She glanced over her shoulder to see that the men were still coming. She turned and aimed. These men were good, adept at crossing open terrain whilst not making themselves easy targets. Well trained and experienced agents. She managed to take one down with a few well-placed shots. The other two hit the ground and returned fire, pelting the rocks around her with alarmingly accurate rounds.

She retreated further among the boulders to avoid being hit. She looked all around, frantically trying to find a good hiding place. If she could conceal herself well enough, she might be able to take these two down, although that still left the sniper to contend with and she'd lost sight of him. She hoped the reverse, that he had lost sight of her, was also true but she doubted it. A scrambling noise betrayed the arrival of the first of her enemies. If only she had some mines on her! She half ran and half skidded down the face of a particularly huge rock and landed hard at the bottom. She saw a narrow gap between two other giant stones and quickly slipped between them. She stopped, slowed her breathing and waited. Again the noise gave the man away as he tackled the boulder she'd just raced over. She peered out and shot him.

She broke cover then, only this time she ran *toward* the body, going for the rifle. If that sniper was still out there she would need more than her pistol to deal with him. She rolled over, snatching up the rifle from the corpse and ended in a squat. The earpiece reported to her that there was nothing wrong with it; it also indicated that she was not being blocked. So why wasn't Kelvin answering? She knelt where she was, rifle aimed, awaiting the second man. She gave him forty seconds. If he didn't appear by then she could safely assume he was coming at her from another direction. A movement made her tense. The man appeared. She pulled the trigger but the rifle didn't fire. The man saw her and ducked out of sight. She retreated again, trying to understand why the gun didn't work.

It hadn't overheated, it *was* loaded and it wasn't in safe mode. *So why the hell...?* Then she noticed the sensor on the handle. She couldn't tell for sure, but she realised it must check the handprint of whoever was using it and it had been pre-programmed only to work for the man she'd just killed. She pondered the possibility of removing the sensor somehow or the man's hand... but she decided she didn't have time. She threw the useless thing away in a direction she wasn't going in, in an effort to at least trick the remaining men into thinking she'd gone another way. She also grabbed a small stone to use as a distraction should she need it later.

"*Kelvin!*" she hissed, trying again. Still no response. She hurriedly climbed up the side of another boulder and then lay atop it, staying low. Carefully she drew her pistol again and waited. She knew if he'd realised which way she had gone, he would be more cautious this time. He would expect her to be waiting for him. She felt a bead of sweat inch its way down her back, made cold by the wind. The man, dressed in dark blue with rifle ready, was cautious indeed. His face hidden by clothing and goggles, he advanced warily. Her eyes narrowed as she thought of learning more about him. Who was he working for? Why was he there? She tossed the stone hard and away from her. It clattered somewhere and the man spun to cover it, his movement well practised and swift.

After a few seconds of silence he moved out from his cover, to see more, believing her to be somewhere she wasn't. She shot him in the back and he went down instantly.

She took care to ascend down *unhurriedly* now. The sniper was still out there, but he had been some way back and it would be foolish to allow injury to herself in such a careless way. She approached the body and rolled the man onto his back with her foot with the intention of frisking him. After making sure he was actually dead and not faking, she removed the goggles and facial clothing. A stranger. No logos or symbols on his clothing. Not surprisingly, there were no documents and no personal belongings. His rifle was identical to the first man's, which meant she couldn't use this one either.

Perhaps these men had been there to interfere with the business deal too; maybe it had been a double-cross. It seemed likely. If you dealt with dirt, then you should expect dirty tactics. She had a choice now: go after the sniper or not? She chose not to, and instead reverted to a previous plan she'd made that she had, at the time, felt she might not need. She whistled sharply, wondering where her ride had wandered off to. She had been gone for over an hour so she could understand that it must have become bored and wandered off in search of food.

She'd been on this insufferable planet for only a few hours but she'd got to the rendezvous site on the back of one of the indigenous lizards. Bounding over a large boulder, with a peculiar roar that sounded more like pressurised gas leak, her mount returned. He was nearly ten feet in height and twice that in length. The saddle was still there, luckily. Her relief was substantial. Sometimes she preferred animals to people; at least they didn't try to be your friend before they attempted to murder you. Only one thing put her off: the smell. However, she had no choice. She clambered onto its back.

"Go!" she ordered, pointing ahead and slapping its back. The direction she went in was of little importance now, so long as she didn't go North, but she knew she had to get away from this place.

The lizard took off abruptly, bounding forward with a surprising speed and agility. Satiah clung on tightly as it leapt from rock face to ground and all over the damn place. Why it couldn't just go in a *straight line* she had no idea. A gunshot made her look around. The sniper had broken cover and was standing atop the boulders about fifty paces away. She lay flat on the creature's back. Another bolt swished by so close, Satiah thought it had winged her for a second. Then he was out of sight as the lizard left the rocks behind. Spooked by the shooting, it was really going for it now. Having no intention of slowing it down, Satiah gritted her teeth and held on for dear life. Hissing wildly, it pelted into the trees, leaving her pursuer far behind. Spiky branches tore at her and she stayed low to avoid the worst of the branches.

The lizard seemed to somehow keep running and running like it would never stop. Only when they were through the trees did Satiah began to relax a bit. She began to pat its back, telling it that she wished it to slow down.

They rounded a corner and the creature finally halted. Satiah almost fell off because of the rapid stop and looked out across the herd of lizards grazing there. It had run all the way home, apparently. She patted the lizard's back in gratification and tried to call Kelvin again.

"Kelvin, if you can hear me please home in on my signal and pick me up," she instructed. No response came. She sighed and called Randal, her direct superior, instead. He answered.

"What's wrong?" he asked, knowing something had to be up. Satiah wasn't one for casual chats.

"I'm not sure but I need someone to come and get me," she replied, downing some water. "I was able to carry out your instructions but before anything else could happen I was set upon by some men coming from the North."

"Ah," he replied, sounding puzzled. *"They shouldn't have been there."*

"Someone forgot to tell them, obviously," she remarked, a little sardonically. "Can you help or not?"

"*Certainly*. I'll dispatch a team right away; they will be there in two hours. I *thought* you had transport of your own?" he replied, curious.

"Me too," she growled, eyeing the sky speculatively. "Thanks." She disconnected and sighed heavily. This place was desolate, no wonder no one ever bothered to colonise it. Something in the distance shone and she leapt down from the lizard's back immediately, thinking that somehow the sniper was back. The flash though was the sun glinting on something in the sky, not a rifle sight lens. An approaching craft. *At last*!

She stood and watched. Her reprieve was short lived. Something was wrong… it was coming down way too quickly. And it was heading straight for her. Realising what was about to happen she started screaming and slapping the lizards closest to her to get them to move out of the way. She pulled out her pistol and fired it repeatedly into the ground and then the air. This had the desired effect and the lizards stampeded madly away from her. She too started to run. The drone of the engines was loud now. She dived down behind some rocks and hoped they would protect her from the effects of the crash. There was a very loud booming noise as it hit the ground and skidded along, leaving a track in the ground strewn with fire and bits of metal from the hull.

She crouched there, her hands over her ears as it screeched past. A wave of dust, dirt and smoke enveloped her. The ship eventually came to rest almost a kilometre away from her, hull steaming, and leaving a trail of fires burning. Coughing, Satiah stood and began to run along the churned up ground to get to it. If there was *anyone* within one hundred kilometres they would have seen that. As she got closer she could see from the smoke billowing out of it that a massive internal fire was burning, and those with any sense would keep their distance in case it all went up. She rushed forward though; she had to see what was happening. Kelvin was in there.

She reached the main door but it was partially buried in the ground. A docking area was still exposed though! She couldn't touch it, it was too cold despite the nearby flames. Sweat poured from her now as she aimed and fired. She hit the manual override control unit, normally used by people trying to access the ship from space. The door slid open and she staggered back with a cry as a fireball erupted out from the doorway. She pulled the breathing apparatus from her belt and put it in her mouth. Smoke inhalation though seemed the least of her problems. She winced in the heat as she edged towards the open hatchway. Sparks flew from the open circuit she'd shot and flames were everywhere. She took a risk and jumped through the hatchway into the fire beyond.

Inside, the heat was almost more than she could tolerate. Blinking the stinging sweat and smoke away as best as she could, she got hold of an extinguishing unit. She began to fight the fire, conscious all the time that she was vulnerable here, and not just because of the blaze and the possibility of the craft exploding completely. She was fairly sure she'd lost any potential pursuers from before, but the smoke from this wreck would attract attention very quickly. Had Kelvin been anyone else (except Carl, her lover) she wouldn't have even considered going in to get him. She needed Kelvin though to help keep her alive. Then she stopped, an idea coming to her. Kelvin wasn't the only thing that had a vested interest in her survival. She stopped using the extinguisher and carefully removed her glove. She reached into her flight jacket pocket and grasped the Obsenneth gemstone.

"I need help, I have to get to Kelvin," she said, in her mind. An orange glow suffused her skin, like an aura. The heat was gone, just gone.

"I can prevent the flames from harming you," Obsenneth assured her, "but I can only do this for a short time."

"Okay," she replied. "Let me know when my time is about to expire." She moved forward, literally walking through the flames. They moved around her, as if she was a substance they couldn't interact with and could only avoid. She hurried through the furnace, more confident now that she could see she was immune to the heat and the flames. She reached the control room which, astonishingly, was clear of the fire.

Kelvin was there. The big robot was inert. He was slumped forward over the controls, his appendages limp and the red lights that were his eyes were out. She rushed to get to him, and tried to see what was wrong. There was no obvious damage. Three hours ago he had been fully functional. His power core was supposed to last for four thousand years.

"Kelvin!" she shouted, pushing one of his arms. There were no external controls on him, there was nothing exposed that she could see either. What had happened to him? He was too heavy for her to lift. Again she appealed to Obsenneth for his help, but he wasn't capable of protecting her from the fire *and* moving Kelvin at the same time. When complete he would be able to, but alone his power was limited. Speaking of power, his was running out. There was one thing left that she could try.

Again, as the controls were down, she had to use the labour-intensive alternatives. There was a chance that she could detach the control room from the main body of the ship, using the emergency ejector system. She was already starting to feel the heat again as Obsenneth's power began to run out. She gritted her teeth as she struggled to pull the lever down. Using her own weight to help she leaned into it, her face going red with effort. With a crash the lever fell into position. There was a violent jolt as, against the odds, the charges fired and the rockets sent them flying up and ahead. Satiah, who wasn't strapped in, was bashed against the ceiling and then the floor, and cried out, clutching her shoulder. She struggled into the pilot's chair and, with hardly a second to spare, got the restraints on.

They hit the ground violently and everything fell silent. Satiah felt her own blood drip down the side of her face. The wound stung as sweat ran into it. She sat there, momentarily exhausted. A distant blasting noise signified the inevitable destruction of the rest of the ship - the fuel tanks, most likely. The sound roused her from her daze-like torpor and she stood unsteadily as the shockwave made the room shudder.

"Kelvin!" she said, kicking his metal leg hard. A voice in her ear startled her.

"Phantom Satiah, this is Phantom Gaulle, respond please," said the deep male voice.

"I'm here!" she called, preoccupied. "Home in on my signal."

"Will do, fair warnings?"

"I don't know, just imagine it's raining," she replied, warning him that there may be enemies present.

---

Eight days had passed since Operation Blacklight had been completed. And while Satiah had been… *away*… things had progressed. Politics had a reputation for being slow and unwieldy, yet this year had been very different. At the end of the Vourne Conspiracy, the current leader of the Coalition had been illegally placed there. Brenda Watt was the Commandment Benefactor, *the leader in other words*, of the whole Coalition. Her predecessor, Balan Orion, had been assassinated. No one really knew for sure *who* had killed him but there were many theories. Vourne had certainly planned to kill him, but there was some evidence that he didn't do it. In any case, according to *procedure*, the leader had to be elected following the democratic process. And so it was that an election was in progress…

––––––––♦♦♦♦♦♦––––––––

Satiah was in an elevator with Randal. It was rising fast as they headed for the visitors' area in Phantom Headquarters back on Earth. She'd been back less than an hour and, although she'd been successful, she'd barely got through unscathed. Apparently everything had gone as planned, though that was hardly her problem anymore.

She was having trouble concentrating on anything, mainly because she was worried about Kelvin. She couldn't get him to work and she didn't even know what was wrong. She'd operated without him before, it was nothing new, but she didn't like doing it. Randal was talking to her and she forced herself to focus on what he was saying rather than all the possible things that might be wrong with Kelvin.

"…serious matter. I mean, I know it's *always* a serious matter and I know that everyone always *says* it's serious, but it *is* serious…" he scowled, conscious of how badly he was explaining himself. "We need a scale of seriousness to enable me to work out *how* serious a serious thing is."

"We have, it's called the risk table," she murmured, so quietly he only just heard her.

"Are you okay?" he asked, turning to regard her properly.

"Aye," she mumbled, clearly not okay. She was remembering her last discussion with him *before* that assignment. The mission he had for her... and he thought she was going to *love*. Randal sighed. He knew Satiah about as well as a Phantom could know another Phantom. So, not well. He knew she had secrets, everyone had them. Normally she was a master at self-control so she must be under some considerable pressure to let her worry show. He sent her the mission file he had started for her.

"In this mission, you're going to find there are many things about it that other agents would kill for," he smiled, kindly. "For a start, you will only be working eight hours a day." That got her attention.

"What? *A standard shift?*" she asked, confused. Satiah couldn't remember being on a job where every waking hour wasn't crammed full of things to do or think about. The idea of only having to work for eight hours at a time seemed too good to be true. What was the catch?

"Just for the next six weeks or so and then you're done," he stated, tapping his communicator meaningfully. She took her communicator out and read the short mission data he'd just sent her.

## (CP) OPERATION SELECTOR (CP) REPORT: Dated at end. Designation (TS). Top Secret. Status Active. Satiah reports...

CP was a mission type that stood for *corrective politics*. Those were rare; indeed, she could only remember doing one of those in thirty years. Operation Raven. The objectives of that mission had been: one, to replace a political party leader with another specifically chosen, and two, to ensure that no rival could remove him. It had been challenging, and not in the typical way. She didn't have to climb mountains, dodge lasers, seduce the unwary or wrestle with carnivorous plants - it had been all about putting pressure on individuals. Gradually bribing, intimidating or, in one case, murdering the potential enemies. It had been long too, taking nearly nine months.

This task, from what she could already tell about it, would be short lived. Six weeks. The election would be over in almost exactly that duration. The timeframe told her that, *whatever Randal wanted her to do*, it had something to do with the election. They left the lift and Satiah realised that someone else would be briefing her on this mission too.

"Are you trying to tell me that when my shift is over, *that's it*? I can sleep, I can… do whatever I want?" she queried, distrustfully.

"Well, there *is* something else of course but, once you have taken care of that, then yes. *The time will be yours*," Randal nodded.

Her mind was racing. She'd have time to fix Kelvin properly, she could… she could get *Carl* to visit her. She bit her lower lip gently as she thought about that. It was risky, bringing him so close to her while she was working. But with Kelvin non-functional, it would make sleeping easier with Carl around… *or maybe not*. Randal was watching her again, wondering what she was thinking. Her expression gave nothing away as she reasserted the cold chill of dispassion over herself.

"I'll believe it when I see it," she grumbled, still not sure what to believe. She didn't want him to get the idea that she thought she owed him anything. Randal laughed, genuinely amused by her reaction.

"It must sound like it's too good to be true," he allowed, reasonably. "Then again…" He thought about it. "Depending on how it goes, you might end up hating it. *Having nothing to do for all that time?*"

She faced him, deliberately not answering his question in a very definite way. They entered a windowless room, only just large enough for the screen, table and group of four chairs that occupied it. He gestured for her to sit furthest in, so that she could watch the door. Field agents always appreciated being in that position. It made them more at ease when they could watch who came and went. That, and it also meant no one could sneak up behind them. Randal, an ex-field agent himself, knew exactly how she felt. He casually sat opposite her and switched the monitor on. It was a blank screen but Randal suspected they would need it later. For several seconds they just sat there, staring at one another.

"Did you see the test results for the new DD41?" he asked, making conversation.

"No, but someone was telling me about it. Wasn't there a problem with the operating systems? Something about them not being able to sense one another in all conditions?" she replied, mirroring his tone with an added modicum of mockery. He smiled, knowing what she was doing. She'd never been into polite conversation. She was a being of action, not civility. Even among her own kind, people like him, she maintained a guarded detachment.

"Would you prefer that I just shut up?" he asked, casually.

Before she could answer with something stereotypically witty, the door opened and they both stood, partly from reflex and partly out of politeness. A tall, handsome man entered, dressed in office clothes. He was carrying several files and a data cube.

"Sorry I'm late. I'm Scott Snell," he said, by way of a brisk introduction. They shook hands rapidly and Scott sat down, flicking open a file.

"*Operation Selector*," he mumbled, as he read. Randal and Satiah exchanged meaningful glances before sitting back down again. Randal knew what Snell was about to say would upset Satiah. He didn't like it either.

"Scott Snell works for the PAI as a *political analyst*," Randal said, eyeing Satiah. Satiah instantly felt a stab of loathing towards the man. Political analysts, or *string-pullers* as they were informally known, were high on the list of people who annoyed Satiah. It was worth noting that *they*, as in *the political analysts*, did not like that epithet at all. They annoyed Satiah because of the ability they had when it came to manipulating governments. They bothered her almost as much as journalists. They were the main creators of propaganda. The inventors of misinformation, made to deceive everyone, *even the people on their own side.* She recognised that while this was sometimes necessary, they nearly always misused *and* overused it. Because of political analysts and journalists, it was impossible for anyone to know truth from fiction. Even the people that *had* to know... *people like her.*

This guy particularly riled her though because he also worked for the PAI. The PAI, or Primary Agency of Investigation, was a sister security agency operating for the Coalition. A much more domineering, pushy kind of older sister who insisted that they were in charge and that everyone did what they told them to do. Well, that was two reasons to dislike this man. Terrible origin, awful profession and… was he picking his nose? Satiah was a bit snobbish, some would say *very* snobbish, but she couldn't understand why anyone would do *that* in company unless they were *trying* to offend other people.

"You're *late*?" she questioned, rudely. Scott looked up. Wasn't time in some way equivalent to money? Isn't that how the formula went? Or was it that most people never made any money while waiting?

"Yes, sorry about that, I was held up," he remarked, noting her apparent dislike of him instantly. He gave her a one-cornered smile, almost a sneer. "So… *you're* Phantom *Satiah*, I've heard so much about you…" Randal rolled his eyes, wishing that Scott would just say what he had to say and get out.

"*Really*?" Satiah growled, leaning forward almost aggressively. "And *who* did you hear it from?"

"*Maybe* we should get started," Randal stepped in quickly. "Crammed schedules and all that." Satiah continued to glare at Scott while he leered back at her. Finally Scott looked away.

"Right, let's do that. What's your view on the election, Satiah?" he asked, directly.

"Brenda is the discernible favourite; she has the majority in pretty much everything. The only problem is that she wasn't elected. She was placed there *because of a coup*," Satiah explained. She was tempted to tell him that she thought it was a waste of time - *the election*, not the coup. It was a waste of time as Brenda was obviously going to win, so going through the motions of an election was pointless. She didn't say that though. "Because *that much* is public knowledge, there will always be those who wish to replace her with a leader that they *did* elect." Or that they *think* they have elected… paradoxically, she seemed to recall that Balan had been concerned about Brenda's popularity too, or so Vourne had said. Balan had never had Brenda's popularity and, *to Satiah's knowledge*, neither had anyone else for a long while.

"Yes," Scott agreed. "And *we, as in the government*, feel that her removal from power now would be… *ill-timed*."

"Her main rival is a man called *Oli McAllister*, computers predict that he has a twenty eight percent chance of replacing her," Randal stated, quickly. "That's a full *eight percent* over the acceptable margin according to the statistics."

"*Wow*," Satiah growled, sarcastically. "*That high, huh?* Why not go the whole hog and round it up from eight to ten making it an even thirty? That's an extra two percent: more scary. That sounds *even more* terrifying." She scowled. "Doesn't sound like much of a threat to me."

"Agreed but, we can't take any chances where *democracy* is concerned," Scott laughed, cynically. She smiled back but not in a nice way.

"And you want me to kill him?" she asked, thinking she could see where this was going.

"No," Randal said, seriously.

"*Of course not*," Scott replied, in mock outrage. "We *must* uphold the illusions of autonomy and egalitarianism. Without them we wouldn't be able to *control* anyone. There would be anarchy, you see. Beings need to believe they have the power and the right to change things and protect themselves. Beings need to think that they can influence the government. Let's be honest… no self-respecting government can afford to let *that* become a reality. Not if they want to be in control. If *you* simply killed the problem, you might shatter the pretence. People would say: *isn't it funny how when things don't go their way, accidents happen until they do go their way?* We would risk losing control." Satiah shrugged. She could see where he was coming from, and this was why she felt the election was a waste of time. The outcome had been decided already, regardless of how the vote went. Regardless of what the citizens wanted.

She actually assumed that even *the next election* had already been decided. He was right in that the myth of democracy needed to exist to prevent a collapse into chaos but… a part of her *liked* chaos. She flourished in it as it made hiding easy… she didn't like order. She detested conformity, unless, of course, it was *her* order or *her* conformity. A double standard maybe but she didn't care. And if the public were *leading themselves* they would only make a mess of things. There were too many sheep, and the few leaders there were could not be trusted to toe the line. Couldn't be trusted to keep their interests aligned on the designated path. Designated by whom? Did that matter? She'd made one grab for power already and it had failed... she'd been fortunate to escape alive. Luckier still to get away anonymously. No one knew what she'd done. No one knew what she was *really* capable of.

"Why not simply *rig the vote*? Isn't that what you normally do?" she questioned candidly.

"It is, *but* the independent enquiry that we set up in order to *prove* that no rigging was taking place was... *infiltrated*," Scott said, looking harassed. While Randal did his best to disguise his smile; Satiah didn't even try to hide her glee.

"*By who*?" Satiah sniggered, amused.

"*It doesn't matter*!" he said, dismissively. The PAI making mistakes *as usual*, she thought. "The public are generally going the way we want them to. Oli is the only one that *could*, according to the computer, cause a problem. If not now, then somewhere down the line perhaps." Better hope that the computer itself isn't up to anything, she thought to herself.

She shrugged again.

"I reiterate, why not just kill him? I'm sure a *terminal illness* or some kind of *natural death* could be more palatable than an assassination..." she began, casually. Randal and Scott were shaking their heads. No, no, that would be *way* too simple *for us*! Why agree to that when we can make *your job so much harder*? Satiah wanted to kick something.

"Brenda is the one we want as Commandment Benefactor. She's agreed to *all our funding requirements* for the next *decade*. No budget trimming, no downsizing and *no more* spending reviews. She's malleable, shockingly idealistic and she has *such* an honest face and trusting nature. She's even popular with the public! We don't want to lose *her* or her popularity. If her rivals start *dying*, people will naturally assume that *she* is orchestrating their deaths," Scott stated, determinedly. Satiah rolled her eyes, starting to lose patience.

"So if you don't want *me* to kill Oli and *you* won't just rig the vote... *what are we doing here*?" Satiah asked, coldly.

"You will infiltrate his movement, as an elite trained security guard, recommended by the government. You will gain his confidence and then... it's up to *you*. You could get him *discredited, persuade* him to give up or... *ruin* his election campaign from within, somehow," Randal specified. "Make certain he does not win but *keep him alive.*" She leaned back in her chair and crossed her arms, thinking about it. So, *no one* would suspect a guard *provided by the government*? And there was *no way* he was going to win, regardless of what she did! Then again, this job *was equal to* six weeks of her doing very little indeed. And *so what* if they suspected she was more than she seemed? They could prove nothing! Then she remembered how she struggled to remain inactive. She would get restless...

"A sex scandal, perhaps," Scott suggested, leering across at her again. "*Very sensational.* The CNC would love it." Her eyes narrowed as she regarded him full on, rather like an angry panther gradually losing patience with a badly behaved rat.

"*Corruption* is always a good one," Randal said, eyeing Scott irritably. Randal was genuinely concerned that if Scott continued to behave like that towards Satiah, she might just kill him - and he wouldn't blame her for it. "Expenses, tax fraud, even some kind of security risk. Possibly a dangerous but unconfirmed connection with the *Federation*. That would be enough for most of his supporters to turn against him."

"Whatever you do, I'm sure that the media can be counted on to pile in with a suitably destructive spin, of course," Scott smiled, pleasantly. "You know the kind of thing. *CB candidate seen with Federation delegate in secret meeting.* It should be easy for someone of your calibre to kick it off."

This was the most awful mission ever! Yet in some respects it was a perfect mission, with all that free time and a high chance of success... and relatively small danger levels. *Keep him alive*? Interesting. She'd already established that *she* was not allowed to kill him, but...

"Is he in danger from someone?" she asked, perceptively. Scott and Randal exchanged a look. "*Apart from* you two, I mean." Scott pulled a face.

"Only about as much as any politician is. We know he has *rivals* and, well... *anything is possible*," Scott admitted.

"Have there been... *threats*?" Satiah asked, as anyone would.

"No, not direct ones," Randal told her.

"Clearly you think he's *in danger* as well as *being a danger*," she stated, wondering why they were dancing around the point so awkwardly.

"It's *unconfirmed*," Randal stated and Scott glared at him. Randal eyed the other man icily. "I'm *not* sending her in blind."

"*Lovely*," Satiah smiled, tightly. "I thought it might be like that."

"We have reason to believe *someone* is working against him… within his own circles," Randal said.

"So you want me to make him fail while also stopping someone else who wants the same thing?" she smirked, keeping her anger carefully under control.

"We don't know who they are or *how they intend* to bring him down," Scott said, seriously. "He cannot *die,* for the sake of our democracy." O the irony…

"No, no, I get it," she said, nodding sourly. She was starting to feel rather gloomy. She tolerated the fact that democracy didn't exist, couldn't ever truly exist, she even used it to her advantage, but she didn't like the idea of taking part in the performance.

"I'll handle it from the CNC side," Scott went on. The CNC, Current News Corporation, was the press. "I can do the usual spiel about constantly redefining what unemployment means as a term. Leaking higher figures so that when the real figures come out they are easier to stomach. And we're doing all we can through negative portrayal to demonise Oli, but his followers are unexpectedly hard to sway. Bottom line: *we need you to bring him down.*"

"Maybe his followers have brains and disregard the news as the distorted hoopla it is *on principle*," Satiah remarked. Scott scowled at her. Randal laughed quietly.

"Can I leave the rest to you?" Scott asked, to Randal. He nodded. Scott departed, leaving the data cube and files behind.

"You know what they call him, behind his back?" Randal asked, his eyes gleaming. She grinned.

"I'd love to," she replied, mischievously.

"Slimy Snell," he told her. She nodded slowly, thinking how appropriate that was. "*You did not hear that from me.*"

"How *fitting*," she smiled, heavily accentuating the *f* in fitting. Her tone was one of disdain. "Can I hurt him?"

"No," chuckled Randal, half inclined to say the opposite.

"Please, I'll do it *quietly*," she giggled, not being serious. No, she'd want that one to scream.

"Now… before we go into discussing Oli in more detail… are you *sure* you want to take this mission?" he asked, straight faced again. Again she hesitated. All that free time was a massive temptation to her and it wasn't like this assignment was anywhere near as dangerous as many she'd done before. Kelvin needed to be fixed and, if Carl was free, it would be perfect. On the other hand, she didn't think it was needed. That computer was massively overestimating the danger Oli presented. It had to be. The *Cult of Deimos* were a real threat that needed to be countered, not *this* upstart. And she hated being involved in politics, as she regarded politicians as one of the worst kinds of people. And she included *herself, a ruthless killer,* in that judgement too. At least when *she* did things, she did them *herself,* often at great personal risk. They just gave the orders for other people to take all the risks. And doing *anything* for *Slimy Snell* did not exactly leave her overwhelmed with joy and fulfilment.

"Do *you* know who infiltrated the PAI's sham of an enquiry into vote rigging?" she asked, suspiciously. He motioned to himself as if clarifying that it was himself that she was addressing. She raised a coy eyebrow.

"Everyone has their own idea about it," he answered, cryptically. "Division Sixteen could be behind it." Ah yes, the infamous Division Sixteen: the newcomer on the pitch of Coalition security agencies. Saying *that,* it was one that had managed to entrench itself strongly in a large number of affairs. She'd worked with them before and, unlike the PAI, Division Sixteen brought a much more cooperative attitude to the table. The PAI, Phantom Squad and Division Sixteen all worked for the Coalition, though sometimes it *really* did not seem that way. Just recently Satiah had killed a PAI agent as, due to the circumstances at the time, they hadn't realised they were on the same side. In *this case,* conversely, she didn't buy what Randal was suggesting.

"So it wasn't *us* then?" she quipped, darkly.

"Always *so suspicious*," he condemned, impishly. She gave her trademark low chuckle to that. "So you'll do it?"

"...Why not?" she smiled, obligingly. "As you say, many agents would kill for a job like this. Minimal risk, fewer hours and a relatively easy task. Obviously the fact that someone else on the inside is trying to bring him down too complicates it a little but... *nevertheless...*"

"Great, because I was not looking forward to *another* briefing with Slimy Snell," Randal smirked. "His behaviour was unacceptable in my book. I hated it when he looked at you like that and I'm sorry."

"I've had worse looks," she smiled, letting it go. "*I'm not exactly known for being oversensitive.* Anyway, the dance has now started, who knows what will happen to him by the end?" Randal raised his eyebrows a bit but didn't comment on that.

A picture of Oli appeared on the monitor. He was a slim man of average height. Her brown eyes studied him quickly, instinctively looking at him as she would a target in a shooting gallery. Oli's eyes were blue and his face bland. By that she meant that just by looking at him, there was nothing there to make him particularly unique in any way. Nothing to say, this is who I am or what I do. He was wearing a custom made suit, again, nothing that stood out about that.

"*No past secrets*," Randal began, knowing that would be the first thing Satiah would go for. "Nothing you can use there." She scanned through the file, noting age, status and planet of origin.

"He's *single* so a sex scandal could be a bit tricky," she mused. Randal rolled his eyes. "Unless you had him hook up with Neo-Remnantists, there's nothing that can be done that would alienate him enough. Unless, of course, you could prove that his partner, whoever he or she is, is a Federation spy."

"It's all starting to sound rather implausible," Randal granted, laughing.

"How do you *know* someone on the inside is working against him?" she enquired, pointedly. "Or is that more of Slimy Snell's intel?"

"We intercepted a *suspect* message. *Nothing solid*. We can't tell for sure but it looked like someone was trying to strike at him in some way."

But Randal didn't know who had sent it... *interesting*. That implied someone was clever enough to stay hidden. Granted, it was only *now* that they were getting serious, but still....

"Does Oli have a double?" she asked, next. Most prominent politicians usually had one. *Some* had several.

"Not yet, as far as we know."

She continued to read for a few minutes in silence while he uncomplainingly waited.

"He's done well to get as far as he has," she noted, more to herself than to Randal. From the start, a *typical* election would take four years. First, Constitutional Elections would take place on all the planets within the Coalition. There were seventy seven million planetary *zones* within the Coalition, each zone averaging around one hundred thousand *individual worlds*. When the constitutional leg was over, it moved on to the Planetary Selection Process followed by the Zonal Ballot. The zones made up seven thousand six hundred and twenty two *Quadrants*. The penultimate stage of the Election was the Quadrant Selection Process. This would determine those candidates that would run *directly* for the Commandment Benefactor's office in the final stage. When that was over it came to the *final stage*: the *Benefactorial Campaign*.

They were just starting the final stage *now*. The last six weeks of mayhem.

Because of the outcome of the Vourne Conspiracy, however, this was *not* a typical election. It had been rushed. Campaigns normally months long had been condensed to days and, in one case, mere hours. So, six weeks to go before the result was in. It was down to one hundred and nine candidates. Brenda Watt was one of those and so was Oli McAllister. She, *the evident favourite Brenda*, had a proportional representation at fifty one percent already and it was said that once you reached *fifty* you could not lose, leaving two eventualities aside: *arrest or death*. Oli had seventeen percent, which wasn't a bad second place considering that there were one hundred and seven others still running. She could understand *why* the computer had flagged him as a threat because *statistically* he was the only other thing above about six percent.

Being thorough, she read through the list of names of those others still running. One instantly jumped out at her: Sam *McAllister*. Her brown eyes rose to face Randal again.

"*Sam?*" she questioned, tilting her head to the side.

"His brother," Randal nodded, confirming her suspicion. She raised her eyebrows. "*I know*," Randal concurred. "It is rare to have two candidates from the same world make it this far in the election. It's *unimaginable* that they should be biologically related."

"*Unimaginable but apparently not impossible. That's* a statistic I wouldn't mind the computer worrying about," she muttered, returning her attention to the screen in front of them. Randal chuckled.

Sam had a representation of naught point three.

"I'm thinking *jealousy*, leaving aside any potential family feuds," Satiah reasoned. "If they're both from the same world it's *likely* that they have mutual friends working on each other's campaigns... *what better opportunity?*" Randal nodded more fervently. It was known that the brothers were not on speaking terms.

"*Exactly* what I was thinking," he stated, seriously. This was partly why he felt Satiah was one of the best Phantoms alive. She was logical, methodical and meticulous in *everything she did*. She wasn't done yet though.

"This guy here... six percent representation, *third place*. He would have good reason to clobber Oli," she went on. She brought up the file. "Brenda's security would be too strong so Oli's an easy target."

Mark. Unlike the others mentioned so far... this was *not* his first election. He'd been in three others. He'd never come close to winning but he enjoyed a solid following and six percent was his highest ever achievement. He could be running out of patience.

"It's never a good feeling to be so vastly outdone by the new kid on the block, is it?" Satiah murmured, going deeper into his record. Randal grinned, enjoying being able to listen in to her analysis. She moved both Mark and Sam onto a list she had started. She took one last look at the candidate list before returning to Oli's information.

Kate was listed as his Public Relations Team Leader. Satiah went into her background too. Kate's name was added to her list. Then there was Malla, Oli's Chief of Security. Again, he went on her list. Then she went into administrative staff, cleaners… *anyone* that would be *there* or *could be near*. She silently read the intercepted message that had sparked off the whole thing.

**I won't rest until this is over. I won't let him get away with this. Oli cannot win the election, he must be stopped. I will use any means at my disposal to achieve this. I will avenge you, my angel.**

Well, it would be hard to explain that away as a joke, Randal had been right to be concerned. Satiah was getting interested as the many possibilities gathered in her mind. She would sleep well that night. Remembering that Randal was still there, she deactivated and took the data cube.

"I start tomorrow?" she asked, casually. He nodded. She moved for the door but he didn't follow and she paused, recalling that earlier that he had said *there was more*.

"I'm sorry to do this to you but you will have *plenty* of free time," Randal began, producing another data cube. Instead of blue, this one was red and she knew exactly what it was. She pulled an unwilling face.

"Oh no, *please, no*, I don't want to do a review *as well!*" she protested.

"This is sitting on my desk, if you remove it I will *remember that favour*," Randal stated, waving it under her nose. She sighed, taking it from him slowly.

"What is it?" she asked, inquisitively.

"An exploding reactor," he told her. "I need you to review the enquiry, as a dispassionate juror would, and determine who or what was to blame. It's all on there." Satiah thought she knew what reactor he was talking about; she'd seen a report about it on the news. As explosions went it had been bad. Thousands had been killed and radiation had contaminated a large area.

"Who else is reviewing it?" she asked.

"No idea, the usual *eight* I suspect," he shrugged, as if it didn't matter. She supposed it didn't really. She'd managed to get out of doing one for years so she imagined it was about time she got lumbered with another one. And, if Randal needed a favour…

"Fine, you owe me," she stated, in a bleak tone. He smiled.

"As does the average citizen," he joked.

"I'm not sure they'd see it that way, what with this *conspiracy* I've just pledged to support," she remarked, amused.

"*This is not a conspiracy*," he stated, feigning horror. "It's maintaining the *security* of the Coalition."

"Yes, they'd not see it like *that* either," she stated, grinning.

"Look at it this way: it's *ten years* of job security for you," he replied, knowing what she would say next.

"A Phantom has no such thing as job security," she reminded him, grimly. Then she smiled and rested her hand on the handle of her pistol. "I make do with this." He grinned in a comradely way.

---

The Vourne Conspiracy, *as far as the public knew*, went something along *these lines*. Balan Orion was the Commandment Benefactor of the *Human Coalition*. It was renamed briefly 'Human' Coalition after being known as the Earth Empire before that. It was one of the many steps Balan took to reshape society during his three year reign. He had not been in power long; indeed, to some, it seemed a bit of a mystery as to how he'd acquired the office in the first place. There was widespread belief that the vote had been rigged to ensure he won. Nevertheless, nothing could be proved, and he became the Commandment Benefactor. That was when the Pluto Major controversy had started.

Pluto Major was a planet right on the boundary between the Colonial Federation and the Coalition. It had been a part of the Earth Empire, yet had taken steps to leave and join the Federation because of the changes Balan was implementing. The people began to hold demonstrations to get the leadership of the world to legislate a withdrawal strategy. The army moved in to reduce the level of violence. In order to 'ease tensions' Balan had ordered Commander Bev Spencer to supervise the military. Meanwhile, the Federation, who had been watching what was going on, began making noises about suppression. Spencer had clamped down hard and had begun a few ethnic cleansing programs in order to remove those who opposed the will of the Coalition from the general population, the relics of which were still there for all to see.

Whether Balan had ordered her to do these things, or she had done of them off her own back, remained a mystery. Things had gone from bad to worse when Brenda Watt, a delegate running in the election against Balan, had visited the world in an effort to resolve the situation. She, unlike Balan, used diplomacy instead of force. She met with the Federation party and the leadership of the world. Then it went quiet for a few days. Suddenly, out of nowhere, assassins struck and Balan was murdered. Apparently there was footage taken of the killing and the fight afterwards. Allegedly, the guards had been inexplicably absent at the time. Most unbelievable of all was what happened next. Spencer returned to Earth, out of choice or not was unknown. It was at about this time when, lying in state, Balan's body was pilfered by persons unknown for reasons unknown.

There was a meeting held in the Mulac Building. The Mulac Building was a large, triangular structure, mainly used for conferences whilst doubling as the Site B for governmental congressional activities, until a few months ago when, during the aforementioned meeting, it had been the site of an explosion. Possibly more than one blast, as people watching from nearby said it sounded like a war had started inside. Craft flew by and shots were fired. Several people were killed but then silence clamped down on the place. No one knew what had really happened in there... or if they *did* they weren't saying. The repair work was ongoing. The exterior was largely restored, but the interior was purportedly gutted from fire and blast damage.

It was public knowledge that the only leader, of the whole of Balan's inner circle, to survive this fight was Phantom Leader Vourne. Commanders Spencer and Grey were dead. Brenda Watt, who may or may not have been present at this meeting too, emerged as the new Commandment Benefactor. Vourne was hunted down and apparently committed suicide before other Phantom agents could apprehend him. His suicide note attracted additional donnybrook due to the suggested notion that the note was not in his handwriting. Since then Pluto Major was released, the army withdrawn, and it joined the Federation. Indeed, it had been what happened on Pluto Major which had aided Ro Tammer's rise within the Federation at about the same time.

So… Brenda Watt was now the new leader of the Coalition. Her first act was to drop the *human* part of the title as a way of demonstrating she was moving in a different direction to Balan Orion. Nevertheless, as always when an administration changes, a period of instability occurred - it was a time when people did a lot of moving around. That was when the arrests, releases and trials began. Everyone knew it was happening, they just had no details. There was no one to interview and no one was talking. Yet each day more people were implicated in the plot against either Balan himself, or Brenda. Basically, it seemed to the public that everyone who was implicated was either dead, incarcerated or missing… never a good sign. It implied institutional murder and all manner of other grievous misconduct.

Above anything else, it meant that learning exactly what had happened was likely impossible. Since the beginning, this scandal had been gaining momentum throughout the Coalition. While lacking the straightforwardness of the Ro Tammer trial, it added fuel to the fire simply because it was so difficult to understand who was who. All the secret services were involved. It had been the birthplace of Division Sixteen from the ashes of the Gushtapar. The Gushtapar had been a private army of Commander Spencer's made up of veterans and fanatics. When whatever happened, happened… those who remained loyal to whoever was in charge now were formed into Division Sixteen.

Pretty much everyone agreed: the Vourne Conspiracy had been kicked off by the event of Balan Orion's murder. His body was still missing which didn't help either. The body of his receptionist had been recovered but the laser gun wounds were of no assistance whatsoever. The Vourne Conspiracy had earned its name as *Vourne* was the last leading member of said controversy to live. There were rumours of immortal involvement, with *Dreda's* name being bandied around. The media speculated endlessly, as did those who relished a good scandal or conspiracy. Yet not much real information was around and mostly everything was being done *behind closed doors*. This wasn't helping the public's scepticism.

And then there was the darker side to all this… the idea that the people who might have been involved were still out there. This election was taking place as a direct result of the conspiracy. A supreme event. Could they trust the current leadership after everything that had happened? What was real, what wasn't, and how could you know? An election had already been in progress when Balan was alive and Brenda had been his most popular rival in that election but, due to his death and the apparent chaos, it had been suspended indefinitely. Brenda, to her credit, had immediately held a referendum: continue with the current election *or* begin another. The public had chosen to begin another and she was, in effect, to run for her own office despite it never *legally* being hers in the first place. Brenda was said to be agreeable to this personally.

All of that was a combination of the official version of what happened and how the public saw it. What had really happened, however, might never be known…

---

Oli McAllister read through his speech a third time. He'd assigned most of it to memory now. Even after all this time, he *still* felt nervous in front of the crowds, whether they were friendly to him or otherwise. He had to believe in himself! That's what everyone kept telling him, anyway. If you didn't believe in yourself, who else would? He was a tall man, well dressed, and had a youthful energy about him. He had that shade of hair that made it hard to work out if it was golden or brown. In the light it was golden; in the dark it looked brown. Under the surface though, this was a man in conflict. His beliefs and his wisdom often clashed in his mind. His mother had once told him that he was a carbon copy of his father.

He believed that everyone should be equal and yet he knew that the hardest workers deserved the highest rewards. He felt that everyone should be given the benefit of the doubt, though he had trouble trusting people he didn't know well. He wanted everyone to be happy but he knew that without sadness, happiness would lose all meaning. He felt that he understood the problems of the Coalition and that he could solve them. He still clung onto self-doubt though, the idea that the power might corrupt him. In trying to repair the damage, not only might he himself become damaged, he might add to it if he was wrong.

Since he was young, he'd learned that he had a knack for solving problems. He was from a well-off family but that could not be said of everyone on his planet. One day, when he'd been a boy, he'd been at home when he'd heard someone crying. It was coming from the heat of the outside. The air shimmered but he never felt it in the air-conditioned bubble that he called home. Yet the sound of someone's misery moved him enough to investigate. He'd gone outside and encountered a young girl, sitting on the pathway. There was a spilt carton in front of her. She was about five and her name was Sally. She'd been sent to get supplies for her mother as her brother was very ill. She'd been in such a rush to get it back that she'd fallen over and accidentally dropped it.

She was horrified by what she had done and plunged into the kind of deep despair that only a child can truly understand. As if the whole world would end and it was *all your fault.* In a habitual act of generosity, he insisted she come into his house out of the heat and gave her some water to drink. While she was drinking that he had set his young mind to try to find a solution. Sally's brother was dying and her mother needed these supplies to save him. Sally had been running so presumably they were needed urgently. He had asked Sally exactly what had been in the bag. She had told him. He had gone into the food store and searched for these items which he knew they had in abundance. The androids always kept it well stocked and organised.

While he didn't have everything she needed by name; he had things he knew were essentially the same thing, similar products. As her need was dire, he packed a case with twice the amount she had originally had and handed it to her. That metal case would not break open if she fell again.

"Take these," he remembered saying to her. "Your mother will know what to do with them." Hope and uncertainty battling within her, she hurried away, promising to repay him in some way. For a while he had wondered. He'd imagined the alternatives playing out. Too late, just in time and the contrasting aftermaths. Failure, grief and death against relief, happiness and life.

It had been the next day when any clue came as to what had actually happened. A tiny capsule of sweets and… a love letter. The letter he still had now. At that time he'd never realised the significance of it but it did explain that all was well in Sally's world. All was well *because* of his help. She'd sent him the sweets because she had nothing else to send, and even though they were her favourites she felt that he had earned them. He had solved a problem and he had made a difference. While this example was hardly the most monumental of achievements he'd ever managed, it was the one he drew on most when he needed strength or reassurance. It had an innocent, uncomplicated charm about it. A simplicity that adult life seemed to be devoid of.

See, the thing was, that girl Sally had one day become his first love. His acts of spontaneous generosity, while not always so easy or as simple as he felt they should be, *mostly* rewarded him. Yet it led him into self-doubt once again when he began to wonder if the praise and rewards he received for his generosity were leading him down the wrong path, the path of only doing things for what you got out of them. He felt sure that *right there* lay the event where power corrupted you. When generosity was no long the motive, it was greed. And no longer was happiness of others the goal, wealth took its place. This, he felt, was why even the best, most wonderful people failed when it came to wielding power. They might start well but it would corrupt them. It would change the way they valued everything. And he secretly feared that it would do the same to him.

When Sally had died in an accident many years later, he'd seen it as a sign that he had lost his way. That he'd not loved her enough. That he'd forgotten how to be humble and that he was aiming too high. Getting so preoccupied with where he was going that he'd forgotten where he was. He'd vowed never to forget that again. He was just a man, trying to do his best, just like everyone else. All of that was why he was now trying to win the election to prevent Brenda from illegally taking what wasn't hers. To prevent an injustice.

"Now *try* not to let them rattle you this time," Kate reminded, levelly. She was talking to him about his speech. Trying to prepare him as best as she knew how. Kate, a spritely woman of nearly one hundred and seventy, had known him since he was a baby. She'd even taught him how to cook. She was only small but she had the willpower of a giant, and she had a gift for encouraging others. She was, however, prone to missing obstacles.

"Unemployment can *easily be resolved* by bi-managerial collateral strategy implementation." She blinked as if suddenly unsure if he was listening or not. "Say it!" Oli repeated what she had said and she nodded in approval.

"You must have *conviction, you* have to believe it, Oli," she told him. "It's all about image! You have to project strength and conviction. People will listen to you and trust you more readily."

"And if they ask me to *explain*?" he asked, a little irritated. She was doing her best but he had a sneaking suspicion that she didn't actually know what she was talking about. *The same suspicion* the last crowd he'd addressed had had of *him*. He didn't see the irony in that *he was the politician* asking *her* to explain to him what *he* was supposed to be talking about.

"Explain what?" she demanded, in exasperation.

"Bi-managerial collateral strategy," he stated, coolly.

"*Oh, pull yourself together Oli*! If you can't get your head around *that* you don't even deserve the right to vote!" she retorted, dismissively. "Put some effort in, put some effort in!" He sighed, waiting for the bluster to end.

"If a manager moves down two notches in command, takes a wage cut and trains their replacement… it creates two new positions for beings to be recruited into. Once recruited, these two do the same as the manager, multiplying the positions ready for others to move into. Then, once a viable workforce has been collected, they all switch around so that the managers end up where they were originally, *and* they have enough people to do the work," she explained, almost losing her way as she spoke. He looked at her dumbly. And what kind of manager would *willingly* take a pay cut to train his own replacement? She waved a small hand in the air as if swatting at an invisible insect.

"Or something like that, anyway! It's *new-age-modern-business-optimisation*."

He didn't repeat the question though in case she tried to explain it again.

"Maybe we should just stick with Brenda's illegal rise to power," he stated, sighing heavily again.

"I've told you before, *that's too negative*. People see it as a personal attack on her, not a reminder that she shouldn't be there," Kate insisted. "Look, just keep doing what you're doing."

"That will not win this election," he stated, intensely. Kate closed her eyes and remained silent for just a moment too long, and that was when he realised she'd given up hope of that.

"She's got *fifty percent* Oli," she uttered, quietly.

"She shouldn't even *be there*! You *know* she shouldn't be there...!" he began, building into a rant.

"It's what the people want!" she yelled over him. "And by *people* I do not mean the public... *I mean the government.*"

"We have six weeks to change their minds," he reminded, optimistically. "Once they understand where we're coming from they will come around to our way of thinking, I know they will."

"It's dangerous, Oli," she stated, worried. "You *know* it's dangerous." Had she heard something or was it simply labrish? Chatter was ubiquitous after all, and no matter *what* anyone says, they usually take at least some of it to heart.

"If they were going to get rid of me they'd have done it already," he smiled, not quite as sure as he sounded.

"Just... I know *you* don't believe what we were talking about the other night but... I'm scared, okay? I never expected we would get this far... I don't know, maybe *I'm* the one who needs to work on their nerves," she said, emotionally. "It's just all that Vourne conspiracy stuff, you know? It's got me rattled. Makes me wonder what they will do next... and what they've already done."

"*No one really knows what happened...*" he dismissed, trying to be encouraging.

"*Something* destroyed the Mulac Building and it wasn't too many cakes, was it?" she stated. They laughed.

"I'm not naive enough to assume they don't hide things. That's one of the many things I plan to stop," he insisted. "With the help of the public, of course."

"It's a dream," she sighed, with a weak smile. Her wrinkled face was invigorated somewhat by the wistful gleam in her green eyes. He'd had that ability since he was a child too: he could make people dream. "A good dream, a noble one, but still a dream."

"Remember what Sally used to say?" he reminded, softly. "Today's dreams are tomorrow's reality. And if you become lost, think of yesterday's nightmare to tell you what not to do today."

"I loved her a lot *dear Sal*, you *know* I did, but she didn't half talk a lot of bollocks, Mr McAllister." They laughed.

---

"So, Commandment Benefactor, can you shed any light on the sudden end of the Vinu-Shintu war?" Deetee asked, with a perfect, media friendly, smile. "Let's just say, a few eyes and visual implants widened when you solved that one." Deetee was a professional journalist. With a quiff of thick golden hair that had earned him the nickname Blondie, and bright blue eyes, he was as photogenic as he was amoral. His bosses at the CNC prized him and what he could do. He was ruthless, uncompromising and didn't let *anything*, specifically the truth, get in the way of a good story. He'd been given the task of interviewing the Commandment Benefactor during the Benefactorial election, one of the most prestigious responsibilities.

Brenda had a bad case of stage fright and sat there on the couch tensely. She was ashamed that she'd only ever *heard of* the war shortly after it had ended. She was just so very busy and had to trust her people to tell her what to do and say. She just had to *remember* what she was supposed to say. She was a poor actress but her blushes and mild stutters only seemed to make her more endearing to the public, or so her aides and administrators informed her, and they kept telling her that she was generally liked. She only had to *learn the script*. She was quite pretty in an intellectual sort of way and despite her strong ideological beliefs in equality, democracy and helping people, she felt a little overawed. She smiled nervously and pushed her shoulder length mousy brown hair behind her ears.

"I really think we should um… leave that to the um… the people *themselves* to resolve. A-after all, once they finally started talking properly i-i-i-it was surprising how little work I actually had to do," she said, stammering slightly. She saw a young Manthor, a lizard from the planet of the same name, thump his tail in support and give her a *thumbs up* sign in her peripheral vision. She was starting to warm up and get more confident now she'd had her breakfast. Deetee never stopped smiling, it was quite unnerving, like his face was just stuck that way… like a mask. Someone's communicator went off in the background and she had to fight to remain seated and not dash off to answer it. Please someone, answer it! *Please*! It was so distracting, it might be important…

"As you know we've been following this election since the beginning," Deetee went on. "Some people say it is a bit of a waste of time! How would you react to that point of view?" Her face flushed red, mildly horrified that anyone could possibly think the democratic process a waste of time.

"I would not be very good at this job if I ignored what the people wanted, and *the majority wanted* this election to take place," she smiled, honestly. "As a leader I really follow the herd, if you see what I mean." Deetee was nodding slowly, that smile still across his lips.

"*As a leader I really follow the herd,*" he repeated slowly, as if in awe and revelation. Then he leaned forward slightly, changing his angle again, each move and each word carefully chosen for reasons of portrayal and association.

"A lot of people are more interested in *how* you got into office in the first place, can you tell me about that?" he asked, his expression still unchanging.

Brenda froze and someone suspended the interview.

"I told you, nothing about the Vourne Conspiracy please, *keep it light* Deetee," ordered someone, sharply.

"She *needs* to answer that, too many people have been asking about it to just gloss over it," Deetee protested. "Now we've got her here in the studio, I hoped to give at least *some* impression of realism about it."

"I thought you were a *good* journalist," someone joked. Ha-ha.

"*All right, all right!*" yelled someone. "Ma'am, would it be *okay* if you answered that question?" Brenda looked at her aide who gave her a slow but reserved nod.

"It's fine," she smiled, timidly. She had a suitable answer prepared.

"Go again, three, two…"

"A lot of people are more interested in *how* you got into office in the first place, can you tell me about that?" Deetee repeated.

"As you already know, I was in the previous election against Balan Orion of the Traditionalist National Party and, rumours of vote rigging aside, according to the poll data, I was well over forty percent. In the confusion, due to my popularity, I was selected to oversee the period of transition we are now ending. I mean, it would be awfully simple for me to sit here and accuse the Orion ad… ad… administration of corruption and that would certainly open a can of worms or two. I've had to take a more pragmatic angle on this and to try to view our society, *the Coalition*, like a g-g-g-giant jigsaw with a few b-b-b-bits missing. And, despite recent troubles, I think I *can* really help get those pieces back," she explained, genuinely believing every word she'd been told to say. She didn't know the words had been chosen to deliberately trip her up, to make her seem more trustable to the people watching, and help them to relate to her. She didn't realise she was little more than a figurehead with no actual power.

She still thought she could make a difference.

The studio audience clapped in apparent support and praise. A few of them, who *actually believed* they could read between the lines, imagined she had simply dodged the question and had not really answered it. Wasn't that what politicians did? Therefore, even to them, she seemed no different from anyone else. She was the perfect leader. She continued.

"These recent troubles I'm gradually getting to, but with the election to run in as well, it would be h-handy if there were a few more of me," she giggled, self-deprecatingly.

"I imagine running this campaign must be tough and I'm going to take this opportunity to *thank you* for putting a brief hold on that

*Operation Selector*

and coming in to talk to us here at the CNC," Deetee smoothly went on. As he said the words thank you, he put his hand over his heart symbolically. "One of your rivals is coming from a different angle again, saying that you are illegally running the Coalition and that you, as the Orion administration did before, are rigging the vote. How would you respond to that?"

Brenda was really shocked by that and glanced up to see what her aide's reaction was. She crossed her arms, a previously agreed body movement to tell her how to answer that.

"I doubt an outright denial would impress anyone," she said, simpering sweetly. "I would remind everyone that the whole reason I was running against Balan Orion in the first place was for similar reasons. The idea of *anyone* abusing or manipulating the election for any reason I find appalling. I can understand why people would think such things were happening, but I can assure you, *I can promise you*, that no such thing is occurring in this election."

"Consider this a friendly dress rehearsal for your up and coming debate," Deetee temporised, slyly. "Another thing I personally wanted to ask you about was your ongoing charity work with the people of Pluto Major. Let's just see something of that..."

A screen behind them began showing images of the usual thing. Children crying, buildings burning, other generic scenes of suffering. These were terrible events, *real* terrible events. *Real people had died* and now... it was being exploited by the media. Used... to manipulate, and to spread fear. Who could prove if these images were even *of* Pluto Major? Who could prove that all this work had actually been done, and that donated money had actually reached them? Who could prove *anything*? The media had won: they had taught people not even to trust their own senses. Of course, their continued domination depended entirely on their performance. One wrong move, one misjudged scheme, and they would be made to pay a dreadful price. Perhaps *that* would be the closest thing to justice, for them to fall for their own propaganda. To believe that they were untouchable was the first step on the road of self-deception which led up the mountain of denial. A place one could only fall from...

Brenda and Deetee watched the screen as Brenda and her team arrived, being depicted not as saviours or anything like that, but as normal people *just trying to help*. Wasn't that realistic? Wasn't that *more authentic*? Brenda, a genuinely selfless person, looked away, a little embarrassed and uncomfortable. When the clip had ended Deetee nodded, as if this was the first time he'd seen the footage - which it certainly was not. He and the CNC had been planning all this for days.

"It's hard to watch," he said, injecting a little false compassion into it. Not too much, don't overdo it.

"*It's even worse to experience*," Brenda stated, a little gloomily. She'd been there and she really had tried to help, but she was starting to see how that generous act was being *used*. She couldn't say or do anything; she had to do what her aides told her to. It was for the best, they said. *We know how to handle it*, they said. You must trust us, they reminded her frequently, and we'll hold your hand through everything they throw at you.

"I can *only* imagine," Deetee said, milking it for *all* he was worth. Not a lot, some would say. "Tell us *more* about your work with the President of Pluto Major. I've read reports of you rebuilding the schools and trying to get industry going again. That's *got* to have been difficult. What sorts of challenges have you been facing there?"

"W-well, w-water was a big one at first. In the fighting, damage had been done; I don't understand the technical side of it, I'm sorry, but the problem was we couldn't get the water *into* the city. We had to do a lot of work on the pipes to make sure the water was safe to drink and that it didn't flood or anything. Then there were the medical issues. I mean, they *had* hospitals but they were overwhelmed and they didn't have the supplies and we had to bring personnel in to help. It was madness at first, just madness. After that, there were concerns about some of the weapons used in the surrounding areas, fortunately nothing too bad was there, but we still had to evacuate thousands and investigate that," Brenda told him.

Wouldn't it be great if they said something *good* for a change? Brenda would agree, she was not comfortable talking about these awful, depressing things all the time. It *had* all happened, and she really *had* helped, but talking about it like this… it felt dishonest to her. She felt like she was exploiting people. She was starting to wish her aides had not talked her out of refusing to do this interview. Yes, it *would* help her campaign and yes, she was *only telling the truth* but… it still felt wrong to Brenda. That communicator was going off again and it was driving her up the wall, someone answer that! Why was no one answering it?

"The charity you have set up, um…" Deetee said, pretending to try to remember the name.

"*Benefits for Pluto*," she provided, as she had been told to.

"Yes, that's it, thanks. I've heard it's raised nearly four billion Essps in a week, how does that make you feel?"

How do you think, you pathetic vulture of a man? If emotional blackmail was a qualification, you would have a doctorate in it, Brenda thought. What he was twisting this into made her start to feel both sad and angry. He didn't play *to the crowd*, he *played* the crowd with a sickly snake dance of sensationalism. Then again, maybe he had help. Chemical help.

"It's not enough, we *need* to keep going," she answered, staying on script. "I mean, Pluto Major is not the only place in the cosmos where bad things have been happening. This is what I mean about *pieces in a jigsaw*."

"I see," he said, adopting a pose that implied that what she was saying was deeply profound. She found it patronising. "So your plan is to develop this, if you will, into a galactic aid movement?"

"I have *many* plans," she smiled, introducing humour just where she was told to.

"*One would hope!*" he laughed, right on cue. They laughed together in that way people do when they know that others are watching. Brenda's ears somehow managed to tune in on that ringing communicator again. She could hardly sit still now, it was like a craving.

"Once again, thank you for taking the time to come in and talk to us about these things; may your day stay positive," Deetee leered.

"No problem," she said, shaking his hand abruptly. The transmission was cut just in time as she leapt up and darted over to the offending communicator. She answered it, and she felt so happy she could weep.

"Yes?" she asked, politely. "Can I help?" Brenda's aide followed her leisurely, a disapproving expression on her face.

"Err, is Shelly there?" asked a man.

"I don't think so; can I take a message...?" Brenda asked, out of habit. The aide grabbed the communicator from Brenda and disconnected the call.

"*Wait*, no..." Brenda began, uneasily.

"We cannot have *the* Commandment Benefactor of the Coalition scurrying around picking up messages for random people like some kind of low level employee," the woman stated, stern and straight-faced. "Now come on, your next appointment is in twenty minutes. *You have a schedule to keep.*"

---

Jinx watched as the two security craft, sirens wailing, passed by many hundreds of floors below. A bitter wind blew that would make most shiver but his bodysuit insulated him against all but the most cutting of air currents. He'd been there over an hour, having first checked out the location for layout and ambush purposes. Two figures, wrapped in cloaks, were approaching from a dimly lit walkway coming down from the floor above. One was carrying something. Jinx gave no expression other than a mild curiosity. He understood why it was like this and why it *had to be* like this. Discussing assassination was always best done away from prying ears.

"Am I to assume that your presence here means you agree to pay in full?" he asked, in a growl. One figure nodded and the other passed him the sealed case they were carrying. Fine, so we can forget all the disingenuous banalities, Jinx thought.

He unsealed it and drew out the first sheet to see who his target would be. A picture of Oli McAllister was inside, along with various other pieces of information.

"I know this man, don't I?" he asked, rhetorically. "He moves in politics." Neither figure said anything. "Any requests?" he asked. Was it to look like an accident? A suicide? What? Again neither figure replied. No preference then.

"I'm assuming you want this done *before* the end of the election?" Jinx guessed, levelly. One of the figures bowed their head in a gesture to the affirmative.

"Right, I'll make contact in the usual way," Jinx told them, as he turned to leave. He strode to the elevator and the second the doors closed he made a call.

Someone answered but no words were spoken.

"It's Jinx," Jinx said.

"Hello," was the deep answer.

"How's it going, Octutin?" Jinx enquired, rather pointlessly.

"Good… good," was the cold reply.

"I've got another job for us," Jinx told him.

"Who is it this time?"

---

According to the message left by one of the delivery androids, her apartment wasn't quite ready yet and it gave an approximate time for her to arrive there. She'd left them some rather complicated instructions with regard to some of her belongings and how she wanted them arranged. Kelvin would be laid out on a table close to other machinery she'd had on standby. The egg, which was supposed to be hatching any day now, was to be stored in a side room where it could be monitored. And then there were all the regular furnishings etc. So, Satiah had four hours to kill. An easy choice of word, perhaps 'spend' would be more apt on this occasion but then when time was spent it never returned. Just like those who had died.

She didn't particularly mind either way as she had wanted to drop in at the Priory for a long time. Years, in fact. The Priory was a bar. Specifically, a private bar above another slightly less private bar. A place especially for Phantoms at a loose end who didn't want to sit around Phantom Headquarters. As a result, it was never full as few Phantoms had that kind of time to burn. She reached the normal bar, the one below the Priory, just as the sun was sinking beneath the horizon. She couldn't see the sunset; there were too many skyscrapers blocking that view from her. As she went through the entrance she passed a hovering advertisement player. She glanced across at it. *The Tragedy of Astyanax, a story about sacrifice and conflict. It asks the question: how can one man ever truly apologise to woman for all the injustices against her from his kind?* She rolled her eyes thinking: that'd be a *long* story.

The bar was about half full, or half empty depending on your own philosophical slant, and Satiah knew what she had to do. She approached the bar and pointed to a beer label called *Priory*.

"One of those, please," she smiled, just as if she could be anyone.

"It's off," grunted the barman. They made eye contact.

"*One of those, please*," she repeated, with just a tad more emphasis. He gave a curt nod and she walked through to the stairs beyond. On the top floor, three flights later, was a door with a security drone outside. It scanned her and the door unlocked for her. She went into a completely different bar: the Priory.

When she'd gone there for the first time, a long time ago now, she'd noticed something. She'd noticed it *before* anything else. Every time she'd ever gone since, it was always the first thing she looked for. It was also the first thing *everyone* noticed upon going in. It was the broken screen on the wall. It was around thirty years ago when she'd first entered that place and it was there even then, as if challenging entropy to come and get it. The screen had been shot; it was possible to see the blackened traces where the laser bolt had cooked the circuitry inside. It was left hanging there as a gesture, never removed, never replaced. Always to remain there. Naturally, the first thing she'd asked the Phantom that she had been with at the time was *why* it was there. He'd told her that the Priory hadn't always been a Phantom-only bar. Years and years ago, anyone could go in there.

The story went that one belligerent customer had insisted on turning up the programme he was watching. He was asked again and again and... Satiah had guessed the outcome. Instead of killing the customer, the nameless Phantom had blasted the screen to get silence. Ever since, it was decided that Phantoms *only* should be allowed in that place. It just wasn't safe for members of the public to hang around in a small environment with Phantoms. Certainly not when intoxicated.

Instead of bar stools or chairs, there were more comfortable furnishings. The music though, she theorised, was supposed to suit the kind of people listening to it. Hard at the same time as fast, while also being in the background and dangerously subtle. A mellow malevolence. Aggressive lyrics being snarled out, mirroring the rapid fire delivery of a machine laser gone haywire. The place hadn't changed much in over thirty years, even if a lot of the patrons were dead. *That birdcage* was new, though. Inside, a particularly large toucan was perched and it regarded her in solemn silence. And which one of us is in *the real cage*, its birdlike features seemed to enquire? She prodded the cage, smiled and whispered a hello to it before scanning the patrons.

There were just two other Phantoms in there at that time and one of them she knew. Phantom Istrum was nursing something dark and potent looking, a pensive aspect about him. He was tall and solid and had the second highest kill rating of all *living* Phantoms. The only one with a higher figure was Phantom Mensa. Satiah, though it didn't bother her much, was ninth on that table. That may seem to some like a long way down; however, she had *successfully* completed more missions than he had. So they were sort of even in her eyes. Randal, it appeared, shared her opinion that the end result was all that counted. How you got there was up to you.

She took her Golden Float, the drink that was fast becoming her favourite, and sat opposite him.

"Essp for them?" she asked, curious. She was interested to know why he was there. Come to it, why anyone was.

"No change on me," he grunted. Then he smiled and they shook hands. "What's up?"

"Nothing *yet*," she mused, sipping her drink. She was careful to avoid gaining a frothy moustache; she only allowed that to happen when she was alone or with Carl. It was a quirk that even she didn't quite understand. Something private. A side to her that only those special to her got to see.

He didn't say more, just leaned back and began to stare into the middle-distance again.

"Everything okay?" she asked, attentive.

"Trouble with the PAI," he grumbled, focussing on her again. "I'm going to write a book about it and call it: *three freighters, two pilots and a broken computer*. Would you read it?" *What's the slogan going to be: expect no mercy?*

"...*Sounds more fun than the Tragedy of Astyanax* ... What's it about?" she grinned, amused.

"The usual. Incompetence, pretence and hubris," he complained, seeming to warm to the topic. She eyed the clock. Okay, two hours, let's see if I can keep him talking all that time without saying any more than *five words*, she thought.

In the end she failed but she only used about fourteen, so it wasn't a bad try. It was clear that she wasn't the only one whom the PAI had irritated lately. They had been after a group of drug smugglers, in order to trace where the supply was coming from. Inventing a strategy to nail them, they had the idea of a false convoy. Inside, instead of the usual payload, would be the operatives. They would board, take control and find out all they needed to know. Unfortunately... due to an apparent *miscommunication*, the convey set off six hours too late. The late arrival spooked the criminals and they fled. No shots were fired and no one was hurt, but at the same time it had ruined months of work. Typical PAI ineptitude!

By the time she reached her apartment, she was a little the worse for wear and staggered badly to avoid tripping over the door seal. She went to the window and peered out at the night lights of the city. She'd always liked that view. Whether it was the drink, or the idea of such a straightforward mission, or just a general good mood, she called Carl. Her bedsit was clean of any *suspicious devices* and he could be her pretend/real boyfriend. By *that* she could explain, should anyone notice him, that he was all part of her cover act. Also, Randal *had* noticed that her pattern had changed and that after years of working relentlessly, she was now taking time off. If she could get Carl to see her *while on a mission*, it would look less suspicious. He answered immediately even though she knew he would be asleep, on his world it was a few hours before dawn. She smiled, pleased to be such a high priority in his life. *But then so she should be!*

"Satiah, *are you okay*?" he asked, concerned.

"I'm bored and you're too far away to jump on," she said, softly. "I want you to come and see me; you've never been to Earth before, I remember, so..." she ran her hand down the wall as she spoke to him, "... I want you to come and see me."

"Wait! *What*? I thought you *were working*?" he asked, confused. "You said..."

"I know, but I think I can get away with it," she shrugged, honestly. "This job is looking like an easy one. A good amount of spare time... time I would like to spend with *you*."

"Are you sure? I mean, you *know* how much I love you..."

"I've forgotten again, you'll have to remind me, sorry," she smiled, mischievously.

"*That's not fair*! You're *not* allowed to seduce me into it!" he groaned, in protest.

"*Sorry*," she purred, making herself sound alluring deliberately. "I suppose we *could* wait months and years until we next meet, but we both know you won't last anywhere near that long."

"Is that a challenge?" he asked, perplexed.

"Come here and find out," she shrugged, completely nonchalant.

"I hate you sometimes," he grumbled, without meaning it. "You like torturing me and making my life so hard!" Her eyebrow rose at his choice of adjective. She shook her head and grinned.

"*Your life... right.* And yet you obviously want me to, otherwise you wouldn't keep coming back," she smiled.

"I would run away if I could but we both know I'm not fast enough," he chuckled.

"So, surrender," she said, in a playful tone. "Maybe if you give in we can skip the rough stuff."

"...*So, so cruel*..." he said, pretending to cry.

"So... when will you get here?" she asked, knowing she'd got him.

43

"I'll be there in four days," he stated, with such certainly she wanted to giggle.

"*Oh, such a bad boy*!" she scoffed, in mock outrage. "You break *so easily*."

"That would be funny if it wasn't true," he said, yawning.

"*Oh gosh*, did I *wake* you?" she asked, as if shocked.

"You *know* you did. You relish my suffering and you strike in the early hours of darkness when you know my resistance is weakest."

"See you soon," she giggled, disconnecting.

---

"Wake up, Satiah," Obsenneth said. Lying on her front, still dressed, Satiah snapped awake, taking in her environment instantly. She realised that Obsenneth had managed to get from inside her jacket into her hand. It was still early, maybe two hours before she had intended to awaken.

"What do *you* want?" she growled, annoyed at the early awakening.

"To enquire as to whether you intend to run that scan I asked you to do..." he answered.

"*I'll get around to it*! You waited thousands of years before you were found, what's the sudden rush?" she muttered. "I need to fix Kelvin first and then he will run the scans while I do my job."

"How long will it take you...?" he asked.

"I don't know what's wrong with him yet," she replied, glancing over her shoulder. She could see Kelvin's bulky form lying inert in the living area.

"Very well... should I sense anything that seems like another part of myself I will alert you," Obsenneth stated. She let go of the gemstone, breaking the mental connection.

Out of self-drilled habit, she rechecked her apartment for anything that might have changed in the night. There was nothing. She rechecked her gun even though she wasn't intending to take it with her this time. In order to help her blend in she was going to be issued with a standard rifle by the security team. It would look very strange for a regular security guard to have her own *personalised* laser pistol. A standard rifle could be tampered with, adapted subtly, which is exactly what she intended to do. So long as it looked to everyone else like there was nothing unusual about it, she could improve it at her leisure. Component checks were always a possibility but she'd check out the levels of scrutiny they had when she got there. Even *the best security*, the *best* defences and the *best* people had their weaknesses.

Phantom Squad had provided her with a transporter that she could use to get to and from work each day. Again, it was something that looked very normal on the outside. She'd been reliably informed, however, that its capabilities were far beyond normal. She washed, took time to ensure she looked tidy and then dressed in her new uniform. A dark blue body suit, designed for durability. It had some light armour around the chest and arms but primarily it left her able to use her natural speed and flexibility. She still kept her blade in her boot and Obsenneth in her pocket. She didn't feel quite right without her pistol on her hip, never did feel quite right when it was missing. She eyed Kelvin as she got ready to leave. Going without him didn't feel right either but, she reminded herself, even if he was in complete working order he couldn't be by her side this time.

The drive there was longer than she liked. Nearly forty minutes. It reminded her of a time when she had been in her early teens, enduring the rigours and the *perils* of Phantom training. She'd forgotten, at some stage during the ensuing decades, what sticking to the traffic lanes actually meant: long queues and *slow* speed limits. Very slow. Several times she caught herself wanting to accelerate, targeting the back of the vehicles around her out of wont and craving to cut loose. Instinctively she kept checking to see if anyone was following her. All of this was completely unnecessary, though it did liven up an otherwise monotonous journey. Finally she reached the skyscraper where Oli McAllister had his campaign headquarters. She parked and then casually wandered over to the entrance.

The robotic receptionist scanned her as she came in.

"Can I help you?" it asked, whirring over the table to come closer.

"Aye," she assented, sighing heavily. "I'm here to see…" She trailed off as if trying to remember, while of course she knew exactly who it was. "…Malla. He's the man in charge of Oli McAllister's security. I've been hired to help."

"One moment please," the robot requested. Obligingly she sat down, crossed her arms and legs and stared up at the advertisements on the wall. *Is one of your friends exhibiting signs of depression? Don't know what to do? Take these…* Satiah closed her eyes, jaded already. She opened them again when the lift chimed. Three people got out, two men and a woman.

As they approached her, Satiah didn't move or even show any interest in them whatsoever. She knew who they had to be and she was playing the role of disinterested professionalism. She'd seen all their pictures when she'd looked into their backgrounds the previous evening.

"Satiah, isn't it?" asked the taller man. He was big, around six foot six and broad with it too. His bald cranium, serious demeanour and green eyes identified him to her: Malla.

"Malla?" she extended her arm. They shook hands.

"Before we start your shift, I want to talk to you first. Your recommendation, while concise, could have been more informative. Let's find a room," he said. She shrugged and nodded. Fair enough, she reasoned. I don't like working with strangers either. But then, it's always the people *we think we know* who are the most dangerous…

That was exactly what they did and Satiah sat at one side of a table. Malla and Shannon, the female guard, sat opposite her. The other man stood outside by the door.

"The first thing I wanted to ask you was about your political opinions. Which party do you support? Why do you support them? Who have you voted for in the election and why?" Malla asked, as she had thought he might.

"I don't vote, haven't since I was young, I distrust all politicians," she said, nonchalantly. This was true but it wasn't why she didn't vote. She knew that the whole voting process was little more than a paperwork exercise as far as the powers were concerned. They always made it work how they wanted, no matter what the public wanted or needed. Satiah was good at this though, and she knew the best things to say would be those closest to what she actually thought. Using *a truth* to hide *the truth*.

"And as for parties, I'm not even sure which ones there are anymore," she went on, eyeing Shannon. Shannon looked disgusted but Malla seemed fine with this.

"People fought *and died* to make sure you have that right to vote," she stated, evenly. Satiah stared at her, right into the depths of her brown eyes.

"I didn't ask them to do that, *did I*?" Satiah replied, stiffly. Malla was quick to wade in and stop this turning ugly.

"It's *fine* Shannon, I'd rather have someone who believes *nothing* than someone who *openly supports our opposition*," he said, soothingly. He turned back to face Satiah again. "Do you think Oli will win or not?"

"I've no idea what will happen," she replied, honest again.

"How long have you been an elite?" Shannon asked, crossing her arms. She *really* didn't like her and it was more than just her political views that were behind this woman's dislike. Satiah wondered what else there could be… and if it was relevant to her mission.

"Five years, seven months and twelve days," Satiah lied, immediately. That was what her cover story said.

"What are your other commitments, aside from your job?" Malla asked, interested. Satiah, slumped there in the chair, the very soul of detachment, shrugged indifferently.

"I have a *boyfriend*?" she offered, as if unsure whether that counted as a commitment. "I think he votes." Carl was from the Colonial Federation and wouldn't be a part of this election, no matter how he felt about the political side of it.

"You *think*?" Shannon asked, sceptically.

"You'd have to ask him, like I said; I'm not at all up to date with who is who. This is how I work: you tell me who you want me to protect, and I will do that for the money you pay me, that's it," Satiah spelt out, still utterly unperturbed. Malla, contrary-wise, seemed to like what he was hearing.

"It's just shift changes and stuff, there could be short notice changes to your hours depending on what occurs," Malla stated. This was only to be expected. Satiah nodded, displaying honestly how careless she was about that.

"Please don't be offended by any of these questions," Shannon apologised, her words somehow lacking sincerity. "It's just that when we hire new people it's unusual for them to seem so perfect on paper."

"I would do exactly the same," Satiah replied, with a smile. "And I'm a very challenging person to *offend*." Again, the truth.

"Everything checks out," Malla smiled. "If you will come upstairs, we can get you kitted out." They all stood and moved out. Satiah could feel Shannon's eyes on her, watching. What was she looking for... other than a fight? Something had made her mistrustful but Satiah felt it was nothing to do with her cover... it was more personal. She knew that she did not know this woman, had never encountered her *before*. So it couldn't be due to anything she had done in the past...

She was given a rifle, an AE20 sub-machine laser. A little better than she had expected, but still not quite up to her high standards. An armband that had a tracker in it, so she could be found on the system *and* access the building alone, was also provided. Then she was led into a large area where a briefing was about to take place. There were about fifty or so people there, a very small number compared with all those supporting Brenda's campaign. She had thousands of staff... even more if you included all the ones she *didn't* know about. Satiah's keen brown eyes swept over the people there. Who amongst these was the enemy? There could be more than one. She moved to stand with the other guards who were clustered together, chatting quietly.

That was when she saw him for the first time. *Oli McAllister*. Kate was standing with him on an improvised stage to talk to everyone.

"Morning team!" smiled Oli, rubbing his hands together. "How are we all?" A chorus of answers sounded from various people. Satiah didn't answer, playing the role of bewildered newbie. Kate handed Oli some files and he scanned through them.

"Okay, some new starters with us today to help give us extra energy. We have *Stan*, a message fundraising support advisor! Stand up, Stan!"

A young man with ginger hair stood awkwardly and waved his fingers in the air. Satiah made a mental note that just because he was *new* didn't mean he wasn't involved.

"That's great Stan, great to have you with us!" Oli went on, seeming to mean what he said.

"And we have a new guard to keep us all safe: *Satiah*!" he announced. "We all wish Frank well in his early retirement and welcome you here with us, Satiah." Satiah regarded everyone coolly and raised a hand almost like she was dismissing them.

"I feel safer already," he joked, casually. Everyone laughed. Everyone *except* Satiah. Her eyes were everywhere, seeking anything suspicious. Her eyes settled on a fire extinguishing unit, colour-coded green. It was out of date by four days. Nothing unusual in that, *one would hope*. Nevertheless, she made eye contact with Malla and pointed to it. He understood what she meant at once and she began to wonder if it had been a test for her *set by him*. The replacement, this one still in date, was right outside the door... She smiled, amused. At least he was *serious*, if a bit amateurish, about security. That didn't mean he wasn't her enemy though, and how many more tests had he set up for her?

Oli was talking again.

"Now we've got to really move on this, everyone! We all know Brenda has a huge advantage on us but I still think we can pull this off," he said, passionately. "We all know she shouldn't be there, we all know it's illegal. I have my speech to deliver later today and none of you will have the time to watch it. I know *it's hard*, I know you've all been pushing above and beyond on this. I want you to know that I will not forget this, and that it means something to me. Please keep it up!"

Satiah had to admit, he was a reasonable public speaker. Suddenly invigorated, the room burst into activity. She had to get closer to Oli somehow, though she doubted Malla trusted her enough to leave her alone with Oli, certainly not yet. She moved over to Malla, conscious of Shannon's eyes on her again, to talk to him.

"Where do you want me?" Satiah asked, grimly.

"Well, just follow Oli around; see that no one bothers him. You and Shannon can keep him out of harm's way together, I'm pretty sure," he said. He must know of the brewing animosity between them, he wasn't blind! What did he think he was doing? Was this another test? Testing her obedience *or* her intelligence, that was the question. Obey my orders and please me, or point out my potential mistake and please me?

"*Shannon and I?*" Satiah clarified, meaningfully. She'd gone down the middle road of questioning the order without specifying an actual grievance. They made eye contact again and she knew she'd guessed right. He was trying to figure her out.

"Shannon's always a bit standoffish at first but, when you get to know her, you'll find you probably like her," he assured her. Don't bet on it, she thought.

"Sir," she said, in acceptance and moved off to obey. One good thing was that it got her close to Oli. She stood close, but not too close, and was rarely more than arm's length away from him for the next few hours. Then breakfast began and another chance to prove herself too.

"How do you check his food and drink?" Satiah asked, to Shannon. Shannon's eyes widened, taken completely off-guard by the question. The hesitation told Satiah all she needed to know. *They didn't*. It's a wonder he was still alive!

"We don't..."

"No worries," Satiah articulated. She had to carefully restrain her condemnatory reaction to this development and not scream at anyone for incompetence. "Are we going to start checking *or not*?"

Shannon seemed uncertain.

"I'll talk to Malla about it," she said, heading away. Satiah turned and nearly bumped right into Oli who was smiling down at her.

"Is there a problem?" he asked, quizzically.

"Not yet, sir," she replied, seriously. "We were just discussing how best to ensure that your food and drink are safe for you to consume." This caught *him* by surprise too, and he instantly looked uncertainly at the drink he had just finished. She took this as an opportunity to build trust and support between them.

"It's *okay*," she smiled and touched his shoulder lightly. "I don't think you're in any danger, sir, but this is what I do. It's my job to..."

"No, no, I get it, it's fine," he said, still flinching from the idea. "It's just something I've never thought about."

"Like I said, it's my job to think of these things so that *you* don't have to, sir," she reassured him. Then she took a step away from him, as if out of respect.

"Satiah, isn't it?" he clarified, as if only just remembering.

"Yes sir," she responded, calmly. Malla and Shannon were coming over and she knew Shannon would not like her talking to Oli like that. She didn't even really know *how* she knew that but it was a feeling, her usually dependable sixth sense reminding her to watch herself as well as Oli.

"It seems with new blood there comes new ideas," Malla said, as he reached them.

"Isn't that the idea of innovation?" Oli joked, without being serious. "I think that..."

"Do you think that checking his food and drink is *necessary*?" Malla asked, directly.

All three regarded Satiah, earnestly. As she searched their faces for the answers she wanted, she could see nothing. No guilt. No anger. They all seemed as they should. She shrugged, maintaining her gruff practiced deportment with ease.

"Up to you, sir," she replied, rigidly. "I thought you already did." Glances were exchanged.

"Well, a decision needs to be made, I'm getting hungry here," Oli chuckled.

"How *can* we check?" Shannon asked, genuinely unsure. "Short of tasting it ourselves first?" Malla thought about it.

"I can get the equipment," he stated, impressed. "Well caught, Satiah."

"Sir," she replied, without emotion. Shannon was staring again. What *was* her problem? Straightforward jealousy didn't seem the answer. She seemed competent and stable; also she was more attractive than Satiah. Dark skinned, curvaceous and perfectly aligned dreadlocks. When she smiled, which she didn't seem to do very often, men would find her very appealing.

"Wow," Oli said, still talking to Satiah, "a pro! I'm glad you're looking after me too. Where did you work before?"

"All over, sir," she replied, vaguely. She threw out some technical expressions she knew he wouldn't understand. "Shadow, base and eagle." These were terms used by some to describe certain types of personnel deployment in convoy movements. "Each job is different and where you were has nothing to do with where you are so… all over, sir," she concluded, starting to realise he was getting even more interested.

"Where *did* you find her?" Oli asked, turning to Shannon.

"She was *recommended*," she said with a tight smile, shifting on her feet awkwardly.

"Were you with the military?" he asked, as Satiah knew he would. Everyone asked that. *Only as much as anyone under fire is, she wanted to quip.*

"Yes, lieutenant, three years, then I left and became a hired enforcer, sir," she answered, following her cover story.

"*Mercenary*," Shannon corrected, with more than a little dislike. Oli didn't seem to hear that remark. Ah… a clue. Shannon didn't like Satiah because of her *vocation*? Possibly. That would also explain her outrage at Satiah's rather amoral view on politics.

"My father was a military man," Oli told her, animated. "We will talk about this later, I have to go over there and talk to the market guys but I promise I will be back." *Be back*? You can't go anywhere without *me*, she thought to herself. He moved off and she and Shannon followed. Satiah carefully kept the other frampold, peevish woman in her peripheral vision all the time. Shannon may not be a danger to Oli, but that didn't mean she couldn't be a danger to Satiah herself.

For the next few hours, she and Shannon followed Oli around constantly. Satiah had to check his meals… which were fine. A little zesty for her tastes, but she couldn't have everything. The speech he gave around lunchtime was okay. Nothing out of the ordinary. Satiah could sense that something behind the scenes was happening though - something sinister. The threat was real, as the old saying went. She just couldn't see it yet. The day felt like a long one, but eventually her shift was over and she was able to return home. *Home...* a place she hardly ever got to visit.

She began work on Kelvin, carefully removing the armour and exposing his inner workings. The power core was there and seemed normal. She ran some of the more routine checks too. She sighed and realised that more hours had passed and she actually had somewhere to be that night. Somewhere she rarely got the chance to visit. She got ready, dressing in a suit. She reviled suits but the woman she had to be that night was not herself. It could have been *once...* and the pretence was still needed, so it served a purpose. That didn't mean, however, that she had to like it.

---

Two percent. It didn't sound a lot, but it meant a great deal. Oli McAllister had gained two extra percent of the vote that day. Point five percent was the usual daily fluctuation but... *two whole percent*. It rekindled his hope. *Nineteen percent proportional representation.* Some candidates had dropped out, bringing his rivals down to less than one hundred now. He knew though that he had only one real rival: Brenda Watt. If he could get that figure up to forty, it might be enough to trigger a second poll between just the two of them. He'd watched the interview with Brenda and Deetee, unsure of what to make of it. Brenda seemed her usual friendly flustered self and had been thrown some tricky questions. As usual she'd slipped through the net and her popularity remained. It would be his turn the next day to face Deetee.

There were a lot of other things going on now too. The Nebular Union, like the Coalition, was going through a period of muddled change. Its government was in chaos and the Premier, though confirmed to still be alive, was missing. The Cult of Deimos had been publicly unmasked and everyone was seeing shadows. The media was doing its best to make it look like an attempted uprising but it was all so confused, it was impossible for anyone to know the truth. Oli knew no more than anyone else about it, but wondered if it would come up in the interview. There seemed to be so much stuff happening all of sudden that even the CNC was having trouble keeping up. It was almost as if, *somehow*, everyone had chosen to act all at once, each acting as the other's distraction.

The Ro Tammer trial rumbled on within the Federation. The second trimester had begun a day previously and the list of individual charges was still being read out, eight hours in. Next would follow the list of victims and all manner of other lists, compounding the strength of said charges. She'd not been in power long, a few months if that, and in that time she'd managed to do so much. Ro herself was unspeaking, unsmiling and apparently unrepentant in the place of the accused. The next trimester, *the third was worst*, would be where the tribunal began their witness examination and all the other procedures they had to do. The media were trying to follow this momentous hearing as best as they could, but what with everything else going on it was reduced to just one of many long running chronicles.

With so much going on it also significantly reduced the chances Oli and his team had to promote themselves. Kate entered his office looking tired but glad that some progress had been made.

"You okay?" she asked, hoping he was in a good mood.

"Yes, today we took a big step towards our goal. We do that *every day* and we will win," he stated, seriously. Mathematically correct but…

"How are *you*?" he enquired, pleasantly. He sipped his drink and she grinned at him as she sat down.

"Have you checked that?" she joked.

"Don't you start," he groaned, rolling his eyes. "I wonder what she will look into next. The air quality in case someone chooses to gas us or something."

"Who *are* these miscreants?" Kate laughed.

"Well, I never criticise anyone who takes their job seriously," he replied, casually. *"And she was right*, technically it's a risk." Then he eyed her. "Just yesterday you were the one saying how dangerous what we are doing is. Maybe you should talk to Satiah about it." Kate eyed him sharply. "*What?*" he asked, looking around in confusion.

"*You remembered her name*, I don't think I've ever known you to do that so quickly *before*," she noted, a little suspicious.

"Well, she made an impression on me I suppose, plus it's the sort of thing one remembers: the possibility that someone is trying to poison them," he shrugged. She smiled a knowing smile as she nodded at him slowly.

"Are you sure that's not the only reason?" she persisted.

"She's military, my father was military, and she's been under my feet all day pretty much, I don't know… what are you asking me exactly?" he asked, hoping he didn't already know. Older people were renowned for their *feelings* and *opinions* on younger people. They felt they knew best and were often comically or tragically mistaken.

"Nothing," she smiled softly, dropping it. "I admit I didn't think we would get two percent. Maybe a few mantissa but never a whole two."

"Even *I* didn't," he chuckled, gleefully. "Seems the optimist *and* the realist were blindsided by that one."

"It just goes to show, you can do all the analyses and exercises in prediction you like and things can *still* remain just as random as static spikes."

"So, by that logic, tomorrow could be the same or *even better*," he smiled brightly.

"Well, it might… *or it might not*. Logic and politics don't belong in the same place," she laughed.

*"Maybe they should."*

"Do you want to go over anything for tomorrow?" she offered.

"I probably should, but I think I'm starting to suffer from information-overload here," was his riposte. All the things he'd read, seen and talked about were in danger of forming a sort of cerebral whirlwind in his mind. Flying around and around, all together and by themselves, making less and less sense with each gyration. He knew he had to prioritise and isolate the most important parts and hope that was what he would be asked about. In plain English: it felt like it was all getting on top of him.

"That's understandable. Personally I find it hard to believe all this stuff is going on at once. I can't take it all in. Yet, I suppose it's just like any other day, I just never noticed it was this intense before," she said, sympathetically. "Do you want me to tell you to try to relax?"

"No," he smiled, resisting being mothered.

"Do you want me to tell you that it doesn't matter what happens now, as the people *who matter* know the truth about how hard you're trying?" she offered, being humorous.

"No," he chuckled, not bothering to tell her that not only *had* she just said that but that *she knew she had*. She stood as if to leave and then turned to regard him sitting there once again.

"If you need a distraction, maybe you should call her."

---

Satiah was doing something she rarely indulged in. Daydreaming. Thinking about Carl and of a few of the things in her life that weren't deadly or terrifying. Escapism was among the purest of sustenances, from which the will to live could gain strength. Her will to live was in high demand, what with her having to live so many lies. Watching the lights of the city flash past sometimes had a heady effect on her, whilst also being calming and centring. She was in a taxi which was flying her to her destination, when her earpiece jolted her from her unusually pleasant reverie.

"Yes?" she snapped, rudely. She didn't like being interrupted... even when she wasn't actually doing anything.

"Oh, hi, you're the agent on Operation Selector?" asked a man. He sounded young and excitable. Oh no, *please*, not another recruit she had to mentor! She thought about lying and saying that it was someone else but in the end decided she couldn't be bothered. It would most likely be a pointless endeavour in any case... not unlike her current mission.

"It's *Satiah*," she told him, grimly. "What do you want? *I'm busy.*"

"Hi, Harrier here, I'm a colleague of *Rainbow's*, he's on vacation now but before he went he left something for me and if I needed help *your name* was put forward. He said that an intellect such as yours was unrivalled and that you owe him a few favours," Harrier explained. A namedrop, a compliment, and bribery - all in less than a moment... she felt sick.

She rolled her eyes. And which adulterer was he on vacation with *exactly*? A few favours? Was he on drugs? Rainbow did *her* favours, *end of*. The idea of the reverse occurring frustrated her greatly.

"I'm busy," she repeated, cranky.

"But you're doing Selector, you should have *loads* of free time, *he said it would be okay*," Harrier went on.

"Look…" she began, preparing to get nasty.

"He said *only you* could help him with this," Harrier stated, quickly. The young man had sensed he was about to lose her attention and so had thrown in his biggest chip. It worked, her anger faded immediately and curiosity flooded in.

"All right, I have *a little* time, what is it?" she asked, interested.

"If you're too busy, maybe I should call back later…?" he began, now just being a pain.

"Don't get cute *boy*. Tell me more," she insisted, hiding her amusement.

"Well… it's a book," he began. What was this? *Charades*?

"By *more*, I meant *something helpful*," she complained, seriously.

"Okay, he's found this book and it's written in a language that no one understands. Not code, *a language*, he said. And I've had a go at it too but it's a nonstarter, I'm afraid. So… I was hoping to pass it along to *you*. I promise, *you solve this*, you get all the credit. It's driving us all insane up here," he elaborated. She simpered silently as she imagined all the analysts in Phantom Squad literally clawing at the walls in frustration. Did this also mean that if she didn't solve it she would get all the blame too?

"I'll look into it but *that's all*," she stated, firmly. "And I will be expecting you to do me some favours too, seeing as he's not there." She did not want this sort of thing to become a regular event. She didn't know how but she'd get Rainbow for this. "Deliver it to my apartment. I'll look at it tomorrow."

"*Great!*" he exclaimed, sounding delighted.

"*Where* did Rainbow find it?" she asked, her eyes narrowing shiftily.

"It was archived, apparently. Under… Vourne. *Yes*, that was who'd stored it. Been in the vaults for a few years…" His voice was drowned out by many different sets of alarm bells going off in Satiah's mind. Why *her*? Did they know? Was this some kind of ploy to trick her into revealing the truth?

"*Like I said,*" she stated, struggling to stay composed. "I'll look at it tomorrow." She disconnected and ran her hands through her hair. Vourne's name being on it didn't help her paranoia but then again, she reminded herself, his name was on a lot of things. Nevertheless, it really had her intrigued now. It made her think about the vaults, deep under Phantom Headquarters, and the billions of things they contained. All secret, most of them deadly in one way or another.

Once, when she was still training to be a Phantom many years ago, she'd had to go into the vaults to fetch something from them. It had been a lifeform that lived within light itself. Specifically, a Runer, a species which had adapted to existing within the wavelengths of invisible light somewhere in the infrared part of the spectrum. It fed on thermal radiation to survive. In any case, the experience as a whole had been an eye-opener. There were a series of giant hatches, she couldn't remember how many. Each one was over one hundred metres in height and the same again in width. And, according to the operator, each led to another dimension used entirely for storage. That was how much stuff they had locked away down there. Of course, none of that stuff was technically there in itself, just the gateways to it. Normally when things went into the vault they never came out again. If they ever did… Satiah knew to beware.

The taxi pulled up in front of a large building. Satiah got out and stood on the broad walkway as it whizzed away. She sighed heavily as she looked up at the construction. This had been a long time coming… almost two years now. She'd been putting it off, leaving it to one side and allowing it to remain in the background. She wasn't afraid or too full of dislike, she just felt awkward. Unhurriedly she went inside and entered the tiny lift. Floor six hundred and nine. Apartment seven. The lift was no slower than normal really, but it still seemed to take its time. Finally, it reached the floor she wanted and she padded out into the corridor beyond. Dressed as she was, and being completely unarmed, made her feel uncomfortable. Yet for the deception to work it had to be that way. She reached the door. Seven. She pressed the chimer and waited.

A man answered. He was tall, thin and elderly. He was way over one hundred and fifty now. His brown eyes and face lit up when he saw her and he smiled.

"*Hello Satiah*!" he said, hugging her.

"*Papa*," she smiled back, her posh inflection giving the second *a* an r-like sound.

"It's magnificent to see you, come on in! You look very pale, I hope you're getting plenty of rest," he was saying, as she entered his apartment. It was just as she remembered it, from the last time she'd been to see her father. Neat. Tidy. A bit small and a few dusty surfaces here and there but otherwise well-kept.

"How are things at the bank?" Ah yes, the bank. Satiah's father *didn't know* what she did or what her life was like. As far as he knew she was working in the Coalition Financial Institute. She'd been working there almost her entire career and she kept the details down to a minimum. With some help from Vourne she had set up a small network of computers to help maintain the ruse of her being there, just in case anyone ever tried to call on her there, or get hold of her. It was rare that anyone did, fortunately. If anyone ever needed her for financial reasons, Phantom Squad would take care of it for her and then tell her what had happened. *She was their secret* and so they had a vested interest in protecting her.

"The same as ever," she deflected, briskly. "How have you been? You must tell me everything."

"The same as ever," he echoed, trying to be droll.

She glanced across and noticed the glass cabinet of antique power cells that he collected. He'd collected those his entire life. She didn't know if there was a name for that feeling you experience when you see something from your past and it makes you feel happy and sad simultaneously. Nostalgia? Melancholy? Comforted? Heart-warming was probably closest to the mark in Satiah's case. It took her mind back to a time when things were simpler. To a time before the darkness came into her life. A time before it had all changed. She reasserted her self-control, as always. Even here, in the company of her own family, she had to be careful. Even here, *she had secrets to hide*, perhaps more so than anywhere else.

"Drink this," he said, handing her a warm beverage. "What have you been up to?"

"A lot of research," she smiled, honestly. "You know - the usual."

"You still on for that promotion?" he asked, sitting down with a relieved sigh. "Always knew you would do well." She cringed inwardly. It wasn't that she didn't feel proud of some of things she had done but she was almost certain that *he* wouldn't be. She sometimes wondered why she occasionally subjected herself to this. It did hurt, no matter how much she prepared herself for it beforehand. Above all else, it was a reminder of what she saw as her own weakness. In her line of work, *caring* about anything other than your own life could, *would* become a flaw. An exploitable flaw. She felt this around Carl too, to a lesser degree. Maybe it was because Carl knew just who she really was that made the difference.

Here she was acting, playing a version of herself that didn't exist, even if it once had. It was also a reminder of how normal people would see her if they knew the truth. They would fear, distrust and loathe her. Imagine, your daughter turns up out of pretty much nowhere and tells you that for the last half a century, give or take, she's not who you thought she was. You had been sharing your home with a professional killer all that time and you never even suspected... Look at those you love now. Do it. *Look at them* and ask yourself... *what are they hiding*? Who do we ever *really* know?

Is this what *everyone* does? Acting out their roles as if under scrutiny? She somehow doubted it. They weren't *all* Phantom Agents. They couldn't *all* feel like this.

"Everything is going well," she allowed, straying from the truth a bit. "What about you?" she asked, quickly turning the focus off herself again. "You've not asked for anything and you know that if you need any money..."

"I'm still not desperate enough to ask one of my own daughters for money," he stated, with a grin. She sat down opposite him.

"Well, if that changes, it won't be a problem," she assured him. "How is my sister?" She didn't actually care, but it was the sociable thing to do.

"Same as ever, although she's a lot happier now the trial is over. She asked after *you* actually, the last time we spoke," he told her.

"Really?" she asked, trying not to sound bleak.

"Why don't you talk to her?" he asked, more softly. "Then you wouldn't both need to use me as your messenger relay system."

"We might one day," she answered, in the same way she always answered *that* question. He didn't know, just like her sister didn't know, that it had been down to Satiah that the trial had ended. They *couldn't* know either, as then she would probably have to tell them who she really was. This was precisely why no good deed went unpunished. You take the time to save someone's life and they repay this anonymous act of generosity by asking awkward questions like *why*. Satiah reminded herself to keep things in perspective. Were their positions reversed then she would want to know too. It was unfair of her to be so *hypercritical* about it. It made her feel like a bit of a fraud, if she was being honest. But then, she'd always had a hypocritical outlook towards hypocrisy.

Her father, as if sensing her disquiet, changed subjects respectfully.

"Any potential suitors on the horizon?" he asked, interested. Again, this was one of his traditional questions. She had thought about telling him about Carl, but it was easier just to answer in the negative.

"No," she smiled, shaking her head.

"I know when you were younger, people always told you to get a job and get up the rungs of that ladder but sometimes I think they forget to let you know that there are *other things* in life aside from careers," he pointed out, as she expected he would. Did she pretend to be amazed by this or exasperated? Neither, she would dish out another platitude.

"Oh Papa, I love how you always look out for me," she stated, and really meant it. Although a tiny voice in the back of her mind was asking: *how* can he look out for you when he doesn't even know who you are?

Well, he knew *part* of her and he loved her and she loved him. Love is such a very tiny noun for a sentiment so diverse and problematical. How could you ever possibly convey how you truly feel about anything with a word so restrictive? She was sure that if *anyone* could elucidate the mechanics of it, it would be Reed. Each letter of the word in all its component-level glory.

"Someone should," her father smiled, warmly. "It is my job, after all." The past gave context to the moment, it had to. Without history, everything is meaningless, even if that history is a sham. But, paradoxically, the most terrible deceptions often have a lot of truth in them. The truth they use to hide behind. Like the sheath conceals the dagger.

"I *do* think of you sometimes, *please* don't think I'm only here out of some sort of *obligation or duty*," she said, putting some effort in. "You *do* know that, don't you? I don't want you to feel like that, okay? I'm just *so busy...*"

"You don't need to explain to me or to apologise," he said, forgivingly. "It was the same with me and my parents too. I know. *I understand*."

There, apology done. The guilt returned to the side-lines of her mind. It would be back soon enough of course, she knew. Was this what love did? Corrupted you with a myriad number of emotional conflicts to dull your objectivity and your reactions? This was why she didn't see him too often, she knew. To stay sharp... and stay alive. The conversation remained easy if a little over-formal. They dined out, at the expense of Phantom Squad, in a good restaurant. There was some laughter, some meaningful words, and plenty of meaningless frivolity. She let him, rather pointlessly, see her home first. He didn't know it but she had his home bugged... just to ensure he was safe!

When she got in she discovered the book Harrier had called her about, on the floor disguised as a parcel. She placed it on the table and then began to get to work. She had a lot to do that night. She was going to break into the campaign office and bug *every* computer, *every* room and anything else she could think of. She'd installed a few during the day but she'd not been able to get around everywhere, and it was hard to do that under everyone's noses. She glanced across at Kelvin, still non-functional. Normally she'd check the building layout with him first but... never mind.

---

"I'm in," she said, her voice a whisper. Octutin was sat in the back of the law enforcement vehicle. The city could have an eerie look in the twilight of midnight. An atmosphere where one would listen out for footsteps not of one's own making. Traffic was present, if infrequent. It was quiet.

The driver's seat and the front passenger seat were occupied by lookalike security men. They were in fact two mercenaries he'd recruited from local sources. Having claimed to have worked with each other before, he trusted these two men to act as his support should anything go wrong. Octutin was small and unimpressive looking in comparison with the mercenaries.

He eyed his communicator as he activated a screen in front of him. On it was a live tracking system, used for construction and demolition planning. He scratched his greying black beard thoughtfully.

"Good," he said, calmly. "Keep going." One of the mercenaries lit a smoke and stared across the road, bored. A picture began to draw itself on the screen… a layout was being inscribed for him so that he could work out the best place to plant the device.

Octutin's silvery eyes glinted in the blue light from the screen, interested. While it was likely, not to say highly probable, that this building would be no different from many others, he wasn't taking anything for granted. There was a crackle of noise on the radio and he tensed out of habit. Nothing happened though, and the picture continued to form at a slow but steady pace.

"There are a few guards," the woman whispered. "They are just doing the regular patrols on the premises, I think."

"You know what to do should any of them spot you," Octutin reminded, casually.

"Of course."

―――――― ·✦✦✦✦✦· ――――――

What had started out as a test had turned into one of the easiest infiltrations Satiah had ever performed. The security here was so sloppy, a baby could have crawled in and no one would have noticed. She'd cut her way in from the roof and, using a lift which should *not* have been active, she'd made her way down to the floor she wanted. Not the floor Oli's team were working on, but the floor above it. She would also do a sweep on the floor below. She began to plant her equipment in hidden spots and sometimes within other machines where they would be difficult to spot. It was very quiet and she'd seen neither hide nor hair of any guards. She wondered if they even bothered to do the ordinary patrols. There *were* card readers on the walls that they would flick to show that they had been there, so she hoped they'd not tried to be clever and connect them all up to one somewhere.

During the day she had counted three guards and she knew there would be less at night. The building owner probably didn't think it was a good use of his resources to pay for the same force at night when there should be no one there. To her disbelief, when she scanned the building, she detected *three* others, two in the reception on the ground floor, the guards she presumed, and one coming up the stairs. Had someone come in to pick something up? That was a possibility. Had they somehow realised *she* was there and sent someone up to check? Unlikely. She jogged lightly down the carpeted corridor and concealed herself in a darkened office by the stairs.

Dressed completely in black, a woman reached the landing area and looked around cautiously. She had a bag on her back and looked *very* suspicious indeed. She whispered something, Satiah couldn't hear what, and began to pad along towards the main meeting area, the place where the morning briefing had been held, and would be again. Intrigued, Satiah slid her pistol out and followed. The woman entered the room silently and then went over to where Oli would be standing when he gave his morning briefing. She dragged a table quietly over and stood on it to get to the ceiling. Satiah slipped into the room without a sound and crept closer, whilst hugging the wall. In the shadows, she was almost invisible.

"You're *sure* this is where you want it?" whispered the woman. Satiah couldn't hear *who* she was talking to, unfortunately. The woman stood and pushed one of the ceiling panels up and aside. Torch in her mouth, she then crouched and took something out of her bag. Satiah tilted her head to the side as she watched calmly, going through her options. Her first instinct had been to take this woman down, a single bolt in her back would be *all* that it would need but… she'd learn more if she waited. If she *let* whoever it was believe that they had been successful in doing whatever they were doing, then she wouldn't scare them off. If she scared them, they would melt away and she would run the risk of them striking again but in a completely different way. Or they might strike again, but ages later when she wasn't around. She thought she could guess that they were going to plant some kind of explosive device in the ceiling which would detonate at a certain time during the day. It was a pretty obvious strategy.

The next question was: should she report this? More to the point, did she tell someone on Oli's team? That presented a double problem - who could she trust to tell, and how would she explain what she was doing there to discover this in the first place? No, they would also have to remain in the dark. The more innocently they behaved, the more unknowing, the less chance that whoever this was would realise that someone was onto them. She didn't need Malla to step up and turn the place into a fort. By now, the woman was placing the primed device into the ceiling. Still Satiah waited, judging the efficiency of this woman and potential enemy combatant by how long this was taking her. She was done in just over six minutes. Device deployed. Fairly skilled but Satiah had both done it and seen it done much faster. Without knowing *who* she was, it was difficult to guess at motivation, but Satiah already knew she wasn't working alone.

The woman, without realising she'd got company, replaced the ceiling panel and pushed the table back into position. She checked the table for any signs of dirt. There were none. After a final glance around, without noticing her silent observer, she retreated back into the corridor as silently as she had come. Satiah followed her again. She was following for three reasons: first, to see if she planted *anything else*, second, to see how she had got in and third, most importantly, to see where she went next. She would scan the building again in case she'd had time to prepare anything else on any other of the floors below. The woman led her all the way to the ground floor, passed the guards in reception and then went outside. As casual and easy as a walk on a beach in a calming breeze.

Satiah had seen many examples of poor security, Collgort-Elipsa being a very recent and memorable one. This, however, was just as bad. This was *Earth*, a place where warships were regularly stationed and the armed forces were regularly billeted. The very *heart* of the Coalition. Although this *was* just an office building, most of the time completely unimportant... this would understandably lead to a certain level of complacency. *Now,* though, it had gained political importance. Satiah saw the woman get into a security vehicle outside and was driven off into the skies. Satiah's eyes narrowed. Were the law enforcement squads involved in this, or was it just a very good imitation? Law enforcement could be seen to have a motive in ruining Oli's chances in the election. He'd given them no economic assurances and that had certainly upset the management. Then again, they'd had that before and had never resorted to breaking their own laws. Satiah returned upstairs, sneaking past the sleepy security once again. She quickly found the device in the ceiling.

She'd not been quite right. Yes, it *was* a device and yes, it certainly *would* explode, but not with great enough force to do any real damage. Purpose... reaction. Terror tactics? What would fear do? Convince Oli to pull out from the election? Having met Oli now, she felt it was unlikely that that would work. Then... she realised *why* placing the device had taken as long as it had. It was wired in to the building's power supply... *the chain reaction...* Satiah smiled. Clever. Why bring your own bomb when there was one already there that they could take advantage of? The building's generator would be the target and that really would be a big bang. It might even take out the surrounding structures as well. In a swift move, Satiah defused the device and began to carefully disassemble it. She would hand it to Harrier and his accomplices... who would then tell her *who* had built it, *how much* it cost and, hopefully, *who bought it.*

She continued for the next few hours, placing her own, much more harmless, devices all over the building. Once she'd done that and downloaded all the messages from all the communicators there, she collected the components of the explosive and departed the way she had come. On the roof, the craft she had arrived in sat there in the dark. Out of habit, she checked to be sure no one had tampered with it while she was gone. No one had. She set off noiselessly, careful to avoid the cameras and eyes of any guards… assuming, of course, that those eyes bothered to open.

---

"We're done," Octutin explained. Jinx nodded slowly, as he listened to the other man over the communicator.

"Any trouble?"

"None, it went about as well as it could. The guards were inefficient, and the standard security systems were minimal and in dire need of an upgrade," Octutin detailed, carefully. "Will you inform the client or shall I?"

"I'll do that," Jinx smirked. "I'll discuss payment with you as soon as I have discussed it with them."

---

Malla was absent that morning, due to an appointment with a specialist arranged sometime ago, *apparently*. It seemed he had a long-term problem with his left eye. Satiah was once again following Oli around with Shannon, remaining vigilant, never forgetting that she could be brushing shoulders with whoever was behind the events of the previous evening. Satiah had instantly thought Malla's non-attendance was suspicious. A chief of security *not there* at the exact time an attempt would be made on a life he was responsible for? Now that did look dirty, didn't it? Also, no one seemed to have any details about the actual medical issue that purportedly plagued him.

Then again, he was not the only one, and anyone with half a brain would claim coincidence. Who wouldn't? She had no proof Malla had done anything *untoward*, of course, but then, as a Phantom agent, she didn't *need* any to take action against him. That was the beauty of not being restricted by the tight margins of standard law enforcement departments. She could do *anything* she chose, provided she could justify it to Randal and then he would defend her against anyone else who questioned her actions. And that *anything* included targeted termination.

She was pleased to see than no one seemed aware of the events of the previous evening. If whoever was behind this *wasn't used to this kind of thing*, they would not behave like a professional. They would be easier to scare off, they would be more likely to make mistakes and the odds were that the motive would be personal. She eyed the ceiling panel above Oli's head as he spoke, imagining what would have happened had she not intervened. It looked just like all the others. There was nothing abnormal about it. She wasn't listening to Oli as he went through his usual routine, addressing his campaign team. Her eyes were everywhere, studying faces as before. The same faces with a few missing. No one looked like they were expecting *anything* to happen. No one looked anxious. Shortly before the bomb had been supposed to detonate, coincidentally or not, two people made excuses and left the room. Satiah made a mental note of these movements. She would find out why later.

Oli concluded with a familiar rallying comment that he seemed to always end these morning meetings on.

"Together we can achieve anything," he said, raising a determined fist. There was a cheer and a few imitated the gesticulation.

"Sir, when you leave here, who escorts you to your accommodation?" Satiah asked when he'd finished. She already knew but she was testing him. Just like she knew that they were watching him overnight too.

"Malla. Although *last night* Corban did it," he answered, not really guessing at the significance of her question. Corban was another of the team that she'd met the previous day. Oli seemed to realise that she wasn't asking that question just because she was new.

"Why? Worried something might happen? Trust me, *this is a democracy*, I don't know where you have worked before but things like that don't happen here." O, you poor deluded man, she thought.

"Of course not, sir," she said, maintaining her usual cordiality.

"By the way..." he said, flushing slightly. "After we're done here tonight, I was thinking of taking the city air. I would like you to come with me."

"Just *me*, sir?" she asked, confused. "Malla..."

"It's not..." he began. Instantly she knew what he was trying to say. "I wanted to... I wondered if you knew anywhere we could go that was worth seeing?" he managed, rather awkwardly. This awkwardness was made all the worse by the fact that Shannon could hear every word and did not look at all happy. Satiah played it carefully, choosing to make it look like she'd not quite grasped what he was suggesting. He was, after all, a visitor to Earth so, if it wasn't for the fact that he clearly had become interested in *her*, he could just be seen as someone who wanted to learn more about the planet.

"Sure sir, I know a couple of places," she stated, in her usual tone. Her tone was almost blank, very official, like she wasn't capable of even comprehending emotion. Her eyes though, they told a different story.

He noticed that she'd apparently missed the point but wasn't sure how to bring it up again. Then someone else started talking to him and it was swept aside.

"Are you going to tell Malla about this?" Shannon asked, to Satiah. Jealous? It must be quite annoying for her to have been apparently overlooked for someone as nondescript as Satiah. Satiah was half tempted to ask Shannon, sarcastically, if she'd finally decided to take his security seriously. She had already decided to keep playing dumb; instead she did what anyone would do.

"No, you can do that," she responded, tersely. Shannon's eyebrows rose a little. She'd not seen that coming. "I was hoping you would form up around us, just out of Oli's immediate sight. I *think* he's starting to find our presence a bit heavy. He must be under a lot of stress and our continual attendance around him could be wearying for him. I've seen it before."

Shannon had no direct response to that. She knew Satiah was smarter than she pretended to be, but as everything Satiah had said was both practical and not at all defensive... it was hard to tell what she was really thinking. She was certain that Satiah knew what Oli had been suggesting, just as she thought she knew *why* Satiah had not just gratefully accepted. Yet why ask Shannon and the others to be there too? It could be a bluff, of course, but… Shannon became aware that she was starting to go around in circles.

"I will," she limited herself to saying, pertly. Satiah now had, or could *potentially have,* a new problem. If Oli was romantically interested in her, she had to find a way of putting him off. Granted, a relationship with him would undoubtedly help her keep him safe and that *was* her mission. But she didn't like him… and *Carl would not like him much either, she was sure.* And obviously there was Shannon too.

Satiah didn't know if Shannon had a thing for Oli or that she just had a problem with *her,* but either way she could present trouble further down the line. So much for trying to stay low key. She could sense Shannon eyeing her up, assessing her, seeking vulnerabilities. She would find none. Satiah though had found three in Shannon. She had a temper, which made her very easy to manipulate; her left knee was still recovering from an injury; and she didn't seem to understand exactly how her own communicator worked. She could use it, certainly, but that morning she had asked Satiah to adjust the settings for her as she wasn't sure how. Satiah had used this opportunity to bug the communicator. While she was not a suspect, she, like everyone else, *was* a person of interest.

———— ✦✦✦✦✦ ————

Later that day it was the interview time. Oli had been in make-up for ten minutes and Satiah had opted to go in there with him while Shannon would be the one to stand nearest to him while the interview occurred. Satiah always avoided being in view of a camera if she could. Her face, while not exactly infamous, was best kept out of the media's eyes. Even if she was only on the periphery or in the background, it was a risk she didn't want to take. Shannon, pleased at her reluctance, had taken the opportunity to make a cutting remark.

"Yes, it would be better for *someone like you* to avoid the cameras," she'd said, maliciously.

"*Someone like me?*" Satiah had growled. Shannon was quick to cover her tracks and hide behind politeness.

"Well, I don't know you *well* but you seem very shy and sometimes being in front of the cameras *can* be daunting. I've seen all kinds of people caught off guard. They just stand there, like they are paralysed with fear. It can be quite traumatising. I've done it before so it makes sense that I should go."

Satiah was quite certain that what she had meant was something along these lines: *I think a wooden hussy of muscle like you would just look ugly. It's a wonder you can string two words together that aren't Yes Sir.* Ever the great actress though, Satiah had only grunted as if she agreed. It was a sign, after all, that her cover act was working. She wasn't going to rise to it yet, if at all. She would keep her mind on the job… something she wished Shannon might do. Kate was talking to Oli, preparing him for the questions that Deetee would ask him. Satiah had seen Deetee before and she'd already decided she despised him. Leaving aside the fact that he was *a journalist,* the man had such an air of self-satisfied superiority it made her want to thump him. He reminded her a bit of Slimy Snell, except that Deetee was more clipped and attractive in that way only *celebrities* can be.

"Are you ready?" Kate asked, hopefully. Oli smiled and turned the chair to face Satiah.

"What do you think? Am I ready?" he asked. Kate was also looking at her. Satiah shifted on her feet, trying to look as puzzled and nervous as she could.

"The perimeter is secure, everyone is in position so… yes sir," she responded, a little earnestly. "Shannon will be on screen with you but, as I have already told you, I will be by the main door if you need me." Oli and Kate shared a glance but nothing more was said. Satiah shrugged off the mild discomfort and concentrated. Was everyone where they should be? Was someone else there who shouldn't be?

"We go in ten," the director shouted. The androids moved into their places, all camera feeds were checked and rechecked. Lighting. Sound. Satiah crossed her arms and vowed to herself that she would *not* allow the discussion that was about to take place irritate her. She detested any kind of political debate and the posturing kinds of showmanship it generated. Really? You're *so* busy being a politician? How the hell did you have time for this interview then? Ruling the Coalition was not something you could just stop doing. This was partly why no one ever saw the people who were *really* in charge. They literally were too busy and far too sensible to ever reveal what they did or even *who they were* to the public. Oli made eye contact with her and she provided an encouraging smile and nod. Luckily Shannon missed that one.

It began. Deetee addressed Oli in his usual soul-sucking, toe-curling style. No, not *style*, that implied there was something *good* about it, *way* was more accurate. He had *a way*. And even that was disgustingly crawly. His smarmy smile and his perfect look… *urgh*… Satiah had to look away. She was already struggling to prevent her mind seeing him as a target on a range.

"Isn't it great that you found the time to come and join us down here in the studio?" Deetee asked, rhetorically. Satiah felt her skin crawling just at the sound of his voice, and focussed on watching everyone around her, *seeking danger*. No such luck.

"One of the first questions I have simply *got* to put to you is: why would you want to run against Brenda Watt after her successful resolution of the Vinu-Shintu war?" Deetee asked, pretending to be all agog.

Prepared, Oli answered.

"I could say it's because I'm sure it was a victory more for her diplomatic team than her *herself*, but instead I just to want to remind everyone that strictly speaking she *shouldn't be* the Commandment Benefactor yet," Oli answered, tactfully.

"Of course, after all, that is part of the reason why this election began."

Deetee nodded, without missing a beat. "Yet some people are saying that it's all a bit excessive and that it doesn't need to happen at all, what do you think about that?" Oli took the time to sip his water. It actually made him very angry that anyone would say that, but he had to stay in control.

"I would remind those people that, as I said before, *legally* we should be leaderless right now. I understand the necessity of having a proxy, but clear leadership needs to be established for the benefit of all. Divided administrations seldom thrive and there *is* dependability in unity. I do not wish to say Brenda hasn't helped or that she's done anything wrong by stepping in; however, I will reiterate that she cannot simply replace her predecessor without a vote. *It's illegal,*" Oli stated, carefully and clearly. Kate nodded and silently clapped at him encouragingly.

Deetee smiled, a devious gleam in his eyes.

"Those are good points you raise there, a lot of people have expressed curiosity as to why it was *Brenda* that did step in, care to comment?" he asked, smiling like a predator.

"*Hold it!*" called someone, from the control room. "Deetee! I've told you *before*, you *can't* talk about the Vourne conspiracy!"

"Did you hear me mention it?" Deetee enquired, sardonically.

"*You* know what you're doing, *I* know what you're doing, *stop it now!*" the director's voice argued, stubbornly. Satiah rolled her eyes but Kate was looking a bit angry.

"It's okay, *we* can answer that! *Isn't that what we're doing here?* Discussing the controversial stuff?" Kate protested.

"Well it *is,* yes..." was the awkward response. Satiah almost sniggered... almost... if only they knew...

"I don't see why *discussing* it is a problem," she stated, crossing her arms. Satiah could, and she was starting to feel a bit sorry for the director. If he didn't *know,* then he might suspect what could happen to *him* if he allowed this discussion to proceed. Forget his job... what about his life?

"Fine, okay, answer *that* but *no more!*" he compromised, uneasy. Kate frowned, still dissatisfied, but she didn't challenge again. Three, two, one...

"Those are good points you raise there, a lot of people have expressed curiosity as to why it was *Brenda* that did step in, care to comment?" That was Deetee, repeating the question as the recording began again.

It was supposed to be live, and as far as the public knew it would be, but it was actually done about twenty minutes in advance of the time it was supposed to be on.

"Brenda's administration has held a lot back about itself, claiming that they cannot disclose much yet, due to the possibility of *ruining the integrity of the investigation*. I can see there is some wisdom in that; however, in order for the election to be run appropriately, the truth has to be known by all. Otherwise it's not a *proper* election. It just adds fuel to the fire for those who believe that we are living in some kind of dystopia," Oli answered.

"Are *you* one of *these people*, Oli?" Deetee asked, jumping in like a greedy vulture. Oli backtracked as planned.

"Of course not, but these insecurities do have their place and when Brenda sits here and flatly refuses to reveal anything, I can quite understand that some among us become suspicious," Oli said, levelly. The studio audience had been told not to be as welcoming/forgiving/ *overwhelmingly for* Oli as they had been for Brenda, and had duly watched in silence.

"Yet you have repeatedly cited before that there is widespread corruption and vote rigging occurring in several places and times through this *and* other elections in the past," Deetee went on, sounding like he was reading out charges now. "Do you still believe that? Do you have proof of these wild accusations?"

Satiah's eyes drifted to one particular member of the studio audience. He was wearing a red jacket and he was behaving *differently* to the others. He was half sitting and half standing as if he was trying to say something or go somewhere, and looked suspicious. She edged forwards slowly, moving towards him in a roundabout way. Why had no one else noticed him? They all seemed completely absorbed in the drama of the interview. He looked concerned about *something*, perhaps afraid, whilst watching the interview like all the others. There was nothing remarkable about his face, but his jacket was on which was another factor that made him stand out to her. The rest of the audience seemed warm enough to not need any layers at all.

He was still shifting indecisively, like he was trying to pluck up the courage to *do something*. Satiah had initially thought that this man was planted there to distract her from someone else, but there were no other suspicious characters that she could see. His apparently normal appearance, however, didn't detract at all from the potential danger he represented. He was large, but not big enough to repel Satiah easily. All the same, she approached with caution, careful to ensure he didn't see her getting closer. Her brown eyes flashed as she took in her immediate surroundings again out of habit, to check for anything that might impede her if it came to a struggle.

"They're not *wild accusations;* they are, however, strong opinions of which I have *no evidence to support* but do still nonetheless believe. It's *common knowledge* that one such enquiry into corruption was itself corrupted by persons unknown. That's no coincidence in my mind," Oli answered. Deetee looked delighted, but the director looked flustered and his hand inched towards the suspension lever again. Kate too was now starting to look worried. She knew she had encouraged this, but it could easily go too far.

"Are you suggesting a cover up?" Deetee asked, his tone professional.

"Perhaps a cover up of a cover up, it's impossible to know as no one will say," Oli stated, flirting with the line now.

The man in the red jacket abruptly stood up. There was something small and black in his hand. The problem with most security was that they were forbidden from making the first move. They couldn't bring a potential enemy down without justifiable criteria. *She could though.* Satiah leapt in, tackling and flattening him instantly to the floor. Panicked shrieks and screams came from everyone around. She began to secure the man's arms by yanking them behind his back while her knee held him down, face to the floor.

"*Don't even think about it!*" she snarled, in his ear. He wasn't resisting her particularly, but she didn't know if he would start to try.

Pandemonium ensued briefly as Oli was moved out by Shannon and two others. The audience scattered, trying to get away whilst also trying to see what had happened. Two security androids approached Satiah and the man she'd subdued. Luckily, instead of filming this altercation, the director cut the power to the cameras. The man was trying to say *something* over the noise but it was so loud that even Satiah couldn't actually hear his words; however, after cuffing him, she'd noticed the black object he had been carrying. It was a book and it was open on the floor, a few pages still moving. A quick scan through it with confirmed to her what she'd just started to suspect.

He'd wanted *a signature* for his collection and, wanting to be first in the queue, was going for it *too early*. She'd thought he was an assassin and all the time he was just a fan. This kind of thing happened far too often for it to be humorous anymore. She backed off as law enforcement moved in and quickly established what she already knew. The man was reprimanded for moving in too early and everyone was allowed to return to their seats. Deetee was furious at the interruption. He'd been gradually manoeuvring Oli into sounding like a madman, as he had been told to, and all that effort had just been ruined as Kate would have had time to make Oli aware of the trap he was slipping into. He glowered at Satiah, conveniently forgetting that if she'd allowed the man to move in then it would have been him who interrupted anyway. Satiah stared dumbly back, continuing to play her part as the overly enthusiastic bodyguard.

"You *idiot*!" Shannon hissed at her. She was glad Satiah had apparently screwed up and was instantly ready to try to capitalise on it.

"The guy looked like a threat," Satiah drawled, as if greatly bored by all this. "Better safe than sorry. I have apologised to him and it's not like he was seriously hurt or anything." He genuinely had looked like a threat and Satiah wasn't worried about anything she'd done. Actually, it only helped her seem all the more like what she was supposed to be.

"And what would have happened if he'd prosecuted us?" Shannon asked, rhetorically. "You could have *seriously* affected Oli's popularity." Even better if so, but Satiah doubted that this would happen as only twenty people or so would ever hear about it. As takedowns went, it had been a little sloppy but, funnily enough, she'd not been trying for finesse at the time. Besides, she couldn't do anything too amazing or it would draw too much attention to her.

"My job is protect him, not make him more popular," Satiah stated, bluntly.

"*Or less popular*," Shannon stated, seriously. Satiah only shrugged, which seemed to infuriate Shannon even more.

Oli came over at that point, which stopped her from saying anything else.

"Are you okay?" he asked Satiah. "What happened?"

"Mistake, sir," she responded, nonchalantly. "Thought it might be a weapon he was holding but it turned out to be just a notebook."

"Well, don't be too hard on yourself. Your timely interruption got me out of a very tricky situation there," he smiled, sincerely. Oh no…

"That was fortunate, sir," she confined herself to saying. "As you know, my first priority is your safety."

"I've noticed," he chuckled, trying to get her to smile or even laugh. She didn't though. She didn't want to.

Not only would her smiling prove she was a human capable of feeling amused, but it would also anger Shannon more and make him even *more* interested in her. She stayed inexpressive which was easy for her to do, even with all this going on. He was still there, awaiting a response, so she had to say something.

"Perhaps next time I will defer such things to my team, sir," she said, a little sheepish. He regarded her analytically for a moment. He suspected that she was acting but she stayed in character anyway - she had to. Thankfully, Kate came over at that point and dragged him away to continue filming. Satiah and Shannon exchanged looks.

---

"Why didn't it go off?" Jinx demanded, not angry but curious. Octutin didn't know. There were obvious eventualities. It had been discovered and removed. The hired operative had lied and hadn't placed it there at all. The device itself had failed to explode for a mechanical reason. There were a few other explanations too. Just because it hadn't gone off at the prearranged time didn't mean it wouldn't detonate at some other time. A faulty timer seemed on the cards. Octutin had checked the device himself before trusting it to the woman he'd hired for the job. Every component had been in optimal condition. Yet surely if it *had* been discovered they would have heard something by now.

"I've been in touch with the operative and she swears nothing was missed. It's a mystery," he told him. There was no point in lying and besides, he wanted to know too.

"We will have to try something else," Jinx replied, ponderously.

"I will look into why it failed to explode," Octutin promised, seriously. "If it was discovered but no one reported it…" It was an unexpected outcome.

"Has Oli done anything to make you suspect that he knows we tried to take him out, but is pretending not to?" Jinx asked.

"No, there have been no changes to his schedule, no changes in staff… nothing like that," he replied. Then he paused. "Actually that's not true, a bodyguard was replaced as he retired but that was the day before the explosive was installed," he corrected himself.

"The day *before*?" Jinx mulled it over. "Any idea who?"

"You'll have to ask the client."

---

"What is it?" Randal asked, tersely. He didn't like Scott at all.

"Oli has gained an extra two percent representation. You might want to have a word with Satiah," he stated self-importantly.

"She most likely already knows," Randal responded, deliberately misunderstanding.

"No, I meant *tell her to do something to cripple him*," Scott quantified.

"She's been there *two days*! She won't have had much time to do much of anything yet, and two percent is nothing," Randal argued, levelly.

"If he makes thirty percent it might be enough to…"

"She'll take care of him, *don't worry*," Randal hissed, disconnecting. He glared at his communicator fleetingly before returning his attention to the screens in front of him.

---

"But that's going to take *hours*!" Harrier protested. Satiah smiled impishly. I know, she thought.

"*You* wanted me to look at that book. It takes time for me to do things and when I'm doing one I cannot do the other, it's all perfectly logical," she explained, with exaggerated patience.

"Okay, okay," he said, caving quickly. "The usual?"

"Yes, all the trigger words plus *anything* that looks like *a forest...*" she advised, authoritatively.

"*What?*" he asked, thinking he'd misheard.

"*A euphemism*! *Forest* is a euphemism *for* euphemism! Don't you ever *read* the code books?" she demanded, haughtily. Sulky silence. She went on. "Anything that *went* outside, anything that came in *from* outside so yes. *The usual.*"

"No one *uses* the trigger words anymore!" he complained, with a sigh. She smiled.

"That's because they *don't* want to get caught," she told him, pointlessly. She disconnected and smiled contentedly. She'd just persuaded Harrier to go through *all* the bugs she'd positioned throughout the office and bring back *anything* incriminating to her. That should keep him busy.

She, in the meantime, needed to prepare for her *date?* She wished this wasn't the case but she'd seen that expression on too many faces to not recognise desire when she saw it. She tore open the parcel to reveal the book Harrier had sent her on Rainbow's behalf. It was old looking, tatty and more than a little dog-eared. She opened it smoothly and regarded the spidery scribble inside with incredulity. It seemed to be a codex with some rather bizarre coloured illustrations inside it. It was made from vellum, according to a note Harrier had typed for her. The skin of an animal. Tanned. Very old-fashioned and odd. While he couldn't tell for sure, Harrier had also said he was sure it was complete. No missing pages or content. Pity, it would have been nice to have one last page casually explaining how to read the rest of it. Some of the pages were foldable sheets. The text *seemed* to be going from left to right but obviously she couldn't be sure.

One picture she instantly comprehended was a constellation. Astronomy was not one of her talents and Kelvin was incapable of helping her this time. Sighing heavily, she had to look up a list and go through it to find out if she was correct. It took her nearly fifteen minutes to find it. Reemus, no. Roomar, no. Ryhore, no. *Satmarrick Constellation.* It looked like a curved sword blade, a scimitar, without a cross-guard. At least, it did to *her*. Yes, it was the place illustrated in the apparently un-readable book. She couldn't believe Rainbow and Harrier between them hadn't figured that one out! So much for the *intelligence* branch. Maybe she was wrong and it wasn't a constellation at all. It *could* be some kind of strange circuit diagram, she supposed. She scrutinised it closely, wishing for the umpteenth time that she had Kelvin's help with this. His eyes were better than hers and he could analyse the image with the aid of the vast array of databases he had.

She looked at the text again. It seemed to be syllabic script mainly, though what resembled letters could also be made out. It was odd in that the longer you looked at it, the more maybes you could see. She knew this was partly because of the way people's minds worked: it was called apophenia. Seeing patterns in randomness, or basically seeing things that weren't there. She thought through several of the lesser known languages that she had heard of. *Tabular C, Cubelike K* or *Crosswise 15*. Some of the larger symbols did resemble those from Crosswise 15. An hourglass-like pictograph also looked a lot like certain mathematical icons.

If she was right about that picture really being the constellation of Satmarrick then it made sense to her for the text, in *whatever language it was*, to be referring in some way to said constellation. So logic would dictate. She counted the lines of text, then the number of words and multiplied them. Thirteen times eleven was one hundred and forty three. Well, that was that idea out then. She'd wondered if perhaps it had something to do with the galactic coordinates but apparently not. That constellation was ranged from 1002-5541 through to 1100-9978 which was nothing to do with 143. But there *were* four ones in those ranges and… she stopped herself and stared up at the ceiling with a wry grin on her lips. No, stop being silly. She made a note of the constellation then closed the book and returned it to the table. She'd have another look later when she had more time.

Now, in one hour she would be on escort duty. She hoped it remained strictly within the confines of the bodyguard role and didn't shift into that of *companion*. She eyed Kelvin, wondering if she had time to…

no, she'd look at him when she got back. She began her ablutions and thought about Carl. She knew, even though he would *say* that he didn't mind, he would be against the idea of her being with another man. She wasn't too keen on the thought herself, ironically. She could use Carl as an excuse to push Oli away if he tried anything with her, she decided. Or she could say she was concerned that Shannon might not like it, which might put him off. She could even indicate that Shannon liked him and thus she didn't want to get in their way. Alternatively, she could just imply that she was of a different persuasion and men were not it.

Then there was tonight. The bomb that had not gone off might make them, whoever they were, try again. Harrier still hadn't finished with the work of identification. Apparently, they had scratched some of the information he needed off the materials she had recovered. Of course they had, they would hardly leave a forwarding address on it, would they? She wondered if they would try something similar next time, or turn to a different strategy. And she'd not checked up on whether Malla had really been to that appointment or not either. Then there was that report Randal wanted her to review. There was always *something* for her to do! Just as well in a way, when she had nothing to do, was when she really went crazy.

---

"It is *not* a date!" Oli objected, for the ninth time. Kate just kept smiling like someone who had badly misjudged their own medication. A smile that said: *it doesn't matter what you say, I know the truth.* It made him want to complete her daily puzzle for her, as he knew that would *really* annoy her. She lived for that puzzle. It was a challenge for her that was completely safe and gave her a sense of accomplishment every day. Something to smile about. No matter what else happened that day, if she'd completed the puzzle correctly, it made her feel better about herself. Sometimes it took her twenty minutes and sometimes she'd be struggling with it all day. He remembered once that she'd failed to complete it, and it had led to a few days of misery and an inability, well, a *begrudging disinclination*, to start another one.

"Well, whatever it is, don't forget *who you are* in the election, the public most likely will approach you," she told him.

"I won't, you can come along yourself if you like?" he offered, maintaining the pretence that he had no interest in Satiah at all. He didn't know that Shannon and a few others would be there. Malla hadn't told him. As far as he knew it was just him and her. He donned a hat in a minimal effort to disguise who he was.

"Very fetching," Kate remarked, trying not to laugh.

"No point in drawing attention to myself," he grunted, regarding himself in the mirror. "How do I look?" She glanced at him and shrugged unhelpfully.

"Well, I use my eyes, but I have no idea how *you* do it," she murmured, tapping a screen to enlarge the text. He chuckled.

"Right, I'm off," he stated, heading for the door. He halted on the threshold, surprised by the silence. He turned to look at her again. "Not going to tell me to stay safe?" he quipped, teasingly.

"Satiah has been here two days. She's passed Malla's tests, brought down some innocent man thinking he was going attack you and watches everything you eat and drink like a hawk. I think if *anyone* could keep you safe, it's her," she replied, seriously. He rolled his eyes.

"I give up," he muttered, leaving.

―――――♦♦♦♦♦♦―――――

"Just don't lumber me with any… *creatures*," Deetee insisted. They were standing on a high walkway, the androids filming. Passers-by were looking at what was going on, but upon seeing the CNC logo, hurried on. The countdown began. Deetee's face assumed its standard smile. If there was a record for the longest-lasting smile, he would have it. This was the filming for the 'Beings on the Walkway Special'. He would address members of the public and see what they had to say regarding the election. This kind of programme, despite being popular according to the figures, was Deetee's least favourite. He hated talking to the public as people tended to fall into two categories. Those that cared and those that didn't. Those that didn't just wasted his time. Those that did

*Operation Selector*

often wasted *even more* with endless rants about whatever pet hate they had. Nevertheless, the viewers always got what they wanted.

Microphone ready, he was given the signal and approached a woman walking briskly along. She saw him coming and glared.

"No!" she yelled, barging past him. Not at all put off, Deetee simply accosted the next person along. An elderly man, minding his own business.

"Hi there, *Beings on the Walkway Special*, do you have any opinions regarding the election?" Deetee beamed.

"What?" the man asked, slightly deaf. Deetee repeated the question more loudly and the old man smiled.

"Brenda Watt has *my* vote," he said, casually. "Last week she actually came down to see us at our community centre and unveiled a new central heating system. It's wonderful. This one doesn't make *any* noises in the night and it *actually* warms the place up, it's fantastic."

It was all Deetee could do not to burst out laughing. There was *no way* he could use this in the actual programme, it just wasn't realistic enough. On he went, asking more and more. Overwhelmingly, the vast majority supported Brenda. She'd been everywhere. Opening *this*, helping with *that*, or seeming to have a reasonable grasp of what people needed. It took him *hours* to find someone who wasn't voting for her. Trouble was that *that someone* wasn't voting at all. They were a tourist from the Nebular Union.

"This is not good for *balance*!" Deetee protested. "We need to get someone who *doesn't* support her but that we can pull apart easily. Yet it seems that there's no one *on this planet* with that point of view, I'm afraid."

Standard Citizen, a new programme *supposed* to reflect the true needs of whatever constituency it was set in, was beginning next week. Deetee had been chosen to act as presenter in that too. In it would be a carefully scripted, liberally performed collection of interviews and statistical reviews which was designed to subtly convince those watching it to vote for Brenda Watt. This was why, if the pretence was to look realistic, they had to find at least a few people who were staunchly against her. Those few would be vilified, and/or made to look ignorant, and finally dismissed as something from the past that no one wants to revisit. It was all part of the plan that Deetee was being paid a lot of money to help implement. He was a master in the use of one of the most dangerous weapons ever created: *words*. It is no coincidence that the term *words* is an anagram of sword.

What Deetee was really looking forward to, though, was the live debate. Obviously it wouldn't be *live* exactly, but as far as the public knew it would be. Brenda would play the victim, which she did well, acting as though everyone was targeting her but, even though she wasn't sure why, she wanted to help them anyway. The other candidates would see through this and become increasingly enraged and make more and more mistakes which Deetee would capitalise on. However, there was one aspect of that debate that no one would have any control over: a representative of the Colonial Federation would be present, along with the Nebula Union. They would probably say nothing as they normally didn't, and this time it was doubted that anyone from the Union would even be there, but it was a potential risk.

———— ✦✦✦✦✦ ————

"Time to get up," the voice said. Brenda blinked, yawned and stretched. Her aide was standing in the doorway, looking at her.

"*Morning*. Right," Brenda sighed, slowly rising. She was groggy. "What are we doing today?" The woman smiled casually.

"Aren't *you* the one who decides that?" she asked. Brenda considered that.

"I still need to go through the economic appraisal," she said, tying her hair back.

"No need, that was done last night," the woman answered. Brenda paused in shock. "It's fine. I double checked it myself," the woman went on. "You have nothing to worry about; long term investments have been made in both education and security. Healthcare remains a concern, along with accommodation but, in alignment with your suggestions, it was decided we would concentrate on the elderly and the workforce."

Brenda frowned. Yes, she *had* told them that that was the way she was thinking, but still it would have been nice to actually oversee the process herself.

"It's good," the woman went on, detecting Brenda's disposition. "Without *your guidance* it might have been *weeks* before it was resolved. Thanks to *you*, people are getting what they need."

"I suppose," she mused, timidly. The aide smiled calculatingly and put her hand on Brenda's shoulder.

"You know what your problem is?" Brenda shook her head. "You've been *overworking*. You care *too much* to let yourself get the rest you need. As lovable as this is, it's *not* healthy. You know you have our full support in all things."

This was true. She always felt so tired and anxious these days. Weren't *those pills* they were giving her supposed to help with that? She'd known that being Commandment Benefactor of the Coalition would be a demanding undertaking but it was both more and less than she'd anticipated. She did trust those around her to help her but she was starting to wonder. They just seemed to tell her what to do and where to be *all the time*. Yet wasn't she the one in charge? They kept telling her *she was,* but she never actually seemed to *do* anything. It felt like she was supervising a system that looked after itself. She was pleased she didn't have to micromanage, but nonetheless it troubled her. Whenever something happened, whatever it was, *they told her* how best to respond to it. They did this by suggesting courses of action and then basically persuading her that whatever option they suggested, was the best. They could find reasons for anything. Plausible reasons.

She'd wanted to make things better and she had promised herself to never lose sight of what she needed to change. Now, though, she was struggling to keep track of everything. There was always *so much* to remember. Maybe she was right, maybe she was just *overworking.*

"You're *right,*" she said, emotionally. "I'm sorry I'm being so difficult. I guess I'm a bit of a control freak." The aide smiled, a knowingly triumphant gleam in her eyes.

"Most good leaders *are,*" she reassured, slyly. "If you weren't taking any of this seriously *I* would be worried." She laughed convincingly.

"You're doing a brilliant job, Brenda. I've *never* known a more moral and kind person than you before. Now, is there *anything* I can get you? Anything at all?"

"Just some water, please."

―――――・▸◆◂・―――――

"Where were you this morning?" Shannon demanded, irately. Malla turned around in surprise.

"You *know* where I was," he frowned. There was a moment of silence. A pause of re-evaluation.

"Did you hear what happened?" she asked, still simmering.

"Are you talking about Satiah…?"

"She's *dangerous. Completely paranoid*. We should replace her," she stated, forthrightly. Malla opened his mouth to answer when he stopped himself and tilted his head to the side.

"I'll talk to her," he said, at last. "I can't say *I* have a problem with anything she's done. She saw right though that business with the fire extinguisher. All right, the guy in the audience *was* harmless, but there was no way *she* could have known that…"

"Be that as it may, I don't trust her," Shannon stated, flatly.

"And what does Oli think?" Malla asked, looking at it from a different angle.

"Oh, he *loves* her," she almost spat. "Ever since she realised we weren't checking his food, he's been completely lapping up *everything* she dishes out." Malla had the sudden urge to laugh at her wording but he hid it well. It didn't seem very appropriate at that moment in time.

"What is it *exactly* that she's done to earn your distrust?" he asked, trying to mediate as best he could. *And your obvious dislike*, he stopped himself from adding. Shannon paused and crossed her arms.

"It's… It's hard to explain. There is *something* about her… *like she's hiding something*. She's just so alert *all the time* but she never expresses any opinions or even vibes. *Like a machine*," she stated, trying to *not* say what she really wanted to. Mercenaries were dogs and could *never* be trusted. And *how* could Oli possibly be attracted to her?

"She's new, that's *why* she's so unfriendly, it's *understandable*," Malla said, trying to defend her while trying not to sound like he was defending her. He recalled saying something similar to Satiah about Shannon, absurdly. "I'm *sure* she'll soften up eventually and then, *when you get to know her*, you'll probably change your mind." Shannon's eyes narrowed suspiciously.

"Have you met her *before*?" she quizzed.

"No," he stated immediately. "You *know* I haven't."

"But you've worked with me for years and, *even though you know you can trust me*, you're *not* taking my word on this?" she demanded. By *word* she meant *side*.

"I *said* I'll talk to her," he said, suddenly in danger of losing his temper. Shannon realised she'd overstepped the mark then, and knew she had to back down for now.

If he needed proof of transgression... Shannon made up her mind that *she* would find some.

---

A smear might be enough. Satiah had already seen a message from the administration to Oli regarding his proposed amendments to the budget. All she needed to do was amend the answering message and leak it to the press from someone else's computer. It didn't have to be anything *too* dramatic. Just something negligible like the ending of the state pension scheme, or the suppressing of the vote rigging investigation. Something a bit heartless, but nothing outright cruel. *She* would then track it down to that computer when a search was ordered but she would afterwards *discover* that it had been done by someone else and *not* that computer's owner. She didn't want anyone to lose their jobs over it, but she needed to put a dent in the campaign somehow. This would also mean that if anyone did suspect that *she* might have orchestrated the leak, it would make no sense as *she* was the one who had originally cast doubt on the first party's guilt. It would look like a plot to drag her into it.

She was waiting where she and Oli had decided to meet. If he wanted to see the planet then that would be what she would show him. Exoth-Tower, Green Stadium, Weavers Walkway, the Mulac Building… Okay, maybe not *there*. She realised, much to her dismay, that these had been all of the places she'd intended to show *Carl*. She'd been promoted! She was now a tour guide apparently! *Sadly, no pay rise.* She reminded herself that Carl was there to see *her*, not the planet. Mysteriously, Oli wanted the same thing… this was most unfortunate. Perhaps… she sniggered as she thought of a new idea. She wouldn't take Oli to all the tourist spots; she'd take him to the red-light region. He wouldn't like that, she was sure. It was the most dangerous area on the planet, which, compared with most worlds, wasn't that dangerous at all. Crime was at an all-time low on Earth.

Alternatively, just stay in character, play it dumb and apathetic, she could just *ask Oli* where he wanted to go. *He'd asked her,* after all. Then again, she'd said she knew places… She'd adjusted the scopes on the rifle they had given her and slung it across her shoulders as a taxi soared down from the skies to park nearby. Oli got out and paid while she advanced over to him. He'd dressed well for the occasion and she wondered what he would think he realised *she hadn't*. She was still in her security uniform. The taxi took off as he turned to face her.

"Hi," he said, eyeing her levelly. If he was disappointed he didn't show it.

"Evening, sir," she smiled, cordially. She'd already seen Shannon and a few others arrive nearby. They were poor at disguising themselves.

"Did you have anything particular in mind about what you wanted to see, sir?" she asked, anxious to keep his attention away from the others.

"You don't have to keep calling me sir," he insisted, pleasantly. "You're off duty now."

"Very well," she replied hesitantly, as if this scenario was difficult for her to comply with.

"What do you think is best to see of this world? Do you live here, by the way?" he asked, as they began to walk rather tensely along together.

"Dunno," she grunted. She looked all around as if considering the question *very* carefully. She hoped this would make him question if she had any personality at all. "Yes, I do live here sometimes. The *Skygates* are pretty active. All the people coming and going all the time. I like to imagine who they are and where they have come from." The Skygates were where all the passenger ships docked to pick up the tourists or off-world workers.

She hoped her words would sound as empty as she thought they were, unfortunately he leapt on it like a conversational lifeline.

"Me too," he said, animated. "It's a big cosmos when you think about it. I mean, we still have *so much* to explore. It really makes you think sometimes, doesn't it? Puts your own problems in perspective, keeps you down to… well… *Earth*." He laughed awkwardly at his own joke. This was painful now, *actually painful*. She wondered if he felt as awkward as she did. No, no one could feel this uncomfortable. It would be rude for her not to respond to his comment, even if the humour was *pathetic*. She knew she'd only make things worse but she couldn't think of what else to do. She smiled. It really was the smallest of smiles, made *strictly* out of civility, but of course he didn't see it that way. He thought he was getting somewhere.

"Good place to be," she stated, indifferently. She raised a hand to get a taxi's attention. Almost instantly one dropped from the skies to collect its new customers. She quickly turned the focus on him; this was starting to get on her nerves.

"Where are you from?" she asked, coldly. Again, taking the bait, he began talking. She had to pay attention, even though it bored her utterly, as it might be relevant to the mission. He started talking about his home world, family and hobbies. Apparently he painted, who knew? *Who cared*?! She glanced out of the mirror, noting that two other taxis were following them. Malla and the others, she presumed. Why would they need *two*? How many people had they brought with them? She had that feeling again… that feeling that told her something was about to happen.

Who else knew that she and Oli were meeting that night? Kate had to know. Malla and Shannon knew. Harrier hadn't alerted her to any chatter that might give away an aggressive intention. There was always the outside chance that this might be someone acting completely independently. A regular criminal who had no idea who he was following. If only she could scan the craft and learn more! It was steadily gaining on them, coming up quite close now. She wondered if whoever it was might flash at them in an attempt to make them stop and get out. She made her decision. If nothing else it would get her out of this long-drawn-out itchy chat.

"One moment," she said, raising her hand to get Oli to stop talking. He turned as if to look around. "*Don't look*," she ordered, suddenly very serious. He seemed to realise that something was going on very quickly, thankfully.

"What's wrong?" he said, edgy.

"Driver!" she called, grimly. "Go left at the next junction."

"That will not take you to your destination any more quickly," the android stated, bewildered. In order to make more money, the computers that drove taxis were programmed to take *the long way* to destinations. It wasn't unusual for locals to know this and counter it by specifying particular directions. Directions they *knew* would get them to where they wished to go fastest. In this case, however, no matter which way you elected to take, *left wasn't correct*.

"Correct, it won't, do it anyway," she responded, slipping the rifle onto her lap. She eyes never left the mirror. As they went left - so did both other cabs. One now directly behind the other. They were all in a line.

"*Satiah*?" Oli piped up. She pulled out her communicator, ignoring him.

"Malla?" she said, softly. She had to figure out who was who. It worried her that she was *the only one* who'd apparently noticed what was going on. Perhaps it had been a deliberate act that the others had failed to notice. They could be involved. Or they could just be incompetent.

"Now where...?" the android began.

"Keep going," she told it, a bleakness coming to her countenance. If she hadn't already, she was sure that at any time now she would tip off whoever it was that they had been clocked.

This strategy of following them made sense as their destination had never been confirmed, so *if* someone back at the office *had* overheard, they would never have known where it was that she and Oli would end up. They might know where and when they were meeting first, though. Malla and Shannon had known, of course. *Shannon had known first.* On the other hand, Oli could have been followed straight from when he'd left his accommodation.

"Satiah?" Malla asked, answering her.

"Where's *Malla*?" Oli enquired, rather stupidly. Did he *really* imagine they would just let him go out without following him? She raised her finger to her lips and shushed him.

"Are you directly behind *our* taxi, sir?" she asked, levelly.

"No, there's a cab between us, why...?" he began. A knowing grimness reached to her eyes.

"All right, *everyone stay calm*," she instructed, in a growl. "The taxi between us is following us. Any ideas, Malla?"

"Are you sure?" That question came from Shannon who was with Malla. A flash of anger was quickly suppressed by Satiah who never liked it when people, *who should know better*, doubted her. Especially when *those people* might be playing for time. Time for *what*, she wondered. She gave Oli a dangerous smile and the look that came to his eyes and face made her think of Carl. The look said: *oh no, what's she going to do now?*

"There's an easy way to prove it," she snapped, suddenly forcing her way forward into the driving area. The android tried to protest but she wrenched out the exposed power cable, rendering it non-functional. Next, she pushed its tiny body away to make room for herself and scrambled into the seat properly. The controls were basic and she quickly overrode the security system. After that she roughly pulled on a safety harness.

"*Satiah?*" Oli asked, panic and incredulity battling it out in his tone.

"Strap yourself in!" she barked, hitting the accelerator.

Oli only just managed to obey that instruction in time as Satiah banked right abruptly and then nosedived towards the ground at a terrific velocity. In doing this she broke about five laws and terrified everyone who saw it. Satiah though was exhilarated. It was the most fun she'd had since she returned to Earth. *Game on!* As she guessed, the taxi between hers and Malla's followed immediately. Malla too began to follow.

"*What are you doing?*" Shannon demanded, livid. Satiah didn't answer as she barrel rolled dramatically all over the place. She was certain that if she presented an easy target they would get hit by something. Oli was petrified as she narrowly missed a walkway and the beings on it as they shot past.

"We see him!" Malla stated, confronted with the proof of what Satiah had said.

"Call law enforcement," Satiah instructed, concentrating. If she was honest, she wouldn't want them interfering in her business but at the same time she had a role to play, and it was the responsible thing to do. Taxis were nippy and responsive vehicles, but she had to assume that her opponent would have either the same or greater capacity. Warning horns sounded as she slipped between two other vehicles at an angle that no normal driver would even attempt. Oli shrieked, the proximity of the near collision scaring him. He'd seen nothing yet! She was expecting shots to be fired anytime now. She kept close to a freighter that began to shift about a bit, nervous at her repentine arrival and neighbouring vicinity. More warning horns blared gratingly. Where was he? *Where was he?*

Suddenly he was right there, skimming over the roof of the freighter, straight at her. Her knuckles went even paler white than usual as her grip tightened and she slammed the joystick to the left. The movement was so abrupt that Oli crashed into the side of the cabin painfully.

"Security are incoming," Malla warned, still just about following. Why was no one shooting yet?

"Any idea who this guy is?" Satiah growled, still working on being as hard to target as possible.

"Not a clue."

"*Hold on!*" she warned, to Oli. She decelerated so hard that they were both thrown forward into the restraints. The chasing taxi tried to turn and slow down but in doing so it flew right past Satiah. She strained to make out anything she could about the driver but the screen was tinted. That told her what she'd already suspected... *it wasn't a taxi.* It was a fake. Just like the imitation law enforcement vehicle that had departed from the campaign offices the night before.

Same people, perhaps?

Pushing the craft to its limit, she darted between the streams of traffic, using them as cover. She flipped over, moving directly into the paths of ships going in the opposite direction. They swerved and scattered, some faster than others before them. Satiah's reactions enabled them to avoid even the slightest of collisions. Oli gasped and could only gawp in shock as the lights and warning sirens whizzed past him at lightening rates. Satiah turned off, or rather swerved out, of the line and into a ship parking area. An android standing in the middle of the area only just leapt out of the way in time as she snapped the barrier clean in two. The other craft was still hot on their heels but had most likely not expected this. Satiah concentrated as she weaved this way and that through the tens of parked ships.

Oli cried out as she went straight underneath a parked freighter and slammed on the breaks. She turned in the seat to see where she was going and began reversing in a straight line as fast as she could. Oli kept low and out of her sights. The other craft came in after her and had to move quickly to avoid crashing straight into the back of them. Satiah, now used to the controls, decelerated again and took them forward and over the same freighter before flying straight out of the parking area again.

Once more they joined the traffic lanes, causing chaos and confusion in equal measure in their wake. Satiah was testing their pursuer to see how good he was... or at least that was the excuse she would give. She *was* doing that, but she was enjoying this too much for it to be the only reason. It was all she could do not to roar with joy as the engine screamed in protest. The lane took them through the inside of a building, not unlike the way that ground vehicle routes would take you under mountains. Continuing to maintain an erratic and unpredictable flight path, Satiah rudder-rolled back and forth between the traffic going their way, and those that were not. She wished she was in something that had more speed and more power, but on occasion you had to work with what you had. Still the fake taxi was just able to keep pace with her.

She could hear the warnings as approaching law enforcement, *the real ones this time*, reached the chase. A side window opened on the taxi and a barrel-like object appeared. Not needing or wanting to see more, Satiah plunged them into another drop. A shot was fired and something hit the side of the taxi, jarring them from the impact. One of the wings was ripped off, sparks flew, but no serious damage was done. Satiah brought them in to land.

"When we hit the ground, get out and run for cover, *don't* look back!" she ordered, making sure she had Oli's attention. Oli nodded blankly, mildly shell-shocked. The other taxi seemed to be running away now that law enforcement had arrived, but Satiah was taking no chances. It could be a decoy, there to distract her *or* law enforcement or *both*, so that the real danger could present itself unopposed. Malla was following her down.

Beings darted out of the way as Satiah brought the taxi in to land. She hit the walkway but kept going, skidding along almost one hundred meters from the momentum. Ten more seconds and they'd ground to a halt. Smoke rose with the clamour from the alarmed crowd. Satiah was already out and running for the entrance to a building, Oli's hand in hers. He was so slow that she was practically dragging him.

"*Quickly!*" she yelled at him, they were sitting ducks on the street. They entered the building just as Malla and Shannon landed outside the building, and they dashed in after them.

"Did anyone get a look at who was driving that?" Malla asked, authoritatively.

"Viewports were tinted, sir," Satiah responded, covering the doorway with her rifle.

"There might have been more than one person in there," Shannon noted. She was wrong, Satiah knew. The way the shooting had happened told Satiah that it was someone *alone*, or else the person that *wasn't* driving would have taken the shot.

Naturally she didn't tell *them* that though. Oli seemed to have to come to his senses and was staring at Malla and Shannon in dawning comprehension. He had probably wondered how they had got there so fast, and then guessed the answer in as many seconds. He could hardly reprimand them for it though, not now *this* had happened. It may have been unclear who had been chasing them, but no one was in any doubt as to who they had been trying to kill. Malla eyed Satiah and decided that he wouldn't be talking to her about anything after all. If she hadn't been there, Oli would have probably died. Then again, if Oli hadn't decided to go out and look around with her, this might not have transpired at all. He reminded himself that speculation was a waste of time.

---

Satiah got back to her apartment in the early hours. There had been interviews, statements, all the usual procedures to endure. An awkward goodbye with Oli, no more awkward than the hello had been, had also tried her patience. She hoped that this experience might help to put him off. She began to work on Kelvin again, scanning him for faults. Head to toe…. nothing. Everything should be working. She put her hand on his cool metallic face delicately. Even though it had been only a short while ago that he had called her very *sanity* into question, she just wanted him to start working again. She'd built him from nothing, and to start again just made her feel tired all over.

"*I wish I knew what is wrong with you,*" she whispered, sadly. "*I promise I will find out and I will fix it.*" She didn't want anyone else to work on him, but with limited time, and her ideas starting to run out, she might have to call in a specialist.

A virus wasn't out of the question. She sat there, going through the lists of the latest viruses that might somehow have overcome his constantly evolving defences. There were seven main suspects. Most were actually harmless, in that they didn't do much damage, they just immobilised everything. They were military, designed to paralyse enemy automated factories without alerting the supervising mainframe. How he might have been exposed to any of these she could only guess. None of them were on any *official* lists, and two weren't actually known to exist yet, they were *theory only*. Next, she tried some operational checks on his body. All results were positive so… nothing wrong there either. It was just his brain that wasn't firing. *She knew some living beings that had a similar problem.*

She detached the head from the body and began to disassemble the shock-absorbent assemblage. It took over *two hours*. Finally, when she was done, she washed: her hands and arms were covered in lubricant, cooling fluid and dirt. She'd have to finish the job some other time, she was tired. Lying in bed and staring at the ceiling for several minutes, too restless for sleep, Satiah reflected on how many times she'd suffered from this form of insomnia. Trying to sleep when you couldn't is something everyone experiences from time to time. You enter a sort of in-between state where you're trying to reach sleep yet are apparently unable to detach yourself from the waking world. There were more than a few people who would have reason to want Oli dead, her own so-called *boss* included. She had to find out where *Malla* had been earlier that day.

Would the leaked tax information she planned to disseminate be enough to ruin Oli's campaign? If it wasn't, what could she try next? She hoped she'd managed to lessen his interest in her. And then there was the book. *Why* had this book been removed from the vaults all of a sudden? Why had it taken so long to be of interest again, assuming it never had been before? Could she trust *any* specialist to work on Kelvin without her direct supervision? Oh… she'd forgotten to review that case for Randal… She fell asleep at that point.

---

That awkwardness was back. That sort of reserved, annoying edginess Oli had around her. It was clearly going to take more than a short chase to scare Oli away from her. Satiah began to realise that it might even have made the attraction stronger. Maybe some kind of warped style of the suspension bridge effect? Just her flaming luck. Maybe she should start picking her nose like Slimy Snell did. No, that was going too far. According to the figures, provided that morning, nothing had changed with regard to Oli's proportional representation.

*Operation Selector*

This was good news for Satiah, but obviously Oli was pushing his team again now. He ended the morning meeting with his usual mantra. *Together we can achieve anything.* Satiah sighed: it was always easier to close people's eyes *after they were dead* than it was trying to open them *when they were alive.*

"We have to assume that someone is trying to kill Oli," Malla stated. Of course! People didn't usually shoot at others for any other reason. Satiah kept quiet, remembering to note if anyone said *anything* about bombs. Malla was briefing the whole security team about the events of the previous evening. They were now all on amber alert. There had been a discussion about hiring more guards to help with no real decision being made. It was a double-edged sword, flooding the place with guards, especially guards you didn't know or couldn't trust. If this attempt had taken place the previous week, Satiah might never have been able to operate as a guard. She was thankful for small mercies. The idea of having to work as some kind of promoter almost made her shudder.

"It is reasonable to assume that, as they failed and were not caught, they will try again," Mall went on. Satiah knew she had to pretend that all this wasn't blindingly apparent.

"Adjusting Oli's schedule would be problematic, sir," she suggested. Shannon shot her an aggravated glance. Yes, it must be absolutely intolerable that the person you hate most keeps coming out with good ideas and you can't think of any.

"We should talk to Oli about it," Shannon stated, crossing her arms and purposely not looking in Satiah's direction.

"I spoke with him this morning," Malla shrugged. "He doesn't know what to do for the best. I think he's still hoping that *he* wasn't being targeted at all." Typical politician, refusing to accept reality in the face of logic.

"That only leaves you, Satiah?" Shannon asked, exhaling sharply. "Any idea why anyone would want to kill you?"

"Only to get to him," Satiah replied, shrugging.

"Law enforcement has offered to help and they apologise for not being able to catch whoever that was last night. It seems it wasn't a real taxi at all, but some kind of adapted model," Malla explained. "From the descriptions we gave, they can't identify the firearm that was used - though, from the damage sustained by the taxi, it's likely a high-powered rifle."

"It would have to be when you consider the range; there must have been about sixty meters between us, sir. A pistol can get that far, but not with that much clout," Satiah agreed. "I wasn't hanging around, and we have to remember that he was also driving at the time. It's fair to assume that, as whomever it was still managed to hit us, it has to be a highly capable shooter."

Satiah went through the incident again in her mind. At the time she had wondered why it had taken him so long to take the shot. Perhaps they had been confused by the fact there were two taxis and not one. Perhaps they'd had to get the gun in the right position for them to use it. The barrel hadn't protruded far, just a few inches. She'd seen it only because she had been looking for it. Anyone else driving by would most likely have missed it. They wouldn't have missed the shot itself, but that wasn't the point. She went through all the short barrelled rifles she could think of. The Seeker 950 was certainly a possible. The barrel of a larger rifle could have been sawn off too.

"We will have to start doing area sweeps *before* the public appearances," Malla was saying. "High ground will need to be watched at all times." They did do that already, to a degree, but as with most things so far, it was very slack. Satiah knew though that a planet-wide city of skyscrapers and walkways was a sniper's paradise. They could hide in plain sight and no one would have a clue they were even there until it was too late. It was almost pointless trying to locate them like that.

"You might want to talk to him about wearing protection, sir," Satiah suggested.

"I have *mentioned* that, but he was worried it might affect his popularity," Malla said, irritated. His irritation wasn't with her, it was with Oli. By 'mentioned' she assumed he meant: *lectured with increasing impatience.*

Oli felt that if his supporters saw him wearing body armour, they would think he was *paranoid*. Malla, and everyone else, saw it as suicidal not to.

"I'm *sure* you've already thought of this, but it occurs to me that you *could* have a portable shield generator operating," Satiah replied, shrugging. "He doesn't even have to know about it and it would make any sniper's life *very* difficult." This was the first time she had omitted the word 'sir' when talking to Malla. He didn't notice.

"He already thinks there are things we're not telling him," Shannon cautioned. There were.

"He must understand that, to avoid putting too much pressure on him, we must do certain things that he is better off not knowing about," Satiah replied.

"Oh he *must, must he*?" Shannon responded, her temper flaring. "He *is* our boss you know, when all is said and done."

"If he dies, all *will* be said and done," Satiah replied, coolly. Malla stepped in.

"The shield is a good precaution. If anyone realises, we will say it's to protect him, should anything be thrown from the crowd. Whatever we do, we mustn't let anyone know someone is trying to kill him," Malla insisted. The political implications were obvious. No one could know outside of those who already did. This was not unusual. If any political figure faces a genuine, unambiguous threat then it is *never* made public. This is done for two reasons. First, it would give away to the assassin that they were onto them. Second, it could be seen by the public as a political strategy to generate sympathy.

"You don't think we're taking all this much too far?" Shannon scoffed. "Where will it end? *Using an android replica of Oli for all public events, just in case?*"

"I'm just saying it's best to take all the precautions we can," Satiah said, firmly. While it was tempting to escalate the situation with Shannon and then give her a... *piece of her mind*, Satiah knew it wouldn't do any good.

"We will," Malla assured her. "In the meantime, I'll deal with Oli." He headed across the room to talk to him, leaving Satiah and Shannon alone. Neither woman looked at the other.

---

"We have another problem." Octutin stated.

"What?" Jinx asked.

"Someone else is trying to kill our target," he replied. "Someone tried to shoot his taxi down last night. Any idea who it is?" Jinx thought about it.

"Tell me what happened," he requested, deeply curious. He wasn't a fan of competition; it tended to get very nasty very quickly. Did whoever this was somehow know about Octutin and Jinx? Had the client got impatient and hired someone else too? If they had, they hadn't said anything. Octutin told him, in detail, what had happened: the apparent social activity that had become a brief but high-speed chase through the skies and walkways of the city. He explained how a difficult shot was taken and only just missed, and then the aftermath. Jinx remained silent when Octutin was finished, thoughtful.

Was someone boxing clever? The unexploded bomb. An apparent prelude to some sort of scheme where they fake an assassination attempt to justify additional security? He'd known people to do all kinds of odd things when they felt threatened; however, this did seem odder than most. And Jinx couldn't be sure that Oli even knew about the bomb. If he knew nothing about their attempt, why would he make up his own? Would an attack affect the vote, perhaps? And if it did, why hadn't he made it public? Jinx had no interest in politics, but he felt that if the attack was made public, it could, in theory, help gain sympathy votes. On the other hand, if Octutin was right and it was a real attack entirely independent of them and their client, then what? Well, the client had to be informed, for one thing, if for no other reason than that *they themselves* might be targeted, intentionally *or* otherwise.

"*Tricky*," Jinx growled, at last. Octutin said nothing, but he did agree as he was aware of all the potential ramifications. "Give me some time to think; in the meantime we go on as planned. I'll put my ear to the ground, see if I can learn anything that might explain who it was that attacked them."

"Will do," Octutin concurred. "I have something in the pipeline. I'll let you know when I can confirm it."

"Great."

"Last night a Neo-remnantist cell struck at the innocent once again. In an attack that has universally been condemned as barbaric, a team of four hijacked a passenger cruiser and attempted to crash it into the Bureau of Democrats on the planet Darpia. The cruiser was shot down before it could strike its target, but the passengers were still aboard and the death toll is over nine hundred so far..." The CNC report was cut off there as Oli deactivated it and shook his head. Darpia was a Coalition world.

"Sick," declared Kate, sadly. "I can never understand why people do things like that."

"And I know this will sound awful, but it may alter the content of the up and coming debate. It will definitely be a problem for Brenda, but then it's a problem for us too," Oli sighed, his head in his hands. He was still reeling from the attempt on his own life. Satiah watched the interaction from the doorway, where she was standing.

"The only spin you can really put on this is that whichever one of you wins this election, your stance on this is the same. Zero tolerance. We can't use it to ruin Brenda's day. Not only would it be in bad taste, but it would also be completely unjustified. You have to maintain your popularity. You won't do that if you get into a blame game with her or anyone else," Kate advised. "She will be facing more heat on this than you though, if that's any consolation." It wasn't.

"Sometimes I just wish *everyone* would stop fighting," he sighed, despairingly.

"We *all* wish that," Kate agreed, softly.

Satiah agreed wholeheartedly that what had happened was wrong, but only because of the cowardly nature of the attack. Against civilians? That's not a fight, that's just wrong. She thought about Carl - if he had been somehow caught up in it! She could see the fear and pain in people's faces and it angered her. Her heart, such as it was, did *really* feel for those who'd died so needlessly and so forlornly. How *dare* they attack *her* Coalition and hurt *her* civilians! Part of her wanted to immediately go out and get revenge but... she had a job to do. Keep *someone else* alive.

She knew that fighting was human nature and to get rid of it, even if that were possible, would mean you were no longer human. It was how things developed, both ideologically and technologically. Most advances in science were acquired during or because of conflict. Besides, she'd be out of a job if there were no threats to civilisation.

Satiah also wondered if the timing of the attack was important. The election *would* be affected by this - there was no doubt about that. It cast some doubt in her suspicious mind. Had it been who the CNC said it was? The second she'd heard about it, she'd asked Randal if he knew anything. He had told her that it *was* a real terrorist attack and that Phantom Squad had no operations to mess with the election. Well, *Selector aside,* obviously. That didn't mean Division Sixteen or the PAI hadn't either *allowed it to happen* or even *organised it themselves*. She didn't like to think they had, but she knew they were capable of it and had done similar things in the past. And then there was the Federation, the Union, and other organisations like the Cult of Deimos that may have had a hand in it too.

Try telling that to the families of those who had died! Even if they *did* believe you, it would only make their agony worse. If that was possible. It was a thoroughly terrible situation, only made worse by the terror and distrust it naturally spread.

After all, the CNC *were* under the government's indirect control. Satiah considered the possibility that the attack *hadn't even happened* and that it could be a complete fiction. After all, with computers and good actors, it was possible to make people believe almost anything, especially when fear and anger were the catalysts. No normal citizen on the planet would or could have seen it happen, and if everyone was being fed the same or similar information, it would quickly be established as truth for most people. Even if disproved later, some would always continue to believe it. Those who still didn't believe would be ostracised in whatever socially acceptable way they could be... those who still thought for themselves, of which Satiah was one herself - a dying breed.

Saying all that: if Randal said it was real, then it was real. He wouldn't lie to her, *he knew what to expect if he ever did,* and he could check with anyone he needed to in order to confirm the validity of the news. As this was real, it would genuinely affect the election as there would be no vote rigging this time around. So, returning to her task in hand, she had to keep Oli alive whilst also ensuring that he did not win. It *was* a remote possibility that, if the Neo-remnantists *were* trying to affect the outcome of the election, for whatever perverse reasons they had, they could be behind the attempt on Oli's life. Randal was convinced the threat to Oli came from within his own so-called supporters somewhere. Satiah thought it was more likely one of his rivals, but… this latest attack, rightly or wrongly, had certainly made her think in other directions.

"There will be a tribute organised *for the victims* and we will need to fit that in with any other plans we have," Kate was saying.

"This will sound terrible, but I hope Brenda doesn't use this as an excuse to end or postpone this election somehow," Oli sighed. There was a silence for a moment: no one else had considered that.

"I'm sure she won't, it would be rather transparent," Kate said, understanding why he was worried about that.

"It's just that I can see her starting some kind of crusade to catch anyone who helped those responsible. And delaying the election until they had been brought to account… that could take *years*," he replied.

"It's more likely that she will try to get this election over as quickly as possible," Satiah interjected. "Precisely so she can focus on that. You and Brenda are very different people but I think you both have in you *what the people want*. A desire to help others. And a shared *loathing* for the cowardly monsters that were behind the attack."

"This is coming from the woman who *doesn't* vote?" Oli remarked, a smile appearing on his face for the first time that morning. She shrugged.

"Just saying," she stated. Oli sighed, shook his head and then looked at her again.

"What do *you* think about all this? The attack? The election? All of it?" he asked. At last, Satiah couldn't help but think, he's starting to trust me. Kate too seemed interested. Satiah played it carefully, adopting a shy air about her.

"*Well, I don't know.* You'll laugh and it's *probably* uninformed so…" she trailed off, and looked away. Oli and Kate exchanged a look and she gave him a nod of encouragement.

"No, come on, I *promise* we won't… *Just tell us*," Oli pleaded. Got you.

"As you know, I don't really know *much* about politics," she lied, adeptly. "But I know these attacks make people scared and angry. The people then blame the government for not keeping them safe. The government is forced into making a gesture or a concession or they change a law or whatever. Right?" They nodded. "Perhaps your best move would be to say that *now* is not the time for an election. If *you* say it instead of Brenda, it *might* make you more popular. People will see you less as a candidate and more as a leader. And if you think she's going to suspend the election then this move, should *you* make it first, might ruin the spin she was planning to put on it." Oli went quiet, considering this. He'd not thought of doing that himself and the idea sounded kind of ethical. In a Machiavellian sort of way.

Kate, however, was shaking her head.

"We would also be playing into her hands if this is what she wants. Then all she has to do is agree and she remains in power for as long as she likes," she argued. "Besides, then we have to answer questions like: *how long* will this be suspended?"

"Like I said, *I don't know much about politics*," Satiah reminded, shrugging again.

"It would be quite a note to kick start the debate on, wouldn't it, though?" Oli asked, grinning roguishly. "I'm pretty sure Brenda wouldn't see it coming."

"Well, I grant you it has a certain *shock tactic value* about it; however, it also *does* open you up to certain criticisms. People might accuse you of using this to cover up for the fact that you don't want to address anything else in the debate, even though *we all know* you do," Kate warned, earnestly.

"So what will *you* do if Brenda makes that move instead of you?" Satiah enquired, trying to hide a smile. "She will open herself to that too then, right?" Oli made a noise indicating that it was not that simple.

"She's *already* Commandment Benefactor. Whether she is criticised or not for making that move, it won't matter because is already in power," Oli explained. Satiah gave him an expression of astonishment, as if she hadn't realised that.

"Maybe I need to read about this kind of thing," Satiah said, as if upset that she couldn't help.

"I can tell you all about it if you like, don't worry, I *won't* blind you with science," he offered, not quite as charitably as it might have sounded. Kate looked as if she was about to say something, but for whatever reason chose not to.

"Great," Satiah allowed, trying not to sound too *for or against* it.

Despite last night's events, Oli had clearly not given up on her yet, but she didn't much like being told what she already knew *far* better than he did. It was all part of the act, of course, but that didn't detract from its tediousness. She'd reviewed all the things Harrier had sent her, but all of it was useless. No one was behaving differently. Malla *had been* telling the truth about his absence, in so much as he was where he said he was. This didn't mean he hadn't known about the device, but *if he did know* he was masking it well. It just didn't sit well with her: the idea he was missing at the exact time it was meant to happen. *Coincidence?* In two days, they had struck twice; this meant they *would* attack again. It was inevitable. This next time though... Satiah had already made up her mind to change tactics. She would no longer remain a reflexive protector; she would switch to an all-out offensive strategy.

She knew - as all Phantoms knew – that in this life, if you wanted someone dead and were willing to do anything to achieve it... the odds were you'd get your wish. The duplicity of that, though, was that it worked *both ways*. If they wanted you dead... Randal had a point about her restlessness. She was finding it hard to just stand by doors and follow Oli around. She needed action, and now she'd convinced herself that just sitting there like a safeguard wasn't going to work, she knew action would be coming her way soon enough.

Drugs were always easy to find if you knew where to look. Shannon had never been an addict and indeed despised those who were, but she'd seen enough to know where to go. With her own Essps she purchased some Zihi, a common opiate that was illegal throughout the Coalition. She would plant it on Satiah somehow and then engineer its discovery. While it would quickly be proven that she'd not *ingested* anything, they would probably assume she was a dealer instead and that should be enough to get rid of her. Careful to ensure no trace of it was on *her* or her things, Shannon had taken steps to ensure it was contained *and* disguised. The last thing she wanted was this to somehow get traced back to her. She felt sure that when Oli believed that Satiah was involved in the drug trade he'd want nothing more to do with her. Malla too would be forced to concede the point that she'd been right all along. Shannon smiled to herself as she flew back across the skies of Earth. Satiah wouldn't be so arrogant for much longer.

---

"His name is Collorah, but he's operating under the name *Red Necromancer*," Jinx stated.

"And he's the one who tried to kill Oli in the taxi chase *last night*?" Octutin clarified.

"Yes," Jinx confirmed. There was a silence as both men thought about the implications.

"…What do you want to do? Team up?" Octutin asked, evenly.

"I'm not splitting that cash three ways, two is bad enough. We will have to take care of him ourselves," Jinx replied, angry.

"All right," Octutin said, unconcerned. "How do you want to play this?"

"First, we have to find him. He failed last night, but something tells me that this guy won't give up so easily and he won't try anything that obvious again. He will be looking for something new…" Jinx reasoned. "Leave it with me. I've got a few more people to speak to."

---

Satiah pulled into the parking area slowly and locked her transport before heading up towards her apartment. It was the end of another shift. She was still getting used to this shift business. It was odd how getting regular sleep felt. She had to remember not to get used to that. She'd had Oli's quarters bugged too, so that she could keep an eye on him even while he slept. His building was better guarded than the office, but *even so...* she'd planned her route and she could get to him in less than twenty minutes. She entered and sealed the door behind her.

"Update me," she said, to Harrier.

"Nothing so far, everyone's quiet," he said, though her earpiece. "I thought you normally did your own surveillance work?" Satiah eyed Kelvin, still inactive on the table. How dare he insinuate something like that? She smiled.

"I don't know *who* told you *that*," she remarked, carelessly. "Let me know if anything happens."

"Will do, anything on that book yet?" he asked.

"No, not a thing," she responded, as if it hardly mattered.

"Let me know if that changes," he said, still annoyingly chipper. "I'll let you know if I see anything so keep one ear open."

"I always do," she replied, cutting him off.

She was tired. Not tired as in physically, she was used to spending days without any real sleep, and her mind was still energetic enough too. No, she was weary of the situation. She was fed up of hearing about nothing other than the election. The rhetoric, the debates, the plans and the news. How they kept going over the same things time and time again. Normally, in her job, doing the things she did, she seldom was exposed to this for any length of time. She wondered how the average citizen coped without going mad! There was no easy escape from the propaganda for them. It was everywhere. Advertising boards, public screens, media outlets everywhere... it was so depressing. She knew that this was partly how it was supposed to work, but still... they were overdoing it. Deetee's face was also everywhere, which didn't help her temper at all.

She focussed on Kelvin again: she had to get him working. She trusted Harrier, but she'd rather Kelvin did it. He never made mistakes, except that time he'd thought she was insane when she *wasn't*, of course, but *nothing was perfect*. Before she had departed that morning she'd left a scanner running, its job to scan every single part of Kelvin. She began to go through the results, trying not to lose hope. If this gave her nothing then she would be out of ideas. That would mean she'd have to take him to someone else. *A specialist*. She'd gone so far as to check out a few of the more discreet ones - those who were private and not associated with any corporations. They were *all* expensive, obviously, but money was of no concern to her. It was their discretion and reliability that she was concerned about. Scan complete. Anomalies found two. *Two*! Satiah's brown eyes went wide with optimism.

Two detailed images appeared on the screen in front of her. Both were components. She went through the explanations and then hissed in annoyance. It said the same thing in both cases. *Unused component located, purpose unknown, origin unknown*. Well, that was *really* helpful! It didn't even tell her if it was wise to remove them or not. She couldn't remember installing either of them herself, but to be fair she couldn't remember most of the smaller parts she had fitted. And she knew Kelvin had installed things on himself in the past. He always notified her, of course, but she'd become too lax. She'd trusted him to know what was good and what wasn't. Granted, he was very good at it, but if he had been wrong…

This development wasn't a complete waste though. She could at least figure out what these two components were. She sent the details off to Harrier. She marked them as urgent but was honest about the fact that it was not related to the mission. She hoped they were not dangerous. She glanced around the apartment. Carl would be there tomorrow evening and she didn't want the place to look like a tip. She knew he wouldn't care even if it did, but she wouldn't be able to sit still, knowing about the disorder there.

That was when her attention switched back to the book that she was supposed to be helping Harrier with. She tried putting a strong light directly under each page to see if anything was hidden there. Nothing. She paused for dinner but continued to stare thoughtfully at the book while she was eating. She couldn't stand an unanswered question: a mystery was something she both loved and hated simultaneously. She couldn't let it go and refused to admit defeat. Throughout her life as a Phantom agent she could count the mysteries she'd never solved on one hand. The ones that she had solved were copious and ranged from the inconsequential to the absolutely critical. She needed mysteries to feed her mind, even though sometimes they gave it indigestion.

After she'd finished eating she retuned her full attention to it. She was briefly distracted when she got a message from Oli, enquiring after her safe arrival at home. *Ironic.* She informed him that she had indeed returned without harm and told him to stay safe himself. The book was weird. She wanted to know more about its source. Where was it found? How old was it? Was it found anywhere near the Satmarrick constellation? Had more than one been written? Who had actually written it? And why was it considered so important that Phantom Squad had sequestered it away in the vaults? She'd give it a few more days and then she'd touch base with Harrier again about it. He might be able to shed light on *some* of those questions.

---

Once again, Oli was stuck on the same proportional representative percentage. Brenda had snatched a few extra as more candidates had dropped out. She was now at fifty three percent. Oli remained on nineteen percent. Fourth day in, and he knew it was still early, but the small gains that Brenda had made were reigniting his insecurities.

"*How* is she doing it?" he asked rhetorically, not for the first time.

"She's doing what you're trying to do. She's helping her citizens solve their problems, and also she got to address the public about the attack yesterday. What she said is literally perfect," Kate explained. "Each word was *so* well chosen." They played the speech of the hurt but strong looking Brenda as she addressed the whole Coalition in the hours after the attack.

"I think we all agree that what happened yesterday was as degenerate as it was tragic. I think you would all e-expect me to say our hearts are with those mourning their loss. My heart is not enough for them, nor should it be. Today I signed a document effectively doubling the android security forces. I know this is not enough either. In a few hours, the remains will start to be recovered from the crash site and returned to their families. And I know... that this is *still* not enough. I will not lie to you. I cannot p-predict or p-prevent some of our enemies from striking. I have let you down so..." She paused there, seeming to be fighting to control herself. Satiah couldn't tell if she was acting or not but the performance either way was compelling. *As, no doubt, it was meant to be.* "... I will do better, I will make up for it," Brenda went on, suddenly very fierce in the face. "Please forgive my failures. I think, I really think, I can... I know we can walk through this fire and reach the o-other side. We *will* overcome this, together in our..."

Oli turned it off, having seen enough. How *did* she do it? How did Brenda *always* seem to say the right things? Do the right things? Now, everything she'd said was the correct thing to say. Politically. Plenty of *we's* and *not enough's*. A fraught confession that *she felt she had failed* only made her more popular, as it seemed so candid. What politician admitted it when they made a mistake? Not many. In reality, it had had nothing to do with her *personally*, and mostly everyone would agree on that. Yet she was the only one held accountable so far. She'd taken it on herself.

And from a more moral standpoint, her speech really did avoid the vexing clichés. She avoided the bland stuff about just saying *their thoughts were with the families* and *how appalling such events were*. That was a script which had pretty much become standardised and therefore, in a way, less meaningful. She'd admitted that saying those things wasn't good enough and the people *liked what they heard*. Being different made it more believable and gripping. The *way* she delivered it didn't count for nothing either. She looked like *it really mattered to her*. Most politicians developed a typically professional way of talking, even a wooden demeanour, for the majority of their interactions. Brenda though was rather conversely a raw nerve: *all emotion*. At least, that was how she *seemed*.

Satiah, typically distrustful of anything *and everyone*, was not moved by anything Brenda did or said. She did notice the change in style, though, and felt that, if Brenda *was* sincere in how she felt then it was good. *Something might even get done.* She also noticed that Brenda hadn't said what she was going to do. *She'd not actually promised anything.* Nothing unusual there either, especially in politics - and telling your enemies, who would also be watching, would be a mistake. How many times had the media given away highly secret information to everyone and ruined many a good plan? Besides, Satiah knew that Brenda was most likely being told what to say by others. She had to be tightly controlled to ensure that everything went as it should. Again, Satiah used this topic to step in closer to Oli and Kate. She had to get them to trust her, yet without them knowing what she was doing.

"Don't let her rattle you, *ignore her*, concentrate on what *you* have to say and do," Satiah told him, seriously. Shannon glanced across at her, annoyed. Since when did Oli take advice from a self-confessed, politically unprincipled mercenary? Even if he *did* like her physically, *for some unknown reason*, that didn't explain *this*. Kate, however, jumped on what Satiah had said. Ever the supportive one, she knew she had to bolster Oli and Satiah had said the right words for her.

"*She's right.* You can't let what Brenda's doing distract you," Kate asserted. Oli smiled and tried to calm himself down.

"What is this? *Stereophonic coaching?*" he guffawed. Satiah wouldn't smile, she was still playing dumb. The only time she would let him see her smile was when something bad was happening. Just to reinforce the fact that she was a *very* dangerous person. Kate laughed, genuinely amused and glad that the tension seemed to have lessened.

"Are we putting you off?" she wanted to know.

"Well…" he began, his eyes very quickly snatching a glance at Satiah. It was so fast, even Satiah nearly missed it and she groaned inwardly. What did she have to do to get him to look elsewhere? She was thinking about deploying the Carl-bomb.

"No, I need *all* the help I can get," he stated, patting Kate's hand tenderly.

"Great, so let's hear *your* speech," Kate said, clapping her hands fussily. "Now, *you remember what I said*, do *not* slag off the security forces. They hate that and frankly it sounds a little vindictive. Plus, with the Vourne conspiracy still rumbling on, it's not the time."

"As an associate of said forces I admit I agree with that," Satiah joined in.

"When I heard what had happened, I was *deeply* saddened. The idea of going through anything like that is just beyond my imagination. There's nothing I can say to convey how I feel about this to you. Shocked doesn't even come close. Instead, I offer all the support I can and implore every Coalition citizen to do the same. It's *important* to remain unified against this force of evil. Do not give in to terror and do not turn on each other, *it's what they want*. Know that we have the greatest weapon, a weapon they do not understand. *Love*."

Satiah said nothing to that. Indeed, at first she'd felt it was bit wishy-washy, and then sickly sweet at the end. Kate made a noise that indicated she was having difficulty with choosing the right words for her response. Oli waited, unsure what was coming.

"It's *okay*," Kate settled on, at last. Oli's face fell.

"But it's not as good as Brenda's," he said, filling in the rest of what he thought she was getting at. Satiah was conflicted here. She wanted to step in and make a disaster of that speech to ruin his campaign, but it would be too obvious and… they might just do it themselves.

"Brenda, whether through some random act or brilliance, has delivered something that only the insane can find fault with. But then, *she had to. She's the Commandment Benefactor*. She's doing this *for real*…" Kate stated.

"*I'm* doing it for real…!" he argued, levelly.

"You *know* what I mean! They take what she says more seriously than what you say because she's *already* in charge. She's doing the job already, therefore… well, she's already in the centre of it," Kate explained. "*You're* still an orbiting body."

"I have to say *something*; I can't just overlook what's happened," he countered. Kate went over the words that he had written.

"Where did this *love thing* at the end come from?" Kate asked, mystified. A pause. Satiah groaned inwardly a second time, this was getting painful again. *Please don't let it be because of me!!!*

"Well, it's the opposite of hate, isn't it? I'm trying to say that *we are* the opposite of *them* and that they can't understand us because we're better than they are which is *why* they hate us," Oli went on.

Kate was silent again for a moment.

"I'm not sure the use of the word *evil* is a good idea," she mumbled, considering. "Just from a *connotation* point of view. If people see *you* say the word, *subconsciously* a few of them might make a connection between you and it and like you less because of that. Also, it makes you sound preachy and judgemental."

"Can you think of a *better way* to describe such a despicable thing?" he enquired, sincerely. Kate leaned her forehead on her hand slowly as she thought about it. Malevolence? Malice? Darkness? This was just what Kate knew they shouldn't do. Get fixated on *words* and forget *the overall message,* but in this case she knew it had to be done *properly.* It almost felt like no matter what they said, they couldn't get it quite right.

"Desperate, misguided, sadistic creatures," Satiah provided, unable to stop herself from helping. They were just taking too long for her tolerance levels, no wonder politicians never got anything done by themselves.

"It's *important* to remain unified against this force of desperate, misguided, sadistic creatures," Oli amended, ponderously.

"*Emphasise* misguided," suggested Kate. He said it again as she had bidden. "Well, it's better than evil." It was starting to sound like a rant but the situation allowed for *some* choice words.

"I'll say it as quickly as possible, perhaps pausing shortly after my initial lines. I will pause before I say *it's important*?" he suggested, tentatively.

"A brief pause would be appropriate," Kate nodded in accord. "Thanks for that, Satiah; you might have missed your calling, you know? You've got a knack for this kind of thing." Satiah nodded in thanks but said nothing.

"Had *you* been in the backseat of that taxi last night you might not say that," Oli remarked. "I've never been so scared in my life." Then you haven't lived at all, Satiah thought as her heart leaped at the memory. She was half tempted to invite him to go driving in an arena with her, just to show him what scared *really* felt like, but then thought better of it.

"I keep telling you not to worry about that. You were safe then and you're safe *now*, it was just a one-off," Kate insisted. Her eyes said she didn't really believe that. And she only said it because she didn't know about the unexploded bomb. Shannon let out a sigh of exasperation so loud that Satiah heard her and, unable to resist, Satiah decided to twist the knife.

"Isn't it time for your lunch, sir?" Satiah enquired, knowing she was a bit early. "I will check..."

"*I'll* do it," Shannon huffed, coming forward and rudely taking the plate that Satiah had just picked up. Satiah didn't smile or react at all but, inside her mind, she was beaming.

Oli too noticed the tension between them, *perhaps for the first time*, and looked puzzled and uneasy. Shannon headed outside resolutely to check and test the food, which was normally Satiah's job. Satiah eyed Oli and Kate.

"Don't worry, I'll check it again *myself* afterwards," she assured, just for fun. Oli shifted uncomfortably and even Kate was starting to look awkward. *Just a little harmless undermining...*

"Very well, good, um..." Oli said, trying to change the subject.

"We still have to go through what's going to happen this afternoon," said Kate, moving on swiftly.

That afternoon they had another speech planned. It was out in a public area and it was to do with the recent upgrading of a medical facility. He was going to state how he would continue to support the service, should he get into office. There would be a time for questions after that, and then they would return to the building to discuss the next day and plan everything accordingly. Oli's day was always packed full of activities, his agenda was rammed, every minute accounted for. There were a number of security concerns. Malla had briefed all the guards, Satiah included, that morning about them. It all seemed pretty standard. Two emergency evacuation routes, barrier control, two team members in among the crowd and all the *stage-management* concerns. Could he be heard everywhere? Would everyone in the crowd be able to see him? What were the usual security activities? The list went on...

Youth were often easy scapegoats for the true villains. The young usually have two traits that make them vulnerable: lack of commitments, and a vast amount of energy which made a combination that, when coupled with their naïveté, made them easily manipulated. Collorah regarded the young faces in front of him. They were angry. *Angry at the world.* Well, they said they were, but really he knew the truth. They were bored, trying to be smarter, older, and they thought this would demonstrate how tough they were. As individuals they most probably all had hidden depths but, when together, mob-mentality ruled almost without challenge. He could have made it political, of course. He might have tried to persuade them it was for the benefit of the Coalition that Oli McAllister died. But he knew the young had a reputation for being completely dismissive of politics. Instead he'd gone for their greed, often the most dependable of sins.

"How many make up your gang?" Collorah asked. The youth he addressed, who *according to him* was their self-appointed leader, answered.

"Fifty seven," he growled.

"At one hundred Essps each, that should be enough to buy you for this," Collorah stated, with a crooked grin. His steely blue eyes gleamed knowingly. "You know what to do and you know what to say if they catch you?" The young man answered with a slang term that Collorah had never heard before. The tone of voice and his facial expression told Collorah that they were in agreement.

"Good," Collorah said. He gave the money over. There was no chance they would dare to disobey... he'd already killed one of them.

Collorah was tall, strapping, and had a poise about him that betrayed his ruthless nature. Black spiky hair ran along his head in a style not unlike liberty spikes or a Mohawk. His gloved hand brushed against the eight-barrelled pistol he had concealed in his overcoat.

As he moved out from the shadowy walkway he instantly became aware that someone was watching him. His first thought was law enforcement, but then he thought a little longer and that didn't seem to be the correct answer. They would have swooped in the second he gunned down the trash. No... this was someone else entirely. It was a quick flash of movement that gave them away, with a very quick step backwards into darkness. Collorah did the same, slipping out of sight and checking his gun. It was ready to go. Confident but wary, Collorah began a purposeful advance in the direction he'd seen the figure move in – an old, now disused parking area for ships. Row after row of concrete and metal boxes, each large enough for a standard sized vehicle. His heavy footsteps echoed loudly as he entered the shadowy shade of the disused place, but he wasn't bothered by that. He slowed to a reduced stride as he reached a corner. He stole a rapid look around.

The blast struck the wall, missing him by a whisker. A shard of concrete flew out from the wall and smoke billowed up. He chuckled darkly to himself as he heard retreating footsteps echoing loudly as the shooter withdrew. Collorah took off after them. Another shot hit the wall ahead of him. He saw the flash and this time returned fire. All eight lasers slammed into the barrier, ripping another chunk of stone free, but the target had moved on. He picked up his pace, cautious of traps. Round and up to the next level they rushed, then he stayed close to the wall and made sure that there were no vantage points from above. Again, shots rang out as whoever it was fired a few rounds to give themselves cover as they darted from one place to another. Collorah didn't return it, he just kept chasing.

Whoever it was moved fast. Collorah ducked behind a burned out vehicle, just as whoever it was sprang out from the left and opened fire. The blackened metal rattled and pinged loudly as the bolts struck it. It was rapid fire this time, no precision, all sweep. Cover fire, in other words. Collorah rolled out and once again answered it with two blasts of his own, ripping further chunks out from the wall. He smiled the smile of a hunter, at first contact with his prey. Scrambling to his feet, heedless of the broken glass on the floor, he pursued again.

This time though, it appeared his prey was not in a *last stand* kind of mood. Collorah heard the engine and only just managed to get out of the way as a transporter sped past, right where he would have been had he not heard it coming. He rolled instinctively as lasers peppered the ground from where he'd dived. Getting back onto his feet, Collorah put twenty-four bolts into the back of the transporter as it sped away into the darkness. There was nothing to be learned from it, it looked like just about a million other craft he'd seen that day alone. Knowing the fight might have attracted the unwelcome attention of law enforcement, he hastily left the area.

---

Sweating hard, Jinx accelerated away from the disused parking area. Somehow Collorah had spotted him and the guy was no slouch. He'd been quick on his feet, smart and daring. Jinx had never expected him to keep coming after him as though he had no fear of what the blackness might have held. It was reckless, to say the least. Or maybe he was just that good. Jinx pulled into traffic and began his evasive route in order to shake off any further pursuit. He put in a call to Octutin, who answered immediately.

"Well?" he asked.

"No, we exchanged shots and I had to withdraw. I don't think he saw me though," Jinx told him. Octutin made a short noise as if cogitating deeply.

"I don't know what he was doing, but he was paying the street gang for *something*," Jinx went on.

"*...I don't like the sound of that*," Octutin stated. "I have no idea what he's planning either. What possible use could he have for them?"

"I envisage we will find out soon enough," he replied. "Have you thought about what we will say, should he succeed in killing Oli?"

"Well, the client won't want to pay us the rest if we never did the job. We don't have to tell them what went down," Octutin reasoned. He knew Jinx would understand.

"We will divide our efforts. *You* concentrate on Oli and *I'll* try and bring Collorah down, or at least distract him long enough for you to get the job done."

---

"Very good," the aide said, encouragingly. Brenda staggered to the back of the vehicle and collapsed inside. She was shaken. She'd had two shocks. First *the attack* and then *the speech* she had had to deliver about it. "I cannot believe how well you handled that."

"I-it was awful," Brenda said, emotionally. "How could anyone do something like that?"

"I'm sure a psychologist could tell you that but I can't," the aide said, without missing a beat.

"What are we going to *do*?" Brenda asked her, directly. "I mean, about the Neo-remnantists?"

"I have made some calls *on your behalf*, and I have to say, the security agencies had all done exceedingly well. They *were* unable to stop the attack, which *is* a horrible thing; they *did* however capture fourteen and kill nineteen more. The ones they have alive are being interrogated as we speak. Rest assured, we *will* find these people and we *will* deal with them..." the aide replied, sincerely.

"When will the trials be held?" Brenda asked, naïvely. "They *need* to face justice. Publicly face it so that everyone knows there is no funny business."

"Shouldn't be too long now," the aide replied, with a sinister smile. Brenda didn't have to know the truth. Brenda wouldn't understand. These people, once interrogated, would be broken, brainwashed and then sent back to their organisation where they would carry out the same attacks *against* their former accomplices. There would be no trial. What would be the point? They were unrepentant, and such a proceeding would only give them a platform from which to spew their hateful bile. They might corrupt the desperate who were always watching these things from somewhere. Brenda was an idealist, a moral absolutist: she would never condone what really went on if she knew. That was why she was the perfect figurehead. That was why she had to win the election.

Brenda sighed and shook her head, a tear falling from her eye. The aide put her arm around her and Brenda began to weep.

"Do they b-blame me? Do they think I'm an atrocious person?" Brenda sobbed. "I-I'm *supposed* to look after them..."

"*Shhh*," hushed the aide softly. "You expect too much of yourself. Perfection is an illusion, Brenda. You have very high standards which should be much admired. *But remember what I said about overworking.*

I think you're just a woman *doing her best* to protect what she loves. You know what else I think?" Brenda shook her head and sniffed loudly.

"I think your leadership skills are unrivalled and with *your help* we can all see this through."

"Really?" she asked, starting to recover herself.

"Absolutely. *Without you*, I don't know what would have happened in the light of that attack."

The aide knew that Brenda had to be convinced of her own supremacy. She had to *totally* believe that she *really was* in charge. The aide and her associates would work *tirelessly* to ensure this became a reality to Brenda. There would be snags from time to time, there always were, but Brenda was leaning on her more and more. Trust levels were building. Soon she would delegate more, she would begin to turn her back and rely on others. They would protect her; keep her safe in her little bubble. Brenda was so suitable, if a little hypersensitive, it was perfect. So long as she was kept popular, so long as she never suspected the truth… then nothing would change and that was all to the good.

---

"It's all gone as planned so far," Scott said. "We thought that the attack might ruin everything, but luckily someone had it covered."

"I can see her percentage has risen a little further," Randal admitted. "That could have happened anyway, though. Other candidates had dropped out."

"How is Operation Selector progressing?" Scott enquired. Ah, so that's what you really wanted to talk about, Randal thought. "I see Oli is still stuck at nineteen."

"So long as he stays there or thereabouts, he will not be a problem," Randal told him. "Keeping him alive is turning out to be a much more important priority. There has been at least one attempt on his life already. Satiah's onto it, so I'm not worried yet, but I thought you should know."

"Let me know if anything changes," Scott said, disconnecting.

Satiah had that feeling she got when things were about to turn sour. She'd had it from the moment she'd stepped off the transporter. The medical facility, a large sprawling complex between skyscrapers, had set up a raised platform near its entrance, and this was to be where Oli would stand to talk to the onlookers. The shield had been set up to counter any snipers that might be watching from far away. The crowd was already starting to gather. Some were medical personnel, some were patients, and others appeared to be members of the public. Somewhere in that crowd two members of Malla's team were supposed to be concealed. Satiah couldn't see them, but wasn't that a good thing?

"Everything okay?" Shannon asked, picking up on Satiah's sudden alertness. Satiah didn't answer immediately. She took the time to check out the walkways above and the proximity of the evacuation routes in relation to where Oli would be.

"Seems to be," she allowed, at last.

Shannon though wasn't convinced. "What do you think?"

"...I think we're going to be rained on." Shannon watched Satiah, like someone would regard a dangerous animal, as she followed Oli. She really did not like Satiah, but she at least conceded that she had good instincts. She seemed to be able to see things that no one else did. So if Satiah was looking around, Shannon did the same. While Satiah's back was turned, however, Shannon was able to bury the drugs inside her holdall.

Oli raised his hands in the air, and smiled a big smile to welcome the crowd. There was some sporadic applause in response. After a few waves and more smiles, Oli began talking. Satiah still could not shake the feeling that something bad was going to happen. Again she scanned the skyscrapers around them, seeking a shooter, or a ship in the sky that might attempt an attack run. There was nothing to see though. She tried to keep one eye on the security team members, knowing that one of them could easily present an unaccounted for danger. The crowd was quiet... perhaps abnormally so. Satiah couldn't know if that was significant or not, but her gut was telling her that it was.

She slowly raised the tip of her rifle, ever so slightly. There was death hiding in that crowd somewhere. She didn't know how she knew but she did. She would have killed for Kelvin's eyes, to be able to see who was armed and who wasn't. Where were the two infiltrators? Oli was still talking, following the established rhetoric, and everyone seemed to be listening. Wasn't it always just as things were looking so normal that something bad happens? She saw it before she heard it. A surge forward. Several collective members of the crowd rushing forward, some slipping between others, some pushing others ahead of them. Satiah aimed but was unsure who to bring down first as there were at least twenty. Instead, she hit the red button on the communicator Malla had supplied her with. A general alarm was given.

It was too late; they were already upon the barrier right in front of Oli, trying to jump over.

"Bring them down! *Stun only*!" Malla ordered. Several guns went off, most in the air to act more as deterrents than actual strikes. Satiah, though, wasn't in the mood for this. She went straight to Oli. Remove him, their obvious target, and the fight would be over faster.

"This way, time to go!" she yelled at him. She grabbed his hand and started to drag him along with her. There was a loud popping sound from behind them. The weight of people had snapped the barrier line, and random youths were rushing in and attacking everyone. CCG, Crowd-Control-Gas, hissed into use, but because of where everyone was, it was hindering security as much as everyone else.

Satiah quickly realised that neither evacuation path they had planned was useable. There were too many people. Instead, she chose a side alley between two buildings and rushed down it.

"*Wait*!" Oli was shouting, at her, "wrong…!" He was trying to stick to the plan, reasonable in many ways but predictable, and in *this case* potentially fatal.

"Trust me!" she silenced him, skipping a longer explanation. Oli, distressed and somewhat confused as to what had gone so wrong so fast, had no hesitation in doing what she said. She'd already saved his life at least once and she clearly had a plan, so he decided it would be best to just do as she said.

They ran down a set of steps leading into a vehicle unloading area. Backing slowly but unstoppably towards them, a large cargo-hauler rattled and its warning lights flashed. Satiah kept going, breaking into as close to a sprint as Oli could cope with. There was a danger of them being pinned against the wall if the android did not see them in time to slow down. They crossed into the next channel between buildings, just before the hauler closed the gap on them. Already out of breath, Oli was starting to struggle to keep up, sweat pouring from him. They reached another open area and Satiah, upon seeing what awaited them there, stopped dead.

Five youths, each armed with club like implements were moving in from all sides. They were laughing, jeering and approaching the point where they would strike. Satiah handed her rifle to Oli.

"If any of them get past me, *kill 'em*," she growled, her eyes telling him that he had to. They were cornered, their only way out was through them. There was no age limit on death, Satiah had been taught from an earlier time. Nevertheless, as a Phantom agent she was obliged to at least give them a chance. Satiah stepped forward to confront them, confident but guarded.

"Back down or die, it's up to you," she warned, without preamble.

Predictably this ultimatum was met by more insults, jeers and a move. Two rushed forward, thinking that this was just the empty bluster of a brave face. They did not expect her to move too. It was not done for their victims to fight back. They either ran or froze, they never resisted. Satiah met their charge head on with a small one of her own. She instinctively opened palmed upward, catching the nose of the closest male. The blow broke his nose and forced the bone back into his brain, killing him instantly. As he went down, she was already on the second. The bat he was wielding hit her shoulder but she shrugged off the blow and employed a neck jab hard enough to fracture his laryngeal prominence. He ended up on his knees, gagging, and blood pumped through his fingers as he clawed at his own throat automatically.

A third was trying to stop himself in his approach now that he saw the fate of his friends. He failed. Stumbling into her, he doubled over as her knee rose, knocking the air from his lungs. With a dismissive shout she deployed the *coup de grâce* in the form of a well practised carotid punch to the back of his neck. He would not be getting up again. The other two, evidently deciding that discretion was the better part of valour, tried to run. Satiah though was not done, she chased. They had hardly got seven metres when she cropped the one she was following. The move, kicking the back of one foot to alter its path and interrupt the running cycle was classic. The foot caught on the back of the other leg as it moved forward and the girl went down hard.

Her hands came out instinctively but she didn't have the experience to try to roll or anything. If the blow from landing didn't daze her, Satiah landing on her back certainly did. Seizing the girl's hands and wrenching them powerfully behind her back, Satiah quickly immobilised her and then secured her. Tentatively Oli approached, and running feet could be heard as the rest of the team converged on them.

"Are you okay?" he asked her, rather pointlessly.

"Aye," she mused, hauling the girl up onto her feet. "We need to talk to this girl, that riot was organised." Oli thought about it. It had happened awfully quickly and he couldn't say what had even set them off. It did look planned, he had to admit.

"You guys all right?" Malla asked, as he reached them.

"Yes, thanks to Satiah, you should have seen her! I don't know how they train elites but whatever they do, they do it well," Oli babbled, motioning to where the bodies were.

"Malla, we *need* to interrogate this girl," Satiah insisted, seriously. "*Before* law enforcement does."

"How do you know she knows anything?"

"I don't but she's all we have got right now. Trust me, that riot was a deliberate attempt to harm Oli," she went on. Malla was nodding in concurrence.

"You and me?" he asked, to her. She nodded.

"Not here… somewhere quieter," she requested, as sirens began to wail in the background.

---

The girl was looking at the floor, displaying no signs of being sorry for anything.

"What's your name?" Malla asked. No response. "Look, you *know* you're in trouble and you will be punished. That's a given. You talk and help us, we might be able to ease that punishment," Malla tried again.

"You can't do anything to me! You can prove nothing!" she yelled suddenly at him. "I have *rights*!"

"We have security footage of…" Malla began.

"*Shut up*!" she screamed, insolently. "No comment." Satiah was leaning against the wall, examining her nails calmly as if hardly paying attention.

"Your parents will find out about this if you don't talk. They will be ashamed of you. *Imagine their faces* and how they will feel when they discover what you have done," Malla said.

"No comment," she repeated, crossing her arms.

"Don't think I'm bluffing, I will tell them," he threatened.

"No comment," she smiled, disrespectfully.

Malla lowered his head slightly and then turned his back on the girl.

"I didn't see a thing," he stated, clearly. The girl frowned, wondering what he meant.

Satiah smiled and slowly moved to stand before the girl. Less defiant now, perhaps sensing what was coming, the girl looked up into Satiah's eyes. Satiah's killer eyes that somehow, on a primal level, conveyed menace.

"Name?" Satiah asked, very softly. But the girl was still too stubborn. She thought she could take advantage of the law. She thought she had rights. *She thought wrong*. Satiah's gloved hand reached forward and patted the girl's face firmly and she gave her a sadistic smile. It was like a slow motion slap… a final warning.

"*You*… You *can't* touch me… you *can't* do that," the girl stated, not so confident now. Satiah's hand suddenly seized the girl's throat in a grip as cold and tight as a constrictor's. The girl tried to scream and resist, but Satiah was far stronger than she was.

The girl's nails couldn't penetrate Satiah's body armour. Her blows were feeble in strength. Satiah's other hand moved in, pinning both her arms against the wall in a well executed move. She flailed and tried to kick and do everything she could to free herself, but Satiah just held on, patiently. Malla tried not to listen, and allowed it to happen because he knew that it had to.

The girl's face was going purple as Satiah slowly choked the life out of her.

"...You're hurting me!" she gasped. "Please... stop...!" Still Satiah said nothing but raised her eyebrows. The expression reminded the girl of what she wanted. You *know* how to stop me: just answer my question and the pain stops.

"Jane," she croaked, finally. Satiah let go and she slumped forward, coughing and gulping in air.

"Why did you attack security?" Satiah asked, her tone *so* calm and unruffled. Her complete lack of anger unnerved Jane even more.

"We were told to," she spluttered, tears in her eyes.

"Who told you?" Satiah asked. Jane hesitated. Satiah's hand formed a fist.

"*Some guy*. He was just some guy! I *don't know*, he didn't talk to me, I just *saw him* a couple of times!" she blurted, thinking Satiah would beat her up. "He paid us to do it."

"If you saw *this guy* again, would you recognise him?" Satiah enquired, eyeing her.

"...Yes, *maybe*. He... he *killed* Daz," she stated, more softly.

"Another of your gang?" Satiah guessed. Jane nodded sadly.

"I was scared of him."

"Then you must want revenge," Satiah continued, as if she was discussing the weather. She made eye contact with the girl. "Leave that gang, get a job and *stop breaking laws*," Satiah spelt out to her. "The only reason I did not kill you with the other three was because I thought you had information I could use. The good news for you is that *you have that information*. You are a citizen of the Coalition and yes, you *did* have certain rights. You forfeited them when I caught you."

Fresh tears welled up in the girl's eyes, all the bravado was gone.

"Please, let me go, I swear..." she began.

"No snivelling," Satiah growled, in her ear. "If you agree to work with us and identify this man, we will release you without charge. If you fail to do this, or lie, I will kill you. Understood?"

"You..." she began, about to say that that Satiah couldn't do that. Satiah's hand was on her before she could finish.

"No, no," she mewed, in the girl's ear. "Don't even *think* of telling *me* about things I cannot do, Jane. Or else..." She ran her finger strongly across Jane's neck to emphasise death. Jane nodded quickly, comprehending instantly.

---

A quick call to Randal prevented law enforcement moving into the situation, and so Jane was left in Malla's hands. When Malla had unsurprisingly asked *why* they had not taken over, Satiah had told him that she had used a few *contacts* she knew to give them a while with her. Malla was more concerned about who had paid Jane and her gang to start the riot, than to worry about how Satiah got law enforcement to back down.

Satiah was also curious about the riot. The tactic employed had been very sloppy. Leaving aside there being no organised coordination, the idea of using a riot as a weapon just didn't sound very smart. There were too many chances of it going wrong. Jane did admit that he, *this guy*, was supposed to have been there. This mystery man. He was supposed to have been helping them and telling them what to do. The result of his absence had been pandemonium.

"I never wanted to be in a gang," Jane sniffed. She and Satiah were at a table, drinking some water. Satiah sighed, recognising and being irritated by the younger woman's style of opening up. Assuming of course that this wasn't all an act.

"*Really?*" Satiah asked, uncaringly. "Saw yourself more as a leading researcher in the field of physics, did you?" The question was heavily laden with sarcasm. Jane sobbed out a laugh. Satiah examined the girl closely. She was much prettier than herself, all golden curls and bright blue eyes. She had been lucky she hadn't ended up somewhere *far worse* than a street gang.

"I... I'm a failure," Jane confessed, sadly. "I just... I screw *everything* up."

"Become a mechanic then," Satiah murmured, still watching closely.

"No one will hire me for *anything*," she stated, rubbing her face with her hands. "This one guy looked at my application and laughed! I have nothing! *Nothing anyone could want.*"

"Oh do shut up and pull yourself together," Satiah hissed, rolling her eyes. "You're in a bad place? Get off your backside and leave! People won't do things *for* you! You want it done? You have to do it *yourself*. Do it well and people will get interested. Most of all, stop being such a wimp. Yes, the cosmos is a tough place, *so what*? Just get on with it." Jane sniffed again but thankfully fell silent. Satiah wouldn't be working in a therapy clinic any time soon, for which she was very grateful. Malla and Shannon entered.

"Oli would like to see you before the end of your shift," Malla told her. "We'll keep an eye on Jane." Satiah nodded and stood before walking out. Great! *Now* what did he want? If this was *another* snack she had to check...

She found Oli alone, sitting at his desk. He *looked* alone too. Vulnerable.

"You wanted to see me," she said, the door sliding closed behind her. Oli eyed her levelly.

"What's happening?" he asked, bleakly. "Malla won't tell me anything."

"We're just asking questions," Satiah said, casually. She strolled over to the other side of his desk. "It's fine, you have no reason to worry about this now."

"I *want* to believe that!" he said, standing and staring out of the window. "It's just seems to me like the world has suddenly gone *mad*." It's always been that way, you just didn't notice, she thought.

"Malla's team did everything right," she stated. "Trust me; you're going to be fine."

"So... this won't happen *again*?" he asked. A loaded question. She shrugged lightly.

"I'm not going to lie to you, Oli," she smiled, manipulatively. "But if it does happen again, we will be here to protect you."

"I just... was wondering if maybe running for this office wasn't such a good idea after all. I mean, what if a lot more beings feel that way about me?" he went on, disturbed.

"It was a set up, Oli," she reminded him. "They were paid to attack you." She wondered if she could use this as a way to get him to pull out of the election. "Do you think that those you love would *want* you to be putting yourself in danger like this?" He glanced down at her.

"I don't know. I never thought about that before." Ambition was a bit like that, wasn't it? Mesmerising and sharpening your focus to such an extent you failed to see anything else.

"Life goes by so quickly. One minute you're alive, and then you're no longer alive. Some think life isn't measured in achievements, but in the time spent with those you care about," she said, as if thinking about it herself. "It is *only natural* that you are *uncertain* right now. *You're in shock.* Don't make any sudden decisions." She had to play this *very* carefully. If she tried to persuade him to give up, it might look suspicious as she was employed to protect him, so why would she want him to stop? On the other hand, if her client was exposed to more danger than she could handle, wasn't it the responsible thing to do? He was certainly troubled. Rattled, most likely. There had been two attempts on his life in as many days.

"I should have done this before…" he said, his face hard to read. This was obviously getting to him now. Satiah had been a Phantom agent for so long that sometimes she forgot that this kind of thing terrified normal people. For her it was everyday life. Literally: life, to her, was all about dodging death. Or at least it had been, until very recently. He was breathing hard and she began to wonder if he might have somehow *been* poisoned or injured after all.

"Before? When you were *younger?*" she asked, not understanding. Surely, the younger you were the less likely it was that you could get into office.

His hands were suddenly on her shoulders and he was staring into her eyes intently. Uh oh. She began to shake her head.

"*Oli…*" she began, trying to tell him about Carl. The kiss silenced her.

# PART TWO

# Transient Killers

Sam McAllister didn't want to be his brother. He'd devoted his life to being not so much the complete opposite of him, but rather *the complete difference*. While Oli had managed to gain a majority on their home world, Sam had maintained a healthy following of his own. Being the younger brother, sibling rivalry would be what most psychologists would blame for their current fractious relationship. They couldn't be more wrong. Their differences were entirely political. Oli was a deep believer in communitarianism and felt that, if he could help get people together, then things would take care of themselves.

Oli didn't see the bigger picture - the bigger picture being that people lived apart for good reason. The likeminded worked with, lived with and reproduced with the likeminded. Why else do you think they lived on different planets in the first place? The second you throw everyone together and act as if their identities, cultural or physical, were secondary to their common purpose… you had a war on your hands. History was testimony to this, a repetition of patterns. Cycles of conflict. Sam understood this. He stood solidly for conformism. Sam stood for unity but only in the individual form. He didn't want worlds to change their allegiances like clothes; he wanted things to stay as they were. Permanently. And he wanted to be in control. He felt he could build up protective barriers and keep the citizens contained safely, to prevent them harming themselves through their ignorance and their greed.

However, until he got into power, none of that mattered in a way. After all, you could promise what you liked until you got into power, so it was always easy to gain popularity simply by lying. Once in power... then the truth would out. Too late, of course. Brenda remained a formidable obstacle in Sam's path, as did Oli. From the start Sam had known he'd never be able to overcome Brenda, she was far too strong politically. Oli, on the other hand, was easier to bring down. He knew that people would suspect him. They were brothers, after all, and the fact that they disagreed to an extent that made civil conversation an impossibility would make his culpability obvious. But then... proof would be needed. Without proof there would only be rumour, and no one with a brain listened to rumours, right?

It was hard to say exactly when he'd decided to kill his brother. Perhaps when they were children and Oli would be praised for something that Sam didn't consider worthy of praising. Perhaps in their youth when the politics crept into their lives. It might even have been the week before, when he had found out that, shortly after running against one another on their own world, they would be doing the same thing but in the final stages of the Benefactorial Campaign. He'd already lost once to this man he was tied to by blood. A second defeat would be a step too far. Too long he'd lived in Oli's shadow, a place he hated to be. It was worse than that, because everyone else saw him standing there too. Held back. Kept down. Silenced and subdued. No longer...

His communicator went off and he answered after checking who it was.

"Can you talk?" asked a woman's voice.

"Hi mate, how are you?" he asked, using a code phrase previously agreed on. It meant: *no, I can't talk right now.*

"He wants to meet," the woman went on. "I will send you the details."

"That's great, I'm fine thanks," he replied, staying on script.

"I will send you the details, come alone," she said, cutting off.

"Okay, take it easy, I will call you when this is all over, we'll catch up then," he replied, to no one.

Shannon looked around as Malla entered the room she was in. He looked unhappy. Nothing unusual there, given the strain they were all under. Oli and Kate were getting the information ready that they would need for the next day: paperwork, agendas... all of it. Malla gestured to her with a nod of his head to get her to follow him. She did, curious and a little excited. Had he found the drugs she had planted? Was he going to ask her about Satiah or what to do about her? They found a side room and, as she expected, he deposited the drugs heavily on the table.

"Is there anything you want to tell me?" he demanded, hotly. That was a question that clearly required a specific answer and it caught her off guard. Surely he was asking the wrong person. Maybe he wanted to know if she'd noticed anything.

"I *thought* you were smarter than this, *Shannon*! All these years! Have you already *forgotten* what this stuff does to you?" Malla ranted, before she could think of an answer. *Wait, what?* Why was she starting to think that he thought they belonged to *her*? Something wasn't right here.

"Where did you find them?" she blurted out, a sinking feeling in her stomach.

"In your holdall during a random check! Technically *Cadel* found them, but fortunately he came straight to me and told no one else!" Malla seethed, levelly. "I hope you appreciate how hard that was for him. You *know* his brother died because of this kind of thing...!" How had that happened? Had *Satiah*...?

"Malla, I *swear* I'm not using," she stated, trying to think of a way out of it.

"No? Just trading? That's often how it starts until you turn into your own best customer..." he began, furious.

"*Malla*!" she hissed, getting serious. An idea came to her, a possible way out of this. "*I promise you*, it's nothing like that. I was *testing* security. I planted it there, in a place I didn't know was being checked, for someone to find..."

"*Why?*" he snapped, uncertainty creeping into his tone.

"Well, Satiah has proven herself so well that I was worried everyone else might start getting complacent," she improvised, hopefully. He let out a breath, still uncertain. She let out a laugh that lacked conviction.

"By all means test me to be sure but *you know me*, I would *never* get into that kind of stuff," she stated, sincerely. That much was true, at least.

He went quiet, his gaze remaining on her, searching for a lie.

"Next time you try anything like that, you *must* at least tell me first," he implored, a little relief in his tone now. "And, since you brought her up, I want to talk to you about Satiah. What *is* going on between you two?"

"Should that be *her and Oli*, not me?" she evaded.

"Whatever it is, *sort it out*. I cannot have animosity between the two people closest to Oli, *especially* not now," Malla warned, sternly.

"Why do you trust her so much? You've only known her for *four days…*" she began, angry now.

"*Why do you think?*" he demanded, raising his voice over hers. "It's pretty self evident! She's saved *his life…*"

"There's something weird about her," Shannon persisted, seriously. "Like, she acts so cold *all the time* but I *know* she's putting on an act. I don't know *why* but *she is*." He looked incredulously back at her. "Okay, not cold but… I don't know, it's hard to explain. *Watch her*. Just keep an eye on her, *please*. I *know* she's up to something."

"…You're jealous!" he stated, in dawning understanding.

"I am *not*!" she denied, immediately. "And I can't believe you of all people thought *that*… that sexist, pigeonholed psychology."

"*All right*, you're *angry* because she's made you *and all of us* look amateurish," he went on, rolling his eyes. "Either way, this has got to stop. We're trying to protect someone's life here…"

"And *why* is Oli so interested in her?" she demanded, almost to herself. "Her bodysuit looks like she's crawled through a mudslide…"

"Okay, enough!" Malla ordered, holding up a hand. "Why don't we just be honest? It's nothing she's said or done, it's because of what she is, isn't it? *You don't like mercenaries.*"

"Neither do *you*," she reminded, levelly. Malla pulled a face.

"True, I don't *normally*, no, but this one seems fine," he stated firmly. "I know I can order her to do anything and she will do it without question. She is always looking for ways to improve how we work. She's spotted dangers before anyone else and she works well with Oli and Kate. What more could you *want* in a bodyguard?"

"That's *another thing* I don't like about her," Shannon admitted. "For someone who *claims* to have no interest in it, she knows a lot more about politics than she told us."

"It's just *six weeks,* Shannon!" he yelled, irritated. "Not even *that* now. Can you not *endure her* for that long, at least?"

"Talk to Oli, tell him to be careful with her," Shannon stated, seriously. "We already know people are trying to kill him and we know nothing really about her past. For all we know, that guy could really have been after *her*..."

"I will ask Kate about her," said Malla. "Oli likes her too much for an accurate opinion, and Kate is very perceptive."

"See, even *you* see that they..."

"I can see that Oli likes her, *a blind man could see that*, but I don't really think she's into him," Malla reasoned. "Unlike *you.*" Shannon lowered her head; there was no point in denying it. Malla sighed and leaned against the wall. "I'm *sorry* he rejected you, I know that it is tough, but that doesn't give you the right to get in his way with her."

"*She's a mercenary,*" Shannon muttered. "Oli couldn't deal with someone like that. He would suffer regardless of how she feels about him."

"You don't know that," Malla reminded.

Shannon was still trying to understand how her plan had failed. She was sure that Satiah hadn't seen her plant those drugs. She had been so careful. Yet *somehow* they had ended up in *her* holdall instead of Satiah's. It had to be Satiah, there was no questioning that. How she'd done it might forever remain a mystery, but one thing was for sure. This was war now. Satiah had made her look like an idiot and humiliated her in front of Malla, and she'd done it without even having to be there. She'd pay for that.

─────── ⋅✦✦✦✦✦⋅ ───────

Randal eyed the message on the screen in front of him. The one that had started it all. It was an encrypted source, though the text was plain for all to see.

**I won't rest until this is over. I won't let him get away with this. Oli cannot win the election, he must be stopped. I will use any means at my disposal to achieve this. I will avenge you, my angel.**

Satiah had already seen this. This one message was why they had assumed the threat to Oli's life came from inside his own campaigning team. They didn't know who it was to, but they knew it had come from planet Earth. Computer analysts had determined it was likely that the threat was from within. Satiah hadn't come back to him yet so he assumed she'd found nothing.

"We all *know* she's your best, no one is bringing *that* into question," Scott was saying, on the communicator. "It's just that she's been there four days and has got nothing to show for it." Randal didn't answer, letting Snell dig his own grave. "Perhaps she needs *help*; we have a team ready for her to work with. You know, to provide her with direction and *support*."

"She works best alone," Randal stated. "Besides, in what capacity would this team work with her?"

"They would support her in a hands on, co-interfacing, multi directional managerial sort of way. It would be pivotal and modular for the purposes of both efficiency and effectiveness…" Scott rattled on. For God's sake!

"*No*. She answers to me alone and she requires *no help*. She will do her job and if she finds she needs help, she will ask for it herself. *She will do whatever it takes*. So long as we leave her alone to do it," Randal argued, refusing to back down. He could just imagine her reaction to any suggestion of plowtering with the PAI. It would feel soiled.

"Naturally I respect that. I'm only thinking of *your* reputation, my friend," Scott laughed, insincerely. "There is a lot riding on this, as you know. We wouldn't want *an intervention* to have to occur." *Since when were we friends? I must have missed that bulletin*, Randal thought to himself dryly.

"Your concern is appreciated," Randal answered, carefully. It wasn't appreciated, nor was it even truthful. "If you can't trust her, then trust me. He will not win but he will live… *perhaps to try again*. The computer never said exactly *when* he would be at his most threatening. Perhaps in the next election?"

"There *is* that possibility," Scott had to concede. Then he laughed. "I'm sure we will soon find out."

───────✦✦✦✦✦───────

Spread across an elaborate couch, dressed elegantly, the very image of luxurious aristocracy, Marisa sipped her crystal glass of Tome. It sparkled, not unlike champagne, and had a light blue haze. Dressed in a white fur-skin robe and a hat of the same material, she exuded regal wealth with a heavy dose of self-centred arrogance. Class is a word meaning a few things, a stylish merit or a grouping of things in common such as attributes or property. It also can mean a societal system of order. After all, humans love labels, so instead of it just becoming a mere grading system, it becomes a method of division. Dividing people up. Segregating them from one another. They are much more easily controlled when they are not all together as one. Classism, as prejudice always is, is the inevitable outcome of categorizing the social order. Marisa considered herself to be at the top of this pyramid of class.

From an early age she'd always felt that she was special. Her rich parents had taught her the value of wealth… and not a lot else. She'd never had to earn money in her life. She understood the economy well enough to make it work for her. Money made money. Yet it was a balancing act and, just like in any act, sometimes the lines changed. If the new lines suited her, then no problem, the party went on. If they inconvenienced her in any way… she did something about it. She sipped her drink with a practised air of indifference. No one was even watching her, but it was a habit she saw no need to escape from. An android entered.

"Your guest is here," it informed her. She sat up, eyeing the time.

"Show him in," she told it, "and we will require refreshments." She slid the hat off, fully revealing her long jet-black curls and green eyes. The door opened and Collorah marched in.

"You're late," she told him. "I have *proper* guests arriving soon; this had better be worth my time."

"Am I the only one you've hired?" he asked, bluntly. She turned to face him, puzzled. She already knew he was not easily intimidated, as she supposed few in his line would be. His lack of respect irked her but she'd already decided that subject was best left alone.

"Of course, why would I hire anyone else?" she answered, the question in her tone. What was he insinuating? She didn't like it when people insinuated things: she felt it was rude. She preferred frank accusations. They were easier for her to work with.

"I was attacked by another operative. As a consequence, I was unable to be where I had to be to ensure Oli's death. I wondered if your impatience had got the better of you," he stated. That's better, she thought. Then she started wondering…

"I'm not *impatient*," she pouted, cross. "Is this some strategy of yours to try and trick me into paying you more money…?"

"No, *as I said before, the fee is agreed*, it was a genuine question," he cut across her. "I can still do this, but it will likely take longer. Not only are Oli's guards more organised than I thought, but with a rival operation going on…" He trailed off, not needing to say more.

"I can wait, just make sure he dies *before* he can be voted in," she instructed. "Who is this rival you are going on about?"

"If I knew I would have said," he grunted. She paused, a brooding look about her. Maybe someone knew what she was doing. Some ally of Oli's that she didn't know about. He didn't have many. Leaving aside how everyone hates politicians, he was new and was threatening them all with a change they didn't want. His death benefited *everyone*… except him, of course.

"What do you think they want?" she questioned. "Are *they* onto *you*?" The *they* was less of a known quantity and more of a speculative marker at this point. He had nothing else, or he would have said, which meant he was guessing. She trusted his instincts and in a way, probability-wise, she supposed it was likely that some kind of resistance to her scheme would occur.

"Possibly. Don't worry, there's no way they could trace anything back to *you*," he assured. *Well done for remembering the only rule I care about, she purred to herself.* Powerful as she was, she knew attracting attention to herself was never a smart move.

"Especially as you haven't *actually* done anything yet," she remarked, provocatively. He didn't rise to the bait.

"I just had to check with you... *before* I take them out too," he growled, with a devious grin. "Wouldn't want to harm an investment of yours." Her eyes narrowed and she made it obvious through body language how much she doubted that.

"Who knows? Perhaps *they* will come after you?" she joked, levelly. As usual, there was no sign of fear from him.

"I hope they do, the hunt is always more exciting when the fight is even," he said, turning to leave.

"Try not to forget your *actual* objective. It *is* why I'm paying you," she called, after him.

The android returned as the hired killer departed.

"Lady Lilith Ring is on her way now," it stated.

"Good," Marisa said, her tone not giving anything away as to how she was feeling or what she was thinking. If someone else was involved then that complicated a very simple scenario: the scenario being how to prevent anyone else being voted in as Commandment Benefactor. Brenda had no plans with regard to altering the rates Marisa's businesses worked with. Her investments and millions were safe so long as Brenda remained in command. She trusted Collorah, he'd worked for her before and he was nothing less than dedicated to whatever his task was. Nevertheless, she'd find it hard to concentrate on the party after that transitory conversation.

"Oh yes... offer her my heartfelt commiserations regarding her recently deceased husband."

---

"No, it's not *enough*," Harrier repeated, sounding frustrated. "These parts are all straight off the black market, probably been there for years. There's nothing on them that the system or I can use to pinpoint either the original manufacturer or even the material owner. They were probably shipped here bit by bit and then assembled planet-side. Hardly anyone is mad enough to send the device anywhere once it's been built." Satiah could hardly concentrate on his words. She was sitting in her transporter, with her hands resting on the deactivated controls, waiting outside the arrivals area for Carl to appear. She should have been elated, excited and at ease. Instead she was really very angry.

Shannon, aka the problem without a number yet, had tried to create extra difficulties for her by planting drugs on her as she clearly lacked the courage to confront her directly. Satiah had slipped them back in Shannon's bag when she had been distracted later. While this neither surprised nor angered her much in itself, it was still an irritant as she knew it would not be the end. Repercussions were as inevitable as waves on the beach. And the longer you had to wait for the wave to arrive, the bigger it would be.

Despite preventing a bomb going off, literally, *and* retrieving it for analysis, Harrier said it wasn't enough. What did he want? A name tag? And *Oli*... How had she misplayed *that* so badly? She had known he was attracted to her, strongly attracted. It had been a good thing in a way, a form of leverage she could use to manipulate him with. Yet she'd chosen not to play it like that. She thought she'd not responded and, if anything, she'd tried to subtly push him away. It just went to prove the old saying that men struggled with subtlety. It is truly lost on some of them. She remembered someone telling her: be direct or they will believe what they *want* to, rather than what is *correct*.

When he had kissed her, before she'd had a chance to tell him that she was in fact already attached to someone else, she'd instantly recognised the quandary this put her in. And not just *her*, but the mission itself. When the moment had passed he had apologised for just doing it without any sort of warning, and stood back to more accurately comprehend her feedback. He was very emotional. That was a given. Leaving aside the fact that he'd survived two assassination attempts after a life of relative safety, he also had been out of a relationship for nearly three decades. Knowing she had to keep the mission in mind, Satiah had been forced to temporise. She had acted stunned and then voiced the opinion that, it was late, they were *very* tired and perhaps, *in the cold light of day*, it would be a sensible idea to reconsider things.

Even *she* knew that that was weak. But what else could she do? She couldn't reject him harshly as it could affect the mission. It could even conceivably lead to his death, if he took it badly. He was under a lot of stress and a thoughtless rejection might be enough to push him over the edge. She had no reason to think that he might be suicidal, but sixty two percent of suicide cases showed no signs of depression before they took their own lives. However unlikely, it *was* a possibility she just *could not* ignore, because of her mission objectives. He had to stay alive.

She couldn't have thrown herself at him either. She was with Carl and had no intention of cheating on him! Granted, he didn't have to know, but there was no point in creating extra secrets for herself to keep when there was another way. Was it cheating though? Her job surely was the first concern here. On the other hand, she was in no way attracted to Oli. There was nothing wrong with him and many people would probably find him very stimulating, but he didn't have the fire she did, or the lazy mischief that Carl did. She decided that should anything further happen between them, it would be strictly on *her* terms.

There was a tiny chance, *a dream really*, that the next day Oli would take her to one side and they would calmly, mutually agree to simply pretend it had never happened. She knew, conversely, when she'd looked into his eyes before she'd *escaped*, that that was as much a fantasy as the idea of them being together in the first place should have been. He had made up his mind that he wanted her. She ran through some potential extraction strategies. Such was the depth of the reverie she had slipped into that she didn't realise Carl was there until he opened the door to the transporter.

She jumped as he opened the door, her hand automatically going for her pistol.

"Woah, woah, easy! It's *only me!*" he said quickly, recognising the move. He raised his hands in a quick surrender gesture. The second he made eye contact with her, he knew something was up. "How come you didn't see me coming miles off? *What's wrong?*" And she used to be such a great actress!

"Hello," she smiled, a little shaky. "Sorry, this mission isn't quite as simple as I said it would be, that's all. How was your journey?" Shoving his luggage in the back, Carl launched into one of his long and somewhat humorous tales of the benign. It was oddly palliative for Satiah just to sit there, listen, and forget her own troubles while she used her imagination to picture what he was rambling about. She didn't even start driving them home; she just sat there watching him. Carl paused, noticing her adoring expression as she regarded him. It was rare to see that, even for him.

"Are you drunk *again?* You look rather spaced out," he asked, chuckling.

She shrugged and leaned over to rest against him. He put his arms around her and squeezed. This was the first time, in a long time, where she felt protected by anything other than herself. It was a moment, a moment she was conscious of. Being held for its own sake, *voluntarily so,* was still a new sensation for her. It felt a little like the rush she sometimes got when gambling on something she had no control over. He rubbed her arm tenderly and kissed the top of her head.

"I don't think I have any wise words of comfort you've not heard before so... *I love you?*" he offered, softly. She smiled.

"Love you too," she replied, and really meant it. No one else could hear her say that and no one could *ever* know. She felt better already, like the utterance of those words had helped remove some of the weights dragging her down. They were still there, of course; nothing had changed except her own attitude.

Sometimes when she had a problem, thinking about something completely unrelated helped her to not only deal with it but find a solution too. Perhaps, circuits crossed, this would be one of those times?

"You know..." she began, knowing he would agree no matter how she phrased it. "...I *was* going to take us somewhere later tonight but I'm thinking an early night might be more sensible?" His hands started to wander, confirming that he understood. See, *some men* understood subtlety... kind of.

The drive back was like a breath of fresh air. She wasn't thinking about the mission, the news or the threatening shadows. She'd not realised how much working *without Kelvin* and having to rub shoulders with so much politics was stressing her out. It was an enemy she couldn't fight in her preferred way - up close and personal with her pistol in one hand and her blade in the other. *Actors on a stage* was a poor metaphor for this situation as it failed to encompass the attention to detail or the true scale of it. There were so many levels, so many implications… it boggled the mind. Yet that was how she felt. Politics can seem like saying one thing, whilst doing another, while thinking about a third long-term plan that no one else should know about. She had a talent for it herself of course, but… it made her unhappy.

As they got into her apartment the first thing Carl saw was Kelvin. "What *have* you been up to in here?" he asked, a little uneasily. Carl didn't much like Kelvin but he'd learned early on that he was part of the package that was Satiah. Kelvin was just another of her tools she simply needed. Like her gun or her boots. She rarely went anywhere or did anything without him performing a function.

"I wish I knew," she breathed, staring down at the mess. "He just - *stopped working* and I'm almost out of ideas, to be honest."

"*Weird,*" he murmured, staring thoughtfully down at the jumble.

"…*And almost fatal,*" she agreed, remembering.

"I know a guy, did some work on the computer on one of the more expensive ships I used to trade in. He has this guy working for him who is a genius when it comes to robotics and computers and stuff. If you want I could give him a call?" Carl suggested.

"Well…" she paused, trying to say no without being rude.

"He won't say *anything about anything,*" Carl reassured, guessing what she was concerned about. "He doesn't even have to know it's *yours,* I'll say it's mine."

"I'll think about it," she said, procrastinating. He grinned, knowing her well enough to understand. He stared at her. "What?" she asked, curious. He said nothing, just continued to regard her levelly. "*What?*" she repeated, more playfully.

"Close your eyes," he requested.

"You're not going to try *that* again, are you?" she retorted, grinning.

"*Seriously*, close them," he stated, rolling his eyes. She sighed as if in great reluctance and closed her eyes for a second, before subtly opening her left eye again.

"*Without* peeking," he stated, guessing she was. She closed it again, trying not to laugh.

"Do you want me to hold out my hands?" she offered.

"No, tell me what you see?" he enquired. She frowned.

"Well, *nothing* mainly because you told me to close my eyes," she replied, smugly.

"You're seeing what my life would be without having *you* in it," he said, with great sincerity. She cringed and let out a belly laugh.

"*Please*, no more, I'll be sick," she protested, laughing.

"Wait there, I've got fourteen more," he said, pretending to search his pockets.

---

Carl opened his eyes and turned over to find Satiah laying there next to him, holding an odd looking book.

"…Morning?" he gruffly articulated. She smiled.

"Sleep well?" she enquired. He pulled a face. "*After* I left you alone," she added with a snigger.

"I think so," he nodded, trying to sit up. Wincing, he fell back down with a sigh and she started to laugh.

"Good thing *you* don't have to go to work," she remarked, getting up.

"I'd never make it to the door," he agreed, still waking up. He blinked hard a few times and yawned.

"I've left notes everywhere for you, *everything you need is here*, be careful - there are a few dangerous things lying around," she told him. She tossed the book aside, having failed again to get anywhere with it. She'd even considered showing it to Kate: she was supposed to be good at puzzles.

"Now, please try not to eat *everything* while I'm gone," she teased, grinning.

"As if I would," he complained, in a hurt tone. "Where do you get all your energy from?"

"That's really one of those deep questions I'm always trying to avoid answering," she replied, adjusting herself in the mirror. He watched, one of his soppy grins on his face. Her shoulders slumped, knowing what was coming. "*What?*"

"You're wasting your time. It's impossible to be *more* than perfect, you should know that by now," he chuckled at her.

"Shut up," she giggled. She hauled on a backpack and grabbed her rifle. She'd now adapted it so that it might actually qualify as something worth using. Another attack could happen at any time now, and she had to be ready for anything.

"I'll see you later?" he asked, even though he already knew the answer.

"I'm looking forward to it already," she chirped, a little derisive. It was hard for her not to mock small talk.

Again, as usual, the journey was a strain on her nerves. She was in no hurry to see or speak to Oli that morning, but she knew it had to be done. Kelvin would have been able to build a psychological profile of Oli by now and he would have capably told her what the least dangerous thing to try was. It was down to her this time. Last night an idea *had* reached her, so it seemed there was something to be said for distracting herself after all. It was a cruel notion but she was angry with him. She would string him along. His maintained survival was an objective *only* until the election was over. After it was over, all bets were off, certainly as far as she was concerned anyway. Five more weeks, she kept telling herself. Just five more weeks of this chaos then she could get back to… well, at least this election would be over. Normality would descend on the government again and it would go back to business as usual for most beings.

She reached the building and parked outside in her usual place. She was a little early and so remained there in the driver's seat, thinking. She wasn't thinking about Oli this time. Well, not exactly.

**I won't rest until this is over. I won't let him get away with this. Oli cannot win the election, he must be stopped. I will use any means at my disposal to achieve this. I will avenge you, my angel.**

Angel? Interesting choice of word as it led to other stimulating words like *avenging* and *guardian*. Of course, romantic partners often, exasperatingly, referred to each other as angels. There was obviously a religious connotation too, but her gut told her that this beatific designation was something personal. It could even be addressed to a child. A dead child, perhaps? Oli had done something, or was being blamed for something, and it was related in some way to the election. And someone wanted him to pay for it. *Any means* told Satiah that death was a probable punishment for whatever the offence, or *perceived* offence, was. Won't get away with what? Oli seemed *too nice*; perhaps he had a darker side that even she hadn't sensed yet.

All that business with the bomb, the shooting *and* the riot… Oli seemed to have more than one enemy. *Was* there another side to him? Her communicator went off. It was Harrier.

"Yes?" she answered, efficiently.

"We know who hired the street gang," Harrier stated, excitement in his voice. "He's known as the Red Necromancer, but we know that's not his real name. He's a hired hand. No interest in politics. Someone's paying him to act, for whatever reason."

"Why would he hire the gang? Do we know his usual methods?" she pressed, intrigued. "Any ideas on location?"

"He's a marksman, no idea why he chose to start a riot," Harrier stated. "I feel obliged to warn you about this guy. He's dangerous." *Well, obviously!* "He's also *expensive,* so whoever is behind him is *probably not* having a cash flow crisis."

"Okay, send me pictures, I need to alert the rest of the team here," she stated, seriously. "I also need you to find him for me. I may have to pay him a visit."

As she entered, Malla was there to greet her. Unusual, she thought. He looked awkward. By way of greeting, she sent him details of the Red Necromancer, feeling ever so slightly concerned he might think it was a joke with a name like that.

"Morning," she grunted to him, as she reached him. "Get my message?" He was caught out, like it was the last thing on his mind.

She frowned. "*Everything okay?*" There were some questions that would always be stupid, but in order to move things along...

"I'm fine," he said, clearly not fine. "I just wanted to ask you if you were having any problems?" That was when she realised what he was talking about. *Shannon.*

"My only problem, *our* only problem, is that someone is trying to kill Oli McAllister," she remarked, avoiding the subject. That seemed to silence him. He began going through what she'd sent him as they rose in the elevator.

"Wow, I've never known law enforcement to be so fast and thorough," he murmured, as he read.

"I was string pulling. Well, *yanking*," she smiled, adopting an air of exasperated vanity. "I had to practically strangle some of my old friends to get it done so quickly. They're so tied up in their own red tape it's a wonder they get *anything* done." She didn't want him to get suspicious about how quickly this had been done, and she hoped the possibility of hurting her own ego might distract him. It seemed to work.

"We owe you big time for this," he stated, thinking about what to do next. "And they think he'll try again?"

"Yes, though probably not using the same method," she concurred. "I know it's a temptation, but I would say that we *shouldn't* hire more bodies." Malla nodded, understanding why.

"I just don't know if we can handle this guy," he stated, worried. "And they have *no idea* who hired him or why?"

"Not yet," she shrugged. "They are looking into it. Can *you* think of anyone? A former employee, maybe? Someone with a reason to hate him?" Malla was thinking back.

"Well, there was *Dean*," he stated, considering. "He was dismissed because he was using the facilities to access pornographic material and to sell his own footage. He *might* have blamed Oli, I suppose."

"When did this happen?" she asked.

"About three months ago," he shrugged. "I can give you the file..."

"That would be useful," she said, as the doors swished open.

"I *really* don't think...' he began. Satiah agreed it was doubtful. Unless Dean was wealthy, it was unlikely he'd be able to afford the Red Necromancer. It had to be looked into, nonetheless.

"Me neither, but we have to be sure," she stated, seriously. "We've still got five more weeks of this mayhem, so that's plenty of time for anything to happen." Malla nodded.

"Thanks again for your help with this, Satiah," he replied, sincerely. "I'm glad I have someone to talk to who knows about this kind of thing. Law enforcement are not always the easiest people to deal with."

"They like it that way."

She entered the main room. Shannon was there and she made eye contact with Satiah. Satiah couldn't resist giving her a knowingly cold smile. *Yes, I know what you tried to do - don't worry, I won't forget it.* Kate and Oli were going through the usual routine as always, but when Oli saw Satiah he almost froze. They couldn't talk yet. Too many people around. In a way Satiah was glad about that, as she was not particularly looking forward to their next private conversation. So, *day five...* and it was already *this tense.* She imagined that by the end of this election, they would all be in need of therapy.

However, it was everyone else that Satiah had to watch. Someone, most likely someone in that very building, had written that note. Even now they were plotting, scheming and planning his death. If not *them*, then someone they had hired. No one was behaving any differently to usual, of course. Why would they?

Sometime soon would be the first live debate. *Live* obviously was an inaccurate description of it, but the title was the title. As far as the public knew, it would be live. Nevertheless, all arguments and scripts were being pored over methodically. The postures, the expressions, and all the subliminal stuff. Satiah knew that it was actually impossible to have an informed opinion on anything due to the incredible amount of misinformation out there - certainly for the average citizen, anyway. It never ceased to amaze Satiah how much effort all these people put into something so farcical. It would be funny if it wasn't so depressing. And each time Oli's eyes found hers, he would stutter, freeze, or almost jump. It seemed he was feeling much worse about that kiss than she was! *Good.* So he should. And interfering with his chances of winning was part of her job, so in a way this did have some benefits.

"*Oli!*" Kate chastised, tetchily. "Will you stay focussed, please? If you freeze in front of..."

"I know, I know," he apologised, tearing his gaze away from Satiah again. "Sorry, can we start that one again?"

"What is your policy on education? In particular: will you *continue* to financially support the adult education programs?" Kate asked, again.

"Education remains an important..." he began.

"See, *right there*, you're really making me quite angry! You're sounding *just like all the others*. You need to be more dexterous, more *unique*! If you want people to listen, and better still, *vote* for you, you need to show them that you can be different," Kate ranted, jumping on him immediately. "You need to show them that you *care* about what they want."

"Maybe you could just *answer the question* too," Satiah chipped in, joining in. *What an original idea.*

"*Exactly!*" Kate agreed, raising her finger wildly. "Keep *any* grandstanding down to a minimum."

"*I only said four words!*" he protested, trying to keep a sense of humour. *They were the wrong four.*

"Sorry," Kate said, making a conscious effort to back down. "Sorry, I was just... sorry. Let's go again." She asked the question again. Satiah eyed her, wondering if her apparent stress had another explanation.

"Yes, investment in education is an investment in our future," he replied, choosing his second answer. Satiah grimaced, the platitude nauseating her.

"Can you expand on that in real terms?" Kate probed. Oli began to throw out some statistics and some general trends. "Where would you say improvements should be made?" Oli again fended that one off with a few examples of things the existing administration had failed to address. A short argument broke out between them over how her question was worded. *Should and could* were the words that proved the most controversial. Satiah had to stop herself laughing at one point.

"Okay, what about the military?" Kate went on, switching topic to try to catch him out. "Last year *billions* of Essps were poured into defence and other associated areas and no one seems to know where any of it went...'

"*That's what I should be asking Brenda,*" Oli muttered. Satiah's eyes narrowed, as she had a very good idea where that money had gone. Perhaps on some of the many ships she'd trashed. And that was hardly Brenda's fault, Balan would have been responsible for those transactions.

"That's a point, but they will *still* ask you because *you are there,* so answer!" Kate was relentless.

"Until the expenditures are justified to me I will not be renewing those contracts. We are *not* at war. We *don't need* more battleships or soldiers. We have far too many as it is, that money would be better invested in agriculture, the health sector or support for the elderly..." he answered. Satiah rolled her eyes. *Yes, like that's ever going to happen*. And for his information they *were* at war... *constantly*. She knew this was why everyone wanted Brenda to win. She had already signed those contracts so getting rid of her, in a way, was completely pointless. The military always come first whether you like it or not, just ask any scientist.

---

Octutin peered over the edge of the roof. The lights were out in the adjacent structure. These buildings were small for those of Earth, only seven hundred floors. The winds weren't constantly strong, but they were cold and blustery. He scratched his beard briefly as, from several of his jacket pockets, he began to assemble the rifle. He was so well practised he didn't even have to watch his own hands; his eyes never left the darkened window. Slowly he raised the completed firearm and stared down the sights at the same spot. The place where the Red Necromancer was staying. A guesthouse unit, reasonable quality, not luxurious by anyone's standings but... adequate. The fact that he chose this type of accommodation was testament to his professional attitude. Work and fun were likely separate entities for this man. Jinx had tried to bring him down and had failed. Tonight it was Octutin's turn.

"We're in position," said the woman. It was the same operative he had used before to plant the bomb. She and a team of ten others had infiltrated the building and were to break in, on his signal, to kill the rival killer. Octutin would bring him down, should he get the chance from his vantage point. His eyes narrowed, troubled by the complete lack of movement from within and the fact that getting this close had been so easy. There was the outside chance that he was simply not there any longer, but Octutin had had people watching all day. They had seen him return from somewhere but had not seen him leave again. He could also be in another part of the building, the bar perhaps. If he was, they of course had a plan for that too. He tightened his grip on the rifle, preparing himself mentally for the kickback.

"Take him," he growled, seeing no reason in hanging around. The door exploded open, sending a chunk of metal flying into the room as the lights snapped on, illuminating the whole area brightly. The team, shouting as they spread out, had infiltrated the whole place in less than ten seconds. Not a shot was fired. There was no sign of the Red Necromancer. In fact, from what Octutin saw, there was no sign anyone was staying there at all. There was no luggage, no clothing… not even food and water.

"He must be in the bar area," concluded the woman. Octutin sighed. He hoped this didn't turn messy. It was dangerous getting violent on Earth, with law enforcement around every corner. They made his life very difficult sometimes. He was about to tell them to move out and set up plan B when the lights went out.

Screams were heard, along with flashes from guns and another explosion. Octutin could only listen as, one by one, each member of the team was killed. Collorah had been hiding inside the wall and had blasted it open after cutting the power to that floor. He had waited until his enemies, believing themselves to be safe, had clustered together before launching his ambush. Octutin heard the crash as something bludgeoned the operative he was listening in to. He heard the crashing sound as her body hit the floor. Everything was over in less time than it took for them to get in. He listened hard as a rustling noise sounded, followed by the sound of someone breathing heavily.

"It's *rude* to try to take someone in their sleep," Collorah growled, into the earpiece. Octutin swallowed.

"Oli McAllister is *our* target, back off or we will be forced to kill you too," he threatened, as anyone would.

"Too late for that, my friend, first blood has been drawn, may the best man win," he stated. There was a clatter and then a cracking sound as, presumably, Collorah crushed the earpiece underfoot.

Hoping that he'd not been seen, Octutin slid slowly out of view and waited in case the other man sneaked up on him. He took apart the gun swiftly, his hands almost shaking with anger and more than a little fear. He entered the building and made his way further up instead of down. If Collorah knew where he was, he could still be waiting downstairs.

"Jinx, it's me, the team's dead. This guy may be beyond us," he warned, levelly.

"One man killed ten and lived?" Jinx asked, doubt in his tone. "How are *you* still alive if it went that sour that fast?"

"Proximity," he replied. "That and a bit of luck, I think. This guy, he knew we were coming for him and he'd set up an ambush. I spoke to him, told him to back down. *He's not going to back down.*"

"*Great...*" hissed Jinx, clearly frustrated. "Did he say who he was working for?"

"Didn't ask," Octutin scoffed. As if he would have just told them?

"...I'll make a few calls. See if I can't get us more friendlies," Jinx replied.

"I think we should pull out," Octutin openly stated. "Sure, it will cost us but better your life than money, right?"

"No, this is personal now, this is our patch. We take him down," Jinx argued. Octutin sighed, pondering the wisdom of disagreeing further. In the end he decided to play it cool.

"All right," he allowed, leaving it at that. "Maybe it would be prudent to take Oli out first, ensure we at least get paid for that." Jinx calmed down as he thought about that. Also, if his target was gone, the Red Necromancer might not be interested in a further fight. Then again, if he was mad, he might just come after them anyway, simply because he could.

"Have you spoken to the client about this yet?" Octutin asked.

"No, I'm meeting them tonight," Jinx replied.

"Mind if I join you?"

"If you insist. I thought you didn't want them to know about you?" Jinx enquired.

"I don't, but I want to see their reaction when you tell them about the Red Necromancer. Just to be sure they haven't hired him themselves," Octutin replied. There was a hiss on the other end.

"*I never even thought of that*," Jinx admitted, angry. "If they have I'll kill them myself."

"You'll have to get in line," chuckled Octutin.

---

"Are you all ready for the debate next week, Brenda?" asked the aide, smiling pleasantly.

"Of course," Brenda smiled, confidently. "I must say I never envisaged being the Commandment Benefactor would be so easy. It's like everyone is doing all the work for me."

"That's what happens when a dedicated staff follow your orders to the letter," said the woman. "Did you remember to take your medication this morning?"

"Yes," Brenda smiled, relieved. "I set up a reminder on my computer." The aide smiled credibly, concealing her own relief within. Those pills were important. They reduced Brenda's anxieties and made her much mellower, therefore... easier to control.

"That was very sensible, we cannot have you getting sick, we wouldn't know what to do without you," she replied. "If there is anything you need, do let me know, I shall be right outside."

"*Thank you*," Brenda answered, gratefully. "You have been *so kind and helpful*, I don't know what things would be like without you there to explain it all."

"Gobbledygook," the aide laughed. "I'm sure you would be perfectly capable without any of us here. You wouldn't have made it this far otherwise."

"Will *Deetee* be chairing the debate?" Brenda asked, awkwardly.

"Yes,' the aide nodded, picking up on Brenda's discomfort. "I think he's horrible too, if you know what I mean, but we can't change that…"

"Of course not, no, a muzzled press is a bad thing. A sign of totalitarianism," Brenda concurred, quickly. "*I just think he's creepy.*" The aide laughed.

"Well, if I were you, I wouldn't say *that* while we are live," she said. Then she chuckled. "Although it might make more people vote for you!"

"O, about those military contracts…?" Brenda began, as she remembered. The aide stiffened for just a second before relaxing again. "Yes?"

"Well, as you know, there was *one left* that I had to sign and I said I was going to read through it…" Brenda said, biting her lip anxiously.

"*What about it?*" the aide asked, a hint of darkness in her eyes.

"Well, I'm *really* sorry but I spilt my drink over it, is there *any chance* you could find me another copy to sign?" Brenda asked, in a pleading tone. "I was just *so tired* I kind of slumped and…" The aide's smile was back, relieved.

"What *have* I told you about *overworking*? I don't want to have to stand over you in your hospital bed and tell you how I told you so!" she said, sternly. "It's fine, I can easily get another one, so you're going to sign it?"

"Well, I was reading it, but to be honest…" She leaned forward confidentially. "I didn't really understand much of it and I was afraid to ask, so yes. Does that make me lazy?"

"Frankly, the military speak their own language and sometimes they don't even seem to understand one another so no, I'm not surprised at all. Balan had trouble with them, as did his predecessor Samantha Reeve. It's not a problem. Most of these things take care of themselves so long as you're there holding the framework together."

"Really?" Brenda asked, mildly amused. She nodded. "Thank goodness, I thought it was just me. I've always been an admirer of Samantha's integrity. It was partly because of her that I went into politics."

"I'm sure, we must chat about that sometime," the aide said. She leaned in confidingly. "To be honest, she was far better at administration than Balan. She was also a lot kinder to us than he was, but I think *so far* you're winning on the kindness front."

"I *am* trying," Brenda sighed. And she was, as it was in her nature. She'd been brought up to believe that treating people how you wished to be treated yourself was the correct thing to do.

The up and coming debate was on her mind, as it was to all who were invited. It was still just her in terms of confirmed attendees. With the constant movement of the proportional representation, it would be a few days at least before it would be clear who she was up against. She didn't know it was entirely staged. She didn't know that all the audience had been carefully chosen, the questions carefully prepared. All she knew was that she had to learn her answers to whatever questions might be thrown at her. It wasn't so much knowing what to say, as it was knowing how to say it, and what words to avoid.

She didn't like being in power as much as she thought she would. She had been worried that it would corrupt her and turn her into the very thing she had fought to replace. Now though, a tiny part of her had started to wonder exactly how much power she actually had. She trusted everyone around her because she was a trusting person. It never occurred to her to think that they were manipulating her.

---

They were alone. Alone for the first time that day. Satiah was ready and she knew how to play it. She done this kind of thing many times before and she was good at reading people. She would trust her own instincts… Oli was staring at her, wanting to talk. She had decided to let him speak first to reinforce the fact that she was not interested. She crossed her arms and made herself look uncertain and defensive. She didn't want to do anything that would make him think she had feelings for him.

"Did you manage to sleep last night?" he asked, tentatively. She *had,* in point of fact… specifically, with another man. *Her* man. The question didn't catch her out, it only made her realise this could take a while.

"You?" she asked, without actually answering. He shook his head.

"*Not really*," he said, with a hangdog and harassed look about him. "I… I couldn't stop thinking about… you know, *what we did* and…" *what you did, she thought*, "…and I was worried about you. I know you're supposed to protect me, but now I don't know if I can let you." *Really?* O you stupid man! She played it cool, shuffled on her feet, made the effort to look *conflicted*.

"This is a place of work," she reminded him, carefully. "What happened was inappropriate. We're in the middle of an election and I don't think it's a good idea for me to be around you if I will distract you." He looked crestfallen.

"I've really made a mess of this, haven't I?" he asked, rhetorically. "I thought you and I… well, I thought we had a connection."

"We have jobs to do," she coolly maintained. "I am concerned that my participation in things would affect you in ways that others might criticise." This was it. The test.

"No one would ever think *that*!" he said, proving that lust was always going to beat common sense. "Please! I don't want you to think you're making my life difficult because it's *quite the opposite*. Right now, I'm not even sure I would be alive if it wasn't for you." Well, that much was certainly true. "And… we don't have to tell *anyone*."

Isn't that how every tragedy starts? A secret? A bad decision? She pretended not to have grasped the circumstances completely once again… and yet all she could see was Carl's face. She wouldn't betray him, not for Oli.

"What are you saying?" she clarified, as if unsure. "I'm… I don't… I *can't* have romantic liaisons with *my clients*. Plus I have a boyfriend, it would be wrong…" she trailed off, hoping that would be enough. It wasn't.

"You felt something, I *know* you did, and if you *really* had a boyfriend why didn't you mention it last night?" he asked, thinking he was getting somewhere.

Because *you* shoved your tongue in my mouth *before* I could stop you, she wanted to scream.

"It was an emotional day for all of us, Oli, because of what had happened - and I think now is an unsuitable time in my life so I can't, I'm sorry," she said, trying to appear decisive. He seemed to back off.

"I... If that's *really* how you feel?" he asked, eyeing her carefully.

"It is," she stated, knowing that saying anything else would be recklessly stupid.

"Then I will not chase you," he said, sadly. She felt a bit bad, but the relief was too strong to be restrained. At least he'd not gone barmy. She took a chance; she had to get him while he was on the back-foot.

"I will talk to Malla tomorrow about people I think would be good enough to replace me..." Satiah began, deviously. This would be how she would secure his support. If *she* made it look like she was *trying* to leave... he would fight anyone, namely Shannon, who might cause her trouble. Besides, everyone always wanted what they couldn't have. Interestingly, when they got it, they often didn't want it anymore...

"*You can't leave!*" he almost sobbed. She'd known he would. He was a civilized man, she supposed. "*Please* don't... look, I don't know if I will even *survive* if you go now. Please, I'll pay you *anything you want* to stay. Please, I... it's *my* fault. I *misread* the situation. I'm not good at reading the signals. I've not been with anyone for such a long time, you see. I *promise* never to do anything you don't want me to," he went on. "Will you trust me? *Forgive* me?" Got you. She uncrossed her arms and tried to once again to look dithery. His eyes were wide, studying her closely. She wondered what he *expected* her to say, as she already knew what he *wanted* her to say.

"I forgive you," she allowed, and then waved her finger at him as she continued. "You kiss me again and I *will* have to walk away, do you understand? My livelihood depends on my professionalism!"

"No, no. I totally get it, many apologies. I just think *you're amazing*," he said, pushing his luck. Well, she wasn't going to shrug off a compliment like that.

"That's because I am when compared to most other beings around here," she shrugged, as if it meant nothing. She extended her hand. "*Friends only?*" she enquired. He took it and shook it firmly as he nodded his agreement. As with Shannon, Satiah knew that no matter what he said, Oli would try again. She'd beaten him back but he certainly would make another advance. If only there was someone else... *oh wait*, there was.

"Besides..." she smiled, manipulatively, "I wouldn't want to get in Shannon's way." The look he gave her, open mouthed and astonished, betrayed the fact that he'd failed to see the reality.

"*Shannon* likes me?" he asked, curious. That was hard to believe after what had happened.

Yes she does, too bad I might have to kill her if she keeps trying to incriminate me, Satiah thought. She shrugged again, keeping up the act.

"I *think* she does but I'm not great at reading signals of that sort either," she said, self-deprecatingly. "*Perhaps* I have got it all wrong..." Kate entered at that moment and they sprang apart as if caught planning to fake his death or something.

"Oh, *sorry!*" Kate exclaimed, her fingers over her mouth in delighted amusement. "I thought..."

"Never mind, we were just talking, no more near death experiences for me," Oli said, recovering well. Not well enough, apparently; the older woman had a knowing air about her, having probably seen many things like this before. Satiah played along as usual.

"His desk was untidy," she stated, lying very badly deliberately. "We were just organising it." It was face reddening, toe curling, an all-out pure embarrassment, whatever you may prefer to call it. And it was just another performance that Satiah had trained for.

※※※※※※

Carl smiled as she arrived home, but he could see how stressed she was. "What do you need?" He motioned to the wine.

"Only you," Satiah said, dumping her equipment by the door. "It was a tense day. Nothing bad happened, but it still frustrated me."

"Does *everything* frustrate you?" he asked, sardonically. His point was: you can't not tell me what's going on and then complain about it.

"*Why can't it?*" she grinned. "It's nothing," she added, very convincingly.

"...Did you want me to call that guy? *About Kelvin?*" he offered, poking a thumb over his shoulder at the mess behind him.

"Still mulling it over," she replied, with a less convincing smile.

"You *do* look fantastic, you know?" he said, regarding her in the doorway. Looks... so deceptive. For a moment she almost thought she would scream. She didn't *feel* very fantastic at that moment. Maybe having Carl to stay might not have been so smart. His mawkish attempts to make her feel better were having the opposite effect. She wasn't sure she was comfortable with him being so close to her work either. On the other hand, she knew she had a tendency to overreact to change, even self-inflicted change. She resolved to give it longer.

"Did you hear anything today? About the Ro Tammer trial?" she asked, changing the subject. Carl, a Federation citizen, something she still found a little awkward, was intensely interested in the trial. Not just because of the outcome, but also because of the legal precedents it would be setting. Ro Tammer was on trial as much for what she had been planning to do, as what she had actually done. The charge of planning aggressive warfare was a new one and it was based on some legal points that were a little ambivalent. Treaties and established practises that were not actual law were the main issues for that charge. A good counsel would easily be able make a mess of things if they delved deeply into the technicalities.

"According to the *CNC*?" he asked, raising his eyebrows at her. They shared a significantly cynical look. Neither of them liked or trusted the news, for obvious reasons. "Well, there's apparently been some sort of *overlooked technicality* that's halted everything for now. So they are kind of stuck between trimesters two and three. This technicality, *whatever it was*, might have something to do with one of the witnesses against her? At least, I think she's somehow pressuring someone. *I know I would be* in her position. She's so screwed if she doesn't wriggle out of it." So... they'd not got *that far* then.

Satiah frowned, thinking about it. It happened all too often to immediately make her concerned but... this was *Ro Tammer*. Carl watched her face closely.

"You don't think she'll get off with it, do you?" he asked, seriously. He was getting worryingly good at reading her these days.

"Anything's possible," she shrugged, as if it really didn't matter to her. "In my opinion, it was a mistake to take her alive. Too late to do much about that now, not with all that fairness-obsessed nonsense around her. It's always annoying when the wrong people seem to have all the rights."

"I still don't know *how* Admiral Wester managed to catch her in the first place," Carl scoffed, shaking his head. Satiah smiled knowingly while he wasn't looking. "The guy is a genius."

Satiah picked up the red data cube Randal had given her. Review duty was an irritating responsibility, but it was something she had a talent for. While off duty from protecting Oli, she would focus on it over the next few days. Harrier would be watching - well, him and his team anyway - in her absence. It had been decided early on that it would look suspicious if Satiah was always around. It was partly the reason why she'd bugged everything. Naturally she would tune in herself from time to time. A little distance from Oli would help too.

"I've never met him," Satiah stated, casually. She slid into the seat next to him and began putting on a headset. He gave her a quizzical look.

"*Not for you*," she said, mock sternly. His hand landed on her thigh. "Be good or you'll be the one who's on trial," she growled, and he let go with a grin.

"Would you arrest me?" he asked, playfully.

"Yes I would, and I'll do it for real if you don't let me get on with this!" she replied, firmly. He nodded, deciding that she probably would, and continued watching the replay from the latest on the trial.

Satiah couldn't resist a quick flicker of a glance at the defendant. Ro was sitting there, but her body language gave no indication that she intended to surrender. Indeed, she looked rather serene. Satiah leaned against him and he put his arm around her shoulders casually. She could tell, just by how long it was taking the file to load, that this review was going to take a while.

It had been called (and Satiah often wondered who it was that gave names to these things) the *Blue-Jurnn incident*. There was an office, ironically one that she couldn't remember the name of, which named all kinds of disasters, natural or not. The names were based on scale and long-term effects although, when they could, they often chose the name of the location most central to said disaster. The only time this could not happen was when something similar had happened in a place of the same name. Sadly, this was apparently more common than one might think. Blue-Jurnn was the name of the plant as well as the reactor itself. It had been, and still was, located on a Coalition planet called Barckain, about one hundred miles north of the identical plant Green-Jurnn. Its destruction had resulted in the deaths of twelve personnel, five medical personnel, and a lot of civilians.

The nearest habitation was over three hundred miles to the west, a sensible precaution set against exactly this sort of eventuality. Not far enough though, apparently... Satiah read a little of the history of the facility, making note of its advanced age and, in some cases, outdated technology. It powered almost every military establishment on the world and provided additional support to the nearest civilian buildings. Next, she went into the backgrounds of those who had worked there, including those who were dead, endeavouring to identify anyone with a motive for sabotage. Just paddling on the surface before she sank into the nitty gritty about what had actually transpired. There was, as she had expected, nothing obvious.

Unlike the last review she'd had to do, she found herself wishing she'd worked with this compiler before. It was logical in both order and delivery, following the timeline in a detailed and impartial way. Satiah knew there were only four ways this could end. Mechanical failure: which might lead to prosecution of either the manufacturer or the installer; force of nature: instigation from an external natural force like a volcano or a tornado; deliberate sabotage: which should require no further description; and finally there was *being error*, a modern legal term to replace the old-style *human error*. Basically, someone made a mistake either through incompetence or negligence. Satiah knew from experience it was most likely either the first or last option, but she would be thorough. Certainly she could discount natural disasters already.

Everything had been normal until, as part of a new company-wide incentive, *oh dear*, they tried to simulate an unstable reactor core and shutdown procedure. Apparently a similar test had been undertaken the week before at Green-Jurnn which had exposed several worrying shortfalls. Satiah switched across to look at *that* report, curious. The procedure consisted of two main stages. Simply put: *warming up* and then *cooling down* or as *they* called them: the elevation mode and the conservation mode. She made up her mind to check out *just who they were* and if any questions needed to be asked about *their* competence. After the test was over, the reactor was returned to its usual output levels. It had to be, as it was a working reactor and the power was needed. The test took two hours and fourteen minutes, an average of about one hour for each stage.

A week later they tried the same thing at Blue-Jurnn and somehow it had ended in catastrophe. A lethal dose of radiation had been released, though quickly contained, and people had died. How? Who was to blame? That was what Satiah needed to decide. She knew seven others would also be reviewing this and would be doing the same thing. They were not allowed to contact each other, indeed they were not even informed of any details regarding identity or location of the other reviewers. This was to prevent conferring and leaks. Based on the collective decision they made, actions would be taken - assuming they reached a viable consensus. Any other developments that might affect their decision would be sent to them individually, if and when they became available. In this case, it was likely that nothing further would be coming her way. This review was only *one part* of the legal process, but it was one of the final and most important stages.

She began to follow the course of the simulation at Blue-Jurnn, being sure to keep an eye on who *was* and *wasn't* present at the time. Stage one began on the hour after a staff briefing. The briefing had been extended, most likely because of the test. She wondered if that had included a run through of the emergency procedures. The briefing usually lasted for about twenty minutes, give or take. This one had lasted over an hour. This was only to be expected, she supposed, given the task they were going to undertake. She knew enough about the workings and the standard operating procedures of a reactor to know what this kind of thing would involve. This was, among other things, why she suspected Randal had chosen *her* to review this. The technical data would be easier for her to follow than many of his other closest agents.

Details are where the devil often lurks, and she approached the report the way she would were she an employee of the facility. Fresh eyes, always useful in themselves, and an attitude of someone open to the interests of the experiment. At the end of the day, in her mind at least, *experiment* was the best term she could find to define such a test. The environment was as controlled as it surely could be, given the state of the facility at the time, and there was no record of anyone saying anything different before the test took place. No protest or objection had been given, from either the people on the ground or the higher management that were not present. No one was there who shouldn't have been and there was no reason for distrust.

The first sign of any trouble had been a marked delay between the initiation of the computer instructed program and the *actual* temperature drop. Nearly twelve minutes... nine minutes longer than usual. This was dismissed, at the time, by the fact that it was warmer outside than it had been during the previous test. Also, the general level of output of the base was higher than that of its counterpart. In order to get the seemingly sluggish reactor to cool down, more coolant was added, nearly eighty percent – so when the reactor finally did react, that brought the temperature down *too quickly* and to a level that was dangerously close to the shut down level. The idea was to simulate a shut down, *not* cause a real one. Satiah could see that this was where things had turned nasty.

To prevent the automatics affecting the simulation in any way, they had been deactivated. This meant, in order to prevent the reactor shut down, they had to do it *manually* by heating everything up again and accelerating the speed of the reaction. Catalysts were applied. As before, there was a delay, which further fuelled the panic they must have then been feeling. Guess what they did? They added *more* catalysts. Suddenly the reaction was swinging out of control as temperatures soared unchecked by any of the automatic controls. Satiah rolled her eyes, guesstimating what would happen next. *Yes, more coolant.* In a desperate effort to bring the reaction back under control all the coolant they had remaining was dumped in it, but it was too little too late.

The test ended there as the automatics and emergency control was brought back online. By that stage, however, there was nothing that could be done to stop the chain reaction. The workers bravely elected to stay behind and shut down as much as they could, in order to limit the explosion, instead of running to the minimum safe distance. Satiah noted that those who had been in charge of the experiment had *not* stayed behind. Evacuations began and the blast *was reduced* to about half of what it could have been by those who had stayed behind. They managed two out of six shutdowns: given the timeframe they had, it was quite an achievement.

So to summarise… In short they had essentially destabilised the reactor and then lost control of it. The workers, now all dead, had a certain culpability almost by default. They were there, they allowed it to happen and they participated in it. But they were dead. It was hard to punish the dead. Those who had been there *exclusively for the test, however,* were still very much alive *and* uncontaminated. They hadn't altered their strategy after the first test, in light of the problems it exposed at the other reactor. But then, Satiah felt sure, part of the purpose of the trial was to expose shortfalls.

She felt Carl kiss the back of her neck.

"Are you coming to bed?" he asked, genuinely curious. She looked up. She'd been reading nearly six hours!

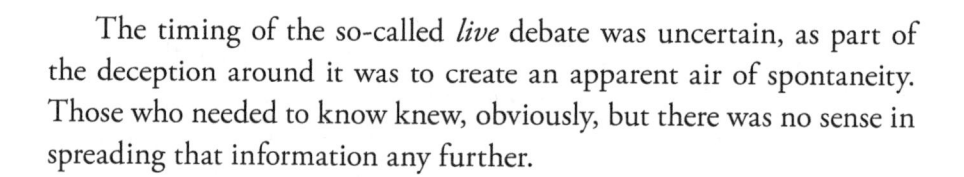

---

The timing of the so-called *live* debate was uncertain, as part of the deception around it was to create an apparent air of spontaneity. Those who needed to know knew, obviously, but there was no sense in spreading that information any further.

"What if they ask me about Neo-remnantist attacks?" Oli asked, seriously. It was bound to come up in the debate, not just because of the recent attack - though that would undoubtedly heighten the general concern - but because it was a very real fear that most people had.

"You must maintain how much you are against them and their methods, then continue to talk about improving the relationships with other superpowers, and working with them with regard to their…" Kate paused, trying to avoid the word destruction.

"*Marginalisation*," Satiah supplied, casually. *She* had been trying to avoid the word *neutralisation*. Oli gave her a grateful smile; she knew he was relieved that what had happened between them hadn't ruined everything. He was glad that they could still talk to, and work with, one another. And Satiah also sensed that he still hadn't quite given up on her yet. Shannon looked on, ever a vibe of thinly-veiled disapproval about her. Particularly when Satiah was consulted for her opinions.

Satiah had relaxed at home for two days with Carl and it had been a much-needed diversion, to say the least. She and Harrier had been watching Oli all the time, of course, and Oli had still been working, but there wasn't any interaction with the public and he had been in the safety of his quarters… *in theory*. No further action had happened. No nocturnal visitors. No riots and no suspicious characters lurking in the shadows. It was all starting to reach the level of expectant disquiet in Satiah's mind.

Something was going to happen; it was only a question of what and when. Satiah was still no closer to identifying exactly *who* was trying to kill Oli from within, but she *was* certain that there was more than one faction. More than one person wanted him dead and they were probably not working with the same side. The methods used so far seemed too varied for the same group of people to be likely to perform. Granted, it could be one person hiring multiple attackers, but where was the money supposed to come from for that?

"You know what bothers *me* about that?" Kate asked, still talking about the terrorist attack. "It's going to sound a bit cynical and heartless but… *of all the times to have an attack*… now, during an election? I mean, I *know* it may be that they are trying to affect the outcome but… the word *distraction* is big in my mind."

"Distraction for another *more dangerous* attack?" Satiah enquired, deliberately missing the point. "Like a feint?"

"No, I didn't mean *that*, though that *could* be the case. I *mean,* to distract the public *from* the election somehow. For some secret purpose. You know, *keep us afraid…*" Kate trailed off. Satiah herself had already theorised about that and, *this time,* it was nothing like that.

"These things are out of everyone's control," Oli smiled, trying to be positive but just sounding guileless. Everything, Satiah knew, was always under *someone's* control. She said nothing though, and smiled as if reassured by his words.

"And remember to not get *emotional*," Kate warned, back on topic. "It's a public forum and people *will* say things that are meant to annoy you. Don't allow them to succeed, no matter how you feel about it."

"I *have* spoken to the public before," he reminded her, amused.

"Yes, but mainly you have been addressing groups of *your own supporters* on your home planet," Kate countered. "These will not likely be as welcoming."

"*Welcoming?*" asked Satiah rhetorically, with grim significance. Even Shannon scoffed in agreement. The discussion went on and on, going over several subjects in all their mundane glory. Satiah reflected on the life of a guard. She knew this would be over for her in five weeks, no matter what happened, but thinking about the idea of doing this all your working life was depressing. Just standing there, listening, watching, and trying not to fall asleep on your feet. This was why security would always become slack. Corners would be cut, reflexes dulled and general awareness atrophied. Staying sharp was key not only to her job, but to her survival. So this assignment presented the subtle danger of stagnation too…

Satiah had that feeling again. The feeling that told her danger was heading her way. She moved away from the door casually, unshouldering her rifle as she moved. Oli's eyes widened as he glanced at her, instantly realising she was alerted to something. Shannon picked up on her unease and began to follow Satiah's example. Kate fell silent mid-sentence as she realised Oli was no longer listening to her. The silence lingered for almost eight seconds.

"*What is it?*" Shannon asked, communicator in hand. Satiah scanned the room with her eyes but could see no menace. A movement, a tiny flicker in her peripheral vision betrayed it to her.

She turned, faced the window and opened fire. Her shooting smashed through the glass and peppered the window-cleaning machine that was hovering outside the equivalent floor of the building opposite. She ducked down just as an answering volley of laser fire began lacing back at her.

"Malla, get up here!" Shannon was calling.

"Get those two out!" Satiah ordered her, motioning to the prone figures of Oli and Kate. They had thrown themselves onto the floor the second Satiah had started shooting. They began to crawl for the door, mindful of glass shards.

Satiah peered over the edge of the next window along.

The window-cleaning unit was now speeding away. It fired again, having seen her. She ducked and then sprinted through the now open door, literally hurdling over the others, still on their hands and knees. Her earpiece was going off, most likely Malla but she couldn't answer as she ran for her transport. She reached the parking area and rushed towards it, the door sliding open ahead of her and the engine revving up, seemingly of its own accord. Oh yes, it was a good job she'd had her vehicle adapted! Who wouldn't? She leapt inside and reversed hard upwards and to the right, before zooming off in the direction the window cleaning craft had gone.

She pulled out into traffic, her eyes flashing as she tried to spot it. She answered Malla now.

"Sniper in the form of a window cleaner, luckily he gave himself away," she explained swiftly. "I'm heading south along the PH429C, no sign yet. My guess is he won't run yet, he will try to blend in. Get law enforcement out here."

"As you say," Malla said, breathless himself. She overtook someone casually, and squinted as she tried to find her target. There was a window cleaning unit three vehicles ahead, but was it the same one?

She continued to approach, taking care not to drive too recklessly. She was soon right behind the other vehicle. It continued on, apparently unknowing, or pretending to be unknowing. She edged as close as she dared, trying to see if there were any signs of damage from her earlier shots.

There was what looked to her like burns on the bodywork. Without warning, the craft braked hard for no obvious reason. Gasping, Satiah swerved violently, almost losing control as she tried to avoid it. The craft then accelerated away in the opposite direction. Satiah spun her transporter, the engine howling in protest at this abusive treatment. Racing after them, whoever they were, she activated the laser guns that the transporter had been modified to include. The window cleaner was really going for it now; having failed to slip away unnoticed, it was pulling out all the stops, frantically trying to get away. Satiah weaved this way and that to avoid other vehicles as she chased.

She spotted the guns before they fired. Two of them, concealed at the back of the craft. She dodged as they fired a steady stream of bolts back at her. She answered with shots of her own. Apparently this window cleaner had nothing ordinary about it, as it shrugged off the blasts without losing control. Sirens were incoming as law enforcement struggled to catch up. Satiah burst forward, drawing up beside the other craft. Jinx, at its controls, ducked as she opened up with her rifle through the passenger window. Glass flew everywhere, cutting into the back of his hands. The wind whipped inside both cabins chaotically. Gritting his teeth, he veered wildly away from her.

"*She's crazy!*" he hissed, fear and anger in his tone. He was jolted hard in his restraints as Satiah then slammed against the side of his vehicle, aggressively trying to force him to one side and into oncoming traffic. He resisted, pushing back. Metal screeched, sparks flew and bodywork crunched and crumpled.

He pulled out his pistol and fired blindly out of the window to try and make her back off. Satiah, staying low in her seat, winced as a bolt burned into the control she was holding. She returned the firing with her rifle. A huge freighter pulled out ahead of them and then, upon seeing them coming, freaked and tried to reverse. Satiah dropped her rifle on the seat and pulled up straight towards the sky. Jinx just decelerated as hard as he could. Satiah continued the same move, doing a graceful looping cartwheel that brought her straight back around to where she was before and allowed the freighter to get out of the way. Jinx, unable to decelerate sufficiently, had to go under it, nearly ripping his own roof off in the process. He glanced behind himself, knowing he was, at the moment, out of Satiah's immediate sight. Taking his chance, he ejected.

Satiah, having passed the freighter, continued to follow the craft as it began to dip towards the ground. To her horror she realised it was going to crash into a walkway. A walkway with *people* on it. She began shooting again, pummelling the back of the craft desperately. It turned from the kinetic force of the blasts, as there was no one at the controls to prevent it. She let out a relieved hiss as it missed the walkway and continued down. She guessed that when she'd been unable to see, the pilot must have bailed. It was the only explanation as to why the craft was just going straight but down in a line with no alterations being made to its trajectory. Law enforcement was on them now and it took some harsh exchanges to explain exactly who was who.

Law enforcement moved in closer to bring down the driverless craft, while Satiah spun around and began to retrace her steps to where the freighter had been. She reached that junction area in seconds and hovered to one side of the traffic as she began a scan. It was pointless. This was Earth. There were people *everywhere*. There was a chance though, that whoever she had been going after had been wounded in the shooting. She began a slow, careful descent to a parking area before getting out. It was empty, aside from a few other craft at the opposite end. Satiah cautiously approached the other two vehicles. Her theory was that it would be likely that her target would want to slip away and how better to do that than steal a parked craft?

Rifle ready, she searched the area between and under them. She did find a parachute that had been hastily concealed there. She smiled as she retrieved it. Maybe Harrier might have more luck with this. Conceivably there might be DNA traces or even blood spatters. She then tried to work out *where* she would run to, if it were her that had landed there.

She would head for the crowds and lose herself in the faceless numbers. She approached the nearest walkway where passers-by were busily going about their business. She knew that the odds were stacked firmly against her now. Her only hope was that he might remain nearby, if only to see who it was that had been chasing him. She began to walk along in the direction of a retail area.

Armed personnel were a common sight on Earth; indeed, most of the civilians were also armed, so a woman walking purposefully down a walkway carrying a rifle was not an unusual sight. There was no blood trail, nothing to follow. No one running or behaving in an untoward fashion. No one with any visible signs of injury. She continued until she was in among the shops, advertisement drones and beings swarming around, looking for bargains. She stood against a building, so as not to present her back to any would be attacker and started watching. She'd give it an hour and then admit defeat. Her communicator went off.

"I think I've lost them," Satiah reported to Malla.

"Where are you?" he asked, casually. She told him where she was and what she was doing.

"Did you get a look at them?" he asked, interested.

"Tall, male and human. I don't think it was the same man that recruited the gang," she answered. Someone tripped and she tensed, thinking it might be some odd prelude to an attack on her but it turned out to just be clumsiness.

"Do you want back up?" he asked next.

"No thanks. Did Oli get out okay?" she asked, uninterested.

"We followed the evacuation plan we rehearsed yesterday, nothing went wrong. I'm starting to worry about this, if you hadn't seen that craft..." He trailed off but his point was made.

"See if you can get footage of the chase," she suggested. She doubted he'd be able to, but it was something he could do other than speculate. "Even if we have nothing on him, we might be able to learn where he came from. Law enforcement will have picked up the craft and that might reveal things too." She didn't tell him that it would actually all be taken to Phantom Squad as an extension of Shogshal Law. Shogshal Law was a little like Marshal Law – this was when the military assumed control of normal channels. The difference was that Shogshal Law was covert and its use was never revealed to the public. Even the majority of law enforcement, military and other institutions were completely unaware of its existence. Intelligence agencies that needed to get things done fast and unhindered by the process of law or bureaucracy were almost constantly using it to expedite all manner of obstacles.

Phantom Squad would be able to take the vehicle and anything else Harrier or Satiah needed from law enforcement using this law. Some people might suspect corruption was going on but most would assume it was either a local solution, created by the command chain specifically for this one occasion, or that someone had just lost the paperwork. Phantom Squad itself would record what happened, just in case. Of course, as far as Malla and everyone else would be aware, law enforcement were the ones they were dealing with.

"I'll get onto that, *be careful*," he said, disconnecting. Crowd watching was tough, even for someone of Satiah's training and experience. The sheer number of beings was a problem all by itself. She tried to focus in on lone, male, individuals. She really missed her glasses at this point, since Alarris had crushed them, and the replacement set were apparently on their way. Those specs would really have helped her sift through the crowd. He'd melted away into the masses. Still, all was not lost, she had the parachute and very soon Harrier would have the vehicle. She decided, instead of going back to Malla and Oli, she'd pay Randal a visit back at headquarters.

---

"How much do we have to pay to get *anyone* to say *anything* negative about Brenda Watt?" demanded Deetee, infuriated. The best he'd managed so far was to find someone that had no idea who was in charge or even that an election was taking place.

"She sometimes has a bit of a s-stutter," joked his assistant. "Just accept it, there's no dirt on her other than this Vourne thing, and we're not allowed to talk about that."

"There's never any juicy stuff anymore!" Deetee complained. "When I was just starting out in this business, if there wasn't anything going on, we'd start something ourselves! Controversial arms deals! Celebrity love trysts! Neo-remnantist hostage situation! We'd invent anything, just to spice things up a little. Generate a bit of excitement. Now you can't say or do anything anymore."

"Yes, but when you guys started overreaching and making those in power look bad, you can see why they got harsh with the press in general. They probably figured, if they're going to spout lies and scandal, then it might as well be *our* lies and scandals. What are you always telling me?"

"*It's not the best kind of truth unless it's got enough spin,*" Deetee repeated, as if recounting an old mantra.

"This election has the spin… just," his assistance assured him. "It might not look it now, but that debate could easily turn into a wildfire. Even if you can't turn it on Brenda, you can burn anyone else you like."

"*That's true*!" Deetee agreed, more cheerful. "We haven't been able to discredit anyone for ages! It would be great to bring a few down."

"Usual rules apply," laughed his assistant, as he bundled some of the cameras back into the transporter.

---

"We *cannot* have this sort of thing happening *on Earth*, of all places," Scott yelled. "Disturbing the peace! Reckless driving! *Shooting*! We were lucky the press didn't see it. Are you *trying* to ruin the crime statistics?"

"I'm sure Satiah had her reasons," Randal sighed, trying not to lose his temper.

"Maybe she was getting bored? Too long without action no doubt factors into her decision making," Scott blustered. The door bleeped, indicating someone wanted to enter Randal's office. Regardless of who it was, Randal was just glad of the excuse to get Scott off of the line.

"Someone's outside, we'll continue this later," he stated, cutting the other man off before he could say anything else. The door slid open.

Satiah entered casually.

"Morning sir," she said, providing the greeting more out of obligation than anything else. It was a positive thing about this mission, that she was so close to home, and therefore so near to a rich supply of resources. Normally she'd be out there on the edge, miles away from help, but not this time.

"*Satiah*," Randal growled, smiling tightly. "I hear you have been *busy* today."

"I think there is more than one faction trying to kill Oli," she stated, instantly. That made Randal pause and choose a different path for the conversation. He knew she didn't have proof but he trusted her instincts enough to let that slide.

"Any idea how many?" he enquired. She shook her head.

"Money is the key to this. We find out who these guys are and we can trace who is behind them. I almost brought one down earlier today but he got away," she admitted.

"Ah yes," Randal said, deciding he'd better at least mention Scott's reservations. "Earth *is* the heart of the Coalition, you know, and it likes to exist in a state of peace and tranquillity." Satiah held his gaze.

"...*Whoops*," she said, at last.

"Look, I know you have to do certain things, but please try to keep the noise down," he requested. "The public don't need to be scared witless *too often*, it's not healthy."

"Scott getting under your skin, is he?" Satiah guessed, with a grin. Randal gave her a withering glance. Without waiting for a smart mouthed retort she moved on.

"I might need... *an extra pair of hands*." That caught Randal off guard. "Just to help go over some of the footage. There is too much for me to get through."

"You have my permission to pick a trainee; I have no senior operatives to spare," Randal stated predictably. She rolled her eyes, no, of course not!

"Fine. *That will have to do...*" she sighed. She knew this would take her perilously close to the realms of being a teacher again and she *really* didn't want that, but this was starting to get overwhelming. With Kelvin out of action and Harrier at full stretch she needed someone else.

And, if her timing was right, she thought she had a certain someone in mind.

"They have got to learn sometime. *You could be really helping someone,*" he replied, understanding how she felt.

"Are they in the usual place?" she asked, as if in defeat.

"As far as I know," he shrugged, lightly. Then he became grave again. "And remember what I said about *keeping it down.*"

"…They started it," she remarked sarcastically, as she left the room. She made her way down to the training areas, deep beneath the surface of the planet. She remembered training down there herself the best part of fifty years ago. The drills, the routines, the rivalries… all of it. She didn't want a whelp though; she wanted someone coming up to when they would be seeking promotion into the ranks of Phantom agents. Someone she could at least rely on not to miss anything. And… there *was* a specific someone she was hoping to find. The door ahead of her swished open as she approached, exposing her to loud instructions being shouted.

"Left! Wait for target! Fire! Weapon malfunction…!"

Several children, probably averaging about twelve years old or so, were being put through their paces by the trainer. Satiah got the attention of the trainer and they had a short discussion. Having found out where to go next Satiah left, heading towards the area where the most advanced trainees were currently situated. She entered another room and was greeted by a deep, concentrated silence. Sat at screens in long rows, youths a year or two older were going through an intense battle simulation. Again, Satiah found the trainer and asked who the most advanced trainee was. Satiah wanted the best. Who wouldn't? And it would be interesting to see how far *she* had come… They discussed briefly what Satiah needed them to do. There were three suggestions and Satiah knew instantly which one she wanted. Satiah then waited outside while the trainer retrieved her choice of trainee.

She heard a door open a few minutes later but didn't look around until a teenage voice started talking.

"You're *her*, aren't you?" asked the girl, obviously awestruck. Satiah slowly turned to stare at the speaker. She was edging forward, toward

Satiah, tense with trepidation. Golden hair, but cut short in a style akin to a finger wave. Pale skinned and blue eyed, she looked far younger than she was. She was wiry in build and a probably a little callow. She had grown up a lot in the fourteen plus years... She bowed her head respectfully.

"Phantom agent Satiah?" Looks meant less than nothing.

"And *you*?" Satiah asked, briskly. She knew how many of the trainees idolised some of the older agents. They were, of course, everything they themselves aspired to be. She'd done that herself when she'd been at that stage. They wanted to be like them, successful, efficient and well respected. The girl stood to attention, clasping her hands behind her back but her expression remained one of intrigue. Wide-eyed astonishment coupled with a hesitant hope. Anxious to be of service and... to be remembered.

"Zax," she answered, firmly.

"How far along are you?" Satiah asked, quickly. She couldn't help playing the role of an intimidating instructor a little, partly to establish dominance and partly just to see how Zax would react. She didn't disappoint.

"Stage nine of twelve," she told her, levelly. So... roughly two more years and she would be looking to become an agent. If she survived, of course.

"Areas of weakness?" Satiah probed, in the same tone.

"Emotional stability and engineering, my best is sixty two percent completions, I will do better," Zax admitted. There was no question of her lying and no point in doing so anyway.

"Areas of strength?" Satiah asked, more softly.

"Combat, problem solving, military tactics, explosives, threat recognition and threat assessment, analytical..." listed Zax.

"Enough!" Satiah interrupted, holding up her hand. She took a step closer. A flicker of Zax's eyes told Satiah that she was successfully unnerving the girl.

"Do you think you could beat me in a fight, Zax?" Satiah enquired, smiling pleasantly. This would be interesting.

"Phantom agents do not..." Zax began, misunderstanding the test.

"Yes, sure, we're not *supposed* to fight one another but... *if we did...* do you think you could beat me?" Satiah asked.

"I shouldn't be able to..." she tried again.

"That's not what I asked," Satiah stated. Zax seemed to relax suddenly and completely and she made direct eye contact.

"There's only *one way* to know," she answered, her voice changing. It was the woman that Zax would one day be, Satiah knew. Creepy. Satiah liked the sound of her.

"All right," Satiah nodded, approvingly. "At your ease. I'm going to explain what I need you for." She did, going into everything in some detail. Zax listened, enthralled. Taking part in an actual mission at her age and rank would really give her a buzz. Even if she only had to do research, which was pretty much what Satiah wanted, if she was successful it would go on her record and might help her later career. It was an opportunity. And at the very least, even if it all ended in failure, she'd got to meet Phantom agent Satiah. That alone would earn her some kudos. Zax, when Satiah was finished, nodded in obedience.

"I will start straight away," she declared, full of enthusiasm and excitement. Satiah smiled politely, handed her a communicator and then turned to go.

"I know... I know *you* don't train many and *that's fine*. If you ever change your mind, *please remember me*," Zax requested, to her back. Satiah turned to face her again, just so that she could be sure that she had heard her but she didn't answer and left. No point in giving her false hope. Still, *she would remember her*. She already had for well over fourteen years. It was interesting to see Zax again... Zax didn't remember the first time. After all, not many actually remembered being born.

++++++

"This is brilliant!" Harrier was saying. "I've found traces of blood *and* industrial markings. Much better, I think this has got the lot." No, *I* found the parachute, *you just examined it*, Satiah thought resentfully.

"Great, *who was it*?" Satiah replied, trying not to snap.

"No idea, I've just started sifting now. It's thrown up seven matches so far so, whoever this guy is, he's on record, but I'm going to let you know when I know for sure," Harrier stated. "Any news on that book yet?"

"No, I'm still looking into that," she replied, seriously. The previous evening she'd dedicated to starting that review for Randal, and she'd not in fact looked at the book again.

"By the way, *nicely manipulated*," Harrier congratulated. "I was just reviewing your discussion with Oli after he kissed you."

"Well, it's good in that he certainly trusts me now," she mused, skipping over the topic she hated. She changed subjects. "By the way, you will be having a helper soon, someone called Zax will be in touch," she informed him.

"Yes, I think she already has been," Harrier replied, puzzled. "Didn't know of a Phantom *Zax* before."

"She's not a Phantom agent, she's a trainee," explained Satiah.

"That will explain why I cannot find her on the register," he mused. "Good, is she?"

"Good enough to fool you into thinking she was a fully trained Phantom agent, by the sound of it," Satiah remarked, scornfully.

"She looked too young but she had an air of authority about her, and she did say *you* had sent her," he objected. She disconnected, laughing quietly to herself.

Malla was waiting in the parking area for her. She swooped down to land near him and then got out.

"Any news?" he asked.

"Not yet, they are running tests," she told him. "I'm obviously not allowed in to see that."

"Obviously," he echoed, in understanding.

"Oli okay?" she enquired.

"They're all a bit shaken up... *me too*," he admitted. "No injuries. I think we may have to revisit getting extra protection."

"You're in charge, of course," she smiled, influentially. "From my perspective, however, it's just more unknowns to watch."

"In four days people have tried to kill him three times – by the law of averages, they have a good chance of succeeding," Malla reminded her.

She didn't tell him that it was actually *four* times. The bomb, the shooting, the riot and then the latest attempt. Each time though, more clues were surfacing. Malla didn't know all she knew, so naturally he would be starting to panic. She needed to reassure him.

"We need to just keep doing what we're doing, law enforcement will help and we're onto them now," she smiled, patting his shoulder. "There is always danger, I know. But we're doing all we can. Why don't you start looking at other security teams now? We can decide who to hire if your mind is made up later. I have a request myself, actually…" she trailed off, mainly to get him to look at her.

"Yes?" he asked, curious.

"I'm going to switch tactics. As much as what I just said is completely true, *I* can't just sit there and wait anymore. I'm going to start hunting them. If nothing else, I may be able to force them to back off. Yet the key to this is working out who it is that we're facing," she said. "In the meantime, I'm going to ask you and Shannon to try and bolster Oli's resolve."

"…How can you hunt them?" he asked, inevitably.

"As an elite, I'm trained to do pretty much everything. Trust me. I will find these people attacking us, even if I cannot find those behind them," she told him.

"Behind them?"

"These attackers are hired hands, I'm sure, they're not our actual enemy. They're a bit like me: mercenary. They have no real interest in it. The money is their only driving factor. That money dries up and they will go away, *nine times out of ten*. It's the motives of those who are employing them that I'm more interested in."

"What are you planning exactly?" Malla asked. He was in charge of her but he'd already decided that Satiah was a resource who worked best when given the maximum amount of room to govern herself. Besides, she seemed to know what she was doing and everything she'd suggested so far had had merit. On the other hand, he knew Oli would want to know where she was even if he didn't actually ask what she was doing. Malla wanted to have something to tell him other than, *don't know, ask her.*

"There are people you can go to. The people who know *operatives*. Most will be ex-military themselves and will know who is around, if nothing else. There is where I will start," Satiah told him. "They will not always know where these people are, but they should be able to put me in contact with them. I will attempt to buy them off, just to see if it's possible to do so. If not…"

"And you will use them to lead you to who hired them?" Malla nodded, slowly.

"I'll try. Most will not just openly tell me, but I'm confident I can persuade them," she remarked, determinedly. Malla had no doubt she would meet with some success. He knew how *persuasive* she could be.

"In the meantime I'm going to move buildings and alter schedules," Malla told her. "Anything to make him a harder target."

"Good," she concurred, sensibly. "Obviously keep me updated in case I have to return in a hurry." He said he would. She would be able to follow their progress through use of those many surveillance devices she had covertly installed, in any case.

---

Elated was not enough, simply *not enough* to describe how happy Zax was at that moment. It was one thing to *meet* a Phantom agent ahead of the time she was supposed to, in this case about a year ahead at the earliest, but it was quite another to be taken from the drudgery of regular drill training and plunged into something real. She'd been given a mission file, a room to work in, contact with Harrier in intelligence and… she couldn't stop smiling. Her instructor had asked her not to smile like that as it was very unnerving to see such glee in someone so young, but she couldn't stop herself. Eager to please and even more eager to impress, she straightaway dived into her task of reviewing the footage. She began from the start, learning who was who as she went.

She forced herself not to try and focus on Satiah herself as she was obviously the last person to suspect, but it was hard not to try and learn things from her. If nothing else, she would have so much to talk about when this assignment was over! As the hours passed, her excitement cooled and she remembered her focus and what she was there for. She began a slow and methodical approach as she sifted through profiles of suspects, records of what had happened and anything else she needed to know. Information came in about the vehicle Phantom Squad had seized from law enforcement. DNA cross matches appeared mere moments on its heels. It was just as fast as she'd dreamed it would be. Criminal profile loading... loading... *Jinx.*

---

Satiah had changed from her guard clothes into her more normal black combat bodysuit. She'd left that silly rifle back at her apartment and had taken *her* pistol with her. She'd also brought her grapple gun and various other tools with her. She would be spending a while dealing with the underworld. While the underworld on Earth was still comparatively safe compared with that of most other worlds, she was taking no chances. Complacency killed too many. Week two, day one, time was ticking... much to her relief. She drove along in her transporter, which had been repaired while she'd been inside Phantom headquarters. She was going somewhere specific, a merchant by the name of Davmav. She'd dealt with him before and she knew he could direct her to the place she needed to find, a place where the seedy underworld operated. A place that was constantly on the move to avoid the diligence of law enforcement.

Her earpiece went off. She answered. An excited Zax explained what she had found out.

"Jinx, he's *known* to law enforcement as a bounty hunter, but also has been linked to assassination and drugs. He was imprisoned briefly about seven years ago for a minor crime, transgression of planetary security zone. Due to him being unlucky at gambling he became known as *inmate thirteen.* This is the man whose blood matches the samples from the parachute you retrieved and some of that spattered within the vehicle brought back from law enforcement. I'm going through his known associates now," Zax reported, breathless with excitement. She had started calmly enough but as she'd continued reporting her enthusiasm had got the better of her, and she'd started talking very quickly. Satiah sighed. She'd not learned how to *maintain* her dispassionate reporting technique yet, but she was still young.

Nevertheless she'd provided good information. *Maybe Harrier could learn something from her.*

"Very good, you have done well," Satiah said, keeping praise to a minimum. "I need you to concentrate on all internal communication from within Oli's administrative team. One of them *has* to be involved. The fact that these assassins can keep on knowing where to find him is evidence of that."

"*You're right,*" Zax agreed, quickly. Satiah rolled her eyes. "I have read the note that you gave me and I will run a search on the word *angel.*" Harrier had most likely already done that, and numerous similar things, but there was no harm in repeating the search. Someone may have sent something *since* he checked, anyway.

"Keep me informed about any developments, *however seemingly minor,* that you encounter. If I don't answer, just leave a message," Satiah ordered, cutting her off before she could respond. Boundaries, young lady! *Boundaries.*

She then called Malla and updated him about *law enforcement's* apparent discovery of Jinx.

"Do you think he is *replacing* the Red Necromancer?" Malla asked.

"No way to know yet. They may even be working together," Satiah answered, shrugging in her chair. She overtook the vehicle ahead, earning her an angry horn blast. She grinned to herself. "As before, just distribute this information among the team. Anyone sees him, *expect trouble,*" she advised.

"I see this one has got form," Malla noted, clearly reading the file himself too.

"Yes," she said, leaving it at that. "I'll catch you later." She disconnected and pulled out of the air-lane in among several rather unkempt looking buildings.

All of this was to the good. Keeping her distance from Oli and Shannon, allowing herself full range instead of playing dumb all the time. She'd all but decided that Malla at least was innocent. He was too straightforward as a man, and had done nothing else to arouse her suspicions. His absence had been coincidence. Shannon too seemed unlikely, as she clearly wanted Oli for herself. Wanted him *alive*. The pair might not be brilliant but Satiah was sure, *with her guidance*, they would be able to keep Oli safe enough. Harrier was monitoring them, as was *she* intermittently. Zax too was now providing another set of eyes so… it should be okay, at least for a little while.

She pulled into a lay-by and descended onto a craft maintenance pad. Two androids ran out to greet her as she got out.

"I want to see the boss," she stated, before either of them could offer any service. "Tell him it's Satiah." One android obeyed and the other offered her a seemingly never-ending menu of services, ranging from repainting to selling and buying of pretty much anything from crates to cruisers. At last, a frightened looking man scurried out to meet her.

"Satiah," Davmav smiled, fearfully. He batted the android away to give them something resembling privacy. "Please, I *am* unarmed. Would you like a drink or anything? I *swear* I got that licence, I don't do that anymore…"

"It's not about *that*," she stated, in a growl. "I'm looking for someone."

"*No one deserves that*," he grunted, before straightening. "No offence. Who's the unlucky fella?" *Unlucky…* Satiah's agile mind instantly jumped on the word, having just heard it from Zax only minutes before.

"How did you *know* it was a man?" she asked, coldly. She knew that was just the way he spoke and that he didn't know anything, but the idea that she might think otherwise frightened him even more.

"I didn't, I swear!" he blustered. "You know I gave up lying to you a long time ago. I'm not stupid, I want to live." She continued to regard him sternly and he scratched his neck distractedly.

"*Err… so…*" he trailed off, uneasy. "Who are you looking for?"

"Inmate thirteen," she smiled, carefully. She'd chosen to use the older nickname Zax had provided. That way if Jinx found out that she was seeking him, he might not think it was because of anything he was *currently* doing.

"I *might* have heard of him," the man said, trying his luck. He wanted a bribe. Her hand slid onto her pistol. She didn't negotiate with anyone unless she had to. He noticed instantly. "*Oh come on!*" he protested, scared. "How am I ever going to prosper if I can't *sell* what I have?" She smiled up at him grimly but said nothing. "Look, you *know* I'd like to help but I have a *reputation* to maintain here, *I'm no grass*." She allowed her smile to vanish and she took a step towards him. He backed away, holding out his hands defensively.

"Okay, okay, how would it be if I tell you all I know about him in exchange for you not killing me?" he offered, sweating profusely.

"You tell me *everything* you know about him. *And* you remember *never* to let him know that I'm looking for him, and *then* I'll *think* about not killing you," she amended, crisply. He nodded, smiling. "*Or anyone he knows either*." His face fell.

"You're no fun, Satiah! At least law enforcement gives me the chance to warn them," he objected, his tone one of dejection.

"*That explains their abysmal arrest record*," she muttered, raising her eyebrow. He laughed hysterically at what he thought was a joke. She gave him a sharp look and he stopped immediately before clearing his throat nervously.

"Need I remind you that I *could* have killed you before? I *could* have put you in a very nasty place for the rest of your natural? I could have done so much to you but I chose not to, out of apathy. But you know what a *bad temper* I have and you know how easily you can make me go away... so go on. *Tell me*." He swallowed.

"I think he's working as a partner now. He is *still* taking up numbers on people. I think he frequents a place called..." he paused, genuinely trying to remember. Satiah waited, not pressuring him anymore. "... Gu... no. Err... Holst's Bar. Yeah, *that's the place*."

"You know his partner?" she asked, interested.

"No idea, sorry. I imagine it's likely that he's a local but I don't know," he answered. Then he straightened in righteous resentment. "I'm a *reformed character* now; they don't belong in my circles. You've got *nothing* on me...!" She put her knee hard into the back of his and had him down on his knees in a split second.

"...But if there's anything I can *ever* do to help *you* I will, *you can depend on me*," he yelped, deciding that trying to intimidate her wasn't the smartest idea. She smiled and ruffled what was left of his hair, before wiping her hand with an expression of disdain on his back.

"Why, that's *very* kind of you," she allowed, backing off and returning to her transporter. The false cheer in her tone was doing nothing for his inadequate fear management strategy.

Holst's bar was an establishment that Satiah was not familiar with, but she knew where it was. The parking was on the roof, under a large holographic display of several solar systems in space, used to promote not only relaxation but also yet another advertisement platform. Zax had provided her with schematics of the layout and general information about the surrounding area. A fight wasn't inevitable, but it was to be expected, and Satiah needed to know everything about not only who she was fighting, but also what else might be there. *And who else...* she had it on good authority, albeit terrified authority, that Jinx *wasn't* working alone. It seemed reasonable to believe that he was working alongside the Red Necromancer. It made sense to assume that, so long as they were still working together, they would remain in close proximity. Or maybe not, they might be playing smart and trying to convey the impression that they didn't even know each other.

The bar itself was on the nine hundred and first floor of a skyscraper, and the floors below were mainly shops, offices and storage areas. The surrounding buildings were all of identical layout. Stairs around the edges, lifts in the centre, all with standard security precautions. Cameras were everywhere but Satiah wasn't too bothered about those. If this had been a Federation or Union world, then they would have presented a serious problem. Here though, within her jurisdiction, provided she could justify it, she could be seen doing pretty much anything and there would be only minimal official obstacles. Arguably, she had less restrictions than ever as she didn't even need to worry about the PAI sticking their noses in - this was technically a part of their plans. Division Sixteen may appear, perhaps, but that was the smallest of chances.

She carefully made her way down the stairs. Injury often occurred in the most mundane of circumstances. Trips from the bed to the bathroom in one's own apartment were a good example. In the dark, the skirting around the bed, trying to be quiet, *crack*! Sound familiar? A warrior of her training had always to be careful. The thump-thump pulsing beat of music vibrated its way out into the entrance area and a security android stood there, watching her. She approached, undaunted. A quick scan would reveal that she was indeed old enough to be there. A computer program hidden deep in the netherworld of coding and AI fabric would prevent it noticing her weapons once her face triggered it. Guns were legal, of course, but going into a bar with one was usually frowned upon. The grapple gun in particular would draw attention.

She entered unopposed into a darkened wall of smoky noise. Lights flashed and dancers whirled around her as she edged inside, trying to spot Jinx. She made her way to the bar, ordered water and took a long slow sweeping look around as any new patron might. Most of these young people should have either been out working, or in higher education institutions, or else a surprising number had taken the same day off somehow… and who precisely was *paying* for these *truancy officers*? So it wasn't that educational standards were falling, they were more sort of dancing around the place like idiots! Oli could talk all he liked about… she let it go, swallowing her anger along with the water. Not her problem.

Her level gaze scanned the others there. She knew what Jinx looked like, or what he *had recently* looked like, thanks to the information Zax had sent her. She also knew that there was a good chance he would recognise her when he saw her, if not as the woman who chased him from the scene before he could strike, then as one of those guarding his target. If he was getting information from within Oli's own office then it was highly likely he would know everyone working there. She glanced at the clock. She was early. It was still light outside, after all. He would probably be licking his wounds, maybe literally, before he chose to take some air. After a failed attempt on the life of his target, unless he was particularly stupid, Satiah hoped that Jinx would need to come up with a new plan. To do that he would most likely have to talk to his partner. Even if they didn't physically meet, messages would need to be exchanged.

Finding a table, facing the door but covered a little in shadow, Satiah prepared herself for a long wait. She busied herself by going through what Zax had sent her a second time, just to be sure she'd missed nothing. This time, she accessed records of those Jinx had done time with, fellow lawbreakers of various disreputable backgrounds. Zax, evidently trying to prove herself, had really gone to town on these reports. Well, she'd looked into links with the Union and the Federation more than anything else. There were a few, but they were the tenuous kind that you would find on *anyone's* records. Things like, once travelled in Federation space, or once visited Union world. Zax evidently harboured suspicions that the other superpowers might be involved in some kind of plot to interfere with the election. Satiah could understand why, but could see that both had too many problems of their own right now to worry about *this*. Besides, Zax didn't yet know about just how the Coalition really chose their leaders.

And other Phantoms were out there to counter the threat of outside intrusion…

So… two killers. Red Necromancer, and Jinx. Hired by whom? *Why*? They clearly were not going to back down easily as they'd already attacked more than once. Granted, they'd come closer to trouble today than they had done so far, which would likely give them pause for thought. She thought back to the note… what was the motive? *Who was angel*? As if Zax was telepathic, she was suddenly in her ear again.

"I've got something," she said, more controlled than before. "An anonymous message, I think it's from the same person. Was sent earlier today, twenty nine minutes point seven seconds after you shot at Jinx." Satiah didn't know if Zax somehow thought she would be impressed by the ridiculously explicit timing she gave, but didn't laugh.

"Let's hear it."

**It seems our enemy has an enemy, but one which we clearly can't trust to do what must be done. Bluntly: the enemy of my enemy can never be my friend. I won't forget you angel, no one should.**

"The weird thing is, I can't find *any* trace of a reply in answer to either of these messages. Now, I *know* a reply might not be necessary and I *know* they might have agreed never to reply to avoid attracting attention, *but...*" She left the sentence hanging and Satiah could see what she meant. It asked no questions so no information was needed, hence no reply. Yet it appeared that whoever it was seemed to be talking in riddles. Satiah couldn't understand what they were talking about. It could be a code, but then why use a code when you're *already* encrypted? The message seemed to be referencing Jinx's earlier attack, the timing gave that away as much as *the enemy business.* It was Zax who voiced what Satiah was considering next.

"Maybe he or she is mentally unbalanced?" she offered, trying to get Satiah to answer.

"*Lovely,*" she breathed. No one she had seen was exhibiting any signs of madness, but so few of them ever did these days. *Except the politicians, of course...*

One thing was for sure, *whoever this was*, angel was their motivation. They needed to find out who this mysterious angel was. It was crucial. Then she could take action. Objective action, purpose reaction. They needed a comprehensible purpose... Something *coherent*. Right now, Satiah and Zax had only a part of the story and it didn't make a lot of sense.

"I will check the medical records of every person who works there, there may be a match even if they used a false name," Zax was saying. "They may have kept their condition a secret from their co-workers, *it happens all the time.*"

"If you say so," Satiah mused, wincing as an extra loud pulse of music hurt her ears.

"Where are you?" Zax asked, curious. "I can't see you on any of the cameras." Satiah explained where she had ended up.

"O sorry, I'll get out of your ear," Zax stated, disconnecting promptly.

The next call she received was a surprise. It was Oli.

"I just wanted to say thank you... *again...* Malla tells me you're out chasing clues with law enforcement," he said, awkwardly.

"That's right," she concurred, keeping her story going.

"Good... I was worried you'd left," he said, uneasy. *O no, here we go again.*

"Leaving would mean I stop getting paid," she stated, keeping it blunt and to the point.

"I thought you'd left because of what happened between us," he said. O... it was *us* now, was it? Why did people always do this? Invent relationships that were not there.

"I thought we had established that we wouldn't talk about that?" she asked, still focussing on the entrance.

"Yes, of course, sorry. Are you sure you don't need any of Malla's team as back up?" he asked, as if verbally tripped up by her words. Oli and Malla were very supportive; it was refreshing to not have to touch-gloves with people on her own side. Well, the people who *thought* they were on her side.

"No, the more people around, the less chance this will have of working," she told him. "Thank you for the thought. I will be talking to Malla about this when I get updates, and he will be able to update you more easily than I." That was the politest way she could think of saying: don't call me again.

"Very well, I hope things work out," he said, taking the hint. *I'm sure you do.*

Just when Satiah thought she could just sit there and concentrate on the task in hand, Randal decided to bother her too.

"How are we doing?" he asked, seriously. Sighing, she brought him up to speed. "Sounds like you're making progress at last." There was nothing critical *or* congratulatory about what he said, it was a mere statement of fact. "Just so you know, Slimy Snell is getting restless. I've told him not to interfere but I wouldn't put it past him to try and insert his own agents in this too." Despite the explosion of anger inside her, Satiah stayed calm and collected.

"Well he'd better let me know if he does, just in case I accidentally kill one of them," she said. It was a fair point. She'd done it before, recently too.

"He *is* aware of *that* escapade."

That got her attention.

"What am I supposed to read into *that*?" she asked, pointlessly. She knew, of course. Another threat. *Revenge.*

"I've got your back *officially*..." he trailed off, his silence finishing the sentence for him.

"But in the real world I'm going to get neck ache again," she muttered, angry. Neck ache from looking over her shoulder constantly. Now, even her own side were gunning for her. *Brilliant*!

"I don't know if any of these PAI agents *knew* the one who you killed," he stated, letting her know what he thought was going on. Exactly the same as what she thought, clearly.

"*Nerva*," Satiah reminded, providing the name. She'd killed him in self-defence, not realising he was a PAI agent when they had ran into one another on a pirate base located on Comet Sunkiss.

"Look, you and I both know how this goes," Randal said, trying to remind her of the correct perspective. "We're partners, fellow agencies working towards a goal of mutual design. If anything untoward happens I would prefer a solid dose of plausible priority or necessary action. Failing that, I would hope that we could escape culpability altogether. Do I make myself clear?"

"You do," she agreed. He was right, of course. Rule number one for a Phantom agent was to survive, no matter what. Even at the expense of the mission, sometimes. And if the PAI tried anything, anything that affected her… she would kill them. Randal just wanted to make sure that no one could prove it had anything to do with her or Phantom Squad. She understood this and concurred in her own mind. No one liked backstabbing.

"Who will it be?" she asked, hopefully.

"If I knew I'd have told you," Randal said, as she guessed he would. "If I find out he's deployed *anyone* I will let you know and I will do all I can to reverse that."

"Thanks," she said, as he disconnected. Well, that was bad news, so much for Slimy Snell; she made up her mind to get even with him when this was done. Wanting her to hurry was one thing, but actively working against her was quite another. She sat there, deep in thought. Betrayal was coming, she could smell it. It had been a while since this had actually happened to *her* instead of another Phantom agent, but she knew what to do. That was when Jinx entered the bar area with two other people. Satiah stayed in the shadows and carefully watched as Jinx and his accomplices ordered their refreshments. She got the bug ready.

Mark looked up from the back seat of the transporter. He was a short man, dark of complexion and manner. The woman, who was acting as pilot and enjoying a smokie, draped her arm out of the window to let the smoke escape as they waited. Mark De-Jool was a politician running for the office of Commandment Benefactor. He knew he would never get it. He knew it was a wasted effort on his part but his supporters expected it. He pushed his jet-black hair back with a chubby hand. His green eyes burned with overweening ambition and a deep bitterness brought about by the prices he had paid to get where he was. A place between old and new... never quite settled. As a young man he'd had a bad case of wanderlust. He'd travelled, always looking for something he could not describe to others - couldn't describe to himself, even. Over the years he came to believe that he was looking for power.

There was no power for him on Earth and there never could be. He just had to settle for what he had, but it was not enough. All the things that others valued more than the planet itself he'd let go of. People who had loved him. All gone now. That cost needed to be balanced somehow! If he never won the prize, he wouldn't even know if it had been worth all the suffering and sacrifice. You had to be in it to win it, but that was the essence of the classic gambler's trap. To lose everything chasing what you could never get on the principle that it would work out in the end. It rarely did. And then there were those he'd hurt to win. Those who were known to him, or just total strangers... guilt and uncertainty joined forces inside his mind to haunt his rationality. Like two serious faced, arms-crossed, observers judging him constantly. It had better be worth it...

"What's the time?" he asked, sombrely. He already knew, of course. He'd just checked. He wasn't sure why he'd even asked: nerves, perhaps. All the things he'd done before paled in comparison to this, a new line crossed further into the darkness.

"Coming up to the time," she sighed, glancing at the clock. "He should be here any minute." Mark nodded and adjusted his position in the chair for greater comfort. He tried to think about something else.

There hadn't been anything else for many years now, and so thinking about something different was difficult for him to do. He settled for thinking about a lake he used to visit as a child, and wondered if it was still there, if it would still seem the same to his eyes.

A transporter lit the darkness as it hovered over the darkened parking area with the usual thrumming noise. It turned and slowly reversed into a space so that it was facing their vehicle directly. Mark let out a breath. He was nearing the end of his career, running out of time. This could be his last chance. That was how he justified these lengths to himself. It was odd, he reflected, how people often grew up and aged into exactly what they had hated when they had first started out. So he'd come to hate himself: a bitter old man. Refusing to accept his own failure. Refusing to give up.

Mark watched as his public rival and fellow conspirator stepped out of the recently arrived vehicle. Mark also got out. The two men approached one another slowly and with the appropriate wariness. Allies they may be for now, but that could change in a second. They moved to look out over the city, the breeze ruffling their hair and causing their jackets to ripple.

"Why do you think they keep failing?" Sam asked, casually.

"That's what I'm here to find out," Mark answered, levelly. There was a brief silence as they continued to look out at the lights of early evening. It was quite picturesque, in an urban architectural kind of way. Sam found himself imagining the distant lights on buildings being those of a control pad close to him. Flashing, flickering and constantly changing. Not unlike the political landscape he lived in.

"I'm going to try and knock them down. This is not what we agreed," Sam stated. Mark shifted uncomfortably. He didn't like confrontation, least of all with hired killers. Sam was right though, they had been paid and they had failed to deliver. Oli was still alive. Worse, unless he was very stupid, he now knew that *someone* was trying to kill him.

"Remember who you're talking to," reminded Mark, trying not to sound as frightened as he felt. Sam shot him a glance.

"Their blundering is costing us both," he argued, calmly.

"I know, I know," Mark said, managing a crooked smile. "We should wait to hear what they say first before we just start accusing." Sam nodded reluctantly. He too wasn't up for chatting to killers about money. To put it mildly: it brought him no joy, but it was a discussion that needed to happen. A deal had been made.

"Are you armed?"

"Yes, are you?"

"Yes."

---

She'd have to try something else this time. Shannon had been stymied. How could she get rid of Satiah *now*? Malla, Kate and Oli all liked her too much. And after that near disaster with the drugs, Malla was being distant with her. Could she get her caught with a member of the press or something? Make it looked like she was an undercover reporter? Shannon groaned to herself. That would never work. The *government* had recommended her! They would easily be able to prove her innocence over anything like that. That really only left her with one option. An accident? Satiah was a professional mercenary and would be hard to get off her guard, particularly with the heightened state of security in general. Did she check her own food? That thought stuck in Shannon's mind. Yes, a deliciously ironic way for her to go...

---

It was about three millimetres long, one across and dark grey all over. The V15 was the latest and most sophisticated form of electronic surveillance, having only recently come off the experimental list. Satiah only had to activate it, and it linked with her tracking system automatically. Equipped with over two hundred different kinds of sensor, it was a definite improvement on the old S series. The S-U8 was good, Satiah never criticized a device that made her life easier, yet it had been surpassed now. And while sometimes equipment from the past could give an advantage, this was not one of those times. Still, you could have the best device in the universe and it would be useless if you couldn't ever deploy it. Satiah subtly took aim and fired the tiny gadget at Jinx's back. It hit his belt and remained there, instantly adjusting to its position.

Satiah leaned back in her chair and tuned in with her earpiece to listen in to what Jinx and his friends were talking about. In the meantime, the device would be taking all sorts of details in that would be useful. Voices, x ray scans of the bodies around it. It could identify concealed weapons and even work out from power signal or weight whether they were loaded. Harrier had got hold of this device for her, and she was allegedly the first agent to use one outside of the testing area. He wanted her opinion regarding its performance. So far she was impressed.

"*I don't know* what's going on," Jinx was saying. "Oli clearly knows for sure now that we're after him, even if he doesn't know who we are."

"I'm more worried about *you know who* than Oli right now," Octutin replied, seriously. "Where are we meeting them?"

"Parking area a few lanes over," he replied, sounding both bored and irritated.

"I've set up the craft you might need," a third man said.

"They won't get nasty," Octutin growled, with certainty.

"They *might*, especially if they *are* the ones who are behind him," Jinx argued. "They might, because we have failed to do what we agreed. In any case, I'm going in ready for anything." Octutin shrugged.

"If he's there, we pull out," Jinx said, in a tone that broke no argument. "If he's there, we *will* bail."

"You won't need to remind me," Octutin smirked. Satiah wasn't sure *who* they were talking about, but it was very curious.

"That stuff arrive okay?" Jinx enquired.

"Most of it," Octutin said. There was a silence as an android waiter unit walked by, searching for empty glasses to retrieve. As soon as it went out of earshot, they continued.

"Which bits are you waiting on?"

"Charges and remotes," he grunted.

"So the important parts then?" Octutin took his turn to grunt in the affirmative.

"Did they say when?" Jinx went on.

"They didn't tell me anything."

"Well, that's typical," he chuckled.

"I looked into that woman, didn't find anything, she's probably just a new security team member," Octutin said.

"Nothing at all?" Jinx asked, puzzled.

"Not even a name, it's like she doesn't exist. She's probably from the Federation or something," he dismissed.

"Yes, *another* migrant," growled Jinx, sombrely. Satiah grinned to herself.

"Did you hear any more about the trial?" Octutin asked, interested.

"*Ro Tammer*? No, they're still dithering over some obscure technicality or other. I didn't really understand it myself," Jinx admitted.

"I find it peculiarly fascinating. How *their* laws are different from *ours*, and stuff like that. The formats, the offences, the timescales... *all of it*. It'd be useful to know in case you ever get yourself caught."

"*That's true*," Jinx granted. "You left out the sentencing."

"Too depressing," he grinned. "What do you think about Brenda Watt?"

"What do I *think*?" echoed Jinx, genuinely surprised by the question. "...She's all right, I suppose."

"Did you vote for her?" Octutin pressed, interested.

"Yes, as it happens, I did. What do *you* care?" Jinx asked, getting shirty.

"Nah, nothing, I was just curious. Given the job we're on... it would be kind of weird if we voted for her main rival Oli," Octutin laughed. Jinx joined him. Satiah too, still listening in, found this exchange somewhat amusing.

"It's got to be a foregone conclusion, this whole thing," Jinx continued. "If they get over fifty, they win. Mathematical certainty. Brenda almost had that on *day one*. All that grandstanding is a load of rubbish."

"It does get on my nerves, because even if you ignore all the posturing and the primness of the thing, you know it's a pack of lies anyway."

Another silence as that line of conversation slipped away into the ether. Satiah heard the clunk as Jinx downed the last of his drink and replaced the glass on the table roughly.

"Let's go," he said. The other two rose. Satiah watched as her tracker began to bleep quietly, following Jinx's movements. She could still hear them talking, even when they were out of sight. Casually she got up and departed too, heading back to her transport. She made sure they were clear of the roof before she came out onto it. She slipped into her vehicle and, without even having to see them, she began to follow. The range on the device was so large that she didn't even have to be on the same planet to overhear their chatter.

She was recording everything, and decided to keep her distance. Normally she liked to move in close, even when she could hear perfectly well. This time, as there were going to be at least four of them, she couldn't risk being spotted. The tracker indicated they had stopped, in a parking area, as they had said. Satiah parked in the building opposite and sat there quietly, still listening in. She glanced across at the empty seat next to her, wishing she had Kelvin there to back her up. Harrier would be listening in to this chatter too, as would Zax. She leaned back, watching the area around her, just in case.

---

Scott smiled tightly.

"You know how it is with them, they always insist on doing everything their way, and interpret any form of reasonable guidance as bullying," he said, as if in regret. The man standing before him, a PAI agent, nodded.

"Division Sixteen are no better, acting like it's their right to just go ahead without any consultation. And then they act surprised and insulted when they foul up and blame us for not sharing intelligence. It's an ongoing problem," Lunell said, agreeing with him. Lunell was tall, lean and dark looking. His eyes, brown and narrow, regarded the smaller man casually. He was a PAI agent who had, until recently, been operating as a mole within an organisation working alongside Division

Sixteen. His cover had been blown due to a chance encounter that had nearly ruined everything.

"Well, the duo I've been bridging with over at Phantom Squad are truly inappropriate in their attitudes. Phantom Leader Randal - *how he ever became leader of anything escapes me* - is holding out on me and deliberately not updating me at the agreed upon times. And his agent, a *woman* called Satiah, is surly, bad tempered and arrogant. Anyway, cutting a long story short, the pair of them are just *unmanageable*. I'm concerned they may threaten our interests in the election through their own incompetence. So... this is why I need you," Scott explained. Lunell nodded again.

"It is my understanding that Brenda Watt is going to win, and that Oli McAllister will lose, but will be allowed to live," Lunell surmised. Scott nodded.

"Exactly right," he acknowledged.

"And my role in this will be?" Lunell enquired.

"Firstly, for now, I need someone on the ground, working directly with Satiah just to be sure that Oli is protected capably. And you will report directly to me," he stated. Lunell paused, wincing deviously.

"And what about Satiah? Am I her superior, equal or subordinate in terms of rank?" he asked, not unreasonably. Scott Snell paused, thinking it over.

"Things are tense enough with her; any additional friction would not help. It's going to have to be *equals*, I think. Just to avoid any... *clashes*," he concluded. "Though, saying that, it's always good to be on hand to provide any *consultation*." He smiled slyly as he said the last word. Lunell understood.

"There is one other thing," Scott added, as Lunell turned to leave. Lunell paused, halting there on the threshold.

"Once the election is over, no one can know how it was orchestrated. *Unfortunately* Satiah and Randal will be security risks... you will have to silence them," Scott instructed. Lunell's thin lips curled into a knowing smile.

"Once the election is over," he echoed, as if in accord.

"Yes," Scott smiled. "I should warn you though that Satiah does have a formidable record so… don't turn your back."

"I never do." As he left he passed another man in the corridor. The man, dark skinned, slim and dark haired, watched him go, then lifted a communicator to his lips.

"This is Division Sixteen agent nine reporting in. Please review the footage I have just sent you and take all necessary steps," he instructed.

"Agent nine, this is Crystal, your network interface supervisor. I have reviewed this footage and will alert Phantom Leader Randal and Phantom agent Satiah to the danger," said a computerised voice. This was no disguise; it *was* Crystal, the most advanced artificial intelligence ever devised. No others could ever rival her as she knew everything about them and how best to contain, destroy or use them to further her own power. She also doubled as the largest virtual repository for all mankind's knowledge. Rumour had it that she answered to only one being… yet no one seemed to know who that one being was.

"Very good."

---

"Thanks a lot for that, Sasha," Deetee smiled, in his usual way. He adopted a welcoming posture, hands open, arms outstretched slightly and relaxed gait. "I'm now going to take you behind the talk, behind the look and behind it all for another edition of *Behind the Times*." Theme music began playing and Zax stood there watching. She had just completed a set of twenty five pull-ups, while sporting a ten kilo weight around her middle, and her arms were killing her. A sheen of sweat covered her as she began her stretches. The ice bath was the alternative but she really didn't fancy that. The music ended and Deetee was back, the smile the same.

"As you know, the year is 58115, but between 58100 and 58109 we were in *the oozies*. Explicitly, *the copious oozies*. Tonight I'm here to talk about how they got that way. Now *remember*…" he said, doing an incredibly dopey sounding laugh as he spoke, "it was *the first decade* since the Common Protectorate War that we *finally* turned the tables on the debt left as the legacy of that conflict.

"The economy was on the up for the first time in seventy six years, industry really was booming," he went on, starting to walk and talk at the same time. "The overall depression in the population as a whole was reducing and…"

"*O shut up!*" Zax hissed, losing patience and deactivating.

"I beg your pardon, young lady?" Satiah's voice came from the speakers nearby. If Zax hadn't already been flushed from her exertions she would have gone bright red with shock.

"Sorry Satiah, *I was talking to Deetee on the screen*," she apologised. "I didn't even know you were there."

"In *that* case, fair enough. Listen, I'm about to eavesdrop on someone else's conversation. I need you to be ready. You weren't doing anything, were you?"

Zax glanced over her shoulder at all the equipment she was supposed to be using.

"No, not at all," she grunted, hiding her reluctance. She'd been sat at a desk all day and it really didn't suit her. She had exercise programs to keep up with and, while she had permission to miss whatever classes she needed to, she didn't want to fall behind too far.

"I'm going to need you to be ready to figure out *who* these people are as I'm assuming they will not be wearing nametags," Satiah instructed. "So, like you did before, *same again*."

"Yes Satiah," Zax nodded, dutifully. She slumped back into her chair and began powering up all the systems again. She was very tired and feared she might fall asleep, so she deliberately sat in an uncomfortable position.

"I'm ready."

---

"She's moving in, we're going to get something here," Harrier said, excited.

"Good," Randal replied, tuning in. About time, he thought to himself. He trusted Satiah but he wished that she would be more inclusive in her plans sometimes, if only for his own peace of mind.

"I've got a call from someone trying to get to you, something about *your suspicions have been confirmed*," Harrier went on.

"Put them through," Randal said, cool as ice.

"Phantom Leader Randal, this is Captain Berry of Division Sixteen. The PAI are targeting you and Satiah and plan to take you out after the election. Take all necessary steps," he advised, before disconnecting. Randal slid his pistol out of his cloak and checked it casually before returning to Satiah's feed. Even though he knew someone was trying to kill them both, it was great to actually be able to keep an eye on Satiah for once.

---

Mark and Sam turned around as the transporter arrived with Jinx, Octutin and the third man in it. Satiah listened in, only able to hear from Jinx's perspective. Engines powered down, sighing noises occurred and then the doors whizzed open. Zax tensed with anticipation, Randal made sure his door was locked, and Satiah just waited.

"What's the problem?" was the first remark. It was a new voice and Zax immediately set the system on a voice analysis program which would search for any matches. If it found a match then they would know who they were dealing with. If there was no match then it would begin to create a new profile automatically, based on what they said, when they said it and accent analysis. At least a planet of origin might be acquired then. In this case, none of that was really necessary. Due to Sam being a public figure, making many speeches in public and doing interviews etc, his voice was instantly recognised and his profile was retrieved.

Zax gulped when she saw it. *Sam McAllister. His own brother*! Zax didn't know that since the beginning Satiah had had him on her list. She issued the information to Satiah and Harrier efficiently.

"Funny, that's what *we* wanted to ask *you*," Jinx replied, clearly ready for the exchange.

"What?" That was a third voice and Zax repeated the process. Again the match was almost instant. *Mark De-Jool*. Another politician running in the election just like Sam and Oli. Zax gaped. So they were working together…

"Who else have you hired?" Jinx accused, in a hostile manner. There was a baffled silence.

"No one, only you," Sam insisted, a little caught out.

"Then why is someone called the Red Necromancer trying to kill us?" Octutin asked, astutely.

Octutin was a fourth voice and Zax did as she had done before, only this time… no match came up. Jinx had a profile, easy to find, mainly as he had done time. This guy was a newbie, certainly as far as official records were concerned in any case. She was feeding all this through to Satiah. Satiah was genuinely surprised. She had suspected Sam, the animosity was well known so who wouldn't? Mark's motives were less obvious but still, in her mind, they were strong enough to make her watch him. The idea that they might be working in concert hadn't occurred to her though. And what was all this about the Red Necromancer working for *someone else*? She'd theorised that more than one party were against Oli but this hinted at three or possibly more factions, all independently after him.

"Who?" Sam asked, as anyone would. If he was lying, naturally he would ask that question to convey the impression he was telling the truth and, by way of coincidence, if he *was* telling the truth it would be the first thing he, or anyone else, would ask. There was an uneasy silence and Satiah began to get concerned. If it came to a fight and Sam or Mark was killed then wouldn't that surely be as bad as if Oli himself had died? In the interests of maintaining the illusion of democracy? She grinned to herself, amused by that thought and the dilemma.

"You've never heard of him?" Octutin confirmed, the scepticism easy for everyone to hear.

"Clearly not," Mark answered, angry. "We do not have the kind of money to waste on *you* as well as *someone else*."

"*Careful, old man*," growled Jinx, in warning.

"Are you claiming that it is because of the intervention of this *Red Necromancer* that you have failed to eliminate Oli?" Sam asked, more diplomatically.

"*That, among other things,*" Octutin muttered.

"Well, if you're not behind him then consider this fair warning that he may be coming after you. He's already said he's going to try to take us out, so why not you too?" Jinx replied, seriously.

"Why would he come after any of *us*?" Mark frowned. "Surely he cannot know who any of us are?"

"Is he *protecting* Oli?" Sam asked, immediately after him.

Jinx had thought about this and he had decided against revealing the fact that they *knew* he was trying to kill Oli. If he told Sam and Mark that, they may cancel the deal on the principle that someone else was going to do the job for them. He was going to pretend that he had thought it was a set up to get him and Octutin killed.

"I don't know what he's doing for sure," he evaded, smugly, "but I *do* know he's come between us and our target. That's why we thought *you* might be having second thoughts." Mark and Sam looked at one another and Mark's eyes narrowed in suspicion.

"If he's moved in then that means *someone* could have found out about what we're trying to do," Mark pointed out. "How could that have happened?" He looked at no one in particular when he asked that question.

He knew that Jinx or Sam might think he was personally accusing them of somehow betraying him. Either one could then hurl the same accusation straight back at him or at one another. There was no evidence that any of them had betrayed each other.

"Well, after all the attempts made on his life that have failed, it's not surprising that someone's caught on to the obvious. They won't know it's *us* but they will know someone is after Oli's blood," Octutin explained. "The fact that *he knows that it's us* even if he doesn't know *who we are* means that he may be trying to rattle us."

"Did he use your *names*?" Sam asked interested.

"He did not," Jinx assured him.

"Then we have no reason to worry so long as he doesn't catch either of you," Mark said, quick to bury the matter. There was another prolonged silence as everyone weighed that up in their own ways. Distant sirens sounded and everyone stiffened slightly until it was clear they were not coming any closer. Octutin gave an uneasy grin.

"So... it remains as it was?" Sam enquired, anxious now to leave.

"...Sure," Jinx nodded, as if in reluctance. The two groups – politicians, and slightly more honest criminals - backed slowly and overly casually away from one another, back to their respective vehicles. Mark left first, his chauffeur driving him away. Sam went next, taking care to go in the opposite direction. Lastly Jinx and the others departed, going back the way they had come.

Satiah didn't move to follow any of them, she knew Randal was listening in and was busy reading the profiles that Zax had dug up. Zax and Harrier too, held on in silence. Randal was expecting Satiah to talk first and so said nothing. After about thirty seconds Satiah frowned.

"Are you all still there?" she asked, in bewilderment. Everyone answered at once and she tried not to laugh. "Who wants to go first?"

"As *Phantom Leader* I believe *rank* gives me that privilege," Randal stated, quickly. Believe what you like, she thought to herself, it's only when you choose to do something about it that the trouble starts.

"Before we go into any of what we just heard, Satiah. *What we talked about before* - the PAI – we've *both* been secretly targeted for elimination. We have until the election is over before their agent acts. His name is Lunell and he will be joining you on your mission to prevent Oli from winning," Randal explained, expecting a hostile reaction.

"...Is this still *mister slimy*?" she asked, after a pause.

"It is."

"Well, then I suggest we obey the first rule of being a Phantom. We survive. And we survive in such a way that ensures our enemy doesn't," she replied, serenely.

"Well, I plan to kill them, however *you* want to word it," he muttered.

"Zax, what have you got?" Satiah asked.

Zax was nervous, even more so now she knew Randal was listening in and there was such treachery going on. But she remembered her place.

As a Phantom she was loyal only to Phantom Squad. Technically, *even the Coalition* was a client, not a potentate. The PAI were an irrelevance if they were not directly an ally or an enemy. Today, apparently, they were the enemy. She began going through the brief histories of Sam McAllister and Mark De-Jool. Neither of them had any criminal record, though Mark had once been suspected of illegal endorsement some thirty years previously. Nothing had been proven and no further action had been taken.

Harrier then took over, providing information on the Red Necromancer, which was almost a repeat of what was known about Jinx. He promised to look into Octutin. Satiah was about to sign off and wander home when Zax asked a question.

"Does this always happen? Is this what it's always like?" she asked, in a tone hard to read.

"Which bit?" Randal asked, outwardly unsure exactly what she was asking about.

"Yes," Satiah said, grimly. "In a way, there is only ever one side in these things. *Your own.* Your true test is learning who to trust and who not to. As long as you're good at that... you stand a fair chance of obeying the first rule and staying alive."

"...*Right*," she said, her tone more determined. That hidden inner strength she seemed to have, made itself known once again. "I will remember that." She signed off.

"...This is coming from a *self-described* bad teacher," Randal stated, with amusement. Satiah cursed herself inwardly.

"And what was *your* answer to her question, exactly?" she asked, pointedly. She wondered if he'd pretended to be clueless in order to get her to answer it for him, but she'd been too quick to stop herself. Zax had talent, skills that needed to be honed and... *she was important.* It would be wasteful to be anything other than candid with her. "I may be a good teacher *in your eyes* but it is not work I excel at." She was tempted to say *and don't particularly enjoy* too. "Watch yourself... where did this information come from, by the way?"

"Captain Berry of...."

"*Division Sixteen*," she interrupted, remembering the man from before. "Nice of them to help us out, wasn't it? I wonder what they want in return..."

"I'm *sure* they'll let us know."

---

"Tomorrow's going to need an axe blow or two to the head before it goes down," Satiah grumbled, as she sat on the edge of the bed. "*I must remember not to use the bladed side this time, too messy.*" Carl nodded, knowing there was nothing he could say, as he didn't really know what she was talking about. There wasn't anything he could do unless she asked so... she just wanted to be listened to. He nodded slowly as he rubbed her back.

"...What did you do today?" she asked, more out of courtesy than interest.

"You mean *after* I spring cleaned the place?" he joked. Both of them knew full well he was allergic to housework. Well, work in general, actually, but so long as he remained inactive for long periods of time the symptoms kept a low profile.

"I made a few calls and got hold of that guy I was telling you about. *You know*? About fixing Kelvin," he said, uneasily. "I've agreed nothing and he's not seen him or anything, I just wanted to get an idea of the guy's schedule."

"I haven't *actually* decided..." she growled.

"I know, nothing's been done or even *talked about*, really. You'll be relieved to know he's available and quite close by. I thought, *knowing how private you are*, if you agreed - because it's ultimately *your decision*, I mean *he's your robot* after all, perhaps..."

"*Get to the point Carl, I'm tired*," she said, smiling wearily.

"If *you choose* to do this, then *I* would go with Kelvin, just to keep an eye on him while you're not there to do it," he suggested, massaging her shoulders a little more roughly. She eyed him doubtfully. He pulled a hurt face.

"Come on, you must trust me *by now*," he said. She pushed him away playfully.

"It's not trust that's the problem," she smiled, shrugging. "It's competence."

"*Charming*," he laughed, not really bothered. He knew how important Kelvin was to her. She put her arms around him tenderly.

"Look at it this way... what do *you* know about robotics?" she wanted to know.

"Nothing," he replied, honestly. "If I did I could sort him out myself."

"And computers?" she went on, her tone the same. He made a noise to indicate the same answer. "So how will you *know* what this man *is really doing?*"

"I can get him to do it half price," he offered, with a grin. She laughed and thought about it. "You..." he paused, staring at her. "... don't have to answer that tonight."

---

Satiah was still having trouble adjusting to this 'going to work at the same time every day' thing. Last night, she had decided, as she was getting nowhere with it, to call someone to help her work out what that strange book was all about. She'd gone through the next part of the review for Randal and then had started to plan out what she would do the next day. Upon instructions from her, Malla had moved Oli's campaign headquarters. This was an irritating but completely necessary step, irritating in that she'd have to replace half the bugs she'd put in, but necessary - not only to confuse the assassins, but to bring them closer to law enforcement. She'd been half inclined to get the embassy involved, but had decided against that because of their lamentable security record.

She dropped down from the lane into the new parking area. This one actually had an android guard which scanned her on arrival. An idea had come to her the previous night. Harrier and Zax had failed to make any progress on learning anything about this mysterious angel referred to in the notes. She decided she would ask Oli himself about it in passing, just to see if he knew something that could help them. In the lift, on the way down to the designated floor, nineteen, Satiah studied the file Malla had sent her concerning Dean. He had been dismissed due to 'inappropriate conduct' and *might* have reason to hold a grudge against Oli.

Malla had compiled an impartial, extensive record, describing in detail the offences committed and an overall history of the man himself: he could be summed up as a petty criminal with small-time ambitions. She was confident he had nothing to do with any of the threats Oli faced. He had mysteriously vanished though. Next came a call she was expecting: Malla.

"It seems law enforcement are trying to help us out and have pressured the government to lend us more support," he explained. *Lunell.* Satiah smiled pleasantly, concealing the rage well.

"I was hoping this might happen," she lied, adeptly. "Do you want me present at the interview or will you and Shannon…?"

"*Of course!*" he insisted. "You're the best we have; I want your *opinion,* at the very least."

"Perfect," she said, easily hiding the bitterness in her tone. She had a plan of how she would handle this but she was more worried about Randal than herself.

Shannon was pouring a hot drink into a glass as Satiah entered the new cafeteria area. It was all white and office-like in appearance. All utility, nothing stylish.

"Oli here yet?" Satiah asked, as she moved to the opposite side of the room. Shannon smiled at her, playing the part of helpful colleague. She'd been doing that more and more since the failed incrimination attempt. She was trying to get Satiah to trust her. Satiah played along.

"He's in his office," she smiled. "Can I get you anything?"

"Thank you for the offer, I appreciate it, but I'm on a diet," Satiah smiled, in a very similar tone.

"Do you want to test Oli's breakfast or shall I?" Shannon enquired, her tone still light and friendly.

"That's *very kind of you,* if you like, you can do it," Satiah smiled, starting to pack spare eating utensils away. Never good to have knives lying around, even if they were packaged up.

She would check the food again *herself*, of course, regardless of what Shannon did. She didn't think Shannon would harm Oli *intentionally* but… Satiah didn't like leaving anything to chance.

"Did you see the news last night?" Shannon enquired. *No, I was too busy spying on the people trying to kill the man you're in love with*, Satiah thought.

"How *is* the trial progressing now? I missed that part," Satiah evaded, deftly.

"No not that bit, the bit about what's happening in the Nebular Union?" Shannon stated. Satiah feigned confusion.

"Must have missed that part too, *why*? What did they say?" she asked, genuinely interested.

"Well, their Head of State is refusing to return to their territory for fear of assassination. I was wondering if it had anything to do with the people after Oli," she said.

Satiah then understood that Shannon was trying to get her to open up about what she and Malla had discussed. Malla was obviously cutting her out of the loop, perhaps deliberately. No wonder she was being so nice all of a sudden.

"*Anything's possible*," she answered, without really giving an answer at all. "What else did the CNC say?"

"A lot of stuff about some cult or something that had attempted to take over the government there. To be honest I wasn't paying much attention at that point, because obviously I was thinking about *our* situation," she replied.

"*Obviously*," echoed Satiah, as if she was thinking deeply about it too. Shannon moved in closer, thinking she was getting somewhere.

"You don't think it's connected, do you?" she asked, in a hushed voice.

Satiah made her eyes wide and held the other woman's gaze. "Have you mentioned this to Malla?" she asked, also in a low voice.

"I thought about it but… have you noticed he's been acting weird recently?" she continued, her tone confidential. *O, very clever*, Satiah thought. She was trying to drive a wedge between her and Malla. Trying to create distrust.

"… Maybe, it's *probably nothing*…" Satiah said, like she was trying to remember something or put it into words.

"*What*?" Shannon pressed, inquisitive.

"Well, he asked me to join you and him in some interview later this morning with a new member of security. He said something about *wanting my opinion*. He's *never* asked for that before… I thought he might be starting to question his own judgement for some reason," Satiah lied, deviously. This caught Shannon totally off guard.

"*Really*?" she asked, her own eyes going even wider.

"It could be the strain of the situation getting a hold of him. I *know* he's feeling it," Satiah sighed, as if in regret.

Shannon was gobsmacked. Why would Malla want Satiah's opinion and *not hers*? They'd worked together for years! Was he still angry with her about what she'd done with those drugs? And, most concerning of all, was he *really* losing it?

"…Maybe," she allowed, unsure exactly what to say.

"When we're with him later, *maybe you should keep an eye on him*; let me know if you see anything… *weird*?" Satiah suggested, trying not to laugh. Shannon nodded, now starting to get rather concerned about her friend. What if Satiah was right and she'd been so preoccupied with her hatred towards Satiah that she'd not noticed what was happening to Malla? It could explain why he was not confiding in her like he used to, and being angry with her, but after what Satiah had said…

"I will," Shannon agreed, after thinking about it. "We're *all* under a lot of pressure and perhaps, as you say, it's starting to get to him."

Satiah watched as Shannon left the room, looking worried. Ironically enough, in an effort to destroy trust, Shannon had created some. *Or so she would think.* Other staff members were starting to arrive now and set up their equipment. No one liked moving, but it had been agreed because it was a sensible precaution. It may also compel the insider, whoever it was, to contact angel and let them know of the change. *Still* no one was acting in a way that got Satiah's attention. *Who* was talking to angel? She knew it had to be one of them. Stan, the new boy? Kate, the Public-Relations Team Leader? Malla, the Chief of Security?

Shannon, the security guard? *Dean*? The list went on and on, nearly ninety people. Surely it had to be one of them.

Satiah subtly checked the food after Shannon had. There was nothing wrong with it. She then took up her post in Oli's new office where Kate and Oli were still going strong. Both, though, were starting to show the subtle signs of exhaustion. Bags around the eyes, a nebulously vacant stare, that sort of thing. Time passed slowly and it felt to Satiah like an olam had gone by when Malla finally called her. She was wondering what kind of gambit Lunell would opt for. She made herself remember that she knew *nothing* about him at all, *as far as anyone else was concerned*, and no matter how the interview went, she could not come down *too heavily* against him. Malla might suspect something if she did. Staying calm, as ever, would prove the key in how to handle this.

Much like the day she had first arrived, Malla and Shannon approached Lunell and led him to a room they would use for the interview. Satiah was to wait inside the room for them to bring him in. Malla entered first, followed by Lunell and finally Shannon. The door closed and Lunell and Malla sat across from one another. Shannon and Satiah stood behind and to either side of Malla. Lunell and Satiah locked gazes for a moment and then looked away. Lunell shouldn't know she was expecting him and technically, whatever happened between them, they couldn't let anyone else know that they knew each other. The look they had shared would tell him that she knew he was more than he appeared to be. She was fine was him knowing *that*. She wasn't sure he would believe it if she showed no sign whatsoever.

Malla took the lead with the questioning.

"Just a couple of questions, hope you don't mind," he said. That remark in itself was not a question; nonetheless, Lunell chose to answer anyway.

"Would it matter if I did?" he smiled, being humorous. "I understand, it's fine, I would do the same." Malla smiled. Shannon watched him closely. Satiah kept her gaze on Lunell and he regarded them all in turn.

"First, I just wanted to ask you about any political beliefs and party allegiances you may have? Also, which way did you vote?"

"*The usual way...* I just selected the box and submitted my answer," Lunell smiled, annoyingly. He let out a quiet and modest sounding laugh while making a dismissive gesture. "No, no, I was originally going to vote for Brenda Watt as she seems to represent a certain stability. Nevertheless, after going through her policies and those of her opponents, I admit... I hesitated. The truth is, I haven't voted yet due to this indecision." He shrugged nonchalantly.

"What about the parties?" Malla went on, nodding slowly.

"What about them?" joked Lunell, smoothly. Satiah decided that Lunell was going to be a problem. Malla grinned.

"Do you have a favourite?"

Lunell paused, as if considering the question very seriously.

"The Traditionalist Nationalist Party has had a lot of bad press, particularly lately. Not only was it the Administration's main powerbase for Balan Orion, but it's got caught up in the Vourne conspiracy - and let's not forget that they still have the taint from Fly's brief rule. So I certainly wouldn't vote for any of their candidates. Brenda herself is Unionist Coalition Party, as you already know, but she isn't their *only* candidate running. Sawma is also running. Hopelessly outmatched by Brenda, of course, and with an election campaign that made less progress than Balan himself did in his relations with the Federation... but *it's another option*."

Sawma was a bit player, the man *did exist* but he was not *really* running for office at all. He had made a few steps in that direction, under the direction of the PAI, to make it *look like* Brenda had competition from within her own party. This was only to give the voters something else to speculate about other than the obvious, a way of mollifying those who wanted to find 'the truth' or to stir up additional but ultimately harmless controversy. He was also a contingency plan for them should they deem it necessary to try and split the vote at any time. Such was the minor status of this diversion, the PAI hadn't even bothered to outline his legislation or provide him with the facility for political broadcast.

Lunell was literally explaining the voting options out there without *actually* giving his opinion, real or otherwise. His tactic worked, and clearly Malla had either lost interest, or didn't realise he'd not actually answered.

"And I must inform you that your new charge has had several attempts on his life already, so this won't be a joyride," Malla stated.

"With respect, if this wasn't of the utmost seriousness, they wouldn't have sent *me*," Lunell countered, with clout. Malla was impressed and then began introducing first Shannon and then Satiah to him. Lunell played his role well as a professional with a sense of humour, nodding politely and saying all the right things at the right times. The interview finished, they all returned to the upper levels and Malla was quick to delegate Lunell's induction to Satiah. A decision Satiah knew would not rest well with Shannon. She wasn't exactly jubilant about it either.

Satiah was about to introduce Lunell to Oli and Kate when he held up a hand for her to halt.

"Satiah, I *know* you're a Phantom agent and I know why you're here. I work for the PAI. I thought you had better know that *from the start* to save you time in investigating who I am and where I came from," Lunell said. The admission, his outright brazenness, caught her by surprise but she didn't let it show.

"Good thing you told me," she smiled, pretending to be relieved. "I might have killed you."

"I didn't want to make the same mistake *Nerva* did," he remarked, with significance. She gave him a look, pretending he had caught her out with his use of that name. He smiled sadly.

"It was his own fault by *all* accounts... *namely, yours*," he continued. He was trying to get a reaction from her but she wasn't going to give an inch.

"It *was* self defence," she growled, levelly.

"Of course it was," he said, in a tone dryer than a desert.

"Are you going to make my life *difficult,* Lunell? If you are I will have you arrested," she threatened. He paused, wary.

"No, we have a job to do here, and for what it is worth I do believe that you're telling the truth about it," he said, casually. "Scott Snell has his own opinion, of course. *He's* who I'm reporting to, *just so you know*."

"This is *my mission*," she warned, pointing to herself to demonstrate. "Get in my way and you might not survive."

"I'll keep that in mind."

Collorah slid though the empty window, having removed the pane of glass. The offices beyond, previously home to Oli's campaign team, were now empty. Another business would be moving in the next day, and he had gone there to try to establish where Oli had moved to. The tables and chairs were still there but all of the screens and other equipment had been removed. They had done it fast; normally it took at least a day. This had taken hours, maybe less. He stalked through the darkened offices and corridors, trying to find anything he could use. When staff moved offices, they always left things behind. He just needed something that would tell him *where* they had gone. He was rewarded less than two hours into his search when he found an empty moving crate... with a location number under the destination designation. He made a note of it, so he could check it against the destination list.

---

Malla looked up from what he was working on. He'd just linked in all the cameras throughout the building and had them adjusted to ensure maximum coverage had been achieved. Shannon was standing there holding two drinks. She offered him one.

"You okay?" she enquired, interested. He took the drink and gave her a nod.

"Yes, fine, what's up?" he asked, casually.

"Nothing, I was just wondering if you needed any help with anything. Satiah and Lunell are with Oli and Kate so... *I'm kind of at a loose end*," she said, simpering slightly. "Lunell was impressive, wasn't he?" She was digging now, trying to understand why he wasn't confiding in her and, more importantly, if he was still mentally competent.

"I'll see what Satiah says," he replied, shrugging. "I thought he was good enough, certainly, but *she's* an elite. She will know best what to look for."

"...Well, let me know if there's anything I can do," she offered, trying again.

"No problem," he smiled, sipping the drink. There was an awkward moment where they both waited for the other person to say something.

"Oli seems to be having trouble sleeping," Shannon went on.

"I'm not surprised, I think we all have a bit of that going on," he said, chuckling. It was an enforced chuckle, as if he was merely going through the motions. Shannon gave up.

"*Are you still angry with me?*" she asked, keeping her voice down. Malla immediately looked more weary and pulled a face.

"No, of course not," he lied, badly.

"How would it be if I said that you were right and that I was *sorry?*" she asked, softly. "I don't want to lose your friendship because of my… *misjudgement.*" She couldn't say mistake… it kept getting stuck in her throat, partly because of embarrassment but mainly because she still felt she was right about Satiah.

"*About Satiah?*" he asked. Wasn't it always about *her*? She sighed, biting back her natural anger.

"Yes," she concurred, as emotionlessly as she could. "You were right, we're all just trying to help Oli, and I was wrong. She's… fine." Malla smiled, seeming to notice her trouble when trying to compliment Satiah.

"*Really*, in what way is she *fine?*" he asked, grinning.

"Don't push it, okay," she sniggered, shaking her head.

"You're lucky I don't make you two kiss and make up," he joked. She made a retching noise. "Look… I *was* angry. I was angry because I thought you were going to do something stupid." She had, but she kept that to herself.

"So you're *not* overstressed?" she asked, letting the real relief show itself in her face and tone.

"Well, no *more* than anyone else here," he shrugged. "I feel a lot better now we've got two elites here."

"Good," she said, leaving it at that. "Are *we* okay?"

"For now," he said, his tone mischievous. "Maybe I should ask Satiah for her opinion."

"I'm not going to dignify that with an answer."

"Two teams, not good," Lunell murmured, thinking about it. He and Satiah were by the door, overseeing Oli and Kate as they worked. She'd brought him up to speed... Well, she'd told him all she was going to.

"And you've no idea at all who it is in here?" Lunell clarified, glancing over his shoulder casually.

"Not yet," she admitted, sourly.

"*Tricky*," he growled, thoughtfully.

"You're *not* going to ask me if I've looked into the use of the word angel?" she asked, haughtily.

"*Now, now*," he smiled, smoothly. "*I* have no issues with your aptitude. Indeed, I have every reason to believe you're doing everything you *can*."

"So why *are* you here?" she wanted to know, crossing her arms.

She knew the truth, of course, but she wanted to make him as uncomfortable as possible. She wondered how he planned to kill her. He carried a gun, but she sensed that he might prefer other methods of dispatch. He was using his own gear, rather than adapting the weaponry provided as Satiah had done.

"To help," he smiled, insincerely.

"How very kind of you," she growled, her anger showing. He only shrugged.

"I apologise if my presence offends you," he said, ever so softly. "I'm only obeying orders." Yes, isn't that what they all say? She smiled tightly.

"Then I have no reason to worry."

She turned her back on him, something she knew she wouldn't get away with doing too often, and moved over to Oli and Kate.

"How are we doing today?" she asked, smiling. She didn't particularly wish to talk to either of them but it was either them or... *him*.

"Still settling in," Kate beamed at her. Kate seemed rather too pleased at the interruption... meaning that Oli was giving her problems. "We were wondering if maybe *you* had any thoughts about this? *Relations with the Nebula Union?*" Satiah's heart sank; she really did not want to get into that.

"*Are you sure?* I was sort of hoping you might just want a refill?" she joked, motioning to the almost completely full flask.

"*Please*," Oli implored. "Neither of us are having any luck with this one, mainly because we don't know if their government exists or not." O, it does, don't you worry about that.

"How far have you got?" Satiah enquired, eyeing Lunell. He was listening in, as she expected he would be.

"Well, trading agreements being discontinued is bound to come up. The lack of communication and possibilities of war will most likely be hot on its heels," Kate listed, sighing with weary disappointment.

"I could just say that, until the situation there sorts itself out - in other words, they work out what's happened and get in touch with us - I can't really answer that," Oli mused. He was right, not very decisive. Too weak. Not that Satiah was meant to be helping them like this. It had been in the interests of building trust between them... *and get them to shut up and get stuff done.* She could almost feel Lunell's eyes on her. She knew what she was supposed to do, and she knew what Lunell expected her to do but...

"I really don't know," she said, accidentally making eye contact with Oli as she said that. "*Sorry.*"

Lunell didn't move in to offer his own opinion. He recognised that his being there was making Satiah behave differently and although it made him interested, he felt sure she wouldn't disobey the mission directive. He wondered if she was worried about making a mistake in front of him. Oli, on the other hand, began feeling guilty because he thought it was due to *the thing* that was between him and Satiah. Kate didn't know he'd kissed her, but she knew something was going on there and so didn't draw attention to it. She thought it was quite romantic, mainly because she didn't know what was really going on.

"You *could* say that as soon as you can contact them, you will do what you can to ensure things stay as they were before they became what they are now?" Satiah went on, deliberately messing up the delivery of that sentence. Thanks for the inspiration, *Brenda*.

"I think we should take a break," Kate smiled, thinking she understood why Satiah had apparently lost the ability to talk sensibly. She stood. Lunell activated the door for her as she paced out. "*Why don't you escort me to the cantina?*" Kate asked, to Lunell. "Oli won't need you both." She thought she was doing them a favour by leaving them alone together. Reluctantly, but with a smile that would make even Deetee seem unwelcoming, Lunell nodded and followed her out. There was another silence.

"I don't know much about Union politics," Satiah said, rather bleakly.

"I'm... *Is this because of what happened?*" Oli asked. *O fraggke-fudger*! Was he incapable of...? Of course he was.

"*No*," she assured, as earnestly as she could. "It's... *actually* I wanted to ask you something..." She could see from his face exactly what he hoped this would be about. Shame she'd have to disappoint him.

"*Okay*," he murmured, uneasy.

"Do you know anyone called angel?" she asked, watching his expression change completely. Hope, confusion and then bewilderment.

"*Angel?*" he repeated, slowly. He was clearly thinking she was trying to somehow sneak up on the subject he wanted to talk about in some obscure way that he couldn't work out yet. "Err no... not that I can recall," he stated, honestly.

"Are you *sure?*" she asked, thinking hard. "Think back, years maybe. By the way, don't tell anyone, *or* ask anyone else about it."

"Well, if I did it escapes me right now," he replied, slowly. "I won't. Why are you asking?"

"It's to do with whoever is trying to kill you," she admitted, seeing no reason in hiding it. "We think it's the name of someone involved. So I thought I would ask you directly, instead of going through pages and pages of your history." His eyes widened ever so slightly due to an elevation in his fear levels, but he hid it much better than he had in the past.

"I *see...* is *that* why you were so nervous just now?" he asked, quizzically.

"Yes, of course, why else...?" she began, not finishing her own sentence. She contrived for surprised comprehension in her manner. "*No, I thought we weren't discussing that?*"

"We're not," he was quick to agree. A little too quickly and rather unconvincingly.

"Really? *I had no idea*," Lunell replied.

"You mustn't tell *anyone*," Kate instructed, levelly.

"But they're such *different* people, I can't visualise it," Lunell stated, as if it was too much for him to grasp.

"*Trust me*, I have nearly caught them a few times now," Kate sniggered, tickled. Lunell's eyes narrowed and a sly smile crept across his lips. So… Satiah was manipulating Oli. He had wondered, but Satiah didn't strike him as the type to use seduction… Not just because she was too nondescript and she wore clothes that concealed mostly everything but because, having glimpsed her equanimity, he felt that she would most likely use coercion or blackmail to get her way. Apparently he had been wrong.

"Aww it was *adorable*, you should have seen their faces when I came in," Kate went on.

"Must have been a picture," he said, thinking ahead. Scott hadn't known that Satiah had bedded Oli. Was that because Randal hadn't told Scott or… *Satiah* hadn't reported it? Meaning the relationship between them *might* be a genuine one and not part of the mission at all? That would give him leverage over her if that was the case, though it would be difficult to prove anything. Phantoms were forbidden from liaisons with *anyone*, it was a well known fact. That might explain why Randal might not know. Yet if it merely was her strategy and not a real liaison… he could get into trouble for challenging her. And either way, Oli might not know she was just manipulating him. Satiah herself would certainly say that she *was*, even if she wasn't.

"Whenever she's in the room, Oli has trouble concentrating," Kate was saying. "Then again, after the last attack, I have a similar problem."

"I heard about that," he said, his mind still on other things.

"I don't know what Oli could have done to make anyone want to kill him," Kate sighed, sadly.

"Politicians always run that risk, *you can't please everyone*," Lunell replied. "So how long have they been seeing each other?"

"Well, it can't be any longer than a week," she stated, a little sarcastic. He laughed.

"True, true."

"Like I said, don't say anything," Kate reminded. He agreed not to.

"They moved," Jinx growled, as he stared through the bino-units scopes. They were on the top of a skyscraper, looking down at Oli's previous offices. Octutin let out a sigh and began to disassemble his gun once again. One day he might even have occasion to use it.

"How do we find out where?" was his inevitable enquiry. Jinx shrugged.

"Surely Sam will be able to learn where his brother is. Or he can get hold of some administrative staff who might know," he said, seriously. Octutin grunted noncommittally. The two of them headed back to the open hatchway, leading back inside.

"Our friendly rival will be in the same position, I imagine," Jinx stated, trying to stay positive. Octutin gave no response to that.

---

Zax activated the last receptor.

"Cam three hundred and seven… it's *good*," she said, quietly.

"I've got the computer monitoring, but keep an eye out," Harrier instructed. Zax stared at all the screens open in front of her. On her big screen, she'd split it into hundreds of tiny squares. She wasn't expected to be able to see everything or to be able to go through every last second of footage. She'd set up search priorities, seeking phrases or certain movements that would tip her off. She knew Harrier was doing the same with a different set of priorities. The second either of them found anything they were to alert Satiah immediately. She returned to her other task… going through the backgrounds of everyone working on Oli's staff. Satiah had already done some, but Zax had been told to check again. She didn't know why she did it… maybe something in her subconscious directed her, maybe not… but Zax caught herself listening in to Lunell and Kate while they were talking about Satiah.

In a rush of panic, seeing how this could cause Satiah problems, she reviewed all footage of Satiah and Oli together. Very concerned after seeing the kiss, and realising that in fact Satiah *was* doing all she could to keep him at arm's length, she called her.

"Lunell thinks you and Oli are seeing each other because Kate told him you are," she blurted, the second Satiah answered.

"...In future, it might be a wise precaution to make sure it is safe for me to talk *before* you just spill everything," Satiah admonished. Zax flushed red.

"I'm sorry..." she said, trying to stay focussed. There was a silence. Zax zoomed in on Satiah; she was literally watching her as they spoke. She was standing in a corridor, looking harassed. Zax wished she could suggest something that might help her.

"I can delete the footage of you kissing him..." Zax offered, rapidly.

"*He* kissed *me*," corrected Satiah, sharply. It really bothered her that anyone would think that *she* had instigated it, seeing as that had been the last thing she'd wanted to happen - but she couldn't change what it probably looked like. Zax winced.

"Sorry, yes, I can..."

"Just let me think for a moment," Satiah said, certain that this might not be as bad as it first seemed. "Lunell will now probably think he has something he can use against me. Now that I know it's coming, I kind of want to see what he tries."

"A denial might not be enough," Zax stated, hoping that Satiah wouldn't snap at her again.

"No," she agreed, her tone low. "I have already given him fair warning about the price of interference. He may not directly approach me, he may go the other way through Slimy Snell to Randal."

"I see, Randal would trust you, right?"

"Yes, and even if he didn't, the truth is that *there is nothing going on*," she replied. "Another lesson for you, when it comes to men *try* to be direct, subtlety isn't always their strong point." Trouble was, in this case, his mental health was important enough to Satiah to make simply rejecting him too risky.

"So what will you do?" Zax asked, trying not to sound too stupid.

"In a way, all this is a sideshow, we need to stay engaged on the killers," Satiah sighed, moving on. "They are the real problem. Them and those behind them."

"What can you do when they, or at least some of them, are backed by other politicians in the election? Wouldn't it therefore be contrary to the mission objectives to do much to them?" Zax enquired. Satiah raised an impressed eyebrow. She'd realised that earlier but it was good that Zax was already learning to be objective.

"It's possible. My hand may be forced, though, and the objectives *were specific only* to Oli, despite all that twaddle about preserving the myth of democracy," she reminded her.

"Why can't we just have them both arrested? We have proof that they are working with criminals, isn't that enough?" Zax asked, not unreasonably.

"I would," Satiah agreed, "trouble is that the people will say it's a scandal designed to ruin the reputations of those running for government. All this mission is really about is making everything look normal when *we* know it isn't."

"...In training they *hinted* that things are never as they appear, but I *never* thought it was *this* corrupt," Zax confessed, sadness in her tone.

"It only ever gets worse, you'll just need to learn to accept it and use it for your own ends," Satiah advised. "Just remember that things are what they are for a reason. It's not crime; it's constitution until it's out of the shadows. Then it becomes incompetence, *not* institutional practise. This is why we fight to keep it in the shadows, but it's not us as individuals: it's the system. The system does not govern your personal actions or thoughts... though it often tries to."

"And *we*, as Phantoms, are *different*?" she asked. Satiah smiled... the young always had to question everything, didn't they?

"Yes," she said, leaving it at that. "We are beyond it all as individual agents. As an organisation we are a part of it, but a self-governed part. At least, we try to be. You will often find yourself questioning the objectives you have been given. That is both natural and good. Choose wisely *who* you ask, and survival and success are likely to be your rewards."

"Is that what you believe, or what you're meant to say?" Zax asked, with a shaky smile. Satiah gave her infamous low chuckle.

## Operation Selector

"I see you're getting the idea," she allowed. "Now keep listening and... keep watching Lunell. What I just said about the killers is true, but you never know when you might acquire an extra one."

"Understood."

It was time to do what she'd planned to do some time ago. She would leak a document in an attempt to damage Oli's popularity. She'd prepared it herself and ensured, above all else, that it would be untraceable. Once he became unpopular enough, in theory, then all these other issues would go away. So she hoped. Satiah had decided to opt for something unpopular but fairly nondescript. Tax reforms, the kind that would penalise the majority of businesses. It would be seen as unnecessary and bad for the economy. It should damage his power base, or at least stop his proportional representation rising. Again... so she hoped.

---

The tracker had fallen off Jinx and deactivated, finally giving Satiah a criticism for the new form of surveillance. It needed a longer lifespan. However, not much else had been learned through it, though it was clear that Jinx had discovered they had changed location, which Satiah knew would mean he would be searching for them. It had been expressed to all members of staff, including Oli himself, that under *no circumstances* were they to inform *anyone* where they were working. She knew this would buy them a few days of peace, although it was inevitable that someone would either say something, or Jinx would find out in some way where they had moved to. Moving again was an option, but there were only a few locations that were fit for purpose. It had to be the right size, have the right security facilities, and be unobtrusive enough to make the constant comings and goings of personnel fade into the scenery. On Earth, such locations that weren't already taken were rare.

Having discovered how Jinx was working and who he was working for, Satiah had switched focus back to the Red Necromancer. Using contacts across the planet, she'd traced him to his accommodation. She'd discovered only carnage. A team of mercenaries lay sprawled on the floor in the main living area, and their bodies were starting to stink – clearly they had been there for a while – long enough to get cold, and vermin to start moving in. She crouched and carefully examined the closest one. Laser bolts, several, in the back. Only one had been killed differently. A powerful blow to the head that would have brought instant death to the woman. The next question of course was, who were they? She sent pictures off to Harrier to find out.

Had they been working for the Red Necromancer? Had they failed him or upset him in some way so he did this as punishment? Or had they been employed by someone else *against* him? Any other eventuality was improbable enough for her to dismiss easily. A flurry of profiles arrived as Harrier identified the deceased mercenaries quickly enough. Most were on record and a few were listed as known associates only, but it was good enough. She decided it was about time someone called law enforcement, if for nothing else than to clear up the mess. She went downstairs into the reception area to question the android on duty.

"Who is the occupant of accommodation unit 1372?" she asked, waving an identity badge before its scanner.

"One moment," it said, running through its search program. "Onkel Fritz," it said eventually. Uncle Fred? *Really?* Satiah grinned despite herself. Why be creative with your cover identity when you could just be insultingly obvious?

"When did you last see him?" she went on.

"Four days, eighteen hours and six minutes ago," it responded. She thought about that… probably *about right* considering the state of the bodies.

"Did he give any indication what his business was or where he was going?" she asked, knowing it would be a wasted question.

"Negative." *Well, there's a surprise!*

Next she perused the security footage and quickly found him. He wasn't hard to spot with hair like that. He even glanced up at the camera and smiled, like he'd known at the time that someone would eventually be looking for him there. A shiver ran up her spine as she saw the look. Part challenge and part joy. He'd left the building, at the time the android had said, and he'd used a taxi. This meant she wouldn't be able to trace his ship. Instead she got Harrier to trace the taxi's movements using the recorded footage of the city wide surveillance system. Twenty minutes later and they'd followed his path to a parking facility where he'd left the taxi and gone inside. Vehicles were going in and out all the time so it was hard, using the same method, to establish which was his. Satiah moved on, going to the parking facility herself.

She made herself known to the android on duty there too and, following the same process, used a picture of the Red Necromancer to enquire after which vehicle was his.

"This human was storing two transporters here," it said. "One is still here. Level sixty four, bay twelve." Satiah calmly went up to investigate, pleased. Finally he'd left *something* other than corpses behind, perhaps even with a mind to returning to collect it at some stage. A transporter was indeed sitting there for her to see when she reached the correct bay. Sleek and grey looking, it bore no sign of being anything other than completely normal. Nevertheless, she approached with caution. A quick scan revealed that it was unoccupied. She got to work on the door and overrode the security locks. It was a basic model that had been adapted to improve its quality. Luckily for her, she was an accomplished infiltrator of many years' experience. It took her less than three minutes to get the door to open.

Inside, the driving area was empty of any belongings, the controls inactive and no sign of any traps. She moved in judiciously, trying to see what, if anything, was under or behind the seats. There was a metallic looking case in the open storage area towards the rear. About a metre across and half that in height. Satiah warily slipped between the pilot's and the passenger's chairs to get to it. It could be a bomb or something, but she had decided it was more likely to be something relatively unimportant. Spare clothes, perhaps? Why else leave it behind? As she made her way towards it, the door suddenly slammed shut behind her, bleeping as it locked automatically.

The engine roared into life as she turned to try and get the door open, and she was flung backwards by the momentum as the transporter, apparently driving by itself, sped forward. She cried out as her head hit the ceiling and her gun clattered to the floor. The transporter shot out of the parking facility, forcing its way through the flimsy barrier with ease. Instead of moving into traffic is just continued upwards… *towards space*. Gritting her teeth, Satiah fought her way back into the driving area and tried first to force the door and then to use the controls. It was no good. The door was locked, coded and strong. The new locking device was far more advanced than the one she'd broken through before, designed to keep her inside. He'd wanted her to get in so he'd made it easy and now she'd fallen into his trap. The controls wouldn't respond to her at all. She couldn't tell if it was operating under remote control or by some pre-programmed routine.

Right then though, she had a much bigger problem. She snatched her pistol from the floor and tried to shoot open the door but discovered, much to her consternation, a thick layer of plate armour was there. Smoke filled the vehicle from her shots, making her cough. Again she tried the controls, this time endeavouring to get to the circuitry. Everything was bolted up more tightly than a Phantom Squad budget, they were *already* in the upper mesosphere, and an alarm siren was wailing at her in time with warning red lights. It was then that she anticipated what was going to happen next. When in space, it would open the doors and windows, killing her almost instantly. She had a breathing device with her but no way of protecting herself from being exposed to space. Desperate, she hammered the control board uselessly with violent kicks in an effort to somehow batter her way through to the circuitry beyond where she hoped she could cut the power.

"Warning, warning, pilot door is unlocking," a voice stated, over the din. She didn't even have time to call for help, she had only one option. She reached into her pocket, grabbing Obsenneth and urging that he protect her from the sub-zero void of space. Just in time he agreed, as the door hissed open and the atmosphere swept out. Her body was encased in a blue aura of protection. As before, when it had been flames, Obsenneth could only save her for *so long*. She had minutes left to live. She tried to decide what to do for the best. Calling for help was out of the question now. She would never be able to explain *how* she had survived without revealing the truth. That was when, much to her relief, the controls reactivated after a few seconds and the doors closed automatically.

Heat and atmosphere were restored automatically, and then the transporter did a U-turn and headed straight back the way they had come. Satiah then comprehended the whole plan: no traps had been necessary *inside* the transporter as the vehicle *itself* had been the trap. Harrier had been right to warn her about this man. He was indeed exceedingly dangerous. How easily she could have perished, *should* have perished. The transporter, having killed whoever was after the Red Necromancer, would then return to the parking facility or… *somewhere else*. It would return to him *with the body* of whoever was trying to catch him inside. He would then know *who* was tracking him and what to expect. It was pretty sound tactics. There was nothing inside that would give her any clues about him were this plan to somehow fail.

Already she could tell she was not being returned to the parking facility. She didn't know where it was taking her, but she guessed what would happen. Should she get out upon arrival if she could? If she couldn't, she could play dead until he got close and then… No, that wouldn't work. He'd be able to tell straight away that she was still alive on account of her not being a solid block of ice. The transporter was now in traffic, driving as normally as anyone else. Again, she tried to use the controls but, as before, they refused to respond. She began work once more to gain access to the circuitry. Unfortunately, *unlike with the exterior door locks*, he'd made it very difficult for her. Thick armour, like that on the inside of the doors, was everywhere. In some places there was even more than one layer. Without something to blast or burn her way in with, she was sure she'd never force it.

She slumped back in the chair, resigned to the fact that she might not be able to get out at all. Could she kick the view screen out? That was when she noticed the tiny black dome-like device resting on the ceiling. An omnidirectional camera, *looking straight at her*. She scowled at it defiantly, knowing that even if he wasn't watching her *now* he would eventually get around to it. *And…* he might now know about *Obsenneth*. That last thought hit her like a blow to the gut, making her exhale hard with anger. She couldn't get out, she couldn't feign death and he was watching her every move. He would know she'd traced him from the accommodation, or at least she hoped he would leap to that conclusion. Then he would think she was just law enforcement, after him for murdering those mercenaries. Could he work out that she knew he was after OIi? But then what did it matter? He would likely try to kill her anyway, who wouldn't?

If he could see her, he might be able to *hear* her too but... She smiled up at the camera as a new idea reached her. She tapped her earpiece.

"Lunell," Lunell answered, not knowing it was her.

"*Lunell*," she smiled, being sure to say his name loudly and clearly. "I need your help, I've run into trouble." She'd expected glee from him, a potential chance to show her up, but instead she received mistrust.

"Then why do you sound *so happy*?" he growled, uncertainly.

"Because you're the *only one* who answered and if you hadn't I'd be out of options," she responded, without missing a beat. Yes, she had sounded a bit too pleased to be believable. She explained the situation quickly to ensure he had the minimal amount of time to dwell on that answer.

"And you want me to shoot you down?" he clarified, very doubtful.

"I need you to prevent this transporter from reaching its destination or, failing that, retrieve me from it before it gets there – that would also work," she stated, grimly.

"... Very well, keep transmitting," he ordered, sharply.

"Will do," she said, nervously eyeing the destination grid. It was impossible for her to see where she was being taken and that being so, she had no idea how long she had before she arrived. She didn't want to call anyone else and reveal who they were, but she had no qualms about revealing the PAI. The Red Necromancer might not believe what he was seeing now that she'd obviously realised she was being filmed. Nevertheless, it would make him think about it. The only question was: could Lunell reach her before the Red Necromancer, or Uncle Fritz as he apparently liked to call himself?

She didn't have to wait long for her answer. Lunell was fast, moving in from the side and eyeing her sitting there. She smiled and waved nonchalantly as if they were friends who just happened to be passing one another on a routine journey to the supermarket. His eyes went cold and hard and she tried not to smile again.

"How do you want me to intercede?" he asked, in her ear.

"Try to..." she began, considering. She was interrupted by the controls as they bleeped in response to some kind of hidden instruction. Without warning the transporter veered into the side of Lunell's.

"What the...?" he began, well aware that *she* hadn't done that.

"Okay, back off but stay in sight," she hissed, irritated. *He* was in control now, presumably having taken over from the computer sometime recently.

Her transporter veered again, this time more roughly, making her crash into the side painfully. She pulled on the safety straps and braced herself to prevent him from slamming her around the inside of the vehicle. Lunell, guessing what was happening, decided to take action. It was an ideal opportunity to kill Satiah in circumstances where he could easily escape the blame. So what if it was a little early? He opened fire, his laser fire cutting into the back of the swerving transporter. Other craft made hasty divergences to escape the apparent road rage attack.

"What the hell are you doing? I said back off!" Satiah spat.

"I'm trying to take out the engines," he stated, in complete honesty. "Might slow you down, even if I can't get you to crash."

"I don't *want* to crash!" she yelled angrily, as the transporter began to move evasively.

---

Collorah had been waiting patiently for his contact to get back to him. He still needed the location that Oli and his helpers had moved to. He was sitting in a viewing facility as if trying to decide which drama to go in and see. He was on Earth, one of the cultural centres of the Coalition, and as he had nothing much better to do, he'd just decided on which programme to see: Smilodon, a thriller about a mutant feline creature which terrorises a tiny jungle tribe when... one of his many alarms activated. He eyed the code and pulled out another device, a hand held computer. An image appeared, revealing the interior of the transporter he'd set up a few days prior. He activated sound and sent it direct to his earpiece. Then he watched as Satiah slowly began to investigate the vehicle.

As planned, when she began to move towards the back and the case he'd planted there, he activated the automatic course designation he'd pre-programmed painstakingly before. He dispassionately observed Satiah as she tried alternately to break out, take control of the vehicle and then, he assumed, prepare for death. Only thing was, when the doors opened and she should have died… *she didn't*. A blue aura appeared to surround her and she had her hand in her jacket pocket. He frowned, deeply intrigued. The craft, continuing to follow his programmed instructions, then closed the doors, re-pressurised and began to return. He stared as Satiah, apparently completely calm, sat there waiting. That was when she'd noticed the camera and scowled at it. His lips twitched with a grim smile.

Then she'd called for help, someone called Lunell, and gave away when he had arrived by waving at him. Deciding that he couldn't allow this to continue, Collorah assumed direct remote control of the transporter and, switching views so that he could see the craft in traffic, attempted to side swipe her would-be rescuer. She began talking again; trying to get Lunell to back off, so Collorah began to try to shut her up by throwing her around inside the cabin. That was when he'd looked up and realised that a small boy was standing in front of him. Collorah smiled pleasantly.

"What game are you playing?" the boy asked, innocently.

"It's called *patience* and it's a very long game, but there is plenty of action," he told the child, shrugging lightly. He handed it to him. "Why don't you have a go, I have a little time, see if you can avoid the shooting," he suggested, highly amused. Excited, the boy began to use the controls in what he thought was a game but in reality was the ship Satiah was trapped in.

"The trick is to avoid all the vehicles and the lasers for extra speed bonuses," Collorah prompted. The boy nodded eagerly.

"How do you know what your score is?" he asked, concentrating.

"*Oh… I'll let you know*," he said, chuckling. He could hear Satiah crying out as she was shaken, lurched and propelled in unexpected directions. She was strapped down, he knew; nonetheless, it would not be a pleasant experience, especially now that her so-called rescuer appeared to be trying to kill her as well…

Satiah groaned as another insane move pinned her against the seat with g-force.

"Lunell, back off, stop shooting, you're making this worse," she growled, levelly.

"What if he simply decides to crash you head on into a wall?" he asked, seriously.

"I really don't think he will!" she yelled back. More shooting. "*Lunell!*" Her eyes went wide as the craft swerved to the right and flipped over as it slid between two parked freighters. Lunell swore.

"That's one hell of an autopilot," he growled.

"It's *not* an auto..." she began. Her words were cut off when she was slammed forward into her restraints as the transporter braked so hard she thought it might snap in two. The metal framework groaned but didn't crack.

Then she was falling. The transporter rocketed directly downward towards the distant street, picking up speed again very quickly. Satiah gritted her teeth, clutching the restraints hard, wondering if he really was going to crash it after all. Lunell followed but stopped shooting. Sirens were sounding now as law enforcement, alerted to the mayhem, were scrambling to catch up and end the chaos. Satiah had one last idea but it could go horribly wrong if she misjudged anything. She turned in her seat as far as she could and blasted the rear view screen. Two shots and it cracked in two. Another and it shattered utterly, the fragments of the viewing port left behind in less than a second. Satiah only just got her arm back around when the craft swept past the ground almost like at the conclusion of a bombing run and began an equally rapid ascent back into the sky.

She undid the straps and allowed herself to fall back over the seat in an ungainly but swift backward roll. Then she just dived out of the window, out into the sky, grapple-gun ready. She was starting to feel sick from all the unexpected and violent motions but she forced herself to concentrate. Lunell narrowly missed her as she fell; he was still following the craft. She waited until she stopped rising and had almost started succumb to gravity before firing at a nearby skyscraper. She hit her target and, as she began to fall, she swung towards the building. She reduced the length of the swing as much as she could but she knew this was going to hurt. She aimed for a window and hoped. Startled faces looked out, first looking confused or disbelieving, then becoming alarmed or shocked at seeing her rapid approach. They dived aside at the last second as she painfully smashed through the window and rolled to a halt on the floor.

She lay there for a second, trying to assess the level of her injuries. Nothing broken... bruises and... *ouch*... a sliver of glass was sticking out of her arm. Actually *quite a lot of of them were. Smashing*! The wind howled in, sending papers flying.

"Are you okay?" asked someone, stupidly. Slowly Satiah rose onto her hands and knees and then to her feet guardedly.

"Window cleaning survey, it's nothing to panic about," she stated, casually. "It seems your windows lack the strength for our new cleaning product. I'll have to discuss that with management." Everyone gaped at her. "What?" she asked, pretending to be mystified at their silence.

"Your *arm*, ma'am," pointed out a man to her left. He nodded at the glass still sticking out of her.

"Oh yeah," she mused, as if she'd only just noticed. "I guess my clothes failed their test too. Bad day at the office."

---

"*Oh no!*" the boy exclaimed. "*My pilot*! She just jumped out! *Is she supposed to do that?*"

"Not really," Collorah responded, hiding his amusement well. He had wondered if that might happen. She couldn't get out of the front or the sides but *the back* wasn't reinforced. She wouldn't have realised until the other vehicle had fired on the hindmost and weakened the area. "I doubt you will lose points for that though." He glanced up as he realised the programme he'd been there to watch was almost beginning.

"Sorry, got to go," he said, casually slipping the device from the child's hands. "You did great; you will be an ace pilot one day."

"Really?" he asked, his eyes wide with hope and pride.

"*Really.*"

Collorah entered the area where he would watch the feature and, while the adverts ran, he crashed the craft himself. There was nothing in it to incriminate him but there was no point in taking inane risks. In theory his signal could be traced, which was why he'd chosen to control it from a public area. He reviewed the whole thing from beginning to end once again, smiled when he saw her use of the grapple-gun, and wondered if she had survived. PAI or not PAI? That was the question. Their involvement in this was unexpected but it did make sense. On the other hand, why had her *friend* been trying to kill her? Assuming he wasn't just a lousy shot. Collorah didn't like second-rate shots. He sighed as the program started and slid the device into his pocket. Food for thought.

---

"Sorry, *what happened*?" Malla asked. He was sitting opposite Satiah as they waited for the medical androids to get to them. Satiah sipped her water through the straw soberly.

"The thing crashed, right into the backside of a transporter," Lunell answered, sagely. "No one was killed, although there were a few minor injuries. A team was dispatched to ensure it stays out of the news, although there is no way it would affect the campaign - in theory." Satiah almost glared at him. A guard should not be thinking in those terms, and even if he was, he certainly shouldn't be voicing it. In a moment of inattention, Lunell had almost blown both their covers! Luckily Malla wasn't really paying attention, as he was examining Satiah's injuries. They were all flesh wounds. A few were deep, but still relatively minor. There was no pain. Her own medication had seen to that much.

She shot Lunell a warning glance and he cooperatively shut up.

"I fell into a little trap, that was all," she smiled, at Malla. "It could have been a lot worse." She didn't add that it could have gone a lot better too. If Lunell hadn't started trying to blast her out of the sky, that last piece of insanity could easily have been avoided. Lunell argued what he had said at the time, that it could have crashed at any moment, killing her. And as it *had* crashed, in the end, it seemed to vindicate his opinion.

"A trap set by the Red Necromancer?" Malla guessed, finally paying attention.

"Is *Oli* safe?" Satiah enquired, curious.

"Shannon and Cadel are watching over him," Malla answered, waving dismissively. "I've got them on constant alert."

Oh yes, *Cadel*, she'd forgotten about him. Angel? He was the main man on duty during the night shifts. It was him that should have seen the bomb being planted the previous week. Had he *deliberately* been looking the other way?

"Good," she allowed, visibly relieved. The relief was genuine. Without any one of the three of them nearby she was concerned that the others wouldn't know what to do if they were attacked again.

"So now he knows you're onto him," Malla went on, thinking ahead. "Will he know who you are?"

"It's possible," she had to concede. "If anything though, that might persuade him to give up." Lunell scoffed quietly and she had to agree with that too.

"What will you do now?" Malla asked. Satiah flicked her eyes in Lunell's direction to make sure that he was still listening. Of course, what else would he be doing? *No, no, you carry on plotting against me; I need to catch up on Block 16, this week Colin is finally getting married but he doesn't realise it's actually his long lost sister!*

"Well, *before* everything turned nasty, I found out that he had had *two* transporters stored in there and he'd departed in one some days ago. I'll have to work with law enforcement to see if they can look back and follow him to wherever he went next," she told him. By law enforcement she did of course mean Harrier. The android arrived and, after testing her blood and noting the self-prescribed drugs already inside her, began to pluck the glass from her wounds. Malla winced as he watched. Satiah smiled at his mild discomfort.

"It's *okay*, I can't feel a thing," she assured him. Next the wounds were closed up, vanishing like they had never been there.

"Don't do it again," the android admonished her, before shuffling off. She poked her tongue out at its back before standing.

"It might be an idea to work with someone," Malla suggested, awkwardly. "I know you can look after yourself, hell I've *seen* you do it, but…" He didn't have to finish. He did have a point but, coming from him… could she trust it? She knew she *couldn't* trust Lunell for a certainty. Malla and Shannon, as well as the obvious problems she had with them, would not be capable enough. She missed Kelvin now more than ever. If he'd been there, not only would she never had had to come to a medical facility to get patched up, but he would have punched his way out of that transporter long before it even reached space.

"Oli is and always will be our main concern, I will look into that and I thank you for your advice," she said, seriously.

He shook his head with a rueful grin.

"I knew you wouldn't want to," he chuckled. "Just be careful." *Great, I'd never have thought of that. Next you'll be telling me not to trust anyone.* She smiled, concealing the inner sarcasm well.

"You know I will." They left the building and headed back to the campaign headquarters. As she approached the entrance, Satiah spotted Shannon watching them from a window several floors up. Shannon waved at her, her expression questioning. Satiah nodded to her, acknowledging the wave.

Malla and Lunell went back to relieve the others and bring Oli and Kate up to speed. Satiah decided that it was time for a meal, she was ravenous. A drink seemed like a good idea too, but she held back on that last one. After checking for poison, something that was starting to become simple routine even for her own food, Satiah settled in a chair to eat. While she chewed on the hot food, her mind continued to chew on the problems she had to deal with. It was almost like the separate processes were intrinsically linked. The closer she got to finishing her meal, the closer she seemed to get to calmer headspace.

A few more days and she'd have to make a decision about that blasted book! She'd left the message and if, for whatever reason, it wasn't acted on, she'd have to return it to Harrier as a non-starter. She still had to submit her answer on that review she was doing for Randal. At least she had now narrowed down, or at least *grouped*, those working against Oli into three separate factions. Well, *four* if she included herself and her own employers. Three that, for reasons to be worked out later, explicitly seemed to want him dead.

Sam McAllister and Mark De-Jool were behind Jinx and his friends. The Red Necromancer was working alone for someone she'd not identified yet. Then there was this *angel* business. The threat from within. Who was it? She still found that she didn't know how she felt about Malla, his absence both explained and yet convenient. His helpful peacekeeping actions and yet subtle watchfulness. And then there was Slimy Snell and Lunell, as if things weren't complicated enough. The Red Necromancer troubled her most of all so far, though. While Lunell was a known quantity, this guy seemed experienced, ruthless and cunning. Always a bad mixture in an enemy. She wondered if they could buy him off. If money was all he was interested in then that could be a simple way out. The negotiation would not be much fun, she knew, but still…

Shannon entered.

"I heard what happened, *are you okay?*" she asked, apparently genuinely disturbed. Oh yes, she was still playing nice.

"I got away with it, I think," she said, finishing the last of her food. "Didn't really learn much, but I'm going to go back to law enforcement later. They *might* have had better luck than me."

"Do you want any of us to go with you?" Shannon asked, possibly with an alternative motive. Satiah smiled.

"That's very kind, but Lunell has already volunteered," she said, avoiding another problem adeptly, the problem being that law enforcement's role in all this was a complete fallacy. Harrier and Zax were doing most of the work but understandably no one could know that.

"Lunell *has* been asking a lot of questions," Shannon informed her. She said it in that way people did when they wanted to be questioned themselves.

"I'm sure he has, those fire exits aren't as obvious as I'd like them to be," Satiah deadpanned. "Just this morning I was thinking about installing some kind of directional arrow system to…"

"No, no, you misunderstand," she said, shaking her head. *Really? You think?* "He's been asking questions about *you*."

"*Me*?" she gasped, as if shocked. "Tell him I have a boyfriend." Shannon rolled her eyes, starting to wonder if Satiah really was that dense after all.

"No, I think he was concerned about how you and Oli work together," she stated. Then Satiah realised that Lunell had done nothing of the sort. Why would he when he already *knew* everything about her? This was all coming from Shannon herself who was still smarting about how close Oli and Satiah were. Albeit by accident.

"Hey, I don't know much about any of this, beats me why he keeps getting me to tell him what I think," Satiah evaded. "It's not like I can refuse to say anything *either*. I *need* this money." Shannon's eyes narrowed almost imperceptibly.

"I'm just saying, Lunell thinks it is *odd* that an elite security guard is giving guidance on political matters to anyone," she said, at last laying out her actual accusation.

"*Me too*," Satiah shrugged, playing along. Then she eyed Shannon as if she was about to confess something. "I don't know what to do about it," she said, as if finally admitting something she'd been keeping secret for years. "What can I do? Have you got any ideas? What would you do?"

Shannon could not believe this conversation. She was making progress, so she thought, just in completely the wrong direction. It seemed doubtful that someone as hard as Satiah would start behaving as if she was out of her depth, even if she was. Particularly in front of anyone. Was she being played? She studied Satiah hard for a few seconds as if trying to make up her mind.

"I would try to distance myself from Oli," she suggested, pretending to really give it consideration. "Not physically, but I mean… *in conversation, you know?*" Satiah nodded intently, giving the impression of trusting sincerity.

"I'll do all I can," she said, as if she'd made up her mind. Satiah couldn't tell if this actually satisfied Shannon or not, but it left her no room to continue on the topic. Well, no room unless she *wanted* to make it obvious.

"I'm only looking out for *you*," Shannon insisted, raising her hands as if in defence. "I don't know *why* Lunell was asking. He may *even* have been thinking of trying to advise Oli himself. *I wouldn't say anything to him about it if I were you.*" No, of course not, as such an exchange could only end with your little deception being utterly unmasked.

"I appreciate it," Satiah said, smiling kindly. Elections were more unpredictable than battles, but this was starting to turn into an election full of tiny battles. "Speaking of Oli, how is he? How are they *all* coping?"

"They're making do. We are all a little more comfortable now that we've switched buildings," she replied. Their safety was only temporary, they all knew that. Shannon shifted self-consciously on her feet. Satiah sipped her water slowly, allowing the awkward silence to continue.

"…Well, I'd better be getting back," Shannon smiled, turning to leave. Satiah nodded nonchalantly.

---

"The second transporter, the one that left days before, departed the parking facility and moved into a large residential zone. I'm sorry to say I lost it," Zax reported sadly. "One minute it was overtaking a tanker and the next… it just wasn't there anymore. I checked all the surrounding lanes. Nothing. I think he was cloaking himself."

"He knew someone would be looking for him, *the trap proved that*," Satiah replied, grimly.

"Do you want an update?"

"I thought that was *why* you were calling," she smirked.

"Brenda's proportional representation has gone up to fifty five percent," she stopped for a moment. "Oli's… O… you're not going to believe this. It's gone *up*. He's at *thirty percent*," Zax stated, astounded.

Satiah's eyes widened. How had that happened? She'd leaked that document which should have seriously damaged his popularity! How could tax reformations like *that* make *anyone* popular?

"How did *that* happen?" she demanded, angry.

"Well, a lot of candidates *have* dropped out," Zax reminded her, uneasily. "And, it seems that your leaked *document* might actually have helped him." Satiah waited, not bothering to ask *how* as she knew Zax would explain. "You see, although its authenticity was *only* questioned by Oli himself, *as well he should have done, seeing as he didn't write it and you did*, the public seem to think it's a mistake. They think *this* because it goes against everything he has ever previously said about tax." Satiah scowled, angry at herself for not researching his actual tax plans more thoroughly.

"Others seem to think it sounds a lot more like what *his brother wants* than what he does, so they think *Sam* is behind it as, in their minds, Sam is close enough to Oli to be able to forge a document like that," she went on. "This is why Sam's proportional representation has lowered still further and…"

"This is why *I hate politics*," snarled Satiah, running her hands through her hair. How… just how…? She groaned. In an effort to ruin his campaign, Satiah had only succeeded in helping it along. Randal would not like that. And now Oli would *know* that someone was trying to torpedo him from within. Okay, she could easily say it was most likely this angel, whoever they were, but it was still irritating. Also, she felt sure, though she was hiding it well, that Zax found this hilarious.

"Are you laughing?" she demanded, tetchy.

"*Me*? No, of course not," Zax said, a little too insistently. A snorting sound that swiftly became a cough came next.

Satiah rolled her eyes.

"I'm glad you think this is funny! I doubt you would laugh so much were I to bring you in here with me to keep Oli safe," Satiah growled.

"I'm *too young* for active duty," Zax protested, uneasy again.

"*You won't be forever*," Satiah reminded. "Now find me the Red Necromancer please… *before* he finds me would be best."

"Yes, Satiah," she replied, not quite able to hide her cheekiness completely. Satiah cut her off, shaking her head, and returned to the main office area. Before she could even get to see Oli, Malla cornered her by the water dispenser.

"It seems you were right about there being someone on the inside, independent of the killers," he said, smiling. He was smiling because their, *or rather her*, plan had backfired. She smiled back hesitantly, knowing that he didn't know it had been her plan at all and that his pleasure in its failure wasn't there to annoy her.

"I don't relish the search for them," she said, sighing. "I looked into Dean's past again and I'm confident we can rule him out. Aside from everything else, he wouldn't be smart enough for this kind of thing."

"Oli's worried about what they might try *next*. This time they misjudged the public but he doubts they will make that mistake again," he continued. He was right, *she wouldn't*.

"Seems reasonable," she concurred, the irritation returning.

"Got any ideas?" he asked, taking a quick look around as everyone went about their daily tasks around them. Satiah too flashed her eyes surreptitiously at them.

She'd been watching these people for days. She knew their names, their jobs and their families. She knew where they lived, she knew their pasts, knew what they ate in the flaming canteen, and *yet*... she *still* couldn't find a link between any of them and anyone called *angel*. Harrier and Zax had also drawn blanks on this one. Whoever it was, it wasn't obvious. As usual, no one was acting suspiciously. As usual, she could see no danger. *Who was it?* She would find out. Preferably *before* anyone else had to die. Snippets of conversations, angles of countenances and a barrage of banal activity was all she had to work with. She made eye contact with Malla again before giving him a shrug.

As she entered Oli's office, Lunell and Shannon turned to look at her. For a second it seemed as if everyone stopped to watch her.

"Sorry," she said, apologising for the interruption.

"It's okay, I think we needed to take a break," Kate said, adjusting herself in her chair for comfort. Lunell nodded to Satiah, taking the chance to move out of there and leave watching them to Satiah. She gave him a curt nod in response.

"Shannon, could you oblige?" Oli asked, motioning to the empty water container on the desk. She smiled, though Satiah knew she really didn't want to leave her alone with Oli.

"Thanks." Shannon left the room and Satiah made her way over to her preferred place to stand, at the side where she could most easily see the door, the window and Oli himself.

"Do you play Gairunn, Satiah?" Oli asked, casually. The question took her a little off-guard. Kate shifted in her seat again, apparently still uncomfortable.

"As in *the card game*?" she clarified, realising how stupid that probably sounded. "No, not really, *why*?"

"It's just that the Sovereign *Sapphire* Tournament is starting this evening," he said. She looked blank, genuinely confused. "It's the biggest Gairunn contest there is? Been going for over a century now?"

"Ah *yes*," she said, as if she knew what he meant. She knew of the game and she supposed they did have leagues and stuff like that, as most sports did, but she didn't know much about them.

"Well, frankly I think we could all use a distraction from this place and, as it's being held here for the first time in over forty years, I was wondering if you wanted to watch some of it with me?" he offered. *O here we go again…*

"I wouldn't *understand* what was going on," she objected, laughing self deprecatingly. "I've not played since I was young," she lied.

"I'll send you the rules," he shrugged. *Thank you so much.* "Malla is coming too so it won't just be us, if that's what you're worried about?" He eyed her levelly.

"No," she replied, knowing she couldn't really say anything else. "No, I'd love to go, sounds like fun, *why not*?" She hated herself right then for not being able to think of a way out of it. Shannon came back in at that point, as if things couldn't get worse, just in time to hear the last of this painful exchange.

"*Fantastic*," he smiled, casually. He knew she would agree to go if she thought someone else would be there. That's why he'd pretended that Malla would accompany them.

Carl had hinted that he wanted to take her there, or certainly that he would go himself… she remembered belatedly. She knew *he* wouldn't be upset or anything; he was so glad to have her with him in any way possible, that he was very accommodating about a lot of things. She, however, *was* upset. She could always fail to turn up, claiming some last minute emergency. But that would just be delaying the inevitable. Besides, despite security, those kinds of places were always dangerous.

Angry losers, troublemakers and any number of those things could easily present a threat to Oli's life. She hoped he would only be a spectator and not actually a player, otherwise she might have to get dressed up just to sit next to him, so that she didn't stand out. On the other hand, it might be better that way as instead of focussing entirely on *her,* he would have to concentrate on the game. She knew this was wishful thinking: Oli didn't have that kind of money. However, Malla would be nearby to act as a hypothetical third wheel…

Kate stood up suddenly, bracing herself on the table with both hands, breathing hard. Everyone turned to look, attention dragged by the abrupt movement.

"Kate, are you…?" Oli began, concerned. With a groan, she collapsed to the floor.

"Get the medics in here!" Satiah ordered, firmly. She crouched next to Kate who seemed to be having some kind of fit on the floor. Foaming at the mouth was the giveaway. *Poison.* Satiah, keen to save the old woman's life, rummaged in her collection to see if she had anything that could help. Sedatives, chemicals for torture, chemicals for pain relief and… she didn't know which poison had been used but she had things on her that could give any poison problems. Her only real concern was the strength of Kate's heart. Shannon was making a call already, using the panic clip as Satiah made a decision. Dilthremolyn would protect the heart, neutralise the toxin and bring down her temperature. Fifty or sixty mills?

One look on Oli's stricken face made up her mind. *Ninety.* She injected her, despite Lunell's muted protest. Lunell didn't know what Satiah was using on Kate, so she could imagine why he was a bit tentative about letting her do it. Instantly Kate stopped thrashing and lay there in a heap, a white fluid seeping from her lips. Shouts from the medical personnel could be heard as they made their way through the office efficiently. Two minutes? Maybe less? That was a fast response time; Satiah would have to congratulate them for that.

"What happened?" asked everyone at once.

"Poison," Satiah explained, grimly. "I think she'll live," and went on to explain efficiently to the medics what aid she had administered.

Kate was carted away with Oli, Malla and Shannon in tow. Satiah went to follow but Lunell grabbed her arm to stop her.

"It's *fine*, I was a little worried about how her heart would cope but as soon as we get her into the facility..." Satiah began, thinking she could guess what he was about to say. He knew nothing of her talents in chemistry.

"*What did you save her for?*" he demanded, his voice hushed but still angry. "If you'd let that poison do its job, *you* could have replaced her as Oli's *main advisor*. There's no one else here he would trust enough. Then you would have been in a much better position to manipulate..."

"I have a role to fulfil here, If I hadn't done what I did it would have looked suspicious and..." she trailed off, in dawning comprehension. She slowly looked up and into his cold eyes.

"*You poisoned her.*"

"Of course," he admitted, freely and without any sort of regret. "She's a good advisor and after this morning's sudden rise in proportional representation, Scott ordered me to take action..." *What?* Rage rose in Satiah as her quick mind read between the lines, filled in the gaps and worked out what stupidity had just occurred. It was one thing *planning* such idiocy but...

"And you never thought to talk to *me* about this?" she snarled, angrily.

"What would have been the point?" he responded, tersely. "If *you* continue to dither and allow Oli to..."

"*I* or anyone else could easily have ingested it too," she growled, levelly. "It was *not* a very controlled environment! What if, for some reason, it had been *Oli* that'd ingested it, *you cretin?*"

"*I* would have prevented *that*," he lied, quickly. *Yeah, right.* Satiah took a quick look around to see if anyone was watching. Everyone was following the medical personnel out. She slid her blade from her boot in a swift move and had it at his throat before he even realised what she was doing.

"That's the second time you've tried to kill *me*," she spat, in his face. To his credit, he didn't flinch or allow his fear to show.

"How is it the *second*?" he demanded. "You've not even established I've tried at all..."

"You fired on me when I was in that vehicle even though I clearly instructed you not to. And now you poison the food and don't tell me beforehand, *what else can I presume?*" she hissed, through her teeth.

"You kill me and you won't live out the election," he countered. She didn't tell him she already knew he had orders to kill her after it was over.

"Are you a gambler?" she asked, undeterred. He gave her a determined smile.

"You Phantoms are all the same," he stated, hatred in his tone. "Paranoid, psychotic pretenders. Thinking you're in charge all the time, exceeding your authority..." Satiah's knee slammed into his groin hard and he doubled over, swearing and gasping. Her free hand smacked him across the back of the head with enough force to knock him down. She replaced her blade in her boot and regarded him coolly as he glared up at her.

"Makes you want to throw up, doesn't it?" she asked rhetorically, her tone bitter. She pointed down at him. "*You do anything like that again and I'll kill you, understand?*"

"*Message received,*" he glowered, red faced. He didn't say it would be obeyed but then she didn't expect him to. Trying to kill *Kate* was well over the line, she knew Randal would agree. Her attempt to lower representation had backfired, actually achieving the opposite, which technically made this latest madness Satiah's own fault.

---

Kate opened her eyes to see Oli, Malla and Shannon looking anxiously down at her.

"*Oh no*, I'm dying aren't I?" she croaked. *Aren't we all?*

"No, close call though, you look a bit like a Cozumel Raccoon," Oli smiled, patting her arm.

"You know that you've *really failed to impress* when someone compares you to a member of the raccoon family," she joked, weakly. "What happened?"

"We think someone tried to poison you, but luckily Satiah had her wits about her, as usual," Malla stated. "Shannon was fast and so were the doctors but if Satiah hadn't jabbed you with... whatever it was..." He trailed off without needing to explain further.

"*Great*... so now they're after *me* too," she murmured, trying to sit up.

"No, probably not, we think they were after Oli again," Shannon said, trying to dispel Kate's fears.

"Well, we can argue all we like about who they were after, but one thing is for sure: *they know where we are again*," Kate sighed, finally succeeding in sitting up. That was, as far as *they* could see, beyond question. Too bad it wasn't true.

"We don't have anywhere else suitable to move to," Malla admitted, seriously.

"We're going to have to check *all the food and drink* from now on, not just Oli's," Shannon groaned.

"Do you think it's the work of the same person?" Kate enquired. "You know, they leak that forged document and when that didn't work they... tried to kill me?"

"Satiah is the only one who might be able to answer that," Malla sighed. "From now on I'm just going to concentrate on keeping us safe and leave the detective work to her. She *is* making progress."

Shannon wanted to say something derogatory to infer the opposite but knew that the mood wasn't right for any sort of criticism aimed at their new *champion*.

"How are you feeling?" Oli asked, sensitively.

"Right now? Thirsty *and angry* in that order," Kate remarked, seeming to be almost fully recovered. The bounce back was mainly because Satiah had been very fast and generous with the damage control medication. Shannon handed her the water, seeming to hesitate as she did so.

"Don't worry," Kate soothed, guessing what Shannon was worried about. "They can't *all* be poisoned."

"*We hope*," Malla mouthed, at Shannon. She made a face at him.

"Did he?" Randal growled, having to hold the communicator slightly further from his ear than usual. Satiah was literally shouting out her fury. Something she rarely did and although he agreed with every word, he wanted to keep his eardrums in good working order, if possible. She stopped briefly to scream at someone else who'd apparently just cut her up before returning unabated.

"*One more thing*, if he pushes me *one more time* I'm going to rip his face off," she concluded, lividly. "Now, what did you want to say?"

"*Me*? O... I was just curious as to *how things were*," he jested. She laughed.

"Sorry," she apologised, restraining her temper. "It's hard enough to do this, without Lunell messing things up even more."

"Well, if it's any consolation, Slimy Snell has been breathing down my neck too," he said. It wasn't.

"I'm on my way to the hospital, just to make sure Kate made it and get an idea of her general condition. If she's out of action there is a chance Oli might want me to replace her. She should be fine, but being the age she is, I am concerned that I might have given her too strong a dose to be good for her," Satiah explained. "I'm still on *three* rival plots to kill Oli, by the way. Well, *four* if you include whatever Lunell tries next, just so you know. This Red Necromancer is going to be a problem, I can tell you that much already."

"Well, I can't offer you back up, there is no one available and even if there was I don't want Snell..."

"... to think we're ganging up on him, *I understand*," she concurred, preoccupied. He didn't mind her finishing his sentences for him, so long as she did it correctly. Since the beginning, he knew that *Slimy Snell's* involvement would cause problems, but he had not anticipated how volatile and sloppy the PAI were.

"After today, it's just twenty days," he encouraged.

"I wish I could say these last two weeks have flown by... but every second has been *like an hour*," she complained, bitterly. "Every hour, a decade... that's how this feels. Just sitting around waiting for whatever *whoever* will try next... If you *ever* tell me I'm going to *love* a job again, I'll resign."

Satiah entered her apartment with a sigh as the door closed behind her. She'd had all she could take that day... all she could take without banging heads together, anyway.

"Drink?" Carl called, from somewhere further in. She could have almost leapt with joy and relief.

"Please! Big as you can carry!" she yelled, dumping her backpack heavily on the floor. As she stretched she could hear him pouring the drinks. Two days without Lunell, Shannon or Oli sounded like the best thing in the universe to her at that moment.

"Satiah...?" His voice was hesitant and she tensed. She made a noise in answer. "You know this *big egg thing* you have in there? Well, it started moving earlier." It took her a few seconds to work out what he was talking about. The egg those strange underwater people had given her as payment for saving them. *Some payment.*

"*O that*! Don't worry about it," she said, leaving her boots behind and going in barefoot. "It's completely normal... So Kelvin assured me."

"Right," he said, smiling at her welcomingly. "Do you want me to leave you alone for a bit?" Her communicator went off to tell her a message had arrived and she glanced at it. It was from Oli and it had a data pack with it... Briefly bewildered, it took her a second to realise that she was reading instructions on how to play Gairunn...

## **CARD GAME RULES**
### *Gairunn - Oolon Standard rules. (Or Five P)*
### *Loopsplit variant & the Gairunn Original*

4 Cards to each player (3-20 players needed). (80 cards per round – 30 rounds per Hand)
600 card deck.

Highest score wins: (50% of round goes to winner & 50 to counter)
Lowest card value is: 16. (168 is the lowest) any lower and it's a FALL
Highest card value is 156. (468 is the max) any higher and it's a FALL

*Hulta Gertrude*

*30 blank cards in deck (30)*
*3 of each scoring card (420)*
*30 extra 16 cards (30)*
*118 extra card values each tenth value (Eg 20 or 80 or 220) (118)*
*2 remaining cards (Echo cards) match the highest scoring card in your hand. Green cards are played & Grey is discarded.*

Computer holds 4 random cards from its own pack at start of each new round After a hand, players may request a short pause (never exceeding five minutes) and players can bail at anytime between rounds.

<u>NEUTRAL RULE</u>: Second highest score neither loses nor wins except in sudden death. (Neutralled) If your score is second biggest you neither lose your bet nor gain winnings. More than one player can have this score without initialising the swing rule.

<u>SWING RULE</u>: if any two players have identical scores, regardless of what that score is (unless it is 2$^{nd}$ highest score/winning 4) then all cards are discarded and a new round begins with the bets staying unchanged (conflicting players only).

<u>SUDDEN DEATH RULE</u>: When only two players remain and reach an identical high score, the computer randomly adds cards to their hand until either they fall or one wins. SECOND VARIANT (apply only to winning hand scores). The offending score is levelled to 100 for all players clashing and four new cards are dealt to each. Then, after going through the pin and pick stages, like normal the computer then shuffles the pinned (red) cards and redistributes them among the players and the highest score wins (fall outs excluded). If the score still ties, the usual Sudden Death Rule is once more invoked. The players get to choose whether to keep the existing score or restart on zero.

Each round one card in all players' hands is randomly barred by the computer (The Pin).

*Players can preserve their cards if they bar their cards after they place their bet then switch occurs where two cards are taken from each player, reshuffled and redistributed among all the players who have not barred their cards. (Any variance on amount of cards is acceptable) (The Pick.)*
*Bets are then placed forward by the players based on their cards (The Price), each player does this in their own time.*
*Each player then declares their score (as does the computer) and the chips are taken/awarded/left. (The Point)*
*Each round the counter goes up with the 50% until either it is won by one of the 4 winning hands or it maxes out at 100,000,000 (any extra money goes direct to the casino). (The Payout)*

<u>*All lose to the winning 4 hands:*</u>
*Score of 450*
*Score of 0 (4 blanks)*
*Score of 400 even*
*Score of 360 (The spin)*

*(Original variant is exactly the same except that some cards cannot be preserved from the switch).*
*(Loopsplit variant is different because in that game it is possible to initiate the sudden death rule at any time during the game (still only between two individuals). It is also only played with 500 cards (100 being randomly removed at the beginning by the computer).*

Satiah groaned as she remembered *why* Oli had sent her that. It was even more annoying because she knew exactly how to play the stupid game in any case. Carl covered the screen of the device in her hand. Her eyes rose to regard him and he pulled an apologetic face.

"Sorry, it seemed to be upsetting you," he said, sheepish. "I prefer to see you smiling, not glaring." She giggled, amused.

"It's fine, just another man wanting to tell me what the rules are."

"*Sexist enslaver,*" Carl condemned, without being serious. "I thought, *as you're off for the next two days,* we could *maybe* go and see the tournament?"

"No problem," she said, patiently. He didn't know, after all.

"I thought it might remind you of that magical night we first met," he joked.

"*Magical*...? I must have hit you harder than I thought," she said, pulling a bemused expression.

His face fell.

"So cruel," he sighed, shaking his head in a playfully sad tone.

"If you don't want cruel, run me a bath," she ordered, waving at him dismissively. "Isn't it my turn to cook?"

"It is," he stated, firmly.

"Okay," she murmured, thinking about it. "*Delivery?*" Cooking was not one of her talents. Rations were not what Carl liked and she had been trying to teach herself a few basic dishes. It was hard doing that in secret. One day she would surprise him with a grand feast and he would be *so amazed*... No, she could see the building burning down right now. Ask her to hunt, skin and kill in the wild and there would be no problem.

The door bleeped, indicating that someone was outside. She frowned and her hand slid onto her pistol. Who could that be? She advanced back out into the hallway, pistol drawn and ready, and her feet making no noise. This was always how she answered doors; it was just easier to suppose the person on the other side meant harm. Paranoid? No, she knew there could be plenty of people out to get her. She activated the unit next to the door.

"Yes?" she asked, rudely.

"Satiah, *it's Ash*, I got your message," came a familiar voice. She checked the screen and indeed it was him. The immortal. The son of Dreda herself. Long red hair, gothic face, tall, bulky frame wearing his trademark black cloak. His eyes were staring right into the camera. She slipped her pistol back into its holster and opened the door.

"Hang on there a second, there is no need for you to enter, I'll go and get it," she stated, casually. She didn't know if he knew about Carl. Reed knew, so it seemed likely that even if Ash didn't know, he would suspect. Being an immortal, possessive of their lofty arrogance, he probably would think all of that was beneath him. Besides, there was nothing she could do to harm an immortal.

Ash waited, looming there in the doorway like the grim reaper itself, apparently unruffled by being left outside. Satiah returned, holding the book she had given up on. As an immortal, she was hoping that he would know of dialects or methods of communication that she, or any normal person, wouldn't.

"Here it is, if you can shed *any* light..." she began, before stopping. Ash's eyes had become narrow and he was staring at her like she'd just grown another head. She followed his gaze to the pocket of her jacket and then she realised what he might be sensing. *Obsenneth.*

"*Ash!*" she snapped, thrusting the book at him. "Here it is." Ash took it, and transferred his gaze to her face. She swallowed, not liking that look at all. She felt like he was looking into her mind. She didn't know exactly what powers he had and was now starting to regret this.

"Is everything all right?" he asked, searchingly.

"No, *of course not*," she retorted, sarcastically. "You *know* I don't like immortals, and also it's annoying that I have to ask for one's help with something that *I* should be able to do myself." He didn't seem very convinced. Did he know what Obsenneth was? What was going on in his mind? This may have been a mistake... her hand began to slowly move back towards her pistol almost imperceptibly. She didn't know why, lasers couldn't harm an immortal, but her body was already slipping into fight mode.

Her brown eyes rose to stare into his unfathomable ones with a hint of challenge.

"... I see," he said, at last. Much to her relief, he turned away, glancing down at the book she'd handed to him as he went. "I will let you know if I have any success," he growled, over his shoulder.

"Thank you," she murmured, watching him go. She slipped her hand into her jacket pocket and felt the gemstone there. She asked a question in her mind, not out loud, trying to understand what might be going on. Ash halted almost in mid-step at the end of the corridor and turned to stare at her. She closed the door on him, unnerved.

# Part Three

# Duel Of The Champions

Week three, day one. Satiah had steadfastly commanded Zax *never* to mention to anyone *under any circumstances* that she had leaked that document. Lunell didn't know. Randal didn't know, and Satiah didn't want to be blamed for the rise in Oli's proportional representation. She was still dismayed at how badly she'd miscalculated the way the public would react. She'd expected instant vilification of Oli, not solidarity and sympathy. Now, they had officially termed it as *Oli's popular support*, publicly stating that his overall popularity had risen to a much higher stature. All because *she* had blundered... she could hear her own teacher in her memory, telling her that mistakes were not for dwelling on, but for learning from. Right now, all that *that* platitude made her want to do was shoot something.

So... she had to take stock of where this left them. Oli was now at thirty percent, his *highest ever* representation, and Brenda was still on fifty five. Technically, Brenda shouldn't be able to lose if the numbers were correct and, *for once*, they were. At fifty five she only really had to wait. It was possible to win an election on fifty, provided your opposition had less than fifty. If they were at fifty as well, then even if a recount didn't solve it, the whole thing would start again. So unless something went drastically wrong in Brenda's campaign sometime soon, she'd already won - right?

Possibly not. These numbers could all change after the debate, as more people dropped out and those who had voted before would be asked to vote again for the final few, assuming they hadn't already done so. There were also other consequences of this latest switch to take into account. *Mark* had risen to *ten percent* after Sam's plummet into one step above minus figures. Mainly because of *her interference,* the public, in whatever form of wisdom that passed for logic in their constrained little perceptions, had blamed *Sam.* In the wake of this, those running for office in the election could easily be seen as *three.* Brenda, Oli and Mark. Everyone else was as good as gone.

Reduced to three candidates, the end was in sight… the debate could take place.

"Do you think it's the work of the insider?" Randal asked, curious. He was talking about the leaked document, the one Satiah had unwisely expected would solve at least *one* of her problems. He didn't know who had done it and so was going through likely options. Satiah was driving to work, at the usual time. Her two days off had been *blissful.* The egg hadn't hatched after all, which was a bit of relief. She still had no idea what she was going to do with that thing when it hatched, or even what it would need to survive. What could she possibly do with an overgrown fish? The only one who *might* know wasn't exactly in an ideal position to step in and help.

Kelvin remained in pieces and she was vacillatingly over the possibility of trusting Carl to get him fixed on her behalf. She'd given the unreadable book to Ash in the hope that he might be able to shed light into its meaning. *That* had nearly backfired too. She didn't yet know for sure if Ash had sensed Obsenneth or not, but she felt certain that *something* was going on there. She'd *tried* to talk to Obsenneth about it but he had been evasive. He had said that it *probably* was not a good idea for Ash to find out about him. Immortals were known to *get funny* about things like him. She remembered the curious silver sphere that Ruby had found on the Orion Observation and Reed's erratic reaction to it. She wondered…

"It seems likely," Satiah dodged, casually. "It's bad for us, but it worked out well for Oli, he's never *been* so popular." Randal sighed.

"It's clear that whoever leaked it had the opposite *intention*," Randal stated, disappointed. "It could have come close to doing your job for you." *Don't I know it?*

"Can't be helped now," she dismissed, vaguely. Randal found her lack of interest... curious.

"Do you know who the insider is?" he asked, thinking she might know.

"The ever mysterious angel or rather *the friend of an angel*? Not a clue yet," she replied, honestly. "Right now, I have bigger fish to fry. Because of *Lunell's* attempt on Kate's life last week, the whole team is *convinced* that the assassins have found us again."

"It would be the conclusion I would reach were I in their position," Randal grunted. "What are you going to do?"

"*Killing Lunell might be a good start*," she mumbled, grimly. "I'm going to have to find a way to reassure them, I suppose. Any news on Slimy Snell?"

"I've had no attempts on my life yet, though I remain vigilant and patient," Randal said, confidently. "Have you finished that review yet?" She rolled her eyes. She'd had a choice: do the review or *enjoy Carl's company*. After careful deliberation, which had taken all of a split second, she'd chosen the latter.

"Shouldn't be *long* now," she smiled, biting her lip to stop herself laughing.

"How long?" he asked. It was all she could do not to explode into a fit of giggles.

"Just give me a couple of days, all right?" she snapped, coming in to land on the roof. "I've gone through all the information, I just need to make a decision."

"Very well," he agreed, reluctantly. "Remember what I said about Lunell, when it comes to it...?"

"Yes, yes, *no evidence*," she said, seriously. "I *have* done this before once or twice."

"And *please* try not to cause any more... scenes," he sighed, exasperated. *Me?*

"*I* didn't *cause* any of them," she retorted, deactivating the drive system.

"Or *finish* any of them," he corrected. "Please, people are supposed to feel *safe* on Earth."

"Yes, I know, I remember the idyllic canard that is this world's reputation," she sighed, adjusting her hair in the mirror. "Watch yourself, Randal. Snell won't be taking prisoners."

"*Neither will I.*"

Satiah entered the office and began to check all the food and drink as a matter of routine. She'd even decided to place a gas detector inside the ventilation system just in case Lunell tried anything else. Lunell was late that morning and looked angry. She expected he and Snell might have had a few choice words to exchange, but it wasn't that.

"Did you disable the power core on my vehicle?" he demanded, in a low growl. She frowned up at him.

"No, I didn't, I don't even know where you park it when you're not here," she retorted, stiffly.

"*Really?*" he asked, disbelievingly. "I just thought it was interesting that after you threatened me last week, this morning *someone* had tampered with my craft."

"It is," she agreed, grinning. "Wasn't me, sorry."

In a huff, understandably, he stalked away, passing by Shannon as he went. Shannon pulled a face and then eyed Satiah.

"What's wrong with Lunell?" she asked, in a low voice.

"Irritable bowel," Satiah improvised, rather childishly. "Either that or it was something he ate which turned on him in the night."

"O," Shannon said, seeming to believe this. "Did you have a pleasant break?" Satiah thought back to the laughs and the intense human contact of the past couple of days. She probably should have done a bit more work but...

"Not bad, yourself?" Satiah replied, aware they were still just playing at being friendly. Her brief time away had revitalised Satiah completely and she was now ready to do battle once again.

"I had some trouble leaving this place behind, I think," she admitted, probably telling the truth. "Still very much on my mind everywhere I go."

"I know what you mean," Satiah agreed, in a matey way. "Listen, *about what you said last week*, how am I going to get out of going to that tournament with Oli?"

"You don't *want* to go?" she clarified. She couldn't quite hide how happy this apparent revelation made her.

"It's not my thing, *besides*..." she trailed off, knowing the other woman would fill in the gaps.

"Try telling him that you have never played before," Shannon suggested. "That's what I would do."

"I *did*, he just sent me the rules," Satiah said, as if disappointed. She showed Shannon the message. Shannon's brow furrowed.

"Hmmm..." she muttered, deep in thought. "I'll get back to you on that. Anything new from law enforcement?"

"They are still tracing the second vehicle," she said. "I don't think they will find it."

"Where does that leave us?" Shannon asked, thinking she already knew.

"In the dark," Satiah answered, in complete honesty.

"I wonder *how* they found us," Shannon hissed, through her teeth. "I keep thinking about that leaked document but there was no way it could be traced *here*. If there was then we would know *who* leaked it." *Yes, Satiah had got that much right.*

"I think it is fair to assume that someone *in here* is working against us," Satiah told her. It was a risk but Shannon was only one step away from that assumption herself... *if she'd not already reached it*. Playing dumb in this case might not be believable and Malla was already thinking that way too. Shannon shuddered and looked around.

"Any theories?" she enquired, as anyone would.

"Only that this is *in itself* only a theory. I don't *know, I just suspect*. There is *no evidence*," Satiah stated. "It *could* have been accidental, *so law enforcement will claim*."

They shared a glance that conveyed their mutual doubt regarding *that* eventuality. Arguably, because of her feelings for him, Shannon was actually the one person that Satiah probably *could* trust to put Oli's wellbeing first. At least for now.

*"What did he do to deserve this?"* she asked, rhetorically. *He unknowingly threatened the powers that be with unmanageable change,* thought Satiah …

"I'm going to chat with law enforcement," Satiah said, authoritatively. "If you could update Malla and then stay with Oli? You and Lunell should be okay, right?" Shannon nodded, secretly glad Satiah didn't want to be around him herself.

"Good luck."

———————— ✦✦✦✦✦ ————————

"*Well done Zax*, Lunell was in a dreadful rage about the power core but then you probably know that already," Satiah congratulated.

"I do. I was watching and listening, *glad to help*," Zax said, obviously smiling. "I *was* careful like you wanted, there's no way he can find out who did it. He will heighten his own personal security in response and it's clear he thinks you did it."

"*Let him*," growled Satiah. "He can prove nothing. Do you have anything else for me?"

"I have discovered that a few of the administrators in the government are making *discreet* enquiries as to the new location of Oli's campaigners. It could be nothing *but…*" she said, ponderously. Satiah smiled. Having learned of the rampant corruption, Zax was now *looking in* at the Coalition for threats as opposed to *looking out* at the Union or the Federation. She would do well to watch all three all the time, *particularly her own side*. Another important lesson for her, never underestimate your enemy but never trust or overestimate a so-called friend.

"I understand, he's been off the grid long enough to warrant a typical level of interest," Satiah concurred. "But anyone not so normal would know that too and would use it as cover for their own enquiries." This was true. Especially in a charged scenario like an election, if anyone disappeared for even a short duration, lots of questions would be asked by lots of people: the media, the rivals, and of course the spectators. Not one of those three groups *should* know about Oli's situation but, given that someone else obviously did, they had to assume that *anyone* could be involved. Thinking anything else would be foolhardy. The media particularly were a danger because of their constant questions and ceaseless endeavours to stick their noses into everything - another reason why Satiah didn't like them, and coincidently, why a lot of them ended up dead.

"Satiah... what would happen if one of the delegates *died*? I mean, with regard to the election process?" Zax wanted to know. Satiah cast her mind back to try to remember what had happened the last time someone prominent had died *during* an election. Plenty had died outside of one. *Balan Orion had been assassinated during an election... he had been Brenda's predecessor. And his remains were still missing...*

"Depends if they have already been eliminated or not. By eliminated, I mean voted out, withdrawn, arrested or disqualified in some other way. I think a few of them were disqualified this time around when they violated rules about trying to sabotage other campaigns. Regardless, if any of those things happen then, *most likely*, nothing will happen - in that, things continue as normal," Satiah explained. "If they *were* still running and died, especially if they were one of the more popular runners... well, it *might* be restarted. This time round, after Balan's death, Brenda held a referendum regarding the decision to start again or not. This was considered, *at the time*, to be the best way to prevent any... *unpleasantness*. As you can see, they wanted a second go."

"So we would have to go through *all this tedium* again?" Zax sighed, disappointed. Satiah smiled, so young and already so cynical. A good quality for staying alive.

A flicker of movement in the mirror made her brown eyes flash up. Oli was coming; she was driving him and Malla to the tournament opening area. The door closed behind him and, wearing something less than a perfect disguise, he approached her craft. A blast of air gently rocked the craft she was sitting in. At that height, with all the air movement, these air currents were almost constant. Satiah took in the statue on the opposing rooftop. An hour glass, made up of thousands of tiny hourglasses. She suspected that it was a relic from the days of the old empire; even now it had a regal, intimidating beauty about it. It showed no signs of corrosion that she could make out at that distance, although she was sure that close up it must have suffered a little. Perhaps it was an object of the protected type... like the Mulac Building... Whatever its status, it was a great spot for a sniper to lurk.

"Goodnight, young lady, and stay *close* to your communicator," Satiah ordered. "I might need you."

"Night Satiah, try not to kiss him again," she snorted, disconnecting before Satiah could yell at her. Satiah sighed with irritation but at this point she was just getting in touch with the funny side. And the game goes on. Satiah opened the door for Oli as he got close. He smiled as he looked in at her.

"How are *you*? I've hardly seen you all day," he asked, casually. *Yes... funny, that*. She tapped the controls nonchalantly and shrugged.

"Well, I've not been on vacation if *that's* what you're inferring," she remarked. "Where's Malla?" She'd expected him and Oli to be leaving *together*.

"O, he said he's going to *meet us there*," Oli explained, somewhat uneasily. He was a *very* bad liar... *he had no business running in an election*. Satiah sighed, knowing instantly what was *really* going on. To get her alone and to make her more inclined to join him, he was pretending Malla was going to be there with them. She would play along for now. It wasn't like there was much she could do other than insist on waiting for him, which would look odd.

"Fine," she said, nodding to him to hurry. "No point in hanging around, let's get going, we're open targets out here on the roof." She had a furry scarf around her upper body, having anticipated she might be driving *just him*.

"You're right," he agreed, getting in quickly and closing the door. She took off without even waiting for him to get into the restraints. To avoid more awkward conversation, she opened her window and turned on some loud music. Then she began to play the game she'd started to play recently. How close can I get to the speed limit without actually going over it?

She knew he kept sneaking glances at her all the time, but she was okay with that - so long as she didn't have to actually say anything to him. They reached a grand opening area for vehicles entering the

Feece-Arena, the facility that had the honour of hosting the tournament. The turnover would most likely be phenomenal. Every facility on the planet had wanted in, back when the tournament had announced its planet of choice. Those behind the tournament, a very wealthy consortium of investors and gamblers, had the pick of the known cosmos as the revenue generated by the tournament was said to be enough to make or break a whole quadrant's economy. Just the entertainments that were hired for members and non-members alike would without doubt break into the septillions. They said that once the members got tanked up, *anything could happen*. It was, as the billboard displayed it, *one hell of a party*.

For once, Oli wasn't staring at *her* - he was in awe of the scale of the place. Despite the huge numbers of people there, there were few queues. The system was efficient and cleverly managed through android and student workforces. The size of the place helped too: the Feece-Arena, which covered nearly ten miles, was over two thousand floors high and a few hundred more deep. Following the directions with ease, Satiah quickly got them to the correct parking area. These areas were so numerous that they were both number and colour coded. She deactivated everything and, without a word to him, got out. She began to throw the furry scarf back inside when a young man ran up to them. He halted upon seeing the weapons she was openly carrying on her belt. Laser pistol on her right thigh, grapple gun on her left and a baton she'd acquired from somewhere even she couldn't remember.

"Err… *Ma'am?*" he began, anxiously. She grunted in acknowledgment as she closed the door and faced him. Oli was coming around to join them.

"Do you have a permit for those?" he asked, sweating now. She crossed her arms and said nothing as she raised an eyebrow at him challengingly. He swallowed. "It's just… *I'm* not asking… It's the *security protocol* you see…" he said, laughing uncertainly. Upon hearing this exchange, Oli began to wonder.

"*You have got a permit, right?*" Oli asked, suddenly doubtful. Her shoulders slumped and she smiled as she showed her pass to him. It was the pass Harrier had provided that gave the false identity details that she needed to continue the charade of her role on Oli's payroll. It was always a good thing when you could get the people who made the real ones to make the fake one too. *Shockingly* they were almost impossible to distinguish between.

"Law enforcement, *sorry*, I had to be sure," he said, much relieved.

"And just *what* would *you* have done had I *not* had a permit? Asked me *politely* to hand them over?" she demanded, in a haughty tone. He cringed ever so slightly and she smiled inwardly. This was fun.

"I have a channel to call if that happens…" the young man said, fumbling with a communicator to demonstrate.

"I'm sure you do," she stated, grimly.

She felt Oli slip an arm around her lower back and he pointed to the entrance with his other hand.

"*Come on Satiah, we're supposed to be relaxing.* I think this is the way in," he said, in her ear. She sighed, allowing him to lead her there. This was *so* frustrating! Making people uncomfortable was one of her hobbies! *Spoilsport.*

"How is Malla going to find us?" she asked, hoping that might remind him of what a fibber he was being. His hand left her back and he adjusted his collar casually.

"I'm sure he'll call if he runs into difficulties," he said, clearing his throat. Did he know *who* he was trying to kid…? No, of course he didn't. The atmosphere inside was quiet. There *were* millions of people in there all coolly moving around, watching the games, placing wagers or drinking. Yet, in order to truly experience the drama of a game, a certain lack of noise was needed. They approached the bar. As she moved further into the room she spotted a man, a familiar man, trying to hide his face from her. It was Davnav, one of her many *contacts*. She smiled, glad to be able to intimidate him some more… whilst touching base, obviously.

"One moment," she smiled, to Oli. She came up behind Davnav and put her hand on his shoulder, hard enough to make him jump out of his skin.

"Well, fancy meeting *you* here," she said, grinning obsessively up at him.

"*Satiah*," he gulped, perceptibly terrified. His hand was shaking so hard his drink was sloshing about in the glass he was holding. "Hi, I'm not doing anything." She leaned in closer.

"*I* never said you were," she purred, in his ear. He let out a noise somewhere between a whimper and a laugh.

"Is... I-Is there anything I can do for you?" he asked, uneasy. Oli came up, wondering what was going on.

"We're thirsty," she stated. There was more to this than simply frightening Davnav. She didn't want Oli to buy the drinks. She was fairly certain he wouldn't try to drug her, but she wasn't taking any chances.

"O, you should have said, *I'll get you some*, what would you like?" he asked, greatly relieved. She shrugged and eyed Oli.

"Well, some wine, Satiah?" Oli confirmed.

"I'll have a Golden," she murmured, knowing it was the latest vernacular term for *Golden Float*. She might as well have *something* to enjoy about this evening.

"O, me too," Oli said, deciding to have the same. Satiah really had to rein in the impulse to roll her eyes. Davnav nodded and headed for the bar.

"You like Golden Floats? He a friend of yours?" Oli enquired, interested.

"Close enough," she shrugged. "Which game did you want to watch?"

"Did you read those instructions I sent to you? I was worried that you might not have had time," he asked, considering.

"Briefly," she stated, technically telling the truth. *About two seconds... How brief could you get?*

"Great, while I wouldn't have minded if you hadn't, and it's not important or anything like that, it could have confused you further if I tried to explain how it worked *while* you were watching it," Oli smiled.

Davnav returned, a glass in each hand. He didn't even look at Oli as he handed them over.

"I've opened a tab for you, it's on me, *please*," he insisted, fearfully.

"*Aww... that's very kind of you*," Satiah smiled, winking up at him. "If only *every* citizen embodied *such* generosity."

"*Yeah...*" he trailed off, looking at the floor.

"Oli, why don't you find us a table while I compensate this man for his kindness?" she suggested, firmly. Oli nodded, a little uncertain, but obeyed. Satiah put her hand on Davnav's shoulder again. He tensed, expecting a punch.

"Any luck?" she asked, all business. "What's the word on the walkways today?"

"Still asking around," he replied, instantly knowing what she wanted. She let go, producing a long bronze coloured rectangular lump of light metal from her thigh pocket, and offered it to him.

His eyes lit up upon seeing it, knowing it was money.

"There's five thousand Essps on here," she told him. "As payment for your continued and much valued support. I never forget favours. *Don't* spend it all at once."

"*Thank you*," he said greedily, almost snatching it off her. "I needed to get my boy a new fuel converter; this will be enough for that..."

"*O no*," she hissed, as if greatly disappointed.

"What? You think a new engine would be better?"

"No, I meant, *o no you've reproduced*," she corrected him, with a playfully cutting smile. He wanted to retaliate but he knew he couldn't - she could see the battle in his expression. She leaned in a little closer.

"*Why don't you tell me how gorgeous I look this evening*?" she pressed, still grinning.

"*I hate you*," he hissed, heading away. She watched him go, her lips twitching with restrained laughter.

Oli was watching all this, looking increasingly baffled. She joined him at the table.

"Sorry about that, *budget cuts*," she smiled, by way of elucidation. "The good news is, *our tab is sorted* so if you want to go really nuts, *by all means do*." A hangover might make the big debate tomorrow even tougher for him.

"I have the debate tomorrow," he stated, awkwardly.

"That's right, you do," she agreed, taking a large gulp of her drink. *Good stuff*. "Malla arrived yet?" He winced. There was a protracted... *something*, in the guise of silence.

"You *know*, don't you?" he asked, a resigned uneasiness about him. Well, that was easy. This guy had even less backbone than Carl did.

"Know *what*?" she asked, putting on a perplexed look. "He's not *already here is he?* Is that what you're saying?"

"I lied," he admitted.

"Well, you *are* a politician," she joked, levelly. "I'd be worried if you didn't..."

"Satiah, I *know* you know what we're talking about," he stated, a little emotionally. Game over!

"What, that you lied about Malla being here because you knew I'd never agree to come if it was going to be just the two of us?" she asked, directly. How could she do this painlessly? If, indeed, painless was the right way to go. Perhaps he needed pain to tell him that this was even more ridiculous than the leaked tax document she'd created. He gave her a rueful smile.

"Yes, *that*... I knew you knew *really*," he said, a little ashamed.

"So what *are* we doing here?" she demanded, allowing her temper to flare. "My position on you or this *hasn't changed*. It *cannot* change."

He looked downcast instantly but she knew how to resist the desire to be sympathetic. Not that she often had that desire anyway, which was fortunate in this case.

"...If that's *really* how you feel?" he tried again.

"It is," she said, in a tone that implied she'd categorically love to nail the lid down on this coffin of a subject.

"It's just that I think you're *incredible*," he replied, deciding to go for broke. "And I don't *believe* you have a boyfriend, nor do I *believe* that you don't feel *any* attraction to me. Your kiss was *too* passionate."

"I can't help how I kiss!" she protested, starting to consider walking out. "And I can't help what you choose to believe, but I really *do* have someone else. Regardless of how I feel about you..." She stopped herself. Mistake, *bad* mistake.

"*See*, I *knew* you felt *something!*" he cried, as if vindicated.

"*No!*" she snarled, through her teeth. A sudden urge to get nasty came over her and she had to force a mouthful of drink down to give herself more time to think. Well, not *force*, more sort of douse. Drown that fiery rage before she said or did something she would regret even more than deciding to play along earlier.

"Look, you're a very nice man but I don't..."

"*Really*, you're going to hit me with *that*?" he demanded, incredulous. He began to mimic a female voice. "*You're a nice guy but I don't see you like that...*"

"Just now you *said* I was incredible, maybe it might be smart to listen to someone who's *so incredible* without interrupting," she countered. This was not going well.

"Yeah well, *you're* not making a lot of sense," he accused. She seized on one last idea... that is to say, the idea *before* the one where she would strangle him, fail her mission and then try to deal with the fallout.

"You know *who else* isn't making a lot of sense?" she demanded, deciding to get overemotional too. She was under control completely but it would seem to anyone else who saw it that the opposite was true. Oli moved to point at himself, raising his eyebrows defensively, expecting her to accuse him of not making sense.

"If you're *so* into *me*, what's going on between *you and Shannon*? Or did you imagine *I hadn't noticed*?" she demanded, cleverly. That threw him completely. "I even told you she still had a thing for you. I told you that because, at the time, I *thought* you didn't already know."

"*What?*" he asked, blindsided by the unexpected allegation.

"I *thought* she was in love with you and *that* I could understand but *I didn't know it was a two-way traffic lane!*" she hissed, fake tears in her eyes. She was making this look very real. Finally, starting to realise he'd taken this too far, he began to backpedal.

"What are you talking about?" he questioned, predictably.

"Shannon told me about *you and her*," she said, dropping the complete lie of a bombshell right there. "She told me that you had hurt her and it would better for me to stay away from you unless I wanted *the same treatment.*" Shannon had never told her this, of course, but she knew from some of the things various people *had* said, that Oli had jilted her in the past. Shannon still wanted him but he didn't want her. Now, her best chance was to make him think Shannon was trying to interfere.

He looked hurt now, crestfallen and betrayed. That typically male look that said: *you weren't meant to know about that*.

"I… It's *true* that at the time I felt and *still do* feel that she and I should remain on different paths, but I have never liked her in that way," he insisted. O, so it's okay for *you* to not feel that way about someone, but when another person doesn't *feel that way about you*, you can't understand *that*? And such ornate wording - maybe Satiah had been wrong, maybe he *was* born for politics after all. She wondered for a second how he would explain himself were it Shannon that he was in front of, before putting that out of her mind. Satiah didn't voice *that* argument, there was no need. She had something better to say.

"I know what you said before about her having feelings for me and she maybe does have *residual* feelings…" he was saying.

"Prove it," she ordered, with an angry nod and a withering smile. She knew it was a near impossible thing for him to do. The only clear way would be for him to compel Shannon to back him up and what were the odds of *that* happening? Especially as Satiah knew Shannon would be strongly in favour of, for whatever insane reason, getting Oli for herself.

"*Maybe she lied*," Satiah went on, adding more onto the pile. Ruthlessly cutting off his possible excuses before he could use them to counter with. "Maybe she and you are still together and she feels threatened by me. Maybe she's made all this up *just to spite you*. Maybe she's just messing with us both for her own personal reasons. Maybe *I've* misinterpreted *someone somewhere somehow*…" She smiled bitterly in victory while shaking her head. "I've heard *plenty* of that before. *Too often to believe it*. How can I ever fall in love with, or even *trust*, a man *with this* hanging over him?"

Oli was staring at her, slack jawed, hardly able to keep pace. Unprepared, men could often easily be forced into retreat by overwhelming drama. Well, if the debate tomorrow wasn't hard enough for him before, the pressure would really be on now. She stood, confident that she'd confirmed the kill, her glass empty.

"And now, *if you don't mind*," she said, holding her head high. "I'm going to get another drink." She spun on her heel with the intention of stalking over to the bar *and* staying there. Inwardly she was quite pleased with herself. It had been tricky at first and she'd almost blundered once, but she felt she'd at last managed to fight him off.

Before she had even got anywhere she almost walked straight into *Carl*. She halted immediately, stunned. One look at his face told her that he *must* have heard at least *some* of that conversation. *Hurt*. He might not know who Oli was but as far as Carl knew *she* was still at the office. That's what she had told him so it would look as if she'd just been caught in a lie. He would have been taken in by her performance too and he would think there was something going on between her and Oli. *What was he doing here? O yes, he had said he wanted to go...*

"*Carl?*" she pronounced, uncertainly. Her instinct to try to use this to her advantage took over. She tried to link her arm in his and turn around to face Oli.

"Oli, *this* is my boyfriend..." she began, seriously. Carl though, slipped his arm free and turned away, visibly not wanting any part of whatever this was. Oli saw this, instead of what she'd hoped he would see.

"*Really?*" Oli scoffed, disbelievingly. "Are you sure? *He* doesn't seem to think so." Satiah chased after Carl, who was already trying to leave and caught his arm again.

"Carl, *please*, there is a *very* good explanation..." she said, feeling oddly powerless. He turned to face her, tears in his eyes.

"It's my fault," he said, so softly she could hardly hear him over her own heart pounding in her ears. "I should have not have presumed... *I'm sorry.*" *What?!*

"*Listen to me*," she implored, increasingly desperate. What could she say? *It's not what it looks like? It's not what you think?* A confused voice in her ear started talking instead, distracting her further.

"*Who's that?*" Zax was asking. She was talking about Carl. *O no...*

"*Carl!*" she called again, as he got free. Why wasn't he listening? *Why didn't he trust her?* "Please, just give me a moment and I'll explain..."

"I may not be enough for you, but *I'm not* ..." he stated, in response. He was stopping himself from saying whatever was supposed to come next. "*I'm going home.*" The anger in his voice and face stung her, it was so unexpected. She didn't think she'd ever seen him look like that before.

This made her rethink things suddenly. Had *he* been having doubts about them? *Why?* She was everything to him, the very core of his world... or so she had supposed. She knew that *she* had had doubts but it never occurred to her that he might have his own. Part of her couldn't believe this at all. What had she done wrong? *What could she possibly have done...?* Then the truth of the matter made itself known. It wasn't anything she'd done, certainly nothing she had done to him. It must have something to do with the restrictions she'd placed on their relationship. She *had* to be in control, all the time, for her own protection and his too but... maybe he'd hoped that might *change* as trust grew. *We* can do this, that and we can talk about this and that but... *there's a part of me you can never know...* And he had wanted more? What did he want? *Why wouldn't he say?!*

She stopped herself, her self control exerting itself automatically. This was not the time or place. Besides, going after him wouldn't help, she needed to give him a little space and escape the emotion of the moment. She also needed to get away from Oli before she decided to just shoot him!

"Okay," she said, choosing not to chase and make things worse.

"*Satiah, what's going on?*" Zax was asking, still in her ear.

"*Quiet, Zax!*" Satiah hissed at her.

She turned to see Oli, still sitting there watching her. Great, now *he* would be thinking that she had *lied* about having someone. Lied to the extent where she'd tried to get an apparent stranger to impersonate a partner. And this man was who they wanted *her* to save...? Her blood began to boil again. This was *his* fault and she would make him pay. But now she had another slightly smaller problem to deal with. She marched out, leaving him alone. She wasn't feeling particularly protective at that moment, least of all towards Oli. She did however send a message to Malla, telling him that he was late and that he needed to get down to the tournament and look after Oli.

"Do I still have you, Zax?" Satiah asked coldly, after making that call.

"You do," she replied, a little nervous.

"Good. *Young lady*, it's time *you and I* had an unobtrusive one-to-one. Stay *exactly* where you are, *I will come to you.*"

Sam had never had a chance of winning: that had been a fact from the start. Nevertheless, his plummet in representation irked him. Someone had leaked a tax document, apparently trying to bring Oli down. The public, annoyingly, seemed to realise that this was forged and, *even more annoyingly*, they had blamed *him* for it. This wasn't just harmful *now*; it may ruin any future attempts he made. He'd called Mark straightaway but he too seemed as baffled at the turn of events as Sam himself. He'd *claimed* ignorance of the document, saying that it wasn't anything to do with any of the plans *he* had for Oli. This had to be someone else, someone else trying to bring him down.

Did Sam believe him? He couldn't decide. So far Mark had been as good as his word, but too many things were going wrong. And, after all, couldn't plans change?

At first he and Mark had suspected Jinx of trying to manipulate them. Jinx had predictably thought the same about them. Scum like him were invariably paranoid, not unreasonably. They had resolved this difference of opinion, albeit temporarily, the other night in the parking area. Mark had done very well out of this sudden switch in representation though, which was why Sam had begun to suspect his cohort of treachery. Mark, just like Oli, had never been so popular. Had he guessed the public would react that way? Granted, it was clear that he was still very much a minority, but he was big enough to gain more attention and therefore potentially more support. Anyone who didn't want either Brenda or Oli would still have a bandwagon to go for. He was now one of the big three.

Sam began to toy with the idea of having Mark assassinated. Preferably *after* Oli, as Mark's capital was still required to pay Jinx for that job. Sam couldn't overlook this easily. The way it had completely destroyed him, and elevated both his brother and his so-called friend, would be hard for anyone to ignore. It couldn't be happenstance. This had happened by someone's design, that was a fact. And *someone* would suffer for it…

Brenda looked out over the crowd that milled around below her in the gathering area. Ambassadors, administrators, politicians, celebrities... the list went on. There were actually fewer of them there than had been anticipated – this was because of the card tournament. Despite this, Brenda was reluctant to join in, crowds worried her. She looked down from the safety of her balcony and was glad of the black glass that separated them. They couldn't see her...and for that she was thankful. She loved to see people, just more on a one to one sort of basis. The aide had said that there was always a small danger of assassination, even for one so popular, which didn't help her level of serenity either.

*"Daunting, aren't they?"* came a voice from behind her. She jumped and spun to see Ash's dark, cloaked form standing a few paces behind her. She'd not seen him since she'd taken power. He looked even more imposing than she remembered. "But then humans do seem to spread very quickly, don't they? Like a virus, or an infestation."

"Ah..." she swallowed, nervous. *"Ash? How did you get in here?* W-what can I do for you?" Ash's eyes pierced hers and she looked away, feeling suddenly very exposed. She knew he had powers, like all immortals, and she didn't like the idea that he could see into her mind at all. She had nothing to hide but that wasn't the point. Everyone had some thoughts that they were not proud of - fantasies, dreams etc. She worried he would see them and think that they were more than they were or something.

"I did *say* I would come to see you, *or whoever rules the humans*, from time to time," he said, coming over to join her. She nodded and made a nervous noise in agreement. He *had* said that. But then loads of people said 'see you later' and they never bothered. His gaze returned to the crowd.

"Reed n-not with you?" she enquired, hopefully. He glanced over his own shoulders slowly.

"No," he replied, in a way that seemed to imply he wanted to say more. It was as if he'd just noticed the small man's absence and was surprised by it, but he said nothing about it. "My mother would have wished me to support *the peace* you have."

"*Dreda?*" Brenda confirmed, a little uncertainly. What was he doing here? What did he want? *Where was her aide?*

"In doing so, I felt I had to make you aware of any potential dangers to that peace," Ash went on, casually.

"D-dangers?" she asked, uneasy. "What dangers?"

"I am not yet certain," he answered, looking doubtful. "Nevertheless, I felt I should give you warning."

"Well, you…. y-your help is *always* appreciated," she said, nodding earnestly. That earned her a cynical smile and she smiled fearfully back, wishing Reed was there. Reed knew how to handle immortals, she didn't. They seemed to have a begrudging respect for the little man, along with almost everyone he worked with. *Where was he?*

"There is a threat but it lacks… *coherence*," he continued, eyeing her.

"A threat to what?" she asked, inevitably.

"Existence," he replied, immediately. Okay, she really had nothing to say to that.

"Perhaps you should alert those who might actually be able to do something about it," she suggested, softly.

"You *are* their leader," he pointed out, amused.

"*Illegally*, yes," she stated, still concerned about stepping on toes. "That's what this election is about. I suggest you speak with the military." He nodded slowly and turned to leave.

"Thank you f-for the warning," she offered, wondering if she had somehow offended him. "R-reed will help you."

"I cannot find him," he answered. He saw no benefit in telling her that he did not trust Reed. His long strides quickly took him out of her sight and she frowned, trying to fathom what that had been about. So… Ash couldn't find Reed… a threat? A threat to existence?

"Ah, there you are," her aide said, making her jump again. *Now* she shows up! "Please, your guests await you."

"O-okay."

---

"So, I'm to erase all evidence of that man *who didn't exist*, forget everything I saw and heard, while also keeping in mind never to give anything away about it to anyone *ever*?" Zax clarified. "And this is on top of never revealing that you leaked that document?

Dressed in her night clothes Zax was sitting cross-legged on the edge of her bed. Her night clothes consisted of a black and white stripy number that would have greatly amused Satiah, were her mood not so prickly. She looked like some kind of giant barcode. Deciding that she'd taken more than enough risks, Satiah had opted to see Zax face to face rather than using any other method of communication. Zax was rather worried at this odd visit, but was not in fear of her life. She was still growing up, of course, but that didn't mean she couldn't be a problem.

"Yes," Satiah ordered. This was an illegal order and they both knew it. So much about this was getting... *complicated.*

"... Then, can I ask you *two* questions, if I agree?" Zax chanced, smiling.

"Why not?" Satiah growled, uncertain.

"Is he *really* your boyfriend?" she asked, wide eyed. "I thought relationships were *forbidden*." Satiah sighed and sat next to her on the bed. If this were anyone else she'd never have handled it like this, but Zax was *special*.

"He is and they are. It was an *accident*," Satiah stated. "Sometimes, in the heat of the moment, there are wild shots."

"*...I think he's great*," Zax said, a little awkwardly. She didn't want to anger Satiah by insulting her boyfriend. "But..." she trailed off and Satiah smiled.

"But not the man for a Phantom agent?" Satiah enquired, amused. "You're right, he's not, but then *who should be*?" Zax flushed red, worried she'd hurt Satiah feelings.

"I'm sorry for what I said about you and Oli, *I didn't know*," she blurted, genuinely.

"O, you mean about the kissing. Right now I'd be more worried about the *murder*," Satiah replied, chuckling.

"He was really quite horrid to you tonight," Zax said, angry. "I thought for a minute you were going to really lose your temper with him."

"It *was* a close call," Satiah admitted. "Now you've seen why I have been trying to avoid being alone with him. I was lucky. His emotions got the better of him and that made him easier to manipulate and trap. A more rational man would have been harder to deal with." Zax nodded, filing everything away in her own 'for use when needed' file somewhere in her memory.

"And your second and *last* question?" Satiah wanted to know.

"Well, it's not really a question *it's... well...* it's more of a *blackmail demand*," she said, uneasily. She felt Satiah's hand land on the back of her neck softly. She swallowed.

"I advise you to think *very* carefully on how you phrase it," advised Satiah, coldly.

"I won't tell anyone about this *or* your man if you agree... *when I'm ready... when I'm good enough...* that you will teach me to be a Phantom agent. Actually, not just *any* Phantom agent, *the best Phantom agent ever*?" Zax asked, hopefully.

Satiah's hand let go instantly. Zax couldn't know that Satiah had already decided that she would teach her *a long time ago*. She'd decided *that* almost before Zax had been born. For a moment there was only the gentle ever present electrical hum that could be heard as they stared at one another in the low light. Satiah had known this moment would come. When she'd last thought about it approaching, things had been very different. Now it was finally here, a tiny part of Satiah felt like crying.

"Done," Satiah growled, burying the flash of emotion with well practised ease. They shook hands and Satiah rose.

"What will you do? About your man?" Zax asked, curious.

"That's *two more* questions," Satiah remarked, without bite. Zax shrugged and repeated the questions. "I have a mission," Satiah answered, bleakly. "Either he will still be there or he won't. If he's *not* I can't go after him until the election is over. If he is... I'll just have to hope he believes the truth."

*"Thank you for not killing me,"* Zax whispered, trying to cheer Satiah up. *Kill you? Dear child… You're probably the only one I don't think I could.* "And good luck."

"I can never have enough of that," she replied, grimly.

---

Life is like a rocket. It starts off very slowly as it rises, you don't know what's going to happen or *if* anything will happen. Then it gets faster and faster, until you don't have time to wonder what's going to happen next. Eventually, when Satiah returned home in the early hours, she found the apartment unoccupied. Carl's bag was gone. A note was there, detailing how she could contact the man he'd suggested she could trust with Kelvin. He'd said *nothing else*. Not a word about *them*. His silence was agony for her. If he wanted to accuse her, then do it. *Please*! If he wanted to forgive her, then by all means, don't delay. If he wanted it to end, then at least do her the courtesy of telling her to her face. Then again… knowing who she was and what she might do if angered… maybe his flight was more understandable.

Satiah sat at her desk fighting back the very real tears and held her head in her hands for a while. She just wanted him to come back! She needed a chance to try and explain what he had witnessed. She should never have brought him this close to her… that had been her real mistake. Her heart had betrayed her before and now it had done so again. Would it always be this way? The people she dared to care about, forced away because of what she was and what she did? What she had been doing with Oli… It hadn't been *real*, it was all an act…! But because of how good she was at lying, hiding and acting… Carl might just assume she was lying to him. *That was assuming he ever came back to her…* then, knowing sleep would elude her, she focussed on that review she had to do for Randal. Ironically, it turned out to be exactly what she needed to cure her insomnia.

She awoke, aching everywhere. She could sleep on the floor, in a pilot's seat, or in a bed, but not in a normal chair apparently. Well, she *could* sleep there too, but it was not worth the morning stiffness and pain. She went for a warm shower, conscious that she was *already* late. She didn't care. She'd realised her affection for Carl was growing, but she'd not noticed it had reached this level. Well, as the old saying went, if it hurt then it had to be love. And it had hurt. To distract herself she checked her earpiece. Lunell had tried to call her, so had Malla *and* Randal. The heat of the water soothed her flesh but failed to do the same for her soul. She made a decision to stop prevaricating and called the guy Carl had recommended. He answered, sounding just as drowsy as she felt.

"Hi," he said, cheerful if a little sleepy. He gave a company advertising/identification patter. "Max here, can I help?"

"Yes," she said. "I hear you're good with robotics and computer programming and analysis. If you agree to my terms then I have a job for you."

"Okay... who are you?" he asked, inevitably.

"That's not important," she replied, bluntly. "*Where I am* is. There are only certain times you can access this asset. Night shift work. And you will be watched, this asset is very important and although damaged it does have material of a sensitive nature."

"*What?*" he asked, all this a bit more than he could take after just waking up.

"Fifty thousand Essps," she stated, firmly. "Is that enough to buy your confidentiality as well as your aid?"

"I'll be right there," he said, suddenly very much awake. "Where and when do you need me?" She told him.

"You get five at the start plus whatever you need to buy parts, and the rest at the end when it's working again," she spelt out. "I also want a detailed reason why the asset stopped working in the first place, to ensure this never happens again." She gave him her location and what time to arrive. He agreed. Next she called Randal.

"You're not at the office, I was worried at first but Zax assures me everything is going according to plan," Randal said.

"That is correct," Satiah smiled, pleased at Zax's intervention. At least Carl was still a secret.

"She didn't however explain exactly what the plan *was*, saying how you felt that she didn't need to know. And that she should be able to work it out for herself," Randal went on, amused. "*So much for not being a good teacher.*"

"I'm sure I'm overrated," she murmured. There was an expectant silence.

"I, on the other hand, *do* need to know the plan," Randal reminded, more seriously. *And you should be able to work it out for yourself too, being Phantom Leader…*

"The plan is what it always was, kill the bad guys, *save* the *slightly less than* bad guy and then reap the rewards of having duped the completely clueless population yet again," she answered, glibly.

"I thought *we were* the bad guys?" Randal jested.

"Well, we're *certainly* misunderstood."

Malla was next.

"We need to talk," he said, without preamble. "The debate is in three hours and *Oli*… he's *not himself.*" *That's good, frankly if he was anyone else it would make her life so much easier!*

"I'll get in when I get in," she responded, rudely. "Let's just say he wasn't the only one to have a bad night's sleep."

"What the hell happened between you two last night?" he asked, directly. "Oli refused to talk about it."

"We had a fight," she replied, seeing no reason in lying. "He has been trying to lure me into bed with him since last week and last night he overstepped the mark."

"*Ah…*"

Satiah paused, having braced herself for an accusation of lying or of something else. Nothing like that came though.

"He's… you *must* understand he's been having a hard time recently. I'm sure he didn't *mean* to do or say whatever it was…" Malla said. Satiah didn't know exactly *why* Malla was saying that. Maybe he was being protective of his friend, or just saying things to try to make sure *she* didn't do anything crazy. Malla needed her and might be worried what would happen if she left. She didn't interrupt.

"People skills are a work in progress with him. He's not *the greatest of touches* when it comes to women, as you probably now know." *Really?*

"We got into a bit of a shouting match," she stated, without going into the actual details. "I worry that some things were said that won't be easy to take back... *that goes for both of us*. What's been happening?"

"Well, he's not feeling at all well. After we arrived last night he'd started on a large collection of bottles and, long story short, he's feeling a little *tired* this morning," he sighed. She smiled at his wording.

"You mean he got wasted and now can barely talk?" she quantified.

"Yes," he allowed, sighing again.

"Give him water, painkillers, bread and something with energy. Settle the gut, numb the head and give the body artificial fuel until it's sorted itself out," she instructed, levelly. *Not that she'd ever had to do that...* "He should be better in a few hours."

"We *hope so*, a withdrawal could be crippling," Malla said. Satiah suddenly felt very hopeful. If he voluntarily withdrew from the election... that would solve all her problems. Well... *some of them.*

"He's considering *that*?" she queried, confused.

"*Kate* was," he explained. "Oli doesn't want to quit though."

"Good," she lied, seriously. "It would waste all of our efforts thus far if he did."

"That's what I said."

"I'll be in soon," she said, noticing how odd the place felt now that she was utterly alone again. Work almost seemed like a welcoming alternative at that moment, rather than to remain there and contemplate the gloom and failure in her apartment. She naturally didn't bother to call Lunell back.

---

When she got there, the atmosphere was already charged with the heat of stress and fear. Business as usual. Malla was the first to greet her.

"I think it might be an idea to stay away from Oli, at least until the debate is over," Malla cautioned.

"I have no intention of even looking at him again," she stated, sourly. He shot her a glance of concern.

"Well, I wouldn't go *that* far. What exactly did he do that...?"

"I'm not *really* in the mood to discuss it, *funnily enough*," she cut across him. "Law enforcement have failed to track the second vehicle down. They think he used cloak technology to cover his tracks." Malla went pale.

"That's *imposing* technology..."

"Indeed. I need to catch up with them today; can I rely on you and the others to protect Oli? The debate itself should be safe enough. *Brenda* will be there so the place will be like a fortress," she went on. He nodded.

"Shannon mentioned something you said about there being someone on the inside," he said, eyeing her levelly. "It reminded me of our previous conversation about Dean."

"Yes, like I said to her, it's *just* a theory..."

"A good one *now*, and I think it's more than a theory, as it explains how they keep managing to find us," he said, seriously. "Have you any idea who it could be?" Satiah was not surprised Shannon had told Malla, but annoyed nonetheless. Even if Malla *could* be trusted, what if someone had overheard their conversation? Then again, it might dissuade whoever it was from trying again, simply knowing that people knew he was there. Assuming it was a he. Still, it had been an interesting test to see what Shannon would do, and Malla already knew of her suspicions. Angel.

She reached the kitchen and Shannon was waiting for her... in the nicest possible way, of course.

"*What happened?*" she asked, all concern and worry on her face. Some of it might even be genuine.

"Oli had too much to drink after trying to make a pass at me," she replied, stiffly. "Have you checked the food?"

"*What?* Of course," she replied, quickly. "*What did he say?*"

"A load of very forgettable stuff. How is he?" she asked, going through her list of things to do.

"*Stuff*? What does *stuff* mean? Not great, he's been very odd towards me, *did you mention me*?" Shannon wanted to know.

"Well, as a matter of fact, *yes*," Satiah admitted, acting awkward. "He rattled me and basically I said *whatever it took* to get him to back off... *it wasn't pretty*. He asked for it though, in more ways than one!"

"Yes, I'm sure he did," Shannon agreed, apparently in honesty. Perhaps his rejection of her could work in Satiah's favour.

"He just wouldn't take '*this cannot happen*' for an answer," Satiah went on. Shannon looked distinctly uncomfortable now, starting to think about being partly responsible for this latest dispute.

"Was he drunk?" Shannon asked, a touch of hope in her voice.

"Not drunk enough to excuse him," Satiah growled. "He accused me of *pretending* to have a boyfriend just to mess him around." Shannon pulled a face, imagining the scene. "If there is *anything* you can do to get him to leave me alone I'd be *very* grateful."

There it was: *the appeal for help*. It was a masterpiece of manipulation. If Shannon had any lingering doubts about Satiah's honestly, they were swept away now. Shannon felt that Satiah had opened up completely to her and much to her shock... none of this seemed to be Satiah's fault. *Oli* had rejected Shannon before and now he was hurting *someone else*... so maybe all this was Oli's fault. Maybe Shannon had been deluding herself about him all this time. Maybe it should be *him* that she took down, not Satiah. How dare he treat people like this!?

"*I'll try*," Shannon promised, deeply thoughtful. Satiah gave her a grateful smile and then hugged her in apparent gratitude.

"*Thank you so much*, you've been *really* kind and supportive to me over this," Satiah lied, adeptly. "It's great to have someone I can trust to talk to about this." Shannon hugged her back, more than a little astonished and impressed with her own deviousness. She thought she was the one doing the manipulating... but only because Satiah had manipulated *her* into thinking that way.

"You won't do anything silly to Oli, will you? *We could be misjudging this*. I'd *hate* to put any ideas into your mind," smiled Satiah, cunningly.

"*Of course not*," Shannon smiled back, as they let go of one another.

Satiah went away, marching down the corridor with purpose. She had to get out there and find the Red Necromancer and Jinx. Lunell intercepted her in the corridor.

"*There* you are," he smiled, not in nice way.

"Not in the mood," she growled, barging past him. He followed.

"I need an update, *what happened*? Oli seems to be flagging somewhat," Lunell asked, excited. "I take it you *torpedoed* him last night?"

"Just concentrate on looking after him, he has the debate later," she dismissed, not even looking at him. He stopped following, glaring at her back as she departed. This was why he hated Phantoms... leaving aside the fact that she'd already physically attacked him once!

———✦✦✦✦✦✦———

Collorah sat up in bed as the message arrived, instantly alert. A set of coordinates. The woman in the bed next to him shifted in her sleep. Collorah didn't waste any time; he activated his computer and got the location of Oli's new campaign headquarters. He began using various systems to access layout plans and schematics to determine the obstacles he had to overcome. He'd had doubts that they'd be able to find out where Oli was hidden when the answer had not been fast in arriving. Then he checked that his new vehicle had arrived and that everything else was ready to go. Finally he got dressed, left the woman her fee and departed.

———✦✦✦✦✦✦———

"The best I can do is give you likely locations," Harrier said, sighing.

"I need something, things are getting tense and I need a result or they might start questioning my competence," Satiah said, calmly. She was driving along the traffic lanes, seeking her targets. Once, when she had been young, a Phantom trainer had once attested with great disbelief that Satiah seemed to have a sixth sense. An unknowable ability to find enemies with seemingly no clues available, or to see danger coming slightly faster than anyone else without a tip off. This time though, her ability seemed to have failed her. She had no idea where the danger was lurking. Well, she knew where a few were, but not the ones she needed to confront. She needed to go on the offensive in a big way, no matter how much it upset Randal.

Was this sudden rise in her aggression anything to do with the events of the previous evening? Well, it *was* possible.

Her mood was dark... putting it mildly. Carl wasn't answering her calls which wasn't helping her temper either. If she could just get him to *sit and listen*, she was confident she could explain it clearly. She had come to the conclusion, on the other hand, that *in a way* this might be a good thing. The first fight was a sign that their relationship was *maturing*... it was just bad timing. *What if he never came back?* She punched the controls savagely as she pulled into a parking area. She got out of the craft and went into the living areas beyond. Inside was another apartment that she owned. She entered, went into the kitchen area, pushed away the table and began to tear up the floor. She removed four metal panels and dragged up a large black holdall. It was heavy and, because of the angle she was at, she groaned as she brought it down onto the table.

Greased and preserved, there to lie in state - perhaps for decades unused - one of her favourite carbines rested. She had come to love the smell of that preserving lubricant over the years. She had several identical weapons dotted around various locations in which she might one day have to use to hide herself. Every agent did it; there was nothing special in preparing for your own witch-hunt. After what had happened with Vourne, she had been on the cusp of fleeing into the shadows, never to return. That time, however, she'd got lucky and no one had realised that she was involved. She opened the bag and stared down at the dulled metal. There it was... *the Repressor*. Well, it was known in all good catalogues as the GPR15... General purpose machine laser. But she called it the Repressor. At 3000 BPM (bolts per minute) this cable-fed, double-barrelled bad boy could squeeze out 50 individual bolts a second.

Weighing in at 140kg (310 pounds) it had a recoil-ratio of 78/100 making it the heaviest thing Satiah could handle. Only the PP7 had a higher recoil-ratio for hand-held arms. This placed the GPR15 as the second largest (30inch – 762mm) double barrelled machine laser in current manufacture. The cable-fed design meant you had to carry the battery or *munition-compass* separately. It could provide continuous fire for 80 minutes. Anything higher was usually found deployed on the wings of fighter craft. After making sure it was all there, she hauled the bag over her back and departed, after leaving the place as she had found it. She deposited the bag in the back of her craft and strapped it down before returning to the driver's seat and taking off again.

If she was stopped by law enforcement then, Phantom agent or not, she'd have a fun time explaining that thing on her backseat.

Her earpiece went off and she answered. It was an animated Zax.

"Is that mechanical monster what I think it is?" she asked, interested.

"What do you think it is?" Satiah asked, carelessly.

"Something in equal parts illegal and dangerous?"

"*My, my, young lady, you must be a Phantom or something with observation skills like that*," Satiah drawled, sarcastically. "Why don't you work on giving me a direction *to point it in*?"

"So Harrier turned up nothing? For someone named after a bird of prey, he's not *great* at spotting things is he?" Zax cheeked, rhetorically. She had a sharp tongue, that was for sure. *Very* disrespectful of authority. Satiah had to agree in this case though, she couldn't wait for Rainbow to get back from his holiday or honeymoon or *liaison* or *whatever the hell he was doing*.

"It's worth noting, however, that *he* is still new, *not unlike your good self*, young lady. And if you think names are so important, *think again*, *I* was named after a Queen from some ancient civilisation. Apparently I am the daughter of a natural satellite too, which makes me wonder just *how* I was supposed to have been conceived." The only reason Satiah actually knew about that was because Carl had sent her a message telling her so, some time back. Zax didn't ask what her own name meant or why she had been named. Registered officially as an orphan, *there could have been no other way*, the Phantom allocation system named her Zax. Satiah knew it was a type of primitive hatchet and… she was no orphan.

"I could *totally* see you as a barbarian Queen," went on Zax, casually. "Screaming down wrathfully at your warrior hordes."

"Try *looking* for my enemies while keeping the *screaming* down to a minimum, please," Satiah reminded, unable to stop herself smiling a bit.

"Am I allowed to ask if you're okay?" Zax asked, more softly. She did have that compassionate side too, Satiah mulled, and she'd have to do something about that. A sense of humour was one thing, empathy however...

"You're *allowed*, certainly, but you should know better than to expect a genuine answer."

"I... *Satiah, I've got a match*! *Your red friend is back*... he's coming from close by where the previous office was..." Zax began, excitement back in her voice. Satiah braked hard, making the craft behind her swerve and hoot to avoid her. She spun around and joined the opposing lane at twice the legal speed.

"Get me to him," she growled, concentrating hard on the traffic.

"...Triangulating..."

"*Come on, faster*," Satiah barked, overtaking over the top recklessly.

"Sending you an image of the vehicle he's using, going through records to find the *previous owner*... He's moving towards *the new office Satiah*, I think he has found out where Oli went," Zax said, very serious now. "Coming in, second lane to *your right*!" Satiah looked up whilst bringing up an image of the craft he was using. There it was, green and battered looking, the transporter drifted past as if completely innocent.

"You're *sure* it's him, I'm about to open fire on him?" Satiah warned, as she swung in right behind him.

"Give me a second," Zax requested. Satiah activated the lasers in the vehicle and they inched out from the bodywork subtly.

Collorah was no amateur and had seen Satiah's approach. She'd drawn attention because of the speed of her arrival. Had it been anyone else he wouldn't have taken further notice, but he recognised her from when he'd watched her trapped in the back of one of his previous vehicles.

"*You again*," Collorah grunted, as he glanced in the mirror thoughtfully. He'd done a scan and could see that it was Satiah although he didn't know who she was - but he knew she was a threat. He'd been planning to deploy a tiny insect to act as his 'fly on the wall' in the new location. He'd not expected to be detected so quickly, and least of all by *her*. Somehow he must have left a clue somewhere, but in a way it didn't matter. Then he spotted the lasers on the front of her transporter and smirked knowingly.

"*I don't think so,*" he said primly, and veered wildly away.

"No need Zax, I suppose he must have a guilty conscience," Satiah growled, taking off after Collorah. There was no point in trying to talk, no use in trying to arrest him… she targeted the engines and opened fire. If she couldn't destroy him she hoped to at least cripple the transporter. She tested his shields with an accurate volley. Collorah went on the evasive, picked up speed and barrel rolled erratically. Then he turned left, flying directly towards a building. He opened fire, using his own concealed lasers, and smashed through a window. He kept firing until he passed out the other side of the building, literally flying straight through it. Satiah followed skilfully. Still under construction, the floor was unoccupied but the supporting girders were in place, creating rock solid hazards for her to avoid.

Collorah joined another traffic lane, weaving in and out quickly to see if she could keep up. Law enforcement would arrive at some stage, that was a certainty. It would make getting away even harder. Collorah initiated a pre-prepared plan and plunged downward, leaving the traffic behind. Satiah capably followed. He branched off to the right and into a subway shaft, equally curious and thrilled when Satiah went in after him, ready for anything. The subway system was mainly for power cables, and other essential passage infrastructure. There was room for vehicles as obviously maintenance had to get in there somehow. Access was restricted but hardly well enforced.

Collorah had already prepared the location he had in mind for an ambush or, at least, an easy getaway. He decelerated hard, knowing she was less than eight seconds behind him. He set the self destruct unit and then sprinted for the cover of some nearby power conduits. Satiah swung in and, upon seeing the craft, halted very quickly. Collorah slipped on some dark glasses to protect his eyes from the flash of the explosion. Annoyingly Satiah didn't get out. A second later, the vehicle exploded violently, sending fire and debris out in multiple directions, but left Satiah's craft completely undamaged. She'd not even lowered her shields, possibly anticipating his trap. That made sense as she had known him to use vehicles to kill. He awaited her next move: he couldn't get a shot at her so long as she stayed inside, which is why he presumed that she was not coming out.

Satiah hadn't actually anticipated the mined craft. As she'd come in and stopped, she'd been midway through a scan of his vehicle when it had detonated. Her shields had saved her. She sat there, letting out a gasp of breath in surprise and relief. She ran a curtailed systems check to ensure she was still capable of getting away and that, if there was any damage, she would know about it before anything could catch her out. Beginning a new scan, this time for her target, she chose to remain inside. There at least she was shielded from attack.

She peered out while she waited, into the shadows. He might have already got away but her instinct told her that this man would be waiting for her. He was bold... and a very good shot. He would know she was alone as she couldn't call for help if she needed to. Zax had fallen silent and Satiah began to realise that the power oscillations from the nearby piping was interfering with her signals. Nothing. Not a blip. No signs of heat or life. Satiah was not convinced; he'd already given away that he had access to the technology required to hide craft from scanners... why not himself? She would have to force the issue. She deactivated the shields, opened the door and slipped out.

Using the bulk of her own transporter as cover she crouched there and drew her pistol carefully. She listened intently even though she didn't expect to hear anything. The hum from the power units was noisy enough to hide the smallest of shuffles in any case. Collorah trained his rifle on the craft, knowing where she was. Through his sights he could see the shadow of her head on the ground. He waited, the excitement making it hard for him to control his breathing. Satiah prepared her grapple-gun and looked around. Not far above and ahead of her was a narrow walkway that led into the darkness of an inspection hatch. Under her own vehicle she threw a distress flare, making it bounce and roll out on the other side. There was a violent crashing noise as, believing it to be a grenade, Collorah fired. In that split second she fired her grapple-gun, and flew swiftly up and over the railing. Another shot narrowly missed her shoulder as she dived to the floor behind cover.

Breathing hard, she sat up with a triumphant grin on her face. She'd *finally* found someone willing to fight on her terms. She rose into a crouch and began work on the hatch entry pad. Collorah hadn't stayed put. Even if she hadn't pinpointed his position by now, it was rarely a good idea to remain in the same spot for too long in a fight like this. Slipping the rifle across his back, he produced his eight barrelled pistol and edged along into the darker shadows. Satiah emerged silently from the narrow tunnel that she had followed in amongst the conduits. Each unit was three times her height and about four metres across. Ideal cover. Trouble was… *he* could be anywhere.

She swung out from cover, pistol raised and ready. More conduits and no targets. She slipped to the side once more to avoid becoming a target herself and crouched low. From her thigh pocket she produced a thin metal tube. She flung it at a nearby power unit. With a clang and a clatter it struck the unit and fell to the floor noisily. She waited, hoping it would attract his attention.

"You'll have to do much better than that, agent lady!" Collorah shouted, from somewhere. Satiah looked around and tried to estimate where he was.

"My mistake!" she yelled back. "Why are you trying to kill Oli McAllister?" She didn't know why he'd chosen to talk to her but she could use that to get close enough to kill him. She suspected he would guess what she was doing, but it was the easiest way right now.

"Is *that* his name? I had wondered." Silence. She looked all around as she crept between the next set of conduits.

"What's your name?" she asked, her eyes narrowing as she focussed on a distant shadow.

"Collorah," was the growl, in response. She swung around, shocked by the closeness of the voice. "Yours?"

"Satiah," she admitted, freely. It was a common enough name for her to get away with telling him that.

"Nice," he replied, seeming to come from the opposite direction this time. At the last moment she ducked between the units again, breaking into a sprint just as he opened fire. Blasts struck several things where she had been and a few even followed her on their ricochet paths. She slipped into a new hiding place.

"Sorry!" he called. *"Are you all right?"* Before she could answer he fired again, this time striking the wall right beside her. In a split second she took in the eight marks of glistening impacts and realised his gun had eight barrels.

She spun, coming around the other side of the power unit and returned fire. Collorah leapt backwards to avoid the shots, though part of his shoulder armour was charred badly. Satiah took the opportunity to change her position and concealed herself behind a different conduit. She wondered how long it would take for the maintenance androids to turn up to fix all this damage. Before long it *had* to start registering, or even affecting some of the things it supported.

"What's the matter, Satiah? Don't you want to come out and play with me?" Collorah chided. "You good girls are all the same, never any fun!"

"I can double whatever it is they're paying you to go away, whoever they are?" she offered, knowing he would be creeping up on her. Of course he wasn't going to namedrop, who would?

"What if I'm doing this for free?"

She leapt out and opened fire. Her shots slammed into the wall and the conduits, sending sparks flying and smoke rising. He wasn't there! She rolled as a barrage of shots came from somewhere further back in the darkness.

"We could chase each other around here *all day* and I don't think anyone is coming to help you," Collorah called.

"What makes you think I *need* any help?" she answered, rigging up a mine on the wall at ankle height.

"It's the smart thing to do when you're so *clearly* overmatched." She scowled, knowing he was trying to provoke her and irritated that he was succeeding.

"Who is behind you?" she asked, changing the subject.

"Can't say, sorry."

Satiah darted carefully to yet another new hiding place, the dim blue and purple lighting making the shadows even harder to see through. Cautiously she peered around to see back the way she had come from. Nothing. She slipped around to look the other way when the mine she had planted went off. Collorah shouted in pain. Satiah spun and opened fire, pelting the area with multiple shots. The conduit exploded a few seconds later and Satiah backed away, fearful of a chain reaction. An alarm sounded and nitrogen gas began flooding in to suppress any fires. Satiah instantly slipped her breathing device into her mouth to prevent asphyxia. It would be several minutes before the gas cleared. She approached the area again, gambling that if Collorah *had* survived the mine, he would be too preoccupied to counter a further attack from her.

She arrived, swiftly covering the area. He'd gone! A clang from above her gave the only clue as she just caught sight of a shaft hatch clanging shut. Using her grapple-gun she rose in the air to the hatchway and blasted it open. Collorah heard the shooting from further down the ventilation system. He was trying to get away now. The mine had wounded him, badly enough to make him realise he'd underestimated Satiah. He wouldn't make that mistake again… always assuming she didn't catch him. He activated a tiny box on the roof of the shaft and then continued on. He could hear her crawling along after him. He reached the exit he'd chosen earlier, and kicked it open, revealing the craft waiting below for him. He coughed as the nitrogen began to catch up with him.

Satiah, hurriedly following, was encouraged when she found his blood inside the shaft. He *had* been injured, as she had suspected when he started to run. She had hoped the mine would get him, but if he had been careful in his approach and armoured then it might have missed him altogether. She spotted the tiny box he had left on the roof of the shaft and blasted it. Black sticky webbing shot out directly across the shaft, effectively impeding her. She swore, pulled her blade out from her boot and began to try to cut her way through. She stopped when she heard a craft speeding away and her shoulders slumped.

"*Brilliant!*" she hissed through her teeth. She wasn't empty handed, however, and returned to collect the blood he had left behind.

## Operation Selector

Deetee had surpassed himself. From the moment he'd first awoken he'd known that this would be a wonderful day. Dressed in a silvery green suit, his golden hair as artificially radiant as ever, he made his way down from control onto the set. A technician passed him his earpiece as he went in.

"How are we doing, Sasha?" he asked, to check that it was working. Microphones were one of the few things in the whole of sentient creation that seemed to have never ending faults and problems. Too loud, too quiet, too scratchy, too muddy, and, worst of all, they had a habit of staying on at all the wrong moments.

"We can hear you perfectly up here," she replied, from the director's room. "The candidates are on their way, they will be there within the hour." Deetee smiled, this time for real. It was *almost* indistinguishable from his media friendly phoney one. It was, however, just a little more crooked. He could see the audience starting to arrive.

Each member had been carefully chosen. Each had had a background check; even their species, gender, race and age judiciously designated. The questions were provided for the debate, to ensure nothing untoward occurred – the correct impression had to be given to the viewer, of course. Too many humans on the show would only anger the 'equal-representation-brigade'. Those who were actually real members of the public had been drugged to ensure they remained docile enough to be managed. The others were actors provided by the government. These actors would be the ones who were meant to ask the questions. Deetee's job was to ensure that the right question was asked at the right time, and that the delegate's answers were suitably trimmed or manipulated into the most pleasing result possible.

He had been told to give Brenda as much support as possible, and to try to encumber the other two as best he could, without making it too obvious he was doing either. It was the job he had been born for. He would be the very soul of honest and sincere journalism. When it was all over, it would be time for a good rosiner of something. Dreaming of success, wealth and luxury, Deetee obambulated around the set in a leisurely manner. He always took a keen interest in who was filming with him. Not because he cared, but because he needed to spot potential rivals. As he roamed the place, he would catch pugils of conversations and get a sense of the vibe. Expectant would be how he would describe it. Expectant with just a dab of enforced professional disinterest.

That was when he caught sight of the one man he respected. Well, *admired* perhaps; he didn't really respect anyone: the media-mogul *Royston Mulac*. One of the richest beings in the cosmos and member of the shadow government, Royston was a man of power. He was tall, broad and had a mane of grey hair. His eyes, which were also grey, were sharp and attentive. He was making straight for Deetee, a regal looking red cloak billowing out behind him as he approached. Deetee bowed his head deferentially and gave him his most sycophantic smile. Royston barely acknowledged the look.

"Deetee," he said, his voice as rich as he looked. "I understand that you have been chosen to present the debate?"

"I have that privilege," Deetee nodded. They began to walk along together.

"I'm going to assume you have already been given your standard restrictions and reminders?" Royston asked, in a way that made it hard to tell if he was being rhetorical or not. Deetee grunted so that it needn't matter which.

"There is a lot more than usual riding on this. It was a mistake to give the public a referendum but *here we are*. Should there be *any* mention of it, or inference to it, you are to steer well clear of *anything* to do with the Vourne conspiracy, is that understood?"

"*That* has been cited by the director, rest assured it will not be a problem," Deetee nodded.

"Keep the weir from bursting with us and you will find yourself elevated considerably *very soon*," Royston replied, with significance.

Deetee's eyes gleamed with gluttony.

"I think we understand each other," Deetee purred. They laughed quietly in conspiratorial tones.

"Understand this too," Royston went on. They turned to face one another. Voices low, expression serious. "Brenda Watt *has* to win this election, *whatever the cost*. If she does, we will have decades of prosperity. *If she doesn't...*" He trailed off and his face hardened. He didn't need to elaborate further. It was Brenda or no one.

"We're still trying to find out *who* leaked that tax document," Deetee mused, pretending to be saddened. "Whoever it was made a very professional job out of it."

"It is clear someone out there wants Oli McAllister to win," Royston growled. He felt that the public's unusual reaction had been predicted by whoever had leaked the document and that it was all part of someone's plan to make sure that Oli defeated Brenda in the election.

"The rumour is that it was *his brother* who leaked the document and that the surge in popularity for Oli was an accident," Deetee speculated.

"*Nonsense*, Sam McAllister wouldn't have allowed anything to jeopardise his own campaign. No, whoever did this had their own agenda, and projected what would happen to Sam and Oli when the obviously faked document was leaked," Royston guessed. His eyes narrowed cunningly. "*Yes... very clever.*"

"To predict that kind of swing would require someone with impressive analytical skills," Deetee said, stating the obvious. "No one foresaw it coming at all."

"The computers apparently did which is why I'm here," he replied, gravely. "Almost everyone was prepared to wave it off. Eight percent over the safety margin didn't seem too bad at the time of prediction. Now this leaked document has appeared it proves that the computer was correct in its threat assessment."

The irony - that it was because of their own interference in the election that it had worked out that way - was completely lost on Royston. Then again, that was because he didn't know that it was Satiah who'd leaked the document, nor did he see that it hadn't been her goal to promote Oli... but to destroy him.

"You're going to be watching the live debate *in person*?" Deetee asked, hiding his nervousness well.

"Of course," he replied, smiling knowingly. "Things often run more *smoothly* when I'm around."

"It will be a pleasure to perform," Deetee said, recovering well.

"I'm sure it will."

"I'm pretty sure Brenda's got this one in the bag," Deetee said, without conviction.

"I was certain she had it last week, but now I'm concerned enough to start taking action myself," Royston replied. "It could be a blip. Elections, *when off the leash*, are known to be rather unreliable. That's another topic I would like you to leave out too... *the vote rigging.*" Well, it would be a little insensitive...

"That one should be easy enough," Deetee concurred.

---

"Are you feeling better now?" Kate asked, as she entered Oli's office. He'd been dressed up and prepared as much as possible but his eyes gave away some of the suffering he was going through.

"I messed up..." he grunted.

"No one expects you to give up; it is after all why you are here..."

"... *with Satiah*," he clarified. Kate let out a breath.

"There will be time enough to concentrate on that after *this*. It's not the final hurdle, but it's the biggest. Once today is over... it's pretty much up to the public," Kate said, trying to bolster him up as usual.

"I acted *so* stupidly," he hissed, rubbing his face with his hands. Kate would normally be fascinated by this, but today she had too many other things to worry about. Not least her own life.

"Would you like me to talk to her?" she offered. She wasn't sure she wanted to get involved, but she needed to get him to perk up. "I'm *sure* I can help."

"...I don't know," he shrugged, helpless. Kate almost rolled her eyes.

"Remember, *together we can achieve anything*!" she smiled, echoing his own rallying call. He gave a small smile accompanied with a huffing noise. "As long as you show that you *care*, in a way, you're doing your best right there."

"I can't stop thinking about her," he confessed, shaking his head.

"I advise you to *try* unless you want them to walk all over you," Kate warned, getting serious. "No one will be there to back you up this time."

Malla and Shannon entered with Lunell in tow.

"We're ready to go," Malla stated, a little gruffly. How many unsettling journeys had *that* been a precursor to?

"How are you feeling, sir?" Lunell asked, all concern and professional sympathy. Shannon said nothing, she just crossed her arms. As Oli looked up, he made eye contact with her briefly. "Much better now," he allowed. It was true... in a way. His head no longer felt like it had an ants' nest inside it. Shannon stared imperiously down at him, still inwardly trying to decide what she would do. She knew Oli well enough to know that he really was all over the place. Whatever Satiah had said to him the night before had really got to him. Her feelings towards him were so scrambled at that moment that she couldn't honestly tell if she loved or hated him. Could it not be both?

Malla and Lunell led the way to the transporter, which was waiting outside. Shannon, Kate and a few others followed them. Suddenly, Oli felt so old, so world-weary. Did he cause such revulsion in Satiah that she would try to pretend that a total stranger was her fictional partner? He knew he was hardly young and he supposed it was inevitable that he would lose his desirability. It was one of the few things he really feared... getting older. He knew he couldn't escape it and he knew it was no different for anyone else but that didn't change how he felt. It wasn't that he felt he was running out of time and that he still had things to do, though that *was* a part of it. It wasn't even the fact that death was at the end of it. It was the idea of no longer being young. Like he'd somehow missed out on something.

Linctus Lotion was a godsend. Before its invention, humans typically lived up to the age of one hundred or less. Now, they could manage twice that, sometimes two hundred and twenty. However, the battle to live longer was never over. Somehow it never quite seemed like you had long enough. He, just like mostly everyone else, had been injected at birth to maximise his lifespan. It was common practise, had been for centuries. It maintained youthful looks and bodies for about one hundred and eighty years. Subtle signs often crept through such as wrinkles and greying hair, but the body itself usually maintained a level of fitness otherwise impossible. The lotion was administered shortly after birth along with all the other immunities, notably that of cancer. Nevertheless, looks didn't equal feelings. Inside, he was feeling the pressure of the years, almost like a weight over his shoulders. Threatening to drag him down.

The ride to the area where the debate was to take place was a short and silent one. Without Satiah around, Lunell and the others were on high alert. Kate, after her recent scare, was almost back to normal. That might not have been the case were she aware that Lunell, the man sitting next to her, was the man who'd tried to kill her.

Watching the skyscrapers glide past should have been calming or at least distracting, but Oli was having trouble focussing on anything. He forced himself to think about the debate and *only* the debate. Once that was over then he could deal with everything else. He made himself think about Sally. She had always been his inspiration for inner strength. He'd be needing all the help he could get.

---

"I've got him," Octutin murmured, as he eyed the screen. Oli's banner was clearly displayed on the outside of the craft. It had to be for various reasons: identification for on-site security, for one; a focal point for his supporters, for another. That and, due to a little known clause in legislation, it was illegal to paint over it or cover it up for diplomatic reasons.

"As we agreed, track it back to the location," Jinx replied, impatiently.

"Deploying tracker," he grunted back. Octutin send the tiny robot spiralling off the ground and into the air. It moved fast and finally stuck to the underside of Oli's transporter. There was too much security for them to attempt anything then, but when the debate was over, he'd head back to his new base. When he did, they would find out where that was and plan their next move.

---

With a jangle of bracelets and other gawkish jewellery, Marisa waved an admonishing hand at Collorah.

"*No!* Don't you *dare* bleed on this panelling, it will cost a fortune to clean!" she ordered, haughtily.

"My apologies," he growled, sarcastically.

"*Help him!*" she spat at her android. It juddered over to him as he sat at a table by the entrance. "*What happened?*"

"The *PAI* happened," he stated, with a small amount of accusation in his tone. That silenced her.

"The... are you *sure?*" she asked, frightened now.

"Positive." He pulled away his armour, revealing a bloody smear beneath. Satiah's charge had wounded him. Three pieces of shrapnel had gone inside him, one dangerously close to his kidney. The other two had just sliced their way through and straight out the other side.

"Do they know?" she asked, immediately thinking about damage control.

"They knew who I am but nothing about you, we actually had a nice little chat before she turned nasty," he muttered, wincing as he was injected.

"She?"

"The PAI agent. *Satiah*, she said her name was, although that was probably a lie," he told her.

"Probably," she agreed. "Tell me everything." He did. "So they were onto you the moment you made a move on Oli's new headquarters?" He nodded. She rested her chin on her fist thoughtfully.

"Their involvement in *his* protection is bizarre... they *should be* protecting *Brenda*," Marisa stated, puzzled.

"That would have been my assumption too," he smirked. "This Satiah is not just lucky, she's good. I had a run in with her before and couldn't understand *how* she managed to survive the vacuum of space without a safeguard. Well, a *visible* safeguard."

"Some special *device?*" she presumed, as if it was that simple.

"Name *one*," he requested, raising an eyebrow. She scowled, unable to.

"*Do I look like a technician?* So *she did the impossible*, is that what you're telling me?" she scoffed.

"Nothing's impossible," he dismissed, shrugging. "I just don't know *how* she did it. The point is, she is playing the role of guard dog for Oli. I can deal with that, but we might have another problem."

"You mean whoever leaked that document?" she confirmed. "How is that a problem of *ours*? Whoever did it evidently wants the same thing we do. *Oli out of the race.*"

"*Do they?*" he asked, with significance. She made a face at him.

"Just say it, I'm not into prolonging suspense," she muttered.

"What if they *knew* this would happen when they released that document? What if they *want* Oli to win and they...?"

"It won't *matter* if he is dead which is *why* I hired you, *if you recall?*" she interrupted, levelly.

"I'm just saying it might get complicated," he warned, as his wounds healed completely.

"It can be as complicated as you like, so long as he ends up dead."

---

"She would never do that," Randal lied, adeptly. "Lunell must have misheard or *misunderstood somehow*. Satiah never threatens people like that."

"That's not what Lunell tells me," Scott went on. "He also said something about her *tampering with his vehicle.*" *Please tell me that's a euphemism.* Randal smothered a grin.

"Good Lord," Randal said, deadpanning disingenuously. "I'm sure wires are crossed somewhere, but I will have a word with her."

"Be sure that you do. She's endangering the whole operation," he snapped, sulkily. With that he cut off and Randal chuckled to himself. *O Satiah, you bad girl, stop bothering the PAI. They don't like it and you're making them cry.* He'd recorded the whole conversation and sent it to Satiah to cheer her up a bit. Randal had no problem with anything she'd done - *yet*. The disruptions for Law Enforcement were regrettable but necessary, and he trusted her to do her job.

A light on his communicator came on and he knew... danger was on its way. He sat up, as he was in bed and his quick eyes saw a flicker of movement pass by the window. He slipped his pistol out and wandered almost lazily over to the side of the door where he waited. He knew this attack, as it was so ham-fisted and had been allowed to progress this far, was not the real one. He watched as someone, very carefully, bypassed the lock on his door from the outside. The door slid open and a woman edged in, pistol in her hand. She was not one of his so he stunned her with a shot to the head. She collapsed, unconscious. By 'one of his', he was of course talking about operatives, not lovers.

"Phantom Mensa," he said into his communicator, quietly.

"Randal," came a cold voice, in response. Mensa always omitted either Randal's formal title *Phantom Leader* or the standard *sir*. It was he who had sent the warning signal alerting Randal to the approach of his enemy.

"The water is coming through as you said, but now I need another bucket. *Do you have one?*" Randal asked, keeping his voice light.

"You've got another drip," Mensa said. It wasn't a question, it was a *statement,* which meant Randal had been right. She was just the decoy and someone else was moving in to complete the task.

"Whereabouts?" A shot went off outside and Randal tensed. A man staggered through the door, smoke coming from his back. With a groan he collapsed onto the unconscious woman.

Mensa ambled through next; gun in hand, his trademark cruel smile on his lips.

"There," he growled, pointing at the corpse. He noticed that the woman was still breathing. "Why did you leave her alive?"

"You know how overly sentimental I am," Randal joked.

"*All clear!*" called Jess, from outside.

"Thank you, Jess," Mensa said, over his shoulder. "What are you plans for *her?*"

"There's no point in interrogation, I already know all the answers, sedate her and put her on a long haul flight to somewhere on the fringes," Randal ordered. "Make it clear she will not be considered a target when she comes back, provided she doesn't do anything stupid." Mensa nodded.

"Very considerate of you," he growled, nudging the corpse off the woman with his foot. "And Snell?"

"Nothing yet," Randal said, shrugging. "If he had any sense he would have stopped this long before now. I just want to see what he tries next. He pushes again, I'll warn him. A third time and he's as dead as that guy."

"Three strikes," Mensa nodded, amused. "Always *so fair*, aren't you?"

"*I try to be.*"

---

"Collorah," Harrier repeated, as he thought about it. Satiah leaned against the wall and stared up into the sky thoughtfully.

"What do you have?" she asked, interested. "This guy is tough, I need to know everything." She'd sent the blood sample to Harrier who was now going through the system to find anything useful. Satiah wondered whether, if she'd given it to Zax, she might have been faster.

"Got it," Harrier replied, after a few more seconds. "Sending you the profile... wow, this guy has some record. Over three thousand confirmed kills..."

"Lunell been up to anything?" she asked next.

"Not that I've *noticed*," Harrier replied. "He's pretty much been doing what you told him to." Satiah frowned, mulling over what was really going on.

She slipped back into her craft and began a leisurely climb from the rooftop she had been waiting on. She moved into traffic and then made her way to the centre for the debate. She had no intention of going inside though; she would wait by the vehicles and study the information on her latest adversary in peace.

"Satiah?" Zax's voice sounded in her ear. "I have some news for you." She sounded... *excited*. Then again, she often did. That was what youths were meant to sound like.

"Good," Satiah allowed, her outwardly easy-going demeanour hiding her inner impatience well.

"Carl is back, he's back in your apartment, bag and all," Zax stated. "I can see him on the camera."

The relief flooded through Satiah and she let out a breath she'd not been aware she was holding in. He'd come back! He was safe! This didn't mean she was out of the woods, by any stretch of the imagination, but it seemed to be a positive step. Zax, however, needed to learn to hide her feelings and maintain poise throughout anything. So…

"O really, *about time*," Satiah answered, with great dispassion. Zax was taken in by this.

"You don't seem very surprised, did he call you?" Zax asked, a little annoyed that her bombshell had apparently been a dud.

"No," Satiah replied, lightly.

"So… you *knew all along* he would come crawling back?" Zax asked, a little put out now. Satiah smiled.

"I did not."

Zax realised she was being played.

"If you don't want to talk about it, you only had to say," she said, a little stuffy. Satiah's smile spread into a grin. Zax was still fishing; only now, she was pretending to be offended.

"I know," Satiah answered, still irritatingly ephemeral in her responses.

"So… you *do* want to talk about it?" Zax pressed, trying to dig further.

"I'm sending you the file Harrier retrieved for me earlier," Satiah said, changing the subject. "You can work on a strategy to help me deal with Collorah." Silence. Zax was now trying to get Satiah to be the one to ask questions. Satiah smiled, seeing right through it. "That will be all." She disconnected casually.

As much fun as playing mind games with Zax was, Satiah was as concerned about Carl's return as she was relieved. She'd wanted it to happen, there was no doubting that but… *why* hadn't he called first? She accessed her security system to check and he was indeed there, watching a programme, apparently at ease. For a moment she just watched him. She then decided to approach him with caution and be ready for accusations. She remembered his anger and how much it had surprised her. She'd seen him frustrated, annoyed and impatient plenty of times but never *angry*. The question returned: what could she possibly have done wrong? *It's my fault. I should have not have presumed... I'm sorry. I may not be enough for you but I'm not ... I'm going home.* Those were his last words to her, she remembered them exactly. What had he missed out? What had he been trying to tell her?

Did their relationship have a future? Had it *ever* had one? Leaving aside the argument about her career not being exactly ideal for an affair with anyone, she considered which was more important to her: Carl or her job. She reasoned that, in a way, it was pointless thinking all this through without Carl to talk to about it. They needed to discuss where they were going and what they were doing. She knew she'd been putting off conversations like that for a reason. And it's not like they'd been together very long, a few months, tops. Was she overthinking all this? Was it just an argument or did it signify deeper things? Didn't they always? Satiah was not someone who spent much time thinking about, never mind discussing, her feelings.

One thing was for sure, she needed to put all this out of her mind and concentrate on her task. She wouldn't get any answers if she was dead. She pulled into a parking position on the roof of the building that was accommodating the debate. She registered with the android on duty, then stayed in the vehicle. She studied Collorah's record thoroughly and then pondered on another question she'd been thinking about. Was Collorah anything to do with angel? She'd noticed early on that he had some kind of tattoo which resembled an angel's wing on his left forearm. It was old, probably decades old, but it was there. It *could be* coincidence. She could find no evidence of anyone calling him angel, or him using that word as an alias, in the file. That didn't mean it hadn't happened though.

It seemed equally unrelated to Sam and Mark and their plans for Oli. She scowled and looked out across the skyscrapers for a moment. She'd heard nothing from Ash about that book yet. She should continue working on that review for Randal - she'd almost finished it - and it would be one less thing to think about if she completed it now. She returned to her place in the review she'd written concerning the

*Blue-Jurnn incident.* After re-reading the crucial points a few times to make sure she'd not left anything out, she at last was able to reach a verdict. It was *being error.* Yet the mistake was not with the personnel *running* the power station. It was with *the people in charge of running the test.* They should have learned from the shortcomings that they uncovered in the previous plant.

They *should* have made sure that no such failings existed at Blue-Jurnn before commencing the test. It may not have prevented the accident, yet they'd clearly not done all they could before the test had started. So the blame would fall on the management who were still alive. She wondered what the other reviewers would say, even though she was sure that no matter what anyone else said, it wouldn't sway her. She glanced up from her screens as another ship came in to land and then returned her attention to them. Once she was happy with her closing statement, she sent it off to Randal with a satisfied sigh. That was when she found the recording he had sent her earlier. She listened into the conversation between Randal and Scott with a snigger or two.

Randal called her at that moment and she answered.

"I've done the review and I've just heard that little chat you sent to me," she told him, by way of greeting.

"The first attempt was made on me earlier," Randal stated, without mirth. She didn't waste time asking after his welfare as he was clearly well enough to talk to her.

"I see," she said, frowning. "What action are you taking?"

"For now *none*, though if he tries it again that will change," Randal asked, still grim.

"Okay, consider me *warned*," she said, in a forbidding tone of voice. Another call was coming in, this one ranked as UU: *utmost urgent*.

"Have to go," she said, instantly cutting off.

"Satiah, it's me!" Zax was saying, rattled. "There's someone else trying to get into *your apartment*! *I think it's the PAI!*" Satiah's heart felt like it had somehow forced itself into her throat, making her feel literally sick with fear.

Royston entered the director's area, which overlooked the stage where the debate was to be held. Several other people were already inside, working on various things. One of them was one of Brenda's aides. He nodded to her and she approached.

"How is *our champion*?" he asked, interested. No one had voiced concern about her yet, but it never did any harm to double-check. There could always be a first time…

"She's doing great sir, her usual self," she assured him. "I was actually going to ask permission to *stop* medicating her, I really don't think it's needed except in times of high stress."

Royston considered.

"I will take that suggestion to the others," he smiled, satisfied. "I think you're right actually. She's so clueless, she's perfect. We must remember to take good care of her." By *care of her* he meant: continue to only let her know what *we* want her to know.

"Here is the script you asked for earlier," she smiled, pleased that he agreed. She handed him a thick metal folder. "Every question and every one of Brenda's answers. Obviously we couldn't write in the other candidates' answers though…"

"*Obviously*," he chuckled. "*Yes…*" He flicked through it casually. "Very impressive."

"Perhaps in future, *with your permission*, we could even control what the opponents say. That is, if you all, in your *wisdom*, decide to go down the route of *not* adjusting the voting figures. We could create our own opponents," she suggested. Royston thought about it.

"We'll look into that," he allowed. "*That's enough bootlicking*," he rebuked her mildly with a wink, not really meaning it. She smiled seductively up at him.

"How accurate is this script?" he asked next.

"The *questions* are verbatim. Deetee and Brenda are liable to wander on and off the exact wording; however, the kernels will be the same," she mused.

"Yes," he nodded, again pleased with everything. Despite the chaos in which this plan was made - *the chaos being the infamous Vourne conspiracy* - things were working out far better than he had envisioned.

A tall man with close-cropped dark hair and a well kept short beard entered. Wearing the white uniform of a Commander, his identity was evident: Merrick Tool. He was one of the five leaders of the military forces of the Coalition. There were four commanders in total and one Admiral. These individuals were also a part of the shadow government. All of this was neatly concealed by the Revised Sanctioned Confidences Statute 58115. Everyone had heard of this act but few grasped its true depths and connotations. He approached Royston and they shook hands.

"How is everything proceeding? Everyone back at the base is keeping their cards close to their chests," he asked, well aware of everything Royston was.

"*No news is good news.* Glad to have you with us, Commander," Royston stated, for reasons of etiquette only. He wasn't surprised to see the military keeping an eye on things too. After all, he felt the same way they did. *Brenda had to win*!

"Everything is ready and we're good to go, sir," the aide smiled. "I have copies of the script for you and others too; I don't have to remind you to *wipe the contents* later, *do I*?" She raised her eyebrows coyly at them. The two men glanced at one another and chortled self-confidently.

"I thought I'd leave mine lying around for a Federation spy to snatch," the Commander muttered, drolly.

"*Really?*" Royston asked, keen not to be outdone. "I was going to sell mine to the highest bidder." They laughed.

―――――♦♦♦♦♦♦―――――

The countdown was entering its final phase… less than sixty seconds. Separated by glass barriers, it was the first time that Oli had seen Brenda or Mark *in the flesh*. They couldn't speak to one another but all three could see one another. In the first booth Brenda and her nondescript aide stood. In the second, Oli and Kate waited, and in the last, Mark, with his support person. Kate mumbled something that Oli missed, and he leaned down to listen.

"What?"

"Will you please *stop* tapping your foot like that, it's *really* irritating," she ordered, tense.

"I'm *scared*," he admitted, stressed.

"Join the club," she countered, unimpressed. The doors ahead began to rise, letting in the noise from the crowd.

---

It was very similar to a moment of silent remembrance, in that almost everything went quiet and most things stopped. Few craft in the traffic lanes, nearly deserted walkways and a strange stillness. The moment the debate began to be broadcast, several minutes later than when it was *actually being filmed*, this suspension of activity occurred not just across the planet but across the whole Coalition. Time, the most famous illusion that there was, could easily be adjusted to be sure no one realised that the whole thing was not *live* at all. Distance could be blamed for poor signals, and interference too made it even easier. Statistically, it was recorded that ninety five point seven nine four percent of the population of the entire Coalition were watching. *No pressure then...*

---

Deetee emerged onto the stage, the very definition of debonair. He'd never been one for understated entrances. His smile concealed a smug vulgarity in its urbane sachet of flashy falsehood. The smile of the snake. As he moved out, the three candidates, directed to their own respective podiums, moved into view too. The music played, the crowd cheered and the atmosphere went through its motions. Social, not meteorological. Spectacle achieved: refined class clashing head on with crass politics in a display of mundane banality. The dancers whirled and spun in an impressive display of carefully choreographed excess and exhibition. *Actors on a stage.* Deetee moved in among them on his pre-prepared path to mix and turn with them. He began to chortle loudly and call out in appreciation as if all this was some kind of unexpected surprise.

He extended his arms to the crowd as if acknowledging them for the first time, still laughing and smiling. As the last female dancer passed him, she took his hand and placed a red flower delicately into it.

"*My goodness!*" he cried, still mostly drowned out by the din. She gave him a dazzling smile and then skipped out after all of her fellow artistes. Deetee gave her a cheeky wave before slipping the flower into his lapel, and once again turned to face the crowd. He feigned gratitude and wonder in his expression as he did this.

"*Thank you so much!* I wish every one of my shows could start *this well!* I'm fortunate the *Galactic-Girly-Giggles* were hired to do that! I'm sure if I tried it myself then the phrase *dance like nobody's watching* would mean something *entirely different!*" he bellowed, at everyone. Well rehearsed laughter was his answer. *Ghastly, just ghastly.*

Brenda, upon entering, made her way to her place. She'd been told to wave at the crowd and she had done so. The noise was so intense after being in the quiet for so long, that she had to stop herself from wincing in mild pain. Her costume, recommended by her aides, had been chosen with precision. An ensemble which was meant to say how friendly and open she was, while reminding everyone that she was in charge and could defend herself if attacked. How exactly you could say all that with just clothes alone Brenda had no idea, but she'd been reliably informed that they had achieved this look. Make up had been modestly applied, she'd not wanted any but after being reminded five times that the Commandment Benefactor only had a best side, she'd relented.

"Try to look at ease no matter what happens," her aide had told her, moments before the glass began to rise.

"Why? *W-what's going to happen?*" Brenda asked, instantly panicking.

"*You're going to win,*" the aide had replied, as if it was obvious.

She reached her platform and smiled out at the crowd pleasantly. At ease, her aide had said, *at ease.* She permitted herself to look across at her rivals. Oli and Mark were both looking as edgy as she felt, and that made her feel a little better. Her only real advantage over them was that she had always known she'd end up in this position, even if she didn't much like it. At the beginning of the election, neither of these men could have guessed that they would make it this far. Deetee, as much as she hated him, knew how to handle the crowd and for that she was much relieved. She loved democracy and she loved that everyone had the right to be there and to ask questions and to vote: nevertheless, the idea of confronting any of them in a political argument scared her slightly.

"I believe they have just released a new album, *watch out for that*," Deetee was still talking. "You will see them later as they will complete the dance at the end of the debate, so... *there's a great excuse for us all to keep the questions simple.*" More laughter. *Ironic laughter*. The worst kind.

"So, it's time to *get serious,* my Beings," he went on. He turned to face Brenda and the others. He altered his facial expression slightly, eradicating the mirth and *somehow* still smiling. Clown-like in its function, his face both revealed and concealed simultaneously. He launched into a fleeting introduction of all three candidates as if to remind everyone exactly who was who. This was supposedly for the benefit of everyone watching but frankly, if they didn't know by now, there was little point in it. In elections *before,* the candidates would introduce themselves, but it saved time and gave them less to remember if Deetee did it for them. Also, as it was an opportunity for him to continue to listen to his own voice, Deetee was only too happy to oblige.

"So, now you know who you're dealing with," Deetee concluded, his eyes gleaming. *If only...* "Here they stand, ready to answer *your* questions!" He raised his hand, subtly reminding the audience *how* they should gain attention if they had a question. Several hands/appendages/tentacles rose. Deetee gave a long impressed whistle.

"Great, glad to see *you're awake out there*, who first? Who first?" He began to move off the stage area and into the crowd. He chose the nearest female human that he liked the look of.

"Yes, what do *you* want to know? Who are you, first?" She introduced herself. Then she asked her question.

"How are you going to deal with the Neo-remnantist extremists?"

"And it's *game on guys,* straight in there *with the controversy,* how *will* you deal with them?" Deetee grinned, darting back to the stage. He approached the candidates. "Who wants to go first?"

Her heart racing, Satiah accelerated hard down the empty traffic lane. She didn't know how long she had, but she knew one thing for sure: Carl was defenceless on his own. She was trying to call him, again and again but he wasn't answering. *She could see him sitting there*, wilfully ignoring the communicator. She could still see him as he heard someone at the door. She'd told him not to answer if anyone called while she was out. She watched as he stared from the communicator to the door and then back again as if unsure what to do first.

"*Pick it up!*" she screamed at the screen, as she pushed her transporter to the limit.

---

"So some might say that you have an extremist attitude *towards* extremism in that you feel that *any and all* extremists should be locked up? Do you include *yourself* in this?" Deetee asked, ever the stirrer.

"With respect, I believe we could be getting caught up in both logical and lexical semantics here," Mark deflected. "What I meant to say was that this *type* of extremism should not be allowed and it should be dealt with harshly to discourage others."

"*In what way?* The judicial system *already* employs the strictest of penalties with regard to charges of Neo-remnantist extremism," Deetee pressed. Mark was looking flustered now, as he'd been easily tangled up in Deetee's web of trick questions.

"This is true," he acknowledged, renewing his composure. "I merely meant to say that the public needs reassurance, and they need to see that something is being done to address this very real problem."

"Brenda, care to weigh in here?" Deetee offered, making her jump slightly. "You must have something to add?"

"*Thank you*," she smiled, kindly. She was always so sincerely polite… another reason why everyone liked her. "F-first I just wanted to say how *appalled* I am that this problem still persists. Z-z-zero tolerance is my only realistic option in the l-long term. My approach, which I've already b-b-begun to implement, will be to empower the security forces with everything they need to confront and contain these offenders. I-I spoke with the law enforcement, the armed forces and the secret services about this *three days ago*. They highlight t-t-to me that I need to tread carefully in the steps I take. What they meant by that is that I *could* inadvertently cause a schism between civil liberties and protective security, should I take the wrong approach. The public is *already* suffering *because* of these attacks. I don't want to hurt them more by t-taking away their rights or their facilities to *prevent more*. Yet, as Commandment Benefactor, sometimes I have to protect my people even f-f-from themselves."

"*I see*," Deetee encouraged, deliberately making it easy for her. "That sounds to me like a sensible strategy but when you said *empower the security forces…* what *exactly* did you mean by that?" His question was designed to look shrewd and probing but in reality it was exactly the question she was prepared for.

"For example, I intend to change the law r-regarding the methods used by security to gather and disseminate information. Currently there are many different departments set up to combat these threats; I propose to combine them to create a u-united front. Currently they do their best, but are sometimes h-hampered by limited communication and sometimes even lack of resources. My law change will give the security forces less restrictions on accessing data, on surveillance and working directly with the Federation and Union g-governments," she explained further. Deetee was leaning on the side of her podium, nodding as she spoke as if in understanding.

"I think we can all see your predicament," Deetee smiled, generously. Mark's face was a picture. He was infuriated that she was getting off *so lightly* after his grilling.

"What about the offenders?" he couldn't stop himself asking. "When you have caught them, *what will you do*? They can't be kept near other prisoners as there is a danger of them converting others into new recruits. People in desperate situations often make reckless decisions, we've seen it time and again. Exposed to ideologies such as these inside prisons, prisoners who were otherwise uninvolved end up joining them when they are released."

The crowd made a disgruntled noise, as if reminding him that he had spoken out of turn. Deetee knew to expect this type of thing;

indeed he would have been surprised had Mark said nothing at all, and smoothly stepped in.

"You do not have to answer that..." he began, to Brenda. She only *had* to answer questions *from the public*, not other candidates. Brenda though had other ideas and she felt it needed to be answered.

"N-no, it's okay," Brenda said, going off script for the first time. "As you know I-I-I do *not* believe in the suitability of capital punishment and it would not s-serve any purpose to let them get away with it with light sentencing. My solution would be to set up remand centres *specifically* with them in mind. That way they will never be exposed to anyone other than each other and androids."

There was a chorus of agreement from the crowd and Deetee was impressed. It seemed they had all forgotten, what with all their frantic scheming, how talented Brenda actually was *without* their support. She was a gifted diplomat with a talent for finding easy solutions to complicated problems. Nevertheless, he was quick to rein in this detour before it got bogged down. She'd effectively crushed any concerns Mark might or might not have had, even if she appeared to have overlooked the financial aspect of it. Deetee suspected that Mark was just trying to trip her up, but the attempt had backfired. He made up his mind to make things *even more difficult* for Mark later on. Now, though, he moved on to Oli.

"Well, Oli, surely you must have something to say about this issue?" Deetee asked, moving to stand by him. Oli was sweating with nerves but he didn't lose his cool.

"In the end you *have* to remember what these fanatics stand for. They will never give up and they will never understand another way of looking at things... least of all themselves," he said, carefully. "There is always more that can be done and there are always things that could be done better. We have to hold our ground and refuse to give into fear because that is what they want." The audience made noises of approval. He'd dodged the bit about what he would do while making them aware that he understood the situation. The problem was that his resolution had been too similar to Brenda's. If he went into that at this stage, it would *look like* he was just copying her. So he'd gone for the *rallying-call-technique…* something he was good at, and it seemed to have paid off. Deetee, who was now bored of this subject, returned to the crowd to find another topic, rather than messing with Oli.

"*You* do not go far enough," Mark hissed, pointing at Brenda. "These people are the worst kind of lifeform. They should be treated as such." Brenda didn't like confrontation, it frightened her, but her beliefs compelled her to engage with him.

"*I will not* turn into what they are in order to defeat them. *We must not* become l-like them," she countered, with a power that astonished everyone. That was the real Brenda, the strong selfless person who wanted everything better for everyone. Even though she was being used, manipulated and lied to… no one could take her moral convictions away from her. She was born to always strive to do the right thing. It was, above anything else, what defined her.

"Will the *honourable* candidate mind shutting up and waiting for the next question please?" Deetee drawled, mockingly. The audience sniggered and laughed at Mark. Deetee found another being, this time a small feathered creature, of a type even he didn't recognise. It spoke, its voice soft and mellifluous.

"Do you acknowledge the danger of populism and, if you do, how will you overcome it?" it asked. Deetee hurried back onto the stage again.

"Any takers?" he asked. Again, as she would with everyone's questions, Brenda would not answer first.

Oli decided to take the plunge and nodded. Deetee smiled the never-ending smile and came over to his podium.

"I could say that there is no such thing as populism and that my presence here is proof of that," he said, wittily. Sporadic laughter occurred and even Brenda smiled.

"But that would be a lie," Deetee chuckled, pleasantly.

"Indeed," Oli answered. "Populism means support for the concerns of so-called ordinary people. Depending on how you define ordinary, *of course*."

"Of course," Deetee agreed, secretly impressed by Oli's technique so far. He was entertaining the crowd while also letting everyone know that he *understood* what he was talking about. If that sounded like something a politician never had to do, well, it wasn't. Too often they had been caught out talking about stuff they didn't have any idea about. Assuming, of course, that that hadn't all been part of the plan.

"In short, what we're talking about here is *everything*, from the clashes between equality and classism, all the way through to communism and capitalism. It *all* factors into populism. If something appeals to a large majority of a population, it in essence becomes a new populism. In so far as it can threaten anything… it would depend entirely on the *thing* itself. So populism is only a threat if the thing that is popular – *with those we define as ordinary people* - is dangerous."

"Define *dangerous*," Deetee requested, trying to find fault.

"Unsafe," Oli joked. A ripple of laughter from the crowd.

"You know what I mean," Deetee clarified, unamused.

"Imagine if Neo-remnantism became a majority ideology, then Neo-remnantism *would be* populism and then that would be when populism becomes *dangerous*," Oli stated, a little smugly. Deetee's eyes narrowed, recognising the trap. If he argued with that, it might look like *he didn't see* Neo-remnantists as a danger, or worse, that *he supported* Neo-remnantism.

As if sensing Deetee's trouble, Oli offered him an easy way out.

"Populism is often seen as a threat to elections. This is because political strategists, not unreasonably, believe people vote for who they want based on what they want," Oli went on. "Say, you're running for office…"

"*You're running for office*," Deetee repeated, being funny.

"… in *your* personal bid for power. *Whatever you say*, there are set policies in place that *you* have to stick to. This is because this is what *you* want to do when you get into office. *Toss whether you're believed or not out of the window for a second*. It follows that the people who want either *those policies* or *what they will ultimately culminate in* will vote for you. If what you're saying you're going to do *could have* a detrimental affect on anything, be it *the economy, the health of the people* or whatever it's going to be… again, this is where *populism* can be dangerous. *What is popular is not always what is good for the people*. That last pearl works well in reverse too." Deetee was silent as he followed the convoluted answer. It was a good rejoinder, and well delivered too. Kate was glowing with pride, he'd executed *that* perfectly. While he had Deetee on the back foot, Oli persisted.

"So, in answer to the question, *yes*, I do acknowledge it. I think that the answers to overcoming it lie in education and accurate communication," Oli said, as if it was nothing important. Deetee couldn't think of a single thing he could do with that. Brenda was making his job even harder now as she was nodding in agreement with Oli. That woman was just too honest for her own good sometimes! Deetee's smiled twitched, just for a flicker, a micro-expression in a micro-second, but he too had deep reserves of inner calm. There would be no point in asking Brenda, so that only left Mark.

"Mark!" Deetee called, pleased to get away from Oli and Brenda and their current good standings. If he discredited Oli on this point he might harm Brenda too. Mark was fair game though, unless he agreed with them, which he almost certainly wouldn't. He didn't disappoint.

"There is no such thing as populism; it is *yet another example* of people inventing problems and giving them impressive names to hide the fact that they are *not problems at all*. Certainly populism doesn't exist as *he* defined it. If you're talking about *an overall consensus*, however, then I agree that could be dangerous, should it be harmful to the state or its citizens. Yet in a democracy the will of the majority rules, so if it did exist it would be unavoidable," Mark stated.

"Didn't you just *relabel* populism as *overall consensus*?" Deetee cut in.

"No – well, yes," Mark tried to answer, unsure exactly which way to go. "I relabelled nothing; I just *redefined where* the danger lies."

"And where does it lie exactly?" Deetee asked, genuinely confused. Sometimes the statements of politicians could sound a lot like the rantings of a lunatic with all the poise and power of a malfunctioning coolant vent. *A lot of the time, actually*. In this case it just sounded a bit muddled.

"*The danger lies* where people are trying to make something very simple *difficult*," Mark stated, starting to get irritated. Deetee made a gesture of outraged disbelief to the crowd, earning him another rumble of amusement.

"Politicians can use populism to enter office, despite never intending to deliver anything they promised, that is where the danger lies. Freighters too slow? No problem, I will make them faster. AIs taking over your job - not an issue, I can stop them. Get me in and I will give you what you want. These are *just a few* examples of how *populism can be dangerous*."

"You can all pick the bones out of that one," Deetee smiled, moving back into the crowd. "*Come on, liven up why don't you*, what *else* do you have for them?" Someone raised their arm to indicate they wished to ask a question. Deetee swooped on them quickly.

"What is going to happen regarding trading between us, the Federation and the Union, specifically the Union?"

---

It had been a shock to see her there last night. She'd *said* she was at the office, wherever that was. Carl knew he was sleeping with a question mark. A mean, uncompromising and dangerous question mark. She was also an alluring, amusing and intelligent question mark who called herself Satiah. She was a Phantom agent who worked for the Coalition, so she had *said*. Then again, she also had said that she loved him and he really didn't know if that was true. Saying that, if she *didn't*, why did she keep coming back? How could he trust what she said to him when he didn't even know who she really was? How could he love a mystery? In his mind she was beautiful and scary in equal measure, and could have anyone she wanted so... *why* did she want *him*? *An overweight ship salesman from Ionar 12.*

He had always feared he would lose her because he didn't think he could live up to her expectations, or even keep up with her ludicrous list of demands. She had remarked on his lack of observation and general clumsiness several times before which, intentionally or not, unconsciously undermined his acumen.

She was *very* officious. Don't do this, don't do that. You can't say this or tell anyone that. You can't go here or there! Inwardly, though he ostensibly accepted this without complaint, and on occasion it even amused him, it was driving him a bit crazy. Knowing as much about her as he did, he was scared of what she might do if he confronted her about *any of it*. She could just walk out and he'd never see her again. On the other hand, she might just flatten him. There was no way to know how she would react. Yet he had seen other sides to her. A gentler, more caring and less violent side of her *did exist*, he was sure of it. *Satiah didn't do negotiating*, he knew that much, and she wasn't like most women he'd known before. She didn't talk about how she felt, not at all. Normally this wouldn't bother him, as he thought people did too much of that, but in her case… it was unnerving. She did things on her terms all the time and that was that.

The shock, for him, had been bumping into her at the tournament *with another man* when she'd *said* she was elsewhere. She seemed to be having a heated argument with this man about something personal. At first, Carl had thought there was something familiar about the guy, but he had become more interested in what Satiah was saying to him as he'd got nearer to them. She looked very angry, which naturally made Carl pay close attention. Now, Carl *knew* she was a great actress, he'd often suspected that she used her acting skills to try to make him feel better sometimes. To pretend she was happier than she was, or more amused than she was. *That* he didn't mind, *funnily enough*.

It had also shaken him when he'd realised how much it mattered to him. He'd not been conscious that he was in love with her. He said he was all the time and he did care, but *love*? He'd been trying to trick himself into thinking it was just because they had fun together that he felt that way. That it was all somehow just in his own imagination and that in reality this was not love, but lust. Well, lust on his part, anyway.

When he'd found her with this man, he'd felt so mad. Angrier than he remembered feeling *for a long time*. Jealous, stupid *and* angry in fact. How could he *ever* have thought he meant anything *to her*? He'd had to get away before she'd done anything to stop him. To his surprise she hadn't tried to stop him, not really. That had also bothered him, on reflection. Surely if she *really* cared she'd have done anything she could to stop him from leaving? On the other hand, nothing like this had happened between them before and maybe she had been as confused then as he was now.

He'd gone back to her apartment, taken his stuff and decided to leave the note behind. He had thought about writing another note, this one to her about them, but didn't know what to say. Instead of returning to his planet, however, he just wandered for some time, still in shock, until he'd found a bar. He'd gone inside and proceeded to get *very* drunk. If that made him a cliché then so be it, he wasn't exactly in the mood to worry about being a stereotype!

The pain he felt seemed almost like a physical one, right in his heart. He didn't want to go anywhere, he just wanted oblivion. Not death or anything permanent, obviously. He needed to just forget about it all for a while. The next few hours went by in a bit of a blur of drink, music and smoke. Then he'd got a call. Not a call from Satiah, she'd been calling him on and off for a while and, as with the note, he still didn't know what to say so he'd not answered her.

This new caller was another woman, though she sounded quite young. She'd refused to identify herself but had claimed to know all about him and Satiah. She'd said that Satiah did really care about him and the man she'd been with was not her lover. He was actually someone she was working with. She also told him that he should go back. Give Satiah another chance. To say all this made him feel even more confused would be an understatement. How did this woman know all this? Was this some kind of trick that Satiah was playing on him?

Deciding that he'd probably have to talk to her again at some point anyway, Carl had agreed and eventually returned to her apartment. He'd half expected to find her there, waiting for him... all triumphant at somehow conning him or proving how predictable he was. She was not. He'd slept for a long while first, too tired and too intoxicated to think straight. He had awoken again and had realised how the pillows smelt like her hair. This did not help in his ongoing battle to stop thinking about her. Angry at himself now, as well as her, he started to watch something to take his mind off... *everything*. There *was* the debate, but somehow he didn't think he fancied that.

That was when the door bleeped, indicating that someone was outside. Almost instantly his communicator started to go off again. He'd memorised her code a long time ago and knew it was Satiah trying to call him. He stood, wondering if she was at the door and wanting to know if he was okay with her coming in. Wouldn't she just come in, though? It was *her* apartment after all, he was just her guest. He looked from one to the other, the door and the communicator, as if caught in some kind of impasse. Trapped by indecision.

Why did he feel like something weird was going on? One of Satiah's many *ridiculous rules* was that he, under no circumstances, should answer the door to anyone. She'd said it was safer that way and that no one could know what or who he was. At that moment, though, he was feeling... disobedient. That memory of her commanding finger being pointed at him made up his mind. This had gone far enough, she wouldn't like it but she'd have to lump it. He was a man and at some stage he had to prove it. He moved to answer the door.

--------♦♦♦♦♦--------

That was a question that only Brenda could really provide an actual answer to, as she was the only candidate there who'd been party to the consultations, such as they were. Deetee made a show of deliberately ignoring Oli and Mark as he approached her.

"A-are you referring to any deals in particular?" Brenda asked the audience member. As rehearsed, the being shrugged.

"I was talking in general terms."

"Well, as far as I know, everything is agreed with the Federation. 'Everything' b-being that all deals will remain on the table. A-as for pricing, as always, there is room for negotiation. I leave that to the designated personnel as much as I can, as they are more familiar with the nature of such deals," Brenda answered, with care. A few glanced around to see that the Federation representative was still watching. He smiled from his booth and gave the smallest of nods to confirm that

that much was indeed true. Brenda noted that no one from the Union was present, as she had been told was likely.

"With regard to the Union, I can't really answer that right now. I'm s-sure you've all seen the news? There was an incident and, since then, we've had no direct contact with the leadership of the Nebular Union. We don't know what happened exactly but, for want of a better phrase, p-please don't quote me saying this because I don't know if it is true, a coup. A coup may have occurred, consequences unknown. We're confident that what footage we have seen discounts the chance that this was any sort of revolution, as all parties involved seemed to be military. Until I hear from the leadership of the Nebular Union, old or new, I can't comment on any of the ongoing trading deals between us and them or the Federation and them. I would hope all is well but it really did not look that way to me," Brenda said, honestly. No one had anything to add to that, as no one else there possibly *could* add to it.

In the director's office, Royston and the others looked on in rigorous silence. Everything was going well so far, but that could change in an instant. The aide returned, looking unruffled.

"Just checked to see if she needed water or anything, and she's fine," she said, updating them on Brenda's condition.

"Good, good," Royston murmured, without looking around.

"I'm concerned that Deetee might be victimising Mark too much," the Commander murmured.

"He has to victimise *someone* or it won't look *believable*!" protested the aide. "He can't touch Brenda, Oli's answers are tricky to pull apart, but Mark seems to hit every tripwire."

"Agreed," sighed Royston, dispassionately. "Makes you wonder how it would have turned out with Oli *and* Sam down there. Brothers fighting one another are something special, after all." He smiled in a brittle way, as if recalling something from his past. Something bad.

Back on the stage, Deetee was once again fishing for a question from the audience. Fewer of them had queries now, as some of the biggest subjects had been covered.

"Will there be any changes regarding the laws around corporate censorship? In particular, within the scope of the arts?" was the next one. Royston eyed the aide questioningly, who smiled smugly back at him. This was *not* a topic he had been expecting.

"*What?*" he asked, incredulous. It seemed his confusion *was* expected, at least to her.

"*Watch,*" she instructed, levelly.

"Anyone wish to take this one?" Deetee asked, as he returned to the candidates. All three of them looked somewhat bewildered by the question.

Oli nodded and Deetee came over to him.

"What are you asking *specifically?*" Oli wanted to know. A man in the crowd lifted a poster up. It was a picture of a rude and offensive nature. Everyone was trying to get a look at it. Oli at last understood.

"We're here to debate *politics,* not the differences between free speech and hate speech," Oli stated, calmly.

"That *is* politics!" shouted someone.

"This is expressionism!" yelled someone else. *What is expressionism? Anything you like it to be.*

"No, it's obtuse and unacceptable. I hope the image is being filtered, young citizens may be watching this!" Oli argued.

"It's ironic!" yelled the someone else again.

"Knowing it's awful doesn't stop it from *being* awful!" Brenda joined in. "In my opinion, *that* is not any type of art I would want hanging on my wall."

"*Here we go,*" smiled the aide, deviously. Royston nodded quickly, watching intently.

"People should be able to say what they like without fear of censorship or accusations of prejudice!"

"Not when it's clear that the sole point of something is purely to *cause offence!*" Brenda countered.

"What about comedy? Doesn't that have an *obligation* to say the difficult thing?" another shouter asked.

"*One at a time please!*" Deetee cautioned.

"I refuse to be drawn into this level of immaturity," Brenda condemned, with clout.

"Comedy is there to reduce tension, not *enhance* it!" Oli argued.

"I don't have a problem with *that exhibit* of expressionism," Mark stated, almost quietly.

"*What?*" Oli whirled on him. Brenda, too, seemed angered visibly by Mark's response.

"It's *art*, it's *meant* to challenge our concepts and perceptions," Mark went on. Art was something that Mark knew a lot about and he genuinely felt that anything, *literally anything*, could not cause offence *if it was labelled as art*. Oli did not share his opinion. "To censor it would be to restrict free speech, something *integral* to the democratic process. Are you saying that's what we need to do?" Mark continued, glibly. There was no right answer to that.

"Good point Mark, are you trying to take away people's right to share their views?" Deetee piled on. Kate had gone red with suppressed rage. She was irritated with Oli for starting to get emotional, like she had specifically told him not to do.

What really annoyed her, though, was the way Deetee kept trying to tear everyone but Brenda down. Like most who noticed that he was unremittingly doing that, she thought he was just wary of antagonising Brenda because she was in charge. No one ever guessed that the whole thing was stage-managed. And those few who ever did would be easily dismissed as conspiracy theorists.

"No, that's *not* what I was saying at all," Oli said, conscious of the trap. It was the only thing he could safely say. "I will, however, say this: how can you tell what *is* and *isn't* art? If you're told something is art, how can you prove otherwise? It would allow people to do or say anything they liked, so long as they presented it *as art*. That's *why* censorship exists!"

"That, and to make money!" shouted someone.

"It's common sense, isn't it?" Mark shrugged, supremely indifferent suddenly.

"*Can we get on with this?*" Brenda asked, sighing. She wanted another question. Neither Oli nor Mark heard her, though.

"Define common sense!" Oli ordered, crossing his arms.

"Reasonable judgement, when it comes to anything practical," Mark said.

"Define *reasonable*," growled Oli.

Back in the director's box, all remained reverently silent as the editors, technical support staff, and the director himself, busied themselves. Everything had to be perfect and everything had to look normal. Perfectly normal. Royston was particularly satisfied with the proceedings so far.

"*Very good*, I knew there was a reason we sleep together," Royston murmured, to the aide.

"I thought you just liked the shameless sensationalism of it," she joked. "I knew if I could just get them to argue, Brenda could breeze through untainted. *Divide and conquer*."

"You are an excellent judge of character. What *would* you have done if it hadn't worked?" he asked, rhetorically.

"You just wait until they get started on tax," she warned, flushing with pride. "*You've seen nothing yet*."

――――――✦✦✦✦✦✦――――――

Doing something that Satiah could only describe as *inspired*, Zax had remotely changed the entry code on Satiah's apartment door. They could both see as Carl, against her orders, tried to open the door to let in a potential murderer. He was unable to do that now, but that didn't mean that the danger ended there. Satiah reached the parking area and leapt out of her craft, engine still running. She ran into the building, hurried down the steps, pistol in hand whilst keeping her footsteps light and quiet. She knew there were at least two of them. Two men outside her door and Carl was *talking to them*. Chatting to them as if they were regular salesmen or something.

"Hold on!" Carl called, somewhat apologetically. He thought he knew the code for the door but for some reason it wasn't working. Grasping how this might be received, he actually tried to call Satiah - who'd stopped calling him only moments before - to ask if she had changed the code. She couldn't have though, as he'd been able to use that password to get in earlier... well, he'd obviously misremembered it somehow. Either way, she would know what it was. That was another thing about her: she had an amazing memory. From time to time, she would claim not to remember something, but he'd started to realise that she might be lying.

Now it was Satiah's turn not to answer. Carl rolled his eyes in irritation. Was she playing games with him now? *You won't answer me, so why should I answer you?*

"No problem mate," said one of the men, as he casually slid a silencer onto the end of his pistol. Satiah reached the landing from the floor above and heard the exchange. She shook her head. *Carl, you stupid, stupid man*! If you'd just *stayed quiet* they might have moved on, thinking it was unoccupied! She made up her mind to just gun these two down when a noise from below her on the adjacent steps made her freeze.

Armed with what looked like the cover of a waste disposal box, Zax was creeping up from below. Was everyone going utterly mad today, or was it just Satiah herself? This could not be happening! Zax wasn't allowed to leave Phantom Headquarters *ever* without permission, and *what was* she thinking? Taking on two experienced operatives with that thing?

Satiah, forced to make her move before she was really comfortable, leapt down directly onto the landing and shot both men dead before they managed to even turn to face her. She then pushed a surprised Zax back against the wall as another man, at the end of the corridor, returned fire.

"*Hello?*" Carl was calling, from behind the door. All the shots were silenced so he'd not heard anything other than two people collapsing. "Hello! *Are you still there?*"

"*What the hell are you doing here?*" Satiah demanded, in Zax's ear. Zax looked worried and instantly regretted her earlier decision to try and help directly.

"I didn't know if you were going to make it in time. I was closer than you and I thought you might be *angry* if something happened and *I had done nothing…*" she began, knowing she'd done the wrong thing.

"And what is *this* supposed to be? *Your new coffin lid?*" Satiah hissed, seizing the lid from Zax.

"I didn't have time to get a gun so I grabbed what was nearby…" she mumbled, bright red now. Her eyes went wide. "*Look out!*"

The third man leapt out from around the corner and Satiah threw the lid at him, as someone would throw a Frisbee. Zax dived out of the way, desperate not to be a burden to Satiah. More silent shooting ensued.

"*Hello!*" called Carl again. "I didn't hear that, are you still there?" Satiah peppered the wall the man was using as cover with shots. Zax rolled and acquired one of the guns the men by the door had been carrying. She too began to shoot but seemed unable to even hit the wall.

"*Guard that door*, young lady!" Satiah furiously ordered to Zax. She dutifully lay down, using the corpses as cover. Satiah sprinted down the corridor, in pursuit of the man.

"Satiah?" Carl asked, recognising her voice. "What's going on? Why didn't you answer me?"

"Shut up!" Zax hissed, kicking the door furiously a few times. "*Quiet!*"

"Who's *that?*" he asked, puzzled. "Has your voice synthesiser broken? *Satiah*! If you think this is funny I can assure…"

"*Shut up!*" Zax implored, straining to hear if anyone else was coming. She could hear footsteps echoing around as people ran, but still no loud shooting. This was a residential area and as both sides were secret service operatives, no one wished to advertise this latest round of treachery. She tried not to think about how badly she had messed up. She hadn't done it to prove herself; she'd done it because she didn't want Satiah to lose her boyfriend. Especially as she had gone to all the trouble of calling him the previous evening to get him to come back…

Satiah peered over the railing just in time to see the man clatter down the next set of steps. She fired four times, almost winging him with the third blast. She had no chance of catching him now, he was too far ahead. Groaning in annoyance, she just stood there for a few seconds, trying to calm herself down. The main thing was that Carl was safe and the PAI had failed to get either him or her. She slowly returned, cautious that Zax might try to shoot *her*, thinking she was someone else. She edged around the corner, after letting her know she was coming back, hand raised cautiously.

"*Did you get him?*" Zax whispered, curious. Satiah shook her head. Her eyes regarded Zax stonily. Zax looked at the floor, not wanting to get yelled at. Now she was calmer, Satiah remembered how well, *up until now*, Zax had been doing. She put a hand under her chin and made her look up.

"Next time, *remember a gun*," she said, leaving it at that. Zax, looking very crestfallen, nodded humbly. "Now I want you to let Randal know what's happened here, to turn my engine off upstairs, and to organise a team to get rid of these." She gave the nearest body a kick. "We're lucky this happened while the debate was on, otherwise there would probably have been civilian casualties. And obviously, say nothing about Carl." She eyed the pistol in Zax's hand. "The sights are out by about three I'd say, that's why you kept missing." Zax eyed the gun too.

"I did wonder…" she murmured. "I'm sorry I did the wrong thing, I won't do it again."

"You will, but so long as you remember what the wrong things are, you should be fine. Now… I would like some *privacy* please…" Satiah moved towards the door. Zax couldn't resist a small cheeky beam when she thought Satiah wasn't looking.

"Don't grin like that, Zax, it makes you look simple," Satiah jested, over her shoulder. Zax gaped.

---

"People are *too easily offended*," Mark shrugged, as if reading from a restaurant menu. "And just because *someone* is offended, that shouldn't mean that *no one* is allowed to make up their own minds about it. *Equality*." Oli hated it when people would use single words to argue whole points of view; *in his view*, it seemed to somehow diminish the intellectual quality of the discussion. It brought it to a dumbed-down level. What Mark meant by saying *equality* was actually something slightly different. He was referring to a specific amendment of the Being-Equality Act, an ages old act of legislation.

"Are you trying to say that if *we all* approach *each other* with *equal consideration* then we should also approach *art* in this way? I would ask *why?* The art itself lacks the capacity to *be* offended and it lacks the capacity to treat anything with equal consideration. Art is not sentient."

"It can be whatever it wants to be, *it's art*," Deetee joked, enjoying the fight.

"The question was: *will there be any changes regarding the laws around corporate censorship? In particular, within the scope of the arts,*" Mark repeated, patiently. "You have not answered it. Instead, you tried to distract everyone by drawing attention to an example of censored art." Oli pointed to himself and feigned blankness. No, *the audience* had done that!

"I propose *no changes* to existing law," Oli stated, sourly. "For anything."

"I think that freedom of expression needs to be looked at very closely. It is clear to me that attitudes need to change. People should become more tolerant to all forms of expression and opinions of others in general," Mark went on. "This closed-mindedness that I can see in our government is harmful to the mental health of our citizens."

"Even if *that form of expression* falls into the categories of hate speech or common indecency?" Oli countered, crossing his arms.

Kate could tell he was really starting to lose his temper now, crossed arms was a sign of intense irritability with Oli. She willed him to calm down and remember what he had to do. Agree to disagree! Let it go!

"Yes, as being less tolerant is violating every being's right of expression," Mark said, also getting tetchy. Brenda was shaking her head and looking awkward. This was just embarrassing. A so-called political debate reduced to a playground squabble about purely hypothetical things. What would it be next? The meaning of all life in the cosmos? She looked hopefully to Deetee, wishing he would intervene, but he was just grinning at them. She knew she should be counting her blessings that at least *she* wasn't looking as stupid as they were, but she felt they were being manipulated somehow. There was a knowingness in Deetee's eyes and she didn't like it.

She pondered the reaction she would get if she just ordered them to stop and Deetee to ask another question. Would that make her a dictator? Her aide had told her to stick to what they had decided, and that would be sensible. Oli though, at last, was coming to his senses. He'd seen Brenda's face and recognised what she was thinking.

"I think we shall just have to let this issue slide *for now*, I'm not convinced we can resolve it in this forum," he allowed, trying to give the subject a rest. Mark smiled, as if in victory.

"Of course," he said. Deetee shrugged.

"Are you sure you covered that significantly…?" he began, trying to kick it off again.

"Another question please, Deetee," Brenda said, quietly but firmly. "I'm sure they have much more to ask and we only have a l-limited time available." Deetee eyed her casually, the smile slipping for just a split second.

"Very well," he acquiesced, with poorly concealed averseness. Royston and the aide exchanged looks. The aide shrugged.

"She's fine," the woman maintained. "Just a little impatient, that's all." Royston raised a doubtful eyebrow but left it at that. In the meantime, Deetee had found another question.

"Drug legalisation. In this case I'm referring to Sicbanan B, will it be made legal, and if so by what parameters?" was the question. Brenda had to fight again not to roll her eyes. Would people never stop going on about this? She could remember *this* debate from her childhood. At the time, there had been a protest march in favour of legalisation. *Well, it had begun as a march and developed into a full-on ramble.* Brenda knew to deal with this one tactfully, but there were only so many ways you could say no. And people would still be offended… *she wondered darkly if one day there would be a 'right to be offended' act.* Not on her watch! Their offence would only cause greater offence in others; it was self-perpetuating.

---

This had been a long time coming. Well, *actually it hadn't*, Satiah knew it just felt that way because her days passed very slowly. She had entered her home, leaving the bodies outside for Zax to deal with. Carl was there, arms crossed, an uneasy expression on his face. He'd seen the bodies. Even if he didn't know what was going on, he knew she'd just killed them. They stood in the hallway, just staring at each other for a few seconds. How to start… Satiah wondered. She smiled, put away her pistol self consciously, and he *didn't* smile back. Okay, she thought, I know where I stand.

"Shall we sit down?" she asked, softly. Carl buried his hands in his pockets and shrugged.

"…Sure, drink?" he grunted, at least being civil.

"No, I'm still on duty," she murmured. Then hastily she added, "*Thank you*, by the way." This was why Phantoms were forbidden from romantic liaisons.

Contrary to popular fiction, most people weren't into sleeping with killers. It wasn't just the ethical implications of murder that put them off; it was more the thought that they might kill *them* too that did it.

He poured himself some water and sat opposite her. The table between them suddenly felt much larger than it was, as if it was a gulf or something dividing them. A barrier separating them, keeping them apart. She resolved to do her best to break through it, even if it was only in her mind.

"How do you want to do this?" she asked, at last. "Do you want me to just talk to you or did you want to ask the questions?" Carl was not looking at her; he was staring at his drink sombrely.

"Who were you with last night?" The question came from somewhere deep inside Carl and he had no choice but to say it the way he did. Accusatory. Satiah took a deep breath, bracing herself.

"Oli McAllister," she said, answering the question straight. Do not defend, do not counter attack, just give him what he asks for, she told herself. His eyes went wide, as he knew who that was and he realised why the man had seemed ever so slightly familiar at the time.

"The *politician?*" he clarified, rather pointlessly. Her face was emotionless and she had no trouble maintaining eye contact. Well, practised liars never did, yet Carl thought he knew her well enough to know the signs.

"Yes." Carl frowned and moved in his seat awkwardly. He knew she hated politicians. Who didn't? They didn't even like each other. So why would she be seeing one?

"Is he...? Are *you and him*...?" he asked, trying to find the right words. He looked like he was going to be sick for a moment.

"No, but he wants me," she said, her tone almost robotic. He stared into her eyes for a long moment and seemed to realise what she was doing. She was being as open as she could. He could ask her anything and she would answer.

"Do you love me?" he asked, almost unable to ask. Unable to hold back her own question Satiah began to counter. It was instinctive, she couldn't help it.

"Yes, I love you. Do you think you're not enough for me?"

He shifted again, even more uneasy now. He began to fiddle with his own fingertips, something she knew he did when scared and trying not to give it away. She wanted to put her hand over them caringly, but held back.

"Why do you want to be with me?" he asked. *Uh oh...* well, she told herself, at least it was progress.

"*Okay,*" she sighed, leaning back in her chair. "*Before* we go into that... to show you what was going on *between me and him*... I'm going to tell you all about Operation Selector. I should tell you that if *anyone* knew that I had told you this, I would be arrested and executed. No trial, no appeal, nothing. *Get it?*" She regretted her choice of ratification instantly.

"You don't have to keep telling me not to do things or say things, I *do* understand what secrets *are*," Carl argued, suddenly heated. "*You're such a control freak!*"

"*O really?*" Satiah couldn't help but rage back. "I'm *not* a control freak! I just expect you to do whatever I say, whenever I say it, exactly how I want..." she stopped herself, realising that she was defining a control freak. She hated the word 'freak' as she felt it was applied to things as a label in a very lax manner. What about control *enthusiast*? Or control *admirer*?

"Yes, *go on*," he said, waving at her invitingly. She was proving him right and he knew it. "Come on, let's hear it."

"I… I just *recommend* a lot," she said, rather sheepishly. He pulled a face of such astonishment, that it was all she could do not to flush red with discomfiture.

"I understand, because of what you do, that there are certain parameters I have to observe in order to spend time with you and I'm fine with those. I just object to being *constantly reminded…* actually," he interrupted himself. It was time to make a stand. Time to get in her head. "*Actually no*, I'm *not* happy with those. *Not anymore*."

"…*Right*," she breathed, not meeting his eyes. Where was he going with this? What did he want? Like she didn't know…

"It's… I *feel* like you're treating me like a chump or something," he accused. "*Are you* treating me like an idiot, or is it *just in my mind*?" She felt like quipping something about him being too stupid to tell which, but she knew the mood wasn't right for that.

"You're *not* an idiot," she stated, meeting his eyes again. "You're *just a little innocent*, that's all."

"*A little innocent*? Compared to *you*, yes I probably am, but it doesn't automatically follow that you can boss me around all the time!"

"I *don't* boss you around all the time, and *every* instruction I give you is for your own good…!" she protested, meaning it.

It was true; she only wanted to keep him safe and secret. She didn't mean to hurt him. Obviously she'd have to re-examine her technique…

"*My own good?*" he argued, sarcastically. "You think I can't *look after myself*? How *did* I survive all that time in my life *before we met, then?*"

"It's… *fine*! So why did you try to let those men in just now?" she demanded, getting angry. "I *expressly* told you not to answer the door to anyone *under any circumstances*."

"Because they were out there! *See*, this is just the kind of *crap* I was talking about… *does it matter?*" Had he forgotten that she'd just had to kill them?

"*Carl*, they were from the PAI and they were here *to kill me*! What do you think would have happened to *you* if you'd let them in? *As a witness…*" she hissed, her tone not so angry. Now she was more imploring. She had to make him see that she didn't think he was stupid or anything, she just didn't want him to die. "I don't mean to bully you or order you around all the time because I think you're incapable, I just... *don't want you to get hurt*!"

"The *PAI*?" he asked, his eyes widened. "How could *I* have known that...? *Hold on*! I thought *they* were a *Coalition* security service?" She sighed and tried to make herself look patient and apologetic. This was a lot easier than she thought it would be, as she felt very apologetic. She knew it must be real, as she didn't feel apologetic very often.

"They are."

"So why were they trying to kill *you*?" he asked, bewildered. She sighed again and held her head in her hands for a moment.

"It's complicated and it won't make much sense if I don't tell you *everything*," she said, sadly.

"How did you *know*?" he asked, suddenly alert again.

"*What*?" she asked, not sure what he was asking.

"How did *you* know they were there...?" He stopped himself, realising the place was bugged. "*Sorry, silly question*."

"I love you and because I care about you *more than anyone else*, I *have* to protect you. I'm good at protecting, but I admit I... I probably need to be a bit gentler about it. I'm not a gentle person," she admitted, a bit ashamed of herself now. She could have been a bit less... *unfeeling* about it.

"*That's true*," he grunted, remembering. She gave him a weary but playful look.

"You *know* what I'm talking about," she hissed at him. He reached across for her hand and she smiled, willingly surrendering it. Barrier broken. I'm safe. *He's forgiven me*!

"Here's the nub of it," he said, awkwardly. "You're the most *amazing* woman I've ever known, and I'm not just saying that. I never met a woman before who, when she's too tired to get up, just shoots the lights out."

"That was a *single occurrence*; I have never done that before or since. At least, not out of *tiredness*, anyway," she protested, mildly. He held up his finger for her silence and she stopped.

"Look at me," he said, seriously. "If we were being compared in terms of physical attractiveness, *I would have no business being with you.* And you're *so strong*, sometimes I feel ever so slightly intimidated, and not in a good way. *Inadequate.* I know you *say I'm not,* but there's part of me that won't believe you. It's like sharing my bed with a dangerous animal. Sometimes when I look into your eyes, it's the scariest thing because I have no idea what you're going to do next." She was trying not to laugh now and she hid it well but he seemed to notice.

"It's not funny," he said, allowing a small smile of his own. "I am constantly worried you'll leave me for someone you like more than me."

She understood. To him, her decision to be with him must seem odd. If she was honest, at first, she wouldn't have known the reasons behind that decision either. She'd just started to *like* him. Looking like he did, he was never going to sweep anyone off their feet with a glance or a dazzling smile. Knowing him, if he tried that, he'd probably trip over something as he did it, fall down a set of steps and end up in a pond at the bottom. But through gradual exposure and contact he'd grown on her over a period of time. That kind of magnetism, in its way, was far more understated and consequently much harder to resist when it got this far. At first he'd meant nothing, then quite suddenly, the opposite was true. He meant everything. This might have been heightened or exacerbated by their initially restricted access to one another; whatever, she was sure a psychologist would have a marvellous time over this.

"I love you because… You make me feel better about myself and I know you will never hurt me," she said, tenderly. Then she smiled softly. *"Not on purpose, anyway."*

"I said I was *sorry*," he grumbled, rolling his eyes. "You're miles heavier than you look, you know, it's your muscles."

"All was forgiven! *Is* forgiven" she said, smiling mildly. "The laughter afterwards hurt me more than being dropped, anyway. That's another reason why I love you. Because no matter *how bad that galaxy out there gets…* you can still make me laugh and that is something I don't want to lose. You remind me what it's like to feel alive, and not just like some cold machine. Today, people are more incapable of dealing with their own emotions than ever, myself included, but you teach me things. Things about myself that I'd forgotten, or worse still that I never knew..." All of that was true, but she felt she'd overdone it and the expression on his face told her that she was correct.

"Are you being serious?" he asked, not being serious.

"*Yes, it's true,*" she promised. "And I *know* you want more of me, don't you? You want to know *who I am* and know me completely?" He leaned away from her, a suspicious look on his face.

"It would... *be nice,*" he permitted, noncommittal. "Do I have to sign any disclaimers first?" She pulled a face at him.

"Sometimes I have done and will have to do *very bad things,*" she told him, a bleakness coming over her. Flashbacks of some of the deeds she'd committed ran through her mind. Some on orders... many not so. "*Coldblooded murder being the least of them.* I don't *enjoy it.* I do what needs to be done... and what I'm ordered to do. If you're willing to stay with me and love me, I can promise that I will love you back with everything I've got... *whatever that is...* but you think I'm pretty? *Inside, I'm not at all pretty.* And I have secrets, *bad ones. I cannot tell you all of them. Not yet, if ever. You would hate me.*"

"...That's okay, I'm not sure I want to know *all* of them," he murmured, very serious suddenly. "How about you just tell me about this Operation *Selector* for now? *Everything else can wait.* At least then I might understand what's going on and... you will have someone to complain to about it. I *promise* I will never say a word to a living soul about this - *other than you, obviously.* I've been on the edge of this *other you* for sometime now and though she scares me... I think I can take her."

"*Are you sure?* Once I fully let you into my heart, I'm not sure I'll be able to let you go... *ever,*" she warned, emotionally. Once she'd decided on someone, she would be in for the long haul. It was her nature. "I'm *very* possessive, twisted and angry but I don't *mean* to be that way... I confuse love with control sometimes... If you can't deal with that then *please... let me know.*"

"...I've survived so far," he smiled, lightly. "And I have to admit I've been very curious about all the things that you've been doing. I may not be capable of much beyond selling ships and making you laugh, but I want to know *you*. If you think I won't love you when I know the truth... *it's highly unlikely*. I *know* you kill. I *know* you steal. I *know* you have a bit of a temper. I know you don't like politicians, journalists... *or chilli*," he said, grinning. She smiled, regarding him solemnly.

"I don't *mind* chilli, just in moderation," she corrected, gently.

"I know your favourite drink, I know you don't care about money..." he paused, beginning to think that he actually might know her better than he had realised.

"What's my favourite colour?" she enquired, crossing her arms demandingly. He pulled a face, ashamed that he didn't know.

"Blacky-whitey-yellowy... *blue*?" he guessed, hopefully. He was trying to get clues from her expression as he listed all the colours, but it was a fruitless exercise.

"Pink," she told him, in a whisper. He began to shake his head in disbelief. "*You tell anyone else that and you're dead*." He held his hands up in capitulation.

"Now... do you want to know about my mission here?" she asked, so quietly he had to really concentrate. Sensing she'd pretty much sealed the deal, she put her arms around him and began to whisper in his ear. The only person likely to overhear any of this was Zax, and Satiah wasn't worried about her anymore. They had their deal, and Zax would one day have to be told a few more secrets too. It took her the best part of an hour to explain it fully.

Carl was astounded, so much so that he suggested half way through that she was making it up. The levels of corruption. The layers of deception. It didn't seem real, but he knew that if Satiah said it was real, then it was. She told him about what she had to do. Who she was working with and how it had all started to get a bit out of control. She told him about the killers, the politicians behind them, and the leaked document that she'd orchestrated herself. As a Federation citizen, Carl figured that they had rigged votes too, but nothing on this scale - so far as he knew. But then, as Satiah pointed out, it happens everywhere all the time. Manipulation. At last, feeling surprisingly good for it, Satiah was done. Her confession was oddly liberating. And Carl was right: it was good to talk to someone about it.

"And *that's* where I am now," she concluded. They sat in silence for a moment.

"...I *had* been thinking about watching the debate but, if it's scripted, I think I'll wait for the book to come out," he said, grimly. "Will you sign my copy?"

"*Do you still love me?*" she purred, in his ear. Her pulled her fully onto his lap and hugged her.

"*O no*, you're not going to turn *all needy* are you?" he scoffed, making her giggle. "I don't think I could stand *that*."

"Tell me you love me," she requested, again.

"No."

"Tell me," she grinned.

"Okay, *all right*, stop nagging! I'll say it *just this once* but then I'm clean for a year," he chuckled. "I love you. Do you love me?"

"No," she teased. "*Maybe* a bit."

"Well, that's a start," he grumbled, with false misery.

"Are *we* still damaged?" she asked, seriously. He hugged her more tightly.

"*We're okay*. So... you *really* aren't even *a bit* interested in Oli?" he clarified, one last time. She rolled her eyes.

"If I wasn't under orders *to protect him*, I imagine that I would most likely have killed him myself by now," she scoffed.

"*That's my girl*," he chuckled. "I'm sorry for being insecure, I... I hadn't realised until last night exactly how much you meant to me. I trust you too, and in future I will endeavour *not* to overreact."

"No apology required. The thought of you with another woman doesn't exactly sit well with me either. Another drink?" she offered, smiling. He nodded, and then grabbed her before she could get off of him.

"*What?*" she asked, haughtily.

"*Pink?!*"

---

"I have no plans to change the law with regard to the legalisation of that substance," Brenda stated, flatly. "I have stated before *the reasons why* and I think we could all go through this one in our sleep. It would lead to c-c-chaos, would be the short answer. It's inevitable. Scientific tampering leading to completely different unnatural drugs that *may* assist in pain relief do not outweigh the potential side-effects. Legal medical research will get the results you want in its own time, where the proper ethics and proper measures are taken to ensure it is all s-safe."

"What about the health benefits?" shouted someone.

"There are many benefits to taking certain elements of the drug, I understand companies have already taken those elements and made them into legal forms of *medicine*!" Brenda said, smiling a bit. "Illegal adaptation of drugs is something we should all avoid."

"Okay, next question!" Deetee swept in, eager to put that one down. He knew what was coming next and if he didn't manage it correctly, it could damage all three candidates.

"Isn't it about time that the planetary type tax system was finally sorted? Is there any need for different planets to be taxed differently based on their type or class or whatever you want to call it? This also affects voting privileges too, shouldn't this be addressed in the name of equality?"

"Planetary tax is based on their status. A, B or P class world. Planet Earth is *A class* and planet Sewjumite is *B Class*," Oli said, answering first. "Now, planets are categorised into one of these three, based on their contribution to the Coalition. This contribution is not just tax, but raw materials, retail products and all manner of other things. *A class* planets tend to have a large and permanent civilian infrastructure with administration, law enforcement cover, and even military investment. *B class* tend to be more colonial in operation, and are established as temporary living areas with a view to maximisation of money making, and not so much on long term habitation. A common example would be mining worlds. P class are protectorate worlds that are not *in* but are *of* the Coalition. It is due to these criteria that the worlds are taxed differently and have different rights regarding any elections within the Coalition."

*Operation Selector*

As usual, Oli was displaying a good understanding of the topic, good groundwork for an actual answer. This was Oli on form now, doing his best to remain dispassionate.

"On an A class world, such as this one, each citizen's vote counts as one. This will always be the case, no matter how many re-votes or recounts occur. A B class world however, due to the fact that is not included as a population centre, only counts as half a vote for each citizen registered there. Therefore, it takes two people for each individual vote. Roughly speaking, the only time that this rule changes is in the unlikely event of an exact tie, and then the half – or 0.5 - figure will be rounded up to one. Protectorates do not have any say in election procedures, but they do pay tax. They pay tax to fund their own protection services from us, a fleet or a platoon, or whatever that happens to be.

"The system is like this to prevent companies and corporations, which own the facilities on B class planets, from manipulating the vote to their advantage. It is because of this reason that I have no plans to alter the planetary class system," Oli concluded. He didn't add that, if they didn't like it, then they could join the Federation or the Union. There were things that had to be done to improve democracy within the Coalition, but Oli really believed that messing with the planetary class system was not one of them. Despite, or perhaps because of, the fact that his answer was not only correct but was also reasonable, the crowd didn't like it.

"But B class worlds *directly* supply the economy of the Coalition; they contribute more than A class planets on average…!"

"Based on *what* research, exactly?" Mark asked, shrewdly.

"It's logical! Raw materials are needed for there to *be* an economy so that the A class planets can support the population, that's how the system is supposed to work," Deetee interjected. "The A planets are where most people live and the B planets are where the hardest work is done. So if the system is really based on contribution then B class should be considered even more important than A class. Metal ore, energy sources both renewable and otherwise, are integral to everything."

"And you think that simply because they provide the food for the industrial beast that they are worth more? *Who* protects them with naval forces? *Who* educates the new work forces? *Who* houses the corporations in the first place? *Who* moves in to *help save lives* in the event of an accident?" Oli countered, still keeping calm.

"The system is as equal as it's ever going to be," Mark agreed. "It's practically synergetic. A mutually beneficial relationship of dependence and security. People will always claim that their work is more important than others, but in this case they are incorrect."

Deetee cursed quietly, he'd assumed that Oli and Mark would disagree, and he couldn't bring Brenda in for obvious reasons. The aide was watching too from the quiet concentration of the directors' room, and was also annoyed.

"*Shame*. I put a thousand Essps on that blowing up like a volcano," she said, disappointed. Royston held out his hand and she reluctantly handed over the cash.

"I told you my dear, *even if it is controversial*, no politician worthy of the name would ever move to change something so elemental. It's in no one's interests. No one with a brain, anyway," he chuckled.

"You were right," she groaned, watching again. "At least Deetee left Brenda out of that one. I fear we may have underestimated Oli." Royston shrugged.

"*It's not over until it's over.*"

───────•••••••───────

"So you still don't know who this angel is?" Carl asked, frowning deeply.

"No idea," she confessed, irritated at herself. "I've been looking, checking up backgrounds, going through potential suspects.... and finding no one." She'd shown him the messages, the first retrieved by Randal and the second by Zax. She slid out of bed and began to dress again as he continued to study the messages.

**I won't rest until this is over. I won't let him get away with this. Oli cannot win the election, he must be stopped. I will use any means at my disposal to achieve this. I will avenge you, my angel.**

**It seems our enemy has an enemy, but one which we clearly can't trust to do what must be done. Bluntly: the enemy of my enemy can never be my friend. I won't forget you angel, no one should.**

Carl focussed on the angel aspects of the messages, unnerved slightly.

"Don't look good, does it?" he said, offering his own contender for the *understatement of the year* award. She frowned.

"It looks damningly suspicious," she stated, casually.

"That a technical expression?" he joked, rhetorically. "I read a crime drama once, a story called *The Apartment in the Orange Zone*, and the guy in *that* faked threatening letters to himself in order to incriminate his rival. Is there any chance something like that could be happening here?"

Satiah paused. Oli sending the messages to himself? She had to admit she'd never thought of that. *Why, though*? He didn't even know that the notes existed or what they said… and he had claimed not to know an angel. *Who did*? Then again, his first love interest Sally was dead so… that would explain why no one is replying.

"No, it's something I hadn't thought of - but unlikely, don't you think? Besides, *I think* you're still jealous," she quipped.

"Well, that's me done," he chuckled, placing the device back onto the table.

"*Nice try*," she said, sarcastically.

"Well, what did you expect? That I would somehow solve everything instantly?" he said, incredulously.

"It would have been lovely if you had," she giggled. "No… thanks for trying though, let me know if you have any other ideas."

"*Well…*" he paused, eyeing her.

"About *the mission*," she grinned, levelly. He grunted in feigned disappointment. "I have to go back, I can't stay in bed with you all day! To be honest, I'm finding it hard to concentrate on the actual mission anyway, now that I have Lunell, Mr Slimy and their friends on my back."

"Yeah, I mean, you'd think they'd at least wait until you completed your mission *before* they tried to kill you," he joshed.

"*Exactly,*" she pouted, playing along. "To be fair to them, *even though they don't know it,* I haven't exactly been doing an exemplary job. It's because of *me* that Oli's proportional representation is playing tennis with the skyscrapers right now."

"There's *no way* you could have predicted that," he scoffed, as incredulous as she had been. "Do you want to watch the debate, see how it's going?"

She gave him a look that implied she'd rather pull her own eyelids off.

"*Just a suggestion! No need to shoot the lights out!*" he declared, shrugging. "You know what? I know I was initially horrified, and kind of still am, but I'm glad you've told me all this. It's kind of exciting, isn't it?" Again she gave him the look. "No, no it's not, you're completely right," he said, quickly. "I don't know *what* I was thinking." She giggled.

"I know, I know, I suppose *sometimes* it is exciting... *when I get my answers...*" she allowed. "But *deadly*. Never forget that last part."

"And *you* like it?" he asked, tentatively.

"I think a part of me *must*, otherwise I think I'd be dead by now," she responded, chillingly. "The first rule they teach any Phantom is that you must survive... irrespective of anything, *even your mission*. Why? Because so long as you're alive, it's a lot easier to kill." He eyed her levelly. "Or not," she amended, more softly. "While there is life there is hope."

◆◆◆◆◆◆

Oli could not believe this. If there wasn't one, then there were a hundred different ways of looking at the same thing. He had *expected* the leaked document to come up in the debate; he had *rehearsed* well-prepared answers to deal with it. He'd hoped that, if it was brought up, it would either be about *who he thought had done it and why,* or it would be from the vantage point of people who thought he'd done it and *someone had leaked it to rightfully expose him*. And, in a way, that second option *had* come up. However, it seemed that *this person believed* he'd created it himself for the sole purpose of framing his brother and making himself more popular in the process. This was annoying because it was something he and Kate had never considered. It was also annoying because he had no idea how to answer this for the best. Kate was looking on, agitated that they'd not thought of this and even more worried about what Oli would say to try to get out of it.

"Well now, Oli," Deetee smiled, clearly enjoying this. "That's quite an *interesting* question, isn't it? Did you *allow* that tax document to be leaked simply to elevate your own popularity as you knew that the public would blame your brother?"

"That is a slanderous thing to ask," Oli blustered. Brenda looked on uncomfortably but glee was in almost everyone else's faces. Deetee knew that for the first time he'd dealt a huge blow to Oli. Oli had answered in a very predictable way which would further convince people that this lie was true. "I can assure you that someone else leaked that file, quite obviously in an attempt to ruin *my* campaign. You can tell by its content that it was *definitely* aimed at me."

"*O my, you little minx,*" Royston gawped, as he looked on. He was impressed by the new spin Brenda's aide had created.

"I was desperate," admitted the aide, levelly. "I had to do *something* and this was the only thing I could think of at short notice."

"It's a *personal attack,* but it's *from the public* and it's a reasonable query for those with cynical minds. Actually, this might be genius," Royston smiled. "It makes the debate look *even more* realistic."

"We'll see," she muttered, not at all confident. It had been a last minute change and those were never a good idea if they could be avoided. Deetee had managed it though.

"It's very difficult to prove a negative, but you have to admit it ruined your brother's chances completely, *regardless* of who leaked it or why?" Deetee smoothly interjected. Oli was almost overwhelmed by the sudden impulse to punch Deetee in the face. He wanted to shout out about how this was all a set up! A deliberate attempt being made by the media just to trip him up. *The slur.* He knew if he did, though, he'd never get anywhere. Quite the opposite, actually.

"My brother and I do not get on, *this is a well known fact,* and I would like to stress *how much* I feel that this is an unworthy subject for this occasion," Oli protested, floundering.

## Hulta Gertrude

"Well, you *would* say that though, *wouldn't you?*" Deetee asked, as if he was discussing the weather. "It's one of those unfortunate things, isn't it? It's almost like the next thing you will say is that *'there is nothing I can say to absolve myself of this without making it look like a lie'*, isn't it?"

Brenda once again did all she could for him.

"Oli does have a point, this is hardly the place for such matters to be dwelt on," she said, stepping dangerously far away from her script. "True or not, right now it's more of a smear than anything else."

"Perhaps it isn't the right place, but it would be *undemocratic* for any of us to *ignore* such a relevant issue," Deetee wriggled. "One politician has already paid the price for it, but how else can we be sure it was the right one?" Brenda knew she should say no more, indeed, she didn't know what else she could say.

"That tax document was leaked by someone employed on my staff and it was done to ruin my campaign. Some think it was my brother who orchestrated it, and that may be true, but there is no proof of any of these theories," Oli maintained, slightly more solidly now. Brenda's intervention, ineffective as it was, had bought him just enough time to recover his composure.

"As you say," Deetee agreed, seriously. "The fact is that, whoever leaked it, it caused your sudden rise in proportional representation. That has happened regardless of who intended what. It *might* look to some like a kind of conspiracy."

"*Probably best if you avoid using the word conspiracy*," the director's voice said, in Deetee's ear.

"It might," Oli allowed, smiling tightly.

"Anything to add?" Deetee asked, eyeing Brenda and Mark. Brenda scowled and shook her head. Mark pondered for a moment before letting it slide. He was hardly coming off very well either and laying into Oli, however successfully, wouldn't help his own popularity. It would just make him look vindictive. The damage had mostly likely been done by Deetee himself, so… move on. Deetee asked for another question.

"What about votes for prisoners?" That was the next question. It was a sign of how bad tempered everyone had become that not one of the three candidates volunteered to go first. It was nearly over, and then Deetee could go into the long prepared dialogue about previous elections and their differences and similarities. "Brenda, you've been quiet for a while, let's hear your answer to that very germane question from the public."

"Currently, once arrested and convicted, a citizen loses all rights. The right to vote in an election is one of those. I don't think that should change. Not ever. I-I-I know there is some discussion about potential miscarriages of justice and th-th-things like that but criminals are not deserving of a voice in our society. It might be something they could take advantage of," she answered.

"Have you considered the consequences of that?" Oli asked, to Brenda. Brenda eyed him in confusion.

"Which consequences?" she enquired, genuinely puzzled.

"Those with *custodial sentences* could be affected. I imagine they might see it as a form of *debeingisation* which could ruin their rehabilitation," Oli argued, levelly. He was trying to make up for lost ground. "I feel you're in danger of confusing *criminal convictions* with *removal from democratic society* which would be against their rights and, as I said, might hinder their path to return as a law abiding, rehabilitated citizen."

Deetee was concerned. Brenda seemed unable or unwilling to counter that sufficiently. She stood there, apparently frozen either in thought or disbelief. Deetee had to move in quickly to cover for her.

"Surely," Deetee stated, smiling his usual smile, "repeat offenders *at least* should have their right to vote taken from them?" He directed his question at Brenda, in the hope that she'd use it to help herself.

"If more criminals succeeded in being rehabilitated, then this would have great benefits," Oli went on, unconcerned. "Reduced reoffending rates and less detention centre overcrowding problems. Improvement in the conditions of said facilities. In any case, *in a democracy*, doesn't everyone count?" Brenda still seemed tongue tied; in reality she was genuinely considering the question and Oli's answer, as it did make some sense in her mind. Again, Deetee stepped in, fearing she'd forgotten what to say. She might even be having some kind of seizure. In either case, he had to defend her.

Somewhere hidden, under the surface of the planet deep down, lights came on - revealing an android copy of Brenda. Ready in case of emergency, this AI would act as a substitute in case there really was something wrong with Brenda. Standby mode was not activated and a countdown began during which her entire history and personality were being automatically programmed. Beside her, in the darkness, there existed copies of Oli, Sam and everyone else running in the election.

Back in the debate though, Deetee was still working on damage control.

"Wouldn't it be *rather expensive* though? Giving these offenders the facility *and* the information they would need to make an informed decision? Think of all those facilities which would need to be upgraded, and the cost of those upgrades. Also, there is another danger. Suppose someone accused of vote rigging is being held there. Could they not manipulate the system?" An angry buzz in Deetee's ear came through as he had mentioned vote rigging.

"No more so than they could anywhere else..." Oli shrugged.

"Indeed, the centres themselves could be considered an easy target for propaganda as their media access would have to be restricted?" Deetee blathered, changing his question adeptly. "It would not be easy to prove the legitimacy of any prisoner's vote either."

"Currently, yes, that would be a concern, but with a *different management strategy* those problems could be avoided," Oli smiled, calmly. Still Brenda was silent, and Deetee was starting to sweat.

"What about how the public feel with regard to *sharing their vote* with those who have turned against them?" Deetee asked, glad to have struck on a new tactic.

Royston, the Commander and the aide all looked on, deeply concerned. Everyone was way off script now.

"Okay, *hold it*," the aide said, to the director. "Suspend it. I need to check on Brenda again, there might be something wrong." She hurried from the room, looking stressed. "Use the nudist running across the screen strategy, I'll be back!"

"If it wasn't for Deetee, *that* could have ended in disaster," the Commander said.

"It still might," Royston glowered. They could hear the crowd roaring in horror and amused surprise as a naked man ran across the platform chased by security guards. This was an agreed upon delaying tactic which was in place so that, should any problems occur, everyone was distracted.

"That Oli is a problem," the Commander went on.

"*He's certainly becoming one*," Royston growled. "I thought we had him just now, but he's pulled this one out of nowhere."

---

"You called that guy about Kelvin?" Carl asked, disbelieving.

"You were right," Satiah said, very deliberately. "And I was being... *overly protective*. He's coming tonight to have a look at Kelvin, and you and I will be here *watching him*. I know there are still some things we haven't talked about, so don't think that it's all going to be magical from now on...? In real life, nothing ever really goes away, but I think this is workable." He nodded.

"So much for you being simple and uncomplicated," he smirked, casually. She shrugged.

"I prefer the term *quirky*."

"I am impressed about your leap into the unknown... sounds *like a plan*," Carl nodded, pleased. "Any chance you could make Kelvin a bit sort of *nicer* to me?"

"No," she stated, flatly. Then she smiled. "Why? What did he do?"

"Nothing... it's just the way he stares at me sometimes and on occasion when *you and me are... you know*? *I feel like he's listening*," Carl admitted. She snorted with laughter.

"It's okay, he's just my friend, that's all, he's not... he's *just* a machine," Satiah assured him.

"Yeah..." Carl murmured uncertainly, as he eyed the inert Kelvin. "I was just your *friend* once too..."

"As much fun as this has been, I *have* to get back to work. The debate will be at an end soon, and I will need to catch up on what happened," she said, touching her earpiece. "Zax?"

"Bodies taken care of, I deactivated your drive as ordered and Randal is aware," Zax replied, efficiently.

"Good," Satiah congratulated, casually. "Anything new?"

"The debate is still going on, I have detected an unusual transmission coming from the debate building," Zax went on. Satiah could hear clicking and scrabbling in the background as Zax tried to learn more.

"O yes," she mused, going through the likely options. Bomb, illegal broadcasting to pirate station and many others.

"It seems to be coming from the parking area," Zax elucidated.

Satiah guessed it before Zax confirmed it. A tracking device.

"Is it on the vehicle Oli arrived in?" Satiah asked, knowingly.

"It is," Zax established.

"I'll tell Malla to ensure that they switch ships on departure," Satiah told her. "Well spotted."

"Thanks... so, is everything okay...?" Zax began. Satiah rolled her eyes and cut her off. She called Malla and told him of the tracking device. He agreed and ordered another craft to be sent through. He did wonder why, if they already knew where Oli was, why they were trying to track him. Satiah told him it was likely that it was the other group who might not know.

"How are things going?" Satiah enquired, in an off-the-cuff sort of way.

"Haven't you been watching?" he asked, incredulous.

"No," she responded. *I'm not into fiction...*

"It's... right now, things aren't looking so great," he explained, not going into detail. "Don't get me wrong, I think Oli's done pretty well, but it's all got a bit tricky."

---

"That's the third person you've sent to try to kill me and Satiah. Don't even attempt to deny it. If you send more they will be dealt with in the same way. Don't make me send someone to kill you, Snell... I'll only need to send one," Randal growled.

"I don't know what you mean," Scott lied. "I've not sent anyone to kill anyone."

"Now I know that's a lie," Randal stated, grimly. "We've all done *that*."

"I'm not going to pretend to know what this is about, but I will start an investigation…" he began.

"Don't bother," Randal cut him off in mid-sentence, bored by his act. "Try anything else… I dare you." This time he cut him off on the communicator.

---

Collorah, in *yet another* new craft, waited on the rooftop of a nearby structure. He knew where the debate was being held, and had decided that he would follow Oli on his way back to his office. Satiah would be there, of course, but then this had stopped being an easy ride a long time ago. He was fully healed now and ready to attack again. He tuned in to watch the debate, not so much for entertainment, but more as a way of figuring out when Oli might be leaving. Unbeknownst to him, a short distance away, Jinx and Octutin were also waiting to pick up the tracking signal. Jinx had thought it best to leave immediately, but Octutin said it would be better to remain just in case, *for whatever reason*, there was a vehicle change.

---

"W-what's going on?" Brenda asked, nervously. The aide smiled, hoping to conceal her inner frustrated rage.

"*Technical difficulties.* I think security captured the exhibitionist. *How unfortunate.* Still, in a way it was lucky, as the interruption allowed me time to come and see you. I was concerned as you seemed to have stopped speaking, despite several things being asked of you, did you need to run through what we rehearsed again?" she offered, carefully.

"No, it wasn't *that*, I'm fine. It's just that I think Oli might have a point about the detrimental effect on rehabilitation programs," Brenda stated. "It is about their rights as beings." The aide's face froze, but somehow she was able not to snap at Brenda.

"This is a complicated issue, *I agree*," lied the aide, still trying gentle persuasion. "Before this started, though, we *did* agree on your stance.

If you want to change that stance then that is fine, but it would be unwise to do it now in the middle of the debate. If people see you as easily influenced, they might start to think you're weak and therefore not fit to be leader."

Brenda's eyes went wide in comprehension. "...I see what you mean," she gasped, clearly torn. "I... *I don't know.*"

"Why do you think they asked such a question in the first place? *They are testing your resolve.* I wouldn't be surprised if *Oli* somehow *made* this happen," the aide said, sensing progress. "Now, you *really* don't want them to think you're *weak-minded*, do you?"

"Why would he *do that*? I don't understand. I've been as fair as I can with him, and I felt *so sorry for him* because of what Deetee was doing..."

"What was *Deetee* doing?" the aide asked, as if she didn't know.

"He was victimising him and deliberately making him look bad for no reason, other than he was *enjoying* the humiliation. That was *bullying* and that was wrong," Brenda explained. "So I did what I could to stop it. *It's what anyone would have done.*"

The aide sighed.

"Of course," she established, very convincingly. "I doubt Oli did anything because *he dislikes you*; I think he did it purely to beat you. Assuming he did - I mean, I *could be wrong*, it just seemed *rather convenient timing* to me." Brenda still seemed torn and unable to decide what to do. She was trapped in a moral quandary over the issue.

"You know, immediately after all that flap about *the leaked tax document?*" the aide pressed. That clinched it.

"*I think you're right*," Brenda gasped, falling for it. "So I-I-I stick to my stance for now, and then maybe I could change the law later?"

"...If you like," the aide growled, before smiling again. "I should warn you, though, that these law changes sometimes take a *very* long time to bring about, and right now we *do have* other priorities."

"You're right, *I have to stay focussed*," Brenda nodded, her determination returning. The aide glanced at the time. Four minutes gone, that left an eight minute safety margin. The nudist strategy could be maintained convincingly for that long though, so no real harm done. No interruption to filming would be required, and the editors could finish the job. Deep under the Earth's surface, the android replica of Brenda deactivated once again and the whole place plunged back into darkness.

"Let's go," the aide beamed, in apparent pleasure. *"Let's get this over with."* She handed Brenda a glass of water for the sake of appearance, and then headed back to the director's office.

"Well?" Royston asked, a little on edge. He wanted to know if there was a problem with Brenda, as did they all.

"It's okay, she's fine," she responded, nodding. "Very easily led, that's all."

"Can't complain too much about that. It's part of the reason why she's got to win," the Commander grunted. The debate was resumed, and no one who was watching would ever suspect the truth. Brenda's reputation would hopefully remain untarnished.

"I still say that *as offenders*, they deserve to lose their citizens' rights as a punishment for breaking the law. It's the start of a slippery slope," Brenda explained, upon her return. "What will it be next? *Their right to freedom is being overlooked due to their status a-a-a-as prisoners?"* Deetee and the audience laughed convincingly in agreement to that. Oli rolled his eyes. "Besides, as Deetee mentioned earlier, it's just not financially viable right now. I'm sorry, but if you do the crime you *must* do the time and *with that*, you must accept the f-f-full weight of the sentence. I fear if we were to allow this right for prisoners to vote, it might start something that would result in jail time no longer being a useful deterrent against first-time offenders. And I'm sure no one in here would willingly support the idea of giving hard-line criminals *any* additional rights at all! If you allow them to have the vote, you also create a risk of dividing the criminal community and ruining *their type of equality."*

"Well, *if you say so*, I bow to your superior judgement on that," Deetee said, trying to seem as if she'd blinded him with science. That last point she'd made did raise a few eyebrows, but was left unchallenged by either Oli or Mark. The financial argument was strongest and neither of them could think of a suitable counter on the spur of the moment.

"It's true, they *already* get to watch programmes *and* they have better food sometimes than we do!" some being shouted.

"They don't have to pay *a single bill!*" a woman concurred loudly.

"Settle down, settle down!" Deetee chuckled, flapping his hand at them. "The debate is meant to happen up here, not down there, or is that also a matter of opinion?" More laughter. Finally, it was time for the last questions. Brenda, though recently reinvigorated, was pleased this was coming to an end. As much as she loved democracy, it could give her a very painful headache sometimes.

"What are you going to do about fake news scaremongering?!" shouted someone. Ah yes, the many layers of propaganda, easily outnumbering the layers of irony, seemed now to be playing tag with one another. It was only sensible to create a lot of *blatantly transparent types of propaganda* to ensure that the *real lies* were less obvious. People would think themselves clever for seeing through what they thought was *the real* propaganda. This was possibly the most caustic question so far, especially when you remembered that the very programme of the debate was little more than propaganda itself.

It was effectively a wheelie in the propaganda world. What was real? What wasn't? How could they ever know? Deetee really had to fight to stop himself collapsing into hysterics. Royston and everyone in the director's box all had a jolly good laugh about it too. The aide received many a slap on her back for what they considered to be a truly hilarious joke. One last kick where it hurts, and democracy is made and unmade simultaneously. In a sense, to prevent democracy from existing, it had to be seen to exist, and therefore it *did* on some level exist. A most tragic circumstance. *Question*: aren't the best prisons the ones which tricked their inmates into thinking they were really free? *Answer*: it depends.

"There are *many* of these fake news outlets and, despite rigorous attempts to suppress these outbreaks of unsupervised propaganda, a lot of it is still getting tangled up with regulated media," Deetee surmised, as he headed back onto the stage. "For the last question, any volunteers?" This time it was Mark who opened the can.

"There seem to be two main types: those who try to replicate the format of the established media, and those who do not. It is against the law to broadcast your own channel unless you have a permit. To avoid this, they have switched to virtual means. It's hard to trace and even harder to prosecute," Mark explained. "It's a common problem and it's affecting everyone, even those *outside* the Coalition."

"Agreed, so what do you intend to do to combat it?" Deetee probed.

"I would try a technical approach. Design Artificial Intelligences to operate as automatic watchers, much like a virus check, to spot and contain these fake news items *before* they can spread and confuse everyone. I understand they already use something similar to protect children when they are in the virtual realms unsupervised," Mark suggested, reasonably. "The place where this is happening is mainly, if not completely, in the *virtual* world. Therefore, that is the place we need to be to fight it."

"See, a lot of people are worried by AIs, that's a separate issue we covered earlier. I say that now, but it is relevant, there could be a danger of the AIs intercepting genuine news," Deetee argued. "This would have a potentially disastrous impact, especially if a weather warning or something of greater importance was incorrectly seized?" *An election result, perhaps?*

---

"This right here is *why* I became a mercenary," Satiah complained, watching the debate through the darkened glass with Malla. "Democracy *shimockery*, all I can hear is *talk, talk and more talk* but they never *do* anything." Malla chuckled.

"They do go on a bit, I'll let you have that one," he temporised. Lunell remained silent, ever watchful. He had not been surprised to see Satiah return, even though he knew PAI agents would be striking at her that morning. They had clearly failed. He'd been ordered to take no action until after Satiah had been confirmed dead and, as she was still very much alive, that plan was clearly not going to happen any time soon.

"Where's Kate?" Satiah asked, curious.

"She's with Shannon in the side aisles where she can see and hear better," Malla told her.

"*Rather them than me*," she murmured, snootily.

"Made up your mind yet who to vote for, Lunell?" Malla asked, casually. Lunell smiled cunningly as he turned to face them.

"Still weighing up the pros and cons. I must say, Oli performed very well, considering some of the curveballs that went his way," he said, changing the subject subtly. His gaze lowered to Satiah. "What about you, or do you *remain* staunchly uninterested?"

"Some people were trying to change my mind earlier, but when they realised how fruitless their endeavour was... I don't think they were too pleased about the price they paid when they got my answer," she remarked. Lunell's eyes narrowed, taking on her real meaning at once. Malla glanced over at them, mildly confused by the exchange. There was a moment of great tension where Satiah and Lunell just stared at one another intently.

Finally Lunell looked away and headed outside.

"What was all that about?" Malla asked, when he was out of earshot.

"His turn to check the perimeter," she lied, adeptly.

"Listen, I'm glad he's gone actually, I know you said you didn't want to talk about it but... *you and Oli?*" Malla chanced.

"What about us?" she growled, after a heated sigh. *"Not that there is, or ever will be, an us."*

"Oli is a very sensitive guy, you know?" he informed her. Her shoulders slumped, *o really?* "As I told you before, he's not had the greatest of track records when it comes to the opposite sex."

"You don't say," she couldn't resist throwing in.

"He's been hurt before," Malla continued, sensing that he was failing in his attempt to somehow repair the damage. "It's not done anything for his confidence; indeed, I think it has made him pretty insecure."

"If he's got *issues*, why did he push Shannon away?" she asked, smoothly. Malla winced.

"Yeah..." he conceded, falling silent briefly. "I don't really know what happened there. I know that he pushed her away but I don't know why. We haven't really talked about it." She huffed.

"*Why not?*" she demanded, sarcastically. "*Everyone loves to discuss their private feelings on their own rejections.* If you're worried that this will affect our professional relationship, don't be. I do my job, no matter what it takes. It's nice that you try to support your friend, but in this case it's a lost cause, Malla. If he wants better prospects with *people*, maybe going into politics was a mistake."

Malla laughed at that. "Is that why you missed the debate," he guessed, "because you hate politics so much?"

"Partly – that, and I was busy doing some *actual real work*," she said. She smiled as she said it to take the sting out of it, and also because she was glad Carl had come back and they were closer now than they had ever been before. "Besides, with the way *the media* is these days, you never miss anything. They'll be jabbering about this for years." Malla had to agree with that.

"Next, they'll be analysing their handshakes, and trying to understand the psychology or political stratagem based on how they shake hands," he joked. Satiah knew he was simply jesting, but *worryingly* that had happened before. Satiah wondered momentarily if how she drew her pistol revealed anything about her personality; however, she doubted her target, even if he saw her do it, would have long to reflect on that.

She laughed, amused.

"They do get so carried away with themselves, don't they? Like *children* with a new game to play," she concurred.

"Analysts analysing the methods of analysis as they slowly overanalyse themselves into... madness," he said, shaking his head. "Who do you think will win?"

"No idea," she shrugged. "I think probably Brenda. She did okay in the debate - well, what little I have seen of it - and she was winning before." Malla nodded sombrely.

"You know what that would mean?" he asked, rhetorically. "It would mean we would have to go through all this again in the next election." Satiah groaned inwardly, she'd not thought that far ahead. The idea of having to go through all this again made her want to retch. She remembered Zax's dismal reaction to that idea too.

"Really?" she asked, hiding her disgust well.

"Well yeah, Oli will certainly run again! Look how close he's got this time. Even if he loses now, he made it much further than anyone ever thought he would… *most of all, his brother,*" Malla said. "Kate will convince him, even if he is broken by this, to try again."

"I don't know why *anyone* would want to be Commandment Benefactor, it must be hell every day," Satiah scoffed. She made up her mind to do everything she could to ensure Oli never gave this a second go. If nothing else, it might get him killed.

"He's a lucky man," Malla was saying. "Maybe he's got a guardian angel or something."

It took every ounce of self-control she had to not whirl on him, gun drawn, at that moment. It could have been accidental, just a figure of speech. Or it could be that he had heard *that word* somewhere recently and he was repeating it because it was in his head. Or… he *could be* or *could know* angel? He knew that someone inside their campaign team was working against them, or trying to. The leaked tax document was conclusive evidence of that. Yet she'd never told him about the angel messages. She had told Oli and he *may* have told Malla, but if that was the case then Malla wouldn't have been stupid enough to drop it into conversation like that.

"What makes you say that?" she asked, prudently. "He's got *two* sets of killers after him, that's hardly a sign of good luck."

"True, but he was a *virtual no one a year ago* and here he is now in the *highest circles* of politics. Yes, that leaked document was used against him, but obviously it actually *helped* him more than it hindered him," he answered, eyeing her. *"Are you okay?"*

A kind of chill seemed to have come into the room as Satiah had gone into fight mode. One wrong move from him and he'd be dead before he hit the floor.

"Headache," she excused, convincingly. "You don't have any painkillers that I may use, do you?"

"Sure," he smiled. "Several packs. Virtually addicted to the stuff these days."

"I know what you mean. You wouldn't be *an angel* and go get them for me, would you?" she asked, ready to strike. She saw no visible sign of significance. No indication that that word meant anything special to him.

"No problem, I'll get you some water too," he said, completely casual. He left her alone in the room. She exhaled slowly and thoughtfully. Was it nothing? She had suspected him once before of course, not of being angel specifically, but when he'd been absent on the day the bomb was supposed to have detonated…

---

"Naturally only the most basic of AIs would be necessary for such a role," Mark went on. "After all, Law Enforcement searches for things all the time, and their AIs adjust the results of their searches based on history and personality. Same could be said for the average citizen's shopping list or choice of accommodation. The fake news outlets have found a way of piggybacking this and then gaining access to all other contacts and propagating itself endlessly. Sometimes in several ways to the same person. I myself have been a victim of this, believe me."

"I think there are more than enough AIs out there already, surely just reprogram one of those ones?" Oli suggested. "That's got to be cheaper than designing and running another one?"

"That is possible, I suppose," Mark acquiesced.

"I for one find it interesting that they are invariably *bad news* items," Brenda noted, smiling. "Unambiguously the kind that report on or evoke prejudices. Perhaps they feel those are more realistic looking than good news items." Oli and Mark nodded, having apparently not noticed this before. "Do you think this factors in with their *believability value*? There is an imbalance there, even in *the correct* media channels. Bad news items almost always outnumber the good. Indeed, I challenge anyone here to provide an example of the opposite occurring."

"Yes, but someone's good news might not be someone else's," Oli pointed out. "I do agree with you though. Perhaps some sort of experiment is in order. We should generate our own fake news, several kinds and several types, to see which is believed the most."

The aide's eyes widened. What did anyone think *they* had been doing for the last thousand years? As always, Deetee was there to step in.

"Well, that sounds like a very sensible array of options there," he said, over the continuing discussion. "I'm sure I can bring *some good news* to all of you here, when I tell you we are officially... *out of time!*" Deafening laughter ended any remaining conversation between the candidates. "First, I want to take a moment to thank our candidates for their time and participation," Deetee said, slipping into the suave script smoothly, "and to thank you all for watching, those of you here in our studio audience, and the great mass of you across the cosmos..."

As he was saying this, the candidates were led away separately. In this case, an altercation was unlikely, but it was better for everyone that they were simply kept apart. The dancers once more ran onto the stage to begin their next number. This would then lead into *Deetee's Election Evaluation Hour*. The aide slipped her arm through Brenda's, all friendly support. Brenda was grateful; her legs were feeling rather wobbly.

"You were amazing, they *love* you," she said, pretending to be in awe of Brenda. She also had to reassure her that she'd done everything right.

"Y-you think?" Brenda clarified, nervously. "I'm s-sorry I nearly messed up earlier..."

"Please no, I will not hear of it, it's not a bad thing that you are passionate about what you believe in," she said, slyly.

"Do you know if the military have had any contact from an immortal any time recently?" Brenda asked suddenly, concerned. The aide eyed her in bewilderment. An immortal? Where? As immortals looked like normal people, they were hard to spot, and very dangerous enemies. There was only supposed to be one left alive. So that had to mean Dreda's son... *Ash.*

"...If they have they never mentioned it to me, should they have?" the aide probed, subtly.

---

Mark entered his craft and immediately got out his communicator. "Well?" he asked.

"Too early to tell," Sam replied, seriously. "I think it's fair to say you were ganged up on. Deetee kept jumping on you all the time and annoyingly whatever he said the crowd seemed to like."

"I was going to ask you about the proportional representation?" he said, bitterly.

"That's what I meant but too early to tell," Sam said. "From early on we knew Brenda had this made. And Oli's time is running out."

"We hope."

---

"As good as ever, I think," Royston concluded. "Brenda was hit a few times but she had to be to make things look realistic. Mark was a buffoon who was capitalised on by everyone, I think. Oli did cause a few problems, but he was damaged badly towards the end and, while he did recover, I really don't imagine he will become any more popular."

"If this somehow fails and Oli overtakes Brenda, we take the next step - *agreed*?" the Commander asked, grimly.

"Agreed!" everyone chorused.

"I will inform the government," he nodded, turning to leave.

"Yes do, and please tell them to keep the celebration as *well managed* as possible, we want it to look true to life. You can't have everyone looking happy, the public might get suspicious. Tell that ambassador... o errrm... *what's his name*? The one who's *supposed to be* Brenda's main *party* rival?" Royston had forgotten.

"Sawma," provided the aide, rolling her eyes.

"Yes, tell him to look *positively grief stricken* when the result is in. We could have fun with him later, should we need to contain Brenda," he smiled, always looking ahead.

"When she wins, I will initiate the plan for the next election," the aide nodded, "and I will start work on her next campaign." Royston nodded. "Very good."

"There is one more thing," the aide said, stopping him as he went to leave.

"What?"

"Brenda said something just now about an immortal contacting the military, have you heard anything?" she asked, curious. He frowned deeply.

"No..." he said. "Any details?"

"No," she replied, unhelpfully.

"...I'll look into it, normally if immortals are around they do not use the regular lines of communication," he stated, still thinking about it. "I'll make a few discreet enquiries."

---

Oli came in and the door swished closed behind him. He ran his hands though his hair and let out a huge sigh. Kate rushed forward.

"It's over, you've done it, it's over, *you were fantastic,*" she said, earnestly. She meant every word, of course, but to some this would sound rather hollow. He slumped into a seat as Malla handed him a drink.

"We should leave..." Shannon began, but Malla shook his head. There was no rush and Oli needed a rest.

"Can I just... sit and *be* for a moment, please?" Oli requested, gulping it down. Satiah and Lunell were standing in the doorway.

"Take all the time you need," Kate insisted.

There was a silence as Oli collected his thoughts and finished the drink. He looked completely drained and almost older, somehow, as if the whole mind-numbing ordeal had aged him prematurely. His left hand seemed to be quivering ever so slightly too. He'd been under so much pressure recently... perhaps he was at breakdown point. To test this theory, Satiah edged a little further into the room to see if, when he saw her, it might push him over the edge. They'd said they wanted him alive, but they'd said nothing about his mental state. His eyes caught the movement, but he remained as he was... too deep in thought to really recognise anything. She moved in further to Malla's side.

"*He looks done in,*" she murmured into Malla's ear. "*Maybe we should give him some space.*" Malla nodded.

"We'll leave you to your thoughts, sir," he said, giving everyone the nod. They all trooped outside, some more reluctantly than others.

"He'll be fine, he's just reacclimatising," Kate insisted. "I know what these things are like. It can take days to recover fully."

"At least they didn't bring up education," Shannon said, consoling her. "I know he was worried about that."

"They didn't bring up elderly care facilities or mention the Pluto Major controversy either," Kate nodded.

"Probably worried about the Vourne conspiracy," Malla grunted. Then, as he remembered, he asked, "Didn't that argument about how much time governmental bureaucracy wastes go on for ever?"

"To be honest, I doubt anyone would want *that* mentioned," Satiah mused, thinking about the Vourne conspiracy. "Even if it's only *halfway true* it looks very bad." Lunell hid his smile, amused. He knew the truth about that... well, most of it. However, he had no idea about the role Satiah herself had played in it. No one there did.

"You can't deny that *some* of what they did talk about was very controversial," Lunell was quick to add. "Particularly dragging the leaked document into it like that."

"*Yes,*" Kate sighed, looking guilty. "I never saw *that* spin coming. It never occurred to either of us to look at it that way. And, worse still, *I know it caught Oli out.*"

"Could have been even worse," Shannon mused, rather pitilessly, "he was fortunate *Brenda* intervened. Lord knows why she did that! Tension, embarrassment maybe, but if she hadn't Deetee could have destroyed him."

"I liked the bit about whether AIs should be allowed to police themselves or not," Lunell mused, thinking about it. "Very paradoxical."

"*My computer says that your computer says that his computer says that mine is illegal?*" Kate repeated, sighing. "Yes, that was a bit of a muddle. I sometimes think that that is the real danger. We have so much information, we can't see the wood for the trees. I'm just glad they didn't go on about people's prejudices too much, that really winds me up."

"*Sounds like my job,*" mumbled Satiah, mordantly. *My intel says that your intel blah blah...*

Malla eyed a message and then glanced at Satiah.

"He wants to see *you*," Malla said, in her ear. She didn't need to ask who he was talking about. She braced herself for whatever it was and nodded.

"No problem," she mused. She and Shannon exchanged a brief glance as she entered. Oli was pretty much where he had been when they'd gone outside. The door closed quietly behind her with an almost inaudible humming sound.

"How do you think it went?" he asked, his voice weak.

"I didn't see most of it," she replied, shrugging lightly. "If it's a review or analysis you require, I'm sure Kate will oblige you."

"It's not... I wanted to say *sorry*," he stated, some strength returning to his tone. "Last night was... well, it's something I no longer wish to revisit and... it *was* my fault."

"Another drink?" she asked, nodding to his empty glass. She was patently ignoring the apology.

"I'm *sorry*, Satiah," he repeated, as if she'd not heard.

"Yes well, we're *all* sorry about something, *your apology doesn't matter to me*," she stated, insensitively.

"Nevertheless, it is unreservedly presented to you," he sighed.

"Will that be all?" she asked, somehow both clipped and menacing.

"When are we moving back to the office?" he enquired, uneasily.

"Whenever you want," she growled, not even looking at him. He couldn't stand it any longer.

"Please... *please forgive me*," he requested, outright. "I can't think, I can't..."

"No," she stated, flatly. All the power was with her now and she would make him suffer for what he had caused.

"Please, I swear I'll do *anything*!" he implored.

"*Anything?*" she asked, tilting her head to the side as if genuinely considering that. An evil smirk crossed her lips briefly before she turned to face him.

"I promise," he nodded, stupidly.

"A promise that is easy to keep isn't worth an Essp!" she spat, spitefully. "How can I know you're being *serious* about your absolution if you're not truly tested?"

"*Please*," he repeated, feebly.

"I suppose… there is only *one thing* you can do, one thing you can promise that will earn my forgiveness," she said, hard as rock.

"Name it," he smiled, hopefully.

"Regardless of what happens, *irrespective* of the outcome of this election… promise me that you will *never* run again," she demanded, with ice in her voice. He frowned, taken aback.

"But…" he began, sceptically.

"*It's only going to get worse*," she warned, honestly. "By taking these steps you're endangering not only yourself, but all of us too. And it's the only way you will get my pardon." She was really twisting that blade now. Cutting directly between his ambitious side and his more selfless one. "These killers will stop at nothing to waste you and *anyone* who stands in their way. I don't know if I can stop them and *frankly* after the way you have treated me, I'm seriously considering pulling out. It's not like I ever wanted to get involved."

Oli was standing now, emotional indecision all over his face. Pity she hadn't done this to him *before* the debate, she reflected dispassionately. He might not have faired the same. Irritatingly, he'd done surprisingly well when she considered everything.

"I can understand how you feel," he allowed, softly. "I… I *can't* promise you that."

"Then I do not forgive you," she smiled, coldly. She turned to walk out.

"Are you leaving?" he asked, bleakly. It seemed this time that he would not compel her to stay. How could he when he knew *he* was the reason why she was leaving? She paused before she got to the door.

"I was hired to protect you until the election is over, and I'll do it, but only for the money," she hissed, with vehemence. She couldn't *actually go*, obviously. Not only would that violate her mission mandate, but it would also give Lunell free range to do whatever he pleased.

---

Shannon knew Satiah would come to the refreshments area after seeing Oli. She was aching to know what he'd said to her this time. She'd still been unable to think of one thing she could do to Oli to pay him back. There were a lot of options but what with everything else going on there were numerous obstacles. Nothing seemed clever enough, anyway. She wanted Satiah there to *thought-map* with.

*Author's note. A long time ago the phrase 'brainstorming' would have been used to describe this but due to reasons of political correctness, the term was deemed too offensive to use. 'Thought-scattering' was briefly used before the telepathic breakthroughs occurred and then everyone finally settled on 'thought-mapping'.*

She and Satiah could plan Oli's downfall together in an *exchange of ideas*. He deserved this and more, of course. Rejecting her - she still wasn't sure why - and now forcing himself onto Satiah. A woman who couldn't walk away because it was her job to stay and she probably needed the money. Why did mercenaries ever do anything? Money. Shannon envisaged that Satiah may have gambling debts, or owe a blackmailer, or something. Mercenaries often got tangled up in eventualities like that. That was why they shouldn't be trusted.

Shannon didn't consider herself a vengeful person. She just had a problem dealing with things when they didn't go the way she wanted. Put another way: she couldn't understand why Oli had rejected her. She had her pride and refused to ask the reason, even though she was dying to know. Satiah though could be useful to her. Satiah could find out that reason for her. She prepared Satiah's usual drink. Water. It didn't take long. She'd seen that Satiah had tablets that she put in anything she drank. Paranoia, Shannon had laughed to herself in the past. After Kate's dance with death recently though, it had not seemed so funny anymore.

Satiah sauntered into the room, looking as miserable as Shannon had predicted. Shannon stood and beckoned to her.

"Here, tell me everything," she asked. Satiah was feeling like stirring at that moment and obliged. She prepared herself for an award winning performance. She sat down next to Shannon and stared at her just for a second. Shannon stared back, unsure what was going on. Then Satiah started bawling, sobbing, weeping, in apparent devastation. Shannon had not expected this at all, not from someone like Satiah. Then again, she supposed, now that she thinks we are friends, she's dropped her guard. Shannon put a comforting arm around the smaller woman and patted her tenderly.

"What's happened? It's okay, it's okay," she repeated, trying to understand what Satiah was trying to articulate.

A good cry could be most therapeutic, even when you didn't really need to do it, Satiah thought absently.

"He...h-h-h-he said h-he was s-s-sorry," Satiah sobbed, into Shannon's neck. As a Phantom agent, you could be forgiven for wondering what use being taught how to cry would have. As masters of almost anything physical, able to completely control their bodies, down to the extent of slowing their own heartbeats at will, a bit of crying was a doddle. She was making herself shudder with her own sobs, rambling incoherently and sniffing noisily.

"Oli said he was sorry about last night?" Shannon asked, softly. Just to be sure she'd heard right. Satiah nodded, still apparently inconsolable.

"He wanted me to forgive him," Satiah went on, snivelling and blubbing alternately. Shannon was not sure why all this was so upsetting so she guessed as anyone would that there had to be more.

"Did he... you know? Try it on again?" Shannon guessed, thinking that that might be why Satiah was in this state.

"N-n-no he... blamed it all on you," Satiah lied. Shannon gasped.

"What? Blamed *what* on me?" she demanded, seeking both clarity and confirmation. "Drink this," she said, thrusting the water into Satiah's hand. Satiah took it, tried to gulp some down, and then sort of accidentally on purpose spat it out all over Shannon as another particularly emotional snuffle took her over.

"Oh no, *I'm so sorry*," Satiah said, still weeping.

"*It's fine*," Shannon growled, containing her own irritation as best as she could. "Blamed me for what?"

"I'll be all right in a minute; do you want me to get you a towel?" Satiah asked, as if she was really sorry for what she'd done. *Satiah? Sorry?* Those two things just didn't go together.

Shannon allowed Satiah to bring her a towel and waited for a few minutes as the tears gradually dried up.

"He told me that the only reason he was interested in me was because he knew you would leave him alone if he was with, or seen to be with, someone else," Satiah explained, knowing full well that Oli had never said anything of the kind. Shannon's face was a picture. Eyes bulging with anger, teeth gritted in a rictus smile of restraint.

"That's why he apologised to me, because he only recently realised that, despite it starting out as an act, he'd started to fall in love with me and wanted my forgiveness," she elucidated. "That was when I decided that I couldn't trust a thing that came out of his mouth. So I said no and then he stared ranting about how *you* had obviously been talking to *me*, and some spiel about how you are trying to make his life even more difficult than it already is and..."

She trailed off, shaking her head.

"You know, now I'm *saying* all this myself, I'm not even sure I heard him right..." Satiah snuffled, expertly delivering the self-doubt tactic. *I mean, I could be wrong but...*

"No, it's all starting to make sense," Shannon growled, her mind reeling but still scheming too. She rubbed Satiah's shoulder softly.

"It's true I once was romantically interested in him," Shannon admitted. She subtly altered the truth herself now. "That was before I realised what a two-faced, egotistical rat he really is." Satiah nodded in apparent agreement.

"He's *creepy* the way he switches between charming and cruel," Satiah concurred, as if she'd only just realised.

"It makes you wonder who else he's done this kind of thing to," Shannon said, trying to be manipulative. "I can't believe he had the audacity to blame everything that he's done to you on me."

"Neither can I, and I was in there when he said it!" Satiah agreed, with one last sniff and a roll of her eyes. "I don't know *why* I broke down just then... it's... *it's just it's got too insane to deal with right now...* I think it's because my boyfriend is *massively* jealous at the moment and was giving me a tough time about it too. I feel like I'm under attack all the time. You're *the only one* I can confide in, the only one who understands and probably the only one who would believe me." Masterstroke! There would be no way that Shannon would ever suspect her now... not until it was too late, anyway. It was all about you, all about her. Even the most talented manipulators could fall for this one.

Shannon made up her mind that she would confront Oli about this. She'd had enough of his, his... she wasn't even sure there was a particular word for his kind of behaviour. People should not be allowed to do this! There should be a law against badmouthing someone behind their back. Okay, so she'd badmouthed Satiah to Malla a few times over the last couple of weeks, but *that* was different! Firstly, she'd decided that she was wrong about Satiah, and that Satiah was just a bystander who'd happened to get mixed up in Oli's web of machinations. Secondly, it was probably because of Oli's conduct that she herself had started to blame Satiah in the first place. Maybe it had all been Oli's doing. Maybe he had been subtly trying to make Shannon and Satiah enemies, just to distract her from what he was really doing.

"We *can't* let him get away with this," Shannon said, levelly.

"*I don't know*," Satiah murmured, coming over all hopeless. "I don't see how we can stop him."

"We will think of something, *after the way he's treated us*, it's only right that he should suffer a little," she maintained.

"If you say so," Satiah nodded, pretending to be easily led. "You mean like, adding his communicator's details to all the subscriptions we can find so that he gets a deluge of messages from loads of random companies?"

"That's a start," Shannon nodded, patting the table as she thought about it. "Easy enough to do and completely untraceable. Thing about it is though, he won't know it was us."

"That's a good thing, isn't it?" Satiah frowned, playing dumb like before.

"I was hoping to make him take a fall and know it was us, but be powerless to do anything about it," she explained. "*The perfect revenge.*"

"What happened?" Lunell asked, coldly.

"Somehow Randal and Satiah were able to repel the operatives I sent to deal with them. What's worse is, Randal at least knows it was me who sent them," Scott replied. "Therefore… I may not try again."

"So how will we proceed?" Lunell immediately wanted to know.

"Never mind that now, how are things going? I saw the debate and it all seemed to go smoothly," Scott asked, dismissively.

"Things are still tense here, I know Satiah is in Oli's head and is trying to mess with him, but he's a lot stronger than we all gave him credit for. I still have no news of the insider, and I know Satiah has been out trying to catch the assassins, but she's had no luck yet… *so she says*," he related. Scott gave a noncommittal murmur in response.

"Okay, well, stay vigilant," Scott said, decisively. "That tax document leak tells me that, *whoever* angel is, they are still alive and active on Oli's staff."

"Will do."

---

"And may I also offer my most unreserved congratulations, your Excellency," Royston smiled, kissing Brenda's hand. "I was assured that this would be the first time in over a decade that an election was held within the Coalition that was so true to our beloved democracy."

"I-I-I haven't won a-anything yet," she chirped back, flustered. A surprise banquet in her honour had been planned weeks before and, in keeping with tradition, the candidate hadn't been told until she was outside. Most of the government, both real and fake, were present, to offer words of their own choice to the woman they hoped would be their new leader for many years to come. Brenda, typically, was a little overawed by all the splendour and reserve.

"It's not whether you win or lose, your Excellency, *it's how you play the game*," Royston smiled, cunningly.

"Your Excellency," a cool voice came to her, as Royston stepped aside. Wearing a slightly more decorative cloak, as opposed to the old-fashioned grey, Randal stood before her. She knew him from when she'd first taken office, and smiled in relief at a familiar face.

"Phantom Leader," she smiled, blinking rapidly as she tried to remember his name. It was important to her to at least try to remember who everyone was. Courteous and efficient. "Robin."

"It's Randal," he chuckled, smoothly. She flushed.

"I-I'm *so sorry*," she began, earnestly. She was not at all impressed with herself for this.

"Close enough, ma'am," he smiled, not at all bothered. "My compliments on your masterly performance today at the debate. You dealt with everything with a firm fortitude, ma'am. If you ever need me, you know where to find me."

"I don't suppose *you* have seen Reed lately, have you?" she asked, trying to sound casual, but in reality she just sounded worried.

"As far as I know he's on Garginth Zee, he's one of the speakers at their annual beer festival, or at least that's what he told me," Randal said, curious. "Did you need him for something, Ma'am?" Only someone as insane as Reed would miss the biggest political event in five years for a beer festival, Brenda thought!

"How well do you know Ash?"

"Queen Dreda's son, the last known immortal?" She nodded. "Not well… is there a problem?"

"Well, *I don't know*," she shrugged. "He said something about some obscure threat but I told him to talk to the military." Randal went silent and stared at the floor for several seconds. She swallowed nervously.

"Leave it with me, ma'am," he said, after a moment of deep thought. He smiled. "Tonight is your night now; forget all that troubles you, at least for a few hours."

"Thank you, Ro-Randal," she smiled, almost calling him Robin again. She sighed, glad he was the last in the queue, and even more pleased that someone might finally be able to do something about that subject which had been bothering her. Her aide was suddenly by her side, as if omnipresent.

"I have requested your order for you," she said, casually. Brenda smiled and winked at her meaningfully. The aide frowned slightly. "My lady?"

"As a reward for all your hard work and support over the days since I first ended up here... I have arranged a chair for you at my side at the table with whatever you may desire for food," Brenda told her, kindly.

The aide was genuinely speechless for a second.

"...No, no, I couldn't!" she said, seriously trying to get out of it. She liked sneaking around in the shadows, not sitting there like a target in the light. Even she though, corrupt and cynical as she was, was really touched by Brenda's unending generosity. How did you ever survive so long, the aide thought to herself.

"You can and you will," Brenda said, firmly. The aide raised her eyebrows at Brenda's assertiveness. "I won't hear a refusal from you, whatever the reason. You deserve a reward and this is half of it."

"Half?" the aide paused, for a moment worried that this could be some sort of trap.

"Tomorrow, *among all the other things going on,* I've had a word with a few of the ministers, and they agreed that you will be awarded the Golden-Loyalist-Insignia. First class. Making you the one-hundred-and-third woman to receive this high honour. You will be officially recognised as a member of the High Congress of the Coalition once the ceremony is over," Brenda explained, loving the look on the aide's face. Utter astonishment coupled with ecstatic disbelief. She had decades yet to go in her career, and the aide had everything planned with the eventual goal of becoming part of that in fifty to sixty years' time - if she was lucky. Now here Brenda was, offering it to her on a plate.

"Are you *sure* I deserve it?" she said, genuinely. She was feeling very guilty now about everything she'd done. Granted, she'd probably have been killed had she not done a lot of it, but still...

"I know I see only a tiny part of what you do," Brenda smiled, kindly, "and without you I'd never have been able to do so well. I wanted to do this now... in case I lose the election."

"...I... I don't know what to... wow... thank you!" the aide managed. She was acting again, having now recovered her composure, but she realised then that Brenda was one of the most decent human beings she'd ever met. And it was her job to be loyal... officially. She wondered what Royston would think about all this. Maybe he already knew and had just been told not to say.

"I know you're always telling me not to overwork so... listen to your own advice," Brenda ordered, kind-hearted. "I have this job to do and you have yours too but... you're still young. I want to know that, whatever happens here, that you enjoy your life in other ways too."

"I can assure you I do," the aide said, a bit shifty looking now. "Well, if you insist! You're in charge, so I can only say yes."

"That's the idea," Brenda giggled. "Do you have anything that I need to know about the rest of tonight?"

"Yes, the fish is terrible, and order two drinks first time around, the second order is always late," the aide rattled off.

"Right," Brenda nodded. "What will you be having?"

"A wonderful time."

---

Collorah watched as craft began to leave the area. He'd seen the end of the debate and couldn't tolerate anymore of Deetee, so had ignored the rest of the programme schedule. He activated the ship he had waiting in orbit. All cloaking devices were on, effectively hiding it completely. It had been on standby computer-compensate mode to conserve power and to prevent any collisions with unsuspecting craft that may happen to be in the vicinity. On Earth, these craft were many, so the danger of a crash was extreme – extreme enough for Collorah to have taken the time to plot no less than three evasion courses, to counter the possibility of multiple ships in close proximity. While it had never had to utilise those sorts of complicated evasions, the craft had been forced to move no less than six times in the past thirty minutes to avoid collisions: a testament to the never ending streams of traffic that dominated the skies at the heart of the Coalition.

As the debate ended, within the space of about a minute, the skies were full again as the conurbation came back to life with renewed vigour.

He glanced at the time, watching the seconds endlessly counting down. How many times had he done that while on a job? The waiting was often the hardest part. It had cost him a lot in general, this particular job, but one of his most recent purchases had all but bankrupted him. The drone sat on the roof of his transporter, ready to go. Made almost entirely of glass, it was virtually undetectable. It wasn't a weapon: it was one of the most advanced types of surveillance units developed by the Federation. It was programmed to find Oli and only Oli. It would then tell him which ship the man was in. He would then follow that ship, confirm that it had reached its destination and then… well, then, he would see.

---

Lunell noticed the redness around Satiah's eyes. The tell-tale signs of crying. It was hard as her hair kept getting in the way, but he was certain she had been crying. She seemed cheerful enough now though. They were getting ready to leave, lists were being checked, farewells said, and equipment was being transferred from the ship they had arrived in to the ship they were leaving on. Just a precaution. He tried to see what Satiah was looking at, hoping it might offer him further insight. She seemed to be watching Malla for some reason. As far as Lunell knew, Malla was not a person of interest. He'd been a suspect, of course, just like everyone was, but she'd said nothing to him about that status changing for Malla.

Oli was still looking no better. Pale, frail, and generally a mite unwell. Kate too seemed to be showing signs of tiredness. No one was behaving in a way that made him suspicious. Except Satiah, of course, but that was not unusual.

"You will feel better when you have eaten something," Kate suggested, handing food to Oli. Oli looked down at it, like he didn't even recognise what it was.

"How did it go?" he managed, as he began to pick at it.

"Well, it could have gone better," she said, with a sigh. "I really think you did as well as you could, given the inane stuff they threw at you from time to time."

"Deetee was a *real* pain," he hissed, remembering. "It's almost like he was turning the crowd against us. Not Brenda, but me and Mark. Not that Mark did much to help himself."

"That leaked tax document did the most damage to you," Kate told him. "Ironically."

"I never thought of looking at it that way," Oli admitted, shaking his head.

"Me neither," Kate said, pulling a face. "I've already started work on damage control for that; a few things you can say to at least prevent further loss of popularity."

"You're thinking about offering to launch an enquiry into finding whoever was responsible for it?" he guessed, levelly.

"It's the only *reasonable* thing you *can* do," she shrugged. "Even if it is a little predictable."

"Please don't make me ask you to define reasonable too," he said, with a weary smile. She smiled; as attempted jokes went it was pathetic, but it did seem to demonstrate a slight lifting of the spirits.

"It's not over yet," she reminded him, meaningfully. "We can still go out and campaign further, anything could make a difference. You never know, Brenda might make a mistake."

"I accept that the potential for that occurrence must exist as a possibility, but *realistically…? Come on?"* he muttered, pessimistically.

"Realistically, you said yourself, you should never have made it this far!" she encouraged. "And *in itself*, just making it *this far* could be considered a victory of sorts."

"When did you get so bold all of a sudden?" he scoffed, in mild admiration. She shrugged.

"I don't know, I just can't bear to see you looking so sorry for yourself," she mused, equably. "And I'm just glad that the debate is over, I've been dreading it since we reached Earth."

"Jumping about for joy would hardly be appropriate, would it?" he muttered, with a real smile.

"Time to go," Shannon said, as she and Malla approached them, "the ship is ready." They nodded and rose before ambling over to the ship.

"This isn't the one we arrived on," Kate noted, curiously.

"*Security,*" Lunell reassured, with a tight smile. Even though he was trying hard not to, it did sound a little sinister, the way he said it. "Relax; we'll be with you all the way."

"All checks okay?" Malla asked Satiah.

"Couldn't have been better," she replied, casually. "Hopefully they won't realise what we've done until we're miles clear."

"*Hopefully,*" he echoed, unaware of her watchful stare. She followed him up the ramp and into the ship casually. It couldn't be him, she was sure. But who else was there? Same questions… same lack of answers.

The android pilot was there to drive them back but Satiah, distrusting it, insisted on piloting herself. It was a freighter, nothing special about it at all. It reminded her a bit of that ruin of a vessel she'd been forced to use for some time upon her return to Phantom Squad. Sluggish, slow and relatively useless. Exactly the kind of ship you wouldn't use for transporting someone who was in fear of their life. This was precisely why Satiah hoped they would not draw any attention. She took her time while checking all systems and fuel. No rush now. Lunell sat next to her in the co-pilot's chair and stretched out casually. They were alone.

"Anything you want to tell me about Malla?" he asked, directly. She glanced up at him, suddenly tense and alert.

"Why? What have you seen?" she asked, instantly.

"Nothing," he replied, honestly. "You seem to be watching him a lot, and I wondered…" He didn't need to finish his sentence.

"Well, I was talking to him during the debate, shortly after you left the room and, during our conversation, he used the word angel," she explained. "It was probably nothing, and I did try to test him by using the word myself with emphasis but… either he's a great actor, or it was nothing."

"What would be his motive?" Lunell asked, considering.

"That's another reason I think it's nothing. He's had plenty of opportunity to do the job already… unless for whatever reason he's not going to do it himself… I don't see why he would have waited this long. No one else has… even us," she remarked, sourly.

He allowed a smile.

"I think you're right about that," he concurred genuinely. "I've made *no progress* on the angel thing either, just in case you were interested?"

"Not really," she said bluntly, as the flight computer reactivated.

"Do you think there's the possibility that all this is some kind of big misunderstanding?" he asked, intrigued. "That those notes to an angel are from some kind of work of fiction that just has an unfortunate inference?"

"That's one option," she mused, not committing.

"Look, I know the leadership think it's a real threat, but you *must admit*, this angel thing has gone nowhere. All we have is a leaked tax document that, for all we know, might well have come from Oli's brother. Aside from that, no internal conflict has occurred," Lunell persisted.

"Not yet, perhaps," she allowed, still giving nothing away.

"Do you think we've done enough to derail Oli?" he enquired, knowing he was risking her anger by continuing to talk.

"I will revisit that when the new figures for proportional representation come though, until then it makes sense to just wait this out," she said, firmly. "That goes for everyone."

"Of course," he smiled, quickly. "Do you wish me to remain with you on the journey?" She gave him a look and he stood up. "Very well, I'll be back with the others if you need me." The door closed behind him and she smirked.

"*That's never going to happen*," she told herself. The only thing she really needed from him was that he got lost! Preferably in a black hole somewhere. She began the leisurely take off, gave the required codes and then slipped out from the building and into the traffic unobtrusively.

---

"It's *still* not moving, they *must* have switched," Octutin said, sure of it.

"*That's great!*" Jinx hissed, infuriated. "How are we supposed to know which one they're *really* using?"

"That one," Octutin said, pointing to a battered looking old freighter as it departed the building.

"That one?" repeated Jinx doubtfully. "How can you possibly...?"

"There's a drone following it," Octutin explained. *"Our friend is back."* Jinx swallowed and glanced around.

"What do we do, I can't see him, he could be anywhere?" Jinx enquired.

"We do what we planned to do, *follow them*," Octutin replied, cool as ice. They took off casually and began to head after the freighter.

"That thing must be incredibly advanced," Jinx was saying, talking about the drone. "How did you see it? Even though I know it's there, I can't really keep track of it."

"Sometimes when light hits glass it fades, particularly when there is more than one layer. The light around it is slightly more shadowy," Octutin explained, "if you look *closely enough*. Granted, it's almost the perfect stealth drone. Invisible to everything except the naked eye… and even that has to be lucky."

"This guy has a lot of cash," Jinx muttered, enviously.

"Or whoever he's working for does," Octutin shrugged. Jinx's communicator went off and he answered.

*"Who's this?"*

"It's Sam," Sam said, in a growl. "I wanted to talk to you about another job."

"Another job?" Jinx asked, as anyone would.

"My associate Mark… it seems he is behind the leaked tax document. Though he didn't leak it to get Oli, he did it to ruin my campaign. I want him dead," Sam explained.

"Will this be *before or after* we kill your brother?" Jinx enquired, a little insolently.

"Preferably after," Sam confirmed. "Although you could collect his half of your payment for that job while you see to him?"

"What's going on?" Octutin mouthed, curious.

"Hold on a second," Jinx said, smothering the communicator in his jacket to prevent Sam from hearing what he said next. "Our employers have finally turned on each other," Jinx said, to Octutin.

"O," Octutin murmured, jaded. He fired a new tracking device onto the back of the freighter.

Once the ship had been confirmed, Collorah took off and began to follow the freighter, knowing it would lead him to Oli's headquarters. He already knew where that was, of course, but it was important for him to know that Oli was actually on the premises. Knowing he had the drone doing the hard part for him, Collorah was free to weave and move around as much as he liked just in case the pilot of the freighter was vigilant enough to realise they were being followed. He did, however, spot that he was not the only one following the freighter. A smaller craft too seemed to be after them. His competition again! He sighed, was life never easy?

---

Satiah had her boots up on the flight console. She was relishing the brief period of solitude and inactivity. The flight computer was doing all the work for her. She glanced lazily at the scanners and her eyes picked out a craft that seemed to be following them. She slowly lowered her feet onto the floor and deactivated the auto pilot. They were still on course, less than ten minutes from their destination. She smiled, assuring herself that no one would mind a short detour. She pulled out of line and began to pick up speed. Next she turned left, moving in the opposite direction from the new headquarters. Lunell noticed it first and called her.

"*Satiah*, what are you doing?" he asked, calmly.

"Nothing, what are you doing?" she replied, eyes still on the rear scanners. She'd lost sight of them already... *too easy.*

She began to power up the shield, expecting an attack.

"Lunell, we're being followed. Don't tell anyone yet," she ordered, as she disconnected. Still, there was no sign of them now... surely she couldn't have lost them so easily. The door swished open behind her and Lunell trooped in.

"How many?" he asked, casually.

"One *so far*," she murmured, nodding to the screen. "I can't see them now, but they were there." To his credit, Lunell didn't doubt her.

"I'll check the hull for trackers," he said, utilising the internal security system. Satiah nodded slowly, as once again she took another turn, again taking them further away. Lunell squinted at the screen.

"I've got something, it's intermittent but it's certainly there," he told her. "Near the engines."

"They must have deployed it shortly after we left the building. We were clean before we took off, I checked myself," she mused.

"Do we get rid of it?" he asked, wondering what she would do about it. Satiah's eyes narrowed as she thought about it. The fact that they were trying to track them indicated to her that they'd not yet learned the location of Oli's new base. So... if she could somehow lead them to think it was *somewhere else*...

"Lunell, is *your craft* aboard *this one*?" she asked, knowing it was.

"Yes."

"How many can it carry?" she enquired.

"Not many, five or six, why?" he asked, unsure of what she was suggesting.

"And Oli's last headquarters, the one we left, is it still *unoccupied*?" she wanted to know.

"As far as I know..." he answered.

"Good," she smiled, casually. "Take Kate, Shannon, and Malla and, if you can, one other, into your ship and then take them back to base."

"What about all the others?" Lunell asked, immediately. "Are you sure you want me to take *Malla* too, and won't they notice us?"

"They might, but two ships are harder to track than one," she shrugged. "I will lead them back to old terrain. I will order the personnel remaining aboard with me to make use of the evacuation plan we had in place there, and to regroup at Oli's base on foot. In the meantime I will confront those chasing us."

"And Malla?"

"Have to take a chance on that, I'm sure *you* can handle him," she smiled, smugly.

"And what about Oli?" he asked, thinking he already knew.

"This will have to look real," she said, seriously. "I'm going to have to dangle him in front of them to make it convincing."

"Very well, I'm not sure he and the others will approve…"

"That won't matter as you're not going to tell them in front of him. Send Oli up here to me *before* you explain to the others what's going on," she suggested. Lunell nodded and then left. Satiah eyed the scanner again. They were there, further back than they had been, but still there. With the tracker on the ship they didn't have to be that close at all, but as they'd already lost one tracker, they were probably making sure they didn't lose a second one. The door swished open behind her and Oli entered.

"Lunell said you…" he began, nervously.

"Yes, sit down and shut up," she ordered, coldly. "We're being followed and I suspect it's the people trying to kill you. I intend to mislead them and then hopefully kill them. *You're going to help me.*" He didn't say a word, but sat down in the seat next to her and began sensibly to strap himself in. He'd been driving with her before, of course.

"Let me know when you're ready to move out, Lunell," Satiah said, into her earpiece.

"I'm ready now," he replied.

"Okay… wait for my signal before you move, I will try to disguise your departure as best I can," she instructed.

"Sounds good."

"Look Satiah, about…" Oli began.

"*Do you really think this is the time?*" she barked, silencing Oli. She turned again, this time going back in the general direction of the way they had come - in a roundabout sort of way. She lowered the ship ever so slowly, as she approached some walkways.

"Now," she commanded. Lunell burst out into view, free of the freighter. His ship was momentarily concealed by the mass of the first walkway. Being smart, he used it as cover before slipping out into the opposing lane of traffic.

"Done, heading back," Lunell said. "Call me if you need support." She didn't answer that… She'd had his *support* before. She checked the rear scanners again. Still there.

The drone remained with the freighter, so Collorah ignored the craft which had tried to disembark without being noticed. He wasn't sure exactly what that was all about, but he thought it was a decoy. Perhaps the other two had given themselves away. It would explain the bizarre alterations in course. He guessed it must be Satiah: she would be smart enough to see them following her. And she had kept Oli with her, as opposed to using the craft to evacuate him. He smiled as he guessed her destination. She was trying to lure them into some kind of trap... this would be interesting to watch. He was proved right about where she was going when they began to approach Oli's old campaign headquarters.

---

Neither Jinx nor Octutin noticed Lunell's departure.

"I'll inform the team, they tricked us into thinking they'd abandoned this place," Jinx hissed, irritated. Octutin was not so sure and he frowned as he thought about it. He'd been over the place himself after they had gone, searching for clues to tell him where they had gone. He'd found none, just like he'd seen no sign that they had faked their own exodus. Something was not right here...

"How far out are they?" Octutin asked.

"Two minutes, if we're quick we can catch them all as they leave the freighter," Jinx said, thinking ahead. Octutin returned to silent thought.

---

"Those of you still aboard, listen up!" Satiah shouted, over the speakers. "We are going to run through an unscheduled old evacuation plan! Once it is over, you will head back either to your personal accommodation, or the campaign headquarters. I feel obliged to warn you that the danger is real so don't linger! I don't care if you run; indeed I insist that you do. Just try not to trample one another along the way!" She shut the unit down, shaking her head slowly. Oli remained silent, much to her relief. She couldn't deal with any of his bleating at that moment! They were still there, and it seemed that they were not even bothering to try and remain unobserved now. Why would they do that? She glanced around at all the other scanners, wondering if they were acting as a diversion for another attack.

The roof of the building was coming up and she had to concentrate in order to land as close as possible to the entrance. If she got this wrong, there wouldn't even be a roof.

"Okay, here we go," she said, unstrapping herself. Oli did the same. She would leave the rest to the autopilot and get ready to run. She'd get into a lot of trouble if it carried on and fell off the roof onto the ground.

"What are we doing?" he asked, awkwardly. *Fishing! Where did he think?*

"We're going to join the rest of your staff," she replied, mysteriously. They hurried down the corridors and reached the others: about thirty or so anxious looking support staff all huddled together. Satiah and Oli moved to the far end where she got hold of the manual hatch release lever.

"When I open this, *you all go for it*!" she shouted, seriously. "Now hold on, we're coming in hot."

Everyone lurched dangerously forward as the ship cut its speed and dipped to skid across the roof. Satiah pulled the lever and the hatchway crashed down, revealing a mass of dust and smoke billowing around. Metal shrieked and sparks arced beneath them. They all jumped out and ran for the entrance haphazardly. It was closed up, of course, but Satiah shot the lock off. She turned and squinted, trying to make out where the assassins were. Two craft were coming in, the one that had been following them, and one other. They were coming in fast, each armed. She knew they were going to strafe the rooftop and sprinted after the others. She heard the lasers open up, pelting the freighter and the rooftop right behind her feet. She dived through the open doorway, rolling down the first set of stairs.

Holes were torn in the roof as the lasers hit the doorway and roof of the stairway. She dragged herself onto her feet and looked down the gap between the stairs, over the fascia. She could see them all, over a floor beneath her, hurrying downwards. She heard as the two ships landed on the roof, saw the end result of the dust wave, and hurriedly deployed a mine. After that, pistol in one hand, she began to dash downward after Oli and the others. Jinx and Octutin held back as the mercenary force they had hired moved in first. That amount of people running down the stairs was impossible to keep quiet and it was plain what was happening. The mercenaries began to follow.

Satiah heard as the mine detonated, sending a wave of shrapnel and debris falling down the stairs. Screams of surprise from downstairs, coupled with screams of death and pain from upstairs. The wave of dust and other wreckage clattered past her, making her raise her free arm to defend her face from the worst of it. A flailing body slammed down hard onto the metal bannister with a bone cracking snap. It rolled onto the steps in front of her and down further, inert and covered in blood. She put a bolt in its back just to be sure. Peering up through the gap it had fallen from, she fired two shots up at the others who were still coming after her. The stairway itself was not damaged enough to prevent them passing, but that mine had taught them to be wary. Dust was everywhere now, making people cough as they ran.

Down she continued, trying to catch up with the others. Laser fire, in answer to hers, flashed past, hitting the bannister and the floor itself. Unless you were positioned at a landing and facing front, though, it was difficult to hit anything. More shooting. She fired back. She crouched and deployed another mine before moving on. They were about thirty storeys down now, only five hundred more or so to go before they reached the evacuation passage. She hoped everyone remembered which floor it was. Octutin grabbed two mercenaries, as he was towards the rear of the group. This was a wasteful strategy, they were chasing and not thinking.

"You two with me, *we'll take the lift*," he said, over the din.

The next time the mine went off, Satiah had not gone very far and was hit in the back by two particularly large bits of rubble. She had armour on, but the kinetic force they bestowed sent her tumbling down the flight painfully. She hit the wall hard enough to knock all the breath out of her. Gasping, she struggled to her feet, while trying to protect her eyes with her free arm, and kept going. She had almost caught up with the others now, who were maybe two floors or so ahead. They were slowing down, not used to all this exercise.

"Run!" she screamed down at them. "*Keep running*! No one said stop!" Oli was towards the rear of the group.

"Have you called law enforcement?" he shouted. What would be the point, she thought grimly.

"Yes, of course!" she shouted back casually. She fired a few more shots as she passed another landing. There was a shout as she must have hit someone.

She paused, another idea coming to her. She eyed the steps above her, analysing their design and the quality of their substance with the competence only a trained Phantom agent would have. All were well made, but with targeted shooting she was able to weaken the whole flight above. She hoped that when enough of them were on it, it would collapse. Unfortunately, that was not what happened. She turned to look up upon hearing the crash, and realised that the stairway hadn't collapsed; instead, it had come away from the wall and smashed straight into the next set. This set, also mildly damaged, was knocked free. Before anyone could react, all of the stairs were falling down to the next floor, knocking those free too, and as they became heavier and faster… it turned into an unstoppable force of rubble, hurtling down towards the ground.

"*Everyone*! Get off of the staircase!" she shrieked, in warning. "*Do it now*! Oli!" she screamed, as she reached him. "Move off the steps!" She smashed into him before he had a chance to move and they both toppled into the corridor beyond, just as everything crashed its way past them. He landed there, coughing and spluttering. The whole building was shaking and rumbling as the staircase collapse continued downwards. Satiah activated her torch and looked around.

"I need a roster count!" she called, into her earpiece. Oli sat up, still trying to see where they had ended up. She hauled him onto his feet roughly, digging her fingertips into his arm harder than necessary.

"Come on, we'll go down the other side," she said, as if nothing unusual had happened at all. As they jogged, it became apparent that although some of the support staff had been injured, none were in a serious condition.

They were, however, still trapped in the building. She ordered them to do what she and Oli were doing. They would move across the floors they were on, over to the opposing set of stairs and then calmly evacuate the building. The doors opened, providing them with cleaner air, and they continued on, less rapidly than before.

"Did you get them?" Oli asked, gruffly.

"Some of them, undoubtedly," she said, thinking about it. "That last scheme of mine didn't work out so well though, as I'm sure you realised."

"Never mind," he said, forgivingly. "I don't think they would have liked it much, and I'm hardly in a position to criticise."

---

"Where are you?" Jinx hissed, into his communicator. They had just managed to survive being enveloped in the blinding dust cloud that rose from the destroyed stairs below.

"Basement," Octutin replied, looking around to check. It was hard to tell in the darkness.

"Staircase has collapsed, we're going to have to go back," Jinx stated.

"I have a route out, don't worry about me," Octutin said. "I'm going to try and catch them before they get to the entrance."

"Law enforcement will be here soon," warned Jinx. "I'll meet you at the agreed location." Octutin disconnected.

"Let's move out," he ordered, grimly.

---

The next staircase, the one Satiah *hadn't* destroyed, was mercifully clear of smoke and debris. It was shielded by the vast majority of the building. Indeed, had she not known about the other one's destruction, she'd have found no clues here. The support personnel were still moving down, ahead of Oli and Satiah. Everyone was going more slowly now, seeing as they seemed to have shaken off their pursuers. Satiah nonetheless was having a hard time resisting the urge to keep glancing over her shoulder. Old habits, much like Phantom agents, died hard.

"So which ones are these, these particular killers?" Oli asked, breathlessly.

"*Does it matter?*" she growled, unable to stop herself smiling. "I think it's inmate thirteen, *unlucky for some, hopefully him this time*, and his mates."

"Not the Red Necromancer then?" Oli muttered, a little relieved. "How did they find us?"

"*Everyone* knew where you were this time, I'm afraid," she shrugged. "I tried to mitigate that with the vehicle switch. Unfortunately it was a predictable tactic which was obviously seen through and countered."

"These things happen," he coughed. As they passed yet another landing, probably around floor two hundred, Satiah paused. Oli didn't ask why, he was just grateful for the rest. She moved into the corridor beyond, a grim expression on her face. He groaned inwardly, now what? Satiah eyed the lifts and realised they still had power. She noted their position. The first was on floor 389, some way above them. The other was at the basement level. There would be lifts that went further down, of course, but they were located elsewhere. She pressed for the lift and gave Oli a whistle.

"No sense in wasting time and energy," she stated, thumbing at the lifts behind her. A great advocate of this new strategy, he nodded quickly in agreement. As much fun as running endlessly down and around was, it was rather exhausting.

"There is a chance that some of them *might* have used the lift already," she cautioned, adjusting her pistol. "If they did, I'm assuming they went to the basement and are going to move *up* the stairs to try to catch you that way. If *we* go *this way*, hopefully we will avoid that, or at least do the unexpected thing."

"What about the others?" Oli asked, thinking of his support staff.

"They are *not* who the killers are after," Satiah reminded. "If I warn them of the danger they may stop, and then Jinx will know something is wrong. This has to look real. I doubt he will kill them anyway as, in theory, it would warn you he was there and thus make you harder to target."

"*...I suppose that makes sense,*" he allowed, begrudgingly. *Well, what do YOU know about it, she wanted to scream back.*

The lift opened and they got in. She pressed for the basement floor and then crossed her arms as she leaned against the wall, like she was just another bored office worker waiting to get into the office. Oli was watching the floor count on display as they quickly descended.

"*You might want to stand to one side,*" she advised, casually. She moved to stand on the other side so that they would not be instantly visible when the doors opened. He obeyed swiftly. The lift finally stopped, though Oli was in no hurry for it to do so at that moment. The doors opened. Satiah rolled out, pistol ready, into the semi-darkness of the basement. Nothing.

"They must have moved on, *assuming they were here at all,*" she said, hoping she was right. Oli rushed out and then hid behind a structural column that she pointed to.

She could hear the distant sirens of law enforcement as they surrounded the building. Better late than never! Now she had a choice. Wait for law enforcement to reach her, or try to get Oli out herself. Normally she would do it herself, but this was Oli so… she smirked to herself.

"*I heard something,*" she whispered, sharply to him. "*Stay down and keep quiet!*" Oli obeyed, not realising she'd heard nothing and that she just didn't want to interact with him any more than she had to.

"Zax, what's my situation?" Satiah asked, into her earpiece.

"*You're taken, but not officially?* I can't speak for *inside* but there's no way anyone's getting out of that place now," Zax said. *Yes…* Satiah had heard that kind of thing too many times before to believe it. And that girl needed to learn some respect. "Is Oli with you, Randal wants to know?"

"He's with me," she muttered, not at all comfortable with the wording. "Is anyone else listening to us?"

"Are you joking?" Zax hissed, levelly. "I'm not *completely stupid*, you know! I'd have to be mad to…"

"*How is Carl?*" Satiah asked, more softly. "You can see him from where you are?"

"...He's fine, just sitting there watching stuff, *very boring*," Zax replied, reassuringly. "I'd be the first to let you know if that changes."

"*Thank you*," Satiah replied. She was sure he was safe, but he was very close to danger... geographically speaking... and it was making her twitchy.

"The support personnel are out," Zax told her. "I'm finding five life readings inside the building... two of which are you and Oli."

"How close are the others?" Satiah asked, inevitably.

"Ten floors above you... moving up further... they must think you're hiding somewhere up there," Zax explained. Satiah sighed and sat down on the floor where she tried to get more comfortable.

"When are law enforcement coming in?" she asked, not pleased by the cold hard floor at all.

"Less than ten minutes," she said.

"*I can't hear anything!*" Oli whispered loudly.

"*Hush!*" she shushed him, fiercely. Bliss in silence. She knew he was probably very frightened, thinking someone was right there with them... and that made her smile.

There had been one other reason why Satiah had not allowed Lunell to evacuate Oli, beside the fact that she needed him as bait. It also meant that so long as Oli was close to her, it made Lunell's job of targeting her more difficult. She called Malla. The reception wasn't great, but it sufficed. His voice was muffled and scratchy, but still comprehensible.

"You guys alright?" was his instant question. She still had not made up her mind about him yet. This was where Lunell might actually prove useful if he found something. She wondered fleetingly if he was listening in... he *probably was*.

"For now, sorry for all the cloak and dagger, had to think on my feet," she said. "How are you all there?"

"Much safer than you, I'll warrant," he responded. Was that a threat? She dismissed it as nothing.

"I'll let you know when we're out," she said, cutting it there.

"They are not here," Octutin stated, thoughtfully. He'd seen all the support personnel and Oli was not among them, yet he had been seen going into the building. That meant either he was hiding on one of the many floors there, or he'd found another way out. Which floor? Octutin had no time to find out. He called Jinx.

"What?" was the curt answer.

"I can't find him, keep watch outside for him, and follow him wherever he goes," Octutin said, seriously. "I'll get out of this." He moved into the corridor away from the stairs with the two mercenaries in tow. He pressed for the lift.

―――――✦✦✦✦✦―――――

The doors closed and Satiah looked up as the lift departed.

"*Zax...?*" she called, sharply.

"They're nowhere near you," she said, overconfidently.

"They could be soon, tell me *exactly* where they are," Satiah replied. Clicking and scrabbling noises came to her as Zax tried to work it out. Satiah though could already see that the lift was coming down as the countdown of the floors was visible to her. Each lift had a screen for all to see right next to the doors.

"*Oli!*" she hissed, urgently. "Get away from the lift, *hide over there!*" Without a word, Oli scrambled clear, unsure but knowing it was ridiculous to argue. Satiah ran over and stood to the side of the lift, pistol ready.

"They're coming down," Zax warned.

"Yes, I know," Satiah stated, sourly. "*How many?* Three?"

"Still three."

"*They'll be a few less in a minute,*" growled Satiah, preparing herself. The lift arrived and the doors swept open. Two men got out. Satiah reacted so fast that both were dead before they even knew they were under attack. She stayed where she was, knowing that a third was still inside the lift. Octutin, after seeing the fate of his hired help, calmly pressed to go up another floor, making the doors close. Satiah realised at once what he was doing.

"*Stay here!*" she screamed, at Oli. She sprinted for the stairs. She was on the next floor in a moment. She skidded to a halt in the corridor just in time to see the lift doors close again. For a second she feared he'd gone back down again, having successfully lured her out of position, and she made for the stairs again. A shot rang out from the obscurity of one of the rooms, narrowly missing her. She dived for cover immediately.

Octutin groaned. He'd made the lift go up another floor *before* he'd slipped out, hoping to trick whoever was chasing him into thinking that he'd done the same thing again. When they came in to check they would either dash off again, or stay where they were... *where he could get them*. The woman had been incredibly fast on her feet, hardly even stopping to look at the lift at all. When she'd changed direction he'd fired, just missing her head. Now he'd lost his advantage, and worse... she knew where he was. She was not law enforcement; he knew that much as they were still outside. They would have heard shots being fired and they would most likely hesitate before coming in. He *had* to get back to the basement to get out. The stairs were blocked, and now someone was between him and both the other ways out.

He considered trying to bluff his way out by claiming that *he* was law enforcement, so he could get close enough to deal with her, but he figured she'd see through that as he'd already tried to kill her. He went through what he had on him, in his mind. Rifle, pistol, ammunition and knife. Communicator, torch, power supply... he sighed, knowing he'd have to fight his way out of this one. He peered out from cover, trying to make out where she'd gone in the low lighting. There was no sight or sound of her... but he knew she had to be there somewhere.

Satiah knew that the smart thing to do was to keep him pinned, as there was no way out, until law enforcement came. Oli was safe, she and this guy were the only other two other people in the building, and he had to get past her to get to Oli or to get out. Yet she probably had a better chance of ending this quickly by herself, as law enforcement would likely try to capture him using long drawn out tactics. She wasn't interested in his welfare. He might have information she could use, but that was dubious. She already knew all she needed to about Jinx and who he was working for. She edged out from the doorway she was using as cover and crept along the wall, pistol raised and ready.

A muffled but still understandable voice from outside startled her.

"This is law enforcement, you are surrounded, no one wants to hurt you, and if you come out now unarmed you will be treated fairly." Satiah rolled her eyes. She continued to edge forwards, wishing she had her specs with her. A shuffle made her stop and crouch, ready to fire. A smashing noise occurred and she spun to her right. A gas canister rolled in, fired in from outside. She slipped her breathing device into her mouth. Octutin chose this moment to rush out. He knew he was out of time and if he didn't go now, he'd succumb to the gas. He fired as he went. She leapt into another room, out of his way, before starting to chase him. She fired as she ran, striking the doors to the stairway as he slammed through them.

Down he went, desperate now to get away. Satiah sprinted after him, trying to get an angle for another shot. He stumbled into the basement and then began a breakneck dash for the pipeline he knew would lead him away from the building. Satiah, though, was too close to lose. He blundered through the darkness, heedless of anything other than her. She'd stopped shooting in case she accidentally hit Oli, and was pumping with her arms as she ran, gaining on him. She finally caught him on the threshold of the pipeline. She leapt onto his back, going for his neck. He tried to turn to shoot her but she was too close and she crashed into his side, sending them rolling over and over down the pipeline. It was a steep incline and they accelerated quickly as they slipped down.

As they went, they grappled aggressively and Octutin lost his rifle, his pistol and what felt like a few teeth as her fists hammered him. He tried to hit back but she was unbelievably strong and agile. At last they hit the bottom, painfully rolling to a halt. He rolled onto his feet, sliding his knife out and trying to prepare himself for another attack as best he could. Satiah was also on her feet, a vicious animalistic snarl on her face. She seemed unarmed but that wasn't making him feel any safer. He slashed at her a few times, trying to get space, but she dodged expertly, ensuring she had the most room to manoeuvre. He tried again, only this time he didn't pull back fast enough and she grabbed his wrist. Satiah turned, twisted the arm against her own elbow and pushed, snapping the bone. Octutin screamed as she flipped him over her, twisting the broken limb still further.

He landed hard on the floor, disorientated. She still had a hold of his arm and she wasn't in any way merciful as she dropped a knee into his chest while still bending and turning, grinding the broken bones against each other agonisingly. Pale with pain, he tried to fend her off with his other arm. She let go, pushed his other arm aside and the last thing he saw was her knuckles as they met his face with a force that didn't seem real. Satiah stood up, panting, as she eyed the unconscious man and then the shaft leading back up. It was a long way, nearly two hundred metres by the look of it, though the lighting, or rather lack of it, made it hard to tell for sure. Her hips and arms were hurting from the fall but it was nothing serious.

After brushing herself down, she began to pace back and forth as she called Zax. She shook her head, sending the dust and dirt flying out from her hair.

"Got him," she said to Zax.

"*Nice*," Zax said, appraisingly. "He *is* still alive, you know."

"Oversight," Satiah smirked, amused. "I thought I might give you a chance to work with the interrogation department. We don't know who this man is, even though we know pretty much everything else. Get that out of him and then hand him to law enforcement."

"Will do."

---

There hadn't been a lot to see, or rather *there shouldn't have been*, but Collorah had seen more than most with his advanced scanners. He could follow heat signatures and see when guns were fired. It had been quite entertaining actually, but it was apparently all over now. His drone had confirmed the whereabouts of Oli's new office as that was where Lunell had gone. Now all Collorah needed was for Oli to return there himself, and all would be ready. Jinx had made his escape with a few others of his team, significantly fewer than before. Satiah was clearly a force to be reckoned with, but Collorah wasn't concerned about her this time.

---

Much to Satiah's amusement, the gas had rendered *Oli* unconscious, which meant her journey back to his headquarters was peaceful and not full of questions or *anything else*. The android saw to what few injuries she had, and gave her access to a supply box. She drank all the water and ate everything. After surviving a battle to the death with anyone, Satiah had discovered long ago that such an event did wonders for one's appetite. The meal wasn't the greatest, just energy foods and ration bars laced with practically every vitamin you could think of. That didn't stop *her* though, not after all that. Oli was just starting to come round as they arrived. As usual, Malla was there to greet her, and this time Lunell was with him.

Oli was still staggering around a bit, so they helped him move into the building. It would be ironic if, after all that, he were to die from a fall or something.

"You caught one?" Malla couldn't help but sound delighted.

"Yes, they'll be interrogating him directly," she said, pleased that for once she had some good news for everyone.

"*Congratulations*," Lunell said, a touch resentful.

"This isn't over yet though, so…" Satiah reminded, quickly putting a stop to any ideas anyone might have, "…now is not the time to relax."

"In a way, it could *heighten* the risk… now you've made it personal," Lunell stated. She knew he was right about that, and that he of all people would know.

They helped Oli into his new office, just as he seemed to be recovering himself.

"Wow, that stuff is very strange," Oli was saying. Satiah, who'd been gassed on many an occasion, had little sympathy.

"Could have been worse," she said, unfeelingly. "You might want to have some water."

"Will that *help*?" he asked, hopefully.

"No," she smiled, tightly. "But it will give you something to do, now that the debate is over." He sighed, and pulled a wounded face. She was in no mood to be sympathetic. She *had* just risked her life for him, after all. *Again*. She plonked the water down before him unceremoniously.

"There you go," she stated, crossing her arms. Oli faced the water, suddenly unable to look at her. "There's a planet more so..." she trailed off.

Oli began talking, still not looking up at her.

"I've been thinking about what you said. I know I've not exactly been the *most pleasant* of people to be around of late. I'm sorry for that, by the way. I do appreciate what you do, not *just today* but the whole time. I know you think this might be me trying it on again, but it's really not. I wanted to ask you, if there was some way in which I could repay you for this? I *understand* how that might sound, given some of our past conversations, but you can't *deny* I owe you my life. I still can't say about the promise, it depends how *all this ends* and..." He paused, expecting a tirade of anger and getting only silence.

"*Satiah*?" he asked, finally looking up.

She wasn't even looking at him. She was staring out of the window, her eyes wide with... fear? He turned to see what she was looking at and froze. Something was coming, he couldn't make out its actual size or shape but it was big. It was almost transparent, like glass, but it looked fuzzy, bleary, like something seen through freshly woken eyes. Everything around it looked normal. It was getting bigger, coming down from the sky at speed. Satiah hit the general alarm. It was too late. She plunged her hand into her jacket pocket as she reached for Oli with the other.

"*Get down!*" she shouted, as she dived under the table.

---

From a safe distance, Collorah calmly exited his vehicle and wandered over to the edge of the rooftop he'd parked on. It overlooked Oli's new campaign headquarters, the place he'd watched Oli arrive at.

He activated the final program in the craft he had waiting in orbit and then leaned on the guard railing to watch. It was a nice evening; all the lights were starting to come on as this part of Earth prepared for night. He slipped a pair of dark glasses on anyway. He couldn't really see it, no one could. Not until it would be too late, anyway. And even though he knew exactly where it was, he couldn't resist looking for it. The ship, cloaked and invisible, came down in a dive, heading straight for the building. He didn't know where Oli would be inside the building exactly, but he felt however that this had a good chance of working, no matter where he was.

Down it came as bidden. He could hear it more than see it. There was a moment, a point in time, where it was visible, perhaps the second before it struck, perhaps not. The craft slammed into the building, ploughing its way through the structure powerfully, flames and dust erupting from all sides around it. Metal sheared, explosions thundered and fires erupted all at once. That was all that could be heard for a few seconds. Sounds of utter destruction. Then the structure began to collapse in places. It seemed that, despite his best efforts, only about half of the building would collapse completely. The ship didn't explode as he thought it might, but nonetheless it had done its job. A wave of dust rose and spread in all directions away from the edifice. Within moments, emergency services began to arrive to contain the fires and ruin. Collorah calmly went down to join them.

# Part Four

# Auribus Teneo Lupum

"Everything about it *screams* Neo-remnantist attack. It's their kind of MO, random soft target, civilian…" Deetee protested, trying to understand why he wasn't being allowed to cover it.

"The target *wasn't random*," the director said, giving him a warning look. "And the attack *was not* Neo-remnantist." Deetee paused, taking in the other man's manner and connotation. This made no sense unless…

"Is it to do with the election?" Deetee enquired, dropping his voice slightly.

"It is," the director nodded. "In what way exactly, though, I don't know. It will receive no press coverage. It is being officially recorded as an accident caused by a malfunctioning navigational beacon. I've already spoken with them and there really is no chance of a mentimutation on this one. They're quite adamant."

"What? No one will…" Deetee began, before stopping himself. Of course they would believe it, the vast majority would anyway. Navigational errors happened all the time.

It had been over half an hour since the unidentified vehicle had devastatingly collided with Oli's campaign headquarters. Emergency services had arrived promptly and with their usual efficiency. They had activated the standard force-fields to effectively contain the area and prevent unauthorised persons from accessing it for safety reasons. While the building itself had only partially collapsed, damage to the infrastructure of all surrounding buildings was a concern. As a result, only those searching for survivors were allowed inside while scans took place to assess the likelihood of further collapses. And there was, of course, the good old-fashioned media blackout.

"You've more than enough to talk about, Deetee, we've been told to leave it alone," the director stated firmly. He knew what the other man was normally like, but where Royston was concerned, even Deetee, as they all did, toed the party line. "It will probably be covered, but only for a short time and *only* as *an accident.*"

"Well..." Deetee shrugged, grinning cynically. "I wouldn't want to upset anyone."

"Congratulations by the way, you've done a fantastic job today. I'm not sure I know anyone else who could have handled the debate so well," the director smiled, jealously. Deetee knew that the director himself had wanted the job but had been passed over.

"It wasn't easy," Deetee smiled, smugly, "although it does help that politicians are perpetually depicted as lying fraudsters."

"It does indeed," the director agreed. They both started laughing.

———✦✦✦✦✦———

"She's not answering," Zax repeated, very worried. Since the moment the accident had happened, she had been trying to raise Satiah. Randal nodded grimly, expecting the worst. It wasn't pessimism, it was realism. Besides, it was always wise to assume, and prepare for, the worst.

"Very well, keep trying," he instructed, his own communicator at his lips. "*Snell*, what have you got?"

"Lunell was outside the building when it happened and he's reported in safe along with Kate, Shannon and several other personnel. No one has seen Oli, Cadel, Malla or Satiah," Scott replied, through the communicator. Lunell unharmed outside, what a shame, Randal thought. "Do you know who did this?" That was what they all wanted to know.

"*Well, it couldn't have been Octutin,*" Zax murmured, quietly but with a certain conviction in her tone. Randal raised a finger of silence at her.

"We're still investigating, we have a theory but it needs to be confirmed," Randal told him.

---

"If Oli is dead, we will have to use the android replica of him," the aide said, as she walked beside Royston. They were in a narrow corridor, out of reach from prying ears and watching cameras.

"*I knew it was too early to celebrate,*" he muttered, with irritation. "Yes, of course. Now the debate is done, it will be easier, although his friends and family will now become problems." Damage control.

"I know. That was partly why we chose to keep him alive in the first place," she reminded him.

"The media have been sorted out, now it's just a question of finding *him*," Royston sighed, dismally. "What do you think his chances are?" The aide glanced at live footage of the building and groaned.

"Not good," she concluded.

---

Having concealed the body of the doctor he had just murdered, Collorah joined the mass of medical personnel getting ready to move in to search the rubble for survivors. They awaited only a safety clearance before they could move in. He had to confirm that Oli was in fact dead, as the explosives within the ship he'd used didn't seem to have gone off yet. There was a danger that they still might... The ship had struck at the exact point where the structure was weakest, as planned, but the bombs had still failed to detonate.

"Come on, *hurry*, they are dying in there, *let us in*!" barked one of the nurses.

"Please remain calm, the situation is under control," an android responded, unhelpfully. Drones flew by, completing scans of the area. Light indicators would tell the medical personnel when they could move in safely. Six blue lights also lit up next to it, informing them that the surrounding structures *were* unsafe and the utmost care had to be taken. Collorah allowed himself to be pulled along by the mass of medical personnel dashing forward. He didn't notice as one drone stopped in mid-air and slowly turned to observe him.

---

"*Randal!*" Zax yelled, over Randal's talking.

"*What?*" he hissed, annoyed at her apparent lack of respect.

"It's Collorah, *look!*" she hissed, pointing to the screen. "He's dressed as a doctor and he's gone into the ruins." Randal paused, thinking it through. That would make sense if he was behind the attack. He would be moving in to confirm the kill. Perhaps Collorah could simply be seizing a straightforward opportunity, but Randal didn't think so. Zax's hands were flying over the controls - trying to control the drone, trying to call Satiah, trying many other things... as well as she could. Zax was young, but she seemed to be certain in her judgment, and even Randal did have to admit it did look a lot like Collorah.

"Keep trying to get hold of Satiah, if she's still alive she *has* to be warned," he said, knowing Zax could probably figure that much out for herself. "I'm going down there; I'll try to get through before Collorah can reach Oli... if he's still alive."

"Yes sir," she said, remembering that she had to be courteous. Again she tried Satiah, but still she was not answering.

---

Shannon stared at the rubble, horrified. She, just like everyone else, was covered in dust and dirt. Absently she thought that all their lungs would need cleansing after this.

"What happened?" Kate was asking. "What happened?" She seemed to be on the edge of going into shock. Unsteady, panicky and confused.

"I don't know, right now *it looks like* a transporter crashed into the building, but I've yet to hear confirmation, please stay calm," Lunell ordered, trying to listen to the babble of voices in his ears.

"*O no*, where's Oli? Where is Satiah?" Kate wailed, suddenly realising that they weren't there.

"Was it a terrorist attack?" someone asked.

"Where's Malla?" Shannon asked, more calmly. She was trying to call him and Satiah but getting nothing.

"All of you, *please*!" Lunell requested, with bite. "*Quiet*! You will learn nothing if you don't listen and wait!"

———◆◆◆◆◆◆———

Satiah opened her eyes. Darkness. Silence. She remembered everything instantly and became aware of something heavy across the backs of her legs. Her hand was still clutching Obsenneth, as shortly before the collapse, she'd called on him to protect her and Oli from being crushed to death. Slowly she pushed herself up from the floor, dimly conscious of the tiny sharp objects pricking her fingers, carefully testing herself for injuries as she moved. Her head swam a bit but it was nothing she wasn't used to. She reached behind her and, with an effort, pushed the piping off her legs. Then she slowly got to her feet, conscious of the likelihood of hitting her head on something in the dark. Once she was certain that she was unhurt, she just stood there and listened for a moment. Nothing.

"Oli?" she called, softly. A groan came from somewhere ahead of her and to her right. She checked herself for her equipment reflexively. Torch, gun, blade… all there. She turned on her torch and looked around at what had been a meeting room. Utter devastation was a term often overused but was nonetheless accurate in this case. Thick clouds of dust danced in the torch beam, looking just like billions of tiny flying insects caught in the light. She squinted and tried to think about *where* the ship had hit the building. A floor or two *above* where they had been at the time, she calculated. Carefully she edged forward; testing the floor as she tentatively placed more weight in each step. A second collapse could happen at any time. *Not that she'd been in this exact situation many times before, of course…*

The flicker of flames began to appear ahead of her as she edged around a pile of rubble. This was where Oli had ended up. She paused as something rattled above her and she tensed, expecting something to fall through. Nothing did, fortunately. Nothing other than a few trickles of tiny pebbly things tumbling through some small gap. She winced to shield her eyes from them as best she could, whilst peering up at the hole in the ceiling they'd come through. More unrevealing blackness was all she could make out.

Oli was lying on his front, still partially covered by the now barely recognisable table. Warily she went over to him, knowing that the floor underneath them would not last forever. It was already slanted.

"*Oli?*" she tried again, pushing the table off him and starting to examine him. He began coughing as he came to.

"W…What?" he asked, unsure which question to ask first. "*Are you okay?*"

"We were lucky," she said, quick to skip over their miraculous survival. She was already conscious of how stuffy it was becoming where they were, and how unstable. That had to mean that they were cut off from fresh air and theirs was rapidly running out. How long had they been lying there? Forty-four minutes… according to her time-meter. It didn't seem damaged so she presumed it was accurate. A lot could have happened in that time, and as they'd not already been rescued, she had to presume that obstacles of the most potent nature were against her.

"Can you move?" she asked, standing again.

"I think so," he said, trying to stand. He paused as he heard a noise. Satiah gave him a look to remind him to be slow and careful when it came to moving around. Not that he could really make out her expression clearly.

"Good, we need to get out of here," she stated, almost robotically.

"Why? Won't it be safer to stay still?" he asked, not unreasonably. The procedure was to remain where you were if safe, in order to give rescuers a better chance of finding you. He knew that Satiah would know that too, but she wanted to move anyway…

"Normally yes, but I don't want to suffocate in here," she replied, dryly.

Now she had to work out which direction the corridor was in, in relation to them. Had she been standing where she'd been leaning before the crash, it would have been to her right but… She moved to where she thought it would be, and began to try to move a girder that had fallen through. Quickly she gave up, it was unyielding in a way that only something weighing hundreds of tons could be. Even Kelvin would not have been able to shift it. Oli was watching her futile efforts uncertainly.

"*O no,*" Oli groaned, suddenly grasping their new peril: stuck where they were and running out of air. Facing a fatally short future of gulping stale air like fish trapped in poor quality water.

"Breathe slowly," she advised, as she tried to look for something she could move. "We have to conserve what oxygen we have left." He nodded, trying to slow himself down. The trouble was that, for obvious reasons, he was starting to breathe even faster because of this disclosure. Satiah flashed her torch up to examine what was left of the ceiling again. It was cracked in several places and curved. It might break apart at any time, being somewhere between craggy and downright unsure of itself. They *had* to get out of there, she decided immediately. Next she checked the floor.

Slanted. Maybe even buckled? She knew it could cave in at the slightest of provocations, and there were already signs of new cracks forming, gradually reaching out across the floor like fissures about to reveal something dreadful beneath. Satiah though knew what was under them. She listened again, wondering if anyone else was nearby, either other survivors, or potential rescuers, which was always possible. How far had they fallen exactly? She knew they *must* have gone down a significant distance, as there was no sign of sunlight and no sounds of activity from outside. No traffic, no sirens… only the silence of the grave. The grave they were apparently buried alive within. Not to dwell on it…

"How long do you think it will take them to get to us?" Oli asked hopefully, following her gaze.

"Too long," she responded, grimly. "No talking, you're wasting the air." Good excuse, she thought distractedly, the last thing she needed was Oli blathering on now.

Using sound in a collapsed building was dangerous as well. Sound causes vibration and, with their position being as unsound as it clearly was, even talking was risky. Another convenient reason to get him to shut up, she weened. This was why, when signalling for help, it was always best to use *light* if you could. Coded flashes, or just a good old-fashioned waving motion to summon rescuers, would do. Of course, she knew no one could see them, that was apparent, but there was another way to look at their predicament. As they were trapped, with no chance of the time-sensitive rescue they needed, another collapse might actually help them if it exposed a way they could escape asphyxiation.

Her earpiece was still working, but was in a state of self-scan, searching for damage. It would be unusable until that scan was complete. This meant she couldn't call anyone and they couldn't call her. Well, they *could* but she'd never know. Knowing how stupid this idea potentially was, she pulled out her pistol and aimed carefully. Her target was the floor; specifically, the floor near where it had collapsed.

"Get ready for a fall," she advised, over her shoulder.

"*What?*" he asked, nervously. She fired. "*No!* What are you…?" She felt his hand land on her shoulder but she fired again. A loud crunch was the next sound he heard and then a scrabbling noise as more debris began to fall further through the hole it had made. To Satiah's relief, nothing else fell through, and now they had a gaping hole in the floor leading to the next level down. She smiled a bit shakily and pushed his hand off her in a cavalier fashion. She didn't like him touching her.

"Come on," she said, beckoning to him. "We can climb down to the lower level." She carefully lowered herself into the hole, torch between her teeth, and dangled there as she looked carefully at the floor. It was a risk, but she did have Obsenneth if she needed help. Her grip began to slip as there was not much to hold onto that she felt she could trust. She dropped, landing in a well-practised squat on the floor below, whilst remembering not to break her teeth on her torch. The floor didn't budge beneath her and appeared relatively undamaged. She looked around and saw that the corridor *was* accessible here. The ceiling of the room didn't look much better than the one above though.

"Are you okay?" Oli asked, tentatively. He was still upstairs. *Okay?* They might never be okay again! She wished he would stay silent, and not just because of their situation.

"Yes, come down, and make sure you try to land *carefully*, it's a big drop," she warned, as she flashed her torch up and down the corridor. Right was completely blocked, no chance of slipping past or over *that* mass of debris. Left, however, seemed to lead somewhere. Her plan was to find a stairway as emergency exits were usually positioned near those. They could then follow that to an exit, and she could go home. Her shift was nearly over and she needed to be home to help Carl and Max with Kelvin. This latest attack couldn't have happened at a worse time. She bet she'd get caught in rush-hour traffic *again* and it would make her even angrier.

A crash came from behind her as Oli landed heavily on the floor with a groan. She winced, concerned by his lack of elegance and carelessness. Just because she'd got away with it, however, didn't mean to say that he would. He was three stones heavier than she was, a whole nineteen kilograms, and she had landed *properly*. She knew everything there was to know about Oli, she had to. From his allergens, of which he had none, to his zygomatic patterns. Zygomatic patterns, for those who cared, were made up of an analysis of all his micro-expressions and facial recognition profiles. A louder groan came from overhead and she looked up as something over them shifted. Dust fell in waves of flakes and powder, threatening to choke them.

"Come on," she hissed, grabbing and pulling him fully into the corridor. They waited expectantly for larger things to fall, but again, nothing of consequence did. Satiah let out a breath in relief.

A light above them began to flicker on and off, briefly illuminating them and the corridor brightly, before plunging them back into their torchlit blackness intermittently.

"*Hello!*" shouted Satiah, interested to know if anyone else had survived. No reply. Apparently not. The only reason *they* were still alive was because of the power of Obsenneth. She wondered briefly, if and when he was complete, how much power he would have. And… what he would give her as a reward for helping him. That was assuming he stuck to their agreement, which he might not do, of course. Nevertheless, as on several other occasions, he'd saved her life so… that earned him something akin to a small amount of trust from her. Well, trust was the wrong word. Respect was a little more precise.

They followed the corridor along to the first turn and discovered that it too was blocked off by a heap of rubble. Trapped again, only in a slightly bigger space than before. And that air would soon be going off again.

"Might as well sit here for a bit, it seems safe enough for now," Satiah said, cross. They slumped against the wall in silence and she turned off her torch to conserve power. She didn't need light to think.

"They nearly got me this time," Oli said, softly. She switched it on again to look at him. "*Still might.*" He glanced up at the ceiling with import. This was meant to be the bit where she would support him, *assure him* that things were *not that bad*. It seemed like such a wasted effort on her part. She didn't bother. She'd been in worse scrapes before. Who hadn't?

"It *was* a close one," she nodded, casually. The shrug she gave inferred that the outcome, *whatever it was*, didn't matter a jot to her. It did of course, she had her orders. On the other hand she *really* detested him now, so…

Oli began to wonder if he was in such an unstable situation that it would end badly no matter what happened. Auribus teneo lupum: holding a wolf by the ears. This was certainly the closest he had come to getting killed so far. This was despite Satiah's recent successful capture of one of his killers. And no one seemed to even know *why* they were going for him!

"When I was young," he began, in a reflective tone. Satiah rolled her eyes. *O shut up!* "I never knew what I was going to do with my life." *Who does? Some people never know! Please shut up or I might have to kill you.* "My father was a businessman as well as a soldier and though certainly ambitious, he *never* specialised…" *Was this man full of bravo-sierra or what?!*

"Oli," she interrupted, seriously. She felt a strong desire to cover his lips and nose with her hand and never let go. "*I don't care.* We may have a good supply of oxygen *now*, but that doesn't mean you have to use it all yourself!"

"Did I tell you that…?"

"*Oli*," she hissed, more aggressively, "just shut up and listen out for help!" He went quiet for a minute, but Satiah knew it was only a matter of time before he began to prattle on again. She thought idly that perhaps this offered a unique correlation with regard to his personality, and his career. Did people who often had trouble keeping their mouths shut end up in politics? No… that couldn't be true. Some people with that exact same flaw ended up as executives, activists and even operatives. *Shame*. As fleetingly irrelevant theories went, that one had a bow tie and everything. She envisaged a future where she would be trapped with him for hours and it made her feel sick. And it really was the case that she had better places to be for once. She was meant to be at her own apartment tonight to help analyse Kelvin… *S'blood*!

"*I want to talk about something*," he announced, eyeing her. *There's a surprise.*

"Can't you do it in your head?" she retorted, sarcastically.

"Until recently, I thought only *one person* hated me, you know, actually *genuinely* loathed me. Now I can see that there are several…" he sighed, staring at her. *Yeah, me included.*

"Who? *Your brother*?" she guessed, slightly more interested.

"Sam, yes…" he admitted. Wondering if she would live to regret it, she decided that in the interests of the mission, it could be relevant and she should ask about it. She already knew Sam was trying to kill him but she didn't really know why. She didn't particularly care either, but if he wouldn't shut up he might as well talk about something that might actually help them.

"Why does *he* hate you?" she asked, with such detachment that it almost amused her. Wasn't making yourself laugh a sign of madness? Well… *only if other people realised.*

"For almost as long as I can remember, we've always fought. Over politics, women and money. Old grudges never forgotten or forgiven… no reason to ever work together. I can't say I ever hated *him*; I certainly don't like him though. He's done all right for himself so… *he's no failure*," he said, clearly trying to sound reasonable. "That's what I could never quite come to terms with, you see. How a man can have all that I consider to be the trappings of success, and *still* be motivated by dissatisfaction, anger... and hate."

Oli didn't know that Sam was behind at least two of the people who were trying to kill him, and Satiah saw no reason in telling him. Especially at that moment. Yet she was feeling nosy about what had caused this feud.

"How did *that* happen? Why do you think he hates you so badly?" she asked, next.

"I think it stems from one particular incident... back when we were young," he replied, thinking about it. Of course, any therapist will always make it *seem* like whatever is wrong with you, *if anything*, has its origins in your childhood. Sometimes they might even be right. Sometimes they should take a look at themselves before they start reciting platitudes to help others... Satiah wasn't a good therapist, not by any stretch of the imagination; she didn't have the required compassion. She did, however, have a natural talent for manipulation.

"Really? *Tell me about it*," she smiled, her brown eyes gleaming in the torchlight with haughty guile.

"Did you ever go on long holidays with your family to, say... *resorts*, like Yellvenna?" he asked, interested. She blinked.

"Yes of course," she cooed, stringing him along. She wasn't even sure *where* that was, but she wasn't going to let him know that.

"Did you ever climb the ancient towers that make up that old shrine that no one seems to know the origin of?" he asked, curious.

"Once or twice," she answered, wondering how best to answer. "I can't say I ever reached the top but I've never been good with heights." He eyed her, as if suddenly seeing her for the first time.

"How far above the ground did *you* get? Eighteen hundred meters or two thousand and twenty?" he asked, seriously. He was testing her. One of those figures was *wrong*... and she didn't know which. Satiah knew what he was doing. She hoped that the whole tower thing wasn't a work of fiction too.

"I was a child, I wasn't really counting at the time, and I was too busy racing my sister. At the time it *seemed* pretty high, but everything seems so big when you are little," she dodged, nimbly. "So what happened?"

"*I was racing my brother* actually, and we were about halfway up, maybe a bit further. The sun was in my eyes. Sweat too. Stinging and blinding, but I persevered; I think most children are like that - more capable of pushing through symptoms like that without quite so much effort. Anyway... I was some way ahead of him so I didn't see how it happened, but I heard him shouting at me to stop," Oli said, thinking back. "I thought *at the time* that he was trying to trick me into stopping so that he could catch up. I carried on."

"Did he fall?" she asked, inevitably.

"No, no, he was just stuck," he replied, sighing. His face altered with emotion as he replayed the moment in his mind. "I was a little taller than him and I don't think he could reach the next outcropping or something like that. I reached the top and waited for him. He never showed up and by the time my parents and I worked out what had happened... he'd been there for about four hours." Satiah tilted her head to the side as she listened, thinking about it.

"He looked at me, *when we finally got him down*, and I remember noticing that it was the first time he ever looked at me with extreme dislike in his eyes. *Real detestation.* Since then it's seemed to constantly burn inside him when I'm nearby. I think he thought I *purposely* left him there like that, just to humiliate him," Oli recounted. "I tried to explain what happened several times, but he persistently refused to talk about it." It might seem like a small thing, but Satiah had known people to murder others for *far* smaller things. And, as she was sure Sam would point out were he there, *she hadn't been there.* How could anyone know how he felt? She would counter with: *why would anyone care?* So, that one event had started an enmity that was reaching its climax now? *How unfortunate.*

"Now the two of us head the largest parties on our home world," he went on. "And we find ourselves in the same election... at odds again..."

"And like before *you've left him behind,*" she couldn't resist saying. It was actually because of *her* that Sam had lost this one. He would probably have lost it anyway but, thanks to her leaked document, she'd delivered his capper. "...How does that make you feel?"

"Not good," he said, visibly mortified. "It makes any chance of us burying this in the future fade before my eyes. It should never have gone like this…" He trailed off, wishing a number of wishes all at once.

"That's what everybody says," she smiled, bleakly, helpfully adding: "I imagine he must abhor you *all the more* now. It's understandable."

"Well, it's irrational…" he began, a little defensively.

"All you had to do was climb back down and check up on him," Satiah said, sensing weakness. "Your decision to continue on up that day has led to all this. *It's so sad* – to know that *you're* responsible for this. If *only* you'd helped him, things would be very different now."

"Don't you think I've not realised that?" he retorted, tears in his eyes.

"But as ever, you're looking forward, never glancing over your shoulder to…"

"Why are you saying these things to me?" he demanded furiously.

"*You – said – you – wanted – to - talk*," she reminded him, emphasising every word very deliberately.

"Look, Satiah, I *know* you're angry with me but…" he was crying now. Satiah stopped listening to him. The air was getting thinner again, she was sure of it. Heat in the back of her throat. Her earpiece had almost completed its self-scan.

"…Can't we just forget *all that happened*, at least until we get out of *this*?" he begged, snivelling. "We might never get out and I don't want to die like this. *Please*."

"Okay," she smiled brightly, as if it had all meant nothing. She stood and began to walk along the corridor, flashing her torch around. There *had* to be a way out, *there had to be*. She must have just missed it before, she told herself sternly.

She crouched in front of a non-functional door and began to get to work. There was still some power coming through, that flashing light proved it. If she could get power to the door, she could open it and they would at least have more air. Trust her luck to get trapped alongside such a whining windbag! She got the panel open rapidly, with some help from her blade, and eyed the circuitry inside. No obvious damage.

She eyed the light above her that was still flickering. It was too high for her to reach.

"Oli!" she called, seriously. "Get over here: I need you for a second." Still sniffing, he came over, wiping his tears away. "Reach up and disconnect *that* side of the light." She handed him her blade. "You can prise the covering off with this. Be gentle, I *don't* want it damaged."

She began to gingerly pull the control pad away from the door, wondering how far the wires would extend. Almost three feet. She'd set everything she could into the opening function. All she needed was power. At last, with her direction, Oli managed to get the light off the ceiling. She exposed the internal mechanism and began to connect it to the workings from the door that she had pulled free from inside the wall. As she connected the last link, a spark flew as power made the leap. The door lurched open a fraction to reveal more darkness beyond, but then it stopped just as abruptly. There was not enough power for more movement. Satiah disconnected and then slid her fingertips through the gap and began to pull. It didn't shift. Gritting her teeth, she braced herself and tried again, this time pulling it towards her and trying to force her boot through the gap too.

It began to edge back with a painful slowness. She kept trying, unwilling to give in. A few more minutes of labour and she'd made a gap big enough to slip through. She flashed her torch inside to find a room beyond. Half of it was a wreck with rubble piled to the ceiling, but there was an open door that she could see leading on. She guessed that through the next door there would be a kitchen.

"Come on," she said, lithely slipping through the gap she'd made. As she put her full weight on the floor, a groaning sounded. She halted immediately. "*Hold on!*" she warned in a whisper, holding up her hand. She slowly began to edge forwards again, in the direction of the next doorway. Each step was a nightmare of weight dispersal and engineering tolerance estimation. She swallowed and, hoping she was right about the strength of what was under her, scampered three quick steps forwards and into the doorway beyond. She paused there, turning to face Oli. He could barely get in, being larger than she was.

"Your turn," she encouraged, beckoning to him with her free hand. "Try to tread only where I trod and *go slowly*." Oli began to do just that, as he nervously glanced at the rubble to his right. He made it across without incident and Satiah slowly turned to flash her torch into the kitchen. There was a lot of rubble everywhere, but there was not so much damage. She led the way into the room.

"Get us some water," she advised, thinking ahead. They might still have hours before they got out and water would be essential. "I'll check the next corridor." She moved into yet another corridor beyond and was confronted by a very odd find. It seemed that the building had not just collapsed but had fallen down too. The whole structure had fallen down beneath ground level, she didn't know how far, and she was now looking into two different infrastructure levels.

A shout of surprise and a crash made her dart back inside.

"*Oli*!" she shouted, worried. She envisaged him having fallen to his death through a crack in the floor, or him having been killed by something lethal landing on him.

"It's okay, I just fell over something," he said, scrabbling around. She raced around the work surfaces he'd been behind and paused. It seemed he'd fallen over a body. *Malla*! She crouched and felt for a pulse. Nothing. Oli was staring down at the body in horror and sadness. Satiah grabbed Malla's torch and handed it to Oli. Malla had been hit on the head; hard enough to crack his skull open. She checked again for a pulse to be sure, but a head wound like that was almost conclusive. He was already feeling cooler.

"He's dead isn't he?" Oli croaked, softly.

"Yes," she snapped. Malla's death was a bad thing to her - *now* it meant that it might be impossible to know if he was angel or not.

"I don't understand how we survived," he wailed, cradling his friend. *She* did, but she couldn't tell him, obviously.

"We have to move on, Oli," she said, putting a hand on his shoulder and shushing him. She squeezed. "It's not safe here. I don't understand exactly *how* but the building seems to have fallen deep into the infrastructure constructions under the ground. I don't know how far we've gone but there could be *hundreds* of floors between us and ground level."

"*It's because of me!*" he sobbed, still clutching his friend. "He's dead because of me!" Satiah groaned inwardly.

"Oli, *listen to me,* I don't know what is holding this structure where it is. I've found an access point that will lead us into the infrastructure. Once we get in there…" She was interrupted by a rending, crashing noise from above. Something crumbled somewhere and the whole place shook. Dirt flooded in from the corridor outside.

"*Oli!*" she hissed, trying to literally drag him along with her. He wouldn't let go of the body.

Now she had a choice here. The place was going to either fall further down - or just implode completely - of that she was certain. If she stayed there trying to save Oli, she might die as well if he wouldn't let go of Malla. If she ran, she could get out herself. No one would ever need to know that she'd even been with him. Yet her orders were to ensure his survival until the election was over. She did the only thing she thought would probably work. She stepped back and pulled her gun on him.

"Oli!" she snapped, her voice almost like a whip-crack. "Get up and follow me." He stared at her as if she'd gone mad.

"…Satiah…?" he began, seeming to come to his senses. She put her torch in her mouth again to free her hand.

"Come on," she growled, grabbing his arm and hauling him along with her. This time he let go of Malla.

She replaced her gun in its holster and flashed her torch at her find. He had to see it to believe it.

"*There!*" she ordered, pointing to the opening. "Climb up into that corridor!" Oli, still sobbing and gasping, grappled and dragged himself up into it inelegantly. The ceiling lowered as he moved and the floor began to drop. Satiah backed away and then took a running leap in after him split seconds before it came down. She just made it, rolling to a halt as Oli watched the building they had been inside vanish from sight, to be replaced with a blackened wodgy *something* and then a scratched metal wall. Satiah too watched, a grim expression on her face. No going back now…

"*What just happened?*" he demanded, turning Malla's torch on her. "I don't understand!"

"The ship must have fallen through the... *I don't know either Oli*, just count your blessings," she retorted, struggling to her feet. "I think this is the infrastructure, but I don't know how far down we are. Some of these places have been abandoned for thousands of years. *We could be anywhere.*"

"What about the air?" he demanded, scared. "What if we're sealed in some place...?"

"I don't know *yet!*" she yelled in his face. "Stay calm! Did you bring any water?" He paused, confused momentarily by the question.

"I... I..." he began. He'd been distracted by Malla and had not got around to getting any provisions.

"*You're useless!*" she sneered, up at him. "I give you *one thing* to do...!"

"That's hardly fair..." he argued, without conviction.

"Do you actually *want* to survive to see the outcome of the election or not?" she asked, sarcastically. "I thought you did, seeing how you put all that effort into the debate, but now I'm starting to wonder if I was wrong about that."

"*Please*, this isn't helping us," he said, backing off. "I'm sorry, *I'm sorry all right?* I just panicked. I ... Malla... I just..."

"*Shut up!*" she instructed, coldly. She turned her back on him and faced the blackness that was their way forward. She was going to get out of this, with or without Oli. The infrastructure, however, went on and on, she knew. Thousands of floors deep and planet wide, it was the secret subterranean part of Earth. A place of forgotten things and perpetual dark where no one ever went. Her shoulders slumped as she considered *how* she could get them out of it. Her earpiece went off, having at last made it back online.

"Satiah? This is Zax; respond please, this is very urgent..." Zax's voice sounded. Satiah's heart leapt in relief. If she could get hold of Zax, Zax might be able to find a way out for them. Plus, it was just good to hear another voice beside Oli's.

"It's me," she said, smiling despite the situation.

"Collorah's down there with you, he sneaked in with the medical staff," Zax warned. The smile vanished from Satiah's face even quicker than it had appeared.

"I need you to tell me where I am," Satiah instructed. "Trace my signal."

"Randal wants to know if you have Oli with you, he's coming down to help," Zax said. Satiah glanced around at Oli who was listening.

"O yes, I've certainly got him with me," Satiah growled, seriously. *As if she could forget him.*

"Satiah…" Zax said, disbelief in her voice. "You're *beneath* the basement level of the infrastructure. How did you guys survive the fall?"

"We're not sure," Satiah lied, worried about what Zax was trying to tell her. "*How many floors down* are we?"

"Ten thousand and eighty three," Zax answered, wincing as she said it. Satiah's eyes widened.

"…*That's quite a long way down*," she muttered, thinking about it. "Do you have blueprints for these levels?"

"No," Zax replied, instantly. "Those I have here only cover the first nine hundred. After that, *according to these*, it's all *sealed off*."

"*Exquisite*," Satiah uttered. "Could you do me a favour?" Zax braced herself.

"Yes," she said.

"Would you mind awfully letting the man looking after my apartment know that I might be a little late and he will have to handle the maintenance himself for now?" she smiling, knowing Zax would understand.

"Of course," Zax said, smiling in admiration. She was very impressed that despite what was happening, Satiah could think of things like that. She wished she would be that cool one day. "If he asks where you are, shall I say you're at the office?" Satiah glanced across at Oli as she spoke.

"Tell him I'm keeping this business alive," she remarked, disconnecting.

"Why are you not asking *for help*?" Oli asked, confused.

"Just give me a minute!" she hissed, waving dismissively at him. How exactly could they not already know that they needed help?!

"Satiah," Randal said, as he answered. "How the hell did you and Oli survive that?"

"We don't know. *Collorah?*" she asked, meaningfully.

"Yes, he came in disguised as medical staff, I'm going to try to reach you but I don't know where to look, obviously," he told her. "Don't forget to keep one eye open for the PAI too, they might use this as an opportunity to take you out."

"Thanks for the warning," she said. He disconnected and she faced Oli.

"*O Oli,*" she smiled, unable to hide her interest in his reaction to this latest development. "The Red Necromancer's down here somewhere too. *Guess why he's here?*" Oli went pale and looked around feverishly.

"He must be *crazy,*" he gasped, fearfully.

"Help is on the way but we're a long way down. We're going to have to get ourselves out of this one."

---

"What do you mean, *late?*" Carl complained, crossly. "I've made dinner and everything!"

"I'm sorry, I'm just the messenger," Zax told him. "She said she loves and misses you."

"*No* she didn't, she *never* says stuff like that," Carl grumbled, without being serious. "She says things like: *where are you, why are you late,* and *how dare you do that, unhand me at once*!" Zax giggled.

"I'm sorry, she's in a bit of a situation but *I can't tell you more,*" she said.

"She'll be a situation all right, when I shove this *vociferous vegetable Vorvorsca salad* in her face," he said, sighing. "All right, well, thanks for letting me know. You're our PA now, are you?"

"*I was promoted.* She also said, you have to handle *the maintenance* yourself," she said, casually. He rolled his eyes.

"Righto," he replied, throwing Satiah's dinner back into storage. He disconnected before slumping into a chair. He shook his head. He'd got up two whole hours early too, cutting his afternoon nap down by half! *Half*!

"*The things I do for love. It's always the man who suffers.*"

"Oli, from now on we're going to have to be *really careful*," Satiah cautioned. "There will be things down here that even I might not be able to deal with. I'm hoping we won't find anything but... let's put it this way... this place, *all these places*, have been sealed off *for a reason*. I'm going to need you to do exactly what I say when I say it. Okay? And no more *hysterics*."

"What kind of things?" he asked, uncertainly.

"I wouldn't like to speculate but... potentially hazardous materials. Radioactive or just plain toxic..." she answered. "Mutant creatures that want to suck our blood." He winced, a bit disturbed by the last one.

"This is *Earth*..." he began, disbelievingly.

"Yes, it is, but this is also an abandoned part of it buried deep below everyone, miles underneath them *where nothing can get out*," she said, seriously. "Imagine *how hungry* it will be if it's still alive."

"That's *not funny*, you're trying to scare me," he accused, irately.

"All right, well, I'm going to try to get out of here, if for nothing else other than to survive. If you want that too then I suggest you come with me," she said, marching away. Her boots made no noise. The dust was everywhere, in thick, black, sand-like piles not unlike soot. The corridor was dark, lit only by their torches. There were occasional sounds coming from the direction of the destruction. Ahead, there was nothing. They had been going forwards and along for about six minutes when they reached a t-junction. She flashed her torch up each way to be greeted by identical looking corridors.

"How long do these stretch for?" he mumbled, bleakly.

"I'm not sure *anyone* knows anymore," she admitted, unable to stop the misery in her tone from being audible. "Some have been here for thousands, even tens of thousands of years. *Some maybe since this planet was rebuilt*. I know we're not at their deepest even here, but we're not far away." He suppressed a shudder and looked around uneasily while considering the history and danger of the situation. Then he sought refuge in hopeful disbelief of her statement.

"*Nonsense!* There *must be* an emergency maintenance elevator *somewhere!*" he insisted, nervously.

"There are probably *many* but I don't know where they are or even if they still work," she disclosed.

The murmur of their voices echoed softly away as their shadows passed through the darkness. She chose the right hand corridor and began to trudge on again, Oli padding after her. On some level in her mind, Satiah had always been interested to see what these places were like. A bit of morbid fascination with the unknown, perhaps, or maybe just the subliminal instincts of a born sleuth, she wasn't sure. This was hardly the time for exploring, but she was curious as to what these places had once been: what they had been used for and who used them. Her enquiring mind was becoming increasingly restless, imagining how these places may have looked back in the day. Thinking about others who had been there… before all the lights went out. Before it was all cast away into the mix of fact, opinion and assumption that was history.

She nearly didn't spot the large hole in the floor ahead. She managed to stop herself from tumbling down by grabbing the wall at the last second. She shone her torch down but the bottom was invisible to her. She glanced up to realize that another hole of equal proportion was there, leading upwards. Again, nothing but the dark. A cool breeze blew down suddenly and despite how muggy it was down there, her hair began to dance about her face and she shivered.

"*Bejabbers!* I wonder… if *that* leads to the surface," she pondered, considering her grapple-gun. There was no question of it ever having the range she'd need to go straight up, if indeed the shaft itself was a straight line, but she could have gone up the wall bit by bit. Well, she could have if she were sure it led to the surface and if she didn't have Oli with her.

"I can't see the top," Oli said, seriously. He mopped the sweat from his brow with his forearm. "It's warm down here, isn't it? I didn't notice it at first but I'm sweating like anything." *Yes, and you forgot the water.*

Satiah swallowed, noting her own growing thirst yet again. Going back wasn't an option. They had to go on. Randal was coming in and Zax knew where they were, if the worst came to the worst they would think of something. Satiah sprang across the gap easily and continued on. Oli followed a little more hesitantly. She could tell the darkness was starting to get to him. He was getting jumpy. He kept hearing things that weren't there, catching spectral nothings in the corners of his eyes. She tried to remember the first time she'd been trapped in an environment like this and what it had felt like. Her hand rested on the handle of her pistol for reassurance.

"I think something's following us," he confided, as she knew he would. *And so it begins.*

"It's your imagination, Oli," she argued, as gently as she could manage. "Believe me, I have been listening and I have heard nothing." The speed of his counter comment was enough to convince her that his fear was getting the better of him:

"No, it's *not*," he insisted in a harsh whisper, starting to show signs of hysteria. "It was like a shuffling noise…"

"Oli, if there *is* anything at all down here with us, it will most likely be so surprised to come across us that I doubt it will harm us," she misled, calmly. "Anyway, *I'm* the smallest, you're supposed to be comforting *me* and *assuring* me that we are in no danger."

"You've done this type of thing before, I haven't," he retorted, levelly.

"Precisely, *so believe me when I tell you that we're perfectly safe*," she stipulated, impatience creeping in. He went quiet thankfully, but then a clang from behind them made her halt in her tracks. Oli didn't even say anything, he just pointed agitatedly back the way they had come with conviction. Well, she had to admit, she *had* heard *that*. Her first suspicion was that it was Collorah, though that seemed unlikely. They were a long way from where he would be. Miles deeper, actually. It was probably just more rubble shifting or something. In either case, whatever it was, standing there and waiting for it to come to them didn't seem like the smartest strategy.

They had passed many closed doors on their way. *You know, those things that things happen behind?* Satiah now decided she had to open, or try to open, at least one of them. Just quickly to see what was inside. How dangerous could it be? She'd resisted this temptation up until now but Oli clearly needed a distraction or he'd turn into even more of a gibbering wreck than he already was. Satiah paused by one and crouched to examine the access panel. It was in bad condition and whatever inscription there had once been had long since worn away. Like something written in the sands of a beach, losing their being to the caress of water, these symbols of a past long forgotten were faded into obscurity by the passage of time.

"What are you *doing*?" he asked, urgent. "*We have to keep going.*"

"We're okay for now," she insisted, firmly. She knew he could hardly leave without her, but if she started saying yes now, it would only get harder to say no later. To her surprise, the door suddenly fell right off of its rusted hinges and would have fallen on her had she not rolled to the side. Torch in one hand, pistol in the other, in a posture known as *the cross-hand*, Satiah entered the blackness of the room beyond. Oli followed and all was silent.

Dust was everywhere, as she had expected. There were crates. Tens of them all stacked on top of each other, all silent and dark as if they were there to wait out eternity. She examined the nearest one, brushing the dust away from its now non-functional display screen. No clues.

"*We should go,*" Oli hissed, at her.

"Not yet," she murmured, unconcerned.

"Satiah, come on, *please*, it's not safe down here," he went on.

"Keep watch if you like," she offered, squinting at the controls. They were ancient. And, absurdly, *solar powered*. Absurd considering where someone had chosen to store them, a place almost as far from the sun as it was possible to be on this planet. Normally, had she not had Oli with her, she'd have forced her way inside one of the crates to see what it contained but this time she chose not to bother.

She turned to see where Oli was standing but he wasn't in the doorway anymore. She returned to the corridor, flashing her torch left and right. There was no sign of him.

"Oli?" she called, a little uncertainly. She checked the floor, looking for their tracks in the dust. He'd not gone in, nor had he gone back that she could tell. She returned to the room, wondering if he'd gone down another aisle or something and she'd just missed him in the dark. She thought she saw something, like someone standing there, in the corner of her eye. She spun around, pistol raised. Just a support beam with a mangled pile of metal in front of it. She hissed, angered by her own edginess.

"*Oli!*" she snapped, angrily.

Where was he? She saw torchlight flash off the wall nearby.

"Satiah?" Oli replied, walking out from another area. "Sorry, I was just…"

"*Don't* wander off, this place is vast," she admonished him, instantly. "Stay close at all times."

"Yes, sorry," he said, uncomfortably. "I was just checking…"

"*Checking*? What could *you* possibly have to check up on down here?" she retorted, irked.

"You said to keep watch and I couldn't see what was down there at the end…"

"I meant *of the corridor*!" she replied, deciding to let it drop. "Let's go, we're wasting time. I thought maybe there might be something interesting in here but there clearly isn't." They returned to the corridor and once again checked both ways before moving on. Satiah felt drawn to inspect everything but she knew to stay on task.

"What's that *stench*?" Oli asked, after several more minutes of silent striding.

"Decay," she replied, having already smelt it. "I'm *not* stopping to see what it might be."

"…Fair enough," he said, seeing no reason in arguing. The smell continued to get worse; Satiah ignored it as best as she could. She imagined ice cold water gushing all over herself to try to take her mind off it. Something had died. Something had died *recently* down here. Her rational mind told her that, in all probability, it had to be vermin. Rats and all manner of other things probably came along here from time to time. There was nothing here they could live on but *they* didn't know that until they got here. What else could it possibly be? Another more distant clang sounded behind them and Oli spun around, almost shrieking in terror. Whatever it was, clearly it was still a long way behind them, perhaps further than ever, but he was not used to this.

"Do you want to stop for a bit, have a break?" she suggested, in an effort to calm him down.

"*No! Are you crazy?* It could be on us at *any time*," he argued, emotionally.

"*Oli...*" she began, taking a deep breath.

"*No! You're not listening*! There's something in here with us and it's going to kill us, it's probably responsible for that reek...!" He was shouting now, really starting to lose it. She didn't want to have to knock him out but if he kept shouting like that he might attract trouble. *What if he turns on me?* She had wondered about that before.

"Hush, *I heard something*!" she lied, again. She would make his paranoia work for her if she couldn't prevent it. She forced herself to whisper and pulled him close. "I think you're right, what do you think we should do?"

"We have to get out of here," he said, a little cooler.

"Okay," she said, trying not to be too patronising. "So we keep going? Is that what you're saying?"

There was a pause.

"Sorry," he breathed, realising what had happened. "*I'm so sorry, Satiah.* I don't know what happened there, I just got it in my head that there was something back there and..."

"It's fine, just *please* try to stay close," she said, glad that it seemed to have worked. Normally, were it anyone more solid, she'd have just told them to buck up and stay serious, but Oli was increasingly unstable. She knew she had to accept at least some of the blame for that. Therefore, being unduly hostile toward him would be counterproductive as long as they were down there.

"The fear you're feeling now is completely normal," she said, giving him some solace. "I myself feel just the same." *Introducing empathy.* "I'm always seeing things, you know? In my peripheral vision? They always look like something they're not. Always. I'm regularly thinking that I hear things but, through experience, I've learned to *ignore* most of these things. It's just... do you want to know something interesting about eyes?"

"What?" he asked, confused by her question.

"Tests have been done on this kind of thing innumerable times. People that are locked up in dark environments will claim that they saw lights or colours or shadows even though it is completely impossible for them to have done so. It's all been documented. It's *natural* for your eyes to do things like that when cut off from their only source of light. Now, I know it's not totally dark here because we have lights with us, but the principle still applies," she said, very soothingly. *That's it, time for rational thought to make a long-awaited reappearance.* "Now, *I know* we've both heard things together and I'm not for one minute suggesting that we both hallucinated the same thing. Instead I'm going to say that, even though we certainly heard *something*, the assumption that it is something dangerous *could be faulty.*" *Technically true.*

"...*Yes*," he agreed, with some reluctance. She continued to try to defuse the tension.

"Some people have a condition called synaesthesia, where the subject's senses somehow become interconnected. They can see sounds or hear colours and all sorts of other combinations. *I don't know the details.* You lock one of them in a dark room and even though their senses are different, they too experience things that aren't there. It's also been shown that you can retain a sense of where your own body is and how it looks while moving even in total darkness. It's instinctive and no one really knows how we do it. The only thing we should really be frightened of is fear itself. Fear clouds judgement and without good judgement we won't get very far."

"Did they do tests like that on you when you were in the military?" he asked, curious.

"*Well...*" she smiled, seeing that she'd made progress. She'd taken his fear off the unknown, turned it into analysis and placed it onto their conversational subject. "*I shouldn't really talk about that*, but yes, they did put us through a few *unorthodox* situations. Of course they were called other names like *movement management skills workshops* and titles like that. They did that because firstly, they didn't want to tip off any participants by suggesting what they might *really* be going to do. Knowing that it was a test of some sort might affect the results of said test. And secondly, I suspect they *also* did it so that *no one who shouldn't would know what they were doing*. Those scientists would go nuts if they thought their data was invalid because someone went into the test knowing that they were being tested."

"Did they do other tests on you too? My father would never answer me when I asked him about things like that," Oli wanted to know.

"Shall we keep going?" she offered, motioning for them to continue walking. He nodded. She was struck with the realisation that this conversation was in itself a bit of a psychological test. Could she overcome his fear using subjects of interest to him? Would fear itself *be* one of those subjects? Lucky for her she was excellent at making up plausible lies on the spot with no preparation or even prior knowledge. "Again, I shouldn't *really* be talking to you about this but… you're not going to tell anyone, are you?"

"No, of course not," he agreed, quickly.

"There was the time I was involved in an experiment concerning sleep deprivation. They wanted to test this new drug, to improve the wakefulness of people in the hours before dawn. Even with all the advancements in technology and physical training, it remains one of the best times to attack someone. Anyway…"

---

Randal looked down into the darkness. The building had collapsed and that had caused multiple collapses underneath it, taking Satiah and Oli down thousands of levels below. How they had survived was a bit of a mystery but Randal knew they were far from safe. He watched as some more rubble tumbled off the edge and descended into the darkness, almost in slow motion, before fading completely from his vision. It had been a narrow escape. If Oli *had* died, the mission would have failed and they would all have been on damage control. Brainwashed clones and replica androids sprung into his mind. Whatever was necessary would be deployed to make it look as if he was still alive. It occurred to him that Oli didn't know how lucky he was.

Knowing that this time he was allowed to answer the door, Carl casually wandered over to let Max in. As soon as he opened the door, exactly as he had expected, Max did a double take.

"*Carl?* What the hell are you doing here?" he demanded, in astonishment.

"I'm just having a holiday," he grinned, as they shook hands.

"How have you been?"

"Same as ever, what's happening?"

"The usual, just the usual…"

"I was asked to take a look at someone's computer, some lady, she was pretty specific about how she wanted me to work," he said, a little confused.

"O *her*! Yeah, she's the local social conscience worker, *very active* in helping out the community," Carl lied, casually. "Come on in; let me get you some beer." Max shrugged, nodded enthusiastically and then dragged his equipment inside.

---

Zax watched the screen as her new drone swiftly descended down into the darkness.

"How far down is it?" Randal asked. She told him. "Satiah has all the luck sometimes."

"At least Collorah will have the same obstacle as us before him," she said, shrugging. "I wonder how he intends to get down there."

"*I'm just as concerned about Snell and what the PAI might try during this.* Satiah said something about Collorah tending to use vehicles so I'm betting that he has a way," Randal growled. In the distance, Zax was starting to see little patches of flickering orange light. *Fires.*

"I think I'm getting warm now," she informed him. "I can see flames. You're going to need protection, I recommend level…"

"*Three,*" he interrupted, with a sigh. "I thank you for your recommendation but I do not need it." She pulled a face but didn't say anything.

"I can't believe they would do that to *their own troops*," Oli stated, outraged.

"*There are laws about doing it on the enemies.* We were the fortunate ones, it could have been worse," Satiah replied. "Some people lost a lot. And I *mean* a lot. I bet you're glad you didn't go for a career in the military now?"

"Somewhat," he agreed, seriously. "And how does this never get out? How is it the media never learns of these things and yet they can find out all sorts about celebrities' lives?"

"*It's a mystery*," she mused, trying not to smile. "Maybe it's just not juicy enough for them to bite on."

"Yes," he murmured, thinking back to the debate. *Deetee*. "If I get into power... I think I would have to do something about the media."

Satiah, despite herself, was interested. Having dreamed often of being in power herself, she too had plenty of designs on them.

"Really?" she enquired, mischievously. "Wouldn't that affect free speech?"

"Well, obviously I'd have to accept them for their role in exposing the truth when needed, but I think they need reining in a bit. They seem to have far too much influence for my liking," he sighed.

"*Careful*," she warned, grinning in the dark. "That right there is the slippery slope to tyranny." She didn't tell him that she'd have had them all arrested the moment she had the opportunity.

"I suppose you're right, it's just all the fake news and stuff out there that bothers me," he confessed, sadly.

It was then that Satiah first became aware of a distant thrumming noise coming from ahead of them. A pulsing, plangent beat. It was obviously mechanical and... vaguely familiar to her. Oli fell silent upon hearing it.

"What do you suppose that is?" he whispered, worried.

"I think it's a generator. Possibly one of the main planetary power reactors," she replied, excited. This was good. The cables would inevitably lead to the surface and if there was anywhere where emergency access was required it would be there.

"You sound pleased," he noted, hope in his voice.

"At the very least we won't need torches anymore," she smirked. "Come on, if we..." She was interrupted by a metallic scrambling noise from behind them.

---

Snell eyed them levelly, the ten strong team of operatives he'd chosen, as they stood patiently in front of him.

"You will infiltrate the undercity area and locate Oli. When you've found him you must bring him back to the surface safely. Satiah may be with him. She's a Phantom agent assigned to protect him. If she is indeed with him, then she is to be killed," Scott instructed, sourly. "Given the scenario, her death can easily be explained away. Once she's been taken care of I'll alert Lunell who can then take the next step."

"Understood," they all agreed, with curt nods. He motioned to the door and they hurried out. The tracking device Lunell had placed on Oli was barely registering, they were so deep. Nevertheless, it was enough to give them a general area to investigate.

---

It may have been what had caused the clanging noises earlier. Its origins were something Satiah could only guess at and even if she'd wanted to speculate, she hardly had time. Coming straight at them out of the darkness was a very badly damaged looking robot. A reprobate unit left to wander around down there by someone, who knew how long ago? Its limbs were flailing as if it had lost control of its motor function, and its mouth emitted a piercing wail as if announcing its attack. Satiah reflected later that it sounded a lot like metal being bent or crushed. Her pistol was in her hand quick as anything, and she put two bolts in its head, but still it came on. Satiah pushed Oli aside just as it crashed into her.

It hit hard enough to hurt and she cried out as she hit the dusty floor with the writhing metal lunatic landing on her. She tried to reach for her pistol as she dodged a flailing appendage. She slid out from under it as it began to rise.

"*Stay back!*" she screamed at Oli. He was standing there, looking helpless, and trying to decide what to do. Satiah couldn't say for sure how the machine could see them as its eyes were non-functional, but it apparently could. She rolled free, trying to locate her pistol in the dust. A metallic arm tripped her and she sprawled onto the ground, coughing in the clouds of dirt and dust. She felt its cold hard fingers tightening around her throat. She tried to push it away but for all its lack of control its strength was undeniable.

Its other arm came up to grab too, but she snatched an exposed cable and yanked, holding the other arm back. It whirred and she growled as back and forth its arm went.

"Get the pistol!" she snarled, through her teeth. "Oli!" Oli began a frantic search on the ground before picking it up and aiming as she and the mad robot tussled violently. Its hand suddenly let of her neck and it balled into a fist. She dodged the first blow but the second glanced off her forehead. Next it formed a star shape in an effort to gouge out her eyes.

"*Shoot it!*" she implored, desperately. Oli fired. He was hardly a step away and yet somehow he missed and the bolt hit the floor, sending up another cloud of dust. He fired again, this time hitting the mechanical menace in the back. Satiah scrambled free, bleeding now but still relatively uninjured.

The robot continued to flail and roll about on the floor as Satiah snatched her pistol from Oli and shot it repeatedly, until finally it seemed to have been successful dispatched. She then slumped against the wall, panting heavily.

"Are you okay?" he asked, urgently.

"...Yes," she allowed, still breathing hard. She chose not to rebuke him about his rotten aim. She considered herself lucky he hadn't accidentally hit *her*! If he *dared* to say *I told you so* she would give him a very brief but memorable accuracy lesson... where *his balls* would be her targets.

"*What was that thing?*" he asked, rhetorically. He knew there was no way she could know. Her main worry now was: were there more of them?

"A bit haywire," she managed, wincing. She touched her injury and eyed the blood on her fingertips. It wasn't bad. She really needed a drink more than anything now. Oli nudged the robot with his foot and he jumped back hurriedly as it juddered for a short time.

"*Leave it alone,*" she ordered, seriously. "It was tough, whatever it was, but we were lucky it was old and out of control. Had it been fully functional..." She didn't need to finish that sentence.

"Can you walk?" he enquired. She almost barked out a laugh as *she'd* been asking *him* that not so long ago.

"Yes," she assured him. "Question is: can I still fight?"

―――――◆◆◆◆◆―――――

The predefined rendezvous area consisted of a small, disused equipment store under a subsurface parking area. A sort of bothy or hut, secluded in a corner, wrapped up in the sinister cloak of amber twilight. Hidden inside this hut, a place no one went, in a building no one cared about, Jinx waited anxiously. It had been a disaster. The mildew, damp and overall rundown condition of the building acted as a metaphor as to how their last endeavour had ended up. Jinx still wasn't sure what had gone wrong. He did know now that, unless a miracle happened, Octutin was not going to turn up this time. He was over two hours late and Octutin was never late. The inevitable conclusion was that he'd probably not made it out of there alive.

Jinx confronted the question of what to do next. Without his running partner he knew he would be unable to complete this job. Besides, he had to avenge his dead friend. He wouldn't take his rage out on those who had killed him though. First, he wasn't sure who they were, and second, they were only defending themselves. The real culprits here were those who had hired him to do the job. He already knew that at least one of them was planning to turn on the other. Sam had contacted him personally to discuss the possibility of assassinating Mark. At the time he'd taken it all in his stride, but now this was starting to smell bad all over. It was common for conspirators to turn on each other once they'd achieved their immediate aims, but it was the timing of this which bothered Jinx.

He'd lost two teams, achieved nothing, and now he'd lost his friend too. Someone was going to pay. He'd only ever had to take steps like this once before. Back then, someone had made the mistake of very clumsily cutting him out of a deal, a deal he had practically masterminded since the beginning. He'd got even that day. Today was looking very much like that day. He called Sam. Sam answered.

"Yes?" he said, concerned. Any communication they had would obviously set off alarms in his mind.

"We need to meet," Jinx stated, without preamble.

"Is Oli dead?" he asked, hopefully. Unusual for a politician to be so optimistic, Jinx thought.

"It's not about that," Jinx explained, sourly. "Just you and me."

If was difficult to say if Sam was suspicious or not. He hadn't advertised it if he was. Who would? Jinx hoped that Sam would presume that he would ask him for more money which... in a way... he would be. He was already several thousand Essps in debt because of this job, and no matter what happened, he needed to deal with that. Also, after this was over, he was getting the feeling that he might not be able to visit Earth again any time soon. He'd need yet more funds to support himself. He knew Mark was substantially richer than Sam, and he suspected that Sam was reliant on Mark's money to be able to pay Jinx himself.

---

Collorah was on a voyage of discovery. Not only had the explosives he'd planted in the ship failed to go off, but the collapse of the building had exceeded his wildest estimations. Somehow, probably due to substandard building materials or general long-term corrosion, parts of the building had fallen through into the infrastructure below. They had fallen a long way, too far to see without the aid of equipment. The structure seemed relatively intact from his vantage point, but he knew it only meant that one floor had remained that way. A scan revealed faint heat signatures everywhere, mostly small fires. Some though were larger and more human shaped and... they were moving. Someone had survived... incredibly.

As he quickly descended towards the remains of the structure, Randal shot past him, literally riding a drone. Collorah would have shot him but he was gone too fast, disappearing into a hole and out of sight. Not for a second did Collorah think he was with the medical team. Satiah must still be alive and she'd called for help? Collorah began to hurry. Satiah was dangerous enough on her own, if she had friends too he knew he'd be totally outmatched. After what seemed like forever he reached the roof and strode out across the ruin to reach the gaping hole Randal had used to gain entry. He crouched and flashed a torch down to see better. How could anyone have survived that? How had she survived being exposed to space without protection? He had to find out.

---

"Take it easy Zax, I almost lost my grip there!" Randal complained. His arms were starting to ache from holding himself there. He'd been hanging on for nearly a minute now and he knew he could hang on for perhaps the same length of time again. He was a strong man, but strength wasn't the problem - it was blood flow to the arms. Normally, if you let go with one arm and relaxed it by lowering it and allowing easier blood flow, you could hold on much longer but, as he was clinging to a drone, he was not in a position where he could easily do that. He gritted his teeth, starting to really feel the strain now.

"Sorry sir," Zax replied, in his ear. She was piloting the drone from Phantom headquarters and, in order to get in ahead of the killer, Randal had opted to make use of the drone's speed and ease of movement. It was actually a crime to use any kind of drone in this way, thanks to some crazed teenagers, but he wasn't worried about that. He did worry, however, that Zax might forget he was there and accidentally crash him into things that the drone itself would normally miss. As he got into the building, he realised they had to go still further down.

"Won't happen again." What was it that it reminded him so much of Satiah's false assurances when she said things like that? She also had that same rintherout gleam in her eyes too, now that he thought about it. A wild unpredictability, which should mean that she'd be a great Phantom agent if she lived long enough.

"Take me to a level *higher* than where Satiah is," he instructed, levelly. "Then I can go down on foot and hopefully meet her as she and Oli come up. I don't want to be chasing after her."

"Sir," Zax replied, in acknowledgement. The drone slowed noticeably. "I'll take you to about nine levels above her approximate location. Do you want me to tell her where you are?"

"Yes, wouldn't want her shooting me dead thinking I'm the PAI," he muttered, his feet now inches from the ground.

"Quite, sir," she responded, as the drone finally halted and began to lower. Relieved, Randal dropped and swung his arms around in relief. Then he pulled out his pistol.

"Keep this drone in the area, we might need it to get Oli out," he instructed, starting down the dusty corridor.

"Sir."

---

She had no idea where they had all come from, but one thing was certain: they were trying to kill her and Oli. Malfunctioning robots formed a line of running metal, hurtling down the corridor after them, fuelled only by some kind of madness. Maybe they had been making the noises earlier, maybe not; it hardly mattered at that moment. As she ran she fired behind her, missing Oli, hitting them in the legs, trying to slow them or trip them. Oli was not used to this and was already out of breath and wheezing as he ran. She took in his condition, recognising the early onset of a stitch. He couldn't keep this up. Randal was calling her and so was Zax but she wasn't in the best situation for a chat. She had to get them away from these things. A door on the right was slightly open and she hoped it led to somewhere other than a dead end.

"In there!" she ordered, stopping and shoving at Oli. He went, too weary and frightened to question it. Satiah took a second to try some more accurate shots but they were nearly upon her in that time. She leapt through the door, slammed it shut and then jammed it. A hammering began on the other side, a pounding of metal on metal as they tried to batter their way in. Immune to both pity and pain, limited only by whatever power source ruled them, she knew they would get through eventually. She flashed her torch around, looking for anything she could use to block the door.

"*Table!*" she shouted, more to herself than to Oli. She jumped over Oli, who was lying on the ground, panting and sweating, and began to drag the rusted excuse for a table over towards the door. Oli got out of the way, still breathing heavily as she wedged it into position. It shuddered under the barrage the door was receiving, and metal shavings and clouds of rust began to fall from it. Satiah looked again for anything else she could use.

There were crates, old chairs, and what looked like metal lockers. She began to build her barrier methodically but with an urgent energy. Oli watched her with admiration in his eyes as she moved and achieved. Finally the door was completely hidden behind a huge pile of lockers, furniture and a few other things she'd come across. Her breathing was still even, just as Oli was starting to recover. They made eye contact and she knew what he was thinking.

"You might wish to consider a regular exercise regime," she suggested, coldly. He nodded as he stood up.

"...Yes," he managed, his voice high pitched from the exhalation. Satiah began to search for a way out. As she'd worried before, there was no other door. She glanced at her makeshift barrier as the never-ending hammering gave way to a regular but much harder slamming noise. They must be throwing themselves against it, having realised they weren't going to be able to punch their way in.

"I *really* don't like this place," Oli said, shaking his head.

"It certainly lacks many of the creature comforts any good tourist would appreciate," she mused, looking up. He followed her gaze. She seemed to be looking up at an aperture of some kind. It was a dirt covered dusty sort of postern, square shaped and, if you were on your hands and knees, big enough to get through. Trouble was, it was shut, *and* it was on the ceiling. Another bang made the whole barricade shudder.

"Lean against it for a moment," she ordered, still staring up. Oli obeyed and watched as, torch in her mouth, she used her grapple-gun and began to rise towards the hatchway slowly.

Satiah hung there for a moment, having a closer look before reaching out to grab the handle. She didn't want to shoot it open unless she had to. The robots were not tall enough to reach it either, but they could get up there if they climbed over one another like ants crossing a river. So she'd rather be able to close it behind them and rely on it delaying them for a while. They might not even notice it if luck was on their side, but she wasn't going to chance that. Oli groaned as he felt the things he was leaning on jolt from another blow. He knew not to call to Satiah and interrupt her, although he badly wanted to know what was taking her so long. He felt everything shift forward a fraction as another robot crashed against the door.

Satiah yanked hard but the door wouldn't open or even budge. She began to examine the edge, doing her best to ignore the racket going on below her. There was no chance she could get her fingertips in there; it looked like it might even have been welded shut. She cursed under her breath. She looked around, edgy, seeking another possible exit. There was nothing. She refocussed on the unyielding metal again and calmed herself down. There was always a solution! She just had to think of it. That was when she noticed what looked like a control panel. It had been so black and dusty she'd not realised it was there. She began scrubbing it with her forearm carefully yet rapidly to see what sort of state it was in. There was a panel with three switches in a line, green, yellow and red from top to bottom. There was also a button-guard to their right. That too might once have been red. With no helpful labels, presumably worn away centuries ago, she had no idea what any one of these controls would do even if they *did* still work. She rubbed it with her fingers, hoping to find lettering that might give her a clue. No luck.

"*Satiah*!" called Oli, worriedly. He was now actively pushing against the blockade to hold it in place. He didn't think it was going to last much longer.

"Ah-huh." she acknowledged, as she removed the cap revealing a big blue button underneath it.

"I might need your help here!" he said, trying to sound reasonable.

"Good," she said, not really listening. She pressed the button. It was tough, refusing to go down but she forced it in and it clicked loudly as it went down. There was a loud crunching sound from above her and she lowered herself a little in case she needed to get away. Thump! Thump! Thump! These sounds came from the hatchway and then it swung open with a screech, revealing cool darkness and a strange, somewhat familiar smell. She flashed her torch inside, a hopeful smile on her lips. A smooth walled tunnel, apparently completely free of dust leading upwards.

"Come on," she hissed, lowering herself to the ground.

"How can we climb *that*?" he demanded, in fright.

"Brace your body against one side with your legs and slide up, *it's easy*, hurry!" she ordered, handing him the cord. He began to climb with annoying slowness while she took his place at the barricade. He couldn't use the gun to raise himself there because then she wouldn't be able to follow.

"*Hurry up!*" she growled, not quite loud enough for him to hear her. He tried to get up into the shaft but couldn't. She watched in mounting panic. Another violent jolt from the door reminded her of their peril unnecessarily. This right here was why politicians were only good for giving orders: because they lacked the capacity to carry them out!

"Satiah!" he cried, pleadingly. "*This isn't going to work*, there has to be another…"

"*Stay there!*" she ordered, trying to contain her fury. *If she had to carry him herself…!* She snatched the grapple-gun and rose once again while he clung to the door itself.

"Get your foot up into the slot between the hinges!" she hissed, impatiently. "Then push yourself up until your knee is about half extended. *Go on!*" There was a clatter from below as something fell from the barricade and rolled onto the ground. The door edged open an inch. With great difficulty, Oli managed the movement. "Now, one at a time, raise your leg and push it against the wall you are facing!" Another crash from below. One more and they would be in.

Trembling with the exertion, Oli managed to wedge himself in the shaft. Satiah stared up at him incredulously. Was he ever going to move? Well, he'd have to! She clung onto the hatch with her free hand and reset her grapple-gun.

"I'm only going to say this to you once, Oli!" she growled. "Open your legs and don't move!"

"*What?*"

"Just do it please," she said, aiming. He carefully slid his legs apart, nervous of falling. She fired her grapple-gun, the cord shot past Oli and stuck in the ceiling at the end of the shaft. She began to rise and, as she moved, she hit the button, causing the hatchway to close behind her.

"Fall to the hatch!" she ordered, "You can stand on it now!" He dropped, and they passed one another in mid-air. He landed hard on the now closed hatch, just as she reached the first corner.

She flashed her torch and was very much relieved to see that it went on. A distant crashing noise informed them of their barrier's fate. Light came from under her as Oli retrieved his torch from his pocket and stared up at her.

"What can you see?" he asked, in a loud whisper. She was still trying to place that smell she had recognised from somewhere. Faint but still there. Not decay this time... more chemical-like...

"Metal, mainly, but we have a path to follow," she replied, hauling herself onto her belly in the next part of the shaft. She then chucked the gun down for him so he could reach her. She crawled a little further along to give him room and sat there uncomfortably. Oli rose and did the same as she had to get in. Then he passed the grapple-gun back to her.

"Now I know why you carry that thing," he breathed, slumping against the side of the shaft. He was exhausted. She slipped it back onto her belt and crawled away without a word.

The next corner looked like a dead end but she knew it just went up again. She'd done this kind of thing a lot, but never with someone else. Talk about being slowed down.

"Oli! Come on!" she said, heartlessly. "This might get up to the surface faster than wandering blindly around those tunnels."

"I'm not moving!" he stated, his eyes closed. "Give me a few minutes at least. *Please.*" Satiah pondered how safe he would be if she just left him there and went on herself. *Oli safe?* Those two words just couldn't get along with one another. She checked her pistol out of habit while she considered what the purpose of this shaft was. It wasn't ventilation and there were no cables, so… now she thought about it, those metal walls were smooth but they did have *a faint grey stain…* the sort of blemish *evaporated liquid* makes on things…

"*Oli,*" she said again, wondering how best to put this. "We might not have much time."

"Satiah, we're quite safe in here…" he began, exasperated. *What was this: role reversal?* That button she had pressed and those sounds she had heard. At the time she'd *thought* it was the hatch unlocking but *now…*

"Oli, it's not safe, *come on!*" she hissed, turning around and going back to fetch him.

"What's wrong?" he asked puzzled. A loud thump silenced them both and Satiah looked back and forth up the shaft, unsure from which direction the danger was approaching from. There it was the distant roar of approaching fluid. Hoping that they could somehow outrun it, Satiah began to crawl forward again.

"This way unless you want to drown!" she said, through her teeth.

She'd said *drown* and that could be a possibility, but she'd not explained the other danger she knew was coming. She'd at last remembered what it was she could smell. The residual smell of almonds gave it away. Sodium cyanide. A tedious little industrial reactant with some particularly nasty properties.

"How ironic, seeing as right now we're dying *of thirst,*" he grumbled, crawling after her. She reached the next part of the shaft that went straight up and realised, if she stood, she could reach the next corner. She dragged herself up quickly and began to scramble down the next shaft. Oli though was not the fastest of people, and she had to keep stopping. At last she reached a hatchway. She could feel blasts of air coming from behind them now, whipping past them as air pockets were pushed out and through a narrow vent above the hatch. That smell was getting stronger… she knew the fumes would be on them soon. This time there was no question about the hatch.

She blasted it open and flashed her torch ahead. Another storage area? She couldn't tell but there seemed to be no danger in there.

"Come on!" she yelled, over her shoulder. She got out and grabbed him as he reached the end. The liquid could plainly be heard now as it rushed towards them. They just escaped its path in time and it jetted out from the hatch onto the floor in a continuous, powerful, toxic flood. Satiah led the way, clattering up a metal stairway noisily. It led to a door. She knew they had time, and the liquid levels might not be able to rise with any significance, but she was done taking chances on anything. Plus the fumes were harmful, which was more incentive than she needed to get the door open. One violent kick and they were out into… another dusty corridor. She slammed it shut behind them before they moved on.

The fact that it looked dismally like the corridor they'd been in when the first robot had attacked them sent Oli into an immediate panic. It wasn't the same corridor; Satiah knew it wasn't, as the dust hadn't been disturbed by their feet yet.

"How did we manage *that*?" he hissed, pale with fear.

"*We* didn't," she said, starting to march on.

"*Wait*!" he hissed, still tired. "I have to sit down for a few minutes, I know you do this all the time and I apologise for slowing you down, but I'm beat." Satiah paused, deciding that they were safe enough at that moment to allow him a short break. Just a short one. He was being punished, after all.

"Zax, give me an idea of where I am now," Satiah said, knowing it was silly to hope for anything good.

"You've risen about twenty seven floors," she answered. "Randal is about thirty floors above you, coming down."

"Ok," Satiah sighed, leaning against the wall. "We need water, any ideas?"

"Well, to find water underground, first find a *y-shaped* stick, place your *right hand* on the ground and…" Zax began, being funny.

"*Zax*," growled Satiah, closing her eyes, *very* unamused.

"Look *up*, can you see any pipes?" Zax said, grinning cheekily. It was all right for her, she wasn't trapped down there with a throat like a desert, and a gibbering idiot who had to be kept alive. Satiah flashed her torch around.

There were several.

"Yes," Satiah said. "Any particular one?" If this was another of her jokes Satiah would spank her.

"Copper coloured," Zax prompted.

"Not a lot of colour down here at all," Satiah said, grimly.

"Hold on..." Zax said. Scrabbling noises ensued. Satiah closed her eyes again, swallowed painfully and waited. "Can you see any plaques or notices anywhere? Maybe a key or a legend or *something*!" Satiah began to wander along, scrutinising the upper walls and the piping more closely. Oli watched her, wondering what she was up to now.

"*No*," she murmured, curious. Zax had made Satiah aware of the absence of notices. It was a strange one, as normally you couldn't move for such indicators.

They should be there, logic dictated it. In an event where androids were unable to fix a problem, an engineer would be sent for and they would need to know what was what. There was a complete absence of any sort of instructions and yet, in a place like this, safety notices at least had to be there somewhere! Then Satiah reached up and rubbed the dust away from the wall. She wished she was a bit taller sometimes, it really would be helpful. A thick cloud of dust moved, revealing something written there. A whiteboard with red letters. *Unit 3333.222.982. Next intersection 150m.* Okay... progress. Satiah already knew Zax had no blueprints of the area but she might have information on that unit.

"It's a current section box, powerline intersection," Zax told her, excited.

"Which way?" Satiah asked, seriously. She turned and motioned for Oli to follow her. He reluctantly stood again and staggered after her.

"I think the way you're going, maybe one hundred and forty steps," Zax said. "If not..."

"If not, then it's back the other way," Satiah interrupted, impatiently.

"Yes," Zax said, calmly. They both had the same idea. At the intersection, hopefully, there would be a first aid box, kept there should anyone be injured while carrying out maintenance. There *should* also be water. There was indeed a cabinet in the wall ahead and Satiah actually ran to it in relief. She opened it with ease and instantly a very faint light came on to help whoever was looking inside to see. There, dust free, were six cold three litre metallic containers. Designed for water storage, the water itself would be good quality for thousands of years. The gentlest of coolant mists hovered around them. If it still had energy to sustain it., the water would be drinkable.

"Zax... you're a lifesaver," Satiah grinned, reaching in to grab one.

"There might even be food in there - well... *vitamin pastes*..." Zax said, trying to sound pleased about that. Satiah shoved one bottle into Oli's chest with a sarcastic smile, before retrieving one for herself. It had probably been there for decades but for all that it tasted beautiful. Cool, clear and very much appreciated. Satiah couldn't help but gulp almost a whole third of it instantly before she had to stop in order to breathe again. Oli was doing much the same. Satiah decided to have a rest herself. There was no sense in tiring herself out. She sat down, her back to Oli. She ripped a gash in a tube of paste and began to squeeze the tasteless goo into her mouth. It was disgusting but it was nutritious and she had nothing else.

"Bon appetite," Zax said, casually. "I bet you would much rather have my *delicious*, mouth watering, fried Banwer though, huh?" Banwers were noted everywhere for their great taste and filling tendencies. Three layers of tasty meat, diligently separated with the most placid of leaf vegetables, encased in two slices of baked material made from dough. Somewhere, typically under the second layer of meat, a variety of sauces could be applied. Satiah would usually have two, mixed together. The shan-pou and the freyloosap and... and *now* Satiah was starting to think about eating it.

Spanking was too good for Zax, Satiah reflected, amused, as she gently poured a little water down her back and then front. Maybe three extra gruelling training sessions would be the answer. She imagined grabbing her by the scruff of her neck and shouting at her to run faster before watching her run around the training area. Yes… it would do her good and get rid of all that excess energy she seemed to have.

"*You* have a sadistic side, young lady," Satiah grinned, knowing what Zax was doing. A ripping sound was her answer, followed by…

"*Mmm*," Zax agreed, clearly eating her Banwer now. "*O my*! Mmm. So… succulent, so *so* good."

"Talking with your mouth full is *not* very ladylike and I hope you choke. I'm going to cut off now," Satiah stated, cutting her off.

"Randal, where are you?" she asked, next.

"Not sure," he admitted. "This place is a nightmare; according to your pet Zax I'm about nine levels above you now."

"See if you can find a service lift," she advised, downing more water. "And keep alert, not all the dangers in here are as obvious as you might think." She explained what had happen to her and Oli.

"I see," Randal replied, steadily. "I'll let you know if anything changes." He disconnected and she turned to see Oli lying there on the floor, staring up at the ceiling thoughtfully. Probably still trying to come to terms with the new direction his life had apparently taken. Well, at least he'd stopped talking, she was glad of small mercies. She began to wash the slight head wound she'd received earlier.

---

"This is one impressive machine," Max stated, swigging his drink. Max and Carl were sat in chairs, overlooking the area Satiah had placed Kelvin. Carl nodded casually.

"Who was the previous owner?"

"No idea mate," Carl answered, honestly. "Someone else took a look at it and she noticed, er…" He paused to try to remember what Satiah had said about what she thought might be wrong with Kelvin. Unfortunately her precise wording escaped him due to more than a few beverages. He passed a piece of paper over to Max with an explanatory wave. Max read through it quickly.

"Two components of unknown origin," Max read aloud, in mock ominous tones. "Unknown purpose, have sent off for analysis, nothing back yet. Who did she send them to?"

"She just sent the details mate," Carl said, pointing. "I think the components are..." he hiccupped, "... in that plastic bag over there. If you're hungry I think I have some salad." Max, slightly drunkenly, moved over to the table and rummaged in the bag. He pulled one out and squinted at it for a few minutes in silence.

"Cheers mate. You know what? I think *this* is one of those new tablet-adaptor thingies," he mumbled, turning it over and over.

"Reckon it caused the breakdown?" Carl enquired, hopefully.

"Nah, this thing doesn't do anything by itself, it's fundamentally a glorified connector," Max dismissed, putting it back in the bag. He picked out the other component – a silver cube with a lead sticking out of one end. "*What the hell is this?*" he murmured, to himself. Carl eyed him casually and waited.

"Hold my beer a moment," Max requested, his eyes never leaving the device.

Carl came over and obligingly held the drink as he watched Max get a hold of Kelvin's head. Satiah had already removed the shock dampening layers so everything was already exposed. Max, using prongs of some sort that Carl couldn't identify, slid the component back where it had been removed from and stared at it for a few moments. Carl tried to look at what he was staring at. He wasn't looking at the offending component anymore, he was looking at something else in there. Max again focussed on the component, wiggled it back and forth a few times, confusion on his face. Carl waited, knowing never to interrupt the expert. He'd had enough practice of that with Satiah.

Max continued to stare for a few moments more, then his eyes widened with dawning realisation. He moved the head again, angling it towards the floor. The component fell forward in its slot into a new position... directly cutting through a... now, what was normally there? If this machine was standing up and walking around, it leans forward for some reason; this thing moves and cuts off... Max let out a breath, and did it a few more times to make sure he was right.

"Well, *whatever this thing is*, if you want this guy to work again, you'd be best either getting rid of it or finding some other place for it," Max recommended. He placed it on the table and both men stared down at it suspiciously.

"And you've no idea what it is?" Carl asked, handing him his drink back.

"I thought at first it might be memory of some sort, but it was in the wrong place for that. It doesn't even have any 55s," Max said.

Carl nodded and grunted as if he had any inkling of what *that* was supposed to mean. Max shook his head again while staring at it, before downing the last of his beer casually.

"Whatever it is, it's the cause of the problem, basically making it shut down every time it moves forward. You can never actually see it happen because of where it is... *very subtle*. It's directly triggering instant power loss and once the damage was done that was it. There *are* some scratches below it where it looks like *some kind of bracket* was mounted in order to prevent this, but where *that's* gone I've not got the foggiest," he said. "And your lady has no clue either?"

"If she has she didn't say," Carl shrugged. "Maybe it's some kind of scanner, I mean, now that I look at it... that wire isn't a wire, it's more like a..." He trailed off, unable to say the word he was thinking of. "Scimitar."

"What?"

"Scimitar... Scimitar. *Emitter*, it looks like *an emitter* to me," Carl managed, eyeing his drink. He nudged Max. "It's strong stuff this, eh? Let's see if there's any more."

"She won't mind?"

"*Nah*, she'll be *fine*!" Carl declared, opening the cooler.

"Shouldn't I at least put him back together and test him first?" Max asked, curious. "She sounded pretty certain about what she wanted."

"We'll do it later!" Carl dismissed, opening another bottle. "Hey, we should go and catch the end of the tournament, want to go?" Carl hurriedly scribbled out a brief note detailing what they had found out about Kelvin. Satiah would be delighted! And, on a more selfish side, it would help to show her that her overprotectiveness might not be such a great thing all the time. *Just saying.* Max took a long gulp of his new drink and then stared ahead decisively.

"I don't see why not."

---

"We're lost, aren't we?" Oli asked again. Satiah sighed. Oli detected her annoyance instantly. "It's not your fault; it's those *useless* wall maps. They aren't any good unless you know where you're starting from." Still she said nothing. "I mean, whoever designed them..." he began again, nervously.

"O shut up Oli," she glowered, irritated. "There *is* a lift around here somewhere, I'm sure of it. Keep listening for sounds."

"What sounds?"

"*Any*!" she articulated, somewhere between a growl and a snarl. The truth was that they were indeed lost. *Only a bit*! She wasn't going to let him know that though, not if she could help it. He was jittery enough as it was, without the possibility of death by starvation entering the equation.

All of this reminded her of something she'd been through about twenty years ago. Back in 96 or maybe 97, it didn't really matter. She'd been working on a mission, Operation Nightfall if she remembered correctly. She'd been tasked with finding a lost expedition. It was an armed military force, but small, and of a reconnaissance sort of nature. She tracked them to a planet called Silles, an uninhabited ball of rock somewhere out in the middle of nowhere. Long story short, it turned out the officer leading the trek had lost his mind and had ran off down a set of tunnels, which ultimately led into the labyrinth of a long dead subterranean city. Instead of just leaving him to it and returning with the remaining survivors, something Satiah had wanted to do, she was ordered to go in and get him back. *Typical*! Well, that city, the way it felt and looked, was very similar to this. A never-ending complex of abandoned networks, some still operating and some not.

She'd found the officer on the seventeenth day. Dead, of course. That was what happened when you lost yourself without food, water or means of communication. Satiah herself had nearly got lost on her way back out too. At the time, it never seemed to have an end. Corridor after corridor. Darkness after darkness. This was different: naturally, it was different every time, but still… when she allowed her mind to wander, it had a wont to dredge up old nightmares. She was on Earth now and, despite the danger, she was arguably much safer than she had been that time. She'd feel much better if she could substitute Oli with Kelvin, though, or even Zax or Randal.

A little voice inside her head, the one her sixth sense sometimes used to talk to her, was… *mumbling*. Trouble? Of course it was trouble, it stayed quiet when anything good ever happened! Her hand slid down to the handle of her pistol, ever ready. Its mumbling was sounding more distinct, like her own voice saying something like… *Slimy Snell wasn't busy right now.* So if he wasn't busy…? A creaky noise came from ahead of them… a lift descending. At first she was relieved, thinking it was Randal. Then she checked herself. No, he'd have called her to inform her of his proximity. No… She was in a great place to be killed right now and the PAI could get rid of her, no questions asked.

"That sounds like a lift," Oli smiled, hoping to cheer her up.

"It is," she said, pulling her pistol out. She pushed him against the wall. "Get ready to run."

"What? *Why?*" he asked. *If you don't trust me by now…*

"Just do it," she spat, unwilling to waste any more breath on the subject. She stood in front of him, aiming ahead into the dark. "Randal, we're not alone anymore," she breathed, in warning.

"How many?" he asked, instantly.

"Unknown yet, I don't even know for sure who they are, but my gut tells me they are PAI," she stated, quietly.

"*What?*" Oli asked, in shock. She kicked herself mentally for her clumsiness.

"*Quiet!*" she hissed, at him.

"*Do what you must,*" Randal said, almost carelessly. "I'll join you when I can."

"Okay," she said. "*Zax?*"

"Got you."

"Anything you can tell me?"

"It's indistinct but from the energy detected I would say... *six*," Zax estimated. "Maybe ten." That would probably be about the size of the lift itself. And more might come down at any time or at another location.

"Okay," Satiah said, swallowing. "*Oli*? Back away, *stay close to the wall*."

Oli said nothing and complied. Slowly but surely, they began to edge backwards. Satiah didn't know if she could take six PAI operatives alone and, as she had to protect Oli, evasion seemed a better tactic. Trouble was... they were being forced away from where they needed to be. The lift. Sounds came from ahead. Clicks and shuffles. What could easily have been a muffled conversation and then lights flickered on. Oli gasped, fearful.

"Keep going," she urged, as loudly as she dared.

"Why would the PAI...?" he began, concerned.

"It's standard law enforcement *code* for *persons alien and inimical*," she lied, quickly.

"*O*..." he said, reassured. "I bet that leads to some confusion."

"Only for those who *don't know*," she replied, quickly. "Let me assure you, if it really was *the* PAI we would have nothing to worry about. *And you heard none of this from me!*"

Oli could never know the truth. They turned a corner and Satiah stopped them upon sight of a door. She knew it wouldn't be long before their tracks were found in the dust. She crouched to work on the lock, torch in her teeth, and Oli hovered anxiously over her. The door slid open and they slipped inside before she sealed it again.

"How do you know there's a way out of *here*?" Oli demanded, wondering why she'd led them into what might be a dead end.

"*I don't*, I'm gambling now," she admitted, levelly. "Start looking Oli, I'll make sure this won't open very easily. At least, unlike before, they will struggle to batter their way in." Oli started to look around, and quickly found another door. It was on the other side of the room, so it was unlikely to lead back to the same corridor.

There was one more thing Satiah could do to save herself, of course. They needed Oli alive and they needed him to believe their lies. If it came down to it, she might be able to use him as a hostage to get herself out. She'd have to explain it away *to Oli* as a calculated bluff, but she was sure she could force him into complying. Despite the fact that he could be problematic, she knew that he probably would trust her if push came to shove… or shot. She got to work on the next door, deciding to only go through with that as a last resort. It might be possible to avoid the PAI altogether, so forcing the situation early could be fatal. Nevertheless, it never hurt to plan for the worst. She got it open and it revealed another corridor beyond.

"Satiah, they have split into two teams of three, I will watch for any more," Zax told her. Satiah smiled, a little relieved. Three she might be able to take out herself, so long as she had surprise on her side.

"Thanks Zax, keep feeding me the new stuff," she ordered. "*This way,*" she added, to Oli. She pointed up and he froze in confusion. All he could see were pipes.

"They will follow our footsteps in the dust," she explained, quickly. She jumped up, caught a pipe and then swung her legs around it too. She flicked her head to get her hair out of her eyes.

"We will climb along this pipe until we reach the next corner and then we will go on as normal," she told him.

"So they won't know which way we went," he realised, grinning. "*That's ingenious.*"

She raised an eyebrow.

"Only if they don't look up," she qualified. She moved along quickly, having done this kind of thing too many times for it to slow her much. Oli, on the other hand, was able to get up but was very slow. He kept mistiming his steps and nearly knocking his own legs off the pipe in the darkness. Satiah reached the corner, went around it, and then simply unwrapped her legs in a very well-practised, slow motion, reverse hanging knee raise. She dropped and spun into a crouch, pistol ready. She then turned on her torch, revealing the endless dusty floor ahead. A grunt came from behind her. Oli had nearly reached the corner.

"Come on, nearly there," she encouraged, curtly. She made sure she was out of his way as he struggled along, teeth clenched and sweating.

"You can come down now," she told him and began to go on. A loud thump and a groan told her that he had misjudged something and fallen. She didn't have to hide her smile in the dark.

"You okay?" she asked, trying not to laugh.

"Yeah," he groaned, as he got back onto his feet. "Just my pride damaged." A thought struck Satiah. How had the PAI operatives known to get off at their floor? They could be anywhere down there, or so the PAI should think. She searched herself for a tracking device, wondering if Lunell… no, it wasn't her, *it was Oli*. It was him they could detect somehow. Lunell must have planted it on him, knowing that she would notice if he did it to her.

"*Oli?*" she began, wondering how to broach the subject. "Did Lunell give you anything recently? A gift, or something you asked for maybe, or a little something for extra security?"

"Yeah," Oli mused, remembering. "*How did you know?* He said not to tell anyone…"

"*I'll bet he did*," she grunted. "What was it?"

"This ring, it's a homing device so he can find me at any time. It seemed sensible enough at the time…" he explained, holding out his hand to show her. She snatched it off his finger before he could say or do anything else. Then she ran back the way they had come and hurled it as far down the corridor as she could.

"What are you…?" he began, totally bewildered.

"Its signal is what's drawing *them* to *us*," she argued, as he tried to grab it off her. "Lunell might be able to track us, but we don't need him, and that signal is making us a target for everything down here. It's probably what drew the robots' attention in the first place."

Oli stopped arguing, seeing the reason.

"I'm sorry, I wasn't thinking…" he began, eager to stay on her good side.

"It's fine, you didn't know," she said, anxious to move on. They hurried quietly along for ten minutes or so. Satiah was confident she could lose them now. They would find the ring and know they had been there and they might even find the dust trail again, but she was at last starting to understand the layout of this place. It was all to do with power dispersal. The generators for the planet were located near the core for safety and accessibility reasons. Yet the conduits themselves were identical, and their routes upwards would probably all be similar too. Her only real problem was not knowing what else was down there with them.

---

"So can you get the time off?" Ash asked again, as he waited. Ruby pushed her long golden hair behind her ears and thought about it.

"This is *not* an ideal time for me right now! I'm *trying* to create a good impression here..." she explained.

"I'm sorry that *all existence* has chosen an inconvenient moment to come under threat," Ash apologised, peculiarly. "There is no immediate rush." *Why did he say things like that to her?!*

"*Wait*!" she said, shaking her head and holding it in her hands briefly. "Say it all again."

"You remember Satiah?" he asked. She shivered.

"...*Vaguely*," she lied, uncomfortably.

"Well, she asked me to translate this," he said, producing the book. She eyed it, enthralled for a moment. Then she shook her head. He'd done this to her too many times for her to fall for it again. He was trying to get her interested.

"No! No, I *know* what you're trying to do," she stated, giggling. "Whatever it is, I refuse to get drawn into..."

"I can't do it without *you*," he said, manipulatively. "I need *your human* mind."

"You are *such* a *liar*," she scoffed, biting her lip in flirtatious amusement. "You just want me as your guinea pig again!"

He put his hand on her shoulder and touched her mind, a mental game of tag.

"Stop that!" she implored, leaning back against him.

"Why?" he whispered, in her ear. "You don't seem too averse to it." She closed her eyes, enjoying the sensations he could make her feel. "*I* know you," he breathed, making her shiver all over. "I know you love an adventure. Come with me again, Ruby."

"...*A-Ash*," she groaned, as he moved away. "This is *not fair*! And, and, what has this got to do with *Satiah*?" He eyed her and said nothing. "*Tell me!*" she cried, knowing exactly why he wasn't. If he thought he could get her to go on another of his voyages again, he would have to... well, he would have to... *o no*... he was giving her one of *his looks*, one of those that made her go a bit weak at the knees.

"You would only be gone for a little while," he said, making it sound all so reasonable. Why did he do this to her? It was *always her*! Just because they were in love, that didn't mean he had to drag her around the galaxy for his own amusement.

"When?" she asked, in defeat.

"Four to six months' time," he said, grinning impishly. Was he joking?

"That's... *okay*," she said, surprised it was that far away. "*Why the delay?*"

"...I will know better later, suffice it to say that the time is not right yet." Well, Ruby was no expert on anything, but she knew a cop-out when she heard one. She put her hands on her hips and tilted her head to the side. As usual, he was hiding things. He *always* hid things. Sometimes she believed he did it just to see if she could dig them out or not.

"Okay," she grinned, with a wink. "*I'm in*."

"Good... and stop undressing me with your mind."

"*Me*? As if!"

---

"O my goodness, *that's dreadful*," Brenda cried, genuinely shocked.

"Investigation has begun, all rescue efforts already underway. We don't think the media know yet," the aide said, casually.

"This could look bad," Brenda acknowledged. "I mean, they might make it look like I had something to do with it."

"It's possible," the aide smiled, calmly. "We have things ready for that eventuality and, in the meantime, we will continue as normal.

Oli *has* survived the collapse, though, so it could have been worse." It was a good thing that Brenda was starting to think like that, the aide mused. Stop thinking about doing things and changing things, think only about how she looked to other people. That was the perfect paralysis for someone like Brenda. Too scared of doing the wrong thing to do anything.

"Can you send a message to him, *from me*, conveying my sincerest condolences for *any* of his personnel who were not so fortunate?" Brenda asked, emotionally. "*It must be horrible.*"

"Sure," the aide nodded.

"How did it happen?" Brenda asked, sadly.

"Looks like a course-plotting failure currently, as opposed to terrorism, but the investigation remains incomplete," the aide answered, tactfully.

"*It's so sad*," Brenda sighed, upset. "All those people."

"Yes," the aide agreed. This had never been a part of what she was involved with, so she could genuinely join Brenda in wishing it had never happened. "I will keep you updated."

"Thank you," Brenda smiled, sounding a little happier.

"If the media *do* learn what has transpired, *don't worry*," the aide said, and meant it. "They always try to use these things to create more trouble, and *the people know that.*"

---

It turned out that it had nothing to do with the tracking device Lunell had planted. It seemed that those PAI operatives were there for a different purpose entirely. *Apparently.* Satiah and Oli had continued on. Satiah was doing her best to use convoluted routes and not just blindly run down the endless corridors. If she *had* been blindly running, they would have missed the next part completely. This might have been for the better. Again, as before, Satiah got them into another room, and this one didn't have another door leading out again.

"There's a control pad over there," Satiah indicated, as she sealed the door as best she could. "See if still works." Oli scampered over to it and eyed the very different looking pad curiously.

Satiah, according to the plan she was working from in her mind, felt that they were drawing close to another lift shaft. If she was right about the layout, then they had to be. Oli began to fiddle with the controls and something clicked. Before he knew what was happening the wall began to move. It slid upwards, slowly and loudly.

"*Oli!*" hissed Satiah, irritated by the racket.

"Sorry," he said, awkwardly. "I didn't think it would still work." When would men learn not to touch things without permission? She darted over to him, flashing her torch into the blackness beyond. The floor was gleaming back in the light, blackly. It was clean, no dust and instantly Satiah began to get worried. What had they found?

When the door stopped moving, silence once again reigned. Satiah let out a breath.

"Okay, as usual, follow me and say nothing," she ordered, beginning to move slowly into the dark area. Ceiling, wall and floor were the same shiny black, and free of any sign of dirt. This was new! Well, either new or very well maintained. She glanced over her shoulder, partly to check on Oli, and partly to see if the wall was still open. They might have to beat a hasty retreat at any time. Oli had gone pale and his eyes were wide and fearful. She tentatively began to advance again. There were no obvious threats ahead after all, and she had to be mindful of those who were following them. Her heartbeat began to fit in with her own footsteps again. She hated it when it did that, but it was natural. There was a door at the end of the corridor they were in, this one smaller and more normal looking. Its control pad was gleaming red and purple intermittently. Whatever they had found, this place was still active.

They reached it, and Satiah eyed it. It was the very latest in design and it was tough. It would be equipped with the very latest of profiles to deny entry. It probably had the trill-codex and everything. So, taking a risk, she shot it. The door swished open but no alarm sounded. She felt sure she must have triggered *something* by doing that, but there was no other way she could get in, and there was no point in going back. They entered, and began to move along a walkway overlooking several aisles beneath. As they moved, lights came on above them to illuminate everything around and... *below them*. Oli happened to look to the left and down before stopping dead and letting out a gasp.

Down there, lined up in long rows, were tens of them. They were him. Men that looked exactly like him in every way. They were laying there; their eyes open but somehow blank, staring straight up at him. He blinked, shook his head, tried to make sense of it. No, he *had* to be seeing things, just had to be. Why would there be loads of copies of him lying down here in the middle of a disused place no one ever went? His hands gripped the railing as he steadied himself. He continued to stare down, unable to look away. As he stared, he realised that there was more. It wasn't *just him* down there. Brenda Watt was there too, or rather... many of her. Like him, she was lying down, well – *they* were lying down. Unmoving, totally silent. As with him, her eyes were open, displaying only the most expressionless of trance-like looks. He opened his mouth but no words came out. And it went on. Beyond her were copies of Mark *and* of his own brother. Was *everyone* who was running in the election down here?

Sweat broke out on his forehead as he endeavoured to process what he was seeing. To make sense out of the nonsense before him seemed impossible. Him, her... *them*. *What was this*? He couldn't think of a single justification that explained this. Mad! Yes, that was it! He'd lost it. Must have. Absolutely gone off the edge and *now* he was seeing things. There was one way to make sure he was just daydreaming all this. There was another person with him who he knew he could trust to tell him what was really there. He didn't turn fast enough.

Satiah brought Oli down with a single, precision, blow to the head. *Talk about bad luck.* Of all the places to run into... a secret PAI base. If nothing else, it explained the hopeless security. Oli lay there unconscious after she'd done her best to slow his fall. Satiah pondered what to do for the best as she looked down at him. She would explain this away easily enough. *O... are you okay? I was so worried... you were hit on the head by something that fell... What do you mean? No, Oli, you couldn't have, there was nothing like that in there. You must have imagined it. Perhaps that thing hit you harder than I realised. Does it still hurt?* No, her real problem now was that she had a lump of unconscious deadweight that she had to protect and somehow get out of there, all on her own, with PAI operatives no doubt already closing in on her. She got out the medication she always had with her, and injected Oli with a strong sedative. That gave her twelve hours.

She knew just where to hide him too. She dragged him, rather unceremoniously, down a metal stairway. Among the inactive androids, some of which were copies of him, he would stand the best chance of going unnoticed. She knew why they were there and, indeed, what purpose they would serve, would any need to be activated. She could already hear the approaching footsteps of multiple agents running closer. It was a sound that used to haunt her dreams. She managed to find an empty ledge to deposit the real Oli and then slipped away into the shadows. She could see the walkway as six operatives trooped in from the way she and Oli had come, and six more arrived from the opposite direction. She calculated escape routes, distances and angles while she tried to decide what to do. The PAI agents were having a discussion and one of them pulled out a communicator.

"Phantom agent Satiah, we know you're in here, we know who you have with you, please come out, we mean you no harm!" a man declared, over the speakers. Ten out of ten for innovation there, she mused. She pulled out a mine, attached it to the wall, and then slunk away, staying in the darkest areas.

"Are you injured? Please let us know where you are!" he requested, trying again. *Come on! Pull the other one!*

"*Randal, I'm in trouble,*" Satiah said, in a fierce whisper. She explained what had happened.

"This changes things," he said, seriously. "I'm about two levels above you, how many of them?"

"Twelve at least," she replied, seriously.

"So we're about even then," he joked. She rolled her eyes. "At least there will be a working lift in there somewhere."

"We will search for you, please do not resist!" the man shouted. Satiah planted another mine and adjusted her pistol. She peered out from between two metal columns. She noted that two men had covered each entrance; meaning eight would be coming directly after her. They would fan out into pairs and begin a methodical yet predictable search pattern. She could avoid them easily enough normally. Trouble was, she had to stay near Oli or risk losing him, to present the obvious problem. She continued to whisper to Randal and Zax about the deployment of the search and about the place she was in. Satiah knew that she would be killed the moment she was seen, so there was no question of even responding to these operatives. She ducked under one large silver pipeline before stepping over another.

She turned a corner and almost screamed. She was face to face with an android copy of Brenda. Tens of them actually. Going all the way back towards the wall where they continued on in a curve and out of sight. The same face again and again, with the same expressionless mien, illuminated in either red or purple lighting. This first one, *this first fake Brenda*, was not only standing up but it was held in place by three appendages coming down from the machinery above. They must have started the activation process on this unit for some reason, before stopping it again. She peered back the way she'd come, pistol ready, debating quickly what to do.

A noise from that direction her made her slip behind the android and stand exactly alike and behind it so that, even if she were seen, she would likely be missed. Two men, rifles ready, emerged from the red and purple lighting near where she had been standing. She held her breath and was conscious of how real the android's hair felt against her face. They were silent and ready for anything as they crept by, seeking her. She made her face as blank as she could so, should they see her, she'd look as blank and robotic as the android Brenda. Okay, she looked nothing like Brenda, but in that lighting anyone might look like anyone at a glance. A light went over her briefly but, as she had hoped, they missed her. A blast and two screams from the other end of the room betrayed the detonation of her mine. She didn't move though.

There was a mad scramble as others ran to check on what had happened. That was when she moved. She slipped out from behind the android and towards the underside of the walkway. Keeping low, to avoid behind seen by either set of guards at the doors, she crept closer and closer until she was right underneath it. She reached up to the underside of the walkway and lifted herself up into its concealing shadow. She held herself there, her arms straining a little. She slid her boots into loose holds there to try and take some of her weight. She waited there and could hear footsteps as someone ran along the walkway right above her.

"Hand him over Satiah, it's over for you!" came another demanding bellow. *Finally done pretending at last, are we?* She pulled a face in soundless mockery. If they wanted him, they'd have to come and get him. And that went doubly for her! To think that she would even consider complying just exposed the true calibre of those she was dealing with. Substandard PAI training! Another explosion occurred as her second and last mine went off. As before there were screams. She let go and, with her grapple-gun, dragged herself upwards quickly, while they were all distracted.

She reached the ceiling and nippily hid herself on top of the piping up there. In the darkness she shouldn't be easily visible, and the heat from some of those pipes might be enough to conceal her, even from heat seeking vision. If she had her glasses or Kelvin, she'd be able to know *exactly* how many of them were left within seconds. Seven or eight, most probably, but she knew she was guessing. Guessing was never good. She began to drag herself along, staying low and shadowy, trying to pick them out. Four were easy to see, those who were safeguarding the two entrances at either end of the walkway. The others, among the darkness of the storage area below, were essentially indiscernible to her.

Satiah was starting to wish Randal had brought others with him. She didn't doubt Randal or anything like that, and *yes,* Phantom agents *were* easily better than PAI operatives, but they were vastly outnumbered. Even a couple more Phantoms would have been enough, she reasoned. She slid her suppressor onto her pistol, deciding that at the very least she could take out the ones guarding the escape routes. With accurate shots, she'd downed all four in about five seconds. There were shouts from below as they saw their comrades fall, but they couldn't yet see her. One body even flipped backwards over the hand rail. Silence fell. She knew they would be calling for help. Who wouldn't? Until

Randal got there, she had to stay, because she knew she wouldn't be able to get Oli out by herself. Not with all this going on.

A thought struck her. Where exactly *had* she left Oli? She remembered stowing him away down there well enough, but it all looked the same now. It would, as all the androids were supposed to look the same as the people they were replacing. She swore under her breath. This was *so stupid*! So characteristic of the PAI to use the situation and try to make Phantom Squad look bad. Well, if anyone was going to get egg on their face this time… a movement attracted her attention in the darkness below, and she aimed. There was someone down there, she was sure. She stopped herself suddenly. What if it was Randal? Conceivably, it might even be Oli? She might have made a mistake with the dosage, or even the type of drug or… stop *it Satiah*! She ordered herself to eliminate all self-doubt and pull the trigger.

She fired. A woman cried out. This time though, unlike before, someone else returned the fire. Due to her shot being silent, there was no way they could know exactly where she was; however, they *had* got the direction right, probably because they had seen how the body fell. This wasn't always the best guide as, unless they were standing still in a tranquil environment, the direction of fall might be deceptive. Shots hit the wall directly beneath her. One even hit the pipe and steam jetted out from the pipe itself. It was only pure luck that it didn't spray up straight into her face. She lay still and quiet as more shots rang out from someone somewhere else. Blam, blam, blam! Silence. Blam. Silence. The jet of steam gradually quietened into a gentler periodic hiss. She could hear the zizz of nearby machine-driven wheels hidden in the wall. She couldn't tell if they had worked out where she was or not, but she knew she'd stayed in one place too long.

She began to crawl along the pipe as inaudibly as she could. The stillness of sudden death had descended on the place now. Those still alive lay in wait for a moment of vulnerability, whether that moment was their own or their enemy's. Expectance. Where was Randal? She peered down again, pistol ready. Nothing moved. Unending silence, save for the noise of the machinery. She was starting to feel the heat from the pipe now too, as superheated water flowed around inside it.

She needed another mine, something to use… She decided to use the baton on her belt and slid it out soundlessly. Then, with the strongest throw she could manage, she launched it across the room end over end. She grabbed her grapple-gun and fired just as it crashed into something on the other side. Rapid laser fire went off as she descended quickly, down into the darkness.

Pistol at the ready, she began to advance carefully, once again making full use of the available cover. She'd lost count of her enemies, never a good thing. Then again, there hadn't been one good thing that had happened in this operation yet, so at least it was consistent. Could inconsistency be consistent, thereby…? Never mind. She was hoping they were still seeking her in the wrong direction but if they were smart, one of them would always be guarding the opposite direction. It was easy for her to think complacently: *it's the PAI and they are never that smart.* She knew though that that was wishful, bordering on reckless, thinking. In a fight for survival, it was astonishing how clever some people could become.

"Four of them," Randal's voice said, in her ear.

"Where are you?" she whispered back, greatly relieved. A gunshot went off.

"Correction: three."

Someone ran out across the gap between two supporting columns. Satiah put them down.

"Two?" Randal guessed.

"Where are the last couple?" she growled.

"To your right… *moving away*," he prompted. She began to move quietly along again, keeping her eyes peeled. "*Where's Oli?*"

"Unconscious, I had to put him to sleep *so he couldn't see all this*," she explained, sourly.

"He's light enough for us to manage," Randal allowed, understanding. A shot rang out, hitting the wall a few metres ahead of Satiah. She crouched and listened hard.

An explosion breathed fire through one of the entrances and everyone stopped.

"What was that?" Randal asked, as it hadn't been him that had caused it.

"*Collorah?*" Satiah hissed, working it out by process of elimination. He had finally caught up with them. Collorah, as if summoned by her thoughts, flew into the room. He was using a v-shaped speed-glider, fast and aerodynamically dexterous, to achieve speed and still present a difficult target. Flames shot out of the thrower he was wielding, burning their way through the narrow passageways. Satiah leapt to one side and was left panting due to lack of oxygen. The last two PAI agents were not so fortunate. Neither died instantly and ran around in flames, shrieking like banshees. Randal, compassionately, shot one dead, but the other vanished into cover, still howling.

Satiah used her breathing device and peered out as Collorah did the same in the opposite direction. She fired at him but the shot passed right by his head, just missing him.

"*Where's Oli?*" demanded Randal, making use of his own breathing device. Satiah was too busy sprinting for safety to answer. As Collorah flew upward to turn around, instead of shooting directly at him, she fired at the piping he'd got close to. Steam shot out, making him cry out and swerve away as she vanished underneath the walkway.

"*Satiah?*"

"I don't know! I'm a bit disorientated!" she admitted, seriously. "Do you have heat seeking vision?" He did, and he started using it. "You get him out, I'll be your diversion," she suggested, easing herself up onto the walkway to try to see where Collorah had gone. He had to be on that side of the room somewhere, he *had* to be.

"What's the matter, Collorah?" she yelled, provocatively. "*Hovering* between life and death?" Another jet of flame was her answer and she ran for the door as he rose out of hiding. She reached the doorway and threw herself forward and to one side as the fire rushed past her. Her pistol skidded away before she could grab it. Collorah flew in after her recklessly. She leapt to her feet and rushed towards him. They collided painfully. She succeeded in knocking him off his ride, and also in knocking all the air out of her own lungs. She almost choked on her own breathing device as she tried to recover. The speed-glider exploded as it struck the wall, sending shrapnel everywhere.

Satiah spun to face Collorah who had ended up opposite her, flamethrower aimed right at her. He pulled the trigger. There was a click and Satiah grinned maniacally at him. In the clash she'd ripped the connectors off.

"Too bad," he growled, dumping it on the floor. "Where is he?"

"Where's…?" Satiah began. She'd been going to ask him to whom he was referring, even though she knew he was after Oli, but he was already rushing at her. She dodged, pushing away the hook punch he'd thrown. An undercut was next and she just managed to avoid it. In response she jabbed at his nose and neck. He was big though, he pushed away the blow she'd aimed at his nose, and shrugged off the blow to his neck with a grunt. He put in a cross punch which clipped and glanced away from the side of her head. She fell against the wall and, as he tried to use the extra room, she caught him with a roundhouse kick in the side.

Elbow and knee blows went both ways for a moment, all instinct and no planning. She forced him to back off with a straight kick to his chest again. He stopped, staying distant, and remained in a fighting crouch. Then he spotted her gun on the floor. He made a dash for it, clearly not liking his odds of beating her hand to hand. She too ran for it. He reached it first but, as he stretched, he took a hard kick to the side. He started to rise, grunting as she struck blow after blow, going for his eyes. He tried to shield his face with one arm, while extending the gun toward her with the other. An open palmed hit to the back of his hand sent the firearm clattering away again. Both of them threw the same punch and both hit each other.

Satiah sprawled on the floor, blood oozing from her upper lip and nose. Collorah, knocked back onto one knee, rose again, fists clenched. She returned to her fighting stance, feet shoulder width apart, knees bent and hands ahead of her, one in a fist and the other open. They circled one another slowly, each trying to find a weakness to exploit. Satiah took the opportunity to take stock of her opponent. A brawler who'd clearly learned the basics of martial arts, but was nowhere near her level. He was bigger, stronger, and heavier, and could take more physical punishment than she could, but she was faster, more flexible and, she hoped, more cunning. She spun, turning her back on him briefly, as she unleashed a powerful back-kick. It took him in the chest and sent him staggering back against the wall, gasping for breath.

He made a sudden movement, aiming something up his wrist at her. She was already moving as the throwing star hurtled towards her. She yelled as it sliced past her shoulder before embedding itself in the wall. She scrambled to get to her gun as he came on again. She rolled over it, raising it as she turned on the floor. The two blasts she fired struck his chest and he fell back, inert. She slumped back for a second in relief before hauling herself onto her feet again. He remained still. She aimed to place the cold-blooded shot, but paused. They were right in the middle of a secret PAI facility. Perhaps leaving him behind and alive might be a smarter idea.

She returned to the room where the firefight had begun, breathing hard. Randal was hauling Oli along almost casually as he headed out. Satiah hurried to catch up. They took an arm each and continued to pull him to the lift Randal had used. Back in the other doorway, Collorah slowly sat up and ripped off the ruined body armour he'd been wearing. He knew he'd been lucky, if she'd shot him in the head... Now that she thought he was dead, it might give him a chance.

---

"*They've done what?*" The man repeated himself. Snell sat there gaping at him.

"I have assembled another team and we'll take them out for sure this time..."

"Leave them alone, that's an order!" Snell barked, seriously.

"Phantoms Randal and Satiah have just butchered *twelve* of my men in a restricted location," the man complained.

"I don't care about your men! What about those androids?" Snell demanded, lividly.

"There is *extensive* fire damage to the whole area..." Snell held his head in his hands. The government would not be pleased that their back up plan had just been cremated!

"Save what you can and then seal it," Snell ordered, standing decisively.

"Sir."

*"They must have Oli with them; why else would they be down there?"* Snell sighed, rhetorically. If they had only called him, this whole thing could have been avoided. Snell could do nothing to them for this. If he did, then they might let it slip that the androids had been trashed. It was self-defence, and even if it wasn't, Snell could not prove otherwise. He doubted the government would care about *that,* their only concern would be that their first contingency plan was now useless, *thanks to him*. It would be his men, the PAI, that would be blamed for this fiasco, however incorrectly. And Phantom Squad would just smile and say: we were doing our jobs to make sure Oli lives, as per your instructions... he slammed his fist down onto the table angrily.

What if Oli had seen the androids? Snell promised himself that he'd never work with Phantom Squad again. He'd get even if he could, but this had gone too far. He'd already tried and failed to ice both Randal and Satiah. Randal had seen right through it, of course, and had threatened him. Snell doubted that the destruction of the android storage area had been intentional and, as Oli was there too, the real danger now would be how much he knew. He couldn't be killed, yet he might know - or at least suspect - that all was not as it seemed. This might not be a problem as, with medical help, they could ensure such ideas were brainwashed out of him. Nevertheless, his survival was the absolute imperative, as they no longer had standby androids to take his place should he die. The last question remaining for him was: did he report the destruction of that facility, or didn't he?

---

"This door was open *before* when I came this way," Randal stated, with conviction. Satiah sighed as, between them, they eased the deadweight that was Oli onto the dusty floor.

"It's completely automated, for blast containment; I *can't* get it open manually..." Satiah began, wondering what to do next.

"I know," he nodded, turning back to face the way they had come. Satiah had a sinking feeling that he was going to lead them back that way. "Zax, give me our location please," he requested. Zax told them. They had risen several hundred floors in that lift but now they needed another... again.

"Collorah is still alive," she warned.

Randal reeled to face Satiah in confusion.

"Why didn't you finish him?" he demanded, annoyed.

"Useful distraction," she explained, shrugging, "*for the PAI.*" Randal sighed. She had a point. "With someone else running around down here, ambushes will be harder to..."

"Yes, I get it," he stated, waving her off. It may have been a mistake. "Get his arm." They lifted Oli again and began to head back the way they had come. "Is there any chance you can wake him up?"

"Well... it was a strong dose, but he is probably still young enough to cope with the wake up dose. I was *enjoying* the silence," she remarked.

"Yes, well, wake him," Randal ordered, letting go. "If he remembers anything about..."

"Yes, I know, *deny, deny, deny,*" she dismissed, going through her collection of needles. "Snell won't like this..."

"He's going to have to live with it," growled Randal, angry. "That man has managed to put a mozz over this whole operation."

"A *jinx*, you mean?" she sniggered, flicking her syringe casually.

"*I know what I mean,*" he muttered, with a reluctant grin. For a moment, a deep silence fell over them as she concentrated and he listened. She slid the needle into Oli's arm.

"Stay quiet while he comes around, I'm going to have to play nice nurse for a few minutes," she advised, frustrated.

"No worries, I'll check a little way ahead, it was safe before but..." he said, not needing to finish. Oli's eyes fluttered open in the torchlight.

"O *thank goodness*, are you okay?" Satiah asked, all apprehension and sympathy. "That was quite a knock, how many of me can you see?" Oli groaned.

"Satiah? What happened? I remember..." he began. She shushed him.

"*Don't worry about any of that right now*, you take a breather," she counselled, controlling the situation. She peered into his eyes, seeking the tell-tale signs of concussion. She'd hit him just right, and his medical history held nothing about abnormalities, but you could never be too careful. He seemed fine, but she resolved to keep an eye on him.

"What happened?" he asked, again.

"Something fell on you," she said in complete honesty. Yes, her gun, held by her, and at the time it had been quite satisfying. "You want the good news?"

"We have *good* news?" he quipped, in feigned astonishment.

"Randal *from law enforcement* has found us; he helped me carry you here. He'll be back soon, you can trust him, and he's *very* reliable. We found a lift and are a lot higher than we were before. We just need to keep going and find another, and we'll be out of here by midnight," she smiled, positively.

"...I had the *weirdest* hallucination..." he growled, struggling to his feet. He was aching all over from his recent exertions.

"*Really?*" she enquired, a little too insistently. He flashed his own torch at her.

"Are you okay?" he asked, seeing the blood around her nose and mouth.

"Of course, what hallucination?" she asked, dismissively.

"I just... I know this is going to sound crazy, but I could have sworn I saw Brenda Watt before I lost consciousness," he told her, with a shaky laugh.

She laughed too.

"I think we need to get you to a medical facility, just for a quick evaluation," she said, taking this in her stride. Don't tell him he's wrong outright, just act concerned.

"No, no, I think I'm fine," he said, chuckling. "It's just stress, overwork and maybe a bit of brain damage."

"There's no such thing as *a bit of brain damage*," she said, as if uneasy.

"Hey, you yourself said I looked okay…"

"I did not and even if I did, *I'm hardly qualified*," she said, sighing. "Although, for what it's worth, I think you'll be fine. I don't want to worry you but we do need to check as soon as we can."

"I know," he said, agreeing.

Randal came back.

"No sign of any…" he began, but wavered ever so slightly when he saw Oli, "… *obvious* trouble ahead."

"*Marvellous*," Satiah was quick to reply, with a smile of congratulation. *Well remembered, boss.* "Any more of your *law enforcement* people coming down to help?" Randal was quick to pick up on what she meant.

"Not that I know of, certainly not yet, they are a bit preoccupied with the collapsed building at the moment," he said, nodding. "Are you feeling up to this, Mr McAllister?"

"*I don't have much choice, do I?*" he chuckled. Randal shook his head and gave Oli a flawless death's head grin.

"Let's go," Satiah nodded, motioning for Oli to go ahead of her.

After several minutes of hushed progress, Satiah realised that with Randal there too, Oli wasn't very chatty at all. Maybe if she could get Randal to hang around some more… a noise from behind her ended that line of thought. It sounded like distant doors opening noisily. She stopped, pistol ready. What could it be? Collorah? or the PAI? Or some other unknown and unexpected terror that lived down there? Randal and Oli stopped too, but neither said anything. They all stood there listening for a few moments.

"Zax?" Randal asked. "You have anything for us?" Satiah could hear the familiar scrabbling of her frantic efforts to be as fast as she could with what they needed.

"Power build ups are all around you… I think you're underneath some kind of assembly line," Zax explained.

"Three fifty," Carl grunted, swigging his drink. Had he *known* that he would only get a sixteen, he'd never have discarded that century. You live, you learn. Fortunately, as second highest score of the round, he'd lost nothing. He glanced at the time, wondering where Satiah could be. He was sure that if she'd made it home, she'd have called him. He had the sense not to gamble with money; instead, he was sitting around a table with three others, all of whom were enjoying a sensible recreational game of Gairunn, as the actual tournament continued on screens all around them. They were playing for peanuts, literally. Carl was doing very well, having secured at least two packs' worth. Max though didn't have such restraint, and was playing on one of the other tables. Judging by the amount of chips he had acquired, he wasn't doing too badly either.

A big win occurred somewhere. A spin, the winning hand of 360. A quiet cheer broke out, along with the inevitable groans of those who had betted against that occurrence. Carl grinned, loving the atmosphere. He thought about Satiah trapped in an office, no doubt held up in a long and boring meeting, having to fetch drinks for the politicians, and grinned. *She'd hate that*! And, though he felt sure that *she thought he would mess it up*, *he* had found out what was wrong with Kelvin. He waggled his eyebrows thoughtfully as he imagined her face when he told her what the problem had been, and gulped down another mouthful. She'd be *so happy* to have Kelvin back... even if Kelvin was a bit of a third wheel. Carl could just imagine Kelvin standing in the background, looming up like a big intimidating shadow. There was still one mystery left though. What *was* that device for? If *even Max* didn't know what it was...

---

They were getting closer. The lights were evidence of that. It had taken hours, but now the corridors they were using were lit and dust free.

"We must be coming up towards the maintenance levels," Randal muttered, thoughtfully. Satiah knew that it was a few hundred floors to go before they reached the surface. All right, maybe not midnight, maybe dawn. She'd been in many places like this before, but the identically interminable corridors made her feel increasingly bleak. She steeled herself, knowing it was nothing more than a mild bout of claustrophobia mixed with apeirophobia. Nothing could be eternal, but the idea of infinity scared her somehow. Ever since she'd known what it was, part of her had been frightened by its endlessness. The idea of being trapped in there until she died wasn't helping much either.

"I had no idea any of this was here," Oli said, to Randal.

"Few do," Randal said, bluntly. "Access *is* restricted, as you would expect, but on occasion things like this happen and someone else finds out about it." Satiah glanced behind them as she had been doing routinely for some time now. Collorah would be coming to get them again. It was just a matter of time. Oli looked completely exhausted now. Her day had started later than his, but he'd not really slept the previous night as he had been feeling the pressure from multiple angles. And angels. She thought more about that. She'd gone back and forth over Malla's culpability since the beginning. His *coincidental* absence on the day of the bomb.

To be fair, those who had planted it, she was sure, were unrelated to angel. So even if he *had* been angel or *had known* angel, not being there that day was still only miraculous happenstance. He'd had plenty of opportunities to get at Oli which he hadn't used. But he *had* said the word angel to her. Back and forth again. So, Satiah tried the opposite approach, which she had also done before. If it wasn't Malla, who else could it be? Shannon was out of the question. So were Dean, Cadel, Stan and apparently all the others... if they were still alive. Malla wasn't the only one this event had claimed. Had they not had that second message to angel from whoever it was, she'd have been half inclined to dismiss the first as some very odd joke.

Had she got this back to front? Could angel be asking questions and these were replies? Zax had unsuccessfully looked into this, as had Harrier, but there was still the slim chance that angel might even be a corporation. The old infuriation returned. How could this be causing her so much trouble? Carl's idea about Oli sending them to himself came back fleetingly too. *Why would he do that?* And she still didn't know who was behind Collorah! Zax and Harrier had done their best to chase the money but had had no luck. That was the trouble with so many beings existing in the cosmos… two people really didn't stand much chance of finding the right one, especially when you factored in false names, pretences and all kinds of transactions flying around in all directions. The best way would be to follow him back to those who were supporting him, but of course he knew that too and would do all he could to prevent it.

And *where* was Ash with that book? Surely all he had to do was glance over it to know whether or not he could translate it! He was an immortal, wasn't he? They were *supposed* to be able to do things like that! That was the whole point in her getting him to look at it in the first place. If he tried to somehow use this against her she'd really lose her temper! He was supposed to be Dreda's son! The least he could do would be to call her and say how he was getting on. And then there was that business with Obsenneth too. Had he sensed Obsenneth itself, or just *her fear* that he had sensed it? She pictured his mysterious brown eyes in her mind, knowing there was no way for her to tell. She made up her mind that, if he ever bothered to return, she'd give no sign of fear next time.

"Picking up life forms ahead," Zax warned.

"Ahead?" queried Randal.

"What's wrong?" Oli asked, tentative. Satiah slipped past him to stand next to Randal.

"How many?" she asked.

"Maybe forty or fifty, yes, dead ahead," Zax quantified. Satiah raised her pistol, as did Randal. There was a turn in the corridor ahead and Satiah remembered that corpse and those piles of garbage they had passed some way back.

"*Subterraneans*, we've entered their territory," Satiah growled.

"By law they have no such thing," Randal argued.

"Agreed, but they are most definitely here though," she replied.

"Subter…*what*?" Oli asked, confused and fearful.

"They used to live on the surface *with the rest of us*," Randal said, as if he knew all about it. "With one sob story or another they fell into the poverty that is down here. Some say they are scavengers, others say cannibals…"

"*Cannibals*!?" Oli almost shrieked. Satiah's lips twitched. Randal had just made that up. He was scaring Oli just to make her laugh. She appreciated that.

"No one *really* knows," she joined in, pretending to be scared herself. "No one ever… *lived long enough to learn the truth.*" Oli went pale and stared in front of them down the corridor.

A figure walked out from around the corner ahead. Hunched over, almost hunchback like, he seemed to be wearing a selection of brown grubby drapes. Long matted hair covered his face, hiding it from them. Satiah was guessing it was a *he* based on size, but it could have been anyone or anything. It stood there, as if watching them.

"Sizing us up," Randal said, telling the truth this time. "Trying to work out if he and his gang can take us."

"You can bring as many fists as you like to a gunfight, won't make much difference at this range," Satiah reasoned. Seeming to realise the folly of attacking, the unidentified life form retreated back around the corner.

"If we go on this way, we'll walk right into them," Satiah said, thinking it through, "and Collorah is behind us somewhere." She nodded to a closed door a little way back and on the right. Randal gave her the quickest of compliant nods and she crouched to begin work on the lock. Oli sighed, envisioning another painful climb to freedom.

In the light it was far easier for her to work and, as most of these locks seemed to be the same or similar, she got it open in seconds. A noise greeted them. A mechanical, regular pounding noise. That factory Zax had told them about…

"Come on, don't forget to watch your head," she directed, moving in. Oli followed and Randal was last, closing the door behind them. No point in giving Collorah, or anyone else, extra clues. They were in an empty office. There was a desk piled high with crudely organised paperwork. Schematics, graphs and all manner of other statistical information. Satiah grabbed one. The company logo was on the bottom left of each sheet. E-Electrics Co. Satiah had actually heard of them, they were big. In a way, that was a given, as only the largest of corporations would actually own a factory on Earth.

"Should we not go on?" Oli was asking, wondering why Satiah was stopping to read anything.

"We will," she murmured, not looking up. She showed her find to Randal and pointed to a specific area on it. He regarded it solemnly. Oli waited, taking the opportunity to sit down for a moment.

"Those are defence sentinel systems," Randal stated, eyeing Satiah. He didn't quite take in what she meant.

"I know. But… if they *make them*… *why not use them*?" she asked, levelly. Randal allowed a smirk of admiration to cross his lips.

"You must excuse the slowness of someone used to desk work," Randal apologised.

"*I'll let it slide this time,*" she joked, with a nod.

"First place is still yours," he said, motioning for her to take the lead.

She reached the next door which was unlocked and not even mechanical. She turned the antiquated handle slowly and then eased it open just a crack to peer inside. A drone like silver disk spun to look in her direction and she shut the door again abruptly. As trespassers, regardless of who they were, there was no question of it not shooting at them. It reminded her of a famous series she'd used to watch as a child called *Drone Battles*, in which small teams of either family members or engineers would make drones to battle one another in a special arena for charity. That defence sentinel looked just like a drone, but it didn't have the range of a drone. It was probably programmed to work only within the facility.

"At least one," she told them.

"At least one *what*?" Oli asked, worried.

"Level?" Randal asked, wanting some understanding of its quality. She shrugged.

"Its motion detectors were clearly okay," she said, grimly. "It may have multiple lasers, so splitting up to try and confuse it may not work." Randal pulled a face.

"Well, we can't go back," he stated, repeating what she had said earlier. "What about this?" He produced a green cube, about the size of a mug, from his jacket. It was a CEMP charge. Conservative electro-magnetic pulse charge. In theory it would, upon detonation, fry the circuitry within the sentinel.

"By all means," she smiled, making way for him. He primed the charge then, as she had done, edged the door open. Again, as it had done before, the sentinel reacted to the movement of the door and Randal flung the charge inside. The sentinel shot it apart before it even got close. Randal slammed the door shut, a rueful expression on his face.

"Too simple," Satiah sighed, guessing what must have happened. "Oli, look for another way out of this room," she instructed, knowing how pointless it was. Oli looked all around incredulously as she and Randal conferred in whispers.

"I could make a call, get the company to let us out," Randal suggested.

"That's the easy way," she objected. "Besides, that could take hours and we don't have hours. Not with Collorah breathing down our necks."

"That thing's pretty formidable for a sentinel, must be one of the latest," he argued. She eyed the diagram she'd discarded earlier.

"The Watcher 4000," she noted, looking for any design flaws. Randal pointed to a gap in the armour where the energy unit was powered up.

"That's *miniscule*," she murmured, considering whether she could shoot it.

"That was no doubt the idea..." he remarked, a little cynically.

"I'm trying to figure out how many shots it would take to bring it down without a precision strike," she contemplated. "You can bet it won't give us a chance to get at its charging area."

"Six or seven," he mused, eyeing her pistol. "With *yours*, maybe less. *Do you have a licence for that?*" She shot him a withering look.

"Only *three* lasers," she said, tapping the picture.

"*More than enough for us*," he muttered. Then he eyed her. "Would a mirror work?" Satiah considered. It was a very old trick and not usually that successful. The idea was to approach the sentinel head on, with the mirror held out before you. It would detect the motion but when it searched for a target it would only see itself. By the time it did a second scan to understand this apparent anomaly, the mirror-wielder should be close enough to get at it. She turned to look at the mirror on the wall.

It was about a square metre in size. She shrugged, pulled her knife from her boot and began to unseal it from the wall. Oli watched them, dumbfounded. Was there a way out behind that mirror? He had to admit he hadn't thought of looking there. She and Randal then placed the mirror on the table carefully. Slowly they both turned to look at Oli.

"What?" he asked, uneasy.

"Want to lead the charge?" Randal asked, casually. He slid two square metal sheets aside on the back, revealing hanging cords. They would normally be used to hang the mirror on a wall without using the adhesive lines along its edges. Oli would be able to then hold the mirror without gripping the sides. It was dangerous but no one else would do. Randal and Satiah were the only ones good enough to guarantee hitting the sentinel enough times.

"*What?*"

After telling him the plan, Satiah and Randal stayed behind him, ready to dash out and separate as soon as he was through the door. Satiah had to open the door a fraction again before getting to her position. Oli nudged it open with his foot and tottered in, holding the mirror ahead of him. The sentinel spun to face him but didn't shoot. Lights flashed as it used all its meagre processing power to figure out exactly how it was looking at itself. Randal and Satiah leapt out to each side of Oli and opened fire. In seconds, after being at the focal point of nearly thirty laser bolts, the sentinel crashed to the floor, blackened and smoking. Satiah remained ready in case another turned up to investigate the noise as Randal helped Oli lower the mirror.

The metallic pulsing was louder now and, as they clattered down a narrow set of metal stairs, they reached the assembly line.

"Keep to the *painted* safe walking areas, Oli," Satiah warned, over the din. She pointed to the floor so that he could see where it was safe to walk. Green was safe, anywhere else wasn't. An explosion nearby made them hurry. Collorah had no doubt taken on the subterraneans.

As Satiah glanced behind them, she saw the silver shine of another sentinel coming after them. She started shooting at it, glad that its limited range prevented it from firing back. Randal turned to see what she was shooting at. Then came another and another. They started running, ducking under pipes and leaping over small lines that rotated constantly to add their contribution to the assembly.

"How many?" Randal yelled, as they went.

"*Too many!*" she shouted back. Oli was struggling to keep this pace up. Lights were coming on now and an alarm was flashing red. He almost fell over, but was literally dragged onwards and back up by Satiah and Randal. A bulkhead was slowly lowering at the end of the assembly line.

"One last sprint!" Satiah bellowed. All three ran towards their ever diminishing escape route. Satiah and Randal took the lead quickly and, though Satiah just beat him there, Randal went through first to check it was safe. Satiah crouched under the lowering bulkhead, frantically beckoning to Oli. He scrambled underneath it and she rolled aside as it crashed shut. Oli lay there gasping for air and wheezing while, completely motionless, Satiah and Randal covered different sides of the room. Oli eyed them and was deeply envious of their physical prowess. They were hardly even panting while his lungs felt completely useless in comparison.

"Storage," Randal mused, eyeing the crates everywhere. "This must be where the completed items are placed ready for shipping." His deep voice echoed slightly in the cavernous space. Satiah made a noise in concurrence as she replaced her pistol in its holster. She crouched beside Oli.

"*Ready?*" she asked, unable to stop herself smiling a bit.

"Ready to die? Absolutely," he uttered, between hoarse gasps. She and Randal hauled him up onto his feet again.

"O you're going to live Mr McAllister, you have no worries there," Randal assured him, trying not to sound too sinister. Satiah gave Randal a warning glare before following the course of a walkway above them.

"We will try up there," Satiah suggested, eyeing the ladder. One by one they used it to reach the walkway which overlooked a vast area.

Satiah reached the door at the end and kicked it open, gun once again ready in her hand.

They were about to go in when the bulkhead door began to open again. Randal glanced down and across to see the shadows of security androids coming in. Black against the beating red of the alarm.

"*I think they know we're here*," he joked, mordantly.

"Shame we wasted that charge of yours," she commented, pushing Oli ahead of her. They closed the door behind them, even though Satiah had busted the lock.

"Keep an eye out for a fire escape route!" she ordered, mostly to Oli. She knew Randal would even now be looking for that. "That's our way out."

"There!" Randal shouted, and pointed.

They hurried up yet another set of metal steps, these went around and around in multiple rectangles. Randal reached the top first and got the door open. Satiah was dragging Oli behind her again, otherwise he would get left behind. Laser fire struck the steps under them as android sentries began to shoot at them from the floor below.

"Come on!" Randal barked, urgently. Outside was a corridor and the three of them staggered through together. The door slammed shut after them.

"I'm… going to have to… *stop* for a bit," Oli declared, slumping to the floor. Randal and Satiah exchanged a look before each going in different directions down the corridor. Oli was glad to leave them to it as he mopped his forehead on his sleeve and tried to ignore the torment of the stitch he'd developed. Even breathing hurt now.

Satiah reached the junction in the corridor and peered around. Where were they *now*?

"Zax, I need a location," she requested. Scrabbling and a muffled yawn.

"You're directly under maintenance, is there a door on the right?" Zax enquired. Satiah moved along a little further before finding it.

"Aye."

"It's a lift."

"I can't call it to me from here," Satiah replied, irately.

"Okay, hold on a moment," Zax replied. More scrabbling. Satiah sighed.

"This way is a dead end," Randal reported, coming back. "I'm bringing Oli to you."

"Acknowledged."

The doors began to open by themselves, revealing the portentous darkness of the shaft inside.

"Young lady, if you think I'm going to *climb up that* then you're very much..." Satiah began, annoyed.

"I'm bringing it down for you, *give me a second*, it's *nearly* three in the morning, *jeez*," Zax complained. Satiah grinned.

"Stay awake and alert, we *will* need you," Satiah ordered, knowing that this would test Zax in yet another way.

"I know," she grumbled, clearly already struggling to stay awake. Cables were moving, Satiah could see them. Randal and Oli reached her.

"Lift is on its way," Satiah explained, briefly. "How far up can this one take us?"

"To floor..." Zax yawned a third time, not even bothering to hide it this time. "... 623...You're almost there."

"Only six hundred and twenty three to go," Randal said, in a droll manner. Oli groaned, wishing it was not that many.

"Try dunking your face in freezing water," Satiah suggested to Zax. "If nothing else, I'm sure it will improve your looks."

"Yes Phantom Satiah, *thank you* Phantom Satiah," was the sarcastic response. Satiah grinned, Zax was learning fast.

"Shouldn't you have a word with her about her impertinent attitude?" Randal asked, casually.

"*I know, very impressive, isn't it?* Never confuse impertinence with honesty," Satiah cautioned. "She gives lip, of course she does, but that tells me more about what's going on in her head than a scripted response ever could. Besides, she's *still* a baby at fourteen and she's missed her beauty sleep. And... if you don't like the answer, maybe you shouldn't have asked the question." Randal grinned at that last bit.

"She'll be fifteen soon," he stated, eyeing her intently. "The age they start to make the jump to agent."

"O... *well, happy birthday*," she muttered, knowing what he was hinting at.

The lift came down in front of them. They got in without waiting for it to stop.

"You all in?" Zax asked, seriously.

"We are," Randal nodded. The lift began to rise and the doors slid about halfway closed. As it picked up speed the strong breeze was welcome.

"I bet a few insurance bills are going to go up," Satiah remarked, with a grin. Randal chuckled.

"These things happen."

"What's the time?" Oli asked.

"Nearly half past now," Randal told him. "*We'll be up in no time.*"

---

"This had better be important," Sam complained, as Jinx finally reached him. The parking area was deserted of vehicles other than theirs. The crisp early morning breeze reminded Jinx of the stubble he needed to shave off at some stage.

"Mark not with you?" Jinx enquired, hiding the bitterness he was feeling well.

"No, you *know* I can't trust him, not since he leaked *that document*," Sam retorted, also bitter.

"So you *know* it was him?" Jinx asked, interested.

"It's *got to be*, look what happened! I've no proof, of course, but then I don't need any, do I?" Sam smirked, pleased at his own wit.

"Not for me," Jinx agreed, careless.

"I need you to take him out," Sam stated, without more preamble. "Your fee still the same?" Jinx had already decided how he would handle this. Sam went around to the back of his transporter and opened the storage area. Jinx tensed, mentally prepared for a pre-planned precision move. Sam dragged a crate into view and opened it, revealing the Essps inside. Jinx, though, wasn't looking at the money. Sam turned to face him.

"I'm leaving this…" Sam began. Jinx pulled out his pistol and blasted him up through the mouth. Sam pitched over backwards, dead instantly. Jinx then carefully wrapped Sam's hand around the handle of the gun before placing it close to the body where it might have fallen had Sam *really* shot himself. Jinx then took the crate and stared down at the body after shutting the compartment.

"*For Octutin*," he stated, before turning on his heel. He placed the money in his own vehicle and counted some of it, partly to ensure it was real and also to have a rough estimate of how much was there. Sam was probably about to depart for home and he was taking everything he had with him, now that the election was lost. Over twenty thousand. That was more than Jinx could have reasonably hoped for. But then Mark was next… Jinx called him.

"Yes?"

"Mark, Sam just hired me to kill you, *something about a leaked document*, I think we need to talk about *another arrangement*," Jinx lied, callously. "It's only fair you get a chance to *return the favour*."

---

After what seemed like hours of searching for the light activation unit, ever so slightly tipsy, Carl had given up. During the process of making a snack, he'd knocked over at least six things, two of which he couldn't even identify. At last, he reached the bed, mumbled an apology to no one and got in. He was asleep instantly, breathing heavily, after his head hit the pillow. He'd had to leave Max behind at the tournament due to a so-called *lucky streak*. That was okay though, he'd have to come back at some point if he wanted to get paid.

---

Zax had to admit that Satiah's idea about keeping yourself awake by immersing the face or head in freezing water had some merits. Once you got over the cold shock, of course. She returned to her desk after doing stretches. This staying awake was hard; all she wanted to do was sleep now. Each time she felt her eyes starting to go, she submerged her face into the freezing water. It was either this, or ingest drugs such as caffeine and she wasn't allowed to do that. An alarm went off and her eyes went wide suddenly. Angel had sent another message!

Zax re- read the last two messages first, just to remind herself exactly what had been said before she checked this new one.

**I won't rest until this is over. I won't let him get away with this. Oli cannot win the election, he must be stopped. I will use any means at my disposal to achieve this. I will avenge you, my angel.**

**It seems our enemy has an enemy, but one which we clearly can't trust to do what must be done. Bluntly: the enemy of my enemy can never be my friend. I won't forget you angel, no one should.**

Then she checked the new one.

**Can you see the news where you are? I'm not sure if it's on the news, but it soon will be if it isn't now. Oli won't have survived that. I think fate has taken care of him as it did you, my angel.**

Zax read it again, confused. Oli wasn't dead. O wait… someone who *thought he was* must have sent it. She called Satiah after ensuring that Harrier was on the line. He was, although he seemed to be having difficulty staying awake too.

"Angel's back," Zax said, by way of explanation. She then read out the message.

"Harrier, see if you can trace it," Randal ordered. He knew it would most likely be a waste of time, as it had the last couple of times, but it had to be tried.

"Whoever sent that has seen the building collapse but is unaware of Oli's survival," Satiah mused, stating the obvious. "That means Collorah is well and truly out of the picture. Malla is obviously not the culprit either."

"Why?"

"*He's dead.*"

"O… no one told me," Zax stated, puzzled.

"It's been a busy night!" Satiah complained, preoccupied. "Oli too couldn't have sent it."

"Why would he…?" Zax began, even more confused.

"It was a possibility!" Satiah hissed over her. She frowned deeply. She didn't *have* another person of interest. Zax waited anxiously for more, but Satiah had dried up.

"...Well, *someone* sent it," Randal stated, irritated.

"*We know!*" chorused everyone, drowning him out.

"You're sure Malla is dead?" Zax queried, unsure where else to look.

"As sure as I would be if I had killed him myself," Satiah replied, with conviction. She remembered she nearly had at one point. Randal raised a doubtful eyebrow at her.

"I explained *that*...!" she began defensively, knowing he was referring to Collorah.

"Who else is there?" Zax articulated. "What about Shannon, he rejected her, remember...?"

"Regardless of *how* she feels about him now, she's too stupid for this!" Satiah dismissed, though not so resolutely. "Besides, I know it's not her..."

"How do you *know*?" Randal asked, sceptically.

"*Who else is there?*" repeated Zax, unhelpfully.

"*I know, all right*? I have an instinct for this; trust me, *it's not her,*" Satiah said, seriously. Randal was about to say something when the lift halted violently, almost knocking them all to the floor. They were then plunged into darkness as all power deactivated.

"*Zax?*" growled Satiah, in the dark.

"*Not me!*" she protested, defensively. "It's law enforcement, they've cut off your section. I thought they might - that's why I didn't close the doors all the way, you should be able to force them." Randal activated his torch and Satiah began to heave at the doors roughly. Such was his state of fatigue that Oli didn't even ask what was going on.

"How far did we get?" Randal asked.

"You're seven hundred and one floors down now," Zax told them.

They clambered out onto the floor they had stopped at. Everything was dark and silent.

"*Fantastic*, back to this again," Satiah grumbled.

Shannon jumped as she made her way back to her temporary quarters - Lunell was lurking there in the doorway.

"Sorry, did I startle you?" he asked, knowing he had.

"A bit," she admitted, shifty.

"Couldn't sleep?" he provided, sceptically.

"Just needed some water but no... I keep dropping off but then waking up again," she told him. He nodded slowly and grinned deviously.

"I understand. We will know more in the morning, in the meantime you can only endure the agony of not knowing," he said, sincerely. She nodded and closed the door on him after she entered her room.

Lunell darted from the doorway and into the kitchen where she had come from. Everything was dimly lit and the communication unit in there showed no sign of being used, but she had most certainly been in there. Snell had just sent him the details of the latest angel message. Some time ago, he'd reached the conclusion that whoever was sending these had to be using a communal machine in order to prevent being traced individually. The timing of the last one made Shannon look very culpable. It was not enough though, not yet. Unlike Phantom agents, the PAI waited for *evidence* before they did anything. And he only had circumstantial evidence so far. Whoever had sent that, believed that Oli was dead - and she might believe that too.

---

While Oli slept on the floor, using a rolled up jacket as a makeshift pillow, Satiah and Randal sat there in the dark, talking in low voices.

"You're running out of people, Satiah," Randal said, trying and succeeding in pressurising her. "It *has* to be someone still alive; it *has* to be someone who doesn't know that *he's* still alive..."

"It's like they are *commentating*," Satiah went on, giving the impression that she was hardly listening. "Telling angel what they think is going on, and that they're not actually doing or planning anything themselves. The last two messages look like that, anyway... I wonder if they were written by different people."

"What?" Randal asked, sensing potential progress.

"Well, it's just that the first message, the one that started all this, was very threatening. Not specific, obviously, but menacing enough to get you interested," Satiah said, thinking about it. "The next one is referring to someone else and is threatening too, but to a lesser degree. Frankly, if the second message had been the first, no one would have paid any attention to it."

"If the second message had been the first it would have made no sense," Randal grunted. She ignored that.

"The third message is the most unthreatening of all, and it's all about a kind of *mission accomplished* theme," Satiah mused. "Which I suppose, if you think he's dead, it must seem like it is."

"*What are you getting at, exactly?*"

"I don't really know," she admitted. His eyes went skywards briefly. "Well, *what do you expect*? Everyone that I suspect keeps being proved innocent, or dying." She told him about Malla and her endlessly changing opinions about him with regard to his possible guilt. This time, Randal agreed with her, and he realised he'd been out of the game long enough to forget just how challenging all this could be.

"It's just *so ironic*, this whole operation. We started this because we wanted Oli to live, and we thought angel was going to try to kill him. We've saved him and stopped multiple attempts on his life from two entirely independent sources. People on all sides of this have died, the PAI are crazier than ever and... we're *still* no closer to learning who angel is than we were on day one. It's almost like *they had nothing whatsoever to do with any of this.*"

"...Are you saying it's something entirely unrelated that seems to coincidently fit in with the timescale?" he asked, interested. She shrugged.

"*It's happened before,*" she said, thinking about a few notable examples. It had. Intelligence was still more about theory than reality in ninety percent of cases. This was why missions happened, to learn the truth. But sometimes happenstance played merry hell with it all, making people leap to false conclusions and leading either to complete disasters - or absolutely nothing.

"Well, that is one great excuse for you not being able to find out who it is," he said, wryly. She scowled playfully at him.

"*You know what I know*, who do *you* think it is?" she asked, directly.

"If it's *not* Shannon then I'm adrift at sea," he said, thinking about it. Satiah's mind ran along what Zax had been saying. Had Malla somehow faked his own death? She'd recognised his clothes, as his face and head were too badly damaged to confirm identity. There were teeth, of course, but it wasn't like she could check those at the time. What state would his remains be in by the time law enforcement or other emergency services reached him? She wondered why he would bother, and how he would have known *when* to fake it, anyway. Collorah wasn't in league with angel. Not directly, even if they both wanted the same thing. And, if he *was* still alive, *where was he*? No! No, no, this didn't make any sense! And Shannon... no, not her either. Satiah was sure about it. Randal had instincts though too, didn't he? Was an impartial, some would say external, instinct more accurate than what she had? She stopped herself right there! Doubting herself, particularly now, wasn't going to help anyone.

"We *made* this happen," she said, bleakly. "This is all of our own design." She was talking about the whole election business, and everything to do with it.

"Well, when you say 'we', you mean *they*?" Randal quibbled. He loathed the PAI as much as she did.

"No, by allowing them to do it, *we helped them*, so no. We," she responded, stubbornly.

"...When did *you* start to care?" he asked, a little coldly.

"It's not compassion, *it's anger* that this is now my problem," she retorted, levelly. "You *know* compassion is not in me. *I don't do love.*" That was an outright lie and she knew it, but her anger gave it credibility.

"Well, whatever it is, we are where we are; while we *could* go back it's easier to go forward," he stated. Time travel was always tempting, but never a good idea. Why was it that when someone like Reed said something like that, an idea would come to her? Randal was saying the right things but she was getting nothing.

And, as if because she'd thought about Reed, a new idea *did* come to her. An idea she wondered why she'd never had before. She didn't voice it yet though. Not yet. It could be wrong. Okay, if they thought it was Shannon, let them. Why not even act as though she agreed with them. Shannon was no friend of hers; besides… she could even use this to draw out the real angel. She stood decisively, and Randal looked up at her sharply as if sensing her sudden inspiration was more significant than an urge to get moving.

"Let's get going, my back is aching," she grumbled, giving Oli a kick. *"Come on, we're moving on."*

---

Nothing had been said about it. Not a word. Brenda was astounded. The aide entered the office, carrying a tray with a small silver box on it.

"Here you are," she said, eyeing Brenda curiously. "I had no idea you liked Drezmach." Drezmach was a metallic plant that fed on oxygen.

"They are supposed to smell nice in summer," Brenda replied. She paused as she eyed the younger woman. "Why are you not wearing your medal?"

"I didn't want you to think it had gone to my head," she shrugged. "Besides, knowing my luck lately I'd probably lose it." Brenda laughed.

"Is there any reason for this apparent media blackout of Oli?" she asked, casually. The aide paused.

"What media blackout?" the aide asked, innocently. She knew, of course, but couldn't say.

"It's just no one has covered Oli in the news, and I thought it might be us censoring it," Brenda stated, smiling. "You yourself told me that we have answers for the questions they might ask, but no one has asked me anything all morning."

"Well, there's a lot going on, what with Sam McAllister's suicide and…"

"*What?*" Brenda asked, spitting out her drink.

"Didn't you hear? He was found in a parking area a few hours ago. *He'd shot himself,*" the aide told her, glad of the distraction.

"*Why?*" Brenda asked, her eyes wide and sorrowful. The aide shrugged, genuinely not knowing.

"I'm no psychologist, but it might have something to do with either losing the election, or his financial problems… *or both*," she said, pouring Brenda another glass of water.

"That's terrible," she said, sipping it more carefully this time.

"Besides, as you know, Oli *was* in hiding, it's probably *his team* that have kept the press away from the incident," the aide said.

"He was?" she asked, confused.

"He was," the aide confirmed. "He, and others like you, no matter how popular, are often at risk of assassination. *It's a sign of the times, I'm afraid.*"

"I wish there could just be peace for everyone," Brenda sighed, staring out at the early morning. "Is that so much to ask?"

"Morally no, but *practically…*" the aide trailed off. "It will all settle down once the election is over, everyone is currently very excitable."

"Assuming I'm still here," Brenda smiled, softly.

"I'm sure you will be," the aide allowed, reassuringly. "Your decision to hold that referendum about the election in the first place is what I think cemented your chances of success."

"It's what the people wanted," Brenda smiled, calmly.

"Yes, *the people*," echoed the aide, a little smugly.

<hr>

For those who care, twelve to thirteen steps are all that you need to make a flight. Satiah wished she could achieve flight right then. And flights were to be no more than sixteen steps too. *How interesting.* So, by that logic, they only had eleven thousand five hundred and twenty steps to go… give or take. It was about an hour before dawn now. Her thighs were starting to burn, so she could only imagine how Oli must be feeling. Randal too was showing the first signs of feeling the strain. She glanced down the gap between the steps, flashing her torch down there. No signs of pursuit from the factory security, the PAI *or* law enforcement.

"I think I'm going to suggest this as a training programme for the trainees," Randal puffed, quietly.

"They'll love you for that," she breathed.

"Why are you so interested in Zax?" he asked, directly.

"*Come on,*" she smiled, having prepared for this question a long time ago. "Even you must see her *potential*. Besides, for whatever reason, the training so far has not dampened her positive enthusiasm. She doesn't approach a task seeing it as just a duty - she still sees it as an adventure too. It's rare to see that kind of passion."

"Agreed, but there are plenty of others who share these qualities."

"What can I tell you, Randal? She was in the right place, *under my nose*, at the right time. I needed someone good and they gave me her," she replied. "Why all the questions? *Don't you trust me?*"

Randal laughed it off. She could sense his curiosity though. Up and up, round and round they went. Satiah was starting to hate planet Earth all over again. Oli gave a cry and fell into a seating position on the steps behind them.

"I'm sorry I... I need another rest," he pleaded. Randal and Satiah halted and both tried to check how far they had to go and if they were still alone. Randal gasped, after hearing what Zax had to tell him.

"What?" Satiah asked. He turned to look down at Oli before inviting Satiah a short distance away from him with a head movement. She followed him out of earshot, uneasy.

"Sam McAllister is dead," he told her. She frowned, unsure which of the several questions she had to ask first.

"When?" she finally settled on.

"A few hours ago, his body was found... *in a parking area,*" he told her, with significance. They both remembered that night they had been watching a secret meeting in a similar place.

She knew what he was inferring.

"Is Mark dead too?" she asked, quickly. Randal shrugged.

"If he is, we don't know it yet."

"Was it a *suicide*?" Satiah asked, perceptively. She waggled her eyebrows at him to show what she really thought.

"This right here is why I trust your gut," Randal said, with a grim smile.

"*So Jinx has gone rogue,*" she mused, more to herself than to him. "Maybe they argued over the money or the job, maybe not. Either way… Jinx will maybe go for Mark too, *assuming Mark didn't pay him to do that to cover his own tracks*, or he will run."

"According to law enforcement, a single shot was heard in the early hours and there were no signs of anyone else being there."

"*Randal, he's hardly going to advertise the murder, is he?* I bet Sam didn't have any money on him either," Satiah smirked, knowingly. Randal nodded. "It was Jinx, I'd swear on it." Randal remembered something Zax had said to him before.

"Well, it couldn't have been Collorah, could it?" Randal concurred, meaningfully. She let out a hoarse laugh.

"It's a good thing we only pledged to look after Oli…" she paused, thinking ahead. Someone was going to have to deliver the news to him. And she *really* didn't want that person to be her. "Do you want me to tell him?"

"It will have to be done gently; he's under a lot of stress…" Randal sighed, trailing off.

"Yes," she agreed, sombrely. Then she grinned, giving the impression that she'd like nothing better than to hurt him. "*Can I tell him?*"

"…No, leave it to me," he said, giving her a disapproving look.

"*Spoilsport*! I would have done it gently," she protested, secretly glad to have got out of it.

Randal approached Oli on the stairs and sat down next to him.

"What?" Oli asked fearfully, knowing something bad was coming.

"I'm sorry Oli, there's no easy way to tell you this so I'm just going to go ahead and say it like it is. Your brother is dead," Randal told him, bluntly. To his surprise, Oli started to laugh.

"You have my sympathies," Randal went on, wondering why Oli was reacting like that.

"It's just, what else is going to happen?" Oli asked, too tired to get up. "Having failed to get me, they go after him instead. In a way this is no surprise to me. *Nothing surprises me anymore.*" Randal sighed and got up, deciding that Oli was clearly in some sort of denial, but was unwilling to engage with him anymore.

Oli continued to laugh until it turned into tears. Randal and Satiah looked down at him, wondering how this latest blow was going to affect him mentally.

"He's still taking it in. He's tired and slightly mad right now," Satiah told Randal. "I was concerned he simply wouldn't believe you."

"Yes," Randal said. "I fear that there might be a real suicide soon." Satiah shrugged.

"I have been half expecting that myself. He does have great resilience though," she stated. "Excuse me." It was Harrier calling her. She went up to the next floor, away from prying ears, and answered.

"What have you got for me?"

"Those two components you marked as urgent, the technical data has just arrived," Harrier answered. "The first component is one of the latest tablet-adapters. The Gen15 according to this booklet."

"What does it do?" she asked, interested.

"Nothing, it's just a specialised adaptor," he replied.

"And the other?" she asked, irritated.

"This one set off a few alarms actually, apparently it's on the secret list, not yet in circulation," Harrier replied, sounding excited. Her eyes narrowed in concern. "It's the RFS, a resonance filter scanner. One of the latest brain scanners. Apparently after tests, these things can actually tell if someone is insane or not. Who did you want it for?"

Satiah was stunned into silence. Kelvin still thought she was mad. The fact that he'd somehow got hold of this thing and not told her about it further supported this theory. She'd submitted to the last test and it had proven her utterly sane. Kelvin still obviously didn't trust Obsenneth and thought he was affecting her mind in some way. She was torn between anger and gratitude. Anger because he still doubted her and was keeping secrets from her, but gratitude that he was still trying to protect her.

Granted, he was programmed to do nothing else, but he did have the ability to alter his own programming. She wondered how she was going to deal with this. Whatever his stimuli were, she couldn't have him presuming that she was crazy all the time. And, despite this rather painful revelation, she was still not able to solve the mystery: neither of these things explained *why* Kelvin was not working. Perhaps, as she had feared when she'd first found them, they were not relevant.

"*Satiah*?" It was Harrier, still awaiting her answer.

"Sorry, still here, what?" she asked, still thinking hard.

"Who did you want it for?" he repeated, sighing impatiently.

"No one in particular, I just wanted to see what it was," she bluffed, quickly. "*This stays between us*."

"*Of course*! So… is there anything else?" he enquired.

"No, thanks Harrier, that was… *useful*." Satiah was surprised how astonished she was, given the amount of secrets *she* had, about the fact that Kelvin had been keeping something from her.

"Any news on that book?"

---

Mark was smart enough to know, as soon as he heard about Sam, what was going on. And, more importantly, what Jinx had in mind for him. He'd play along at first, but he had his team ready. If Jinx thought he could trick him into lowering his guard then he was dead wrong. Everything had been so simple at first: kill Oli McAllister. That was it; as aims went, it had been an easy target. At least, it should have been. Mark was realistic enough to know that, Oli or no Oli, he stood no chance against Brenda. Earlier, Oli's absence may well have made a difference, but not now. Certainly not after that catastrophe of a debate. It was time for losses to be cut. Jinx had clearly decided to make the first move; Mark had no doubt it was Jinx who'd taken out Sam. O, he'd been clever enough to make it *look like* suicide, but Mark could see what had really happened.

The way he'd said *return the favour* on the call had also given Mark a warning. He'd sounded angry but controlled. He'd sounded like a man just about to commence his endgame. Mark had to assume that Jinx would predict his plan, to be on the safe side.

"You're sure you want us to do this, sir?" the man asked. He was standing there, beside the doorway, a pistol in each hand.

"It's for the best," he said, conscious that this man *knew* how this worked. He was paying him to kill a former employee of his. Okay, Jinx was never an employee, perhaps *associate* would be a better term. They both knew that he was already thinking: how long before I become that *disgruntled former employee* myself?

"If he wanted to talk to me about how to deal with Sam, then *Sam wouldn't already be dead*," Mark told him, hoping to use reason to win him round. The man smiled tightly, his blue eyes narrowing.

"I've got two on the stairs, one in the building opposite and one in a vehicle outside. Your transporter is out the back," the man told him. "It's textbook. We wait, then you give the signal to let me know if we take him or not."

Mark nodded. "And if Jinx shoots first?" he asked. He shrugged.

"He won't. He will want to get in close and make sure you're dead and that there are no witnesses. He will most likely also want your money... another reason to come on in and explore. Also... I have a request," he said, a little smugly.

"Name it," he said, expecting him to ask for more money.

"Can I keep his body?" he enquired. Mark frowned briefly, puzzled. "He's wanted in several places, dead or alive. I intend to claim his bounty."

"O... yes, of course," he allowed. He had forgotten about that. "So is *that* what you are? A bounty hunter?"

"*I'm an entrepreneur*," the man said, waving off the question with some rather amateur theatricality. "A flexible guy who can be *whatever* I am hired to be. Assassin, bodyguard, BH, mercenary, *escort*... pretty much everything. The universe is overpopulated, got to do your part, *right*?"

"*Yes*," Mark murmured, not at all impressed. "The highest bidder and all that?"

"Exactly."

*Bayler* had been a last resort. Known locally as *the skull merchant*, a name that didn't inspire much confidence, Bayler had been recommended locally as the go-to guy for this kind of job. He had arrived within the hour, with a team of people he claimed were dependable enough, so that did lend some badly needed credibility to his nickname. Mark had been watching him closely, only to find Bayler watching him just as closely. He had short ginger hair and very pale blue eyes. Almost grey, actually. Bayler was clearly a performer; Mark thought he liked to put on a show… to anyone who was willing to watch. He swaggered a little as he walked too. Yet his underworld contact had stated that Bayler was not as he seemed. He was as ruthless as he was efficient. He just didn't like to seem that way… particularly to his potential victims.

"Do you know Jinx then?" Mark asked, not liking the silence.

"I've never had the pleasure of meeting him face to face," Bayler replied, with that rather insane grin he used a lot. "Heard he's a nice guy but everyone *always* says that." Jinx? A nice guy? Was this man drunk?

"Indeed," Mark agreed, not sure if that was true. Bayler suddenly turned serious and Mark briefly glimpsed the real man behind the act. He was listening to something, no doubt another member of his team.

"He's coming," Bayler warned, in confirmation. "He's on his own… get ready boys, party time."

"What do you want me to do?" Mark asked, curious.

"*Let him in,*" Bayler replied, as if it was obvious. "I can't easily shoot him through the door." Mark obligingly deactivated the lock.

The door opened with a click and Jinx entered, pistol undrawn. Mark swallowed nervously. This was it.

"Jinx, I understand Sam has betrayed me and you wanted to talk about it?" Mark asked, managing to keep his voice even. It would be interesting to see how Jinx was planning to play this. He didn't seem at all wary. But then he didn't know that his doom was standing so close by.

"Something like that," Jinx smiled, coming closer. As he moved further in, Bayler aimed his guns, ready to strike. But he wasn't aiming them at Jinx.

"Don't move, *Mark*," Bayler said, winking at him. "Jinx isn't so great at hitting moving targets." Mark gaped, instantly realising his mistake, this was a set up. Somehow Bayler and Jinx were working together. No wonder Jinx hadn't been at all cautious. Jinx grinned knowingly.

"Not good at trusting the right people, are you, Mark? But then that's normal for a politician," Bayler jeered, tickled.

"Look, we can talk about this…" Mark began, starting to panic.

"That's another thing you all do way too much of. *Talk*," Jinx sneered, ripping his pistol free of its holster. Mark tried to leap for cover, but was killed before he even cleared the desk as both men gunned him down. They high-fived one another almost casually afterward. Jinx crouched to be sure that Mark was gone.

"Did he tell you where the money is?" Jinx asked, casually.

"*Yeah…*" Bayler began, as he struck Jinx over the head with the butt of his pistol. Jinx fell to the ground, unconscious.

"Is the money in his vehicle?" Bayler asked casually, into his communicator. "Great, so the word on the walkway was right all along, and inmate thirteen is indeed *here*. His old gambling buddies will be *just thrilled*. Get up here and give us a hand. Mark has got his cash stashed here too… it would just be plain wrong to leave that behind. *Like I said… party time.*"

Mark hadn't been so smart after all.

---

"You're *sure* this is the right floor?" Satiah asked, again.

"Yes, I swear!" Zax huffed. "Now can I *please* go to bed?"

"One second," Satiah smiled, pleased to annoy Zax for once. Randal and Oli were still a few flights below her and she had apparently reached surface level. She crouched, wincing as her thighs screamed out their protest. She got to work on the lock. The door slid open, revealing… a walkway and a building across a road. The icy breath of night air washed over her. She smiled.

"You can go to bed now, we're out," Satiah confirmed. She peered back inside. "*We're out!*" She looked around, trying to work out exactly where they were… somewhere she didn't instantly recognise. There was a line of traffic several hundred metres above her.

She managed to get the attention of a taxi, which swooped towards them. Randal and Oli staggered out, looking a bit disorientated, and more than a little messy. The taxi halted at their level and the android inside opened the doors. They all got in and Satiah ordered a course to the nearest medical facility. Once there, all three of them were checked over and healed of all wounds. Satiah was surprised at how little damage she had actually sustained down there. At the time, it had felt much worse. She noticed a few other Phantoms hanging around, no doubt to reinforce Randal. She went to see him. He was standing next to Oli, who was being scanned. They moved to one side.

"No brain damage," he said, reassuring her.

"*Are you sure*? He *is* a politician," she quipped, wearily. He eyed her.

"Maybe you should get some sleep," he suggested. She nodded. "I'll contact you later."

She departed and began to go through her messages. A lot of questions, basically. The usual. Where are you? Are you okay? Where is Oli? She didn't answer any of them. Oli was safe and Randal would take care of him, at least until tomorrow, when she could rely on Lunell and Shannon to take over. She felt so tired, she wanted nothing more than to get some well-deserved sleep.

She finally reached her front door at about nine. She opened the door and stared in astonishment at the mess. Bits of Kelvin were everywhere, along with empty beer containers and... *was that her dinner?*

"*Carl*," she murmured, in disappointed exasperation.

Too tired to even bother to try and work out what Carl had been up to, she immediately went for a shower. She'd been wanting to get that dust and dirt off her since she'd first awoken down there, and it was a relief. The warm water soothed her and made her yearn even more for bed.

She reached the bedroom, wrestled some of the cover away from the comatose Carl, and then fell into her own slumber. Yet her mind remained restless, going over everything while she slept, dining out intellectually and subconsciously on the series of happenings and ideas she'd had. She was dimly aware of being pulled into Carl's warm arms at some stage, but she couldn't tell when that was. It was almost evening when she finally awoke again. She reached out for Carl but found only bedding. She sat up, upon realising she was alone. The place was… *tidy*. Carl was standing there in the doorway, watching her.

"What's going on?" she asked, rubbing her eyes sleepily.

"Nothing," he smiled, clearly hiding something. She yawned and raised an expectant eyebrow. He shifted on his feet and refused to meet her eyes.

"Then why do you look like you might, had I caught you stealing my underwear?" she asked, curious.

"I'm sorry, we got drunk and trashed your apartment, we didn't mean to do it, it just sort of happened," he said, quickly. "But, on a positive note, Max *found out* what was wrong with Kelvin! Hear me out! It was some kind of scanner thing and it slipped out of its position because the bracket was missing…"

She giggled.

"That's okay, it doesn't look too trashed," she noted, guessing he must have cleared away most of the mess while she was still out of it.

"I was trying to clear it up before you came back, but I gave up, knowing you'd probably find out anyway," he confessed. She flopped back down with a loud sigh.

"So you're trying to tell me that while *I* was struggling miles underground to stay alive, battling all kinds of inhuman menaces and challenging the very limits of my own ability… you and Max were having a party?" she chuckled. *"Boys will be boys."*

"I *was* worried, but Zax told me you would be late and I had to handle the maintenance thing myself," he said. He came over, carrying Kelvin's head. As best as he could, he explained what Max had told him the night before.

"Where *is* Max?" she asked, frowning. She half expected him to crawl out from under the bed, wearing a toga, with cocktail umbrellas lodged in his hair, or something equally ludicrous.

"No idea, I had to leave him behind at the tournament," he replied, honestly. "He was fighting the dragon and I was trying to avoid knocking anything over." She rolled her eyes.

*"You sound like a lunatic, Carl,"* she sniggered, mock sternly.

"He was playing this guy *called* the dragon," he elaborated, seeing her confusion, "and I was too drunk to stand." He sighed. "And… we sort of… *ate your dinner.*" She smiled forgivingly.

"Wow, you guys *really* live life in the fast lane," she said soothingly.

"You were underground?" he asked, confused. "Not at the office?" Satiah told him what had happened.

"I'll get you some breakfast," he declared, after hearing all of it. In the measurement of a night of suffering, she'd clearly won. She'd just stretched out and prepared for a nap, when her eyes snapped opened and she stared at Kelvin's head suspiciously.

"…If you still think I'm crazy, you're very much mistaken," she growled at the inert robot.

"Did you say something?" Carl called, from the other room.

"No!" she replied, her eyes never leaving Kelvin. As if to punish Kelvin for his lack of faith in her, she wrapped the covers around herself and wandered out to the kitchen… leaving his head behind. She perched precariously on a stool while Carl bustled around. He seemed to know his way around well enough.

"So…" she said, as a precursor. He paused in mid step as if she'd just yelled at him to freeze. "I'm no closer to figuring out who angel is. My boss thinks it's Shannon, my gut says *no*, but I know for sure now that it couldn't have been Malla."

"Sounds to me like you need to worry more about Collorah and the PAI than angel," he said, seriously.

"That's a point," she allowed, sipping the juice he'd given her. She could get used to this.

"No, *that's* a pint," he joked, pointing at her drink. She smirked up at him in a 'you're so funny' kind of way. "Did you hear about Sam?"

"Yes, it *wasn't* a suicide," she told him. He dropped something in the cooling unit and shook his head.

"You just *can't trust* the CNC these days," he muttered, as if that in itself was news. "You said him and Mark were working together, so was it Mark?"

"Very good," she giggled, biting her lip. "You're not at all bad at this."

"Thank you, *very* patronising, *and* you're dodging the question," he said, waving a playfully admonishing finger at her.

"You see right through me, don't you?" she asked, flirting shamelessly.

"Only when you let me," he shrugged. He dumped a large plate of food in front of her. "You're not allowed to leave the table until you've finished the last morsel," he went on.

"This isn't the table," she whispered up at him, as if he didn't know.

"It's a figure of speech."

"No, it's a work surface."

"I give up."

"Jinx killed him," she said, with certainty, staring up into his eyes. He waggled his head in a disbelieving way.

"How do you know that? I buy that it wasn't a suicide because I know what he was up to, but how can you know Mark didn't do him in?" he asked, levelly.

"My gut tells me," she said, shrugging. He leaned in, moved the blanket aside and put his ear to her belly. She giggled, ran her fingers through his hair and started eating.

"Nope, nothing," he said, after a few seconds. He replaced the cover and faced her. "Sounds hungry though. Do you want to be left to your meal?"

"No, I've discovered you are good to talk to about this, which basically means I'll never let you leave now," she said, honestly. "You might help me figure it out."

"So Jinx backstabs Sam," he said, making a dramatic stabbing motion with his hand. She nodded. "Makes it look like a suicide to…?"

"… cover his tracks, and assuming Mark wasn't in on it too, not to alert Mark to his betrayal," she replied, downing more juice.

"Why did he kill his own employer?" he asked, next. Even he could guess at some of the reasons.

"Didn't agree with his opinions about breast feeding in public," she remarked, shrugging. He grunted as if in agreement. "My power of deduction tells me that it was most likely the money."

"And your gut tells you? Or it is too busy eating to care?" he remarked.

"Um… the second option," she said, thinking about it.

"If it *was* Jinx, why *only* kill Sam? Surely if he had an issue with Sam, why not Mark too?" Carl suggested.

"Yes," she agreed. "Assuming it was Jinx acting alone, and he wasn't working for *Mark* to kill Sam." He tilted his head as if trying to physically look at something from a different angle.

"How much do you get paid again?"

She eyed her earpiece and, as usual, everyone had been trying to get hold of her. Zax, Shannon, Lunell, Oli… the list went on. She sighed drearily.

"The price of being so popular," he said, trying to cheer her up. He rubbed her back fondly. "When do you have to go back?"

"I'll talk to them all and then… hopefully Lunell will be okay until tomorrow," she smiled. "That's the beauty of shift work; you're restricted by hours… though I've gone above and beyond slightly." She called Zax first.

"How are you feeling?" Zax wanted to know, annoying energetic and cheerful.

"Let's save the hard questions for later. I'm guessing that you called to tell me that Randal has moved Oli and his personnel to a new place of safety," she fathomed.

"Commandment Benefactor Brenda, are we supposed to call her that now, or only after the election is over? Anyway, she's graciously agreed to put them under her protection," Zax explained. "All of this is strictly mum, no one can know, obviously. Not only would it expose Oli yet again to danger, but it could also potentially hit Brenda's campaign."

"That's conceivable," Satiah acknowledged, downing the last of her juice. She held it out for Carl to get rid of. He did.

"Harrier reports that Lunell and Snell are up to something, but whatever it was seems to have been put on hold," she went on.

"*How reassuring*," Satiah mused, mordantly. She was losing track of all these safe locations.

Next she called Shannon.

"How are you?" Shannon asked, instantly.

"I'm okay, how is Oli?" she asked, behaving naturally.

"Well, he's alive and he's here…" She paused and Satiah waited, knowing something important was about to be said. Randal thought angel was Shannon and Satiah didn't, but she was out of suspects. "… Listen… how well do you know Lunell?"

"Not that well, why?" Satiah asked, intrigued.

"He's… it's *probably nothing*," Shannon began, uneasily. *Here we go.*

"You're starting to sound like how I feel," Satiah joked, just as a normal person might. "Tell me, what is it?"

"Last night… I tried to call someone using the general communicator in the last building… when I went back to my room, he was standing there in the corridor… I think he was watching me," she told her. Ah… perhaps this was why Randal was thinking it was Shannon.

"Watching you as in watching you, or watching you like, *watching you*?" Satiah asked, trying to get to the bottom of this.

"I don't know, but it made me feel uncomfortable," she replied. Satiah paused, wondering how to deal with this.

"Has he ever done anything like this before?"

"No, not that I've seen," Shannon replied.

"Who were you trying to call?" Satiah enquired next, being thorough.

"Malla," she answered. "I… *I didn't know then.*" Her voice shook and Satiah remembered she'd only recently learned of her friend's death.

"O… *I'm so sorry Shannon*, I didn't know him well, but he was always very nice to me," she said, honestly.

"Can you come see me? For a drink or something?" Shannon asked, abruptly. "I… I need to talk to someone." Satiah was both reluctant and intrigued at the same time. She had hoped to spend all that night with Carl to thank him for his interesting method of solving the problem with Kelvin.

"Sure," Satiah smiled, not meaning the kindness in her tone. Just because she thought Shannon wasn't angel, and just because she felt sorry for her, didn't mean she liked her. First, she had to speak to Lunell and get his opinion. He may have found something out.

"I'll come to you; my place isn't very presentable right now." Lunell answered immediately.

"Satiah, this *is* unexpected," he drawled, sarcastically.

"What did you see last night? What was Shannon doing?" she asked, directly. He paused.

"I don't know if I'm honest. I know what *she said* she was doing, and I know where she was, but as to what *she actually did*... I can't confirm one way or another," he said, noncommittal. She rolled her eyes.

"What do you *suspect*?"

"I think she's the insider we've been looking for," he replied, outright. Okay, exactly as she had supposed.

"The timing is there," she allowed, trying to make him think she wasn't too contrary to the idea. "What's the motive, do you think?" Indeed, the timing of Shannon being there couldn't easily be overlooked.

"Why Satiah, I didn't think you Phantoms *cared* about that sort of thing... *or* evidence," he said, trying both his luck and her patience.

"Do you think it would be because Oli rejected her?" she provided, letting that go. It made sense so long as you ignored her personality.

"Yes," he answered, a little carelessly. "It's almost textbook. The scorned woman and all that. I'm sure *you* understand?"

"But you can't *prove* that she is angel, can you?" she replied, not letting him get to her.

"...If I could I would have acted already," he responded, coolly. That much was true.

"Must be frustrating for you," she smiled. "Would it interest you to learn that she just spoke to me to tell me that she thinks you might be harassing her?"

"*It would*," he allowed, not remotely bothered. He had been doing his job, after all, and Satiah couldn't deny that.

"I'm going to talk to her tonight and I will try to get her to confess if I can," she lied. She knew he would lap this up even though, despite all this, she *still* didn't think it was Shannon. Despite the rejection, the timing was *still wrong*. If she hated him all that time, why would she wait for the election at all? *Her perfect revenge*? It was a long shot.

"Make sure you record it," he advised. "We need to be able to demonstrate it was her." *It's not her*, she wanted to scream.

"Of course," she said, smiling artfully. Carl was watching her face closely and drew away when he saw that look. It was one of her *scary* looks. She grabbed his hand to stop him getting away and disconnected.

"What *are* you up to now?" he asked, uncertainly.

"Whatever happens I *have* to reassure Shannon," Satiah explained. "*She's the only one left.* Malla, Cadel and about half of the whole security team died in the collapse. I'll try to get back as soon as I can…"

"Hey, I'm just happy to be here," he said, grinning. "Do you want me to get Kelvin going?"

"*Erm…*" she began, unsure how to start with that subject.

"You can trust me," he assured her, sincerely. She smiled.

"It's not *you* I'm worried about," she said, still indecisive. She hadn't told Carl about Obsenneth. It was on the list of things to gradually tell him about so as not to rattle him too much. As a consequence of this, he had no knowledge of Kelvin's apparent hidden belief that she was under its influence or that she was losing her mind, and that this was why she was hesitant about reactivating Kelvin.

Carl was looking from her to Kelvin and then back again, dawning realisation on his face.

"There's something you haven't told me, isn't there?" he asked, comprehending. She made a noise of reluctant agreement.

"Are you going to tell me?" he asked, curious.

"…I have to go and talk to Shannon," she said, evading the subject poorly. He sighed, crossed his arms and grinned down at her knowingly. "What?" she asked, sassy and amused. "*What?*"

"Nothing," he said, lightly. She pulled a face at him before marching back to the bedroom. "He's not dangerous, is he?" Carl asked, after her.

"Not to you," she replied, over her shoulder. She hadn't called Oli back.

---

Shannon's apartment was eerily like her own, Satiah reflected. Only without all the junk lying around, and Carl, obviously.

"Wine?" Shannon offered.

"You got any Golden?" Satiah asked, eyeing her. It was obvious that she'd been crying. Satiah had cried in front of her before so, oddly, Shannon apparently felt it was okay to cry in front of her too. They sat at a table, facing one another. Satiah took note of an already empty bottle on the work surface. Shannon had clearly started without her. Bleeding heart? Maybe she was angel after all.

"*Thanks* for coming over, I didn't... I didn't think you'd want to *so soon after what happened*," Shannon said, seriously. Satiah, although not a particularly compassionate person, had to be wary of developing sympathy for Shannon at this stage. They were *not* friends - Satiah, at least, was simply pretending. But Shannon seemed to have really started believing in their 'friendship'.

"How long had you known Malla?" asked Satiah, patting her hand gently.

"Must have been... thirty four years, just over. He was a good man," she told her. Satiah didn't say she was sorry for her loss. As others had most likely already said that, it was pointless. Besides, she wasn't.

"Cadel too," Satiah noted, reminding her that Malla was not the only one to have lost his life. Shannon snivelled. "Malla was very supportive to me; he was particularly helpful when I was investigating Dean's dismissal."

"*Dean?*" Shannon asked, as if confused. Had she forgotten who Dean was? Fog of grief, Satiah dismissed it as such.

"Yes, he used to work for Oli's team but was dismissed when..."

"What are you talking about? Dean *wasn't dismissed*, he just disappeared," Shannon said, casually.

Satiah was stunned into silence.

"*What?*"

"Well, he was probably dismissed *too* after he didn't come back, but he *just vanished* about..." she paused, as if trying to remember.

"Three months and three weeks ago," Satiah provided, suddenly very alert.

"...Yes, something like that..." Shannon said, before stopping. She recognised the change in Satiah's posture. "*What's wrong?*"

"*...I don't know,*" Satiah replied, trying to think. "Can I show you something?" Shannon nodded. Satiah brought up a picture of Dean, from the profile Malla had given her to check, and showed it to Shannon.

"Who's that?"

Shannon eyed the picture.

"No idea, never seen him before, is he one of those people after Oli?" she asked, perplexed. *Huh?*

"*That's Dean,*" Satiah stated, her other hand very close to her pistol. Shannon gave her a look as if to say: *are you going mad?*

"That's not Dean," she replied, baffled. She began fiddling with her own device. Satiah waited breathlessly. What was happening? Shannon showed her a picture. It was a picture of the victorious team, Oli's team, dated four months ago, of Malla, Shannon, Oli, Kate and several other people.

"Second right at the back," Shannon prompted, seriously. Satiah's quick eyes found the man immediately and, to her shock, she realised that she recognised him.

*Scott Snell.* Mr Slimy was standing right there in that picture, less than a metre from Oli himself, smiling gamely along with the rest of them. Satiah went cold all over for a second, before a fiery rage flooded in. The PAI had been watching Oli for months, *since long before* he'd even started the election. They might even have helped him take power on his home world!

"O..." was all Satiah could manage. Well, at least it certainly removed Dean from her list of suspects regarding angel. He'd never really existed in the first place. All that time wasted! These records would have been doctored by the PAI, inventing all that twaddle about inappropriate images and incompetence. But if all that was true... why hadn't Malla been equally puzzled by the change of information? He had known Snell as Dean, not this other guy! But then, Malla had not been the one to dismiss Dean. According to the data, however worthless it might be proven to be, *Cadel* had.

"Where are you going?" Shannon asked, as Satiah almost ran to the door.

"I just need to check something, I'll explain when I get back," she replied hurriedly. Satiah leapt into her transport and recklessly sped all the way to the PAI building. She was intercepted in the doorway by a receptionist.

"Can I help you?" she asked, firmly. Satiah gave her a look and she almost shrank back.

"I'm here to speak to Mr Slimy *please*," she bit out. The woman's lips twitched, betraying the fact that she knew exactly who Satiah was referring to, but couldn't admit it.

"Who are you here to see?" she asked, preparing a visitor's pass.

"Scott Snell," Satiah clarified, through her teeth.

"And you are?"

"*Very angry.*"

"I need a name for the form," the woman pleaded, unsure whether to laugh or not.

"Phantom agent Satiah," she replied, calming herself. She gave her serial number too. The woman was fast in producing the pass. She smiled brightly at Satiah as she handed it over. She'd probably get in trouble for this, but it would be worth it.

"Level seventy four, wing four, room ninety," she said. "May your day stay positive."

"*Same to you,*" Satiah growled, moving to the lift. When she was gone, the receptionist snatched up her communicator.

"Hey Val, you will *not believe* who just came in here...!"

---

Snell looked up as the door to his office opened and Satiah strode him. He frowned.

"Phantom Satiah, how did you...?" he began, wondering how she'd got in so easily. She suddenly leapt over his desk; feet first, grabbed him by his lapels and slammed him against the wall.

"*What-have-you-done?*" she snarled, furiously. She thumped him into the wall in time with her words.

"Satiah, I must protest…" He was silenced by a punch to his gut which left him without breath.

"I *know*, all right? I know about *you* working on Oli's team under the name Dean!" she stated harshly, still holding him there as he tried to breathe. He tried to fend her off but she was strong and he wasn't. This whole operation was an attempt to cover up the PAI's failure in preventing Oli ever getting as far as he had. *And* to shift the blame if it all went wrong…

"We… we had to ensure he lost to his brother in… the constitutional election," he explained, trying to breathe. "The computer said…"

"Only you fudged it, *didn't you*? *That's what all this is about*! Oli should never have even been running in this election at all, *should he*?" she growled, repeatedly shaking him against the wall like a rag doll.

"Not officially… no one was meant to know… about that mission. We made a mistake… we underestimated his popularity…" he wheezed, ineffectively trying to fight her off.

"Yes, and when you couldn't stop him *or his brother* from turning up in this election, you dragged us in to clear up *your mess!*" she hissed, seeing it all now.

"How did you find out?" he demanded, outraged.

"I found out through *doing my job correctly*!" she retorted, about to put a knee in his groin.

"*Satiah*!" Randal called, from the doorway. "*Enough*, let him go!" She turned to look back briefly. Randal raised a commanding eyebrow and motioned to his still undrawn pistol. She roughly released Snell with a shove.

"Ah, *Phantom Leader*, thank you for calling off your dog…" Snell began, relieved.

"I would be *very* careful what you say, Snell, or I might just let her carry on," Randal snapped, lividly. "You should have told us *everything* at the start and you know it." There was a silence as Snell slowly pulled his chair back up and sat down at his desk sombrely.

"…What do you want?" Snell muttered, negotiating.

"*Pull Lunell out*," Satiah spat, in his ear. "Let me handle this *myself* to ensure it is done properly." Snell sighed and glanced at Randal before nodding reluctantly.

"Agreed, anything else?" he asked, next. *Actually, since you asked...*

"Why did Malla not realise you had altered Dean's history when he handed me the information?" she pressed, demandingly. "And if you just disappeared, how would he know to lie about it?"

"Hacked the records and Cadel was paid to tell Malla the cover story," he said, with a tiny shrug. Satiah had thought so but she had wanted it confirmed. There had been other options. She nodded to Randal, telling him that she was finished.

"You *stop* holding things back from Phantom Squad, *stop* interfering in our business and *stop trying to kill us...*" Randal listed, his tone as cold as it was ruthless.

"...As you say," Snell growled, glaring up at Randal. They'd got him cornered in his own den and he knew it.

"... in exchange for us staying discreet about your previous *failed* effort to remove Oli and his brother from the race," Randal concluded. "*And* staying quiet about your *failed* attempts on our lives." Snell nodded, sourly. Randal smiled tightly and nodded to Satiah.

"After you," he said, wanting to make sure he didn't turn his back on her with Snell there. Satiah glanced down at Snell who slowly turned to look back into her eyes. She shunted the files on his desk childishly, scattering them on the floor before marching out. Randal sniggered and gave Snell a pseudo salute before following her outside. They left the building and didn't speak until they were on a walkway.

"*You knew*, didn't you?" Satiah asked, turning on Randal. He shrugged.

"I *suspected*. The rarity of this mission type alone was enough to arouse my suspicion. But I had no idea *what* they were hiding exactly," he explained.

"No, you just waited for me to find out *for you*," she noted, with a little bitterness.

"It *is* your job," he reminded, coldly.

"I know," she acknowledged, allowing a small smile. "It has wasted a lot of time though."

"That's the PAI for you," he joked. "It must have felt good to give Slimy Snell a bit of beating though, mustn't it?" She smiled.

"O… he's been asking for it for *such a long time*," she concurred, still not satisfied.

"I'm sorry I couldn't have given you longer, but I was worried about you permanently damaging him," Randal quipped.

"It would be the closest thing to justice he would ever know," she muttered.

"You're probably right about that."

―――― ✦✦✦✦✦ ――――

"What was all that about?" Shannon asked, as Satiah returned.

"It's okay; I made a mistake, that was all. I had the wrong picture," she said. "It freaked me out a bit, I thought… *I don't know what I thought.*"

"I can imagine," Shannon allowed, forgivingly. "*Where were we?*" Satiah took a big gulp of her Golden Float.

"*Reminiscing.*"

"Yes," Shannon nodded, sadly.

"Malla was a very loyal person," said Satiah, out of nowhere. "He had nothing but good things to say about anyone. *Even Oli.* He didn't deserve to die like that in there." She would try to gently turn the subject around to Oli as, if Shannon actually was angel, it might be what she really wanted to talk about.

"Do you think… *whoever is trying to sabotage Oli*… died in the collapse too?" Shannon asked, eyeing her.

"It's a possibility," Satiah replied, carefully.

"So you don't think that." It was a statement this time, not a question. "*Me neither.*"

"*I don't know, Shannon,*" Satiah said, pretending to be struggling with her own emotions. "I wish I did. I don't think we have the kind of luck where they would be cut out of the picture so easily."

"I was thinking… Angello might be the man we're looking for," she said, seriously.

Angello was a Publishing Coordinator, working on Oli's campaign. He'd been around long enough to be the culprit, but it was too obvious. Satiah had discounted him on day one, yet it was interesting that Shannon had picked the only member of staff to have the name angel in their name. Even more interesting, considering that *she didn't know* the recipient of the messages was called angel. Was the real angel sitting there in front of Satiah, trying to divert her attention? Or was it just Shannon getting desperate and grabbing at straws? Still Satiah's instinct refused to accept Shannon as angel.

"*Really?*" Satiah asked, playing along. Who knows? Shannon might have seen something.

"He seemed very anxious all day, but then… I suppose we all were. And he had an argument with Kate and Oli about the size of the logo," she detailed, without conviction.

"An argument?" Satiah repeated, with observable intrigue.

"Well… *a discussion*, it wasn't *that* heated, but it was a bit tense. I think there was a question about a design that had already been approved or something," she explained. "Whatever, it led to an exchange…"

"I'll ask Kate about it, anyone else?" Satiah asked. Shannon shook her head, sniffed, and then buried her head in her arms. Her body was shaking with silent sobs. Satiah tried to comfort her.

"It will all be okay," she assured her, unsure exactly what to say for the best. Out of clues, out of suspects… angel remained as mysterious as he or she had at the start. That was when she got a call from Lunell.

"It's Lunell," she mouthed, taking it outside. Shannon, despite really wanting to listen in, stayed where she was. Satiah reached a walkway and stared out across the lights of the cityscape.

"Saying goodbye?" she asked, as she answered.

"Two things. First, I just wanted to say that I had *no idea* what Snell had done before with regard to *any* previous missions involving Oli McAllister," he stated, grimly. She scoffed silently to herself. Denying it seemed rather pointless. "And second, I know I have been pulled off this assignment. But… I have a lot of leave to use up and I have decided to stick around."

Satiah scowled. She'd seen this coming, naturally, but she'd hoped that she'd be wrong.

"*You're off the assignment*," she reminded, needlessly. "I would stay out of this if I were you."

"Well, *you're* not and we both know you wouldn't," he replied, without missing a beat.

"You cannot expect me to trust you or work with you," she retorted.

"Why would I? You haven't bothered so far," he pointed out. "How's it going with Shannon?"

"What did I just say?" she asked, irritated. Was selective deafness a qualification you needed to be part of the PAI?

"You can't handle this *all by yourself*," Lunell insisted. "You need me."

"Only about as much as the common cold," she retorted. "If I see you tomorrow…"

"*You'll do what*?" he growled, his tone suddenly savage. "Gun me down right in front of Oli? I doubt *even you* are *that* reckless." *Was that a challenge?* She restrained her competitive grin.

"You should already know by now I have other, *far more subtle*, ways of taking people down," she threatened, also allowing her temper to show.

"We could solve this if we work together," he snapped, infuriated by her.

"Work with the PAI? *After everything that Snell did*? I'm surprised you don't just resign," she argued, levelly.

"*I* had nothing to do with that," he bluntly objected. "In any case, you have no problem about what he did, you just don't like the fact that he never told us." *Us?* How dare he even use that word!

"And why should I believe that? Indeed, how can you *prove* that? I agree this assignment has gone nowhere fast, but now I know what the PAI have been doing in the background I'm not in the least bit surprised," she ranted.

He sighed and went quiet for a moment, obviously collecting himself.

"Well, I'll be there," he growled. "Whether you like it or not."

"Better watch your back then, huh?" she menaced, unintimidated. "This is your last chance to walk away."

"*Not going to happen,*" he replied, grimly. *Well, she'd tried.*

"In that case... I'll see you in the morning," she said, suddenly becoming cheerful and chirpy in manner. It might unsettle him. She disconnected, seeing no sense in continuing the conversation. Maybe Snell had ordered him to leave, maybe not - either way he was staying and would be trouble for her.

---

There was one more surprise in store for Satiah that night. She'd been expecting it, in the sense that it was a likely possibility, but nevertheless it was astonishing to hear.

"Mark's dead too. *Murdered.* They've activated an android to take his place," Randal told her. "In a way we were lucky, as Mark has little in the way of family or friends. It's an easier charade to play."

"Jinx?" she asked, sourly.

"Most probably," he replied. "There is some talk about it being down to a guy called Bayler, but..." She nodded.

"I wonder why he didn't bother to try for the whole suicide thing again," she reflected.

"There could be plenty of reasons," Randal said. "It's good news for us. It means three threats are down to two. Collorah and angel."

"They didn't get Collorah?" she asked, bleakly.

"You should have ended him there and then," Randal stated, unforgivingly.

"You know why I didn't," she replied. "I'm going to get some rest." She cut off and went back to the bedroom.

"No closer then?" Carl asked, as she snuggled up next to him. She shook her head.

"Watch this space though; we're just over half way there... I'm guessing we'll get a few days, maybe weeks and then, right before the result is in..." she trailed off, without needing to finish.

"I now totally understand why you have so many trust issues," he chuckled. She giggled.

"*Trust issues*? You sound like a student," she told him.

He turned the light out and pulled her close.

"What are you going to do?" he asked, in her ear. She didn't know but, for the first time, she didn't mind admitting it.

"I don't know yet," she murmured, already half asleep. "*Purpose... dictates... reaction...*" Carl listened as her voice slowly faded into sleep. Her breathing, deep and even, was all he could make out. He lay there wondering. Kelvin was fixed now so... what was her problem? Why didn't she just reactivate him? Deciding that he might be better off not knowing, having heard a few of her secrets already, he too slipped away into the oblivion of deep sleep.

───────✦✦✦✦✦✦───────

Week three. Day four. Another day, another new building to check, another blasted evacuation/extraction procedure to memorise! *What an exciting life she did lead.* Satiah arrived at her usual time and reported to Shannon. Shannon was now acting head of security so, in a way, it was fortunate that they had created better terms between them, albeit temporarily. Lunell was there, as he had promised.

"We lost seventy four in the collapsed building, that's including Malla and Cadel," Shannon said, with enforced dispassion.

"That's pretty much half the security team, and a third of Oli's campaign team," Satiah surmised, grimly. "Malla and I often discussed the pros and cons of bringing in extra hands. Now it looks as if we must." Shannon nodded.

"I found a company he'd been considering in his notes," she said, handing a computer to Satiah.

Satiah ran her eyes over it. Three-Stripe-Security. They had good recommendations and the name meant nothing to Satiah, so she presumed they were legit. She made a mental note to get Harrier to run a check on them at some stage.

"How many are you thinking of hiring?" Satiah asked her.

"How many do *you* think?" Shannon asked, sincerely. It was a bit of a dilemma. Too many people, strangers with unknown motivations, might be more trouble than they were worth. On the other hand, at least thirty were required to adequately protect Oli.

"One unit should be enough, depends what Oli has in mind," she said, ducking the question.

"How many in a unit?" Lunell wanted to know.

"Thirty," Shannon provided, after Satiah effectively blanked him. Shannon picked up on this; a blind person could have done, but she didn't know what she should do about it. She supposed she should get to the bottom of it and try to resolve it as quickly as possible. That was now part of her job.

Yet Satiah was now the only friend she had, ironically. Malla and Cadel were dead, and Oli… well, she still couldn't decide where she stood. After everything that had happened, she didn't feel she could victimise anyone. They'd all been through too much now. Shannon, despite the previous night's drinking, hadn't quite been able to overcome the feeling of impending doom that had been over her since the day before. Somehow they had been able to keep Oli alive against some impressive odds, but their luck had to run out eventually, her mind told her. It also told her that things could always get worse. A stray thought occurred to her, the kind scientists could most likely spot on their old fashioned motion-energy-encoding models, a thought about her future. The idea of Oli winning the election, however unlikely it seemed at that moment, and her having to watch and protect him for years.

She didn't know if she could live through years of this kind of pressure. It might destroy her… in more ways that one. Perhaps now was one of *those moments.* One of those epiphany-type, life-changing reflections that don't always arrive in time to do much about them. She made up her mind. She was quitting this job after the election and going to find something that didn't bring her this level of misery! She'd just have to ride it out until then.

"That *should be* plenty," Lunell said, with significance, "though our enemies have exceeded the *should be's* plenty of times so far."

"If it were down to me, I'd take Oli off world," Satiah remarked, sourly. "In fact, now the debate is over, staying here is not essential... *if it ever was.*"

"Oli wants to stay," Shannon stated, inflexibly. Satiah merely shrugged.

"*He always wants what is bad for him.*"

"Be that as it may, we have a job to do," Shannon snapped, without meaning to. "I..." She paused, forcing herself to calm down. "I'm sorry," she breathed, closing her eyes and sighing heavily. "Do you want me to go to him and try to persuade him to leave?" Satiah shrugged, like she couldn't care less.

"No," Lunell said, casually. "He needs to concentrate on his campaign right now; besides... it would not look good from his supporters' point of view."

"Since when should that matter?" Satiah argued. "We're talking about saving lives here. Maybe even our own. Just because slinking away might look bad, you think it warrants madness as an acceptable alternative?"

"*It's Oli's decision,*" Lunell smiled, knowingly.

"Lunell," Shannon asked, trying to be diplomatic, "would you mind running a quick check on everything?" Her way of making him leave was so transparent it was almost laughable. Whatever was going on between Lunell and Satiah, Shannon trusted Satiah the most now, and Lunell being there, saying annoying things, was clearly irritating Satiah and making what should have been a simple enough discussion difficult. Lunell gave her an eloquent look before nodding.

"*Absolutely,*" he remarked, his word loaded with all kinds of significance. He was contesting her leadership skills, telling her that he knew she was trying to get rid of him, and also implying he was smarter than she was, all at once. Both women watched him leave. As soon as the door closed, Shannon collapsed into a chair, almost exhausted by the conversation. Satiah continued to stand, seemingly unmoved and fresh as ever.

"What is it between you and Lunell?" Shannon asked, exasperated.

"I don't trust him," Satiah told her, completely honest for once. "And you shouldn't either."

"You think he…?" Shannon asked, her eyes widening.

"No, he's *not* the insider. As a matter of fact, I think he thinks *that you are*," Satiah responded, cunningly. "Why else would he challenge you like that?" Shannon scowled in incredulity.

"That's crazy," she stated, outright.

"Look at it from his point of view. You're about the only one left alive of the security management," she said. "No one else has proven culpable, so…" she didn't need to finish her sentence.

"*But it's not me!*" Shannon declared, incensed.

"*I* know that and *you* know that. This is why he and I are at odds right now. That, and the fact he keeps trying to make me look incompetent," she said, hiding her own snigger well enough. Shannon held her head in her hands. What the hell? Had she caused this earlier when she'd been trying to discredit Satiah?

"Don't you believe me?" asked Satiah as if hurt, piling on the pressure. Shannon looked at her.

"I do," she said. "I *know* you're not incompetent and I know that because of everything you have done since you got here. If I've ever been anything other than welcoming then I sincerely apologise." Satiah knew what was going on. Shannon was feeling the stress and, increasingly desperate and isolated, she was being forced to confide in her more and more. If only the apology, however heartfelt, had actually touched Satiah. It was too little, too late as far as she was concerned. Shannon had repeatedly tried to make her look bad. Had things been different and Malla still alive, Satiah had no doubt that Shannon would still be trying to bring her down.

"If I were you, I'd find a way of proving that you're not the insider to Lunell before he chooses to do something about it. I'm guessing the only reason he's not already confronted you about it is because he has no real proof," Satiah went on.

"How… *I know why he thinks it's me!*" Shannon stated, in sudden realisation. She told the story of the communal communicator again and then looked at Satiah.

"Is that why you were interested in what that was about last night?" Shannon asked, grim. Satiah had prepared for this.

"I knew Lunell had seen you there because you had told me you thought he was stalking you. As soon as you said his name, it confirmed to me that he'd started to suspect you as the insider. So when I asked you about it, I was more interested in what Lunell had been doing there in the first place, than I was about you being there. We all get thirsty from time to time."

"O…" she said, suddenly seeing her point. "So… what do you think he was doing there?"

"I think he might be getting desperate and was trying to incriminate you regardless of your innocence," Satiah shrugged. "Another reason why I wanted to speak to you, so you would have someone to help you corroborate your story."

"*What evidence could he possibly have?*" she groaned rhetorically, clinging to the lifeline that Satiah had prepared for her.

"It made sense, I already knew he'd run out of ideas," she replied, patting Shannon's shoulder. "It's nothing personal."

"And he's mad at you for defending me?" Shannon asked, for clarity. Wasn't it strange when fiction mirrored truth?

"That, and the fact we've had a few clashes over the way to run things around here, yes," Satiah answered. Shannon closed her eyes. The tension was like a living entity in that room. It could smash glass and make flowers wilt with a breath.

"I hate this job." That was, Satiah realised, one of the most honest things Shannon had ever said to her.

"Hire these guys," Satiah advised her. "Send them to me when they arrive, I will brief them. Tell Lunell to stay with Oli and Kate. Also, see if you can get an idea for the rest of the campaign schedule." Shannon nodded.

---

It was less than an hour before her shift was due to end and Satiah had one more thing to do. Harrier had come back to her about the security firm to deliver a squeaky-clean reputation and a history of reliability. The new team had arrived promptly, led by a tall gaunt man called Aaron. He had previously been a soldier, a mercenary and, rather bizarrely, a financial advisor before this job. His team had dispersed around the floor to take up their positions. Satiah entered Oli's new office where he, Kate and Lunell were. The discussion between Kate and Oli halted immediately as she moved over to the desk.

"Aaron and his deputy will be alternating between days and nights," she announced, formally. "They are reporting directly to me. I asked Shannon to distribute a rough outline of the up and coming campaign tasks. *That was this morning...*"

"Well, it's a bit complicated, Satiah," said Kate said uneasily. "We're not *entirely sure* what we're going to do yet, let alone when we're going to do it..."

"It doesn't have to be *gospel*, just a loose itinerary will do," Satiah replied, seriously. "I'll write it for you *if you like*, but we need to know these things."

"We've been talking about it all day," Oli explained, sighing. "Take a look at this."

He slid a computer over to her which was airing a program hosted by Deetee, going over the debate with a fine toothcomb. Sam's death was also mentioned.

"*How distressing*," she said, with a smile that didn't reach her eyes. "You're relying on the CNC to show you how well you did?"

"Look, we can't say what our next move is yet, never mind anything that comes after," Oli replied. Satiah decided to drop it. She knew enough about Aaron and his team to know that they wouldn't care so long as they got paid.

"Okay," she said, lightly. Kate and Oli shared a meaningful look. "Was there something else?"

"We were wondering if you had any ideas about where to go from here?" Kate asked, levelly.

"Yes, *any* input would be appreciated," Oli agreed, sighing. Satiah couldn't stop herself from eyeing Lunell as he stood there, darkening the doorway.

"What did you originally plan to do?" Satiah asked, wondering how to deal with this.

"We had a series of public appearances planned but…" Kate said, leaving it at that.

"I'm assuming you don't want to have another interview with Deetee?" she asked, unable to stop herself grinning.

"Not particularly," Oli replied, bluntly.

"It would just give Deetee more chances to making Oli look bad," Kate concurred. "His brother's death complicates things too. Especially because of that leaked document. This is bound to affect Oli's popularity. There was supposed to be one last…"

"So? *Follow the script*! Isn't there a script you have ready for just these sorts of situations?" Satiah replied, flustered and getting dangerously close to one of her volcanic rants. *"My brother's passing was not about me, although as I'm going to talk about its effect on my campaign, it will look like I think it's all about me, but I tell you it really isn't!* Look, I'm *just* a mercenary, Kate, I don't understand this stuff." Carl had called them 'volcanic' after she'd kicked off about politics one night. She remembered his words and they calmed her a bit. *Only a woman like her could make words sound as hot as magma.* "You owe it to your supporters to *do something* but *I've* no idea what. I'm just here to make sure no one else gets hurt, all right?"

"We will need another day before we can give you a rough plan," Kate said, shrugging. "We're still working on what to say if anyone asks us about the destruction of our headquarters." *No one will mention that, because no one knows that it was your headquarters*, Satiah wanted to scream at them. It had been suppressed, but they didn't know that, obviously.

"Okay," Satiah said, washing her hands of it. She couldn't force them, and it was nearly time for her shift to end, anyway. This was one of the few operations where she really could, in all good conscience, wander home and ignore some of it. "You've already met Aaron and his team, but you might want to think about introducing everyone at tomorrow morning's meeting?"

Oli and Kate nodded at that.

"You know, just so that *everyone knows everyone else*?" Satiah explained, to make it clear. "With new people around, infiltration is easier, so everyone *needs* to be on the look out for strangers." They nodded again. As she looked down at them looking up to her, she suddenly wanted to laugh. This was a man who wanted to rule the whole Coalition, and his most trusted advisor… and they were looking up at her now the way some of the youngest Phantom trainees did when they didn't know what to do. Gormless was not a word she often used yet, at that moment, she couldn't think of another one more appropriate for them. No wonder everyone had decided on Brenda: for all her naïve ideology, at least she knew good advice when she heard it.

Lunell was watching, his eyes gleaming expectantly. He thought she was going to use this as an opportunity to derail Oli completely. What would be the point? Oli McAllister was almost finished anyway. His brother's death seemed to have kicked him to rock bottom, despite his initial reaction to the news. They were hardly close, but what with everything else it had just been another blow to a badly flagging man. The silence extended as they both waited for her to say more.

"I'll see you both in the morning," she said, bearing her teeth in a tight smile.

She, not in the mood for any sort of pingle or argument with either them or Lunell, marched out without another word.

# Part Five

# The Hang Fire

"Good morning, my name is Sasha, in the headlines today..." Music began, steady and attention grabbing in style, just to get the viewers' pulses going. "Item one, elections *now and then*. Deetee takes us on a trip down memory lane and brings us a comprehensive chronicle of elections past and present. Item two, fuel costs set to rise again after deal between Eco and Kittinger folds. Item three, the probe into the probe into the vote rigging was launched today, although experts remain untroubled and doubtful of its necessity. Item four, in a sensational swing, in what may turn out to be the trial of the decade, Ro Tammer fires her own defence counsel and opts to represent herself in court. More on that later. First, we go to Deetee live outside the Mulac Building, *hi Deetee*."

"Thanks Sasha," Deetee smiled, nodding slowly. He gave his customary and rather dopey sounding laugh. He was indeed walking along one of the three famous high walkways, linking the three towers, and overlooking the top of Mulac Building. He maintained his dapper appearance and irritatingly upbeat manner. "As usual, there has been a lot of excitement, this is normal in an election, and *as usual* there has been controversy. Today I'm going to be talking to you about what *wasn't business as usual* this time around. First though, let's go back in time and consider what an election is really about." Light classical music began to play and next to him there appeared a deed type of document.

"Signed by nearly three thousand leaders, the Great Constitutional Charter of Democratic Liberties was sealed and first upheld to create the Earth Empire in 31977, over twenty six thousand years ago. While we no longer call ourselves an empire, many of the clauses and the statutes of this unique document remain as important today as they were when it was first written, the citizens' right to vote being just one of hundreds," Deetee went on, before walking out of the camera range like he was actually going somewhere. Next, he was standing in a literary facility with one of the keepers standing next to him. Before them, in a hermetically sealed glass container, the charter itself lay. For the purposes of the so-called *natural look*, Deetee and the keeper looked like they were already in the middle of a deep and captivating discussion.

"Wow, so what you're telling me is that you have *actually* touched this?" Deetee asked, acting enthralled and fascinated.

"Yes," chuckled the keeper, pleasant and quiet.

"What did it feel like?" Deetee said, before laughing at his own joke and waving it off as they had planned. "No, no, seriously… What does it mean to you? You know, to just reach out and touch a part of history?"

"Well, when I first started working here, I didn't actually believe it could be the real thing. I mean, for a document to have survived that long is maybe not so rare, but to have gone all that time without even being altered once is a lot rarer. That being said, we all know democracy is the thumping heart of our society. To be able to take care of this historic document on a daily basis really means something to me."

"It sure is a lot bigger when you get this close to it," Deetee nodded, with the same smile as always. "The images out there somehow don't do it justice, do they? So how exactly do you take care of it?"

"Well, I change the access codes every day, check that the equipment around it is functioning correctly and, once in a while, supervise a more thorough analysis. It's just the same as mostly everything else we have on display here," said the keeper.

"That's incredible! And how long does that take?" Deetee enquired, his expression never changing.

"About three minutes usually, assuming everything is okay."

"Three minutes, *that's fantastic*. You get to spend three minutes with this document, how does that feel?" Deetee asked next. Gradually lowering the average intelligence of the viewer was an art, and asking dumb questions was surprisingly effective.

"It's just *beyond* describing," the keeper answered, as he was supposed to. "Just knowing that all those people got together and created it to make life easier for everyone, out of the goodness of their hearts, is mind-blowing in itself. I often like to imagine being there as they signed it. The atmosphere must *really* have been something."

"No doubt," Deetee agreed, as he began to move away. "So as you can see, the past is pretty much the present and future all at once." *What did he just say?* "The first election within the Earth Empire saw riots, burning effigies, attempted assassinations and all sorts of mayhem, whereas today nothing like that happens. We have evolved to form an unequalled example of democracy. Now, I'm not saying we're perfect, but we're getting better all the time. Let's take a little look at the last election."

Deetee, now seated at a desk, held up a picture of Balan Orion, the previous Commandment Benefactor - the tyrant who was assassinated and whose body was later stolen by people unknown for reasons unknown. Deetee didn't mention that though.

"A member of the Traditionalist National Party, Balan was a born diplomat of considerable courage and inspiring leadership," Deetee said, skipping over the truth without a shred of shame. "He often championed underdogs such as the elderly and the unemployed. He was a gifted debater, proving time and again his lucidity and firm grasp of the subjects in question. If he had a fault, which everyone must have obviously, it could only have been that he was too compassionate. Nevertheless, all good things must come to an end. At the time, the Coalition was under economic pressures virtually unseen before, and Balan knew this had to be addressed.

"So his campaign was mainly centred on big investments in new trading deals. He knew, right from the word go, that if nothing changed, then there was a strong chance that the Coalition might go into recession. A depression of a depression, if you will. His strategy lay in getting the right people around the table to talk about the future. It was a time of reform, after all. But what about the man *on the inside*? Who was Balan Orion really? To answer that, we're going to have to take a look at where he came from, how he grew up and, most importantly, how his upbringing turned him into such a powerful leader."

Next, Deetee was standing next to a woman in an administrator's uniform.

"Can you sum up Balan Orion in one word?" he asked her. She pulled a face, emphasising how difficult that would be.

"Challenging," she settled on, as rehearsed. They laughed together for a moment. "No, I don't think that's possible. I worked with him for about six years, on and off. He was a dignified man but he had a heart of gold. But, just like a lot of people, without his morning brew, he couldn't get a lot done."

"It's interesting that, once you become someone *that prominent*, more and more people seem to forget *that you're just like them*, don't they?" Deetee went on.

"Fame has a way of making that happen," she agreed.

"When he first joined the party, I heard that something funny happened," Deetee asked, his smile somehow growing. "Can you elaborate?"

The woman smiled back. "Well, it happens a lot more than people think, but when you're initiated into the party, you have to wait outside until someone lets you in. That day, the man who was supposed to let Balan in was absent due to sickness, and... well, we sort of forgot he was there," she explained, giggling. "He waited I think for about two hours, and it was just as we were coming out from session that someone noticed him... and the rest is history."

"So he was a patient man too?" Deetee laughed. She shrugged.

"Polite," she amended, as she was supposed to.

"So, on that day, where had he come from? What was his background?" Deetee asked, sounding interested.

"Balan was born on Raindrop, a planet that has a bit of history when it comes to prominent politicians. Balan included, nearly ninety Commandment Benefactors were born there," she began, launching into the script. "It has both beaches and universities that are famous galaxy wide. Balan was born as one of twins and, despite a relatively unremarkable childhood, he excelled as a young businessman. He got involved with shares and his community government. He was quick to race up the ranks and, decades later, he became president of the planet."

"Did he always intend to run for Commandment Benefactor?"

"Yes, I think so. He was driven to succeed."

"How would you say this election compares with the last?" Deetee asked.

"Well, it's hard not to take a broad view but we're in a very different place politically now than we were then. I suppose you could say the campaigns were run in two main camps last time around. You had two different solutions to the same problem. This time around, it was more about trying to stay on the same road and not lapse back into indecision. Balan ran with a view to *improving* the economy in the long term, while still protecting the core business model. His opponent, Torkmire the Fourth, was an advocate of more short term fixes and continued cut backs. I'm guessing that that might have been why we had a landslide vote. The people were tired of the procrastination."

"I see what you mean."

"This time around it's a little less clear cut. Brenda is Unionist Coalition Party, so she's more liberal and has a much softer style than Balan had. I must say her campaign has been a masterpiece from its beginning, to where we are now. She has actually had much more solid opposition than Balan had too, so it's been interesting to watch. Much more work to do, but she's coped phenomenally well, considering the enormous pressure she's under. It's a bit of a dirty topic right now but Pluto Major, though largely overlooked in the debate, has been a major thorn in her side. Still, she tends to sit back and answer questions, whereas Balan would grandstand about what he intended to do regardless of specific enquiries. In the end though, it's just two ways of doing the same thing.

"The opposition in both cases has been soundly trounced. Balan had, and Brenda has, sizeable majorities in the proportional representation. I'll just show you the figures while you're here. Brenda is comfortable now at sixty-eight percent. Hardly a landslide, but definitive enough for a concrete victory. I know there's always the chance everything could change on the last day, but that's never happened before and I don't see it happening this time either. Balan enjoyed a ninety six percent majority when he got into office. So, as you can see, the numbers are vastly different, but more people have voted this time than last time, so that makes a difference too."

"According to my research, things have been largely consistent after the Common Protectorate War," Deetee noted.

"That's true," she agreed. "That was a time of great political upheaval."

Back in the same office as before, Deetee stared into the screen, trying to look intuitive.

"We are in a unique position where we can look back on so many elections where a lot of people were concerned that betting syndicates were manipulating them. Analysts often tell us that an election can be more lucrative than a whole year of business as usual. Certainly more money changes hands in that time per second than at almost any other. In order to get to the bottom of this I am going to have to see an expert." Stock footage of him walking down a corridor purposefully was used, as he said that last sentence to give the impression of real movement. "I'm going to meet a professor of statistical analysis, he's been watching electoral rolls for years… if anyone knows the truth about this, it's him."

"Morning," Deetee smiled.

"Morning," replied the stern faced man.

"I just wanted to ask, before we start, where these theories came from?" Deetee asked, feigning mystification. The man removed his visual aids from his eyes, folded them neatly in two, and regarded Deetee the way a teacher might a promising student.

"The truth is that there are always rumours of this kind of corruption," he replied. "They are groundless, of course; there is no chance that any of them are really workable. In order for the syndicates to alter an election in any way, they would require too many people working with them. It simply would never happen; it's not realistic that it wouldn't be noticed."

"Isn't it true though that millions of people are betting on the outcome of the election before it even starts?" Deetee asked, his tone one of malignant disapproval.

"There is no law against doing that; in any case, it would be impossible to enforce. A little flutter is harmless enough. The only hypothetical danger is if the syndicate wants to improve their own odds of winning unlawfully. That's the danger most people are worried about. Like I said, though, it's improbable."

"Would you say that syndicates are powerless to affect the outcome?" Deetee asked, outright.

"Absolutely, the whole idea is a bit ludicrous. A good plot for a work of fiction, perhaps, but it doesn't stand up for one moment in reality."

"Ah, but what about the Songuary Institute?" Deetee asked, as if he had unleashed something really serious. The man shrugged.

"That was a one off. Besides, that institution wasn't a betting syndicate, it was a fraternal organisation made up of individuals in key positions and, most importantly of all, *they got caught*. Their plan to alter the votes by hacking into the computer system was as poorly executed as it was conceived. It was the kind of thing you can imagine them cooking up one evening at a particularly riotous party. Apparently, law enforcement was watching them the whole time," he answered, as planned. Deetee laughed.

"Some people copy others, so the public will always see it as a danger, no matter how unlikely," he pointed out.

"Technically, it is," the expert shrugged. "This is why whole departments are set up precisely to counter schemes like this."

Back to the Mulac Building again.

"You see, some people just love the smell of a bit of collusion, it adds drama to what could be a rather dull event. The young particularly are often the biggest group of voters that can't easily be predicted. Older people tend to campaign for a certain stability with regard to keeping things the same. Young people are all about change, but they never seem to be able to agree on which change. This is why they are the political equivalent of a wild card in the Gairunn deck. Often the young are seen as uneducated or deluded when it comes to politics and are dismissed by older voters as such. Yet, if you're just counting who says what, then they are no different from anyone else." The scene changed to a walkway somewhere on the planet.

"What do you think of Brenda Watt?" Deetee asked, thrusting the microphone into a teenager's face.

"Who?" she asked, confused. Deetee faced the camera and pulled a cringing face. He then approached another.

"Brenda Watt?" the male responded, considering. He looked a bit shifty for a moment, before smiling nervously. "Yeah, she's the best." Deetee looked directly into the camera again and this time he shrugged in a *'well, what can you do?'* sort of way.

"It took me a while, but on the edge of a college campus, I bumped into this guy," Deetee continued. "What do you think of Brenda Watt?"

"She came across really strongly in the debate," the teen answered, thinking about it. "I got the impression that underneath all the pomp and everything, she's a nice person."

"There, now *that* was a little better," Deetee said, once again in his office. "I'm not going to tell you how many people I had to ask before I got that last response, but I still say it is unfair to paint all youths with the same brush. Uninformed they may be, but they are still a crucial factor in the election process. However, now we have to think about a different question: how can we tell if someone votes more times than they legally have the right to? To answer that question, I'm going to meet another administrator." Deetee walking down another corridor. He presses the control pad next to the door at the end.

"Come in, Deetee," says a woman's voice. Deetee pulls a slightly amazed looking face at the camera. *O my, how did she know it was me?*

They greeted one another and Deetee sat opposite her.

"How can you tell if someone votes unlawfully?" he asked, casually.

"We have several methods of checking," she answered, smiling indulgently. "Virtual footprints are the most common way we can see who has said what and when."

"But what if they use *someone else's computer* to do it?" Deetee was quick to challenge.

"We can still trace that, and the AI is smart enough to know who is who," she told him. "It's been tried many times before, but the culprits are always found out and punished. It may not sound like a big deal to some, but it is an offence, and fines are only one of the many sentences that…"

There was not an eye roll in existence that was strong enough, or capable of, conveying the level of boredom she was feeling right then, Zax was sure. Standing by the screens she was exercising at, she worked up a sweat battering the stuffing out of a punch bag. Which is sadder? Not being able to watch something and simply enjoy it? Or only being able to see what someone else wants you to see? The more she watched programmes like this, the more she understood why Satiah got so angry sometimes. It was all just a huge, elaborate smokescreen. Please kill me now, Zax thought as she switched it off.

## Part Six

# The Closest Thing To Justice

Week six, day two. Rain hammered on the windows of the apartment, making a ceaseless sound that vaguely resembled white noise. It was early, shortly after dawn, and Satiah had just completed her exercise routine. It would be at least two hours before she had to leave for work and, now that she'd washed, she couldn't just sit there and wait. She knew Ash was coming. He'd called her the previous evening and she'd told him he could meet her in the morning. Gracious of him, she'd reflected, she had thought he'd suddenly turn up unannounced to try to catch her out. He'd not said anything about the book at all, despite her questioning him. She was just grateful that he was bringing it back. Obsenneth was in its usual place - her flight jacket pocket. Her jacket was inside a thick metallic crate, in a corner of the tiny room opposite the bathroom and across from the bedroom. Storage was what she mainly used it for, but for now it served another purpose.

She hoped Ash wouldn't sense it. She'd taken other precautions too because, as anyone would, she'd fathomed that putting it in a thick box might not be enough. She'd alerted Obsenneth to Ash's arrival and told it to do whatever it could to hide itself. She'd acquired a generator and activated it to create a separate power source, which she hoped might distract or confuse Ash. It was in the same room, already running quietly. He was an immortal and she didn't really know the extent of his powers and... who was she trying to kid? She had no idea what he was capable of. In case these precautions were still not adequate, she'd decided to temporarily invest in something she'd never used before and knew very little about.

Harrier had been helpful by providing her with this special something: an Empirical Wave Extinguisher, otherwise known as an EWE. Rare and expensive, it was strictly on loan to her. Absolutely had to be back before the end of the week… mainly because no one knew it had gone yet. She'd not stolen anything, she'd just borrowed it for a while. Used in specialised laboratories and occasionally in medical facilities, the device was able to create a void in mental energy for as long as it had power to do so. In effect, it could make someone's mind go completely blank. They would become a zombie, completely unaware, almost as if they were in a coma. No memory, no self-awareness, and no consciousness. Their bodies would shut down instantly as the mind no longer told them to breathe, no longer told the heart to beat… silence. Anyone being worked on would have to be on a life-preserving machine before the EWE was activated.

Why would someone ever want to wipe another's mind completely? Well, a couple of reasons are instantly there. If they had seen something they shouldn't have, or learnt something they shouldn't have, and all other methods of erasing this have failed… also, in some strange medical conditions such as certain forms of mental instability, it might be necessary to use it. Once the machine is turned off, assuming the body has been sustained by external means, everything returns. The subjects would be themselves and completely unharmed. They would have no memory of the experience either. How could they? All of this was technically on the secret list, but Satiah had come up with a theory on how it could help her. She had set up the machine to affect the inside of the crate where Obsenneth was hiding, the idea being to create a void, if you will, of all cerebral energy in its near vicinity. Ash wouldn't be able to read it if it effectively wasn't there, right? She hoped not. She worried that there might be a slight danger that the EWE may affect Obsenneth itself and somehow kill it, but Obsenneth had assured her that there was no danger of that.

"O well, it's your life," she'd muttered, as she'd slammed the lid down on Obsenneth. "Don't say I never warned you."

She went through a quick mental list. Obsenneth in crate, crate sealed, generator on, EWE active, Carl asleep in bed and, maybe most importantly of all… her own mind ready to defend itself. Hiding Obsenneth would be a waste of time if Ash somehow took her over and learned everything that way. She had no extrasensory abilities whatsoever. No telepathy, no telekinetic powers and a very bad sense of humour. She didn't know if that made her more or less vulnerable to Ash but she'd researched how to avoid being hypnotised in the hope that the key to resisting his mind lay somewhere there. She saw them approaching on the cameras, Ash with Ruby this time too. Satiah wondered why Ruby was with him on this little visit. She got the room ready and waited, pistol in her holster just in case.

She tapped on the screen of her computer to stop it from fading into the darkness of rest-mode. She put her boots up on the table, adopting a pose of polite disinterest. She didn't want to give Ash any clues as to what she was thinking or feeling. She hoped this would work… if it didn't she wasn't sure what would happen. If he really could see into her mind then this psychological charade was pointless. Ruby would be easily fooled either way and maybe, if she was desperate, she could use Ruby against him. He cared for Ruby for whatever reason, and that was his weakness. Maybe his only weakness. And she had Carl… She steeled herself emotionally, preparing herself for Ash to try to trick or unbalance her. There was a bleep at the door. They were outside.

"Hi Satiah!" It was Ruby talking. "It's us, are you there?" Satiah opened the door, using the control pad on the arm of the chair next to her.

"Morning," she said, rather coldly. "Refreshment?"

Ash and Ruby halted on the threshold of the room Satiah was sitting in. Satiah noted that Ruby was carrying a bag over her shoulder. The book?

"Yes please," Ruby smiled happily, as Ash answered to the negative. Satiah raised her eyebrows. "Just for me," Ruby clarified, after exchanging glances with Ash. They moved fully into the room and sat in the chairs opposite Satiah.

Satiah rose and strolled into the kitchen area. Everything totally comfortable and normal... honest. Ash was actually checking the place out while looking like he wasn't. His mind searched and searched in vain. Where was it? That power he had sensed before...

"I really wish they would find a way of making that troposphere purer without the rain," Ruby complained, making enforced conversation. She was most likely trying to take Satiah's attention away from Ash. That must be why he'd brought her along... a distraction. Satiah delivered the drink to Ruby with what passed for a warmish smile, before sitting down opposite them.

"Any luck?" Satiah asked, getting straight to it. There was no sense in prolonging this with pretences of sociability. Ash, who had been staring into space, a look of concentration etched on his face, made rapid eye contact with her. Satiah felt something in her mind, like a soft prod in the skull. He was trying to see in there, trying to find her secrets. She relaxed and didn't fight it, thinking that he was expecting her to fight him and therefore he would be ready for that.

Instead, she thought about things that made no sense. Babble of an intellectual sort, in other words. Anything she could think of, from well-known paradoxes, and rainfall in reverse, to nursery rhymes. *If I were to tell you that the next thing I say will be true but that the last thing I said was untrue, would you believe me? I am lying to you, everything I say is false.* He stared harder, seeming to be straining now. She could feel him, almost pressing against her - it was actually quite unpleasant, like someone staring at you while you are unclothed.

"Satiah?" Ruby asked, trying to get her attention away from Ash. They were obviously working together. "Did you hear what I just said?"

*You can accumulate money by spending it. The only rule is that there are no rules. The only thing I can't resist is temptation.*

"Rain..." Satiah whispered, so intent on thinking about random nonsense that she could hardly speak. She could feel the beginnings of a sweat on her forehead.

"Yes, the rain," Ruby said, a little nervous now. She knew that Satiah was aware of what was going on and she was really starting to wish she'd not let Ash talk her into this.

I know that I know nothing.

"You wish it would stop..." Satiah managed, still running through a mental obstacle course. No one goes to that place, it's too crowded. Then, just as she thought she'd run out of energy, and she was on the verge of fainting, she thought she heard Reed's voice. It had the quality of the whispery voice of someone's last breath. She didn't know how she knew it was him but she did. Was it memory? Was it actually him talking to her somehow?

What was he saying? Mirror his mind Satiah: think his thoughts as if they were your own. If you were Ash, what would you be thinking? Satiah grasped what he meant instantly, despite the fact that she couldn't remember him ever saying that to her in her life. She would, instead of tiring herself out trying to lose Ash in thinking about gibberish, only think about what Ash was thinking about. She tried to wonder what he, the son of Dreda, was thinking about. She saw stars in deep space, the ravages of time, and the corrosion of distortion... it was a whole new level of frightening, even for her, but she persevered. Ruby was dying, she was ageing, she wouldn't live forever like him, and that was why she was so precious to him. Satiah made an image of Ruby's face in her mind. She began to make it age, and then she pushed the image back at Ash...

Ash let out a sigh and looked away, apparently giving up. Satiah made no sign of how relieved she was. Or how tired. That had been exhausting. She had a lot of questions about it, but she knew she had to keep going. Act normal.

"Well, not forever," Ruby continued, a little more at ease. "Just while I'm walking about in it... this drink is delicious, by the way."

"Any luck?" Satiah repeated, more firmly this time. Ash regarded her as if he couldn't decide what to say. He turned to Ruby and gave her a nod. She brought the book out of her bag and placed it on the table.

"What if I told you that I was sorry and that I had not managed to make any progress, and perhaps it's simply the balderdash it looks like?" Ash asked, his scrutiny back on her. Again, Satiah was quick to think only about what he was thinking as she answered... which was very hard to do.

"I would be disappointed," she said, a little stiffly.

"Why do you keep doing that?" Ash suddenly asked her, clearly losing patience. Ruby now looked a bit worried as she realised that somehow Satiah was giving Ash trouble.

"What are you talking about?" Satiah replied, innocently. There was a pregnant pause.

"It's a lovely apartment," Ruby uttered, uneasily. "How long have you lived here?"

"Long enough," Satiah said, almost snapping at her. "Ash, did you translate that thing or not? Eight words, all but one consisting of only one syllable. It's a simple enough question, even for you." A flash of anger occurred briefly in his eyes, but he kept control. He didn't like being criticized by humans. He knew she was just trying to manipulate him, but that didn't make it easier for him to resist ranting at her about how humans were ruining everything.

"Where did you say you found the book?" he asked, casually. She'd not told him before, but only because she hadn't known where it had come from herself.

"I didn't," she replied, honestly. She didn't bother to ask again, Ash already knew what she wanted. She instead sipped her drink, the very soul of indifference. What next? Check her fingernails for dirt she knew wasn't there? Ruby, now very uncomfortable, was staring imploringly at Ash. She really didn't want to be there. That was one thing she and Satiah had in common at that moment. Ash was again looking all around the room, not even bothering to hide the fact that he was searching for something.

"Can I help?" Satiah asked, eyeing him in a way that implied she was starting to think he was becoming ill. One final time, Ash regarded her, trying to see into her mind. Pleased to have found something that effectively dissuaded him, she just thought about what he was thinking about again. She knew she could affect him by showing him Ruby as a corpse, but she didn't go that far this time. She just focussed on reflecting what his own eyes saw.

"I'm sorry," he said. "I was just thinking."

"I know," she said, with a creepy smile. He saw the look and smiled back. *Uh oh. He knows. He just won't force it for whatever reason. Maybe Ruby being there was a good thing, after all.*

"It's an instruction manual on the maintenance and construction of a device beyond your understanding," Ash told her, flatly. Satiah sipped her drink again, gaining more time to think about that and what she would say next. By his use of the word your, she understood that Ash was referring to humans in general, not her specifically.

"This device - is it located somewhere in the Satmarrick constellation?" she enquired, lightly. Another brief flash of something in Ash's countenance meant she might have guessed right.

"What gave you that idea?" he asked, as if baffled. He knew the answer to that too. See! We humans are smarter than you think! You may be the son of Dreda but I am a good Phantom agent.

"O, you should know us humans well enough by now, Ash, sometimes we just get ideas out of nothing," she replied, carefully. Don't get overconfident, don't overplay this, she told herself repeatedly, that's what he wants me to do.

"No, it's not, the book doesn't give its location," Ash told her. Another mistake, he'd revealed it still existed.

"So this device exists then, does it?" she deduced, smartly.

"The only thing I can say for sure is that it might once have existed," Ash replied, not giving anything more away. Satiah nodded knowingly. Perhaps it had been a mistake to involve Ash, and not just because of Obsenneth.

She moved to take the book, and Ruby reached out to grab it too. They each grasped it at the same moment. Satiah glared at Ruby. Ruby smiled shakily before meekly releasing her grip on it.

"How interesting," Satiah said, watching Ash closely. "Thank you for looking into this for me. How exactly did you translate it?"

"There are some questions that we immortals cannot answer," Ash replied, mysteriously.

"Can't or won't?" Satiah asked, arching an eyebrow at him.

"My advice to you would be to report back to your superiors and tell them that you have failed to gain any insight into that book," Ash stated, all formal suddenly. "It's not worth them investigating further." Really?

"Come on, you can do better than that," Satiah goaded, confidently.

"I can but I won't," Ash stated, standing. "Thank you for your time, Phantom Satiah." Ruby also stood but Satiah remained where she was, staring intently at them. Ruby wouldn't look at her, not directly. Ash, however, was fearless and even derisive as he glared into her brown eyes.

"...It was a pleasure," she said, finally. Ash had said all he was going to and, as lucky as she'd been in being able to evade his mind reading abilities, she knew she couldn't force him to do anything. The door opened for them and they walked back out into the corridor beyond. The door closed and Satiah stared at the wall in silence as she thought about it more. Slowly she picked up the book and flicked ponderously through it once more.

---

"So?" Ruby asked, in a pantomime whisper. "What did you learn?" They were in the lift, descending towards the ground floor.

"Very little, unfortunately," he admitted, with a groan. "She was resisting me and I couldn't do anything more without hurting her. Her mental barriers were stronger than I remembered... I was almost through, then something else, something stronger, interfered. She had been preparing herself for me, of that much I'm sure. In any case... whatever it was that she's found had either gone, or had been hidden... knowing Satiah it's in all probability hidden. I know I didn't imagine it last time, and her mind gave away to me that something was indeed there to be sensed. Something of great and terrible power. Something no mere human should be playing with. It seems I was right to make a copy of that book after all." They shared a look.

"Okay, you were right!" she scoffed, pouting. "I was wrong! Happy?"

"Not particularly," he answered, honestly.

"Do you think she will do what you suggested?" Ruby asked, next. "About reporting a no-no to her superiors?"

"No," he replied, shortly. "Not for a second."

---

Since the destruction of Oli's second campaign headquarters, he and his team had been placed under the direct protection of Commandment Benefactor Brenda Watt. Until the election was over, technically she wasn't actually the Commandment Benefactor, but she was the only one who had command of such extensive resources. Interestingly, since moving into the complex otherwise known as The Grand Bulwark of the Coalition Assembly, there had been no further attempts on Oli's life. Not even one? He was pretty secure in there as it was one of the most heavily guarded locations in the universe. The Guard of the Benefactor were barracked across the square, an elite unit of former Gushtapar troops who protected the Commandment Benefactor personally. They were unmistakable in their latest red and bronze uniforms. There were never more than one hundred of them, but there never needed to be. Brenda was secretly terrified of them, even though they were there expressly to protect her (or whoever the Commandment Benefactor was).

The Grand Bulwark of the Coalition Assembly dwarfed almost every other individual structure on Earth. It was over fifteen times larger than the Mulac Building, its rather aged antecedent, and had until recently been decorated in the style of the emblem of the Human Coalition: light green lines, wavy and overlapping, with the occasional three golden stripes. Upon the insistence of many, including Brenda herself, in the name of the new Coalition, a new emblem was chosen. Three jagged lines of red, separated neatly by thin lines of elegantly regal bronze. Flags of this design flapped in the wind in hundreds of spots all over the twelve towers. Eleven smaller towers acted as a ring, encircling the largest in the centre. A huge ball of brightness burned in the air above the highest tower's triple spired summit: its energy screen. Constantly active, it was the first line of defence and formed a glowing orb for all to see, an aesthetically pleasing gesture of power in the guise of elaborate decoration.

Unlike before, the new emblem was instantly adopted by mostly everything from warships to documents. It was a way of moving on and helping everyone to forget about the Vourne conspiracy. It had even made its way onto the official Phantom dress uniforms. The new look gave Reef Tower, the large one in the middle which was named after an epic underwater battle on a missing and possibly fictional planet, a brand new and imposing appearance. Brenda, the first person to enter after the redecoration work, stared in awe at her new home. Her aide hovered next to her as always, also looking around in wonder.

"T-t-they really did themselves p-proud this time," Brenda was saying, gaping up at the ceiling.

"…Yeah," the aide said, staring up almost dumbly too. The whole place looked a lot like the interior of some kind of giant basilica. No, a super-cathedral. So much pride in every curve, every illustration… it was breathtaking to behold.

"I'll never be able to do speeches in h-here," Brenda giggled. "Well… I would need a b-blindfold. I just want to stare and stare." The architecture was indeed superb. It would have to be to outdo the Mulac Building.

"I bet it's really draughty," the aide muttered, turning her attention to the polished marble floor. It was so well done; she could see her own face reflected in the floor. She let out a sigh and smiled. It was hard not to believe the golden age myth that was growing around Brenda lately. Everything fresh, new and impressive looking. An economy expanding and soaring interest rates. Unparalleled since the times before the Common Protectorate War.

"Excuse me, I have a call," Brenda said, touching her earpiece. She wandered a few paces away, her heels clipping crisply as she went and the aide turned her back respectfully.

"O… D-Dohead, how are you?" The aide looked out of the window, a four storey high pane of reinforced glass. She could see right out across the cityscape; though Earth was known galaxy wide for such views, this had to be one of the more remarkable ones. Certainly one of the rarer ones, as public access to the Bulwark was restricted.

"O, no, Oli is fine. No, I've not spoken to him; I was giving him space to deal with the sad passing o-of his brother…. why yes!" Brenda giggled. "No… No, I don't know i-i-if I've won yet… where are you? Sounds like quite a party… a beer festival? Is that still going on, it's been weeks? O, that's nice of him to r-remember, tell Reed I hope he is positive…" She laughed again. "What's h-he doing in the thermal spring? …Okay… yes, I will see you soon."

The aide turned to face Brenda again.

"Everything okay?" she asked.

"Yes, i-i-it's good to see that not everyone in the Coalition is completely preoccupied by the politics of this election," Brenda smiled, cheerful. The aide subtly checked her communicator, which was connected to Brenda's and observed that, for some reason, the call had failed to record. That meant she couldn't listen to it later. Odd.

"Who was it?" she asked, genuinely curious.

"Dohead Rens, he s-sometimes takes care of a few legal things for me," she smiled, flushing ever so slightly.

"The Dohead Rens? That famously eccentric lawyer?" the aide confirmed, a little surprised.

"He's n-not an eccentric," Brenda said, a little defensively. "He's lovely." The aide realised she'd never seen Brenda look quite like that before. The aide also realised that Brenda had practically swooned.

"And famous," the aide smiled, shrugging. "I didn't know you knew him."

"Him and his friend Reed," Brenda went on. "The pair of them are as m-mad as each other. Guess where they have been this entire election?"

"A beer festival?" the aide guessed, quizzically. Brenda nodded.

"P-pair of lunatics," she sighed gently, and with great fondness.

"Five days, ma'am," the aide reminded, sensing that Brenda was weary of the election. Who wasn't? "Five days more and you will, at last, be legally, officially… finally, universally recognised as Commandment Benefactor of the Coalition. In the meantime, it's important the public can see you being active. Do you have any suggestions?"

"You're asking *me*? What about the schedule?" Brenda asked, baffled.

"Completed," the aide shrugged. "We're miles ahead, but it goes against the grain to stop now. The navy have voiced concerns about the growing number of warships and activity of the Federation. Apparently Admiral Wester has given his Captains permission to chase pirates anywhere… even into our territories."

"Very well, I will s-speak to them," she smiled, with a sigh.

He was going to lose the election, he knew it. He'd already lost so much. Malla, Cadel, his own brother... and Oli knew they weren't the only things that he had lost in this race. His pride, his self-respect, and his faith in humanity. He'd sunk down in depression before, but never this far. All because of this race. This race that many would say he needn't have bothered running. Why did he bother, it was always a forgone conclusion? Oli looked out across the office, now not so full and certainly not so enthusiastic. Did they blame him? Everyone there – friends, colleagues or acquaintances -had lost something or someone too. He hadn't set out for those things to happen, but that somehow didn't equate too well against all that death and disaster. You'd have to be a monster not to feel some responsibility.

All this, and he still knew very little of the truth. He'd not been told that his own brother had been behind some of those attempts on his life. He didn't know that he'd never stood a chance of winning in the first place. He didn't know that this whole thing had been planned. He didn't know that Mark had been replaced by an android to cover up the fact that he was dead. The idea that he was just a minor distraction for those who were really in charge never entered his wildest nightmares. All he could see was the damage. The damage to himself and the hurt done to others. Satiah's words came back to haunt him. It's so sad. To know that you're responsible for this. Everyone was avoiding him. Satiah refused to so much as greet him if they passed one another in the corridor. Shannon, too, was keeping her distance. Kate had been kind and understanding at first, but his inability to focus any more, and his tendency to dwell on depressive thoughts, had finally driven her away too.

He had one final interview with Deetee scheduled. An epitaph, the media had jokingly and somewhat hurtfully named it. He'd even seen images of a memorial stone, with his name and the dates of his presidency on it, being banded around as personal messages. People could be so unnecessarily unkind sometimes, to say nothing of those still out there trying to kill him. The deluge of freezing rain outside was doing nothing for his mood either. Indeed, it acted as an unwanted metaphor and reminder of his own washed out feeling. Win or lose? His only real desire was that it would all be over.

Satiah had wanted him to promise never to run again. At the time he thought it was because she'd wanted to hurt him. She did - and it had - but now he could see that maybe she'd had another reason. The price of ambition was too much to make all this a fair exchange for a man of good conscience. Power remained the evil masquerading as the necessity it always was. He knew he didn't want power for power's own sake, he wanted it to make things better - but the toll it exacted, even before he'd acquired it, was too much. Had Satiah known this? Was her hurtful ultimatum actually a way of protecting him from himself? It was impossible for him to know. All he could think about was Sally's face.

---

"I'm going to have to disappoint you, Harrier," Satiah said, for once sticking to the speed limit. She was on her way into work. The rain was making everything difficult. "I have made a little progress with the book; however, I can only discuss it with Rainbow. When is he back?"

"Ah…" he said, the wind taken from his sails. Becalmed.

"Furthermore, I suggest you put it back in the vault where it will be safer," Satiah went on. She didn't think Ash would try to steal it from her, but then he was an immortal and did not care about law or humans in the same way most other people did. "Now, any progress on our mystery insider yet?"

"No more messages, unless Zax has found something, it's been well over a week now and we still have nothing," he reported. "I don't know why, but I get the feeling that whoever it is might have moved on."

"It's a possibility," she allowed, not thinking that herself. "We, however, do not have that luxury. We stay, and keep going until this election is over. Stay vigilant, Collorah is still out there, regardless of angel, and he will come at us again if he thinks he can get at us." She disconnected. Over the last week or so, she and Collorah had been playing cat and mouse throughout the city. Satiah, of course, was playing the part of the cat, being the one who did all the chasing. She was trying to find him and drive him out, that being a much more effective strategy than simply waiting for him to strike. Zax had buried herself deep in financial data, seeking anything that might look like Collorah was receiving monies. She had little or no chance of finding him, but someone had to try. She'd also followed his known associates and sought out people that typically hired him or his rivals. She had a list of over one hundred names and was gradually eliminating them. Satiah hadn't disturbed her.

Satiah pulled into the entrance lane and a light began to flash as she was scanned. She eyed the Repressor, still on the backseat. Would they notice that? As she moved forward into an entrance area, thankfully out of the rain, two men approached and one knocked on her window. She lowered it. Dressed in the new red and bronze, she recognised both men as Guards of the Benefactor. Brenda's personal soldiers. This man was clearly an officer too, as he sported a Captain's insignia. She braced herself, wondering what this would be about.

"Is that yours, Phantom agent Satiah?" the man asked, his voice low. He was pointing to the weapon on her backseat.

"Yes," she growled, leaning back in her seat. She sighed, expecting a protracted argument. She was pleasantly surprised when the man smiled and raised an eyebrow.

"I'm sure it's safe enough in your hands, ma'am," he said, stepping back. "In you go."

She stared back at him, gaping in incredulity.

"You're just going to let me...?" she enquired, unable to believe her luck.

"We all serve the Coalition here," the man said, unconsciously standing to attention. "My men have been informed of your purpose at this juncture, and have been told to give you any assistance you require." She stopped talking and nodded, thinking how incredibly sensible that was. *Makes a change!* He pointed to the weapon again with a grim smile.

"With that thing, ma'am, I doubt you will need us though," he added, as a joke.

She smiled, deciding she quite liked this man, and wondered if all of this new guard were of the same mind. Indeed, it made a pleasant variation when compared with departments like, say… the PAI.

"We will see," she permitted, shrugging lightly. "So are your men here all the time?"

"Two hour shifts, wherever Brenda is we are. She's just moved in," he explained, waving his hand in the direction of Reef Tower. Satiah glanced over in its direction for a second, before returning her focus onto him.

"You're very trusting of me," she smiled, using her charm.

"I trained with Division Sixteen ma'am… Berry was my last officer there," he admitted. "So I know of you already. You're a bit of a celebrity on the quiet. Berry told me that without you, Division Sixteen and Phantom Squad might have seriously… misunderstood one another."

"I know Berry a bit," she smiled, digging. "I don't remember you though."

"Captain Maguire, ma'am," he told her, with some pride. She smiled, having already clocked the new insignia on his tunic, and they shook hands through her transporter window. "Eben to my friends. Short of Ebenezer."

"It's Eben then," she smiled, softly. This was a useful man to be friends with.

"What do you think of Brenda then?" she asked, convivially. Then she laughed. "Vote for her?"

"I would, ma'am, she's very generous; you should see where we're billeted. Velvet curtains, thick warm carpets, and the facilities are like nothing I've ever lived in before. Food that's unbelievable. Rank has its privileges, I know, but even the normal guards are living in extravagance here."

"You'll have to sneak me in one night and show me what you mean," she grinned, coquettishly. "Saying that, I suspect that, compared with what you're used to, a lot of things might be considered luxuries." Eben blushed.

"That's certainly true," he said, not sure what else to say.

"Relax, Eben, Phantoms are not allowed romantic liaisons, so I'm not going to pounce on you," she grinned, giggling softly. "Thank you for not saying anything about my friend on the back seat."

He saluted her and she gave him a comradely nod before driving on, back out into the rain and up towards the top of the nearest tower. She'd been parking there since they'd moved in. Compared to Reef Tower, despite its size, this tower somehow seemed much less imposing. It was called West Tower. Each tower had its own name; West, Reef, Philipirous, and Carman, to name a few. Satiah wasn't sure why this tower was named West as it didn't even face west, but she had been reliably informed that there was some obscure reasoning behind it. Indeed, there were veiled reasons behind the names of all of them! She'd just not been informed of what those reasons were yet. The entrances were down low and it was impossible to fly straight out of them because of the shield. She pulled a ubiquitous looking black cloak around her, instead of the phantom grey she often donned, and then got out into the rain. She scurried across the landing area, splashing through the biggest puddles as she went.

The building was designed such that, as rain fell, it was made to go down certain channels and create a waterfall and a fountain on the lower levels, that were both peaceful and spectacular. A door opened for her and she rushed inside. Shannon was there, waiting. Satiah, making a few clicks of irritation and mild disgust, removed the soaked cloak and dumped it into the arms of the waiting android.

"Morning," she said, pushing her hair away from her face. "Lovely day."

Shannon grunted and tried to give her a smile. Satiah didn't have to be clairvoyant to understand what was wrong.

"How is he?" Satiah sighed. Oli was moping around the place, had been for the last week or so.

"Still the same, utterly useless," Shannon replied, without real scorn. Everyone knew he was a man who had lately been sent reeling from multiple psychological blows. "Even Kate's given up on him now."

"You want me to give him a kick?" Satiah suggested. Shannon shook her head.

"He needs more than that I think, any news?"

"Collorah still eludes law enforcement," Satiah replied, shrugging. She didn't have to make any pretence about how disappointed she felt. It was true. He had evaded them… and everyone else. "There is some suggestion that he may have left the planet."

"Good riddance," Shannon muttered, clearly still under pressure.

"I don't believe it for a second though," Satiah continued, seriously. She was always careful to ensure that she never seemed to side completely with whatever fiction she'd concocted for law enforcement. It made it look more realistic if she disagreed with them every so often too. "And just because of our new friends outside and in, that doesn't mean we can become complacent."

Shannon, unable to raise the energy to argue, nodded glumly.

"You're right," she groaned, standing with an effort. "I'll go and check the new perimeter." She didn't know it, but Shannon was still the main suspect despite Satiah's rigorous and constant defence of her. They had been on the verge of bringing her in and putting her through interrogation, but Satiah had dug her heels in and refused to allow that to happen. She didn't care about Shannon's wellbeing, obviously, it was just the fact that she knew, deep down, that Shannon was not related to angel. Trouble was, Satiah could offer nothing else for them other than that she was sure it wasn't Shannon. Harrier had been listening in night and day, but whoever it was had said nothing since the last message.

**I won't rest until this is over. I won't let him get away with this. Oli cannot win the election, he must be stopped. I will use any means at my disposal to achieve this. I will avenge you, my angel.**

**It seems our enemy has an enemy, but one which we clearly can't trust to do what must be done. Bluntly: the enemy of my enemy can never be my friend. I won't forget you angel, no one should.**

**Can you see the news where you are? I'm not sure if it's on the news, but it soon will be if it isn't now. Oli won't have survived that. I think fate has taken care of him as it did you, my angel.**

As nothing else had been sent since, was it not possible that whoever it was had left and not realised that Oli had in fact survived? Perhaps they themselves had died at some stage? And there was something else too, something else no one had really discussed properly yet: that angel had been taken care of by fate, which could only really mean that they were dead too. So someone was talking to the dead. This theory would also explain why angel had never replied. Carl had also given her something else to think about too - something mission related. He'd told her that Oli had implemented some law changes on his own world shortly before the election started. One of these changes had to do with the suppression of certain forms of AI. Carl had suggested, and she couldn't believe she hadn't thought of it herself, that it might be a computer that was trying to kill him.

There was no proof, of course; it was, as ever, just a theory. It made her start thinking that maybe this particular AI might think Oli was planning on exterminating all artificial lifeforms and had decided to do what it could to stop him, even trying to kill him. So angel might be another computer system which had been destroyed or turned off, and whatever was trying to talk to it was another AI. It was a bit strange, Satiah recognised that, but she couldn't deny it was possible. It also explained why she'd failed to find anyone that had a motive. And if it thought it had achieved its wish, it might have deactivated itself. This would explain why nothing else was sent, even after Oli emerged unharmed a day later. She knew Randal would be tempted to see it as a creative excuse for her not being able to discover the real culprit. Blame it on the system, she could hear him saying in her mind.

So she did what she had done every day since she'd started: she went on a patrol of her own, alone. She'd check to see what everyone was doing and if there was anything suspicious going on. Less than a week now, and this would be all over, one way or another. It was ironic though, as now she was starting to get used to it: seeing Carl every day, Oli finally leaving her alone, Shannon no longer plotting against her... okay, Collorah was still out there and she still needed to keep going, but the whole thing was starting to be a lot less stressful. She did, however, promise herself never to get this involved in another election - ever again.

"And who told you about this threat?" asked the distorted voice.

"Brenda, but she was told by Ash," Randal explained, quietly. Silence. "I've seen nothing, but I thought I'd better let you know, nonetheless."

"No, you did the right thing," was the reply. "I'll see what I can find out... did she say anything else?"

"Well, she wants to talk to you," Randal reminded, a little exasperated. "You do pick great moments to wander off."

"I have been busy!" was the defensive response. "Ash isn't the type to go around spreading rumours unless he was sure of his facts. I think we should assume this is something real."

"I'll keep an ear to the ground at this end, let me know if you need her," Randal replied, in agreement.

"Will do."

"I think you should come back, just to keep your eye on the ball, so to speak," Randal replied.

"How do you know I'm not already there?"

---

"So you have no idea where he's hiding?" Marisa asked, sighing. They were in a restaurant, surrounded by other customers.

"I know exactly where Oli is," Collorah stated, coldly, "I just can't get to him. It's too heavily guarded." Marisa's eyes widened when he told her where Oli was being housed.

"Wow," she managed, at last. "I see your problem."

"Brenda has the combined might of the whole Coalition behind her. If I try anything I'll be flattened," Collorah explained. "Also, even moving around is difficult for me now. That Satiah keeps following me and searching for me all the time."

"Are you saying she's better than you?" Marisa asked, manipulatively. "Or are you just scared of her?"

"I'm saying it's not just her and me anymore. Brenda is right next door," Collorah stated, angry now.

"So what is your plan, or did you want to bail?" she replied. Oli was clearly losing the election, but it wasn't over yet and she didn't want this to happen in the next election as well - so she saw no reason in giving up.

"I have one more idea but it's going to cost you," he replied, trying to see how far she would go. She eyed him warily.

"What?"

"I need one of these," he said, slipping a small computer over to her. She connected it to hers and began to look at what he wanted. Her eyes rose to regard him and then lowered again.

"An A class Emulator Android," she read, quietly. She didn't need to ask how he intended to use it. These androids could look like anyone and talk like anyone. They were often used for stunts in place of actors or occasionally fooling the press so that someone very rich could slip out of the back door unobserved. Collorah could use this to get close to Oli.

"What's your plan exactly?" she asked, unwilling to admit how clever she thought this idea was.

"I can get hold of the very latest combat programming, and I could replace a member of staff with the android. It would go in to work as if it was the real person and then…" he didn't need to finish that sentence. It was likely that the android would be destroyed, but as long as it couldn't be traced back to her that was of no importance.

It was expensive, even for her. Yet it was a great idea with a high chance of working and a low chance of either of them being caught.

"Who will you replace?" she asked, interested.

"Someone that is relatively unimportant. There's a guy who works there, Stan I think his name is… he is just what we need," Collorah answered. She nodded slowly.

"What about Satiah? If she's so good, won't she spot this android?" she asked, seriously.

"Not if she's chasing me," he replied, letting her know the other half of his plan. He would act as a diversion for the android, drawing Satiah away from Oli and leaving the way clear. It was inspired.

---

"If he has left the planet, he's slipped past everyone," Zax replied, seriously. "I'm convinced he's still here. I know it's been five days since the last sighting, and even longer since he tried anything, but I imagine he's lying low, maybe waiting for something he needs before he strikes." Snell, Randal and Satiah, all sat around the table with her, nodded. Snell was looking much deflated since the recent events, knowing now that as far as influence in this went, he'd been reduced to naught.

"No news on angel?" he asked, gruffly.

"I still say it's Shannon on the logic that she's the only one left…" Randal began.

"She's not the only one left, there are at least thirty people who have been there since the start that are still there now," Satiah argued, stubbornly.

"After what Lunell saw…"

"Lunell is no longer working on this operation," Satiah was quick to jump in again. "Even if the guy refuses to leave, I still do not include him in anything. Besides… I looked into what he said and have concluded that Shannon wasn't doing anything improper."

"What exactly was she doing in that room with the communicator?" Randal asked, grimly.

"She says she was getting water as she couldn't sleep and seeing as he saw her with a drink, this does seem to back up her account - it was just bad timing," Satiah insisted.

"So if it's not Shannon, who do you think it is?" Snell asked, quietly. She glared at him, but couldn't blame him for asking that, nor could she give a good answer.

"I have no idea," she was forced to admit.

She wasn't going to go into the various and increasingly dubious theories she'd been toying with. It would make her look even more clueless.

"I suggest you take another close look at Shannon," Randal said, promptly. "Even if you get nothing, we're going to have to bring her in anyway. Too many of us think she's involved somehow, even if she isn't angel."

"I'm telling you it's not her, and I'm asking you to trust me," Satiah pleaded, not getting emotional. Dispassion was key to compelling those in authority to trust your viewpoint more. The more detached you seemed, the more credible your testimony would appear to them. It was a lesson she hoped that Zax would pick up on. That aside, Satiah really needed to get them to hold back and give her more time. Snell and Randal exchanged a look. Snell shrugged, a little disgruntled. He held no sway in this anymore.

"It's up to you," he said. "Naturally I'll support you… whatever the outcome." Randal gave Satiah a long and hard look. She faced him down, not giving an inch.

"All right - forty eight hours, after that…" The silence was deafening.

"I understand," she acknowledged. He'd done the best he could for her. He and Snell stood, Zax tried to stand as well but Satiah pulled her down and remained seated herself. The two men left the room and Zax let out a sigh, glad they were gone. She was still nervous around those in high command positions, but she was young so that was understandable.

"What do you want me to do?" Zax asked, knowing she'd been kept back for a reason.

"Who do you think it is?" Satiah asked. Zax shrugged. "Come on, you must have a suspicion?" Zax's eyes narrowed, unsure if this was a genuine question or another surprise test. Was Satiah really that desperate that she was asking her? Deciding in the end that it didn't matter which, as her answer was the same either way, she finally said what she thought.

"Shannon is who they are going for… but I'm thinking… Kate," Zax answered hesitantly. Satiah raised an eyebrow.

"Come on, qualify it?" Satiah probed. Don't stop there!

"I just… she's done nothing wrong, nothing suspicious at all. That in itself I find suspicious. She's been there since the beginning and she would have thought Oli was dead before, when the building collapsed, as she couldn't know he was with you and still alive. So she could have sent that message. She has been heavily involved in steering Oli, whether it be his performance or other things… I…" Zax fell silent, trying to put it simply. "If it was me and I knew it wasn't Shannon then I would look at Kate. Everything circumstantial, apart from what Lunell said he saw, could apply to Kate as much as it could Shannon."

"And Lunell didn't actually see anything, it's what he didn't see that's the problem," Satiah replied, thoughtfully. Zax nodded.

"The truth is, I think, Randal and Snell are out of patience and are looking for an easy answer," Zax whispered, knowing how disrespectful that might sound. She tried to take the sting out of it. "It's understandable; they have to hand in reports too." Satiah tutted scornfully.

"If they want something easy, they should just trust me," she muttered derisively. "In the meantime, I want you and Harrier to concentrate on finding Collorah. I have to take him out of this; right now he's just a dangerous distraction for me."

"Well, I didn't say this before, because I knew you would want me to tell you first..." Zax paused, looking ever so slightly proud of herself. She waited. Satiah too waited, refusing to be drawn into asking what it was, or strangling her.

"I have discovered that something particularly rare and expensive has just been purchased. It was done privately so I have no idea who bought it but... I know the name of the ship it's arriving on," she said, her eyes gleaming with pride. "It will be here in two hours and I thought you might want to be there to meet it."

"Tell me and I might consider not pouring that water over your head," Satiah smiled. Zax rolled her eyes.

"It's one of those A class Emulator Android models... you know? The ones that can impersonate people almost perfectly," she went on. "And it's coming in on a freighter called Neptune's Beard today." She slid a data crystal across to Satiah. "This says exactly where and when. Only half the money has arrived, I'm guessing the other half will be paid on delivery, or on confirmation that it works." Satiah smiled, impressed.

"You know what I'm going to ask you to do now, don't you?" she enquired, sliding the crystal back across to Zax meaningfully.

Zax frowned.

"You want me to be there instead of you?" she guessed, puzzled.

"If Collorah is there, he might recognise me. You are a stranger to him and, well, I think it's about time you played a slightly more active role. I'm asking you to identify who is behind Collorah, learn where they are and then return to your desk to find out all you can about them."

"Don't you want me to work out what their plan is?" Zax asked, still a bit confused.

"Isn't it evident? They plan on using that thing as an infiltrator to get close enough to Oli, disguised as a friend, to kill him that way," Satiah replied, seriously.

"We don't know that..." Zax objected, uncertainly.

"Trust me," Satiah assured her. "It's something I might try. Low risk to them, high chance of success... okay, it's expensive, but so is Collorah himself. For whoever this is, money is clearly not their problem."

"No, it's Oli who is the problem," Zax mused, thoughtfully. Satiah made eye contact with her and raised her eyebrows commandingly. Zax regarded her levelly, unsure what she was asking. Satiah rolled her eyes, giving up.

"Get going," ordered Satiah, shooing Zax away dismissively. "Record everything and don't get any big ideas. You have done well, don't ruin it." Zax dashed from the room excitedly. This was it! Her big chance to prove she was ready! Satiah sighed patiently and held up the data crystal that Zax had just run off without. Zax returned, a little flustered, snatched it from Satiah and departed again. Progress at last... but still no blasted angel!

★★★★★★★

Shannon looked up as Lunell entered the room. She had been avoiding him lately, or at least making sure she wasn't alone with him. Apparently that was no longer an option. He regarded her with a knowing look that she didn't care for. She and Satiah had discussed what she should do if cornered by him: first, she should hit a switch on her communicator which would start recording and sent a message to Satiah directly for assistance. Then she should try to brazen it out. She technically outranked him, which was the key to resisting him unaided, but Lunell would still be difficult to deal with.

"Lunell," she said, when he all but barred her exit path.

"Shannon," he smiled, pleasantly enough. "I've not spoken to you for some time, how are you coping?"

The question almost made her drop her guard, it was so casually and innocuously asked. The gleam in his eyes, one of scrutiny, reminded her of what he assumed and what he intended to do. It was a wretched feeling to know that someone suspected you of something you hadn't done... but you couldn't prove it. A kind of fraught helplessness. Again, as she had done a lot recently, she wished Satiah was there to back her up. Saying that, she bet Lunell would never have approached her at all had Satiah been there. Those two really did not like one another.

"We all have our own ways of dealing with the stress of this place. I used to exercise but recently I've not been sleeping too well and that's affected my fitness sessions too... we just have to hang in there," she said, honest but wary.

"True, I've been distracting myself by putting in calls to home every so often, checking up on my mother, she's fallen ill recently, you see," lied Lunell, adeptly.

"I bet that doesn't help you forget your stress much!" she remarked, seriously.

"You ever touch base with your family?" he asked, lightly.

"Not for years," she replied, honestly. She was starting to wonder where he was going with these questions. "I have a cousin on this planet somewhere but we've not spoken for decades."

"So you've not connected with anyone recently?" he asked, as if saddened. "That must be tough."

"I'm used to it," she replied, starting to try to get away. "Excuse me, I have to check on a few things." Lunell let her past, much to her surprise. Trouble was, he was interpreting this effort of hers to escape him as a sign of culpability.

As she went down the corridor, Satiah approached her hurriedly.

"What happened?" she asked, seriously.

"Where were you?" Shannon hissed, thankful that she'd at last turned up. "Lunell just came up to me." She explained what had happened and Satiah listened.

"He was digging," Satiah said, stating the obvious. "So long as he doesn't accuse you outright, you shouldn't have a problem."

"Even then I shouldn't, as I'm innocent," she retorted, a little hurt that Satiah hadn't said that.

"Of course," Satiah responded, unhelpfully. Shannon was getting increasingly snappy these days.

"I'm sorry, he just rattled me a bit, that's all," she admitted, crestfallen.

"Where's Kate?" Satiah asked, out of nowhere. Shannon blinked at her, wondering if she'd actually heard anything she'd said at all.

"With Oli…" she said, slowly.

"I see."

"Why?" Shannon asked, eyeing her. What was she up to?

"I haven't seen her this morning," lied Satiah, casually. "Will she be in there long?"

"Probably hours," she shrugged, not really knowing for sure. "They usually are."

"Okay," Satiah smiled, as if it was nothing. "You check the patrols are still moving around. I'll be back later." Shannon watched her go, more than a little confused. One minute she was so personable and the next she was almost unreadable, it was most befuddling. Satiah though was not her concern. Lunell was.

---

Kate was staying in the building with Oli and some of the others. Satiah made her way up to the accommodation area, after dismissing the guard on that level - she wanted to do this unobserved. She wandered along the corridor until she reached the room Kate was currently using. It was locked, but Satiah knew the security override code and used it to get in. The room was generic in design, compact, adequate to use, but hardly homely. Single bed, two storage units, adjoining bathroom, an inactive computer, an empty drink container and a half eaten snack. Satiah got to work.

First she checked the bed, all the clothing on it and inside the pillows. Nothing there. Under the bed: same story. She wasn't even entirely sure what she was looking for but Zax's suspicion needed to be investigated. Shannon's room would be next. Neither storage unit was locked. One was full of clothing and the other completely empty, save an unopened bottle of alcohol. Satiah frowned, took it out and gave it a more thorough examination in the light. Why was it there of all places? It was still sealed as if it had just arrived, so presumably it was being saved for something special? It was as costly as it was rare. A possible reward for Oli after the election? Then she found the note.

It was for her! The note said: To Satiah, for saving all our lives any number of times while risking your own. Satiah scowled down at it distrustfully. She always distrusted praise, no matter who it came from or was directed to. It was a lot like a compliment, in her experience, usually used to lower defences or to act as the first part of a request. Did Kate know she was searching her room somehow? Had she just guessed? Was she planning on giving this to her later in public? Satiah's brown eyes missed nothing as she searched for a hidden camera that wasn't there. She replaced the bottle in the unit and shut it in again. That was weird.

Finally she turned her attention to the computer and activated it. No password was required... Satiah was starting to see why Zax was so suspicious of this squeaky cleanness that Kate seemed to have. She'd been poisoned once and nearly killed a number of times, and yet still she hadn't bothered to protect her own computer... Satiah went through her messages and correspondence. Nothing incriminating to find there. She ran a search for angel and found nothing. No contact by that name, and no messages with that word included. Increasingly frustrated, Satiah began a search of the less obvious hiding places. Inside the lights, under the carpet, behind and under the storage units and various other locations, only to end up with nothing yet again.

Taking care to leave everything exactly how she had found it, Satiah returned to the corridor over an hour later. She went through Shannon's room too with the same result. Both of them were clean. This was getting her nowhere! When she returned to the corridor a second time, she had intended to leave but stopped herself. She had one of her feelings. An instinct she had no name for was compelling her to remain. She turned to look at the door at the end. Oli's room. She'd checked all these rooms before their occupants moved in as a matter of protocol and there shouldn't be any clues in there, but… she'd searched everywhere else. Why not?

---

Tall for her age, Zax was worried that the top of her head might just be visible. Positioned in a dark corner of the parking area, in a very unremarkable looking transporter, Zax was hunkering down in the driver's seat as best as she could. She'd already placed her bugs all over the hanger area. She had a hat that she planned to pull over her face so that if anyone did see her it would look like she was asleep. Everything was already recording; she'd checked and rechecked the volume and everything else. She couldn't afford to mess this up and let Satiah down. The freighter was due in less than half an hour now, so all she had to do was wait, listen and then follow. Surely she could manage that? She forced herself to stay objective and not to get carried away by the excitement. It was hard though, she was carrying a real gun for the first time, and it was oddly compelling to fiddle with it.

---

The door swished open and Satiah entered. Oli had a larger space than everyone else as you would expect, he was the candidate after all. Desk, three storage units, his new computer, bed, bathroom, several pairs of shoes littering the floor. She sealed the door behind her and advanced silently into the room. She started with the bed, once again going through everywhere it was possible to hide pretty much anything. The search was yet again fruitless. Storage was full of clothes and little else, the computer unused and the desk… She sat down at it and instantly realised it was locked. She went through all the details of his profile in her head. She tried his birthday, his account security number and all manner of other personal codes to get in. None of them worked.

She scowled, considering just shooting her way in and dealing with the fallout later. Then, it occurred to her.

She tried the date Sally, the woman he'd once loved, had been born on. It worked and the drawer slid open invitingly. Inside were many papers. It seemed to be mainly copies of speeches, some were his and some were his opponents'. Nothing untoward about that. She began skimming through them, still not entirely sure what she was looking for. The bleep of a message arriving distracted her. It came from the new computer she'd overseen the installation of the previous evening and she tapped the screen to get it to come back online. It was probably a company welcoming message or something that often arrived shortly after you'd installed it. What she saw on the message screen actually gave her a fright. She stared at it, dumbfounded for a moment.

**How are you my angel? How's your day?**

A pulsing blue light, indicating that whoever had sent it was actually there awaiting an answer, was what snapped Satiah back into the real world. So... someone was calling Oli an angel? The sender had no identification, coming up maddeningly as unknown contact. It could be a coincidence; after all, Satiah had only asked Oli if he *knew* an angel. Some kind of million to one against miscommunication. They happened a lot... apparently. She'd never asked him if anyone ever called him an angel. It had simply never occurred to her. But if the original messages were for him then they made no sense... that blue light was still on. Slowly, after glancing over her shoulder at the closed door, she leaned in and began to type out a reply.

**I could be better, what about you?**

Satiah had gone for a casual theme for her response, her plan being to slowly lure this person into revealing more. A wavy line appeared as whoever it was began to answer. Satiah waited, holding her breath without meaning to. If only she could find out who this was...

**Not bad considering my husband is dead.**

Ah... Satiah had not been expecting that in reply. She paused, wondering how best to respond to that. How would Oli respond? This was assuming all these messages were meant for him of course. Who else would it be for? It was his computer! The records said he was single and he had certainly behaved as if he was, so who the hell was this? And what could she say? Was this some kind of on the spot revelation? Did Oli know about this already or was whoever this was trying to catch him out? And, if he never got the original three messages...? They had been intercepted, so why wasn't this one being intercepted too? She gave Harrier a quick call, brought him up to speed, and told him to trace whatever this was before she lost it.

"It's because this is a new computer and no one had set up any filters on that interface yet, that's why it's getting through without alerting us," Harrier explained, rapidly. By no one he meant her. "Keep them talking for me, long as you can."

"No worries, I'll just do a strip tease," she responded, sarcastically.

"Seen it... disappointing ending," he deadpanned.

"Better than just being disappointing," Satiah hissed back.

**It's hard maintaining the pretence of normality, after something like that, isn't it?**

She'd said that in an effort of cover all the bases. The death could good or bad for this person or for Oli. Conceivably even to them both together. Whether the grief was real or contrived, the pretence of being normal would have to be there somewhere in most cases. She'd opened up the possibility that she, in this case pretending to be Oli, could even be talking about his own work as much as a dead husband. She had deliberately asked a question too in order to keep the dialogue going. Wow, this was an awkward conversation. That wavy line was there again, letting Satiah know whoever it was wasn't done yet.

**I can't believe you finally gave in. I thought you were never going to answer me. I love you so much. That's why I couldn't stop myself, please forgive me. You forgive me, right?**

Satiah was starting to wonder how to respond but another message came in before she could.

**Those things I said before... I was hurt, you must understand, I thought you hated me. I thought you had rejected me. And I couldn't take another rejection. I'm so sorry. I love you.**

Satiah pulled a face of utter disbelief while reading this. She had to step in at some point, or whoever this was... well, she didn't know for sure but they sounded a little emotional. Probably female, but anything was possible.

**Of course I forgive you, I couldn't ever do anything else, and you know I love you. What did you say before?**

Satiah had to work out what they were actually talking about now. The wavy lines were back, more was coming. Satiah waited, tense.

**Really?**

Really what? She rolled her eyes, wondering how long this would go on for. It was a bit of a risk answering with just one word, this person might think she was using a mirror technique, but Satiah had to say something. And it made sense that Oli would probably forgive whatever this was as he had no knowledge of the original three messages. Then again, whoever this was didn't know that.

**Yes.**

**Really? Really?**

Was this flirting or not? Satiah couldn't tell. A suitable question occurred to her and she answered with it.

**Surely you can expect forgiveness from an angel?**

She waited again, speculating on what nonsense she'd get this time. She hoped Harrier might be getting somewhere tracing this, as she felt sure that she wasn't. She tapped her earpiece to get his attention.

"Whoever they are, they're clever, they're using multiple relays to bounce the signal, and it could take hours to work out exactly where..." Harrier began. Well, if they weren't smart we'd have figured out where they were a long time ago!

"Is it on this planet?" she asked, quickly. "The other messages were, and were they not from Oli's campaign headquarters?"

"So far as I can tell, yes," he replied, "keep digging..."

**Who are you?**

Satiah swore. Well, that didn't take long. In order to give Harrier more time, she knew she had to keep them talking. She would play dumb, it was the most sensible strategy and would probably keep the exchange going longest.

**What do you mean: who are you? I'm your one and only angel.**

Come on Harrier!

**Prove it! What did you do when I told you that you and I are destined to be together forever?**

Okay, starting to get really tricky now. Er... throw up?

**Can't you remember?**

Satiah was seriously running out of ideas now.

**I know you're not Oli and you know what? Oli's going to die for this!**

Well, if there had been any confusion about what was going on here, it had only really increased because of this. At least in Satiah's mind. She was just glad Harrier was getting all this too, she wasn't sure it would be believed otherwise.

**We all are... including you.**

Satiah had decided it was time to throw in a warning of her own. The reply took a little longer to come this time, as clearly whoever it was didn't expect to be threatened.

**I see what's going on here! You're Sally, aren't you? He told me you were dead.**

The door suddenly slid open, the lock sparking into uselessness and Satiah rolled away from the computer, gun ready. Lunell just managed to dive out of the way as she fired.

"It's me!" he barked, angrily. You should have knocked!

"Decided to take me out, huh?" she asked, trying to keep on eye on the computer. "Mr Slimy switching sides again, is he? You must think I'm stupid!" She typed out a quick counter reply while keeping her gun pointed at the doorway.

**Sally is dead, you're next, love from Oli's avenging angel. Death kisses.**

"Satiah! I swear I'm not going to try to kill you!" he retorted, from outside. And the award for the most pointless cliché goes to Lunell!

"Come on, you can do better," she fired back. His gun tumbled in through the open doorway as a gesture of surrender.

"And the other one you think I don't know about?" The second pistol followed a few seconds later. "Enter slowly."

Slowly, his hands in the air, he edged out from cover. Surprised but still distrusting, Satiah did not lower her pistol.

"I never wanted to be against you, we're on the same side and we need to solve this," Lunell replied, grim.

"Be useful for a moment then. Where's Shannon?" she demanded, seeing an opportunity to prove that Shannon couldn't be angel.

"She's been with Oli and Kate; I've been trying to get her alone, why?" Lunell asked, curious. "Finally starting to realise the truth?" Satiah smiled glibly and swung the screen around so that he could read it.

Whoever it had been was gone now, but the rest of the text remained. While Lunell read though it in mystification, Satiah reconnected with Harrier.

"Well?" she asked, hopefully. "We've been looking at this the wrong way. Oli himself is angel and he never replied to the three previous messages as they were intercepted by us. This would explain why he..."

"He never told us about anyone called angel," Lunell finished, for her. He was still reading but it seemed he was in agreement. "And... Shannon couldn't have sent these messages," Lunell went on, with a groan of revelation. "She's with Oli and Kate and I have their whereabouts confirmed." He held up his own computer so that Satiah could see the screen. They were indeed still all together, and had been all the time.

So, Shannon had been proven innocent at last... trouble was, so had Kate and that meant they were still no better off as to figuring out who this was.

"Any luck with the signal tracing?" he asked, sitting on the bed and casually picking up his gun from the floor.

"This planet somewhere, although that may change now that I have said those things," she replied, still wary of him. Lunell nodded. "Why did you come up here?"

"I noticed it wasn't being guarded so I thought I would investigate. Had I known you were here I probably wouldn't have bothered," he replied, seriously. "Did you dismiss the designated guard?" She nodded. "I'll get him back," he grunted, pulling out his communicator.

"The second I sat down opposite her, I knew something wasn't right about her," Oli sighed. "I mean, she already knew who I was. And where I worked, and it made me uneasy."

Satiah and Lunell had barged into his office a few minutes ago, ordered Shannon and Kate to leave, and then explained what had happened. It seemed he didn't know who she was either, but he knew what she looked like.

"She was small, substantially smaller than Satiah anyway, maybe five three? Long wavy dark hair and big grey eyes. She had a kind of weird smile, creepy weird rather than endearing if you know what I mean?"

"Where did you meet her and when?" Satiah barked, a little harshly. She was seething now, absolutely furious that he hadn't thought to mention any of this to her or anyone else before.

"As you know, I've not been seeing anyone for a long time, and Malla suggested I try typhlotic-dating," he replied, actually laughing a bit. "I thought it was a stupid idea but I had nothing better to do at the time, so..."

"Get on with it," she hissed. "I have wasted more than enough time on this already." He scowled at her but obeyed.

"It was nearly two months ago now," he answered. "As soon as she started talking, I kind of knew she might be trouble. She started going on about star signs, saying we were destined to be soul mates or some such baloney."

"So she was trying to tell you she was in love with you?" Lunell asked, trying to get to the point.

"She wasn't trying, she did tell me that several times, I thought she was just free with terms of affection like that," he shrugged. "In any case, I just knew getting involved with her might not be the cleverest idea in the world so I made a polite excuse and left."

"And that's the last time you saw her?" Satiah asked, quickly. He paused and she could guess what was coming.

"Well... I think so..."

"What do you mean, you think so?" she snapped, eyeing him lividly. "You must know one way or the other."

"Look, Satiah..." he began, awkwardly.

"Just answer the question!" Lunell joined in, also losing patience.

"I may have seen her a couple of times, just around, you know? In crowds where I have been speaking, once even in that corridor," he said, pointing. Lunell and Satiah turned around as if to check it was still empty. "I just thought I was mistaken. I don't understand…"

"This person, clearly disturbed as she finds you attractive, is the person who wrote threats down and actually sent them to you. These messages never reached you as law enforcement intercepted them and then told me about them after the first attempt was made on your life," lied Satiah, cunningly. "Malla and I have been looking for this person for weeks and all the time it was your deluded stalker!"

"She hired the Red Necromancer?" Oli gaped.

"Not exactly," muttered Satiah, grimly. "I'm pretty sure that that was someone else."

"Someone else?" he echoed, looking even more unsettled.

"How would she have got in here?" Lunell asked, calmly. "You just said you saw her in that corridor - when?"

"Well, it might have been her, I'm not positive…"

"*When did you see her?*" Satiah repeated, seeing what Lunell was saying.

"Well, a few days ago, it was when you weren't here," he replied, shaking his head. Satiah and Lunell eyed one another, each trying to think what to do for the best.

"Okay," Satiah sighed, trying to calm herself down. "When you saw her, why didn't you say anything?"

"It might not have been her!" he repeated, with agitation. "All the cleaners look the same to me."

"They just hired a team of cleaners a few weeks ago, and one of them used to work for Cadel," Satiah said, instantly making the connection. "A woman named Connie." Oli's eyes widened either with amazement at her deduction, or of further alarm, Satiah didn't know which. Nor did she care.

"She's been here since the day Oli's team arrived, but she was injured when the building collapsed and returned to work a few days ago," Lunell replied, joining her in her deductions.

"This can't be the case, if she's been here all this time I would have noticed and recognised her for sure," Oli said, puzzled.

"Really? Even if she changed her hair style, wore different clothes and blended in with the crowd?" Satiah asked, raising an eyebrow. "If she did all those things, are you sure you would notice a person you've only ever met once? Besides, you did just say that you weren't sure?"

Oli considered and was persuaded that she was right. Typically, Satiah was right about these things.

"Do we arrest her?" Lunell asked, eyeing Satiah. "She's been here all this time, she could have killed him at any time, so why hasn't she done it yet?"

"That's because he wasn't answering her, so she couldn't be sure if he knew she was there. Now that has changed," Satiah replied. "She knows that someone knows she's here."

"The original messages make even less sense to me now, than they did at the start," Lunell admitted, thinking about the original three angel messages. They both started reading them.

Was it coincidence? Could it be possible that another person had sent the first three and Connie had just decided to call Oli angel? Angels did have a symbolic role when it came to star signs, Satiah reflected.

"...I don't think it's her," Satiah stated, conflicted. "It's just not the same... to me, it's looking as if someone entirely different was writing it. I mean, look at the style of it! One is clearly talking *about* Oli while the other, Connie, is talking *to* him."

"We'll give her to law enforcement and they will learn the truth," Lunell said, a hardness to his voice. She nodded, knowing what he really meant by that. And, unfortunately, if Connie turned out to be a coincidence, that would mean they were back to square one. Satiah swore and kicked the chair aggressively. Lunell saw and winced in understanding.

"It's never as simple as that," he told her, as disappointed as she was. She regarded Oli.

"Tell no one about this conversation. If anyone asks anything about this, then refer them to me or Lunell," she instructed, coldly. He nodded.

Collorah and Marisa were in disguise, but their voices had given them away. They had arrived about ten minutes ago and were waiting outside the loading area, in full view of Zax. They were talking about the possibility of them being traced, ironically enough. Collorah's voice was on record and was easy to find as a result. Marisa's was not so easy, but she'd given a brief speech at a funeral three years ago and that speech had been recorded. The voice matched and so her identity was confirmed. As she listened in, Zax diligently went about the business of creating a profile for Marisa. She was a millionaire socialite originally from Hangoul and was currently residing on Earth, known for her investments in military hardware...

There was the motive. Oli, had he by some oversight managed to slip into power, was planning on cutting defence spending, among other things. This would affect Marisa's profit margins considerably. Unaware of the fact that there was no chance he would ever win the election, Marisa had clearly decided to take matters into her own hands. She'd hired Collorah and here they both were. It also explained how this much money could be called on at short notice without anyone batting an eyelid. Technically Zax knew she didn't actually need to follow them now, as she already knew where Marisa was currently living. Yet what if that was a lie and she was in fact based somewhere else? Just in case, she thought she'd better follow anyway.

Neptune's Beard, the freighter, was just pulling in at that moment — a few minutes early, but that suited everyone just fine. Zax watched as the boarding ramp descended and the pilot came out, computer in hand. Marisa went to greet him while Collorah stayed where he was, probably keeping watch. Zax continued to observe as the delivery was made and a man, very nondescript, stepped out of the cargo area. He, or rather it, had to be android. Collorah led it into the transporter they had arrived in. Marisa and the pilot were still talking. As Zax removed the headset and began to make preparations to leave, a hard knock on her window made her jump. She looked up and Collorah was standing there, eight barrelled pistol aimed right at her. She froze, instantly starting to think about the consequences of being caught.

"Out," he ordered, grimly.

Satiah and Lunell burst into the room where Connie was meant to be staying. It was empty.

"I checked her pass on the computer, she hasn't left the building yet, and she arrived at her usual time," he informed her.

"Search this room," she ordered, as she moved back out into the corridor. As with the other rooms, she wasn't exactly sure what might be found, but it was sensible to search. Lunell moved in and began to destructively search the room. She decided she'd make sure he was the one who had to put everything back when he was done.

She leaned against the doorway and casually glanced back up the corridor. That was when Connie appeared, nonchalantly trooping down the corridor towards her room. She stopped dead when she saw Satiah.

"Scratch that, she's here," Satiah growled, to Lunell. Then she addressed the other woman. "Ah, is this your room?" she asked, as if unsure. "Someone reported a broken light fitting and…" Not buying this, and probably guessing who Satiah was, Connie turned and fled. Satiah sprinted after her.

Connie made it to the lift and the doors closed just before Satiah could get to them. She watched as the floor count went up. Lunell bounded past her, taking the stairs and racing up them energetically. Satiah though, upon seeing that Connie was most likely heading for the top, simply called for another lift. Up she went, calmly adjusting her pistol to stun as she rose with only the annoying lift music for company. At last she reached the top and cautiously slipped out into the corridor beyond. There was nothing yet on this floor, all the rooms were still empty. She pressed for both lifts to go down, in an effort to try to trap Connie on this floor. She could always use the stairs, but then maybe Lunell might be there to stop her.

A strong breeze made Satiah start to hurry, fearing she was already too late. She reached a balcony and Connie was there, on the wrong side of the railing, looking very much as if she was going to jump.

"Don't do it," ordered Satiah, unable to hide her astonishment. Connie was weeping.

"It doesn't matter anymore!" she suddenly wailed. "He never loved me, did he?"

"Do you mean Oli?" Satiah chanced, subtly trying to get close enough to grab her.

"Stay away!" she shrieked, backing away and getting very close to the edge. "I'll do it, I swear!" Satiah extended a persuasive hand.

"Don't throw your life away, least of all for him, it's not worth it," she said, trying to sound pleading. In reality, she was wondering what would happen if she tried to jump Connie.

"My life isn't worth it!" was the typical counter.

"Why's that?" Satiah asked, deliberately trying to get her talking again. She had alerted Eben. He had responded, telling her to stall for as long as she could. She'd had training in how to deal with potential suicides and knew the key lay in continued communication and false fellow feelings.

"No one wants me! No one has ever wanted me! I'm no good! So now... I shall throw myself away!" she bellowed, tearfully.

"I want you," Satiah growled, levelly. "I need you to answer some very important questions. Someone is trying to kill Oli and until recently I thought it might be you... am I right?" Connie sniffed, seeming not to understand.

"... I see what you're doing! You're trying to trick me!" she spat, at last. "Do you like feeling powerless? Do you like the feeling that even with your gun you can't stop me doing this?"

"If I were trying to trick you I would not be so obvious," Satiah argued, smiling more kindly. She extended her gloved hand out to her again, imploringly. "Come back to me, we can talk about this. When we're done, if you still want to end it all, then I will not stop you." Connie looked down at the ground, back at Satiah then at the ground again.

"I... I am no good," she repeated, less sure of herself now.

"Go on, trust me," Satiah said, having to say it louder than before because of the buffeting gusts. She took a cautious step forward towards Connie. When Connie didn't move, she took another. That was when Lunell finally caught up.

Darting out from the doorway, Lunell aimed his pistol at Connie. Satiah tried to get him to lower it but Connie screamed and hurled herself from the edge.

"I said don't!" screamed Satiah, impotently. Connie was gone in the blink of an eye. Lunell stopped and slapped his hand against the wall in angered defeat. Why Connie jumped was a bit of a mystery, Satiah would later reflect, as surely, if she didn't want to get shot, why was she okay with falling to her death? She imagined that as she was clearly suicidal, she probably wasn't thinking rationally anyway.

Satiah rushed to the edge to look over, as she noticed something: the screams, Connie's screams, weren't getting any quieter...

As she reached the edge, she found the woman suspended in mid-air. She kicked and screamed out her frustration before dissolving into tears of feebleness. Eben, driving a specialised transporter, slowly edged around the corner of the tower and into view. He'd caught Connie in a gravitational field and was holding her there, stopping her from plummeting to her death. He gave Satiah a wink and a lopsided grin.

"Did you want her for something, ma'am?" he shouted, over the engine and the winds. Satiah bit her lip, put her hands on her hips and nodded with a triumphant smile.

---

Follow your story to the death if you must, was all Zax could think. Collorah did not believe what she was telling him. That she was really into spaceships of all kinds and was an amateur ship-spotter who had a huge collection of serial numbers, engine types and ownership codes. That she had only been interested in the freighter, and not who or what was in it. That she only carried a pistol because her father had insisted. She could see he didn't believe it - his expression and his mocking laughter gave that much away.

"No, honestly, I was just looking at the freighter," Zax insisted, as convincingly as she could.

"How did you know it would be here to look at?" he asked, in a threatening voice.

"I didn't, I always wait here for ships to arrive, I was just…" Zax tailed off, wishing desperately that Satiah was there too.

"What's going on, Collorah?" Marisa asked, blundering into the conversation abruptly. "Why are you threatening this girl?" He motioned to the gun Zax had on her hip.

"That's why," he replied, compellingly. "That, and her being here at all. She claims to be just ship-spotting…"

"Honestly, that's what I was doing," Zax repeated, with a faltering smile. "It's a hobby." She made up her mind that if she was lucky enough to survive this, she needed to work on both how to lie well and also to think of better lies to tell.

"No, she's law enforcement or something," Collorah growled, grabbing Zax's shoulder in a painfully strong hold. She yammered as anyone would about the pain.

"Nonsense," Marisa stated, disagreeing for whatever reason. She pushed Collorah's hand away from Zax, for which Zax was greatly relieved, and stared hard into Zax's soulful blue eyes.

"It's okay, I know why they sent you," Marisa smiled, as if amused. Zax didn't have to play dumb this time; she had no idea what she was talking about.

"Um…?"

"I'll pay you double if you report back to them and tell them that I'm thinking of investing in the android business," said Marisa firmly. Zax was finally starting to get the idea. Marisa thought she was an industrial spy. That she'd been sent there by the company to see who had anonymously bought their specialised android. A lifeline!

"I… don't know what you mean…" Zax said, deliberately lying badly. Marisa smiled knowingly.

"How much do you want?" she asked, thinking that Zax was trying to barter.

"I shouldn't…" said Zax, pretending to waver. Collorah was really making her feel very frightened, so she ignored him. Pretended that he just wasn't standing there, watching her. She focussed completely on Marisa.

"I hate they way they corrupt such young people by making them do this kind of thing," said Marisa sympathetically, shaking her head. "Find another job as soon as you can, you could do so much better. How much?"

"They told me if I didn't do this... I would be fired," whimpered Zax, starting to make herself look like she was holding back the tears. Marisa smiled understandingly; Collorah though still looked unconvinced.

"How much do they pay you a month?" Marisa asked, levelly.

"I'm only an assistant market researcher," she improvised, with manufactured shame.

"How much?" Marisa asked again, with something that might even have been compassion.

"Twelve hundred and sixteen Essps after tax," Zax said, making herself blush. To her amazement, Marisa handed her a bronze Essp bar.

"There is two thousand on this, quit and find yourself a better job," Marisa instructed. Zax could not believe her luck. She kept acting though, nodding with all the shame she could muster. Marisa smiled and then nodded to Collorah.

"Come on, we have work to do," she ordered, seriously. He didn't move though, as Zax walked off. Zax, avoiding his stare, slipped back into the transporter. Suddenly, his hand landed on the controls in front of her to stop her from using them. She jumped a little.

"Whoever you are, today was your lucky day," he said, very deliberately. Slowly he removed his hand from the controls. Zax felt a cold shiver run down her back but she didn't wait around for more. She sped off, out of the parking area and into the traffic. Taking no chances, she began a very long and very indirect journey back to Phantom headquarters. Satiah would no doubt be cross with her for getting spotted, but at least she had made it back alive and with the information Satiah wanted. She pondered how that gun had nearly cost her everything and that she might have at least thought of concealing it. She had hoped she was ready and that she had what it took, but what if she didn't?

Putting Connie through a full interrogation might have been considered by some as excessive. Yet, due to her own actions, absurd and potentially harmful as they were, she had caused a lot of trouble. She'd broken down almost the second they had got her in there. Spilling everything she had to spill instantly. No, she had not sent those three messages to Oli. Yes, she had stalked him, tried to get close to him, but she hadn't wanted him to die despite what she'd sent to Satiah before. She was unbalanced, had a history of mental instability and had been off her medication for almost three months. All in all, it was a sad and rather frustrating business.

Satiah sat in a quiet room pensively, having just reviewed what Zax had been up to, and waited there for her to report back with a tiny grin. They had what they needed to know. Marisa. They had a good idea of what Collorah was planning, and they knew he would have to strike before the election ended. A very sheepish looking Zax came in after awaiting permission to be let in. Satiah glared imperiously at her.

"Report," she instructed, her tone low but icy with unreal condemnation. Zax stood to attention and started talking.

"Marisa identified, location found and plan predicted," she summarised, leaving out the fact that she had nearly got caught.

"How did he know you were there?" Satiah almost shouted.

Zax squirmed ever so slightly but stayed composed. She had expected this.

"I don't know," she admitted. "I was there first so they couldn't have seen me arrive."

"You were nearly killed," Satiah said, eerily soft again. "There would have been no one there to save you and you made a mistake."

"I will do better next time," she assured, strongly. Satiah smiled forgivingly.

"Perhaps I let you off your leash too early and perhaps it was a bit reckless, but lessons learned?" she responded.

"I will..." Zax began, thinking Satiah wanted her to tell her how she would improve herself.

"No, my lessons, not yours," Satiah interrupted. Zax was confused by this.

"Today I learned a great deal about you. If it's any consolation, I have no idea how Collorah spotted you either, as you did everything you could not to be noticed. Sometimes that happens, you live, you learn. Sometimes things that absolutely should not happen… happen. I learned that you can not only lie well enough to convince most, you're capable of adapting to a situation and recognising an escape strategy when you see one. Your story about ship-spotting was weak; luckily Marisa thought you were something you weren't. I am pleased by that part of your actions. Your quick work with the profile was good; you have a talent for finding and researching targets effectively. Despite how out of your depth you were… you never lost your cool and that is perhaps the most important thing of all."

Zax listened to all this keenly. If she'd wanted confirmation that Satiah really was going to train her and that it had already started in a way, this was it. She also wanted to know her errors and how to avoid them in the future to prove to Satiah that she really was the best. To hear that Satiah was at all pleased with her was a huge relief. She worried constantly in the back of her mind that she would fail and be cast away.

"Your mistake was to have a back story that was only marginally more convincing than claiming that you were a dinosaur trainer…" Satiah went on. Zax badly wanted to laugh at the comparison, but knew she shouldn't so she held it in. "… and that your purpose in being there was to survey it as a potential egg storage area." Zax's shoulders were beginning to rise and fall a bit faster than they should if breathing normally; she was really struggling to hold it in, Satiah could tell.

"This is not funny, Zax," she stated, knowing that it was. "This points to a serious flaw in your ability to create good cover for yourself. You will have to work on that. In the meantime, so that you learn properly from your mistake, I'm going to have to punish you." Any desire to laugh vanished instantly and she held her breath. Satiah cleared her throat and held out her hand. Zax frowned, not understanding what she meant. What was that supposed to mean?

"The money," Satiah prompted, with a cruel smile. "Sorry, but I'll have to confiscate that." Zax gaped, realising that she wasn't being punished as such; she was in fact being robbed. She had no choice and so, with reluctance, she handed the Essp bar over.

"Hurts, doesn't it?" Satiah smiled, mock sadistically. Zax nodded morosely. "Next time you're able to take advantage of someone like that, don't get recorded doing it," she spelt out, as one final bit of advice, "or your boss will want his or her cut."

"Yes, Satiah," she agreed, obediently.

"Well, for a first effort you did rather well, not brilliantly but well enough, I think," Satiah smiled, more kindly. She put the money on the table and turned away to activate the computer. Zax saw her chance and gingerly sneaked closer to steal it back.

"Put it back, Zax!" Satiah said, not even looking around. Zax went red and almost stamped her foot in frustration. How did she do that? How did Satiah know? She'd made no noise at all. She replaced the money with a rather pathetic 'err I was only looking' expression on her face. The computer came on.

"Now, back to our other problem," Satiah went on. "Let me bring you up to speed with what you missed." They sat opposite one another, the money all but forgotten.

Zax couldn't believe what had happened.

"So this woman Connie has been stalking Oli all this time and no one realised?" she gasped, in wonder.

"To be fair, we did have a lot of other things to think about," Satiah murmured, with a nod. Zax nodded back at her.

"You know, I did see her watching him a few times but I dismissed it because I couldn't think of a motive," she admitted. "Plus it was only a few glimpses, so I thought it might be sexual attraction."

"It probably was," Satiah replied, thinking about it. "However, all of this means that both Shannon and Kate are back to being suspects… however remote that possibility."

"But you searched both their rooms and found nothing! Harrier's been watching them and has seen nothing, *you* have a feeling that Shannon is not angel or working with angel, and you have Lunell's story that she and Kate were with Oli when the latest messages came through!"

"And we still have no idea who angel really is," Satiah growled, annoyed. "Tomorrow is my last day, my last chance to prove Shannon is innocent before Randal and the others put her through full interrogation."

"You don't like Shannon," pointed out Zax, honestly.

"No, but the desire to watch her being tortured for answers that I know she doesn't have doesn't exist within me either," mused Satiah. "Besides, it will be a waste of time and effort on everyone's part." Zax leaned back in her chair slowly and went over the increasingly fewer options.

"What about Kate, how does your gut feel about her?" Zax enquired thoughtfully.

"I don't know," Satiah replied, running her hands through her hair. "All I know is that it's not Shannon."

"Maybe… you're sure Connie didn't lie?" Zax asked, clutching at invisible straws.

"Connie's idea of reality is a bit blurry, but yes," Satiah replied. "She's telling the truth, as far as she sees it, and if she was lying, she's had ample opportunity to strike at Oli already. The fact that she hasn't tells me she's not angel *or* working with angel."

"Then it has to be either Kate or Shannon," Zax insisted, planting her elbows heavily on the table.

"No it doesn't, there are still over twenty other people who have been there since the start," Satiah retorted, about to go into her list. "There is Stan…"

"Yes, but they…" Zax stopped herself. She smiled. "This is senseless; we're going around in loops." This whole thing was indeed becoming a bit of a vicious circle, Satiah had noticed.

"What are you going to do?" Zax asked, curiously. Satiah eyed the younger woman levelly.

"What I always do… push," she replied, seriously.

"Push?" asked Zax, needing more than that.

"Until I get a reaction out of someone," she elaborated. "I was toying with the idea of planting proof of culpability on someone to see who relaxes after they've been taken out of the picture."

"What? Pretend to arrest Shannon to see who gets careless afterwards?" Zax confirmed, nodding slowly. "It could work."

"Yes, and it might not," Satiah replied. "I'll sleep on it tonight." Zax stifled a giggle and blushed. "Enough cheek, young lady," Satiah grinned, without bite.

---

"I don't get it, he's fixed, why don't you just turn him on again?" Carl asked, puzzled. "Is it because I'm here?" Kelvin had been put back together again and looked exactly like his old self, but... Satiah had not yet reactivated him. "I know I said I don't like him, and I don't, but he's yours and if you need him...?"

"I can't be in here with you *both* turned on," Satiah joked. Carl, though, wasn't to be so easily distracted.

"Come on, what's going on?" he asked, wrapping her in his arms.

"More secret stuff, I'm afraid," she admitted, awkwardly.

"You've not broken him again, have you?" he asked, with a chuckle. She smiled and traced his faint laughter line with her fingertip.

"No," she said, wondering if he'd got that new line because of her.

"Do you want me to drop it?" he asked, softly.

She considered telling him about Obsenneth, but Zax might be listening in. She did trust them both to keep yet another secret, but something told her not to. They didn't need to know. Everyone who knew, or seemed to know - in this case both Ash and Kelvin - had given her trouble. Not overt trouble, not exactly, but trouble enough to make her uneasy around them. She didn't know if the same would happen with Zax or Carl, but she didn't want to chance it. Not until she'd learned more about Obsenneth itself, in any case.

"I worry that if you know all my secrets I will be boring," she said evasively.

Carl sighed, giving up for now, but she knew he would revisit the subject. He'd do this on and off strategy that gradually wore her down. She reminded him of her various plights again, to gently wean him off the topic of Kelvin - about Shannon, angel, Marisa and the rest. He was sympathetic. And that was when, out of nothing, she worked out what she could try next. He sat up and stared down at her with significance. She remained where she was, putting it down to men and their never-ending desire to stare at her.

"You want to think of me just like this in the future, huh?" she asked, grinning.

"You've got that look about you again, the one I told you about," he said, ever so slightly nervous. "The one where I have no idea what you're going to do next."

"That's funny, I just worked out exactly what I'm going to do," she smiled, amused.

"See, this is why you're scary," he said, settling back down again.

"I am *not* scary!" she protested.

"Tell that to Oli," he quipped. She giggled.

"Sometimes I could be a bit scary," she allowed.

"Like, when you're startled, or exposed to anything that exists which isn't you," he went on. She shrugged a little and then had to reposition her pillow.

"If you were in my situation, what would you do?" she asked, sleepily.

"Think how lucky I am to be in bed with me," he stated, with conviction. He then feigned comprehension. "Oh, you mean about your mission?" She giggled again.

"As you know, sometimes I can leave things on the back burner a little too often," Carl said, phrasing that carefully.

"You mean you're taking into account your rampant lethargy?" she corrected. Carl pulled a downcast, injured sort of face.

"What was that for?" he demanded, in a pained tone. She grinned.

"Sorry, reflex! Continue," she said, smiling.

"If you're going to behave like that, I'm not sharing my incredible insights with you," he stated, mock seriously. "And will you stop hogging the cover, I've got less than a quarter of it over here now!" A brief tug of war ensued. "I'd do your chemical pinch on Shannon, that way you could find out if it was her or not without her having to endure all the nasties of a formal interrogation."

"I may do that as well," she said, surrendering it finally and wrapping herself around him instead.

"I see what you did there, very sneaky," he replied, grinning.

"You are warmer," she said, as if excusing the whole deception. "I couldn't just ask you to hold me, you might have refused. Now you have no choice." He sighed in a long suffering way.

"You're boiling," he complained, sadly. She gave a sleepy groan in response. He shook her gently. "Stop pretending you're asleep. You're fooling no one."

"I love you," she cooed, softly.

"That's not going to work either," he chuckled.

"Never interrupt me when I'm talking in my sleep," she replied, still refusing to budge. "Don't worry, I won't get any closer."

"Only because it's not physically possible," he grumbled, closing his eyes. He gently poked her ribs. "Just a polite reminder that it's your turn to make breakfast tomorrow." She didn't answer and he knew he'd be the one doing it, most likely…

◆◆◆◆◆◆◆

Shannon's apartment had a certain bleakness about it. Satiah had broken in to search, and knew it wasn't in her own mind. She knew the code for the door, having subtly watched Shannon inputting it on her previous visit. She'd looked everywhere else and in the interests of covering herself, she knew she'd have to check. At least then, no matter how things ended, at least no one could say she'd not been thorough. She went through everything keenly. Shannon didn't live on Earth, she resided on Oli's home world, but she'd needed a place to stay while looking after Oli on Earth. Satiah had been planning to go to her actual home and search that too, but Lunell had told her that he'd done that a few weeks ago. She had attestation that he'd told her that too, just in case he tried anything funny later.

She had obviously been inside Shannon's apartment a couple of times before now, usually to give comfort, or to talk about how things were away from the prying ears and eyes of Lunell and Oli. Things that both of them could easily do without. Being watched all the time was something people had to live with, regardless of whether they ever got used to it or not. Cameras, motion detectors, listening devices... everywhere. Fact of life. Their association, Shannon and herself (Satiah wasn't sure if a fake friendship which one person may or may not believe in had a name), had become closer. In a way, it had had to, mathematically speaking, there were less people there to associate with. More private thoughts had been confided, whether true or not. Satiah didn't know how Shannon actually felt about her, or whether her part in this interaction was genuine or not. It had certainly come out of a falsehood but, especially after learning that she was a suspect, Shannon's behaviour and attitudes had seemingly changed for real. Satiah was aware that even if she didn't truly like her, Shannon had been forced into relying on her for pretty much everything.

It was something Satiah had been used to for decades: going through the most intimate things of other people's lives. Details, snippets of deeply personal information, secrets... all were open to her. She maintained an objectivity that put detachment a long way behind her. Shannon wasn't very family orientated; at least, that was what she would have people believe. Yet, hidden amongst financial files lurked a tiny computer unit that had thousands of images, clips of footage and even messages from family members. Satiah went through all that with little interest. She allowed the financial side of Shannon's life to take more precedence, as money was a far more common motivation than family. Certainly when it came to the murder of an outsider. Oli wasn't part of Shannon's family, no matter how much she'd once wanted him to be, so it seemed reasonable to assume that any grievance could just as easily be lucre orientated as it could be family. Shannon had no debts, no signs of fiscal instability. She was planning a vacation on a well-known paradise world for after the election was over. She'd made no secret of that holiday, it was her lifeline to sanity.

Her and half the cosmos, thought Satiah.

One thing she had expected to come across, but hadn't yet found, were signs of her former attraction to Oli. Apparently, Shannon really had moved on at last. After taking care to return the place to how it had looked before she started, Satiah departed. This was done not out of respect, but simply to conceal the fact that it had been searched. When she was back in traffic she made a call.

"Reporting in," she said, as Harrier answered. "Shannon is clean and not working against Oli."

"Clean she may be, but you don't know..." he began, casually.

"I'm going to pay Marisa a visit now," she interrupted, having easily anticipated his reservation. "Angel is a threat I know of but can't counter. Collorah is a threat I can now oppose directly. Is there anything political that concerns Marisa that I need to know about? Should she accidentally die...?"

"No, so long as no one knows you did it, you can take her out," Harrier replied.

"I wasn't planning on taking her out, just bringing her in," Satiah replied, firmly. "We still don't know if she's working alone or not. It's not out of the question that angel could have something to do with her and we need to eliminate that possibility."

"True, but either way you don't have to worry about repercussions," he replied. "Not from our side, anyway."

"That's a first," she grumbled, mordantly. Half of her had prepared for the eventuality that Marisa would be in some way connected to the PAI, or something equally inconvenient.

"I sent you and Zax the plans of her estate, didn't I?" he asked, seriously.

"Yes," she nodded.

"Aren't you even going to wait until it's dark?" he asked, a little incredulous.

"I'm busy tonight!" she objected, adopting a whining tone. "Oh by the way, those two parts I wanted you to look at, you know, the gadget bits...?"

She paused to be sure she had his attention.

"...Yes?" he asked, curious.

"Did you delete any reference to them?" she asked. She'd already asked him this, but there was no harm in double-checking. The amount of people caught out by forgetting or not bothering to cover their tracks properly only ever rose, and she intended to remain excluded from their number.

"Yes," he sighed.

"Good, I'll talk to you later," she replied, cutting him off. That morning, as there were no longer daily briefings or political discussions to be had, or even to listen in on, Satiah had spent the time learning the layout of her next target.

Marisa's estate, located on the roof of one of the many skyscrapers, was five floors high and enjoyed a garden on the outside, along with a pool and various other frills. Security drones acted as guards, although she did have a team of security androids and people too. Who didn't? Harrier and Zax between them had hacked into the security system and would be ready to hit the button on Satiah's command. Cut the power, disorientate everyone, and then swoop in to grab Marisa for interrogation. The only real problem would be Collorah. He probably wouldn't be there, but they couldn't know for sure. If he was, Satiah doubted she'd be able to get to Marisa. Zax had just completed a fly-by using her own drone and couldn't see any sign of him, but that meant nothing.

Satiah send the confirmation code to Zax, she would deactivate the drones. Satiah would have to handle the rest, but she felt pretty confident of success - so long as Collorah didn't intervene. A frontal assault, in broad daylight, with no warning, might seem risky, but she was confident in herself. A big part of it was surprise. There was only one way in and one way out. She intended to use that way as a bottleneck and a way of trapping Marisa.

"Drones are down," Zax reported, her voice low and expectant.

"How long before they notice?" she asked, about to start her personal countdown.

"They're checking already, you have about three minutes," Zax replied, efficiently. Good, easily long enough. "You've got thirty androids and six security personnel opposing you, and obviously Marisa herself. Good luck."

Bringing herself in to land in among the trees so that she'd be hidden from any window view, Satiah checked her pistol out of habit. She then calmly got out, opened the back door and dragged the Repressor free of its bag. She attached the restraining strap and, with gritted teeth, hauled it over her head so that it rested just below her hip. She pulled it back, higher until it was almost chest height. It was the only way she could get her hand far enough under it to reach the handle. A brief examination later, and with one minute to go, she attached the munition compass last of all. A red light flickered on, letting her know that it was ready to unleash a hell all of its own.

She held the compass in one hand and, with difficulty, elevated the gun with the other. It was heftier than she remembered and she wondered how many bruises it would give her when she used it. She gently tapped the trigger to test the safety. It was off. She marched quietly but purposefully forward, through the dense array of vegetation some might call a garden that acted as a privacy screen to passing drones. In less than a moment, she was emerging into a courtyard overlooked by the estate. It was… so peaceful. So serene. She smiled and raised the Repressor. Good morning, Marisa.

---

Collorah had had to change his initial plan. Stan, his new target, was out of his reach - probably close to Oli, under Brenda's protection. So he'd been forced to use some of his contacts to come up with accurate biological data relevant to Stan. If the android couldn't have the body to scan, he'd re-create the physical identity using raw data alone. The android itself just stood there, shimmering in the background while he waited. Its artificial skin had reverted back to factory settings due to lack of information. Collorah busied himself with contingency programming. If this was going to work, the real Stan had to be removed from the picture as early as possible. If this didn't happen, however, the android would need a series of adaptable instructions to follow, to carry out its orders successfully. Besides, he intended to take Stan out himself. Collorah's presence and apparent flight would be the distraction required to get Satiah away from Oli.

---

Zax stretched in her chair. Her back and arms ached from being seated in the same position for too long; until now it wasn't something she'd had much experience of. Her eyes were tired and she felt like she was on the edge of a headache that never seemed to quite arrive. Satiah had told her that she was still growing and needed her sleep, but Zax had stayed up far later than she should. She'd convinced herself that Kate was the one that was connected to angel, and all she had to do was find some evidence to show Satiah. It had quickly become an obsession to prove that, though she had much to learn, she had the potential that Satiah wanted. She was reviewing every piece of footage she had of Kate. All seven hundred hours, give or take. It would be a gruelling task for anyone, but Zax forced herself to use every bit of spare time.

She concentrated on the times when Kate was alone and might not realise she'd been observed, or times when other things of significance had happened. Times when all eyes would have been anywhere but on her. On the day when the building had collapsed, a message was sent to angel. Where was Kate when that message was sent? Everyone had been busy - too busy to watch her. Where was she? Zax tracked her movements from immediately after the collapse. She was with Shannon and Lunell, and then they were sent away from the area, shown to their temporary accommodation and... the time the message was intercepted... ten seconds. Kate was in her room, without a camera. Zax watched the closed door that led into that room, eyes wide. Two seconds... Zax actually held her breath, still staring at the closed door. Message sent. Message intercepted.

Three seconds passed. The door opened and out stepped Kate holding... a personal communicator. Zax froze the image and zoomed in as far as it would go. The screen was facing away. Zax growled out her frustration. It had to be her! It had to be! The coincidence was too much for Zax to ignore. She forced herself to calm down; she had to be alert in case Satiah wanted her for anything. She saved that part of the footage to show Satiah later, to see what she said. She might know of something that may explain this sequence, although Zax couldn't imagine what that explanation would be. She needed more, in case Satiah felt this was not enough. Rewind to when the second message was sent. The day Satiah had been spying on Jinx and Octutin. The day after she'd first brought Zax into the operation. She relived the moment in her head.

"I've got something," Zax had told Satiah. "An anonymous message, I think it's from the same person. Was sent earlier today, twenty nine minutes point seven seconds after you shot at Jinx."

At the time she'd been a bit baffled that no one was replying. They had been intercepted, but they did eventually get through - they had to, so that it would prevent anyone from becoming suspicious. She'd openly wondered if the person they were searching for was mentally unstable. She once again went through Kate's medical records. She activated voice control as it was faster.

"Hi, voice recognition, trainee Zax," she said, to get past security.

"Hello Zax, I'm Crystal, how can I help?" answered a female voice.

"I need to review some material. Kate's medical records for Operation Selector," she said, quickly.

"Loading," Crystal replied, as the screen began to change.

In a moment it was all there.

"I'm trying to establish if there is anything in here that may support a diagnosis of mental instability," Zax explained, sipping her water. "I have checked before, but I was wondering if anything has been erased since its creation?"

"It is worth noting, trainee Zax," reminded Crystal, in the same tone, "that any manipulation of this data would require specific rights to achieve." Zax scribbled a note down on a pad in front of her. A scan began. Zax watched as it happened, intrigued. She'd heard of Crystal, the ever-dependable AI, but had never worked with her before. It was said that Crystal was cannier than any living being and would often come up with creative ideas all by herself. Now Crystal was already giving Zax an idea for potential co-conspirators. Not that she needed or wanted any additional suspects at that moment, but it was nice when a computer could do that.

"Thank you," Zax chirped.

"There is a note here about a head injury, it was here before," Crystal stated.

"It was nearly seventeen years ago," Zaz said dismissively.

"If the skull was damaged, it could take a long time - or another smaller injury - before brain damage occurs," Crystal argued.

"What kind of brain damage are we talking about here?" Zax asked, frowning.

"I have an example of a male patient here. Subject received a head wound on a construction site that resulted in two skull fractures. He was healed that day, but the second skull fracture was smaller and went unnoticed. Sometime later, another injury resulted in that fracture finally impacting the brain. The bone entered the brain gradually and began to cut off his senses until he was unable to feel pain or..." Crystal explained.

"Trust me, Kate may be crazy, but not because of something like that," Zax said. Then another thought occurred to her. "Wait, scratch that!"

"You wish me to cancel...?" Crystal began.

"No, I just had an idea. This accident she had all that time ago, tell me about it," Zax requested, looking at it another way. She smiled as she began to think she might be getting somewhere. What if Kate was schizophrenic, or even had a split personality? Zax had an idea that some of the symptoms might be similar. That might explain why Kate showed no signs of guilt or culpability, because she might not even know what was happening herself. She might be aware that she was losing chunks of time, but what with everything else that was going on, perhaps she'd put that down to being overtired or simply misremembering what the timings were... or something... Crystal was, very methodically, explaining all about how the accident happened.

"Did anyone else die in the accident?" Zax asked, trying to skip everything.

"Kate's sister was killed..." Crystal began.

"This sister have a name?" Zax interrupted, unable to keep the excitement from her voice.

"Cathy... but Cathy's nickname for Kate was angel," Crystal answered. Zax smiled a exultant smile and punched the air with her fist. So what was going on? Could Kate have another personality, perhaps multiple personalities, and one of them was her dead sister? Was her dead sister trying to kill Oli? So why would she want him dead? Had Cathy known Oli? And what was Cathy trying to tell Kate? Did this mean that Kate had effectively sent these three messages to herself? In order that she didn't miss anything out, Zax compiled all that information alongside the footage she'd saved earlier. She tapped the table in front of her as she thought hard. Agitated. How could she prove this?

"Are you still there?" Crystal asked, breaking the silence.

"Yes!" Zax yelled, mildly irritated as the distraction. "Can you tell from a brain scan if someone has Dissociative Identity Disorder, or is schizophrenic?"

"Yes, but we would require a scan of her brain now, not a blueprint from seventeen years ago," Crystal informed her.

Zax did a quick read through of the information about the condition. Symptoms of schizophrenia included: hearing voices, confusing thoughts... Zax briefly considered if she might need to check she herself was ok... delusions, hallucinations... what was the difference? Well, Zax discovered, a hallucination meant seeing something that wasn't there, while a delusion, on the other hand, was seeing something that was there... wrongly. Disorganised speech was another sign, along with catatonic or disorganised behaviour. After observing so much of Kate recently, Zax tried to remember if she'd noticed any of these things. Kate was organised, Oli was the disorganised one. Did she stare into space for extended periods of time? Go into trances or anything? Was that when she became her dead sister, or when she heard her dead sister talking to her? Was she talking to the dead sister as well? Zax held her head in her hands. Satiah would not like this idea, it was too over-complicated, too messy, and she would like it nice and simple.

But this, plus that footage, must surely be worth investigating further! Surely she would say that? Guess who it would be that had to do that extra investigation? Zax sighed, knowing Satiah would make her do it, and returned to the computer.

"Any history of hereditary madness?" she asked, dismally.

"None."

"Any criminal history?"

"None."

"Anything of any interest at all?" she demanded, angry now.

"Please be more specific…"

"Forget it," she sighed, giving up.

"Forget… erasing all data concerning…"

"No! Stop! Don't delete anything!" Zax hissed, frantically. "Just leave everything alone for a second. Stay!"

---

"I thought you were lying about that machine," Ruby stated, a little shocked.

"No, you are the one who likes to make things up as you go along. I, on the other hand, only deceive when I must. Everything I told Satiah was true, except for the part that it might once have existed… as you know, I'm almost certain it still does. And we will have to find it before the humans do," he stated, grimly. "Technology like that should never have been created. It's almost impossible to unlearn knowledge. In this case, if we can find it before them, we can ensure they never learn of it," he went on. She began to mimic him in silence as he spoke. When he turned to see what she was doing she stopped and pretended to be listening closely to him.

"What about this other power thingy you were going on about?" she asked, genuinely puzzled.

Now it was Ash's turn to mimic her.

"Power thingy?" he repeated. "Going on about? I thought you were slightly better informed than that!"

"You've told me nothing!" she declared, shaking her head. "You never tell me anything! You just say patronising things like: 'I'm sure you can think of a reason for that', or 'you've already been given the answer to that'! You remind me of one of my old managers who I hated sometimes! He would write a message to everyone, telling them not to write messages to everyone! And loads of other preposterous…" Ash swung around to face her directly, suddenly serious.

"What do you mean by that?" he asked, a little dauntingly. Ruby froze. What do you mean, what do I mean?

"Err... just saying," she mumbled, not sure what she'd done to warrant that kind of reaction.

"Satiah was saying things like that in her mind," he muttered, staring off into the middle-distance. She followed his gaze nervously for a few seconds before facing him again.

"What?" she asked, inevitably.

"I told you, she was resisting me. It was just her at first, but like I said, someone else intervened," he replied. "Her strategy to prevent me seeing what was in her mind, was basically to think as fast and as nonsensically as she could. She was tiring and I knew all I had to do was wait..." He trailed off.

"Until help arrived," Ruby concluded, softly. He nodded grimly. "Was the help this strange power source you are scared of?"

"I'm not scared..." he began. She crossed her arms and raised her eyebrow at him disbelievingly. "I am wary of it," he allowed, resentfully. "And, as a matter of fact, no, it was not the power that intervened. It was strong, whatever it was, strong and slippery." Ruby made a disgusted face.

"Sounds delightful."

---

There wasn't anything understated about Satiah's attack. The Repressor, the second she pulled the trigger, began slowly but surely to dismantle the building. Laser fire of incredible speed and power chewed up the walls and the door in a storm of powder and shrapnel. Satiah had to brace herself to ensure that she didn't fall over or lose control of it, as the recoil was phenomenal. Teeth gritted, she swung from left to right and back again. A few wild shots were fired back in her general direction, but nothing to be concerned about. Androids and people alike were cut down instantly as they ran out of the mansion to try and confront her. To Satiah, the constant jolting from the gun felt like she was drilling into the ground, or something equally unforgiving.

After less than twenty seconds, the wall began to fall away, exposing the interior of the structure. Satiah continued shooting, as the dust cloud slowly rolled out past her.

"One target remaining," Zax said, in her ear. Marisa. Satiah stopped and silence reigned. That gun made a serious racket. Getting it off would be tricky, so she simply undid the strap. The Repressor crashed to the ground next to her. It had done its job well, though her hip had another opinion. She then pulled out her pistol and began a cautious approach towards the remains of the building.

Marisa, covered in sweat and dirt, peered out from where she'd hidden herself, terror in her eyes. The dust cloud was so thick it was hard to see anything, but she was just glad the shooting had stopped. Satiah picked her way quickly through the rubble and into the part of the building that was still standing. Marisa knew she couldn't fight, and running didn't seem to be a real possibility either. She did the only thing she could do to keep some dignity. She slowly stood and raised her hands.

"I'm here, whoever you are! What do you want? Money or revenge?" she asked, trying to keep her voice from shaking. Satiah emerged from the dust, her pistol the first thing to break out from the realm of menacing shadow.

"Neither," she growled, suspecting a trap. "You move ahead of me, don't make me have to carry you back to my vehicle." Marisa nodded in defeat and began to move ahead of Satiah, back the way she had come.

"Look, we can talk about this," Marisa was saying, in fearful mutterings. "I'm sure, whatever you want, we can work something out."

"We will," Satiah replied, carelessly. As they reached her transporter, Satiah stunned her and then shoved her unconscious body in the back. She retrieved the Repressor - best not leave something like that lying around - and then drove back towards Phantom headquarters.

---

Marisa awoke, strapped to a gurney at an obtuse angle, her head higher than her feet. Her head, feet, hands and middle were all firmly restrained. Zax was standing nearby, her hands clasped behind her back. She looked down at Marisa coldly but didn't say a word... as instructed. Despite her youth, her stare was quite unnerving, especially to a stranger.

"You? Who are you? What do you want?" Marisa asked, scared. Zax just continued to stare without saying anything. Marisa was smart enough to know it was meant to scare her, but was unable to stop it succeeding. A door opened and Satiah wandered in, reached Marisa's right side, crossed her arms and stared down at her.

"Who do you two work for?" Marisa asked, her throat dry.

"Do you know anyone called angel?" Satiah asked, watching her closely. Marisa was confused. She didn't, she'd not heard that name any time recently.

"No," she said, hopefully. Satiah and Zax walked behind her, where she couldn't see them, for a silent consultation.

"Is she lying?" Zax asked, seriously.

"No," Satiah responded, just as intensely. "Not about that, anyway. She's of no further use to us, report this to Randal and then he can decide what is to be done with her. In the meantime, I'd better be getting back."

"I'm very wealthy, I'm sure we can come to some arrangement!" Marisa yelled, nervously. Both women ignored her. Zax told Satiah of her latest theory concerning Kate. Satiah didn't interrupt, she just listened.

When Zax was finished, she awaited Satiah's outlook.

"It's very... creative," smiled Satiah, a little patronisingly. "I think you're starting to go down the route of getting the facts to fit the theories instead of the other way around. This often happens as possibilities become increasingly elusive."

"But the name!" Zax persisted, levelly. "It's too much of a coincidence, and you told me, you said coincidences don't exist!"

"Er... they don't. This is more... more of a fluke," rambled Satiah, thinking about it. Zax eyed her dubiously and it was all Satiah could do not to laugh. Zax had clearly been working very hard and that was not to be discouraged, but it was all so incredibly unlikely.

"A fluke?" Zax repeated, doubtfully. "Okay, well, what about the footage of her with her communicator? That a happenstance or something else?"

"Watch your tongue, young lady," Satiah growled, sternly. Zax straightened and exerted her self-control. Satiah thought about it.

"Give me a moment," Satiah said, returning to Marisa. "Where's Collorah?"

"I don't know, but I can find him," she offered, instantly. "Is that what this is about? You work for Oli? I can call him off!"

"Please do," Satiah ordered, unstrapping one of her arms. At gunpoint Marisa was handed a communicator. She called Collorah, he didn't answer so she left a message. Satiah smiled as she returned Marisa's arm to its confinement.

"Now what?" Marisa asked, tearfully.

Satiah ignored the question and returned to Zax, who was still waiting.

"All right… show me," Satiah requested. Zax smiled and led the way. Soon they were back inside Zax's room and reviewing the footage together. Satiah had to admit it looked promising.

"Well?" Zax demanded, a little haughty.

"It's the same problem as Shannon and Lunell, there's no proof she was calling anyone," Satiah responded, thinking about it. "I grant you it does look very suspicious though. I just… don't get the motive."

"I told you, she thinks she's her own dead sister!" Zax repeated, starting to sound a little crazy herself. Satiah crossed her arms and leaned onto the table thoughtfully. And what possible motive for killing Oli would her dead sister have exactly? Zax continued to pace up and down behind her, unable to stand still.

"…A brain scan will confirm if there is anything untoward going on," Satiah murmured, after more thought.

"So bring her in, we can do it ourselves," Zax demanded. Satiah shot her a glare. Zax paused. "You know? If you think we need to," she added, more respectfully.

"I really don't think it's her…" Satiah sighed.

"Well, it has to be someone there," Zax said, starting to sound like Randal. "You say you know it's not Shannon. Okay, fair enough. But how can you know it's not Kate too? You're nowhere near as close to her." She did have a point, but Satiah's sixth sense remained obstinate. It wasn't Kate. All this stuff about accidents and schizophrenia was... interesting, and Satiah could see why Zax thought she'd got something... and maybe she had, but... it still didn't feel correct.

She glanced across at Zax who was breathing hard with the effort of not exploding. She knew she had less than twelve hours now before Randal and the others formally ordered her to arrest Shannon. If Snell had only, for once, got it right before, then none of this would have been necessary! That was the PAI all over though: creating more problems than they ever managed to solve. If she wasted those twelve hours trying to prove a sane person sane, then she would not be happy. Yet Zax had to learn these things, and Satiah's previous idea of arresting Shannon herself was the only other thing she could think of. On the other hand, if Zax was right (and Satiah hadn't actually said she was wrong yet, even though that was what she thought), then it would solve everything.

And when the truth came out, the truth that Satiah envisaged - that it was neither Kate, nor Shannon - what then?

"Come with me and bring a gun," Satiah ordered. Zax blinked, for a second wondering if she'd misheard, and then hurriedly gathered a holster and pistol she'd prepared previously. Satiah eyed her choice of firearm casually. The PL15... nothing remarkable about it, but solid enough to learn with, she supposed. She did still have smallish hands, so until she'd stopped growing, it was better holding off on deciding which would be her tools of choice. Without a word, they returned to Satiah's transporter and flew off.

"We're going to have to do this fast," breathed Satiah, as they accelerated. "Right or wrong, I only have so long to prove Shannon is innocent."

Zax nodded.

"Snatch Kate?" Zax guessed. Satiah nodded. A communicator went off and Zax answered it.

"Marisa?" Collorah asked. Zax grinned.

"It's for you," she sniggered, cheekily. Satiah glowered at her before answering.

"No, it's Satiah I'm afraid, we need to talk," she replied, curtly. "I know what you're planning to do and I know who hired you to do it. Marisa is now my prisoner. If you give up now, I'll let you go, can't be any fairer." There was a pause.

"...You're bluffing," he chuckled, grimly. "I have no idea who Marisa is, and besides, I've already been paid and... well... I'm professional enough to do what I've been paid to do."

"You mean you don't care about her?" Satiah said. "That's okay, neither do I. I'm pretty sure you care about yourself though. If you go ahead with this, I too will finish my job this time. I'm a professional too. And my job is killing you."

"...You talk very tough," he noted, obviously sneering.

"I've already beaten you twice," she reminded. "Just saying."

"You can't kill what you can't find," he retorted, disconnecting. Technically not true, an atomic blast for example would do it, but she understood his point.

"Trace the signal?" Satiah asked. Zax and Harrier would already be zeroing in, she hoped.

"Parking area, disused, he won't still be there though," Zax answered. "He obviously doesn't trust Marisa."

"Neither would I," Satiah shrugged. They pulled into the entrance area of The Bulwark.

---

Brenda watched as the image of Admiral Wester of the Colonial Federation loomed up large in front of her.

"Benefactor Watt," he smiled, cordially. "I apologise for you having to fit me into your no doubt overflowing schedule."

"It's still Brenda o-officially," Brenda smiled, a little self-deprecatingly. "The election is not over yet."

"My mistake, Brenda," he said, although she suspected it hadn't been. "How can I help?"

## Hulta Gertrude

"I-I will get straight to the point, Admiral, as neither of us h-have much time to waste over fri-frivolities," she said, trying to maintain a stolid countenance. "The fact is… well… your ships have been spotted in our territory recently. One even threatened a freighter which challenged them. I recognise you're clamping down on pirate a-activity and I have no problem with that. Indeed, I would encourage you; h-however… I have certain responsibilities with regard to keeping Coalition citizens safe within my territory."

"I see," he said, more seriously. "I had heard nothing of this. I admit my Captains all have standing orders to pursue pirates wherever they go and it is not stipulated specifically that Union or Coalition territory is exempt from this order. Do you have the ship's name?" Brenda did not and her heart sank a little. She didn't know for sure if Wester was lying to her or not, but it sounded an awful lot like an evasion.

"I regret I do not," she replied, honestly. "Like I said, nothing bad happened, as such. It's more about the fact that they shouldn't have b-been there."

"If a Federation warship finds itself in Union or Coalition territory without a viable pirate target, it must immediately declare itself and dock at the shipyard of the Coalition or Union navy's choice. That's the rule," Wester reminded. "If this was not done and a ship was in your territory without a target then yes, I would admit the Captain acted wrongly. I would hesitate before I disciplined them though, there may have been special circumstances that prevented them from following the protocol."

"Forgive me for my ignorance in these matters, Admiral," Brenda smiled, ever courteous. "But what circumstances would those be?"

"Damage to his ship may have factored into this equation, whether it be navigational or communication related," Wester replied, clearly ready for that question. "He may have even believed he wasn't in your territory and thus saw no need to let you know he was there."

"Then I feel duty bound to warn you that in order to help you catch these pirates, regular border patrols have been introduced," Brenda smiled, a little less polite and a lot more assertive. "I must give my citizens peace of mind that they will not be fired upon within Coalition territory."

"Of course," he smiled, not in the least put out by this.

"Patrols are to be tripled," the aide whispered, into her communicator. "They are to be given special orders with regard to confronting Federation ships."

"Very good," was the reply. "The PAI reports that the Federation is still continuing its ship building and recruiting programs."

"I'll pass that on," she said, frowning slightly.

"Have you heard anything from the Union?" Wester enquired, changing the subject.

"No, radio silence continues, you?" she asked.

"The President says no, and I know I've heard nothing," he replied. "The CNC seem to be thinking along the lines of a coup. And I saw you in the debate saying something similar."

"I said…" she began, smiling.

"I know you said you were only repeating what you'd heard," he chuckled. "Will that be all?"

"Y-yes Admiral, thank you for returning our call," she said. He bowed his head slightly before vanishing into static. Brenda turned to look at her aide.

"Well?"

The aide shrugged.

"You've done all you can at this juncture," she replied. "You handled it wonderfully." Brenda smiled in relief.

"Do you think he was telling the truth about not knowing anything about it?" Brenda asked, more sceptically.

"So long as it doesn't happen again, that shouldn't matter," the aide replied. "Those patrols are in position." Brenda blinked.

"That was quick," she said, a bit startled.

"Brenda, you have in your control the best armed forces in existence. Efficiency is a word not capable of conveying how exemplary they are," the aide said, smiling confidently. "They are utterly dedicated to you. Your orders, whatever they may be, are what these guys live for."

"What's going on here?" Shannon demanded. Satiah had one arm and Zax the other; together they were guiding a very confused Kate along between them.

"One last health check," Satiah growled, unwilling to waste time. "You're next, by the way." Shannon looked bewildered by this. Zax gave her a smile and a nod as she passed by without a word. Lunell looked on, though he knew what was going on.

"What's going on really?" Kate asked, not believing the medical explanation.

"We're going to give you a free brain scan," Satiah told her, levelly. There was a moment where Satiah and Kate just stared at one another and then Kate realised what was going on.

To be physically and forcibly led away, even arrested, in front of everyone like this, was more traumatic than it might first appear. People would always think, without fire there could be no smoke, that she was guilty of something. When tainted like that, even when later proven innocent, people changed the way they looked at you. It was almost like, to them, that you had become another person and could never return to being what you were – in their eyes, at least. It reminded her of a time when she had been little more than an infant and, due to various circumstances at the time, she'd had to stand up in front of a crowd of her own friends and explain why she had turned up without the correct uniform. Humiliation had a variety of flavours, but it always left you feeling hollow and empty, not unlike a great nameless sadness. And, even years later, a brief memory alone could almost make the whole experience repeat itself in your mind, making you squirm and cringe almost as much as you had at the time.

"You think it's me, don't you?" she asked, horrified. There seemed to be little sense in any other explanation. Their grim expressions, formal manner and general behaviour were confirmation enough. Satiah saw no reason in denying it.

"I don't, law enforcement here thinks it might be," Satiah said, blaming Zax openly. "Either way, we have to check."

"You're wasting your time, but if it will bring an end to this insanity then I'll..." Kate began, flustered.

"Interesting choice of word there, Kate," Zax said, keenly. Satiah couldn't hide her smile. Zax had a long way to go but she had the embryo of strength in her. This may indeed turn out to be a fool's errand, but for Zax this was as much about learning how to fight for her views, as it was about being a good investigator. Her challenges wouldn't just come from her enemies, but her so-called allies would want to clash with her too.

They got Kate inside the transporter and sped away.

"I swear that I would never willingly do anything to harm Oli," she ranted, sharply. "What ever gave you the idea that I would do such a thing, for goodness sake...?"

"It's a process, just play along and keep the yammering down," Zax snapped back. Satiah raised an eyebrow, knowing that Zax had only done that for her benefit. To show how tough she could be.

"Excuse me, where is my legal representation?" Kate demanded, angry at being spoken to like that.

"You won't need any."

"Satiah, come on, you know me, will you please explain to this upstart that..." Kate appealed.

"This has to be done, Kate," Satiah spoke soothingly over her, maintaining the pretence of someone who cared. "I'm sorry, if there had been any other way and all that..." She turned right abruptly.

"Wait, where are we going? That way is..." Kate asked, now even more worried and confused. Satiah gave Zax the nod.

"Bag her," she said. Zax nodded and clambered into the backseat before, ruthlessly and roughly, pulling a black cloth over Kate's head. Kate continued to protest, although she didn't physically resist. None of that was strictly necessary, but Satiah didn't want to advertise Phantom headquarter's location if she could help it. Kate had by now realised that this wouldn't be on the books at all, and she didn't know if that worried her more or less! Fear was making her want to be sick. She heard the vehicle stop and was led briskly down corridors, into lifts and she couldn't tell what else, into a room. Then she was lain on a bed of some sort, and she could hear thrumming sounds.

Zax eagerly awaited the results, while Satiah wondered what she would do when she discovered she was wrong. As she predicted, the result came through as a negative. Zax groaned and then eyed Satiah.

"Sorry," she said, downcast. There wasn't anything else she could think to say. She'd been so sure that she was right, in spite of the doubts. Satiah didn't have to say: I told you.

"Well, it had to be checked," she said, instead. "Now while I'm taking Kate back, you…"

"Can get back to my room and start looking for angel again," Zax finished for her, looking glum. "Okay." A new idea materialised in Satiah's mind and she smiled deviously.

"And one more thing, I need a favour - Snell may be of help," Satiah said, to Zax. "I need a package delivered to a certain location. Tell him to call me for details."

Zax frowned in confusion, while watching as Satiah helped Kate outside, without giving her anything more to work with. A package? What was Satiah planning now? How was she ever going to learn if Satiah taught her like this?

"Well?" Kate asked, a little emotional.

"Look me over closely, and you won't see any regrets," Satiah quipped, knowing that Kate couldn't see a thing from under the cloth. "I knew it wasn't you and I had told them several times, but they wouldn't take no for an answer, so I had to prove it."

"That's a relief," she said, visibly relaxing. "Everyone else is going to think I'm up to something now."

"Yes, they are," Satiah agreed, with significance. "That is why you're not going back."

"Huh?"

"With you out of the picture, the real culprit might drop their guard and reveal themselves," Satiah explained, casually. "At the least, they'll think we are no longer looking for anyone. Especially if I go back and tell everyone it's you that's been trying to kill Oli all this time."

"…Even if this works, what happens to me? Where do I go?" she asked, seeing no path ahead other than cooperation.

"You will be moved to a safe location and held there until the election is over," she said, casually. Then she added, "Or perhaps longer, depending on what happens." She didn't tell Kate that she would be released as soon as it was over anyway, because that was when the operation came to an end and Satiah would no longer have to care about any of this.

"It's all a bit blunderbuss though, isn't it?" Kate asked, critically. "I mean…"

"Are you questioning my tactics?" Satiah asked, sudden heat in her tone.

"No, not at all," Kate said, giving up. Satiah grinned. Kate was right though. Just because someone had been apparently caught and blamed, didn't at all mean that the real guilty party would just drop all pretences and relax. She was hoping that they might at least poke their head out from their hiding place to try and see what was going on. Maybe get a touch complacent. There was a small chance a mistake would be made. Too much information given, too much asked for, or too much already known. It would only take one word. A lot of people gave themselves away like that. Satiah herself had done it once or twice too, and could therefore attest to its likelihood and potentials.

━━━━━✦✦✦✦✦━━━━━

"No! Not Kate," Shannon gasped, shocked and completely aghast. "I would never… I mean… How did you find out?"

"I didn't, law enforcement did," lied Satiah, unable to stop herself paying very close attention to Shannon. She still didn't think it was her, but she was starting to get to the stage where she was doubting herself. Shannon still looked baffled.

"How…?" she trailed off, shaking her head. "I think they are wrong, somehow they've got it wrong. I know Kate, she's never been anything other than a good friend." Satiah shrugged.

"They didn't say," Satiah said, shrugging. "I couldn't believe it either, but it would explain why we never found the killer among us, and as we all never even thought about it being her… doesn't that make you wonder?"

"Maybe, but… she was poisoned that time!" Shannon reminded.

"She might have done that to herself to avoid suspicion. I mean, would you suspect an apparent victim of the insider?" Shannon was starting to at last get used to the idea, but Satiah was now even more convinced that it wasn't her.

She took the time to look around the room at the various huddles of personnel who were all talking about what had happened. Which one of you? Shannon followed Satiah's gaze and her eyes settled on Angello. She felt guilty for having started to think it might be him. As usual, no one was acting in a way that could be described as anything other than perfectly normal. Given the circumstances, that in itself might even be regarded as suspicious. Lunell was in among them, probably still searching too. This was ridiculous, Satiah realised. How could someone be able to hide so completely? Was there a way they could be lured out? This person was clearly not going to attack Oli in person, certainly not with everyone else nearby. This situation was starting to remind her of an operation from years ago. On a long haul trip, a case had been found containing a gun and a picture of one of the people there. A target. And Satiah had had to try to work out for whom the case had been put there.

After much deliberation, she'd decided on a crafty approach. Instead of announcing its discovery or even warning the person in the picture, Satiah had placed the case in the middle of the busy area within the ship, a place most people congregated. She'd then positioned herself above it where she would wait for someone to take it. She'd not even informed security of her plan, as they too had been suspects. A guard had picked up the case and, as she'd been about to shoot him, he'd called out to everyone in the room to see who it belonged to. That was when the real owner had said it was his, and thus revealed themselves. Short of getting Oli to fake his own death, Satiah couldn't think of a way of using that idea in this case. It was about the correct bait… the right impetus that could compel them into exposing themselves. Now, wasn't that a thought?

Lunell gave her a nod and, knowing what it would be about, Satiah nodded back and they exited the room.

"What's going on?" he asked, the second they were out of earshot.

"You don't believe it was Kate then?" she grinned.

"You know I don't," he responded, shrugging.

"I'm trying to use Kate to get some idea of who it really is," she explained, seeing no reason to lie about it. Lunell paused, considering this tactic carefully. He made a thoughtful noise.

"What about Shannon?" he asked, at last. "Still no signs of guilt?"

"No, there's nothing," she replied, shaking her head. Lunell pulled a face that made it obvious how fed up he felt about this. She could understand, she felt the same way.

"I am seriously considering asking for permission to arrest everyone here and interrogate them one at a time until we get this solved," he stated, with anger.

"That would be one potential solution," she allowed. "Assuming we're right about that person still being alive and still working here." Oli wandered out into the hallway at that moment, and they instantly went quiet.

"Satiah?" he asked, grimly. "What's going on? You must know it wasn't Kate, it couldn't have been! She was even poisoned…"

"I don't know what evidence they have or even how they worked it out," Satiah said, holding up her hands. "I have told them that I think they're mistaken, but they think they have something."

"And they wouldn't tell you what it was? That's outrageous; I'm going to call my lawyer…" he began, starting to search his pockets for his communicator.

"No need,' she smiled, quickly. "She has plenty of representation already. Everyone is doing everything they can, okay? You just go back to preparing for this last show with Deetee."

"I can't, my assistant has been arrested!" he hissed, sarcastically.

"Then I will take her place," Satiah responded, rolling her eyes. "What topics are we going over?"

"All of them," he replied, sourly. "Though I doubt we will need to."

"Fine," she replied, shortly. She didn't want to spend any more time with Oli, particularly alone, but in order to carry on this absurd charade, she had to step in. They went over some likely questions and responses for a few hours. Oli, she could tell, was not looking forward to this interview. She wondered if he remembered what she'd asked him to do before. No matter what the outcome of this election was, running again would mean she'd never forgive him. She took comfort from the fact that his defeat was inevitable now. Brenda had all but won. She wouldn't like to imagine what might have happened, should it have gone differently. As it was, this could have all been so much easier but, thinking about it, it could have been so much worse.

There were positives to be taken from this too. She'd finally been able to check on Zax. Carl and she were closer now than they had been before, despite the near break up. She'd been able to fix Kelvin, even if she didn't know whether she'd ever use him again. The trouble was, even if it registered in his computer mind that she was angry with him, he couldn't feel the shame she needed him to.

Randal would owe her one for that review she'd had to do. So, glass half full? Another look at Oli and she wished it was completely full and within her reach so she could drink it. He was almost broken now, she could tell. Spiritually and emotionally. One more push would be all it would take. She couldn't find it in herself to pick a fight with him though. She was tired of this mission, and decided to just ride it out without complaining.

---

"It's not her," Lunell said, with finality. Scott and Randal eyed him levelly. They were standing on the walkway that Connie had tried to throw herself from the day before. It was early evening, and the lights of the cityscape were engaged in their battle to outshine the dying sun's rays.

"So if it's not Kate and it's not Shannon, where does that leave us?" Scott asked, rather pointlessly. It was self-evident where it left them. Nowhere with nothing.

"Without a suspect," Lunell said. "You want my opinion?" Neither Randal nor Scot answered, so he went on. "We continue to guard Oli until the election is over as planned, and then we stop regardless of angel and whoever it is working with them." Randal shrugged, knowing it was Scott's pronouncement. Scott pondered for a moment.

"Collorah is still out there, obviously, but his instructions were to take out Oli before the end of the election. If he succeeds after the election is over, what is the consequence?"

"Nothing we can't handle," Randal replied, having already thought about that possibility.

"Are you positive that you have no further leads on angel? What about Satiah?" Scott asked, unwilling to admit defeat.

"She's still guarding Oli and trying to find angel," he said. "She's holding Kate and pretending that she's the insider we've been looking for, in an attempt to trick whoever the real enemy is into making a mistake. She doesn't think it will work though."

"We've tried everything else," Scott hissed.

"If we can keep him alive until the end, whatever happens to him after that is no longer our concern," Randal stated, not wanting an extension to this mission. It was taking up a surprising amount of his time and it wasn't the only mission he was working on.

At any given time, Randal would be overseeing as many as two hundred operations at a time. He often managed only four hours of sleep a day - not enough, he would be the first to admit. As a Phantom Leader, one of only three, he was greatly overstretched. There were several senior Phantom agents, one of which was Satiah. He knew she would want promotion. It would mean she would be able to give orders, rather than just take them. Mensa didn't wish to move up the ranks. Both Satiah and Mensa loathed the additional responsibilities and other duties, but he was sure they wouldn't take too much persuading - duties such as interacting with politicians and other government officials on a regular basis. Randal understood and felt the same way. In the days before the Vourne conspiracy, there had been over ten Phantom Leaders. Fourteen, if his memory served him well. The purge had taken its toll on the organisation. That was why he was forced constantly to ask people like Satiah to work not only as operatives, but as teachers too.

"Indeed," Scott nodded. "I can square that with upstairs easily enough. Very well... it's agreed."

"Good," Randal smiled, but didn't go away. He knew they were not plotting against him and Satiah any more, but he wanted them to think that he might not believe that. He'd send a message to Satiah, explaining the outcome of this meeting. She'd been invited, of course, but typically, she had rudely declined. He passed the minutes - the recorded data in other words - to Zax, with instructions to send it on to Satiah in the morning. He stared out at the city, starting to wish he'd refused his own promotion. He'd taken it out of a sense of duty as much as anything else. He wondered how long Oli would survive after Satiah stopped protecting him. The odds did not look good.

---

Kate looked up as the android came in with her food and water. A screen flickered on, displaying Zax's face.

"You okay in there?" she asked, casually.

"About as well as one could expect to be, locked up and pretending to have been arrested,' Kate responded, sourly. "Is this how law enforcement works normally?"

"No, we're having to use our imaginations a lot more these days," Zax remarked, as though it hardly mattered.

"So I have to stay in here until the end of the election?" Kate qualified.

"That, or we get a breakthrough," Zax agreed.

"And when I am released, what am I going to tell everyone?" she enquired, morosely.

"I'm working on that," Zax smiled, confidently. "I suggest you try to make use of this time to rest and relax as best you can. Don't worry, I know you won't find that easy." She disconnected before Kate could reply to that.

---

With the data collected, Collorah could now implement his plan. His contacts had also revealed that Oli still had one final appearance to make outside of the Bulwark: an interview. He also had its time and location. It would be there that he would strike. Going up against the Bulwark would be suicide, even with the android. The android itself now looked identical to Stan. It had his memories and all other data required to pass itself off as him. Collorah had provided it with a gun and had also implanted an explosive device within it. That would be activated, should the gun not be enough. He began pulling on his armour, knowing to expect another clash with Satiah. She was right: she had beaten him. He felt he had the measure of her now though, and knew that the trick to finally beating her would be at a distance, rather than getting in close. He adjusted the rifle and rechecked the sights. Perfectly aligned. It would soon be time.

---

"If he brings up your brother's death and the leaked tax document, you're going to have to do your best not to overreact, though a certain amount of emotion will be expected," Satiah said, eyeing the list in front of her.

"What?" he asked, baffled. "Care to elucidate further on that?"

"The audience will expect you to show some sign of compassion," she reminded, levelly. "It's well known that you were not close, nevertheless..." she trailed off.

"You think Deetee will...?" Oli asked, wondering if Deetee would be so insensitive.

"Of course he will, that man has no concept of right or wrong,' Satiah muttered, seriously. "He will certainly talk to you about your defeat in the vote."

"It's not over yet!" Oli objected angrily.

She met his eyes with her own stern gaze.

"If that's how you want to play it then, by all means, hide in denial - but I think everyone would respect you more if you accepted the inevitable," she stated, coldly. He sighed, and for a moment thought about challenging her on the point, but he knew she had no liking for him and, he thought begrudgingly, she was correct. He had already lost this race; they just hadn't crossed the finishing line yet. His brother hadn't crossed the finishing line all those years ago... and now he couldn't.

"What are your plans regarding your future?" she asked, gravely. He couldn't look at her as he answered.

"I… I will run again in the next election. I've got much further than anyone ever predicted. My people would expect it. And I still believe I could do a better job than Brenda," he replied, strongly.

Satiah locked her anger away inside a tiny part of her mind. She'd half expected him to do this. Either his ambition, or his dislike of her trying to stop him, was fuelling this. Most people did shove back when pushed… however long it took them.

"I see," was her response, deliberately given without significance. He turned to face her.

"I'm truly sorry Satiah, but I can't give up, not after all this… in a way, it's because of all this that I must go on… even if that means you can never forgive me," he explained sincerely. He didn't know how she'd react to that, but he didn't expect the low chuckle that came from her.

"That's okay Oli, it really is," she said, as if trying to hold back laughter. "You can't win them all." He frowned at that remark, not sure what to make of it. He knew he should be feeling relieved. Relieved that she hadn't raged at him, or started to cry, or just pretended not to hear, but this… it was unnerving.

"So… you're not angry?" he asked tentatively.

"The days when I may have invested any sort of emotion in your actions were only ever in your own mind," she remarked, rather cuttingly. "You have the right to run again, there's nothing anyone can do to stop you doing that… legally. I just honestly believed you would decide, after all this death, pain and violence, that it might be a smarter move not to repeat it. But then I remembered that you're a politician. You never do the smart thing." He gave a half-hearted sneer in response, before turning his back on her to look out at the city.

"What else is there?" he asked, his voice forced and professional.

"If you have any warnings about, or for, Brenda, Deetee will probably ask you about them," she said. "Kate has requested that you'd better not say anything that might insult or smear Brenda. And after the way she supported you in the debate, I'd say you owe her that much anyway. Kate's recommended that you…"

"Can't you just bring Kate back?" he demanded, turning on her suddenly. "She's done nothing wrong and with respect, she'd be far better at this than you are." She smiled levelly at him. In a way, if she'd just arrested his entire campaign team on day one it would have solved everything. Randal would never have allowed it though, because of maintaining the precious illusion and all that, but still... Oli was at the end of the line now, she could tell. It had all got a bit too much and now that he'd been almost completely isolated, he was lashing out.

"I would if I could, believe me," she answered, amused. "In any case, she has recommended that you stick to what you agreed with her before. Remind everyone of the dangers of...of... oh, whatever it is you go on about." She was deliberately pretending not to remember what he often said, just to annoy him.

"Get out," he ordered, in a hiss. "I can't believe I was ever attracted to someone like you." She half expected him to stamp his foot in petulance, like a child who had been refused a treat.

"Neither can I," she agreed, shrugging. She stood and stretched just to show how unbothered she was by this latest exchange. "Shall I send Shannon in?" He was about to snap to the affirmative when he stopped himself and looked pained.

"No... it's fine," he responded, in a tiny mumble. "I'll... I'll do this myself."

"Sorry, say that again?! I never heard a politician say that before," she quipped, as she left the room.

---

"Well?" Carl asked, the second she walked into the room. Now he was completely in the know, he wanted to know if anything had happened. She smiled as he held up an Essp bar.

"Kate is... not guilty," she declared, theatrically. He groaned deeply and thumped the table in disappointment before sliding the bar across the table to her. "Isn't it unlucky to bet on the outcome of this kind of thing?" she asked, grinning.

"Maybe, but who said it was unlucky for us?" he replied, shrugging. She laughed. There was a little beat of silence. "You okay?"

"No..." she confessed, disappointed. "It's only frustration because I feel as if I've lost this contest. I feel as if I've been routed by angel." He put his arms around her. "Like, everything I try, or even think of, they are one step ahead all the time and I don't like it."

"It's not over yet," he said, kissing the top of her head softly. "You still got..." He paused as he realised how little time there actually was.

"Three days," she articulated, her voice muffled slightly.

"... Some time left," he modified, optimistically. "And you have got a plan?"

"Not the best one I've ever had," she admitted, seriously. "Getting everyone to believe it is Kate - just on the off chance that someone might let their guard drop - reeks of desperation."

"Come on, you know that everyone makes mistakes, there's always a chance," he encouraged, loyally. "Anyway, all you have to do is keep that twerp alive for another three days and then kick him goodbye." She giggled.

"Are you still jealous?" she asked, smiling.

"Of a guy who gets to spend all day with you, of course!" he announced, with comic gusto.

"Good," she murmured, closing her eyes. "You know... I could get used to this. Having you this close all the time is better than I thought."

"But you're okay with me not doing anything, right?" he asked, mock concerned. He was talking about the housework. She deliberately misunderstood the question.

"Can you do *anything* right?" she asked, grinning.

"Ouch. Why are you so mean?"

"I can't help it." Her communicator went off. It was Mr Slimy. She answered with a grin. "Did you get my instructions?"

---

Week six, day five.

"If there was ever any doubt about the outcome of this, you've just delivered another body blow to Oli," said Lunell in a low voice. Lunell and Satiah were inside the Bulwark, walking up the steps to the next floor.

"What wrong with him now?" she asked, carelessly.

"He's gone off his food, he's not talking to anyone… he's just sat in his office, staring into space," Lunell replied, seriously.

"We've just got that final interview to do," she explained, ignoring his answer. "If I know anything about Collorah, he will strike at us then, using this android. Our problem is that, despite the fact that we know what he's going to do, we don't know who the android will be disguised as." Lunell nodded.

"It is his best chance."

"It's even conceivable that it's already here and active among us," she went on. Lunell's eyes widened slightly, he'd not thought of that.

"Don't worry," she said, seeing the look. "I'm almost certain that it's not. Nevertheless, we need to stay vigilant."

"Do you want me to inform the others?" he offered.

"No, no, I'll do that," she said, thinking about it. "You stay close to Oli." Lunell nodded. They entered the lobby area of the next floor and separated. Shannon looked up as Satiah came in and smiled welcomingly.

"Three more days!" she said, in greeting.

"Aye," Satiah grunted, as she dumped her rifle heavily onto the table.

"Any news?" Shannon enquired, as Satiah knew she would. It would be odd if she didn't.

"They, for whatever reason, are not including me on anything at the moment," Satiah dodged. "I think they're concerned that I'm too close to Kate or something."

"Oli is not happy," Shannon sighed, looking strained. "He refuses to believe that she is the one. To be honest, I still can't believe it either." Satiah nodded sympathetically, but just shrugged in a 'what can you do?' sort of way. "Can't you get one of your law enforcement contacts to say something?"

"I've tried," Satiah replied, earnestly. "I don't want to irritate them any more than I already have. I'm sure they will let us know what's happening soon."

"I know," Shannon agreed. "I should just be happy that I'm not a suspect anymore, I suppose."

"That would be what I would think," lied Satiah, casually. Then she smiled deviously. "Of course, if it really is her, it's always possible that she wasn't working alone..." That got Shannon's attention.

"What? Where did that idea come from?" she asked, concerned.

"It's just..." she paused, dramatically. "...I don't know. I guess it's because I think if they're right about Kate, someone who no one ever suspected, who else might we have missed?" Shannon was looking all around at everyone again with renewed alertness.

"And if they are wrong..." Shannon went further. Satiah nodded conspiratorially.

"Exactly."

"So... if we think Kate is innocent, that that means the suspect is still here," Shannon said, rather pointlessly. "Who would you think it is?" Satiah pulled a face of confusion.

"Well... it would have to be someone in here," she replied, rather dumbly. "Everyone else is dead."

This time both women looked around as if it would do any good. Satiah remembered her first day, when she'd first seen all these people in the flesh. In her mind she revisited all the old theories about Malla, Dean/Scott, and Shannon too. In a way, it could almost be her first day again for all the progress she'd made on this. They were fewer in number now, these people, and far less busy than they had been that day. She remembered the fire extinguisher being out of date, and when she'd found out that they were not even checking Oli's food. Same faces, same people... yet one of them was duplicitous and therefore two-faced. It was always the pauciloquent ones you had to watch, after all, and be ever on the lookout for. They would of course have known they were being sought, and hopefully would be thinking they might be safer now. For the life of her, Satiah could not spot any difference in any of these faces.

"You know what?" Shannon asked, snapping Satiah out of her grim contemplation. "I can't wait until all this is over."

"Oli plans to run in the next election," said Satiah grimly. "It will be like a reunion as much for the dead as the living."

"He's not!" she gasped, her eyes wide. Satiah nodded sadly. "Has he lost his mind?"

"You know how I look at politicians," Satiah remarked, jokingly. Shannon sniggered briefly at that.

"I'm starting to see why," she replied, in concurrence. Then she sighed decisively. "Well, he'll have to hire someone else next time. I'm not going to go through all this again. Would you?"

"Depends what the pay is like," Satiah replied, with a shrug.

"I mean, he's nearly died at least five times," Shannon stated, with incredulity. "If I were him, I think *I* would be thinking that I was on borrowed time as it was… I definitely would not run the gauntlet a second time."

"He might not give up even after the second time around," Satiah pointed out.

"Did you decide if you were going to vote this time?" asked Shannon, genuinely curious.

"After the way he's behaved, I couldn't vote for *him*," Satiah replied, thinking about it. "I hate Mark, so… I suppose it would have to be Brenda. I won't bother though, she doesn't seem to require my help."

"I wonder what working for her is like," Shannon pondered.

"Interesting," Satiah settled on. They laughed together, but not for real. Her earpiece went off and Satiah moved away to answer it. It was Eben.

"The transporter for Oli is at the gate," he informed her.

"Okay, thank you Captain, hold it there - we will be right down."

---

"I have been doing tens of these interviews," Deetee said, smiling as always. "This is one I think everyone is waiting for. Now, some people, from the very start, have been asking: why do we need to do this when you will clearly win? I know how you feel about upholding the values and principles of democracy, so I'm not going to ask you that question.

Instead I'm going to ask you how you feel right now?" Brenda, all prepared, gave a big 'cat that got the cream' smile.

"I-i-it's not over quite yet, so I'm just waiting for the result while d-doing my job, I guess," she said, nervously. She knew what to say, and she was getting better at remembering her cues and lines and things, but she still worried that she would mess it up somehow. "So... in a word... tentative." Deetee nodded slowly, reminding her of one of those old-fashioned children's toys.

"A lot of people have been asking me to find out more about you as a person. Less of Brenda the Commandment Benefactor and more of Brenda the woman so, in an unmatched twist, today we're not going to be talking about politics. Today we're going to be talking about you," Deetee explained, ever the entertainer. "Think of this as a first date, if you will," he joked, getting an amused reaction from the ever obliging studio audience. "What do you like to drink? Do you have a favourite activity?" Brenda knew she had to fake a laugh at this point. She managed it but it never reached her eyes.

"I'm very busy, please contact my aide," she ribbed. "No... I'm water all the way, I don't d-drink intoxicants and my favourite activity..." She paused to give the impression of having to decide. "I used to be really into gardening before politics took over everything. I created a sort of green zone in a warehouse my father owned, and I would lose myself in there for hours."

"Do you believe that talking to plants helps them to grow?" Deetee asked, as he was supposed to.

"I do, but I fear that when I do it they just go to sleep," she said, keeping it light as instructed. "I generally don't talk all that much, but I would play them music."

"My brother does that," Deetee added, deceptively. "He thinks they prefer more instrumental genres."

"I don't know anything about music, I'm so hopelessly out of touch these days," she replied. Getting in touch with the human side is o so important these days... and fashionable.

"You come from quite a big family, don't you?" he asked, seriously.

"I have six sisters, all of them older and wiser than me… and they never fail to p-point that out," she said, dotingly. "They brought me up too, as my mother left when I was less than two."

"That must have been hard on them, well, hard on you all?"

"It was." Blah, blah, blah…

⋆⋆⋆⋆⋆⋆

Moving targets were harder to hit, it was true, but in this case it was only when Oli moved that he presented a target at all. Inside the Bulwark he was almost as untouchable as Brenda. They had sent out a dummy first, in a transporter, to confuse anyone trying to follow him. Standard precaution. Anyone with half a brain would see through it though… especially if they bothered to look through the windows. They would find it almost completely empty.

Surrounded by at least twelve escorting vehicles, one of which was part of Brenda's personal guard, the second transporter slowly pulled out into traffic. Oli was encircled by Three-Stripe-Security members, along with Shannon and Lunell. Aaron was doing a fantastic job; so far he'd not forgotten anything. Satiah knew that because she had double checked everything herself. Not that she had any trust or controlling issues…

It was as a result of these non-existent issues of hers that she was actually present on the transporter. As there was no way Oli was going to win, it was now all about simply keeping him alive. She stood by the viewport, leaning casually on the guardrail and looking out at the passing cityscape. Aaron went over to her.

"All good," he grunted, his voice sounding alert and wary.

"Wonderful, I expect there to be an attempt any time now," Satiah informed him. "Be ready." The big man nodded to her and paced away, his maroon coloured armour clinking and clicking as he went. Shannon was next, attracted by the clandestine looking exchange.

"What's going on?" she asked, her hand on her rifle.

"Be ready," repeated Satiah. She wondered if Lunell would come over as well, though frankly he shouldn't have to be told to be ready.

Unlike when they had been going to the debate, there was very little excitement now. It was all obligation and longing for the end. Her earpiece bleeped to let her know someone was after her.

"All on," Zax said, talking about her systems. "I'll alert you if I see anything."

"Very good." Next was Randal.

"I'm in meetings all this afternoon, but call if you want me," he instructed, seriously.

"I will," she stated. There was a pause as, while waiting for Brenda to depart, they were held outside the entrance area. Everyone was tense, wondering if this was more than it seemed - deliberating over the possibility that this had all somehow been set up in order to keep them out in the open.

They all watched as Brenda's ship, elegant and painted in the style of the new emblem, moved out from the vehicle. Two fighter craft accompanied it as normal. It moved out of view quickly as it was the only craft legally allowed to fly outside of the traffic lanes and as fast as it liked. It was a source of great pride to those who had worked on that ship, Satiah knew. Almost everything within it was handmade, crafted by expert tradesbeings, and not mass produced. Satiah understood duty and she appreciated those dedicated to it even though she knew, deep down, she was of a different mould. She played lip service to it, of course, on a daily basis pretty much - but in her mind she knew her own life was her first concern, regardless of anything else. Regardless of *anyone* else? That she was no longer sure of.

The ship began to move forward again and she took a moment to glance over at Oli. He looked resigned but determined, if such a combination was possible. He also looked a bit lost without Kate there, constantly whispering counsel in his ear. Aaron and his men were moving to take up their positions all around him. Satiah touched the handle of her pistol casually as she went to stand some distance behind him. Slowly the light of day was cut off by the roof of the building, making it look like a wave of darkness creeping along the floor towards them. A siren began to wail.

"Moving in... Next one along... one, three, three, seven, ten, three, two..." a voice was saying. It was the pilot letting them all know what was going on.

Satiah exchanged a quick look with Shannon, who was between her and Oli.

"We move," Aaron growled, leading the way. They all filed along the corridor towards the landing ramp as the ship slowly parked in the designated zone. Satiah's eyes were everywhere, seeking threats both obvious and subtle. This was the moment when they were at their most exposed. The only thing between Oli and death were about four bodies of flesh and blood. No walls, no energy fields... just people. Satiah, had she been tasked with assassinating him, would likely have chosen this moment to attack. The door opened as the ramp lowered ahead of them. No one was talking, everyone was uneasy. A flash from an adjacent building almost made her reel to fire on it, but it was just the sunlight. The door opened and two guards, facility staff, entered. Satiah hoped they were only what they seemed to be, and nothing lethal. She glanced up, checking that the cameras were on. They were.

Moving through the doors and into the corridor beyond gave everyone the opportunity to sigh with relief. Granted, they would have to return via this route too, but they had passed the most dangerous area without a hitch.

"Very good, stay alert," Aaron's voice came through everyone's ears. An administrator came jogging along the corridor, computer in her hands. Her identity badge was on display to ensure everyone knew who she was.

"Hello," she chirped, cheerfully. "Oli?"

"Hello," he said, eyeing her circumspectly.

"We're almost ready for the interview," she said, going straight into it. "We're going to stop off at cosmetics first, get you ready and camera friendly. It's great to have you here by the way, good trip?"

"Brilliant," he said, in a tone that implied anything but. She didn't seem to be listening to him, though.

"Great," she said, carelessly. "Here is your building pass; the rest of your team can pick up any more they need from my office. That's floor seven hundred and two, room eighty. We're also going to have to go through a building evacuation plan in the event of an emergency…" Oli stopped listening, as clearly she hadn't heard anything he had said. Shannon was listening. Satiah remained alert, and never forgot to count everyone every so often. It would be easy to lose someone for a second and then gain someone else who looked identical. She envisaged that that would be how Collorah planned to switch the android in. A quick snatch and replace… could be done in as little as five seconds. Lunell too was on the lookout, recognising the dangers.

Satiah approached the woman and got her attention easily.

"I need you to update me on the security of this building," she stated, formally. "Shields, access changes, that kind of thing." She handed Satiah her computer while she continued to lecture Oli. Everything was in order. Satiah almost wished it wasn't. This was all going far too well for her liking. She made eye contact with Aaron.

"Register," she instructed, grimly.

"Sound off!" he called. One by one everyone answered as they had been told to do. Everyone was still there, if a switch had been made, it had gone unnoticed and they'd done all they could so far. Aaron politely awaited any further commands she might have.

"Very good, carry on," she smiled, professionally.

A drone flew past the window but Satiah recognised it as Zax's. Drone use in Earth airspace was prohibited but, as with many things, Phantoms were exempt. It sported its own serial code, broadcasting constantly to law enforcement. Oli was bundled into cosmetics for any make up that would be needed. He would normally have used the time to go over what he was going to say, but as Kate wasn't there, he merely sat there, strangely silent. Shannon and Satiah stood in the doorway, keeping an eye on him.

"It's become like a military operation, this," joked Shannon, as they watched members of their own team patrolling the corridors.

"Aye," Satiah agreed, with a sigh. She was trying to stop herself clock-watching. Counting down the hours until this was all over.

Gate four, leading from the commercial subway lane into the basement, had been inactive. The cleaning team were late. The guard on duty looked up from his personal computer as an arrival light flickered on. Rolling his eyes, he tossed the computer onto his desk, stood, stretched and then wandered out towards the gate. The access code was given and the gate began to rise. The man crossed his arms and watched as the large conveyer edged in, warning sirens wailing. A man jumped down and approached him.

"Hi, sorry we're late," Collorah said. He was dressed as a cleaner. Several other men scrambled out. Some began dragging out the bodies of those they had killed and replaced earlier from the vehicle.

"Hey, what...?" began the man, seeing what was going on. Collorah shot him dead.

"Get these out," he ordered, motioning to the bodies. "I want to make sure we can leave this way if we need to. You four are with me, and the rest of you make sure this is in lockdown."

---

Zax frowned and called Harrier.

"I was just about to call you, is it about camera AS33?" he asked, clearly having spotted it too.

"Is it me or is it on a loop?" she asked, excited. "Showing the same footage over and over?"

"I thought so too, let Satiah know there will be intruders in the basement if there aren't already," he said, seriously.

"Basement level near gate four, we think Collorah might have got in," Zax warned, again forgetting to wait for Satiah to talk first.

"Right, thank you for the warning," she replied, levelly. "Watch for their progress in the building, do not alert anyone else, I want to draw him in as close as possible. He cannot have enough people to take on and beat us all. The main danger will be the android, Collorah will be acting as its distraction, I'm sure."

"What will you do?" Zax asked, wondering how Satiah planned to deal with this.

"In a way, there's only one thing I need to do - I have to watch the same thing I have been watching since day one...?" Satiah said, hoping Zax would be able to work it out.

"...Oli?" she offered, hopefully.

"Oli," Satiah smiled, pleased she'd got that far at least. "Everything will continue as normal, so Collorah doesn't know we're onto him. Is that package where I asked you to put it?"

"Yes," she nodded, quickly. "You still haven't told me what's..." Satiah disconnected, knowing she had actually just told Zax what was in it, and faced Lunell and Shannon. Aaron, as if somehow detecting that he should hear this, loomed over her shoulder as the conversation began.

"Are they done with Oli?" Satiah asked, with intent gleaming in her eyes. *Soon we all will be.*

"I think so," Shannon replied, peering over in his direction.

"Right, we've got about ten minutes before the attack..." Satiah began.

"What attack?" Lunell asked, immediately. She waved her hands to get silence.

"The attack we don't know about," she replied, hitting every word with extra emphasis. Shannon looked baffled, but Lunell and Aaron seemed to take this in their stride. "We need to get Oli into the studio as quickly as possible," Satiah continued. "Once there, where everyone can see him, we can wait. Now, I need to be alone with Oli for a second, just to get him ready too."

She slipped between them and closed the door. Oli regarded her in bewilderment.

"What?" he asked hotly, unsure what else to say.

"I need a favour," she stated, without any emotion.

"If you think that I'm going to help you with anything..." he began, making a grab for his hobbyhorse. He was silenced and turned pale with fear when, in that moment, she pulled her pistol on him. She had had to do this once before, to get him to leave Malla's body behind, and it had worked well enough then. She was not in the mood for an argument, least of all with him.

"I wasn't asking," she growled, commandingly.

Several minutes later, they were moving towards the studio, Oli in the centre of a mass of human shields.

"Well, I don't know what the make up team did to him but I can't see any difference," Shannon complained. He'd been in there over fifteen minutes and he looked no different, in her eyes, than he had when he'd gone in.

"I don't think you're meant to," Satiah replied, knowingly. "I want a clear line of attack at Oli; I don't want anyone getting in the way."

"So you keep saying, but I don't understand," Shannon stated, in mild protest. "If no one stops them before they get close, he might be killed."

"It has to be this way because I have no idea who is going to make the attack," Satiah explained. "If we get this right then we eliminate all threats to Oli, get it wrong and they hide away again. Putting it bluntly: this is a trap." Shannon sighed, letting it go, knowing that this was a poor time to start to distrust Satiah again.

Moving forward into the studio area, Satiah slipped in to personally escort Oli to the stage area... just to make sure he went to the right place. A clear path was left as she had instructed. Deetee was there, going through some of the details with Sasha. Shannon watched as Satiah whispered some words into Oli's ear and he gave no visible reaction to them at all, even when she strolled off the stage to take up her position.

"What's wrong with him?" Shannon asked, when Satiah reached her.

"I've not finished writing up the list on that yet," she remarked, seriously. Shannon watched Oli sitting there, perfectly still and without expression.

"He's not drunk or something, is he? He looks odd," she persisted.

"He knows what I anticipate will happen; did you expect him to leap around in glee?" Satiah responded, coolly. "Don't watch him, watch everyone else." The team were still milling around, trying to find places to sit and watch. Shannon did just as Satiah said and began to seek anything suspicious. Satiah rested her hand on her pistol casually. Her stern brown eyes watched with the patience and keenness that only a Phantom agent could. Taking in everything and everyone... not once but twice. Twice? She focussed in on something that she knew to look for: Stan. He was sitting towards the back, only... he was also sitting near the front. There were two of him, as she had feared; the android had manage to infiltrate the group without being noticed. That had to mean that one of them was the android and one was the real Stan. Which one? Until it made the move she couldn't be sure.

Her fingers slowly gripped her pistol and slid it free of its holster. She kept it pointing down and close to her so as not to worry anyone. She tried and failed to remember how Stan had been dressed earlier; the idea being that the one dressed differently had to be the target. No one else had noticed him and why should they? They would only see someone they knew. The only problem would be if someone had just spoken to Stan and then immediately saw the other one. If a few minutes passed, they would forget, or simply assume they'd bumped into him again. As an infiltrator, the android might be programmed to avoid the person it was impersonating to prevent that, otherwise, it would try to kill Stan too - but it couldn't do that in a crowded area as it would prevent it from carrying out its mission.

"I've got it," Lunell said, in her ear. He was on the other side of the room. "It's Stan."

"I know," she replied, in a murmur.

"I'm going to try something," he said, instantly.

"No!" she hissed, wondering what he was going to do. Shannon glanced at her, a question in her face. Lunell was already moving, however, blatantly ignoring her heated instruction. He was heading for the one near the front, probably believing, not unreasonably, that it was a better place to strike at Oli from, and therefore it was most likely the android that was sitting there. She flashed a glance at the one at the back.

"What is it?" Shannon whispered, concerned. Satiah didn't answer as Lunell reached Stan.

"Stan, you have an urgent communicator message," Lunell lied, as he got the man's attention. Stan frowned in confusion as anyone would. "This way," Lunell said, moving towards the doors before Stan had a chance to ask anything. Satiah was hurrying forward now, having guessed how Lunell planned to test if Stan was an android or not. The other Stan either hadn't seen, or was pretending not to have seen himself being led outside. Satiah had the uneasy feeling that it might be the one at the back, simply because it apparently hadn't noticed itself moving out of the room. If the Stan at the back of the room was real and he had seen himself leave, he would have reacted. He wasn't moving at all though, just sitting there, staring ahead as though nothing was happening. Besides, if Lunell had got the correct one, why was it allowing him to lead it away from its target?

She got outside just as Lunell was about to shoot Stan in the back.

"No!" she hissed, trying not to let Stan know what was going on behind him. "It's the other one!" Lunell, to her surprise, paused and didn't shoot. He glared at her.

"Are you sure?" he demanded, replacing his pistol.

"Well..." she began, when Stan turned around. He was holding the communicator and looked even more puzzled.

"They seem to have gone," he said, calmly. "Did they say who they were or what it was regarding?"

"Afraid not," Satiah smiled, politely. "So sorry to have dragged you out, we will let you know if they call back." Stan eyed them both warily, just for a second, but said nothing and headed back inside.

Satiah followed him in and glanced to see where the other Stan was. He'd gone. She turned as if to check on Oli, who was still seated on stage with Deetee, apparently oblivious. Lunell was looking everywhere, trying to find the other Stan too. Satiah suddenly thought of something and hurried to the back where he had been seated. There he was... lying on the floor, stone dead. No one had seen him fall as they were all looking forward. She didn't know quite how it had been done but it could have been done the second he sat down, or even when the android returned to the room. If he'd been dead a while it would explain why he didn't react when the android originally left he room.

Satiah turned, pistol ready, just as Stan, the one they had just let back into the room, raised a gun of his own. Bang! Oli toppled backwards off his chair, having taken the full force of the shot to the chest, to land on the floor behind it. As the howls of shock and terror began to sound, another two shots rang out. Stan went down in a heap, smoke rising from the two wounds as everyone else ducked for cover. Satiah lowered her pistol slowly after making sure the android was not going to be getting up any time soon.

Lunell watched as everyone rushed to the stage, except for Satiah.

"No one panic!" she ordered, in a loud clear tone. "The situation is under control!"

"What about Oli? We need to get him to the medical staff quickly; there might still be a chance..." Shannon began, very confused and a little angry that Satiah wasn't even bothering to come over and check on him. Everyone watched as, very slowly and deliberately Satiah approached the stage. She stepped up onto it and kept coming until she was literally standing over Oli. Without saying a word and before anyone could stop her, she fired two shots into Oli's neck, sending the head of the android rolling away in a trail of smoke.

"We need to get him here to do his interview," Satiah said, into the silence. "Lunell?" Lunell, knowing where Oli was, jogged lightly away to fetch him.

Everyone was still staring in amazement at Satiah.

"Shannon, if you could clear up this mess I would be grateful," she said, as if nothing had happened. Then she slowly started to walk away. Despite Stan's regretful demise, this had actually gone better than Satiah had planned. The android, before she'd shot it, would have recorded Oli's death. Collorah, upon seeing that, would imagine his task over. He would leave and she wanted to get him before he slipped away. She wouldn't have long.

Shannon, though, darted after her and caught her arm, angry at Satiah for not including her in the plan, and even angrier that she hadn't even told her where the real Oli was.

"Listen!" she hissed, lividly. "I understand there are some things you can't tell everyone, but as chief of security I do have certain responsibilities."

"Understood," Satiah said, very deliberately shrugging out of the other woman's grip. "Excuse me." Shannon could only look on in perplexity as Satiah began to sprint away down the corridor.

Lunell entered with a very badly made up Oli. Putting it kindly, he looked like he'd been tile-sleeping all night. The crate the android had been held in, the same crate Zax had had delivered, was where the real Oli had rather roughly been hidden in at gunpoint. Satiah had spoken with Snell, knowing that he already had androids of Oli that she could use, and had borrowed one for the occasion. That was how he apparently looked no different than usual, as the android had never been made up at all.

"What is going on? Where's Satiah?" Oli was asking. Deetee looked absolutely furious, having recovered himself.

"What do you think you are doing? This is most unprofessional, I have to say, you were lucky we hadn't been online! Look at what you've done to my studio..." he ranted. It was the first time, Oli thought rather abstractedly, that he'd ever seen the man when he wasn't smiling.

---

"The cameras are returning to normal," Zax informed her, her tone a little petulant.

"That's because he thinks Oli is dead," Satiah answered, as she waited for the lift.

"How did you expect me to know it was an android in the crate?" Zax asked, unable to hold it in any longer. "I'm not a mind reader!" Satiah smiled and the lift arrived. She moved in and asked for the basement level.

"I thought such an idea would be obvious even to you," she replied, smugly.

"Well it wasn't," Zax replied, sulkily. "...It was a good plan," she said, clearly finding it hard to give praise. Satiah pretended not to hear.

"Sorry what did you say?" Satiah asked, grinning.

"You're not getting a replay," she declared, still miffed. Then her tone softened. "Take care against Collorah."

Satiah disconnected and, when the lift had arrived, she darted down the corridor. She didn't know exactly where Collorah was, but she knew he would be backtracking. He would have come in as a plan B just in case the android failed, and also to serve as a distraction if necessary. Though destroyed, as far as Collorah knew the android had succeeded, and so he was retreating. It wasn't long before Satiah found her first body. It was the administrator who had come out to greet them upon their arrival. She'd been shot and left there, splay limbed, on the floor. Satiah continued on, in too much of a hurry to check any others she found. Collorah didn't leave survivors. Her count had just reached fourteen, mainly guards, when she saw people just turning the corner ahead of her. She padded quickly along, pistol ready, in silent pursuit.

There was no question of accidentally hitting facility staff as they were all dead already, so Satiah didn't even bother to check for non-combatants as she opened fire. Two of the mercenaries were dead before they hit the floor, and a third ran for cover but didn't make it either. Annoyingly, ahead of the others, Collorah had been protected by them. He and one other had made it into door alcoves which afforded them enough shelter. They fired back as Satiah slipped into a doorway of her own. The bolts slammed into the metal, making thumping noises and filling the corridor full of smoke. Satiah crouched and fired again.

"You hold her here, I'll get the others!" lied Collorah, guessing it was Satiah who had managed to somehow find him so quickly. He had no intention of fetching help: he just wanted to get away, but needed someone to remain there to hold Satiah off, and give him time to make his escape. Satiah would have put him down if she'd been able, but the remaining mercenary kept up a continuous barrage until Collorah was out of sight, preventing her from chancing even the nippiest of ganders out from her cover. She crouched, felt for the grenades she carried and then, with a casualness that made it look like she could have been throwing away a pamphlet about politics, lobbed it over her shoulder. The firing stopped as the man broke cover to run. The blast sent fire in both directions and took out the wall on the left of the corridor entirely.

She rolled out from cover and, pistol raised, began a cautious approach toward the bend in the corridor. The sprinkler system activated, along with a warning alarm and good old nitrogen gas. She slipped her breathing device into her mouth. She heard running steps and, guessing that the gas had forced him into retreat, tore after him. His best hope was to lose her; he couldn't know that she already knew exactly where he was going. An announcement occurred.

"Warning, all personnel please initiate evacuation plan V13," a robotic voice repeated, over and over. The secondary lighting system came on, red and green. They were getting close to the gate that Collorah and his people had used to get in.

The remainder of the team had gathered by the entrance and, thinking it would be Satiah, shot their own comrade as he ran through. Satiah heard, guessed what had happened, smiled and then tossed another of her grenades. There were a few precious seconds of warning shouts, and then it went off. Satiah ran through, diving over a barricade they had made to hold back anyone that came after them. They were running towards a ship that was taking off without them, and this allowed Satiah to pick them off with ease. Collorah took off down into the subway. Satiah groaned, annoyed that he had got away, but Zax's drone sped past her, hurtling after Collorah.

"I'm locked on," Zax said, in Satiah's ear. "Wherever he goes, we will know as soon as he gets there." Satiah was about to answer her with a congratulatory remark when a shot narrowly missed her. She dived out of the open.

"Freeze! Do not move!" voices repeatedly shouted at her. She glowered. Android security forces. If she surrendered or tried to fight then they would stun her, take her to a cell somewhere and then interrogate her - pointlessly. She doubted it would go that far, but it would still delay her. That left her with only two options. Run - or hide?

"What's going on?" Zax asked, concerned.

"I'm going to have a gentle stroll in the subway," Satiah replied, grimly making her choice. "Wish me luck." Satiah broke from cover, sprinted madly towards the gate and leapt down into the darkness, a hail of stun bolts hitting mostly everything except her.

Despite everything occurring down on the lower levels, the interview took place, and continued without interruption after a slight delay at the beginning when everyone was made up again. The destroyed androids and Stan's body had been removed, and everyone had retaken their seats.

"It's stating the obvious to say that your campaign outlasted even the most optimistic expectations," Deetee was saying, while smiling. "When you started this, what were your expectations?" Oli, composed but beneath the façade emotional, sipped some water before answering. Here it was, the talk about the election he'd most likely lost. He'd not just lost, but probably would be soundly beaten by Brenda. He genuinely tried to put himself back into the mind-set he'd had at the very start. All those weeks ago, before he'd ever even arrived on Earth. He remembered his old rallying call he had used to invigorate his team.

After the grandeur of the Grand Bulwark of the Coalition Assembly, his presidential office on his home world seemed somehow… childish. Outclassed in every category. Moving in had felt so good, he thought he'd made it. And then… the chance of running for Benefactor had come and it had all changed. What once had brought him strength, happy recollections, or just positivity, had been reduced to the significance of a good article in a magazine. Nice to read, but somehow no longer really applicable to his life. Had he become so obsessed with reaching higher things that he'd lost all interest in everything else in his life?

"When I started…" he began, not even bothering to try and follow the script he and Kate had worked on. His voice was quiet, but strong enough to be heard. For the first time in a long time, Oli was talking from the heart.

"…I was on a different world, thinking different thoughts about different things. I was a different man. My expectations were basically dreams," he smiled, sadly. "I wasn't being realistic, I just let myself get carried away with fantasies about power, change and futures that I could make for everyone. Ambition? Yes… that played its part, certainly. A desire to stop all the things that I considered needed to be stopped. My expectations were about as broad spectrum as anyone can imagine. I'm not sure that even I can know their limitations."

"Did you think you would win?" Deetee specified, a little vexed by the unusually long-winded and ambiguous answer. He was used to well-thought out answers that had words he could target and prise open. He'd been trained to pick politically correct answers to pieces. What he was getting wasn't very precise. Oli's eyebrows rose slowly and he seemed almost to slouch. He looked... depressed.

"It was, and arguably still is, a possibility," Oli said, again not giving Deetee anything he could reasonably use. "I think everyone who ran thought they had a chance. There was even a time when I thought I might get into office, yes. I'm prepared for defeat, indeed I was prepared for defeat before I even started. It was one of the first things I considered: the possibility of being unsuccessful. Odd that people say unsuccessful instead of using the word fail, isn't it?" Deetee frowned, unsure if the question was for him to answer or not. Oli went on. The guy was, for want of a better word, rambling.

"I have lost," he admitted, staring off into space. "My brother too." He didn't make clear if he was saying that he had lost his brother or that his brother had also lost the election: both of which were true, but Oli wasn't following any sort of structure now. He was in his own world. Indeed, he'd almost forgotten he was doing an interview with anyone, he was so self-absorbed.

"Friends and family. Both of those things have been hit hard in this election... I never stopped to think about them, no matter what the outcome," he babbled on. "The worst part of all this is... if I had won, I would have probably forgotten the cost." Deetee was bored. What should have been one of the most viciously cutting interviews of recent times had become a tedious monologue about feelings.

"I see," Deetee allowed, starting to wish this was already over. "Will we be seeing you again? Will you try again? A lot of people think you will, simply because of how close you came."

"I'll run again," Oli said, suddenly seeming to wake up. "There's not a doubt in my mind about that. I've come too far, lost too much to give up on this now. My followers expect it." Deetee smiled, pleased that Oli seemed to have perked up a bit. Perhaps there was some sport to be had after all.

"Had Brenda not been running in this election, who do you feel would have won?" Deetee asked, interested.

"Mark would have been in with a chance. I dare say that Sawma would possibly have prevailed. I would have certainly had different challenges," he went on, a little more engaged. He was, at last, warming to this dialog. "This time around, Sawma didn't seem to make any impression, but with Brenda in the limelight it makes sense. They are in the same party, after all.

"This election was unique, though, in other ways. It was almost a shotgun-election, to coin a phrase. Born from a referendum that clearly made life difficult for Brenda," Oli rambled on, stepping dangerously close to censure of Brenda. He was inches away from stating outright that Brenda had wanted the referendum to end with the result that no second election was necessary. This was not true, and Brenda would be one of the first people to point it out. The original election, the stand off between Brenda and Balan Orion, had been a terrible mess, undoubtedly - Balan's untimely demise being just one wrinkle in the face of the whole thing. The Pluto Major controversy, the Vourne conspiracy... the list went on. "It was done in record time; the last stage was the longest, instead of the shortest like normal. So, purely the mechanics of this election were drastically different from what everyone, even Brenda, is used to. Nothing quite like it had ever happened before either." Deetee's smile turned devious.

"Do you think Brenda only called the referendum because she thought it would secure her position and prevent another election?" Deetee asked, outright. This question, while at one stage hotly debated, had been allowed into the public arena for one reason only: too many people had openly wondered about it. If they left it out, it might confirm to some that they were all being taken for a ride.

"No," Oli answered, even though he felt sure that she had thought it would. "No one predicted that outcome correctly. I mean, six months ago, would you or I have imagined sitting here right now, talking about this?"

"I would not," Deetee said, a little disappointed. "These interviews remind me of post-contest talks, where scores, participants and locations are compared and analysed. If Brenda hadn't gone into politics, where do you think she might have ended up?"

"Charity seems to be a big thing about Brenda. I saw your programme where you discussed her work on Pluto Major and her plans for helping the movement gain momentum for further projects. Where she would be within that area, I can't say. Of course you are aware that the two of us have never interacted socially so I don't have the best grasp of her personality. I have seen that she has generosity, and principles similar to my own. I have also seen that she does have an inner strength," Oli answered, carefully.

"Part of your researching of the opposition, no doubt," Deetee chortled, talking about the programme.

"That's exactly what it was. I don't know if I was ever considered a big enough rival for her to look at me," Oli said, so unknowing. Granted, it hadn't been Brenda herself that had taken such an interest in him, it had been those who were really in power. The ones no one ever knew about. Nevertheless, they had been very worried about him at one stage.

"You have both been compared by a number of analysts, and your policies do often align, but with some noticeable differences," Deetee observed. "In a way, the whole idea of you two being on opposite sides of any argument seems vaguely nonsensical, so some of my sources have commented, what do you feel about that?"

"It is true that some of our ideas align," replied Oli, nodding. "We will all, no doubt, find out more in four or five years when we face off a second time."

"I'm sure we will," Deetee smiled, with finality. "Thank you for your time."

---

The subways, used mainly for conveying only cargo, were poorly lit, cold, damp, and home to a wild and blustery plethora of air currents. Having escaped the androids, Satiah now was walking slowly along, wondering how she was going to get out and onto the street. Another blast of air, caused by the movement of vehicles possibly miles away, whipped her hair around and made her shiver. Water dripped constantly, which seemed to add another layer of cold to everything. She glanced over her shoulder and saw lights. Cursing under her breath, she fired her grapple-gun into the ceiling and rose up to get as flat as she could against it. A second or so later, a freighter passed under her, only inches away. She lowered herself back down, exhaling slowly as she went. Less than three days now, come on, buck up! She went on, seeing no reason in hurrying yet. If Zax hadn't called, it meant Collorah still hadn't stopped. He may even be off the planet already.

Just as Satiah reached a hatchway and emerged onto a walkway, slipping in among the crowd seamlessly...

"He's gone to the Mulac Building," Zax reported. "I think he's going to change vehicles before he leaves."

"That would make sense," Satiah replied, pushing through those too slow for her. "Is my transporter coming to get me?"

"On its way," she replied, efficiently.

"I'm going to have to cripple his escape ships first," Satiah went on. "So long as he doesn't know I'm there, I'll have an advantage."

"There are at least two others with him, they must have been guarding the ships for him," Zax informed her. Satiah glanced around as she heard the thrumming of an approaching ship. It was hers.

She darted through the gaps between people, and leapt up and in as it slowed. She closed the door, scrambled into the pilot's seat, and then accelerated away.

"How are things with Oli?" she asked, thinking about angel.

"No sign of anything odd now, Oli is a bit dazed I think, but that's what happens when everyone is out to get you, I suppose," she responded. "They will be returning to the Bulwark any time now."

"Good. Let me know when they get there, or if anything else happens in the meantime," Satiah instructed, cutting off.

---

Brenda and her aide switched off after Oli's interview was over.

"I-i-is it weird that I feel sorry f-for him?" Brenda asked, sadly.

"Someone always has to lose," the aide reminded her, softly. "Anyway, it's clear he intends to try again." Brenda smiled.

"Yes, I'm looking forward to that," she said. The aide raised a discreet eyebrow, but said nothing. "He brought a lot of good ideas to the table and, as apparently everyone thinks, we do seem to be quite similar on some policies."

"Yes..." the aide remarked, unsure what else to say. She changed the subject. "I know the result isn't in yet officially, but I wondered if asking your permission to commence preparations for the celebration would be acceptable."

"You c-can always ask," Brenda told her, smiling. The she looked uncertain. She didn't want to even think about celebrating until the result was confirmed. "Well..."

"I ask only because there is so much to do, that any delay might cause problems," the aide qualified. "The fly-by alone will take hours to orchestrate."

"I get a fly-by?" Brenda asked, a little awestruck.

"Of course you get a fly-by, it's tradition. Besides, how else can the military welcome you?" the aide laughed.

"Quietly?" Brenda offered, hopefully.

"Not a chance, you're lucky they lost the responsibility of the firework display this time around to the public transport division," she stated, seriously.

"So long as they are not late," Brenda giggled. The aide laughed, genuinely amused.

"I wouldn't say anything about that in your speech, they are likely to not appreciate that sort of wit," the aide stated, grinning.

"I w-wouldn't, honestly," Brenda said, supping her water.

"Do you remember how loud it got when Balan was elected?" the aide asked, casually. "The military, who were doing the display, broke the sound barrier and who's to say how many windows." Brenda guffawed, and covered her face with her hands.

"Yes, they did get a bit c-carried away, didn't they?"

"Relax, we will keep it respectful this time around," she assured. "You need to think about what you're going to wear."

"O p-please no, no more elaborate costumes," Brenda protested. "Can't I just wear my robes?"

"You can, but everyone will expect something more."

"How about a funny hat?"

The door bleeped.

"Phantom Leader Randal to see Brenda," Randal's voice sounded, from outside. Brenda opened the door. Randal paced in. He glanced meaningfully at the aide.

"It's fine, she's my right hand," Brenda smiled.

"I've been checking everything. I've spoken with everyone I can think of and… basically, we have no idea what Ash is talking about," Randal stated, seeing no other way of putting it.

"Oh," she said, unsure quite what to do next. "What did Reed say?"

"Reed is away at the moment," Randal confirmed. "I've left a message for him: no doubt he will have something to say when he gets back to us."

"So… in the m-meantime?" Brenda asked, casually.

"In the meantime, we carry on as normal," he shrugged. "I'm sure that if things were really that bad, Ash would have told us more. It may be that all this is just a theory to him and the warning was more of a general thing than a specific alert. Also, in the meantime, you expressed an interest in closer ties with Phantom Squad?"

"Yes," she nodded, pleased. He sat in the chair before her desk.

"My door is always open," he said, as everyone always did. Was there any point in having a door if it never moved?

"Since what happened," she said, referring to the Vourne conspiracy, "I understand y-you're very thinly stretched?"

"It is true that I have a certain resource problem, currently. The problem should gradually get better though, once the next few years have gone by and the next generations start contributing," he shrugged. "It's funding more than anything right now."

"I have spoken to the military about budgeting recently. I'm not sure why, but it never really came up in the debate, and I can offer you a few more trillion Essps," she told him. Randal's eyes gleamed knowingly.

"I'm not sure either," he lied, adeptly. "It is my understanding that we account for less than two percent of government military spending, which takes up less than thirty percent of the government's overall spending?"

"Yes," she nodded.

"What about five percent?" he asked. "I've spoken with the PAI and they felt confident that they could absorb a reduction for the next year." Brenda blinked, and even the aide looked momentarily mystified.

"They did?" Brenda asked, trying not to sound too disbelieving.

"Yes, I know what you're thinking, but it's really all about new beginnings," Randal shrugged.

"And Division Sixteen?" Brenda asked, eyeing her computer to refresh her memory.

"They are not funded by the government, they are financially independent," Randal said.

"Of the government?"

"Of the Coalition entirely," he clarified.

"So who funds them?" the aide asked. Randal eyed her, a warning in his eyes. She picked up on this and said no more.

"No idea, not my department," he replied, inscrutably. "I'm just here to talk about Phantom Squad, the sister agencies are not in the remit yet."

"W-well..." Brenda began. She shrugged. "If the PAI are in agreement with this, then I have no problem with it, it will not affect anything else that I can see." He smiled.

"No, it's only a reshuffle of the same Gairunn deck," he assured. "A lot of things still need to be replaced after what happened... happened."

"Yes, I understand," Brenda nodded, seriously.

"The other thing was the intelligence report," Randal continued, casually. "Federation ships have trespassed on our territory eleven times in the last few weeks. Eight times they announced themselves and followed procedure, three times they didn't. President Raykur remains at death's door. The Ro Tammer trial seems to be bogged down."

"So, no changes?" Brenda asked, sagely. He shook his head.

"None of any significance," Randal said. "We've sent two agents into the Nebular Union, but neither has been able to find out much of anything yet."

"This is that C-Cult of Deimos thing you told me about, isn't it?" Brenda asked, hoping she'd remembered correctly.

"They are involved, certainly," he agreed. "No word yet on the fate or actions of the missing Premier."

"W-we n-need to know if that changes," Brenda said, casually. "Not just because of the security risk, but the trading companies could be trouble for me if I don't help them."

"Understood," he nodded.

"Anything else?"

"No."

"Thank you for coming to see me, I know you're really busy..."

"It's fine, Brenda, we're all busy," he smiled, holding up his hand. "You don't need to apologise for doing your job."

"Thank you - and thank you for trying to find out about what Ash said," she smiled, grateful. He stopped in the doorway as one last thought occurred to him.

"Do I have your backing if I need another Phantom Leader? Three of us are not enough," he requested, seriously. She shrugged.

"Do you have someone in mind?" she asked, casually.

"Yes."

---

The Mulac Building, once a place of great governmental activity and more recently institutional murder, was currently disused and undergoing intensive restoration, refurbishment and repair works. Its three towers, standing in their triangle, were still iconic of the old Empire and of the Human Coalition. Since the last days of the Orion administration, it had remained empty - somewhere between derelict and rebuilding. Now that the Bulwark had been officially completed and opened to Brenda, there was some talk of simply turning the Mulac Building into a tourist attraction, or even a luxury hotel. Mostly covered in protective sheets, it was impossible to see what was going on inside.

That was what had made it such an impeccable hiding place.

Satiah had never been inside the building before. She'd flown over it a few times, stood outside it once, and seen pictures of the interior on plenty of occasions. It was those pictures which she used from memory to try and create a mental picture of the layout within. She'd once even rescued Vourne from the top of one of its towers, saving his life from Mensa. That was as close as she had come. Now she regarded it coolly through the viewport of her transporter. Collorah might have someone looking out for him if he wasn't doing it himself, so as she approached, she used a group of parked vehicles as cover, and headed towards it. She wouldn't use the main entrance. It was boarded up, for one thing, but that would most likely be where the guard would be positioned. She darted across the open ground between the vehicles and the wall of the building. Using her grapple-gun, she rose up towards a window.

Well, it would have once been a window, now it was blocked off by a thick plastic sheet. Satiah hung there, then slid her blade from her boot with her free hand and cut a long, straight shard from top to bottom through it, pulling herself quietly in. It was dark inside. She could smell the mould and the damp. She edged towards a door that led into an equally dark corridor beyond. She turned on her torch cautiously and took in the scene. Laser damage, now months old, littered the walls and ceiling. In places, there were holes where explosions had occurred. Blood stains, now dry and faded, were here and there too. It had been a hell of a fight, after all. There was some graffiti here and there, and she glared at one bit of it. If they were going to artistically mock the new emblem of the Coalition, why couldn't they illustrate it correctly?

She padded softly along, knowing that it would take her hours to search the whole building. The corridor was blocked by a layer of metal mesh that was reinforced by railings behind it. She peered down, seeing that a hole in the floor was the hazard this was guarding. It seemed to go down for about three floors. She hurried back the way she had come and found the metal stairs that led both down and up to a landing between floors. Knowing that Collorah intended to leave, he would need a ship. It made sense to assume the ship would be on the higher floors somewhere. Perhaps in a place where the roof was missing? She crept up the steps, listening carefully. After four floors or so, she peered up through the bannisters and used her grapple gun to raise her up faster.

She reached the top of that section of stairs, but she'd not reached the top of the building yet. Signs of the battle that had been fought here were not so prevalent this high up, she noted. The worst of the fighting must have taken place in the area where the government would meet. She found a window: she hoped this one would face inward. Again, using her blade, she made a square hole big enough for her head and peered out. Far below her, on the roof of the interior, she could see a ship. There were lights on down there and a few people. Irritated, but glad she had found him at last, she had to go all the way back down stairs, going past the floor she'd entered on, and onwards almost to the bottom.

The ground floor, conveniently signposted, was where she needed to be. The roof of that floor might have been destroyed in the fighting, but she wasn't sure; or Collorah could have been using this as his base the whole time, and removed it himself. She saw a light ahead and edged towards it. Peering around the edge of the doorway, she found herself looking at a large stockpile of ammunition. There was also water and food, together with other general supplies. Yes... Collorah had been using this place to hide out for a while. The renovation work - carried out by androids - might not be in this area of the building, which could explain why he'd gone undetected for so long. She slipped past the doorway and on towards a more distant light. She correctly deduced it would lead into the area where the ship was.

A quick look told her that there were three exits, including the one she was standing at. She considered if it would be possible to somehow, without alerting anyone as to what she was doing, seal off all but one of them. It would be easier for her to trap Collorah if there was only one way in or out. There were at least four other people there and she'd not seen Collorah himself yet. She slipped inside the area, closed the door behind her and sealed it. Creeping around the edges and staying in the shadows, she made her way towards the ship. She had to ensure he couldn't just drive away. It would be all to easy for that to happen. The ship he was planning to use was unfortunately armoured and there was nothing she could do to sabotage it. Not with what she had on her, anyway.

She heard Oli's voice - someone was watching the interview! Ah… she'd forgotten that he might hang around for a bit just to see the aftermath of the killing. Or, in this case, the complete lack of aftermath. A heated discussion began almost instantly.

"How did he survive? The android hit him perfectly! No one, at that range, could have lived," Collorah stormed. No one had any immediate answers.

"We won't be able to touch him now," someone said.

"I know!" raged back Collorah.

Satiah grinned to herself. She casually attached her suppressor onto the end of her pistol, and tried to see if she could get a shot in. Collorah was watching the interview, probably trying to think about next moves. He was only just visible to her, as another man was standing between her and him. Close enough. She fired, taking down the first man instantly. Collorah, with impressive reactions, was able to duck, and dived aside with a shout. Satiah put two of the other three down. The last one had gone into hiding behind the other side of the ship.

"You did this, Satiah!" Collorah yelled.

"I did warn you!" she yelled back. Then she changed position. She got into an area where she could cover both the ship entrance and the nearest exit.

The furthest exit was still a problem, but she was gambling on them thinking she had that covered too.

"It was an android, wasn't it? Or was it a clone?" Collorah guessed, smiling to himself. Satiah grinned again.

"Maybe, good girls keep their secrets!" she responded. She threw a grenade over to the furthest entrance and it went off. Taking his chance, the remaining mercenary used this apparent opportunity to make a dash for the ship entrance. Satiah brought him down quickly with a single shot to the head. She had expected the move. A clatter made her roll to safety as a grenade, this time thrown by Collorah, landed close to where she had been standing.

"Why don't you say all this to my face?" he shouted, trying to get her to talk. Satiah tried to see where he was. He'd found cover and he was still close enough to the ship for her to have to guard against a sprint for freedom.

Collorah waited for an answer, even though he was pretty sure he wouldn't get one. He peered out from where he was hiding, rifle ready. Stillness. Silence. He knew she had to be somewhere close, where she could prevent access to the ship. Why had he stopped to see how Oli's death would be announced? He should have just left while he had the chance. He'd wanted to know though - to get that final confirmation, that he'd finally earned his pay. He'd had to see that Oli was dead. Satiah, it seemed, hadn't been bluffing after all. He reached into his pocket for the remote he had, and activated it.

Satiah turned as the ship's engines began to start noisily. If he could control it, then he could get it to come to him and she'd be unable to stop him getting away. She pondered her options and was about to call Zax to get the navy involved when a better idea occurred to her. The door to the ship was open... and the ship was only small, even if it was armoured so... a well placed grenade might cripple it. She took her two remaining explosives and cast them both inside before making a dash for the nearest entrance. The blinding flash, making even the dark walls bright as day, preceded the sounds of the blasts by microseconds. As she dived out of the room she heard the third and final blast as the ship's fuel ignited.

Ears ringing, and blinded by smoke, Satiah found a wall and, coughing and spluttering, stood up shakily. She slid her breathing device into her mouth and began to pick her way through the wreckage, back into the area she'd just hurtled from. Collorah was unlikely to have survived that, but she was taking no chances. Fires and debris were everywhere. She'd not heard it somehow, but part of the building had collapsed because of the explosion. Collorah, who'd been waiting for his chance to dash into the ship, had seen the grenades go in. He'd tried to get as far away as possible but had been caught in the blast wave and rendered almost unconscious. He slipped a head mask on and struggled to his feet.

Something had hit his leg, and he was unsure if it was broken or not, but the pain made itself known to him in the form of an agonising shooting, stabbing sort of sensation every time he put a little weight on it. He limped tentatively forward, rifle raised. Satiah emerged from the doorway and leapt backward again before he had time to aim and shoot. He threw a grenade in after her, but she threw herself into a side room before it detonated. The force of the blast knocked her against a wall, and something bashed into the side of her head. She hit the floor and rolled onto her back with a groan, delirious from the blow. Her whole body felt numb for a moment and she couldn't move with any real control. Collorah, a pained expression on his face, limped into the room, rifle pointed at her. Where was her pistol? She couldn't feel it in her hand...

"Got you," he growled, with finality.

A shot went off, and Satiah instinctively tensed, expecting to be hit. It was Collorah though that shouted, dropped his rifle and turned around to reveal the wound in his back. A second shot, again from the unseen gun, hit him in the face. Collorah went down, almost landing on Satiah. Feebly, Satiah sat up, still a bit dazed, and waited for whoever it was to step in. She expected it to be Lunell, and she wondered weakly if he would try to kill her too, once he'd confirmed that she was still alive and Collorah wasn't. It would be all too easy for him to claim he'd found her dead already.

Through the clouds of smoke still billowing about, looking very pale and scared, Zax entered. She was holding the pistol extremely tightly, much more tightly than she needed to, and every move she made was tense but standard. After the first kill, a moment in which some psychological trauma is unavoidable, the training Phantoms went through focussed hard on the immediate checking for other targets, the idea being to overlook the first kill by making sure you are not the second. She covered first right and then left twice, following the training routine.

"Clear," Zax said, almost to herself. It was a call to any nearby agents, letting them know that the area was safe. She lowered the gun but didn't drop it. She stared down at Collorah's body for a few seconds, eyes wide, breathing hard. Satiah got to her feet unsteadily and leaned against the wall for support. Her head wound would need to be seen to. She didn't have double vision, but she might be concussed as could already feel the start of a headache coming.

"Zax!" she said, loudly.

"Phantom Satiah!" Zax said, assuming the stance of attention. She was doing her best to hide how she felt, but uncertainty and fear like that was impossible to conceal completely.

"It was kill him, or let me die," Satiah told her, intently. "And I may speak for myself… but you made the right choice and thank you." Though she was unaware of it, Zax had just repaid a debt she didn't even know she had. For her life had once been under threat, a long time ago. And it had been Satiah who had uncharacteristically played the role of saviour that day. Zax said nothing; she just stood there like an android yet to be reprogrammed. The best thing to do would be to continue as normal, Satiah knew. It was important that Zax did not dwell on this too long.

"Thank you for saving my life. And now, it's time you explained what you were doing here in the first place?" Satiah asked, anger in her tone. She didn't want to start yelling, her head hurt too much for that. "And you can do that while you help me to the hospital!"

Zax snapped out of shock and darted over to help Satiah walk.

"I asked Randal's permission!" she insisted, allowing Satiah to lean on her.

"And he let you?" Satiah asked, a bit surprised.

"I'm not sure, he never answered," Zax replied, sheepishly. "I left a message. I thought it best that I got here as soon as that ship exploded, I thought you might need help getting out." Satiah, though it hurt her, started to laugh.

"You do realise you've earned yourself a very severe castigation for leaving the building without permission and interfering in an operation," Satiah chuckled, unconvincingly.

"I didn't look at it that way," Zax replied, that cheeky grin reappearing again. "You see, it turns out that my being here saved my future teacher's life and now she owes me a favour. And that favour can be used right now to get me out of trouble." Satiah grinned.

After several minutes they were able to get out, using the way Zax had come in. Zax then drove her back to be examined by the Phantom medical centre. The mild concussion was healed, along with the broken finger she'd not even realised she had, and the multiple cuts and bruises she'd incurred. The standard advice, which Satiah thought ridiculous considering her job, was given to her by the android on duty. Be more careful in future. Really? Are you really telling me to be careful, Satiah thought?

Zax was waiting for her outside. She held up her communicator for her and beamed.

"Randal for you," she smiled, her eyes gleaming with immature mischief. Satiah answered, while eyeing her in suspicion.

"Yes," she answered, insouciantly.

"Satiah, what have you done to the Mulac Building?" Randal shouted, livid. "Do you have any idea how much that will cost?" She rolled her eyes and sighed, eyeing Zax who was still grinning. Whoops.

---

Week six. Day seven. It was over. If anyone cared, the result appeared: 74% Brenda, 22% Oli and 4% others. Brenda was now the official, legal, Commandment Benefactor of the Coalition. The parade, the fly by… all of it was just hours away. Satiah drove Oli to where his ship was waiting. Even though Collorah was dead, the invisible threat of angel still cast its unwanted shadow over Oli.

"Well, thank you for keeping me alive, if nothing else," Oli said, having to force his own civility.

"Thank you for paying on time," she remarked, levelly. She parked near the ship where Shannon was waiting outside. Oli moved to get out, when Satiah caught his arm and forced eye contact.

"There's no such thing as democracy, Oli! It's a myth, don't run again, *it will kill you*," she warned, completely candid. He eyed her as if she was mad.

"Satiah, I refuse to believe that. You're too cynical, that's your problem, you're too negative," he argued, shaking his head. She'd tried. She wasn't sure why she had bothered, but she had tried. She let him go.

"I would tell you to take care of yourself, but I know you can't do that, so I'll settle for good luck," she said, her tone prickly. He paused before closing the door.

"I really am sorry, Satiah, for some of my behaviour towards you," he apologised. "But I think you're even now, right?"

"Human costs can't be counted," she told him, grimly. "They can be felt though."

Unsure of what to say to that, he waved a casual goodbye as he closed the door and made his way across the platform towards Shannon. That was when Kate came rushing up to join them. She'd been released, and while Shannon had been told the truth -that it had all been a deception to try to lure angel out of the shadows – Oli had not. Satiah watched the reconciliation, whilst holding the bottle of strong alcohol Kate had given her, and Oli turned to look over at her as she watched. She didn't smile at his hard stare; she just lifted the bottle in a slow mock toast. Job done... Adieu. She glanced behind her to check all was clear before slowly backing out into the traffic lane and flying away.

---

Zax looked at herself in the mirror. She'd released her hair from its old style and had let it hang loose. It would flow freely now and would look better when it got a little longer. She'd felt it was time for a change. She wasn't the same person anymore. She'd crossed a line now and she knew it. Yet she'd secured her future well, she reflected, and as Satiah had said, she had made the right choice. Nevertheless, it would take her a while to stop thinking about Collorah's face. Lying there on the ground dead... because of her. Satiah entered the room behind her with purpose.

"Oli's gone," she told her, needlessly. "Do you have my mission report?"

"Yes," Zax said, passing the handheld device to her. "Is it good?" Satiah went through it.

"Not bad for a first effort," she mused, still reading. She began to adjust it a bit here and there.

Then she looked up and regarded Zax with more scrutiny. She took in the new look without comment, guessing what it was really about immediately.

"I find that everyone has their own way of coping," Satiah said, softly. "If you've made it this far, you're going to emerge stronger from the experience."

"I'm sorry, it's silly; I mean, it's what I've been training for all my life, I..." Zax said, realising how odd this might look.

"No, it's not silly. It's very... the fact that you're feeling this and are conscious of the fact that everything has now changed is very..." Satiah felt her own voice catch and she fought for control instantly, "... grown up." Zax looked confused. "As long as you never enjoy it, you're only doing what you think you must or what you've been told to do then, in the eyes of Phantom Squad at least, it's legal."

"I know," Zax said, a little puzzled by all this.

"Look," sighed Satiah, actually taking Zax's hands in her own and sitting down. "You took more steps forward today than I intended and..." she looked up, right into Zax's blue eyes. "This is probably late in coming... no, it is too late but I'm going to say it anyway. The brightest flame burns quickest, Zax, before we start this... enjoy this time of peace. It will probably be your last. I know it's all you want, to start... I was the same myself. Don't do what I did and grow up too quickly, do you understand?" Zax was clearly in student mode again, trying to learn what Satiah was telling her, trying to understand the lesson. Satiah expected her to say that she understood even if she didn't - most people would. But Zax failed to comply with that cliché. How could a child understand that childhood should be sacred? Innocence was only truly understood when it was gone.

"...I'm sorry, I don't understand what you want me to learn," Zax admitted, crestfallen. Satiah was pleased that she had actually admitted it.

"Thank you for telling me that you don't understand, Zax," Satiah said, very deliberately. "I didn't, you see. When my teacher tried to teach me this lesson I said that I did when I didn't. It was my first mistake."

"So... what is the lesson?" Zax asked, a little impatient. She wasn't aware of the swirling emotions in Satiah's heart so, to her, Satiah must just look and sound a bit weird. "What must I study?"

"Being a child is a precious thing. You're sheltered from the pain that knowledge brings. The agony of the truths that you must one day know. Your time as an adult has already started. It's started too early and we can't change that, but you still have a little time before you work with me. In that time that you wait... I want you to be happy," she said, still fumbling with her words a bit. "Just concentrate on nothing serious as much as possible."

Zax pulled a face that gave away that she had no clue what Satiah was talking about. Satiah gave up and hugged her. She'd already grown up too far! Innocence was gone now and it made Satiah almost ache with sadness. Zax patted her back. Was it irrational to want to give someone the childhood you never had? Was it crazy to try to protect someone from hurt when you knew that the hurt was a necessary evil to help them grow?

"Are you crying?" Zax asked, feeling Satiah tremble. Satiah let go and stood a bit abruptly. Zax took a step back in surprise. Satiah's face was a mask of detachment, ever a master of deception and control. Now was not the time for this.

"No," she said, a little too quickly. She forced herself to relax and be sensible about this. Things were what they were; living in a fantasy world wasn't going to help anyone. "I will be in touch," she said moving towards the door. "And try to stay out of trouble in my absence." Zax was indignant, even though she knew she shouldn't be.

"Of course! I'm a good girl too!" she called after her, uncertainly.

Randal had his own way of reading Satiah's reports that never failed to unnerve her, but this time she knew she didn't have that much to worry about. He would make little noises or look directly at her while she sat there watching him, as if making sure she hadn't sneaked away while he was busy.

(CP) OPERATION SELECTOR (CP) REPORT: Dated at end. Designation (TS) Joint PAI operation. Top Secret. Status Active. Satiah reports… Timescale: six weeks. Objectives: 1 protect Oli McAllister from attempts on his life, and 2, prevent Oli McAllister from winning the election by any means besides murder and any form of statistical alteration. Vague but threatening message identified concerning an individual named angel acted as initial impetuous. Suspects identified Jinx, Octutin, Sam McAllister, Mark De Jool, Marisa and Collorah. See attached files one to six. Two separate groups with the same aim and both completely independent of angel.

Multiple suspects eliminated throughout course of assignment in effort to uncover angel. See reference pack one and two. Failed to identify or locate angel. Location of campaign displaced three times. Election statistical analysis provided for proportional representation charts, see reference pack three. It seems clear to me that had this operation not taken place, Oli would now be deceased. However, it is also just as clear that he would never have become so popular without our intervention.

To summarise: Oli lost the election, remains alive but plans to run again in the next election so the statistical danger, however remote, remains. Collorah deceased. Cadel deceased. Malla deceased. Sam deceased. Mark deceased. 107 other casualties listed in reference pack four. Octutin incarcerated. Marisa incarcerated. Jinx unaccounted for. Angel unaccounted for. For further information, please find attached Lunell's report. Dated. Report ends.

Zax had, on Satiah's instructions, kept it brief and left out a few of the more awkward issues. Scott Snell's previous fiasco and Lunell's attempted poisoning were just a couple of examples. She had also used Satiah's name so that Randal didn't know that Satiah had, very illegally, used an untrained Phantom to write her report for her. It was a skill that Zax hadn't been taught enough about, so Satiah had decided to improve her curriculum herself. It also meant that Zax would write it for her. Randal already knew of most of these matters, but it had been part of the agreement with the PAI that all inconsequential foci were swept under the carpet. As usual though, Randal always found something to complain about.

"So you failed," he said, a bit stiffly. "You never found out who angel was."

"Unless you're about to tell me some insane anecdote about how it was really you all along and this was just some sort of test then yes, I accept that," Satiah replied, smugly. He sighed and leaned back in his chair. "Besides, objectively, I think I broke even."

"Well, you left out all that chaos with the PAI which displays a great and much appreciated economy with the truth," he noted, seriously. She frowned; she'd been expecting an argument, not an acceptance. "I feel vaguely like I have not been as kind as I could have been, giving this to you. It seemed like an easy enough task at the start... talk about snowballs." Don't they all?

"So... two favours?" she chanced, thinking she'd got away with it.

"Yes... but I think I can repay one of those now," he said, smiling at her. It was a nice enough smile, but Satiah had the uneasy feeling she was not going to like what was coming. It did seem that whenever he tried to do something kind for her it backfired disastrously. Last time, he'd given her this mission and, if she'd not wanted to be with Carl, she wasn't sure that she'd have taken it on. Political missions were the worst! Except for when they weren't. Satiah reflected that that slogan needed to be improved.

"As you know, we're low on numbers these days and..." Randal began.

"I'm not training anyone else," she said, quickly, thinking she could see where he was going.

"No, I wasn't about to ask you to. Sometimes we need to have people around who have the authority..."

"I'm not doing anything else in politics, not for a long time, I want to do something else," she interrupted, again believing she'd seen what he was driving at. "I wash my hands..."

"Will you just listen!" he growled, irritated. Satiah frowned, now perplexed. "I've spoken with Brenda and she agrees that we need more Phantom Leaders." There it was... Satiah almost gulped. Promotion!

"No, not me!" she blurted, shaking her head. She managed to produce an unconvincing laugh to try to make it sound less startled and more casual. She wasn't sure that she pulled it off. Where was this coming from? "I am not the best choice..."

"Why not?" he demanded, impatiently. He thought he was doing her a favour. Not so long ago, she'd have bitten his hand off, but she'd changed. She'd gone in that direction once before and it hadn't ended well. Granted, she'd survived relatively unscathed, but nonetheless she had no desire to relive the experience.

"I have a terrible attitude, I don't like talking to people like Brenda and her underlings, I couldn't deal with the responsibility," she listed, with composure. Inwardly, she was desperate to dissuade him from this. Randal was listening closely and staring at her in disbelief. Clearly he'd never dreamed that she'd turn this offer down. He was smart enough to know that these reasons she was throwing out at him were not the main reason behind her refusal.

"Satiah... what's your problem?" he asked, directly. She waved a hand at him, trying to disguise her panic.

"I have many problems! Just give it to someone else!" she dismissed, levelly.

"You're the only one I think is suitable," he explained, persuasively. "Mensa, while undeniably a gifted killer, is too unpredictable and doesn't really have the diplomacy skills needed."

"What about Istrum?" she tried again. If she became a Leader, she'd have next to no free time and she wanted to see Carl as often as she could. And then there was Obsenneth to consider...

"The PAI don't like him."

"They don't exactly like me either," she pointed out, smiling ruefully.

"True, but you have leverage on them, same as me," Randal argued, still not sure what was really going on. Seeing that she had no easy way out of this, she did the only thing that she knew would stop this in its tracks.

"Randal, no! If you force this on me, I will leave," she stated, standing up. "I mean it."

Randal realized she was being deadly serious and knew he had to let it go. Satiah was, though he never told her this, his most successful agent. She was, on average, the best. She had incredible instinct, intelligence and just about everything else you could want in an agent.

"...All right, please sit," he said, standing up himself and moving a little distance away from her. Seeming to regain her self-control, she sat down again. He poured her a drink and handed it to her before pouring one for himself, wondering what this was really about. She sniffed at his liquid repast distrustfully. He raised an eyebrow and gave a short chuckle.

"It's not drugged."

"I should hope not, that would be rude." The joke eased the tension a bit, even though he still couldn't figure out what was causing this.

"I won't force this on you," he said, defusing the potential bomb. "But I need support, I really need it and I trust you."

"It's very nice of you to think of me," she allowed, a bit cynically. "I... I still think someone else would be better."

"If you don't want to be Leader, you don't have to be... I can invent a new position, one special to you, to place you in-between Leader and agent, how do you feel about that?"

"What's going on?" she asked, interested. She had to try something else, if she kept refusing, he'd get her in a corner eventually. Force her into making a choice she knew she'd regret.

"That's what *I* was going to ask *you* next," he said, seriously.

"I don't want promotion," Satiah stated, firmly.

"I can see that," he chuckled. "Why not?"

"I'm not ready for it," she lied.

"I think you are."

"Do you have people you're starting to worry about?" she asked, cryptically. If he distrusted others, then that might explain why he was zeroing in on her, and she could deal with that by suggesting that she investigate those he distrusted. He would have already thought of that himself, and maybe had engineered this whole promotion thing as a way of initiating this investigation. A way to stir the pot. She knew that many others would have wanted this promotion. It was ironic that he offered it to her, the only one who didn't actually desire it.

"No," he told her. "This isn't about trust. It's about resources." Well, that was that idea dead in the water.

"Then does it matter who you promote?" she asked, carefully. If trust wasn't the issue and management was, then it was only a paperwork issue. Something that could be solved by pretty much anyone.

"How does Bladess Satiah sound to you?" he asked.

"…Rather weird," she replied, wishing Randal didn't drink such strong stuff. The smell alone was enough to get her drunk, she mused.

"It's a title from years ago…"

"I know what it is, we axed the Bladess system decades before I was even born," she stated, knowing the history. "Bladess Phantom agents were agents with the authority of Phantom Leaders, so that if a Leader was needed but none was around, then they were a back up."

"It's yours if you want it," he sighed, giving up.

"I'll take it… only if no one other than you knows," she said, being difficult.

"That could be tricky to enforce," he muttered, unsure.

"Then no deal," she smiled, casually. She gave him the type of cheeky grin Zax often gave her. "You want me and I have no idea why so… I'm being tricky."

"And I have no idea why you don't want it," he remarked, sourly.

"If a lady doesn't hold back some mystery, you would get bored," she commented. "Maybe I could call in one of your favours now, the favour being to leave me where I am?"

"We'll discuss this again later, when you've had some time to mull it over. Dismissed, Satiah," he remarked, standing again. After she'd left, frowning, Randal sat at his desk and began work. There was something going on that he didn't quite understand and he was starting to think he had been somewhat precipitate in burning that file about the Vourne conspiracy. The one about who had killed Dass and why. The one where Satiah could have been on either side.

"This is okay, right?" Carl asked again. "You're not going to get into trouble or anything?" Satiah, deciding that it was the only part of Earth she could show him that not many others would ever see, had taken him to the Priory. If anyone asked, she'd just say he was with her. She smiled, and his hand stroked the back of hers.

"I'm always in trouble," she replied, with a shrug. There was something that was bothering her though, and it had nothing to do with Selector. It was something about the Priory. Something had changed since she was last there six weeks previously.

"Are you still mad about angel?" he asked, thinking he knew what was up.

"A little," she admitted, sighing. "It's not often that someone gets away. Still, probability says it's got to happen every now and then. The truth is, Randal - he's my boss, by the way - was trying to promote me," she explained, glad to be able to talk to someone about this. "I think I got out of it. I had to threaten to resign to get him to stop."

Carl's eyes widened.

"You don't want promotion? Why?" he asked, not accusingly, just curious.

"I just don't," she smiled, enigmatically. "I prefer to stay where I am for now." He chuckled and shook his head slowly.

"In any other business I'd say you were crazy and maybe you are, I've not decided yet, but I don't imagine your job getting any better," he said. "I know you hate politicians, even the ones you kiss."

"He kissed me," she giggled, knowing that he was just teasing her.

"Yes, sorry, my mistake," he said, winking mischievously.

"I am just glad that whole election is over, maybe after a few years the CNC will stop talking about it," she sighed, still grinning. "It really made a very easy job very difficult."

"...I didn't put you off, did I?" he asked, concerned. "By being here, I mean?"

"Completely," she smiled, seductively. "I could hardly think straight just knowing you were nearby."

"You know what I mean? Is my being here affecting your work?" he asked, directly.

"No," she stated, flatly. "I thought it might at first, but… it worked out well enough. I'll let you know if that changes." That was when it occurred to her. The last time she'd been there, in the Priory, there had been a bird cage over by the bar with a toucan inside. It wasn't there anymore. She frowned and stood. Carl began to look for somewhere to hide but she stopped him by smiling nonchalantly.

"No, no, it's fine, I'm just going to ask the barman something," she replied. She stood and wandered over to the bar.

"I'm still leaving with you, right?" he joked. She waved over her shoulder at him.

"Excuse me, what happened to the bird?" she enquired, casually. The barman eyed her as if trying to decide if she was drunk or not.

"I'm sorry? Bird?" he asked, baffled.

"Yes, I was in here about six weeks ago, and there was a toucan in a cage right there," she replied, seriously.

"Okay, I wasn't here six weeks ago and I don't know what you saw but, to my knowledge, there has never been a birdcage in here," he replied. "Or a toucan." Satiah stood there, trying to understand this. It shouldn't matter, surely? So what if a toucan was there or not? Why was this bothering her?

"Thank you," she said, moving back to Carl. She sat down again, looking into the middle-distance.

"Shall we go home?" he asked, seeing that something was under her skin.

Satiah found herself telling him all about it on the way back to her apartment. He didn't doubt her story or even ask why it mattered, which she thought was good of him. She couldn't answer either question herself yet, anyway. It sounded ludicrous. When they reached her apartment, she decided that she was going to have it out with Kelvin. She needed to get him to stop thinking she was crazy. She would need him in the future, she was sure. Carl remained in the living area while Satiah activated Kelvin in the storage room.

His red eyes burned into her brown ones as he powered up. The big robot stood upright, towering over her. All repairs were perfect. She didn't doubt either the technician's work or her own, but it had been in the back of her mind – a nagging concern that he might not ever work again. She met Kelvin's gaze evenly.

"Don't even bother to run your methodical error finding check system," she ordered, in a low angry voice. She held up the device in front of him. "I know all about what you were doing. I know you still think I'm crazy! Neither is a reason not to tell me what you're doing." She had no idea how he would respond to this accusation and at first got only silence. It was nearly thirty seconds later when he finally answered her.

"Satiah," Kelvin said, in his usual monotone. "I did tell you." Before she could ask when, he played her an audio recording of their conversation. A conversation she simply did not remember. It was recorded the day before he had broken down. He listed the components he was installing and their purposes and there she was, acknowledging and agreeing to these adaptions. Satiah frowned deeply, still unable to recollect this otherwise mundane interaction, trying to work out if he'd somehow manufactured this. He could replicate her voice, she knew he could. He could alter the metadata to make it seem completely genuine material. But he was supposed to be unable to deceive her…

"I… I don't remember that," she said, trying and failing to not be rattled.

"Obsenneth is affecting your mind Satiah, it must have made you forget in order to create distrust between you and I," Kelvin stated, very quick with an explanation.

"No… no, that's not… why?" she demanded, uncertainly.

"We don't know," he replied. "I am sure you are sane, Satiah, your current behaviour demonstrates this. I only ever obey your instructions and follow your programming. I am incapable of any other function… you know this."

"I know!" she snapped, coldly. "But how do I know you haven't found a way to bypass that?"

"If you no longer require me, then disassemble me," he responded. She was torn now, unsure what to do. Someone was messing with her, and it was either Kelvin or Obsenneth and she didn't know which. And what about that toucan? Was that somehow a part of this too? Was she hallucinating as a side-effect of whatever mind alteration that may or may not be going on? Kelvin had the capacity to kill her and he wasn't trying, indeed he was encouraging her to protect herself by destroying him if she couldn't trust him. Yet he was clever, she'd made him clever, this could be some kind of bluff.

"How...?" she stopped herself. There was still one way to sort this out. Ask Obsenneth if he had indeed influenced her memory. He would deny it, most likely, even if he had, but she had to ask. She pulled out the Obsenneth gemstone and reached out with her mind. Logic may give her an answer. If she asked Obsenneth and he lied, whether he implicated Kelvin or not... no, that was no help at all. It would come down to the question she hated: who did she trust the most? Both had saved her life more than once. Both knew most if not all of her secrets. Yet she didn't love either of them. She didn't owe either of them anything. They were, in the end, superfluous... at least, she kept telling herself that.

"Satiah," Obsenneth said, in her mind.

"Have you altered my memory?" she demanded, unable to stop herself sounding afraid. "I need you to tell me if you have, and if you lie to me or I even suspect you are lying, I will hand you over to Ash."

"Yes, I did hide one memory" he said, with a nonchalance that threw her.

"Why?" she asked seriously, in horror.

"Kelvin is a machine and does not understand us, Satiah. I thought he intended to destroy me or you, most likely me. So, in order to protect us, I had to create doubt between you and Kelvin," he admitted, without a shred of shame. "The mechanical failure was genuine though, I was not responsible for that." That made sense in a way as, had Kelvin never broken down, the odds were that the deception might have been more effective. Kelvin would have tried to monitor her mind and she might not have given him the chance to explain.

Satiah paused, thinking about what to do next. She had to assert control over him.

"If you affect my mind again in any way, or I even suspect you have, our deal is void, understand?" she asked, wrathfully.

"Certainly," he agreed. "It was only self-preservation that compelled me to act in such a way. Should I ever feel so inclined in the future, we will discuss it more openly?"

"Good, that is reasonable... and what about that toucan?"

"The bird that vanished?" Obsenneth asked. "That was not me." She believed this, as he'd already admitted to the other accusation. He could so easily have denied it. However, this had shaken her trust in him. If he meant her harm then why keep saving her? He needed her alive. But he wasn't afraid to influence her mind without her knowing. Curious.

"So it was once there?" she clarified, to be sure.

"It was."

She replaced Obsenneth in her pocket and turned to face Kelvin, a little ashamed of herself for ever doubting him.

"Okay, it was Obsenneth, I'm sorry," she said, a bit cross. "We can trust him, he's promised that so long as you don't try to destroy him, he will not mess with my mind again. You may continue with your start up programs now... and one more thing, when Carl and I are together, please look the other way. You're making him uncomfortable."

"Your apology isn't necessary," Kelvin replied, as she knew he would. "And your new instructions are registered."

"You're getting it anyway," she smiled, casually. "I'm going to need you to upload a lot of data, and then you will need to run some scans for me. I estimate they will take several months because of their size, complexity and our schedule..."

# Epilogue

"...And in other CNC news, President and Benefactorial candidate Oli McAllister was found dead this morning at his residence. Authorities refused to comment about the circumstances of his death. They have issued an official statement to the public, asserting that at present they believe it to have been of natural causes, and they have no reason to suspect foul play. The investigation continues..."

Randal, upon hearing that, downed the last of his drink and glared at the screen in front of him. It was confirmed. According to classified records, records even he shouldn't have access to, the results were clear. Zax was Vourne's biological daughter, there was no mistake, and he had double-checked. It had not been the result he was expecting. When he'd run the scan he'd expected Satiah's name to come up. Satiah's profile was unlisted, however. Someone had unlawfully expunged it.

He stood and turned the light out as he left the office.